THE PENGUIN CLASSICS

FOUNDER EDITOR (1944 – 64): E. V.

EDITORS:

ROBERT BALDICK (1964 – 72), BETTY RADICE,   ES

FRANCOIS RABELAIS was born at the end
fifteenth century. A Franciscan monk turned Bened
abandoned the cloister in 1530 and began to study me
Montpellier. Two years later he wrote his first work, P.
which revealed his genius as a storyteller, satirist, prop
and creator of comic situations and characters. In 1
published *Gargantua*, a companion to *Pantagruel*, which c
some of his best work. It mocks old-fashioned theo
education, and opposes the monastic ideal, contrasting it
free society of noble Evangelicals. Following an outbu
repression in late 1534, Rabelais abandoned his post of d
at the Hotel-Dieu at Lyons and despite Royal support his book
Tiers Livre was condemned. His last work, and his boldest,
Quart Livre was published in 1551 and he died two years later.
For the last years of his life Rabelais was persecuted by both
religious and civil authorities for his publications. His genius
however was recognized in his own day and his influence was
great.

J. M. COHEN has translated nine volumes for the Penguin
Classics; these have been works by Cervantes, Díaz, Galdós,
Montaigne, Pascal, Rabelais, Rousseau and St Teresa of Avila.
He also edited the Penguin anthologies *Latin American Writing
Today*, *Writers in the New Cuba*, the *Penguin Book of Spanish
Verse* and the three Penguin books of *Comic and Curious Verse*.
He compiled the *Penguin Dictionary of Quotations* and has pub-
lished *A History of Western Literature* (Pelican, 1956). J. M.
Cohen was born in 1903 and has been writing and translating
since 1946.

THE HISTORIES OF
GARGANTUA AND
PANTAGRUEL

By François Rabelais

Translated and with an Introduction by
J. M. Cohen

PENGUIN BOOKS

Penguin Books Ltd, Harmondsworth, Middlesex, England
Penguin Books Inc., 7110 Ambassador Road, Baltimore, Maryland 21207, U.S.A.
Penguin Books Australia Ltd, Ringwood, Victoria, Australia

—

This translation first published 1955
Reprinted 1957, 1963, 1965, 1967, 1969, 1970, 1972, 1974

—

Made and printed in Great Britain
by Richard Clay (The Chaucer Press) Ltd,
Bungay, Suffolk
Set in Monotype Bembo

LIST OF CONTENTS

THE SECOND BOOK

The Third Book

The Fourth Book

THE FIFTH AND LAST BOOK

TRANSLATOR'S INTRODUCTION

RABELAIS stands prejudged. He has given to the languages of the world that single adjective coined from his name which has come to represent him in the minds of all those millions who have never opened his book. Of course François Rabelais was a *Rabelaisian* writer; that is to say one who mentioned human functions which, after his day, were referred to, by imaginative writers at least, in a far more guarded way, until James Joyce, his counterpart and admirer in our own age, put them back into literary circulation. But this is the least part of Rabelais' achievement. There are *smutty* writers in plenty, obscure figures of the Renaissance or the eighteenth century whose works figure in the catalogues of antiquarian booksellers under the heading 'Curious'. Rabelais' outspokenness was of another sort. He was a man intoxicated by every sort of learning and theory, who had at the same time the earthy commonsense of a peasant. His mind would reach out in pursuit of the wildest fancies, and when he had captured them he would relate them only to the three constants of this life: birth, copulation, and death, which he saw in their crudest physical terms. There was in the mind of this loose-living monk no twentieth-century conflict between the two sides of his nature, the scholar's and the peasant's. They played into one another's hands. Nor was he conscious of any inconsistency between his professed beliefs and the often pagan workings of his imagination. François Rabelais was a whole figure, chock-full of human contradictions, which he attempted neither to reconcile nor to apologize for.

'Rabelais plays with words', wrote Anatole France, 'as children do with pebbles; he piles them up into heaps.' Now if it were possible at this late date to give the word *Rabelaisian* a new meaning, fairer to the reputation of the writer François Rabelais, it should be made to denote the writer who is in love with his medium, the man for whom words call up associations, in contrast to the man who employs them to express previously conceived notions. The characters of Gargantua and Friar John, and of Pantagruel and his company, are built up from what they say. All are loquacious talkers, and all are inveterate parodists. The stories they tell, the actions they perform, their comments and asides, are conceived one and all in terms of literature. Let me take as a random example Gargantua's speech to the defeated enemy after the victorious conclusion of his campaign against King Picrochole. The opening is modelled on a speech by the Emperor Trajan reported by the younger Pliny. But into it are woven references to Charles VIII's conquest of Brittany, to Charles V's imprisonment of Francis I after the battle of Pavia, and to an imaginary incursion by the Canarians, the name of whose king suggests some associations with ancient Carthage. But the true origin of the wars between Grandgousier and King Picrochole – of which this is the conclusion – lies in some events in Rabelais' own early life. They are a dramatic and exaggerative representation of a long feud between the writer's father and a neighbouring landowner over some fishing and water rights on the River Loire, which was bitterly fought out at law. Even the names of the minor characters in these chapters of *Gargantua* are those of the lawyers and others who took part in the suit. There seems even to have been an actual Friar John who acted as legal agent for the monks of Seuilly, who were involved in it. Now all this miscellaneous material, much of which he owed to a visit to his old surroundings immediately before writing his book, was imaginatively welded and recast by Rabelais in the form of a Ciceronian harangue in the grand style affected by his fellow humanists. It is true that Gargantua's speech seems to enforce a certain moral. He says clearly enough that there should be no resort to war except for the gravest reasons and that the humane treatment of defeated opponents pays in the long run. But the point of the matter lies not in the content but in the language. Here again the comparison is with Joyce, the great modern master of comment by parody.

As in Joyce's case, even a contemporary reader would have caught only some of Rabelais' references. Later scholars have painfully explored many of the minor sources of his material. But to enjoy Rabelais there is no more need to identify the possible associations of every phrase, quotation, and place-name, than to have read Professor Livingstone Lowes' meticulous examination of Coleridge's previous reading before attempting *The Ancient Mariner*. So the account of the Picrochean War, with its campaigns and orations, all conducted in the miniature landscape of Rabelais' native Touraine, with every

hamlet promoted to the size of a fortified city, can be enjoyed for its
sheer mastery of language and associations and as a parody of any of
the classical historians over whom one has sweated at school; while
the voyages in the later books make similar fun of the narratives of the
classical explorers and of the pioneering navigators of Rabelais' own
day. One needs, as I have said, no comprehensive knowledge of his
sources. Many of the quotations are there only to tease, and nothing
would amuse the spirit of Rabelais, in whatever limbo he may be,
more heartily than the sight of a literal-minded reader hunting up and
speculating on his every allusion to his curious learning.

Rabelais' inspiration is primarily literary. For his material he resorted to books, quoting, parodying, assembling, contrasting, and
mocking authors great and small, famous and obscure. There is no
single Rabelaisian style, as there is not a single Joycean one. Purely as a
story-teller, François Rabelais is as clumsy as any of his contempo-
raries, in that sixteenth century when the skilled writing of prose
lagged so far behind the craft of poetry. Only too often for his translator's pleasure he merely strings his narrative together on a series of
thens and *ands*; and his sentences are sometimes so rich in half-related
dependent clauses that his true meaning is in danger of escaping his
reader. But once he is caught up by his passion for words, once he begins to catalogue, to pun, to travesty, to etymologize, to pile up his
pebbles into monstrous and misshapen cairns; once he begins to list
the Library of Saint-Victor book by preposterous book, or to arrange
in parallel columns the games which Gargantua and his friends played
in their unreformed youth; then we have the true Rabelais. Again
when he attempts to describe the indescribable, to outline, gesture by
gesture, the argument conducted in dumb-show between Panurge and
the scholar from England – who may have been intended for Sir
Thomas More – or to elaborate the judge Bridlegoose's justification
for arriving at his decisions by the fall of the dice, a practice which he
defends with copious legal quotations; or to twist the omens to
Panurge's satisfaction, when every one of them prophesies his inevitable cuckoldry; here where Rabelais' special quality of intoxicated
ridicule, of exuberant, exaggerative mockery, is engaged, here we
have one of the world's great writers; the authentic scholar who
ridicules scholarship, the enemy of that conventional medieval learning, for which, beneath his scorn, he feels such an instinctive affection.

And here once more the comparison with Joyce suggests itself. For the minds of both these mockers of the Church and its teachings were shaped for ever by the priestly schoolmasters of their youth. Indeed, there is no schoolman's argument, such as he would have heard from the Franciscans in his boyhood, that the mature Rabelais did not delight in playing with, no branch of the old learning so perverse or so abstruse that it did not attract him, even when, as a faithful follower of Erasmus, he was compelled to condemn it. One is even left wondering how many of the means of divination practised in Panurge's quandary he had not himself experimented with, at least in his youth.

For François Rabelais, like all true satirists, was more than half in love with the objects of his satire. As Cervantes, setting out to mock the ballads and stories of chivalry, in fact composed a book more romantically adventurous than the material he parodied; as the Reverend Mr Barham in his *Ingoldsby Legends* showed himself at least as fascinated by medieval revivalism as the Southeys and 'Monk' Lewises at whose expense he was having his fun; as Thomas Hood in his comic poems guyed that very Romanticism that he had himself practised in his early and serious poetry, so Rabelais clearly delighted most in just that curious learning at which he directed so much of his rumbustious artillery.

If we look for the figure in English literature who reminds us most closely of him, it may be Joyce, it may be Sterne or Ben Jonson, all three of whom are Rabelaisian in the new sense that I have tried to give to that word. But certainly, despite superficial resemblances, it will not be Swift. At first sight, Rabelais' preoccupation with the human functions, sexual and excretory, may suggest that kind of physical disgust which we find in the Dean of St Patrick's. Only Swift perhaps, among writers in English, could have described the manifold forms of hideous death dealt out by Friar John to the invaders of the abbey-close; only he would have been glad to invent the hideous trick which Panurge played on the wretched sheep-dealer in the Fourth Book. But Rabelais lacked that ready dislike for humanity which characterized the Dean. When he permitted himself to write brutally, it was invariably out of verbal intoxication. The slaughter of Picrochole's men was an excuse for the employment of the complete vocabulary of anatomy; the drowning of Dingdong and his fellow drovers was simply the conclusion of a dispute between two puppets, the whole point of which lay in their repartee. Rabelais does not create characters, and therefore has no compunction in putting them to a violent death. Four of the five personages who play the parts of Pantagruel's companions were lifted bodily from an obscure poem by Teofilo Folengo, an unfrocked Dominican who wrote under the name of Merlin Coccai, and to whom Rabelais refers several times. Panurge, indeed, who is almost the hero from the Third Book onwards, is modelled on the buffoon Cingar of Coccai's work. Not only was Rabelais so uninterested in the invention of characters as to be willing to lift his personages from other books, but he made no attempt either to keep them consistent. The resourceful Panurge, with his mastery of a dozen languages and his heroic story of his escape from the Turks, is hardly the same person as the blubberer in the ship during the great storm, or the coward who invariably sheltered behind Friar John's stout figure. Of all Rabelais' characters only the friar is invariably recognizable by his mannerisms; by his refusal to swear live oaths, that is, and by his repeated references to his breviary, which is both his prayer-book and his bottle. The rest of the company make contributions to the discussions which are almost interchangeable, and Rabelais seems to forget for whole chapters on end that some of them – Carpalim, the swift runner, and Eudemon, the courteous page, for instance – are there at all.

Rabelais is not concerned with individuals; he is not sufficient of a Renaissance man for that. What he draws is the picture of an age or, to be more exact, of a time when two ages overlapped, the new age of research and individualism, with which he was in intellectual sympathy, and the age of the fixed world-order, to which he owed emotional loyalty. If Joyce portrayed the Dublin of a certain summer day in the year 1904, Rabelais just as thoroughly, though far less methodically, gives us the whole of French life in the two decades before 1550. In his distorting mirror he shows them perhaps more accurately than a historian, for he sees them from the standpoint of a giant: a broadvisioned giant who was the creator of giants.

In his *Pantagruel*, the second book of the series though the first to be written, we take a look at the scholastic education of the time, and find it condemned in Gargantua's letter to his son, which sets out the intellectual ideals of the humanists; we see something of the University of Paris, of its controversies and its libraries; we take part in some

student pranks which Rabelais' Victorian translator preferred to leave
in the original French; we are present at the great argument in dumb-
show, and we go overseas to witness certain heroic wars against the
giant Werewolf and King Anarch of the Amaurots, which last parody
the same kind of heroic tales which afterwards gave Cervantes his subject. The incidents of this book are only roughly tied together. But, as
Rabelais himself wrote, a good workman puts every piece of timber
to its use, and in *Pantagruel* he touches for a chapter or two on all
kinds of other matters: on the law's delays, on the prevarications of
lawyers, on the Euphuistic jargon then fashionable among students,
who never used a simple French word if a new-fangled Latin deriva-
tive could be found to take its place, and on the fates of the illustrious
dead in a limbo where Xerxes hawked mustard and Alexander darned
breeches for a miserable livelihood.

   Gargantua, its successor, was written to take the place of the *Great
Chronicles of Gargantua*, an anonymous popular success which had
given Rabelais his first idea for *Pantagruel*. In this story of that hero's
father, even when using some of the incidents of the original *Chronicles*,
Rabelais was far more serious in his satire, and far more deliberate in
his references to the contemporary scene. So vigorous, indeed, was
his attack on the scholars of the University of Paris in his first edition
that he was forced, when he reprinted it, to temper his language, and
replace the term 'doctors of theology', which pointed directly to the
Sorbonne, by the more general term of sophists. Here Rabelais
showed himself to be the loyal disciple of Erasmus, whom he quoted
in an unashamed attitude of hero-worship. So critical was he, indeed,
of the priesthood, and particularly of the monastic orders, of which he
had bitter knowledge from within, that he made guardedly friendly
references even to the Protestants. But though he objected to their
persecution, Rabelais never came near to joining the Reform movement. The Abbey of Thélème, the place of retreat for both sexes,
whose motto was 'Do as you will', and the constitution, construction, and praise of which occupy the book's last chapters, would
have made no greater appeal to Luther or Calvin than to the Catholic
hierarchy. It was a purely secular organization whose highest ideals
were learning, good manners, and liberal feasting. As an invention,
however, it is more elaborate and more original than anything in
Pantagruel. Similarly the educational digressions of the second book

are far more systematic than those of the first, and the Picrocholean campaign too is far more elaborately worked out than the rather facile parody of the war against King Anarch. It has been said, indeed, that a visitor to the country around Chinon, the home of Rabelais' boyhood, can trace their whole strategy with the same ease as Uncle Toby reconstructed the sieges of the Flanders campaigns in his own garden.

But there are more serious issues raised in this second work which any reader will wish to resolve before going further. One has to decide quite soon what importance Rabelais attaches to his request in the prologue to *Gargantua* that his readers shall chew his seemingly flippant work as a dog does a bone, in order to extract the marrow of its true meaning. Now Rabelais makes a great deal of fun of the art of transcendental interpretation throughout his work, and no sooner has he made his point about the marrow than he withdraws it. Could Homer or Ovid, he asks, possibly have intended all the allegorical meanings that were extracted from their works by later commentators? Homer, he assures us, certainly had no such ideas in his head when he dictated his poems at the only possible time of day for literary composition, that is to say over his meals. So having first asked his reader to look into his tale of Gargantua for hidden significances, Rabelais almost immediately pleads to be read only as an entertainer, on the score that he, like the great writers of old, composed his book only during intervals between his potations and with no thought of conveying more than lay on the surface of his chronicles. Now this is really an attempt to have it both ways: to acquit himself in advance of any accusations of heresy or free-thinking, and at the same time to give his reader the broadest hint that his criticisms were meant to be taken seriously. The explanation of this tactic lies in the political atmosphere of his day. But, as will be evident from the details of his biography, such attempts to protect himself profited him very little. It was clear to everyone that he was making serious criticisms of laws, customs, and institutions, and it was no good his disguising himself as a boon companion, bent on providing only pure entertainment. The entertainment probably always came first. Not only was the criticism there as well, however, but his verbal mastery made it doubly damaging.

There are really no hidden meanings in Rabelais. An occasional contemporary allusion may be cryptic, but there is no need to break the bone to get at it. Only in his references to wine and drinking must we be careful not to take him quite literally. For clearly if his repeated recommendations to drink and feast, which culminate in the Bottle's final oracle *Trink*, referred only to the juice of the grape, there would have been no point in Rabelais' continuous attacks on the religious orders for their over-indulgence at table. For François Rabelais the headiest liquor of all was the liquor of learning, and the most exhilarating feasts those at which learned men met for the exchange of ideas. I do not suggest that this is the whole meaning of his cult of the vine, which permeated his entire writings. Wine for him was the symbol also for the uninhibited interchange of affection between man and man. If we are to judge by his attitude to women in his works, Rabelais went to them only for the crudest gratification of his senses. It was to his own sex that he looked for comradeship, and this comradeship clearly came more easily where food, as well as books and conversation, were shared. On several occasions in his life he took part in those mighty banquets of the learned which were the Renaissance counterpart of our hardly more abstemious week-end conferences. But there is no reference to love in the whole of his great books. His monastic upbringing, even though his observance of his vows was of the loosest, seems to have cut him off from the friendship of women. We hear of an illegitimate son who died at the age of two, to whom he was deeply attached. We know nothing of the child's mother. Nor was he capable of inventing any but the earthiest of female characters. Pantagruel imagines no Dulcinea to whom he can address his vows, but merely promises his father that he will marry in order to produce progeny. Rabelais omits to make him do so. Panurge too, though bent on marriage as a safer alternative to the seduction of other men's wives, which so often runs him into the danger of a beating, is prevented from making a selection by the justifiable fear of being made a cuckold. For cuckoldry, he learns, is the certain concomitant of marriage. Rabelais appears to take the lowest view of women, whom he considers to be entirely governed by their whims, as is clear from a pessimistic disquisition on the nature of the female sex which comes in the Third Book.

This continuation of the tale of *Pantagruel* is almost entirely devoted to the question of his servant Panurge's proposed marriage, and to the various methods of divination attempted in order to discover whether he will make a successful choice. Giants and heroic deeds are forgotten. Here, for the first time, Rabelais has a continuous theme. True, he does not fail to make his usual attacks on monks and theologians, lawyers, and philosophers; his old enemies *the hobgoblins*, who stand for the Franciscans, are not spared a barb or two. But now the giant humanist Pantagruel becomes little more than a foil for the buffoon Panurge; 'terrible deeds and acts of prowess "yield to" heroic deeds and sayings'; and the dark subjects of divination and cuckoldry usurp the place of rhetoric and war. The Third Book is not only structurally the best; it is possibly also the most consistently entertaining. But by the end Panurge is no nearer to the resolution of his doubts than he was when he first laid aside his codpiece, put on his plain brown coat, and hung his spectacles over his ear. The Third Book, therefore, leads straight into the Fourth, in which Pantagruel and his friends set out to consult the Oracle of the Bottle, as final arbiter in this vexed question of the virtue of Panurge's putative wife.

The voyage in search of this Bacchic oracle takes the form of a journey to China by way of an imagined North-west Passage, and the series of islands at which the travellers call gives Rabelais the opportunity of satirizing in allegorical fashion a number of abuses, each of which is to be found in its purest forms in one of the ports at which they touch. It also gives him an opportunity of writing a great storm scene in imitation of that in the first *Aeneid*, though influenced by his old favourite Merlin Coccai. This is a magnificent piece of literary bravura, remarkable for the thoroughness of its nautical language. Rabelais had taken the trouble to find out the name for everything. In only one detail does he betray his inexperience in deep sea navigation, for the ships in which the travellers sail are Mediterranean galleys with sails in addition to their oars. In this book there are references to all sorts of contemporary and classical expeditions. The giant whale was accurately noted down from a seaman's description, and the presentation of little penknives from Perche to the delighted natives is also an obviously first-hand touch; Cartier, who had practised this kind of trading, had discovered Canada in 1534. But events in Europe were also reflected in the happenings on those north-westerly islands. The voyagers meet a ship bound for what must be the Council of Trent, and as a result run into bad weather, while the Chitterlings who are literally cut to pieces by Friar John stand for the Swiss, who had recently been defeated by Francis I. The attacks on Papimania require no explanation; Rabelais was a convinced Gallican, and this was a moment at which an attack on Papal power seemed politically permissible. The results of this boldness will be recorded in the second part of this Introduction.

The Fourth Book, in its comparative scrappiness, perhaps shows some slight decline in Rabelais' powers. The repeated mockery of Panurge's cowardice becomes a little tiresome as the voyage continues. The Fifth Book, which continues the nautical theme, and which was not published until after Rabelais' death, seems to have been clumsily patched together by an unskilful editor.

Chapter Sixteen, for example, in which the travellers inspect the wine-presses, is obviously not in its proper place, since Chapter Seventeen opens with the company telling Pantagruel their adventure with the Furrycats, which has occupied Chapters Eleven to Fifteen; and Chapter Thirty-three bis, which was not in the old editions but has been added from a MS. in the Bibliothèque Nationale, belongs to quite another context. It seems to have been intended as part of the description of Panurge's wedding, which was announced at the end of Book Three, but which never came to be written. The list of dishes which were to have been served on this occasion has been transferred by recent editors to the Lanterns' feast. I have omitted the chapter altogether. What is more, the final chapters, with their mathematical and allegorical account of the Temple of the Bottle, are so dull that it would be charitable to ascribe them to another hand. Pantagruel could hardly have thought it worth while coming so far merely to inspect an early example of a building lit by indirect lighting and constructed on the plan of a heptagon set in a circle, to demonstrate some mathematical formula which is never properly explained. The Fifth Book, however, patently contains much that is of Rabelais' best, especially the incidents on Ringing Island, with their fresh satire on the Church hierarchy, and their deeply felt plea for those who, like their author, were consigned to the cloister, regardless of vocation, by parents unable to provide for them in any other way.

*

François Rabelais was born at an uncertain date between 1490 and 1494 at Chinon on the Vienne, a town which he several times celebrates in the course of his work, and in the immediate neighbourhood of which much of the action of these great chronicles takes place. His father appears to have been a well-to-do lawyer and landowner, and to have given his son his first education at the near-by Benedictine monastery of Seuilly, of which Friar John made such a valiant defence. He may have got some further teaching from the University of Angers, and it is probable that he was accepted as a novice by the Franciscans of La Baumette, outside that city. Here he would have studied theology and in due course have been made a priest. Of this early part of his life little is known. Only from the internal evidence of his writings do we learn of his impatience with the old scholastic learning in which he was instructed and of his pity for those who were consigned by their parents to the monastic life in youth.

Nothing exact is known of him until 1520, when for unknown reasons he became a Franciscan friar. The Franciscans had the reputation of being the most obscurantist of all the orders, but no sooner did François Rabelais enter the friary than he decided to learn Greek. To these Franciscans the New Testament was, in words frequently repeated by Friar John, mere *breviary matter*, to be taken on trust. The new brother wished to read it in the original language. Teachers in Greek were at that time few in France, but Rabelais was able to get the help of local friends, and he with one fellow friar began to study. His superiors, however, confiscated his books. The faculty of theology in Paris, alarmed by Erasmus's commentary on the Greek text of St Luke, had forbidden the study of Greek in France. Rabelais decided to transfer himself to the more liberal Benedictines, a move for which an authorization was necessary from the Holy See. The Benedictine abbot to whom he turned for help was a great prince of the Church who spent very little time in his monastery. He arranged the matter for Rabelais, and took him as his own secretary and as tutor to his nephew. Together with his patron the new monk travelled in the region of Poitou, made friends among scholars, and began to write verses. About 1528 he came to Paris, where the old learning was in conflict with the new humanism, of which he was a disciple, also with the Protestant heresy. Here he left the Benedictines and took orders as a secular priest. In 1530 he inscribed himself in the Faculty of Medicine of Montpellier University, and three months later was made Bachelor of Medicine, which proves that he had known something of the subject before. What is more he could read the texts of Galen and the other fathers of his profession in the original Greek, whilst the rest only knew them in Latin versions. In 1532 he was practising at Lyons, where he began to publish translations of medical works. He was by now corresponding with the most famous of the humanists, including Erasmus himself. In this same year in which he was appointed to an ill-paid medical post he published, under the anagram Alcofribas Nasier, *The Terrible Deeds and Acts of Prowess of Pantagruel, King of the Dipsodes*, a sequel to the popular chronicles of Gargantua, of which, as he tells us, more copies had been bought in two months than all the Bibles that would be sold in the next nine years. The book, with its strange mixture of conventional horseplay, satire on the University of Paris, and serious advocacy of a humanistic education, speedily became popular. In October of 1533 it was condemned by the Sorbonne as obscene. But by this time Rabelais had gained a most influential protector in the person of Jean du Bellay, Bishop of Paris, who took him to Rome as his doctor, where he was called on some business concerning the English King Henry VIII's suit for divorce. Here Rabelais stayed for two months, which gave him sufficient time to inspect the city's monuments and even to assist in a little antiquarian digging. In the meantime he had published a second and revised edition of his *Pantagruel*, which was followed, a few months after his return to Lyons, by his own version of the Gargantua story, in which he hit back hard at his enemies in the Sorbonne. A few of the episodes were taken from the *Grandes Chroniques*, but most of the material was new.

Such was the indignation of the pilloried theologians that François Rabelais was forced temporarily to go into hiding. Du Bellay, however, had been made a Cardinal in the interval, and he took his physician back with him for a second stay in Rome, which was then divided by the rival faction of the French king and the Emperor, both of whom were trying to put pressure on the Pope. Rabelais himself had to approach the Papal Court to obtain absolution for his *apostasy* in quitting the Benedictine habit for that of a secular priest. He obtained a letter authorizing him to attach himself to any Benedictine monastery and to practise medicine. On his return to France, his patron attempted to turn this letter to Rabelais' great profit. Du Bellay appointed him physician to a monastery which was about to be secularized, and where he would have enjoyed the pleasant post of lay canon. But his fellow canons resented this intrusion. So he returned by way of Lyons to Montpellier, where he took his doctorate. After moving for a while between these two cities, he found himself unexpectedly prosecuted for having sent a letter to some suspected person in Rome. By the end of 1537, however, he had attached himself to the Royal Court. Francis I had now openly taken sides against the Reformers, and Rabelais, as an official personage, had consequently to make his peace with the Sorbonne. This compelled him to withdraw his attacks on the doctors of theology when – as has already been noted – his two books were reprinted a few years later.

Francis I having conquered Piedmont, Jean de Bellay's brother Guillaume, Seigneur de Langey, was made governor an took François Rabelais with him to Turin, where he added to his medical duties that of official historiographer to his master. His account of the Seigneur de Langey's campaigns, composed in Latin, is unfortunately lost. In 1541 Rabelais returned to France with de Langey, and on passing through Lyons made arrangements for the expurgated reimpressions of his books. To his great distress he found that his humanist friend Étienne Dolet had just had them reprinted in their original form. A few months later he returned to Piedmont with the Seigneur, who died in 1543. Reference to the scenes about his deathbed will be found in the Fourth Book.

In 1546, with his two earlier books still under the Sorbonne's interdict, Rabelais published his Third. The subject-matter was entirely different from that of his two condemned books. Here was no satire against the theologians, but instead dissertations on a far older and less dangerous controversy, that of the nature of women, which was a fashionable and much argued subject of the time. Here were no giants, and no terrible deeds, but a vast display of miscellaneous scholarship, which should have annoyed no one. The Sorbonne, nevertheless, condemned the book, on the plea that it was stuffed with various heresies. Rabelais went to Metz, an Imperial City, where he was given the post of city orator or secretary. He found the emoluments insufficient, however, and turned to his old patron, Cardinal de Bellay, who took him to Rome, where, as Cardinal, he had been invited to reside. On his way through Lyons, Rabelais left the first eleven chapters of his Fourth Book with the printer. These, at least, were harmless, since they contained nothing but comic stories. Now, in addition to his salary as doctor, Rabelais enjoyed the revenues of two parishes the livings of which his patron had given him, and here he worked on at the Fourth Book. But his detractors would not leave him in peace, and he suffered attacks from a monk who wrote under the Latin name of Putherbus, and an equally violent denunciation by Calvin. But he was safe. For not only had he still influential patrons, but the new King, Henri II, who had succeeded his father, Francis I, in 1547, had adopted an anti-papal policy, which allowed Rabelais to enliven his Fourth Book with the visit to Papimania and the sardonic praise of the famous Papal lawbooks, the Decretals. But no sooner had the Fourth Book left the printers than the King and the Pope composed their differences. Consequently, the new work suffered the same condemnation as its three predecessors. What happened to Rabelais is not known. There were rumours that he was in prison, and he certainly resigned the two parishes which the Cardinal had given to him, and which he had probably never visited. In April of the next year 1553 he died in Paris.

It was nine years before the first sixteen chapters of the Fifth Book were published under the title of The Ringing Island. The complete edition in the form that we now have it did not appear till 1564. How much of it is by Rabelais is a question that still puzzles the scholars. On the one side there is all that display of erudition that we expect; on the other the lack of certain characteristic touches, such as Friar John's repeated references to his 'breviary stuff'. The description of the temple is, as I have said, dull, and may be an addition by the editor. Again, the satire is more openly anti-Papal than that of the earlier books, and might argue that the work had been written after the outbreak of the Wars of Religion, and consequently after their alleged author's death. To the translator, however, there appears to be no strong contrast in style between the Fourth and the Fifth Book, nor does the quality of imagination or the nature of the references and quotations seem radically different.

*

This translation has been based on the text and commentary of Jean Plattard, published in five volumes in the collection 'Les Textes Français'. That is not to say, however, that I have on every occasion accepted his readings or his notes. I have sometimes consulted other editions, including Duchat and Lefranc, and have often followed the guidance of Rabelais' scholarly Victorian translator, W. F. Smith. As for earlier translations, I am often in debt to Urquhart for a phrase. His version, completed by Motteux, is far from literal. In fact it often seems more like a brilliant recasting and expansion than a translation. This applies only to Sir Thomas Urquhart's own work. Motteux's version of the Fourth and Fifth Books is no better than competent hackwork. Like Urquhart, he frequently departs from his original. But where Urquhart often enriches, he invariably impoverishes.

Smith's version of 1893 is a painfully exact exercise in the Victorian Tudor style, valuable, however, for its excellent battery of notes. Thinking it his duty to reproduce his master's sentence forms exactly, this great Cambridge Rabelaisian often matched obscurity with obscurity. When he makes the Prior of the Convent exclaim against Friar John as he bursts into Chapel: 'What will this drunken Fellow do here? Let one take me him to Prison. Thus to disturb divine Service!' one cannot help feeling that he and his monks richly deserved to lose the harvest of their abbey-close. Smith's *Rabelais* deserves to stand on the shelf beside H. E. Watts's *Don Quixote* as a monument of excellent scholarship devoted to a faulty theory of translation.

J. M. C.

February 1954

THE HISTORIES OF
GARGANTUA AND PANTAGRUEL

[THE FIRST BOOK]

THE MOST FEARSOME LIFE OF

THE GREAT GARGANTUA

FATHER OF PANTAGRUEL
COMPOSED MANY YEARS AGO BY
MASTER ALCOFRIBAS
ABSTRACTOR OF THE QUINTESSENCE

A Book
full of Pantagruelism

ADVICE TO READERS

Good friends who come to read this book,
Strip yourselves first of affectation;
Do not assume a pained, shocked look,
For it contains no foul infection,
Yet teaches you no great perfection,
But lessons in the mirthful art,
The only subject for my heart.
When I see grief consume and rot
You, mirth's my theme and tears are not,
For laughter is man's proper lot.

MOST noble boozers, and you my very esteemed and poxy friends – for to you and you alone are my writings dedicated – when Alcibiades, in that dialogue of Plato's entitled The Symposium, *praises his master Socrates, beyond all doubt the prince of philosophers, he compares him, amongst other things, to a Silenus. Now a Silenus, in ancient days, was a little box, of the kind we see to-day in apothecaries' shops, painted on the outside with such gay, comical figures as harpies, satyrs, bridled geese, horned hares, saddled ducks, flying goats, stags in harness, and other devices of that sort, light-heartedly invented for the purpose of mirth, as was Silenus himself, the master of good old Bacchus. But inside these boxes were kept rare drugs, such as balm, ambergris, cardamum, musk, civet, mineral essences, and other precious things.*

Just such an object, according to Plato, was Socrates. For to view him from the outside and judge by his external appearance, no one would have given a shred of an onion for him, so ugly was his body and so absurd his appearance, with his pointed nose, his bovine expression, and his idiotic face. Moreover his manners were plain and his clothes boorish; he was blessed with little wealth, was unlucky in his wives, and unfit for any public office. What is more, he was always laughing, always drinking glass for glass with everybody, always playing the fool, and always concealing his divine wisdom. But had you opened that box, you would have found inside a heavenly and priceless drug: a superhuman understanding, miraculous virtue, invincible courage, unrivalled sobriety, unfailing contentment, perfect confidence, and an incredible contempt for all those things man so watch for, pursue, work for, sail after, and struggle for.

Now what do you think is the purpose of this preamble, of this preliminary flourish? It is that you, my good disciples and other leisured fools, in reading the pleasant titles of certain books of our invention, such as Gargantua, Pantagruel, Toss-pint, On the Dignity of Codpieces, Of Peas and Bacon, cum commento, *&c, may not too easily conclude that they treat of nothing but mockery, fooling, and pleasant fictions; seeing that their outward signs – their titles, that is – are commonly greeted, without further investigation, with smiles of derision. It is wrong, however, to set such small store by the works of men. For, as you yourselves say, the habit does not make the monk; some wear a monkish cloak who are the very reverse of monkish in-*

*side, and some sport a Spanish cape who are far from Spanish in their courage.
That is the reason why you must open this book, and carefully weigh up its
contents. You will discover then that the drug within is far more valuable than
the box promised; that is to say, that the subjects here treated are not so foolish
as the title on the cover suggested.*

*But even suppose that in the literal meanings you find jolly enough non-
sense, in perfect keeping with the title, you must still not be deterred, as by
the Sirens' song, but must interpret in a more sublime sense what you may
possibly have thought, at first, was uttered in mere light-heartedness. Have
you ever picked a lock to steal a bottle? Good for you! Call to mind your expression at the time. Or did you ever see a dog – which is, as Plato says, in
the second book of his Republic, the most philosophical creature in the
world – discover a marrow-bone? If ever you did, you will have noticed how
devotedly he eyes it, how carefully he guards it, how fervently he holds it,
how circumspectly he begins to gnaw it, how lovingly he breaks it, and how
diligently he licks it. What induces him to do all this? What hope is there in
his labour? What benefit does he expect? Nothing more than a little marrow.
It is true that this little is more delicious than great quantities of any other
meat; for, as Galen says in his third Book,* On the Natural Faculties, *and in
his eleventh,* On the Parts of the Body and their Functions, *marrow is
the perfect food concocted by Nature.*

*Now you must follow this dog's example, and be wise in smelling out,
sampling, and relishing these fine and most juicy books, which are easy to
run down but hard to bring to bay. Then, by diligent reading and frequent
meditation, you must break the bone and lick out the substantial marrow –
that is to say the meaning which I intend to convey by these Pythagorean
symbols – in the hope and assurance of becoming both wiser and more courageous by such reading. For here you will find an individual savour and abstruse teaching which will initiate you into certain very high sacraments and
dread mysteries, concerning not only our religion, but also our public and
private life.*

But do you faithfully believe that Homer, in writing his Iliad *and*
Odyssey, *ever had in mind the allegories squeezed out of him by Plutarch,
Heraclides Ponticus, Eustathius, and Phornutus, and which Politian afterwards stole from them in his turn? If you do, you are not within a hand's or a
foot's length of my opinion. For I believe them to have been as little dreamed
of by Homer as the Gospel mysteries were by Ovid in his* Metamorphoses;
a case which a certain Friar Lubin, a true bacon-picker, has actually tried to

prove, in the hope that he may meet others as crazy as himself and – as the proverb says – a lid to fit his kettle.

If you do not believe those arguments, what reason is there that you should not treat these new and jolly chronicles of mine with the same reserve, seeing that as I dictated them I gave no more thought to the matter than you, who were probably drinking at the time, as I was? For I never spent – or wasted – any more – or other – time in the composing of this lordly book, than that fixed for the taking of my bodily refreshment, that is to say for eating and drinking. Indeed, this is the proper time for writing of such high matters and abstruse sciences; as Homer, who was the paragon of all philologers, very well knew, and Ennius, the father of the Latin poets too, as Horace testifies, although a certain imbecile declared that his verses smack rather of wine than of oil.

There is an upstart who says as much of my books. But a turd for him! How much more appetizing, alluring, and enticing, how much more heavenly and delicious is the smell of wine than the smell of oil! I shall be as proud when men say of me that I spent more on wine than on oil as was Demosthenes, when he was told that he spent more on oil than on wine. To be called a good companion and fellow-boozer is to me pure honour and glory. For with that reputation I am welcome in all choice companies of Pantagruelists. It was said against Demosthenes by some envious wretch that his Orations smelt like the rag stopper of some foul and filthy oil-lamp. Interpret all my deeds and words, therefore, in the most perfect sense, show deep respect for the cheeselike brain that feeds you on these delicate maggots, and do your best to keep me always merry. Now be cheerful, my dear boys, and read joyfully on for your bodily comfort and to the profit of your digestions. But listen to me, you dunderheads – God rot you! – do not forget to drink my health for the favour, and I'll return you the toast, post-haste.

CHAPTER 1: *Of the Genealogy and Antiquity of Gargantua*

FOR knowledge of the Gargantua's genealogy and of the antiquity of his descent, I refer you to the great Pantagrueline Chronicle, from which you will learn at greater length how the giants were born into this world, and how from them by a direct line issued Gargantua, the father of Pantagruel. Do not take it amiss, therefore, if for the moment I pass this over, though it is such an attractive subject that the more often it were gone over the better it would please your lordships. For which fact you have the authority of Plato in his *Philebus* and his *Gorgias*, and of Horace, who says that there are some things and these are no doubt of that kind – that become more delightful with each repetition.

Would to God that everyone had as certain knowledge of his genealogy, from Noah's ark to the present age! I think there are many to-day among the Emperors, Kings, Dukes, Princes, and Popes of this world whose ancestors were mere pedlars of pardons and firewood; as, on the contrary, there are many almshouse beggars – poor, suffering wretches – who are descended from the blood and lineage of great Kings and Emperors; which seems likely enough when we consider the amazing transferences of crowns and empires from the Assyrians to the Medes, from the Medes to the Persians, from the Persians to the Macedonians, from the Macedonians to the Romans, from the Romans to the Greeks, from the Greeks to the French.

And to give you some information about myself, who address you, believe that I am descended from some wealthy king or prince of the olden days. For you have never met a man with a greater desire to be a king or to be rich than I have, so that I may entertain liberally, do no work, have no worries, and plentifully reward my friends, as well as all worthy and learned men. But I comfort myself with one thought, that in the other world I shall be all this, and greater still than at present I dare even wish. So console yourselves in your misfortunes too, with as good thoughts or better, and drink lustily if you can get the liquor.

Now to return to our muttons, let me say that by the sovereign gift of heaven, the antiquity and genealogy of Gargantua have been preserved for us in greater entirety than those of any other, except those of the Messiah, of which I do not speak, for it is not my business. What is more, the devils (that is to say detractors and hypocrites) prevent me. It was found by Jean Audeau, in a meadow of his near the Arch Gualeau, below l'Olive, on the way to Narsay. Here, as they were cleaning the ditches, the diggers struck with their picks against a great tomb of bronze, so immeasurably long that they never found the end of it. For it stuck out too far into the sluices of the Vienne. Opening this tomb at a certain place which was sealed on the top with the sign of a goblet, around which was inscribed in Etruscan letters, HIC BIBITUR, they found nine flagons, arranged after the fashion of skittles in Gascony; and beneath the middle flagon lay a great, greasy, grand, grey, pretty, little, mouldy book, which smelt more strongly but not more sweetly than roses. In this book was found the said genealogy, written out at length in a chancery hand, not on paper, nor on parchment, nor on wax, but on elm-bark, so worn however by old age that scarcely three letters could be read.

Unworthy though I am, I was called in to inspect it and, with much help from my spectacles, following that art by which letters can be read that are not apparent – as Aristotle teaches – I translated it, as you may see in your pantagruelizing: that is to say, as you drink to your heart's desire and read the fearsome exploits of Pantagruel.

At the end of the book was a little treatise entitled *Corrective Conundrums*. The rats and moths, or – to be more truthful – some other venomous vermin, had nibbled off the opening; but the rest I have here put down, out of reverence for antiquity.

CHAPTER 2: *The Corrective Conundrums, found in an Ancient Monument*

> ai ? . . . great conqueror of the Cimbri
> V . . . ing through the air, in terror of the dew,
> ' . . . his arrival every tub was filled
>) . . . fresh butter, falling in a shower,
> = . . . ith which, when the great ocean was bespattered,
> He cried aloud; 'Sirs, please to fish it up,
> His beard is almost clotted with the stuff;
> Or, at the least, hold out a ladder to him.'

Some said to lick his slipper was much better
Than to gain pardons, and the merit greater.
But up there came a crafty rascal, sliding
Out of the hole in which they fish for roach,
And said: 'For God's sake, sirs, let's not do that;
The eel is there. He's hiding in this pond.
You'll find him there (if we look closely down),
A huge stain in the bottom of his hood.'

When he was just about to read the chapter,
Nothing was found in it but a calf's horns.
'I feel', said he, 'the bottom of my mitre,
So cold that round it my whole brain is chilled.'
They warmed him with the perfume of a turnip,
And he was glad to stay beside the hearth,
Provided someone new was put in harness
Out of the crowd of awkward customers.

What they discussed was then St Patrick's Hole,
Gibraltar and a thousand holes besides;
Was there a way to close them to a scar
So skilfully that they would not have a cough?
For it appeared to everyone unseemly
To see them gaping so at every wind.
Perhaps if they were neatly fastened up
They might be fit to offer up as pledges.

This point was settled and the raven plucked
By Hercules, from Libya returning.
'What!' exclaimed Minos. 'Why am I not summoned?
Except for me the whole world's been invited,
And they expect me freely to provide
Oysters and frogs for them, and gladly too!
Provided that they spare my life, I give
Their sale of distaffs to Old Nick in person.'

Then to defeat them came Q.B., who limps,
Under safe-conduct from the mystic starlings,
The sifter who is cousin to great Cyclops
Put them to slaughter. Each one blew his nose!

Few heretics were born in this waste field
That were not winnowed on the tanner's mill.
All of you, run there, give the cry, 'To arms!'
You will find more there than you did last year.

Soon after that the bird of Jupiter
Made up his mind to back the weaker side;
But seeing them in such a fearful fury,
Feared they would hurl the Empire down pell-mell,
And so preferred to steal the empyrean
Fire from the stump at which herrings were sold
Than to put through the Massoretic gloss
The air serene, against which men conspire.

All was concluded then with sharpened point
In spite of Ate and her heron's thigh;
Who, as she sat there, saw Penthesilea,
Taken in her dotage for an old cress-seller.
Everyone cried out: 'Hi, you charcoal hag,
What business have you here? You're in the way.
Why, it was you that pinched the Roman banner
That had been drawn up on a parchment scroll!'

And Juno too beneath the rainbow's arch,
With her great hawk, was laying snares for birds.
They meant to play a dirty trick on her,
Which would have caught her out at every point.
It was agreed that of these free provisions
Two of Proserpine's eggs should be her share,
But should they ever nab her on the spot
She should be tied up on the Whitethorn hill.

Seven months later – minus twenty-two –
He that of old annihilated Carthage
Came courteously amongst them, and proposed
That they should take his heritage, or rather
That it should be divided into parts
According to the law of equal shares,
Distributing a snack of broth to each
Of his assistants who drew up the deed.

The year will come, marked with a Turkish bow,
And spindles five and the bottoms of three pots,
On which the back of a discourteous king
Peppered shall be beneath a hermit's cloak.
The pity of it! For one tricksy woman
Will you let all those acres be engulphed?
Stop, stop; no one shall imitate this mask.
Retire and join up with the serpent's brother.

When this year's over he that is shall reign
In peace and company of his good friends.
No violence nor insult shall prevail,
And everything you wish for shall come true,
And the thanksgiving promised long ago
To the Heavenly Host shall peal out from the belfry;
The breeding-studs that were perturbed before
Shall take their triumph on a royal palfrey.

This age of hocus-pocus shall go on
Until the time when Mars is put in chains.
Then there shall come a time surpassing all,
Delightful, pleasant, matchless, and most fair.
Lift up your hearts, go forward to that feast,
My loyal friends all; for he has quit this life
Who would not for the world return again.
So much shall time gone by be called for then.

And lastly, that man who was made of wax
Shall by the hinge of Jack o' the Clock be lodged.
The jangling Jack that holds the sacring-bell
Shall be addressed no longer as 'Sire, sire!'
If only one could pick one's cutlass up
There'd be an end of all this buzzing rot;
A hank of packthread then would be enough
To sew up all this storehouse of deceit.

Translator's note. There is very little sense in this riddle, though some critics
have found in it references to the Pope, the Reformation, and to certain wars.
We have not the answer, and probably there never was one. It is merely a
parody of a kind of puzzle popular at the time.

CHAPTER 3: *How Gargantua was carried eleven months in his Mother's Belly*

GRANDGOUSIER was a good jester in his time, with as great a love of tossing off a glass as any man then in the world. He had also quite a liking for salt meat. For this reason he generally kept a good store of Mayence and Bayonne hams, plenty of smoked ox-tongues, an abundance of chitterlings in their season and beef pickled in mustard, a supply of botargos, and a provision of sausages; though not of Bologna sausages, for he feared Lombard concoctions[1] – but of those from Bigorre, Longaulnay, La Brenne, and Le Rouergue. In the prime of his years he married Gargamelle, daughter of the king of the Butterflies, a fine, good-looking piece, and the pair of them often played the two-backed beast, joyfully rubbing their bacon together, to such effect that she became pregnant of a fine boy and carried him into the eleventh month. For so long and even longer women can carry a child, especially when he is some masterpiece of nature, a personage destined in his time to perform great deeds. As witness Homer, who tells us that the child which Neptune begot upon the nymph was born at the end of a full year, that is to say in the twelfth month. For, as Aulus Gellius says in his third book, this long period befitted the majesty of Neptune, since it took that time for the child to be perfectly shaped. For a similar reason Jupiter made the night he slept with Alcmena last forty-eight hours; for in a shorter time he could not have forged Hercules, who cleansed the world of monsters and tyrants.

My masters, the Pantagruelists of old, have confirmed what I say, and have declared the birth of a child born of a woman eleven months after her husband's death not only to be possible but also legitimate. See Hippocrates, *lib. De Alimento*, Pliny, *lib. vii, cap. v*, Plautus, *in Cistellaria*, Marcus Varro, in his satire headed the *Testament*, in which he claims Aristotle's authority on the subject, Censorinus, *lib. De die natali*, Aristotle, *lib. vii, cap. iii et iv, De Nat. animalium*, Gellius, *lib. iii, cap. xvi*, Servius *on the Eclogues* in explaining the line of Virgil, *Matri longa decem.* &c, and a thousand other madmen, the number of whom has been increased by the lawyers, *f. De suis, et legit. l. Intestato, para-*

1. An allusion to the Italian habit of poisoning.

grapho fin, and *in Authent. De Restitut. et ea quae parit in xi mense*. What is more they have scrawled it into their Bacon-pinching law, *Gallus, ff. De lib. et posthu., et l. septimo ff. De Stat. homi.*, and into certain others which at the moment I dare not name; on the strength of which laws widows may freely play at the close-buttock game with all their might and at every free moment, for two months after their husbands' decease. So I beg of you, all my fine lechers, if you find any of these same widows worth the trouble of untying your codpiece, mount them and bring them to me. For if they conceive in the third month, their issue will be the dead man's legal heir; and once the pregnancy is public they may push boldly on, full sail ahead, since the hold is full, after the example of Julia, daughter of the Emperor Octavian, who never gave herself up to her belly-drummers unless she knew that she was pregnant, after the manner of a ship, which does not take on her pilot until she is caulked and loaded. And if anyone reproaches them for allowing themselves to be thus sported with in their pregnancy, seeing that animals never allow the covering male near them once they are big, they will answer that beasts are beasts, but that they are women and fully understand the grand and jolly little rights of superfetation; as Populia answered of old, according to Macrobius's account, in the second book of his *Saturnalia*.

If the deuce doesn't want their bellies to swell, he must twist the spigot and close the hole.

CHAPTER 4: *How Gargamelle, when great with Gargantua, ate great quantities of Tripe*

THIS was the manner in which Gargamelle was brought to bed – and if you don't believe it, may your fundament fall out! Her fundament fell out one afternoon, on the third of February, after she had over-eaten herself on *godebillios*. *Godebillios* are the fat tripes of *coiros*. *Coiros* are oxen fattened at the stall and in *guimo* meadows, and *guimo* meadows are those that carry two grass crops a year. They had killed three hundred and sixty-seven thousand and fourteen of these fat oxen to be salted down on Shrove Tuesday, so that in the spring they should have plenty of beef in season, with which to make a short *commemoration* at the beginning of meals, for the better enjoyment of their

wine. The tripes were plentiful, as you will understand, and so appetizing that everyone licked his fingers. But the devil and all of it was that
they could not possibly be kept any longer, for they were tainted,
which seemed most improper. So it was resolved that they should be
consumed without more ado. For this purpose there were invited all
the citizens of Cinais, of Seuilly, of La Roche-Clermault, and of Vaugaudry, not to forget those of Le Coudray-Montpensier and the Gué
de Vède, and other neighbours: all strong drinkers, jovial companions,
and good skittle-players.

Now, the good man Grandgousier took very great pleasure in this
feast and ordered that all should be served full ladles. Nevertheless he
told his wife to eat more modestly, seeing that her time was near and
that this tripe was not very commendable meat. 'Anyone who eats the
bag', he said, 'might just as well be chewing dung.' Despite his warning, however, she ate sixteen quarters, two bushels, and six pecks. Oh,
what fine faecal matter to swell up inside her!

After dinner they all rushed headlong to the Willow-grove; and
there on the luxuriant grass they danced to the gay sound of the flutes
and the sweet music of the bagpipes, so skittishly that it was a heavenly
sport to see them thus frolicking.

CHAPTER 5 : *The Drunkards' Conversation*

AFTER the meal they began to chat in that same place, and then
flagons started to circulate, hams to trot round, goblets to fly, and
glasses to clink. Draw! – Pass it over! – Fill it up! – A mixture! – Give
it to me without water, like that, my friend. – Toss me off that glass,
neatly. – Draw me some claret, a brimming glass. – An end to thirst! –
False fever, will you not begone? – God bless me, my dear, I can't get
my gullet working. – You've caught a chill, old girl. – You're right. –
By St Quenet's guts, let's talk of drink. – I only drink at my own
times, like the Pope's mule. – And I only drink from my breviary-
flask,[1] like a good Father Superior. – Which came first, drinking or

1. A breviary-flask, of which we shall hear more, seems to have been made
after the shape of a prayer-book, for drinking on the sly. Rabelais himself possessed one.

thirst? – Thirst. For who could have drunk without a thirst in the time of innocence? – Drinking, for *privatio praesupponit habitum*.[1] I'm a Latinist. *Foecundi calices quem non fecere disertum?*[2] We poor innocents drink only too much with no thirst. – As I'm a sinner, I never drink without a thirst, if not a present thirst a future one. I forestall it you see. I drink for the thirst to come. I drink eternally. For me eternity lies in drinking, and drinking in eternity. – Let's have a song, let's have a drink, let's sing a catch! Where is my tuning-fork? – What! I only drink by proxy. – Do you wet your guts to dry them, or dry your guts to wet them? – I don't understand the theory, but I help myself out by the practice. – Enough! – I moisten my lips, I wet my thirst, and I gulp it up, all for fear of dying. – Drink all the time and you'll never die. – If I don't drink, I'm high and dry, as good as dead. My soul will fly off to some frog-pond. The soul can't live in the dry. – Waiters, you're good at transubstantiation, turn me from a non-drinker to a drinker! – A perpetual sprinkling for these parched and sinewy bowels of mine! – Drinking's no good if you don't feel it. – This stuff flows into the veins; the pisser will get none of it. – I want to wash the tripes of this calf I dressed this morning. – I've taken some ballast into my stomach. – If the paper of my bonds drank as well as I do, my creditors would have a fine job when the time came to make out their titles. – That hand of yours is spoiling the shape of your nose. – Oh, how many more will go in before this comes out! – To drink out of these shallow bowls is enough to break your girths. – This is what's called a flagon to catch flagons. – What is the difference between a bottle and a flagon? – A great difference. For a bottle is stopped with a cork, a flagon with a cock. – A fine difference! – Our fathers drank deep and emptied their cans. – That's shitten well sung. Let's drink! – That fellow's going to wash his tripes. Won't you keep anything for the river? – I drink no more than a sponge. – I drink like a Templar. – And I *tamquam sponsus*, like a bridegroom. – And I *sicut terra sine aqua*, like the parched earth. – Give me a definition of ham. – It's an act that compels drinking; it's a pulley. By means of a pulley-rope you lower the wine into the cellar; with the help of ham you bring it into the stomach. – Now then, some drink, some drink now! That's not filled

1. A philosophical tag: a lack can only be defined if there has been previous possession.
2. Whom has the flowing bowl not made eloquent?

up. *Respice personam; pone pro duos; bus non est in usu.*[1] If I could climb up as well as I can put it down, I should have been high in the air long ago. – This is the way Jacques Cœur grew rich. – This way the brushwood grows beside the ditch. – This is how Bacchus conquered India. – This is the science that won Melinda. – A little rain allays a great wind. Long gulps break the thunder. – If my tool pissed urine like this, wouldn't you like to suck it? – I can keep it down. – Page, come here. Let me write myself next in your list. – Throw it down, Will! There's another pot still. – I appear as appellant against thirst; it's an abuse. Page, draw my appeal up in due form. – A drop left in the glass? – Once I used to drink it all up; now I leave nothing. – Let's not hurry; let's knock it all back. – Here are fine tripes, incomparable *godebillios* from that dun ox with the black stripe. Let's curry favour with them for Heaven's sake, and for the good of the house! – Drink or I'll ... – No, no! – Drink, I beg of you. – Sparrows never eat unless their tails are tapped; I only drink if I'm wheedled. – *Lagona edatera!*[2] There isn't a burrow in my whole body where this wine doesn't ferret out my thirst. – This stuff whips it up fine. – This stuff will drive it out for me, altogether. – Let's proclaim to the sound of flagons and bottles that if anyone has lost his thirst he needn't look for it here. Long suppositories of drinking have made him drop it out of doors. – The Good God made the planets and we clear the plates. – I have the Gospel word on my tongue: *Sitio*, I thirst. – The stone called asbestos is not harder to assuage than my venerable thirst. – Appetite comes with eating, said Hangest of Le Mans, and thirst departs with drinking. – Is there a remedy for thirst? – It is the opposite of that for a dog-bite. Always run after the dog and he'll never bite you; always drink before a thirst and it'll never come to you. – I've caught you napping, and now I'll wake you. Eternal waiter, guard us from sleep. Argus had a hundred eyes to see by; a waiter needs a hundred hands, as many as Briareus, to pour out unwearyingly. – Let's wet our whistles, lads. It's fine to have a thirst. – White wine! Pour it all out, all of it, in the devil's name! Fill it up, right up; my tongue's peeling. – *Landsmann, trinke!*[3] Your health, lad. Good luck! Good luck! – Well, there now.

1. See whom you are pouring out for. Enough for two. The past tense is out of use. We're drinking *now*.
2. Bring me drink, my friend (Basque).
3. Drink, old fellow (German).

That went down well. – O lachryma Christi![1] – That's from La Devinière, from the *pineau* grape. – Oh, this good white wine! – I swear it
goes down like silk. – Ha, ha, a fine taffeta stuff, well woven and of
good yarn. – Courage, my friend! – We'll not be beaten at this game,
I've made a trick. – *Ex hoc in hoc*; from my glass into my mouth.
There's no deception. Everybody saw. Hm! Hm! I'm a Mast Paster. –
Oh, the drinkers that have a thirst! – Page, my dear boy, fill this up
till it spills over, if you please. – Wine red as a cardinal's hat! –
Natura abhorret vacuum. Nature abhors a vacuum. – Would you say
that a fly had drunk out of this? – Toss it off like a Breton! – Down in
one gulp. That's the stuff. – Swallow it down. It's a fine medicine.

Translator's note. It is possible to distinguish a number of voices among these
drinkers. But Rabelais did not identify them.

CHAPTER 6: *The very strange manner of Gargantua's Birth*

WHILST they were pleasantly tattling on the subject of drinking,
Gargamelle began to feel disturbed in her lower parts. Whereupon
Grandgousier got up from the grass, and comforted her kindly, thinking that these were birth-pangs and telling her that since she had been
resting under the willows she would soon be in a good state. She
ought to take new heart, he said, at the coming of her new baby. For
although the pains would be somewhat severe, they would nevertheless be quickly over, and the joy which would follow after would
banish all her pain, so that only the memory of it would be left.

'Have a sheep's courage,' he said. 'Bring this boy into the world,
and we'll soon make another.'

'Ah,' she answered. 'It's easy for you men to talk. Well, I swear to
God I'll do my best, since you ask it of me. But I wish to heaven you
had cut it off!'

'What?' asked Grandgousier.

'Ha,' she said. 'Just like a man! You know what I mean well enough.'

'My member?' he said. 'By the blood of all the goats, send for a
knife if that's what you want.'

'Oh,' she said. 'God forbid! God forgive me, I didn't really mean
it. Don't do anything to it on account of anything I say. But I shall

1. An Italian wine (Christ's tears).

have trouble enough to-day, unless God helps me, all on account of your member, and just because I wanted to please you.'

'Take heart,' he said. 'Don't you worry, but let the four leading oxen do the work. I'll go and take another swig. If any pain comes on you in the meantime I shan't be far off. Give me a shout and I'll be with you.'

A little while later she began to groan and wail and shout. Then suddenly swarms of midwives came up from every side, and feeling her underneath found some rather ill-smelling excrescences, which they thought were the child; but it was her fundament slipping out, because of the softening of her right intestine – which you call the bum-gut – owing to her having eaten too much tripe, as has been stated above.

At this point a dirty old hag of the company, who had the reputation of being a good she-doctor and had come from Brizepaille, near Saint Genou, sixty years before, made her an astringent, so horrible that all her sphincter muscles were stopped and constricted. Indeed you could hardly have relaxed them with your teeth – which is a most horrible thought – even if you had copied the method of the devil at the Mass of St Martin, when he wrote down the chatter of two local girls and stretched his parchment by tugging with his teeth.

By this misfortune the cotyledons of the matrix were loosened at the top, and the child leapt up through them to enter the hollow vein. Then, climbing through the diaphragm to a point above the shoulders where this vein divides in two, he took the left fork and came out by the left ear.

As soon as he was born he cried out, not like other children: 'Mies! Mies!' but 'Drink! Drink! Drink!', as if inviting the whole world to drink, and so loud that he was heard through all the lands of Booze and Bibulous.

I doubt whether you will truly believe in this strange nativity. I don't care if you don't. But an honest man, a man of good sense, always believes what he is told and what he finds written down. Is this a violation of our law or our faith? Is it against reason or against Holy Scripture? For my part I find nothing written in the Holy Bible which contradicts it. If this had been the will of God, would you say that he could not have performed it? For goodness' sake do not obfuscate your brains with such an idle thought. For I say to you that to God nothing is impossible. If it had been His will women would have produced their children in that way, by the ear, for ever afterwards.

Was not Bacchus begotten by Jupiter's thigh? Was not Rocquetaillade born from his mother's heel, and Crocquemouche from his nurse's slipper? Was not Minerva born from Jupiter's brain by way of his ear, and Adonis from the bark of a myrrh-tree, and Castor and Pollux from the shell of an egg laid and hatched by Leda? But you would be even more flabbergasted if I were now to expound to you the whole chapter of Pliny in which he speaks of strange and unnatural births; and, anyhow, I am not such a barefaced liar as he was. Read Chapter three of the seventh book of his *Natural History*, and don't tease my brain any more on the subject.

CHAPTER 7: *How Gargantua received his Name, and how he gulped his Liquor*

WHILE that good man Grandgousier was drinking and joking with the others he heard the horrible cry made by his son as he entered the world, and bawled out for 'Drink! Drink! Drink!' Whereupon he said, 'Que grand tu as.' – What a big one you've got! – (the gullet being understood); and when they heard this the company said that the child ought properly to be called Gargantua – after the example of the ancient Hebrew custom – since that had been the first word pronounced by his father at his birth. The father graciously agreed to their suggestion; it was most pleasing to the mother as well; and to quiet the child they gave him enough drink to break his larynx. Then he was carried to the font and there baptized, as is the habit of all good Christians.

And they ordered for him seventeen thousand nine hundred and thirteen cows from Pontille and Bréhémont for his every-day supplies of milk. For it was impossible to find a nurse to satisfy him anywhere in the country, considering the great quantity of nourishment that he required. Certain Scotist doctors have nevertheless affirmed that his mother suckled him, and that she could draw from her breasts fourteen hundred and two pipes and nine pails of milk at a time. But this is improbable, and the proposition has been declared mammalianly scandalous, offensive to pious ears, and distantly redolent of heresy.

In this state he lived till he was a year and ten months old, at which time, by the advice of physicians, they began to take him out, and a fine ox-wagon was made for him, to the design of Jean Denyau. In this he travelled around most merrily to one place and another; and they made a great show of him. For he had a fine face and almost eighteen chins; and he cried very seldom. But he shat himself every hour. For he was amazingly phlegmatic in his actions, partly from natural character and partly for accidental reasons connected with over-indulgence in the new wines of September. But he never drank a drop without reason. For if by chance he was vexed, angry, displeased, or peeved, if he stamped, if he wept or if he screamed, they always brought him drink to restore his temper, and immediately he became quiet and happy.

One of his governesses told me, on her Bible oath, that he was so accustomed to this treatment, that at the mere sound of pint-pots and flagons he would fall into an ecstasy, as if tasting the joys of paradise. Taking this divine disposition of his into account, therefore, in order to cheer him up in the mornings they would have glasses chinked for him with a knife, or flagons tapped with their stoppers; and at this sound he would become merry, leap up, and rock himself in his cradle, nodding his head, playing scales with his fingers, and beating slow time with his bottom.

CHAPTER 8: *How Gargantua was dressed*

WHEN he reached this age, his father ordered clothes to be made for him of his own colours, which were white and blue. So they set to work, and clothes were made, cut, and sewn for him in the fashion of the day. In the ancient records, which are in the Chamber of Accounts at Montsoreau, I find that he was dressed in the following manner:

His shirt required thirteen hundred and fifty yards of Chatelleraut linen, and three hundred for the gussets, which were square and put in under the armpits, not gathered. For the gathering of shirts was not invented until sempstresses, having broken the points of their needles, began to work with their other ends.

His doublet took twelve hundred and nineteen yards of white satin, and his points fifteen hundred and nine dog-skins and a half. At that time men were beginning to fasten the hose to the doublet, instead of the doublet to the hose; for the latter is unnatural, as Ockham declared in criticizing the *Expositions* of Master Breechesman.

His hose took sixteen hundred and fifty-seven yards and a third of a light wool material, and were slashed in the form of ribbed pillars, indented and notched behind, so as not to overheat his kidneys. And through the slashings was puffed as much blue damask as was needed. Note besides that he had very fine leggings, well proportioned to the rest of his anatomy.

His codpiece took twenty-four and a quarter yards of the same stuff; and its shape was that of a bowed arch, well and gallantly fastened by two fine gold buckles with two enamelled clasps, in each of which was set a huge emerald, the size of an orange. For (as Orpheus says, in his *Book of Precious Stones*, and Pliny, in his final book) this fruit has an erective virtue, and is encouraging to the natural member. The vent of the codpiece was eighty-one inches long, slashed like his hose, with the blue damask puffing out in the same way. But if you had seen the fine wire-thread embroidery, and the charming plaiting in gold-work, set with rich diamonds, precious rubies, rare turquoises, magnificent emeralds, and Persian pearls, you would have compared it to one of those grand Horns of Plenty that you see on ancient monuments, one such as Rhea gave to the two nymphs Adrastea and Ida, the nurses of Jupiter. For it was always brave, sappy, and moist, always green, always flourishing, always fructifying, full of humours, full of flowers, full of fruit, full of every delight. I swear to God it was a pleasure to look at! But I will tell you a good deal more about it in the book that I have written, *On the Dignity of Codpieces*. On one point I will inform you now, however, that not only was it long and capacious, but well furnished within and well victualled, having no resemblance to the fraudulent codpieces of so many young gentlemen which contain nothing but wind, to the great disappointment of the female sex.

His shoes required six hundred and nine yards of purple velvet, and were delicately slashed in parallel lines, with pom-poms of uniform size at the joints; and their soles were made up of eleven hundred skins of brown cows, cut in the shape of cods' tails.

His cape took up two thousand four hundred yards of blue velvet dyed in the grain, embroidered all round with fine scollops and in the

middle with pint pots in silver thread, looped together by gold bands
freely studded with pearls; in this way denoting that he would knock
back a pretty pint in his day.

His belt was made of four hundred and fifty and three quarter yards
of silk cloth, half white, half blue, if I am not much mistaken.

His sword was not Valencian, nor his dagger from Saragossa. For
his father hated all drunken hidalgos, the devil's own infidels. But he
carried a fine wooden sword and a dagger of boiled leather painted
and gilded as finely as anyone could wish.

His purse was made of an elephant's member, which had been presented to him by Herr Pracontal, proconsul of Libya.

His gown took up fourteen thousand four hundred yards, less two
thirds, of the same blue velvet, all flowered in gold in a diagonal pattern; which, by true perspective, gave the impression of a nameless
colour, such as you see on the necks of turtle doves, which marvellously rejoiced the eyes of beholders.

His hat required four hundred and fifty-three yards and a quarter of
white velvet, and in shape it was wide and round, conforming to the
size of his head. For his father said that those hats made after the
fashion of the Spanish Jews, like the crust of pastry, would one day
bring misfortune to their close-shaven wearers.

For his plume he wore a fine large blue feather, taken from a pelican
of the land of savage Hyrcania, which hung daintily over his right ear.

As his hat-medallion, he had a fine piece of enamelled work set in a
gold plate weighing a hundred and thirty-six ounces, on which was
displayed a human body with two heads turned towards one another,
four feet and two rumps – the form, according to Plato in his *Symposium*, of Man's nature in its mystical beginnings; and around it was
written in Ionian script: ΑΓΑΠΗ ΟΥ ΖΗΤΕΙ ΤΑ ΕΑΥΤΗΣ.[1]

To wear about his neck, he had a chain of gold weighing fifty-one
thousand two hundred and six ounces, made in the shape of great
berries, among which were worked large green jaspers, engraved and
incised with dragons, surrounded by beams and sparks, after the
fashion of King Necepsos of old. It fell as low as the navel of his
stomach, and this was beneficial to him all his life, as Greek physicians
will understand.

For his gloves sixteen hob-goblin skins were used, and those of

1. Charity seeketh not her own [profit].

three were-wolves for the trimmings. They were made in this manner by the order of the Cabalists of Saint-Louand.

For rings (which his father wished him to wear in order to revive this old mark of nobility) he wore on the index finger of his left hand a carbuncle the size of an ostrich egg, very chastely set in Egyptian gold. On the middle finger of that hand he had a ring of four metals welded together in the most marvellous fashion ever seen, so that the steel did not rub the gold or the silver press on the copper. This was all the work of Captain Chappuis and his good assistant Alcofribas. On the middle finger of his right hand he had a ring made in a spiral shape, in which were set a perfect orange ruby, a pointed diamond, and a physon emerald of inestimable value. Hans Carvel, chief jeweller to the King of Melinda, reckoned their value at sixty-nine million, eight hundred and ninety-four thousand Agnus Dei crowns; and the Fuggers of Augsburg priced them just as highly.

CHAPTER 9: *Gargantua's Colours and Livery*

GARGANTUA'S colours were white and blue, as you may have read above, by which his father meant it to be understood that he felt a heavenly joy. For white signified to him gladness, pleasure, delights, and rejoicing, and blue anything to do with Heaven.

I quite realize that on reading these words you will laugh at the old boozer, and consider his interpretation of colours most ungentlemanly and infelicitous. You will say that white stands for faith and blue for steadfastness. But without getting excited, annoyed, heated, or chafed – for this is dangerous weather – be so kind as to answer my question. I will put no other constraint upon you, or on anyone else whatever; but merely tell you a saying of the bottle.

Who is exciting you now? Who is pricking you? Who is telling you that white stands for faith and blue for steadfastness? A mouldy book, you say, that is sold by pedlars and ballad-mongers, entitled *The Blason of Colours*. Who made it? Whoever he is he has been prudent in one respect, that he has not put his name to it. For the rest, I do not know which surprises me more, his presumption or his stupidity: his presumption in daring, without reason, cause, or probability, to prescribe by his private authority what things shall be denoted by what colours; which is the custom of tyrants who would have their will take the place of reason, not of the wise and learned, who satisfy their readers with display of evidence; or his stupidity in supposing that without other proofs and valid arguments the world would regulate its practice by his foolish impostures.

In fact (as the proverb goes: Squitty arse never lacks for shit) he has found some fools surviving from the time of high hats,[1] who have believed in his writings and, in accordance with them, have shaped their maxims and proverbs, caparisoned their mules, dressed their pages, quartered their breeches, embroidered their gloves, fringed their bed-curtains, painted their standards, composed their songs, and – what is worse – perpetrated impostures and foul tricks clandestinely among chaste matrons.

In a like darkness are involved those vainglorious courtiers and jugglers-with-names who, when they wish in their devices to signify *hope* (espoir), portray a *sphere*, put birds' *plumes* (pennes) for *pains*, *aquilegia* (l'ancholie) for *melancholy*, the *horned moon* for a *waxing fortune*, a *broken bench* for *bankrupt*, *non* and a *corselet* (un dur habit) for *non durabit*,[2] a *bed without a tester* (lit sans ciel) for a *licentiate*: such an absurd, stale, clownish, and barbarous collection of puns, that anyone henceforth attempting to use them in France – since the Revival of Letters – ought to have a fox's tail tied to his collar and his nose rubbed in a cowpat.

With as good reason (if I should call it reason and not raving) I could have a *panier* painted to show that I am much *pained*, and a *mustard-pot* to stand for the *tardiness* of my heart. A *piss-pot* will denote an *officer*; the *bottom of my breeches*, a *jar full of wind*; my *codpiece*, a *lance in rest*; and a *dog's turd* (estront de chien), *the firm lance within* (tronc de ceans), wherein lies the love of my lady.

The sages of ancient Egypt followed a very different course, when they wrote in letters that they called hieroglyphs – which none understood who did not understand, and which everyone understood who did understand, the virtue, property, and nature of the things thereby described. On this subject Orus Apollo has composed two books in Greek; and Polyphilus has gone further into the matter in his *Dream of Love*. In France you find this method used in the device of the Lord Admiral, which was first borne by Octavian Augustus.

1. A fashion of the fifteenth century.   2. It will not last.

But my little skiff shall sail no further among these unpleasant gulfs and shoals; I return to land at the port from which I came. But it is my hope one day to write more fully on this subject, and to show, both by philosophical arguments and by accepted authorities, approved by the whole ancient world, what colours and how many exist in Nature, and what may be conveyed by each – always providing that God preserves the mould of my cap – that is my wine-pot, as my grandmother used to call it.

CHAPTER 10: *Concerning the significance of the colours White and Blue*

WHITE, therefore, stands for joy, solace, and gladness; and this is no false meaning, but one established by firm right and sound title; as you may verify if you will set aside your prejudices and listen to what I am now about to explain.

Aristotle says that if you take two things opposite in kind, such as good and evil, virtue and vice, cold and hot, white and black, pleasure and pain, joy and grief, and so on, and if you couple them in such a way that one of one kind logically agrees with one of the other, it follows that the second of the first pair agrees with the second of the second. For example: *virtue* and *vice* are opposites in one kind, and so are *good* and *evil*. If one of the first pair of opposites agrees with one of the second, as do *virtue* and *good*, – for it is well known that *virtue* is *good* – the remaining two – *evil* and *vice* – will do the same, for *vice* is *evil*.

Once this logical rule is understood, take the two opposites, *joy* and *sadness*; then the two, *white* and *black*, for these are physical opposites; so, therefore, if *black* stands for *grief*, *white* will rightfully stand for *joy*.

Nor is this significance based on a mere human interpretation. It is accepted by that common consent which philosophers call *jus gentium*, universal law, valid in all countries.

As you well know, all people, all nations, and tongues – I except the ancient Syracusans and some Argives who had perverse natures – when wishing to make external display of their grief, wear black clothes, and all mourning is expressed by black. Now this universal agreement would not obtain if Nature did not give some argument and reason for it, which everyone can at once understand for himself without further instruction from anybody – and this we call the Law of Nature. By white, according to this same natural induction, therefore, all the world has understood joy, gladness, solace, pleasure, and delight. In times past the Thracians and Cretans marked days of joy and good fortune with white stones, sad and unfortunate days with black. Is not night mournful, sad, and melancholy? It is black and dark through privation. Does not light make all Nature glad? It is whiter than anything which exists. As proof of which I could refer you to the book of Laurentius Valla against Bartolus. But evidence from the Gospels will satisfy you. In *Matthew xvii* it is said that at the Transfiguration of Our Lord *vestimenta ejus facta sunt alba sicut lux* – and his raiment was white as the light – by which luminous whiteness he conveyed to his three apostles the idea and image of the joys eternal. For all men are gladdened by the light, for which fact you have the word of an old woman who had not a tooth in her head but still said, *Bona lux* – Bless the light. And Tobit – in chapter v – when he had lost his sight said in answer to Raphael's salutation: 'What joy can I have who see not the light of heaven?' With the same colour the angels testified to the joy of the whole universe at Our Saviour's Resurrection (*John xx*), and at his Ascension (*Acts i*). And in such raiment did St John the Evangelist (*Apocal. iv and vii*) see the faithful clad in the heavenly and beatified Jerusalem.

Read the ancient histories, Greek and Roman alike. You will find that the town of Alba (the first pattern of Rome) owed its foundation and its name to the discovery of a white sow. You will find that if any man, after scoring a victory over the enemy, was permitted by decree to enter Rome in triumphal state, he did so on a chariot drawn by white horses; and so did he who received an ovation; for by no sign or colour could they more surely express the joy of their coming than by white. You will find that Pericles, Leader of the Athenians, ordered that those of his men-at-arms to whose lot the white beans fell should spend the whole day in joy, solace, and repose, while the rest fought. I could quote you a thousand other examples and references to this effect, but this is not the place.

However, by the use of this information you can solve a problem which Alexander of Aphrodisias considered insoluble: 'Why the lion who frightens all animals by his mere roar and noise, fears and respects only the white cock'. For, as Proclus says, in his book on Sacrifice and Magic, it is because the presence of the power of the sun, which is the organ and storehouse of all terrestrial and sidereal light, is better symbolized and represented by a white cock, as much on account of the creature's colour as for his properties and specific quality, than by the lion. He says further that devils have often been seen in the shape of a lion, and in the presence of a white cock have suddenly disappeared.

That is the reason why the *Galli* (that is the French, who are so called because naturally they are white as milk, which the Greeks call ΓΑΛΑ) like to wear white feathers in their caps. For by Nature they are joyful, frank, gracious, and kindly, and have for their sign and symbol the flower that is whiter than any other: the lily, that is.

If you ask why Nature intends the colour white to stand for joy and gladness, I reply that the analogy and conformity is like this: As externally white distracts and dazzles the sight, manifestly dissolving the visual spirits, according to the opinion of Aristotle in his *Problems* and to writers upon Optics (and you will find the same by experience when you cross snow-covered mountains, and complain that you cannot look steadily at them, as Xenophon reports happened to his men, and as Galen explains at length, in his 10th Book *On the Parts of the Body and their Functions*),—so internally the heart is dazzled by exceeding joy and suffers a manifest dissolution of the vital spirits, which can be so heightened that it is deprived of its nourishment, and consequently life is extinguished by this excess of joy, as Galen says, in his 12th Book *On Practise*, in his 5th Book *On the Seats of Illness*, and his 2nd *On Symptoms and their Causes*; and that this happened in former times is testified by Marcus Tullius, *lib. i Quaestio. Tuscul.*, by Verrius, Aristotle, Titus Livius – after the battle of Cannae – by Pliny, *lib. vii. c. xxxii* and *liii*, by A. Gellius, *lib. iii, xv*, and others, by Diagoras of Rhodes, Chilo, Sophocles, Dionysius, tyrant of Sicily, by Philippides, Philemon, Polycrata, Philistion, Marcus Juventius, and others who died of joy; or, as Avicenna says (*in ii canone et lib. De Viribus cordis*) of saffron, which so rejoices the heart that it robs it of life if too great a dose is taken, through excessive dilation and dissolution. On this point see Alexander of Aphrodisias, *lib. primo Problematum, c. xix*, which concludes the case.

But come! I am going further into this subject than I intended at the beginning. So here I will pull down my sails, consigning the rest to the book which is to be entirely devoted to it, and will briefly say that of course blue signifies heaven and heavenly things, by the same symbolism that makes white stand for joy and pleasure.

CHAPTER 11: *Concerning Gargantua's Childhood*

FROM his third to his fifth year Gargantua was brought up and disciplined in all necessary ways, such being his father's orders; and he spent that time in the same manner as the other little children of that country: that is to say in drinking, eating, and sleeping; in eating, sleeping, and drinking; in sleeping, drinking, and eating.

He was always rolling in the mud, dirtying his nose, scratching his face, and treading down his shoes; and often he gaped after flies, or ran joyfully after the butterflies of whom his father was the ruler. He pissed in his shoes, shat in his shirt, wiped his nose on his sleeve, snivelled into his soup, paddled about everywhere, drank out of his slipper, and usually rubbed his belly on a basket. He sharpened his teeth on a shoe, washed his hands in soup, combed his hair with a wine-bowl, sat between two stools with his arse on the ground, covered himself with a wet sack, drank while eating his soup, ate his biscuit without bread, bit as he laughed and laughed as he bit, often spat in the dish, blew a fat fart, pissed against the sun, ducked under water to avoid the rain, struck the iron while it was cold, had empty thoughts, put on airs, threw up his food or, as they said, flayed the fox, mumbled his prayers like a monkey, returned to his muttons, and turned the sows out to hay. He would beat the dog in front of the lion, put the cart before the oxen, scratch where he did not itch, draw the worms from his nose, grip so hard that he caught nothing, eat his white bread first, shoe the grasshoppers, and tickle himself to make himself laugh. He was a good guzzler in the kitchen, offered the gods straw for grain, sang *Magnificat* at matins and thought this the right time, ate cabbages and shat beet, could find the flies in his milk and pulled the legs off them, scrawled on paper, blotted parchment, got away by his heels, played ducks and drakes with his purse, reckoned without his host, beat the bushes and missed the birds, and took the clouds for brass frying-pans and bladders for lanterns. He would draw two loads from one sack, play the donkey to get the bran, use his fist for a mallet, take cranes at the first leap, think a coat of mail was made link by link, always look a gift horse in the mouth, ramble from cock to bull, put one ripe fruit between two green, make the best of a bad job, protect the moon from the wolves, hope to catch larks if the heavens fell, take a slice of whatever bread he was offered, care as little for the bald as for the shaven, and flay the fox every morning. His father's little dogs ate out of his dish, and he ate with them. He bit their ears and they scratched his nose; he blew at their rumps and they licked his lips.

And d'you know what, my boys? May the drink fly to your heads! That little lecher was always feeling his governesses, upside down, back-to-front, and get along with you there! And he was already beginning to exercise his codpiece, which his governesses decorated every day with fine garlands, lovely ribbons, pretty flowers, and gay silken tufts. And they amused themselves by rubbing it between their hands like a roll of pastry, and then burst out laughing when it raised its ears, as if the game pleased them. One of them called it my pilli-cock, another my ninepin, another my coral-branch, another my stopper, my cork, my quiverer, my driving-pin, my auger, my dingle-dangle, my rough-go stiff-and-low, my crimping iron, my little red sausage, my sweet little cocky.

'It's mine,' one would say.

'It belongs to me,' said another.

'What about me?' cried a third. 'Don't I get a share in it? Gracious me, I shall cut it off, then.'

'What,' said another. 'Cut it off. Why, that would hurt him, Madam. Is it your way to cut off children's *things*? Why, then he'd be Master Short.'

And so that he should amuse himself like the small children of the country, they made him a pretty weathercock from the sails of a Mirebalais windmill.

CHAPTER 12: *Concerning Gargantua's Hobby-horses*

THEN, so that he should be a good rider all his life, he was given a fine great wooden horse, which he made to prance, leap, curvet, plunge, and rear at the same time, to pace, trot, canter, gallop, amble, go like a nag, a trotter, a camel, or a wild ass. He made it change its colour, as monks do their tunics according to the Saints'-days; bay, sorrel, dapple-grey, mouse-dun, deer-coloured, roan, cow-coloured, zebra, skewbald, piebald, white.

He himself made a hunter out of a large log, and another for every day out of the beam of a winepress; and he turned a great oak into a mule with trappings for his room. What is more, he had ten or twelve more for relays and seven for the post. And he put them all to sleep near him.

One day the Lord of Bread-in-bag came to visit his father with great pomp and retinue; and on the same day came the Duke of Free-meal and the Earl of Wetwind. In fact accommodation was rather short for so many people, the stables especially. So, to discover if there were any empty stables elsewhere in the house, the steward and outrider of the Lord of Bread-in-bag applied to Gargantua, then a youngster, asking him privately where the war horses were kept. For they thought that children readily give every secret away.

Whereupon he led them up the great staircase of the castle, passing through the second hall into a large gallery, from which they entered into a great tower; and as they were going up yet another stairway, the outrider said to the steward: 'This child is fooling us. The stables are never at the top of the house.'

'You're mistaken there,' said the steward. 'For I know places, at Lyons, at La Basmette, at Chinon, and elsewhere, where the stables are at the very tops of the houses. It may be that at the back there's a way out on to the hillside. But I'll ask him more exactly.'

Then he inquired of Gargantua: 'Where are you taking us to, my little man?'

'To my great horses' stable,' he answered. 'We are almost there. We have only these stairs to climb.'

And, conducting them through another great hall, he led them to his room, saying as he opened the door: 'Here are the stables you're asking for. There's my gennet. There's my gelding, my coarser, and my hackney.'

Then he loaded them with a great lever and said: 'I make you a present of this Friesland. I had him from Frankfort, but he shall be yours. He is a pretty little horse, and a great stayer. With a tassel goshawk, half a dozen spaniels, and a brace of greyhounds, you'll be king of the hares and partridges for all this winter.'

'By St John,' they cried. 'We've been nicely taken in. He's wished the monk on us this time.'[1]

'No, that's not true,' said Gargantua. 'The monk hasn't been here for three days.'

Now how do you think they should have taken that? Should they have hung their heads for shame or laughed at the joke?

As they were just coming down again, thoroughly abashed, he asked: 'Would you like an Obbly-oy?'

'What's that?' they asked.

'Oh, that's five turds to make yourself a muzzle.'

'From now on,' said the steward, 'if ever we are hung on the spit the fire won't burn us. For in my opinion we've been done to a turn. Ha, my little fellow, you've tied straw in our hair all right. I shall see you made Pope one of these days.'

'That's what I think,' answered Gargantua. 'But then you'll be a popsy-wopsy, and this gentle popinjay will be a ready made popelin.'

'That's true,' said the outrider.

'But guess how many stitches there are in my mother's smock,' said Gargantua.

'Sixteen,' guessed the outrider.

'That's not Gospel,' said Gargantua. 'For there's a scent in front and a scent behind. And cent and cent – you added up wrong.'

'When?' asked the outrider.

'Then,' said Gargantua, 'when they made your nose into a tap to draw off a measure of dung, and your throat into a funnel to pour it into another vessel, because the bottom of that one was out.'

'Bless my soul!' exclaimed the steward, 'we've struck a talker. God keep you from harm, my chatty fellow, for you've got a ready tongue.'

Then as they were hurrying down beneath the arch of the stairs,

1. He has tricked us.

they dropped the great lever that he had loaded them with. Where-upon Gargantua said:

'You're devilish bad riders. Your cob's let you down when you needed him. If you had to go from here to Cahusac, which would you rather, ride on a goose or lead a sow in a leash?'

'I'd rather drink,' said the outrider.

As he said this they entered the lower hall where all the company was; and when they told them this brand-new story, it made them laugh like a swarm of flies.

CHAPTER 13: *How Grandgousier realized Gargantua's mar-vellous intelligence, by his invention of an Arse-wipe*

ABOUT the end of Gargantua's fifth year, Grandgousier visited his son, on the way back from his victory over the Canarians, and he was filled with joy, as such a father would be at the sight of such a child. Whilst he kissed and embraced him he asked the boy various childish questions of one kind and another, and he drank quite a bit too, with him and his governesses, of whom he most earnestly inquired whether they had kept him sweet and clean. To this Gargantua answered that he had taken these precautions himself, and that there was not a cleaner boy in all the land.

'How did you do that?' asked Grandgousier.

'By long and curious experiments,' replied Gargantua. 'I have in-vented a method of wiping my arse which is the most lordly, the most excellent, and the most convenient that ever was seen.'

'What's that?' asked Grandgousier.

'I shall tell you in a moment,' said Gargantua.

'Once I wiped myself on a lady's velvet mask, and I found it good. For the softness of the silk was most voluptuous to my fundament. Another time on one of their hoods, and I found it just as good. An-other time on a lady's neckerchief; another time on some ear-flaps of crimson satin. But there were a lot of turdy gilt spangles on them, and they took all the skin off my bottom. May St Anthony's fire burn the bum-gut of the goldsmith who made them and of the lady who wore them! That trouble passed when I wiped myself on a page's bonnet, all feathered in the Swiss fashion.

'Then, as I was shitting behind a bush, I found a March-born cat; I wiped myself on him, but his claws exulcerated my whole perineum. I healed myself of that next day by wiping myself on my mother's gloves, which were well scented with *maljamin*.[1] Then I wiped myself with sage, fennel, anise, marjoram, roses, gourd leaves, cabbage, beets, vineshoots, marsh-mallow, mullein – which is red as your bum – lettuces, and spinach-leaves. All this did very great good to my legs. Then with dog's mercury, persicaria, nettles, and comfrey. But that gave me the bloody-flux of Lombardy, from which I was cured by wiping myself with my codpiece.

'Then I wiped myself on the sheets, the coverlet, the curtains, with a cushion, with the hangings, with a green cloth, with a table-cloth, with a napkin, with a handkerchief, with an overall. And I found more pleasure in all those than mangy dogs do when they are combed.'

'Yes,' said Grandgousier. 'But which wiper did you find the best?'

'I was coming to that,' said Gargantua. 'You shall soon hear the whole story. I wiped myself with hay, with straw, with litter, with cow's hair, with wool, with paper. But

> Who his foul bum with paper wipes
> Will on his ballocks leave some chips.'

'What, my little rascal,' said Grandgousier, 'have you been at the pot, are you trying to rhyme already?'

'Oh yes, my lord king,' replied Gargantua. 'I can rhyme that much and more, and when I rhyme I often catch the rheum. Listen to what our privy says to the shitters:

> Shittard,
> Squittard,
> Crackard,
> Turdous,
> Thy bung
> Has flung
> Some dung
> On us.
> Filthard,
> Cackard,
> Stinkard,

---

1. The opposite of benjamin, or benzoin; an Arabian gum.

> May you burn with St Anthony's fire
>> If all
>> Your foul
>> Arseholes
> Are not well wiped ere you retire.'

'Would you like any more of this?'

'Yes, indeed,' replied Grandgousier.

'Well, then,' said Gargantua:

RONDEAU

> Yesterday, shitting, I did know
> The profit to my arse I owe;
> Such was the smell that from it slunk
> That I was with it all bestunk.
> Oh, had but then someone consented
> To bring me her for whom I waited,
>> Whilst shitting!
> I would have closed her water-pipe
> In my rough way and bunged it up,
> While she had with her fingers guarded
> My jolly arsehole all bemerded
>> With shitting.

'Now tell me I'm not clever! God's bum, I didn't invent a line of it. I heard that fine lady over there reciting it and I kept it in the bag of my memory.'

'Let us return to our subject,' said Grandgousier.

'What,' said Gargantua. 'Shitting?'

'No,' answered Grandgousier. 'Arse-wiping.'

'But,' said Gargantua, 'will you pay me a puncheon of Breton wine if I catch you out on the subject?'

'Yes, I will,' said Grandgousier.

'There's no need to wipe your bottom unless it's mucky,' said Gargantua, 'it can't be mucky if you haven't shat; we have to shit, therefore, before we wipe our arses.'

'Oh,' said Grandgousier, 'what a good head you've got, my little fellow! One day very soon I'll get you made a Doctor of Gay Learning, by God, I will. For you have more sense than your years. Now please go on with this arse-wiping talk of yours and, by my beard, instead of a puncheon you shall have six casks. I know something about this good Breton wine, which doesn't grow in Britanny at all, but in the fine land of Veron.'

'After that,' said Gargantua, 'I wiped myself with a kerchief, with a pillow, with a slipper, with a game-bag, with a basket – but what an unpleasant arse-wiper that was! – then with a hat. And note that some hats are smooth, some shaggy, some velvety, some of taffeta, and some of satin. The best of all are the shaggy ones, for they make a very good abstersion of the faecal matter. Then I wiped myself with a hen, a cock, and a chicken, with a calf's skin, a hare, a pigeon, and a cormorant, with a lawyer's bag, with a penitent's hood, with a coif, with an otter. But to conclude, I say and maintain that there is no arse-wiper like a well-downed goose, if you hold her neck between your legs. You must take my word for it, you really must. You get a miraculous sensation in your arse-hole, both from the softness of the down and from the temperate heat of the goose herself; and this is easily communicated to the bum-gut and the rest of the intestines, from which it reaches the heart and the brain. Do not imagine that the felicity of the heroes and demigods in the Elysian Fields arises from their asphodel, their ambrosia, or their nectar, as those ancients say. It comes, in my opinion, from their wiping their arses with the neck of a goose, and that is the opinion of Master Duns Scotus too.'

CHAPTER 14: *How Gargantua was taught Latin by a Sophist*

THIS discourse concluded, that good man Grandgousier was beside himself with admiration, as he considered the fine sense and marvellous understanding of his son Gargantua. And he said to the governesses: 'Philip, king of Macedon, recognized the intelligence of his son Alexander by his skill in managing a horse. This horse was so fierce and unruly that no one dared mount him, since he threw all his riders, breaking one man's neck, another's legs, another's skull, and another's jawbone. When Alexander considered this problem in the hippodrome (which was the place where horses were exercised and trained), he observed that the horse's wildness was caused only by his fear of his own shadow and, climbing on him, forced him to gallop into the sun, so that his shadow fell behind him, in this way making the beast amenable to his will. By this the father realized the boy's divine intelligence, and afterwards had him very well taught by Aristotle, who at that time was the most highly esteemed philosopher in Greece.

'And let me tell you that from this single discussion which I have just held before you with my son Gargantua, I recognize that his understanding springs from some divine source, so acute, subtle, profound, and assured do I find him in his answers. He will certainly attain a sovereign degree of wisdom if he is well taught. Therefore I wish to entrust him to some learned man who will instruct him according to his capacities, and to this end I will spare no cost.'

Accordingly they appointed as his tutor a great doctor and sophist named Thubal Holofernes, who taught him his letters so well that he said them by heart backwards; and he took five years and three months to do that. Then the sophist read to him Donatus, Facetus, Theodolus, and Alanus *in Parabolis*,[1] which took thirteen years six months and a fortnight. But note that during all this time he was teaching Gargantua to write the Gothic script, and that he copied all these books out himself, for the art of printing was not yet practised. Also he generally carried a huge writing-desk weighing more than seven thousand hundredweight, the pencil-case of which was as big and stout as the great pillars of Ainay, while the ink-horn hung from it on great iron chains, capable of carrying a ton of merchandise.

After this the sophist read him *De modis significandi*,[2] with the commentaries of Bang-breeze, Scallywag, Claptrap, Gualehaul, John the Calf, Copper-coin, Flowery-tongue, and a number of others; and this took him more than ten years and eleven months. And Gargantua knew the book so well that at testing time he repeated it backwards by heart, proving to his mother on his fingers that *de modis significandi non erat scientia*.[3]

The sophist read him the *Compostum*, on which he spent sixteen years and two months, at which point his said preceptor died. In the year fourteen twenty he caught the pox.

After that he had another old wheezer named Master Jobekin Bridé, who read him Hugutio, Hebrard's *Grecismus*, the *Doctrinal*, the *Parts of Speech*, the *Quid est*, the *Supplementum*, Mumble *on the Psalms*, *De moribus in mensa servandis*, Seneca *De quatuor virtutibus cardinalibus*,

1. These were the stock medieval text-books.
2. The stock grammar.   3. Grammar was no science.

Passavantus, *cum commento*, *Dormi secure* for festivals, and several more works of the same dough; by the reading of which he became as wise as any man baked in an oven.

CHAPTER 15: *How Gargantua was put under other Pedagogues*

MEANWHILE his father observed that although he was really study-ing very well, and spent all his time at his lessons, he was making no progress at all. What was worse, he was becoming quite sawny and simple, all dreamy and doltish.

When Grandgousier complained of this to Don Philippe des Marays, Viceroy of Papeligosse, that gentleman answered that it was better for the boy to learn nothing than to study such books under such masters. For their learning was mere stupidity, and their wisdom like an empty glove; it bastardized good and noble minds and cor-rupted all the flower of youth.

'To prove this,' said Don Philippe, 'take any young person of the present day, who has studied only two years; and if he has not a better judgement, a better command of words, better powers of speech, bet-ter manners, and greater ease in company than your son, account me for ever a boaster from La Brenne.' This proposal greatly pleased Grandgousier, and he ordered it to be carried out.

That evening Des Marays brought in to supper a young page of his from Villegongis, called Eudemon, so well curled, so well dressed, so well brushed, and so courtly in his behaviour, that he was more like some little angel than a human being. Then said Des Marays to Grand gousier: 'Do you see this young lad? He is not twelve yet. Now, if you will, let us see what difference there is between the knowledge of your old-time nonsensological babblers and the young people of to-day.'

The idea pleased Grandgousier, and he commanded the page to state a proposition. Then, after demanding permission of the said Viceroy, his master, with his cap in his hand, with an open counten-ance and ruddy lips, and with assurance in his eyes and his gaze fixed in youthful modesty on Gargantua, Eudemon rose to his feet and be-gan to praise and extol him, first for his virtues and fine manners, secondly for his learning, thirdly for his nobility, fourthly for his physical beauty, and in the fifth place charmingly exhorted him to show his father every reverent attention for being at such pains to have him well taught. Lastly he begged Gargantua in his kindness to engage him as the least of his servants. For he desired no other gift from heaven at that present time save that he should have the good fortune to please Gargantua by doing him some welcome service. This speech was delivered by him with such fitting gestures, with such a clear enunciation, and so eloquent a voice, in such ornate language and such good Latin, that he seemed more like a Gracchus, a Cicero, or an Emilius of the olden times than a youth of this age. But Gargantua could keep no better countenance than to burst out bellowing like a cow. He hid his face in his cap, and it was no more possible to draw a word from him than a fart from a dead donkey.

At this his father was so infuriated that he wanted to slay Master Jobelin. But the said Des Marays prevented his doing so by eloquent persuasions, with which he plied him to such effect that his wrath abated. Then Grandgousier ordered that the sophist should be paid his wages, and that he should be made to throw back a pot or two in fine sophistical manner; after which he could go to the devil. 'At least for to-day,' he said, 'he will be no great expense to his host if he does happen to die as drunk as an Englishman.'

When Master Jobelin had left the house, Grandgousier consulted with the Viceroy as to what master they should choose for the lad. They decided between them that the post should be given to Pono-crates, Eudemon's tutor, and that they should all go to Paris together to learn what the young men of France were studying at that time.

CHAPTER 16: *How Gargantua was sent to Paris, of the huge Mare that carried him, and how she destroyed the Ox-flies of La Beauce*

AT this same season Fayoles, fourth king of Numidia, sent to Grand-gousier from the land of Africa the greatest and most enormous mare that ever was seen; and she was the most monstrous too, since you know very well that Africa is always producing some new mon-strosity. She was as big as six elephants, she had her hoofs divided into toes, like Julius Caesar's horse, and pendent ears, like the goats of

Languedoc, and a little horn on her rump. For the rest, her coat was of a burnt sorrel with dapple-grey spots and, what is more, she had the most fearsome tail. For it was as large, more or less, as the pillar of Saint Mars, near Langès, and as square; and its tufts were as spiky, in every respect, as blades of wheat.

If this description astounds you, you will be even more astounded by what I tell you about the tail of the Scythian ram, which weighed more than thirty pounds, or about that of the Syrian sheep, to whose rump (if Thenaud speaks true) they have to fix a little cart to carry it, it is so long and heavy. You clods from the flat lands possess nothing to compare with that. This mare was brought by sea in three caracks and a brigantine, to the port of Olonne in the Talmont country; and when Grandgousier saw her he said: 'Here is just the beast to carry my son to Paris. Now I swear to God, all will go well. He will be a great scholar in times to come. If it weren't for the beasts we should all live like scholars.'[1]

The next day – after drinking, as you will understand – they started on their way, Gargantua, his tutor Ponocrates, and his servants, together with the young page Eudemon; and as the weather was calm and temperate Grandgousier had dun-coloured boots made for his son; Babin calls them buskins.

So they passed joyfully along the highway, always in high spirits, till they came above Orléans, at which place there was a great forest a hundred and five miles long and fifty-one miles wide, or thereabouts. This forest was horribly abundant and copiously swarming with ox-flies and hornets, so that it was an absolute brigands' lair for the poor mares, asses, and horses. But Gargantua's mare handsomely avenged all the outrages ever perpetrated there on the beasts of her kind, by a trick of which they had not the slightest inkling beforehand. As soon as they had entered this forest and the hornets had opened their attack she threw out her tail, and at her first skirmish swatted them so completely that she swept down the whole wood. Crossways and lengthways, here and there, this way and that, to front and to side, over and under, she swept down the trees as a mower does the grass, so that since that time there has been neither wood nor hornets, and the whole country has been reduced to a plain.

At the sight of this Gargantua felt very great delight. But the only

1. This is a well-known saying in reverse.

boast he made was to say to his people: 'I find this fine'. (*Je trouve beau ce*); from which saying the country has ever afterwards been called La Beauce. But all they got for breakfast was empty air; in memory of which to this day the gentlemen of La Beauce break their fast on yawns, do very well by it, and spit the better for it.

At last they arrived in Paris, in which town Gargantua refreshed himself for two or three days, making merry with his people, and inquiring what learned men there were in the place just then, also what wine was drunk there.

CHAPTER 17: *How Gargantua repaid the Parisians for their welcome, and how he took the great Bells from the church of Notre-Dame*

SOME days after they had finished their refreshment, Gargantua went to see the sights of the town, and everyone stared at him in great wonder. For the Parisians are such simpletons, such gapers, and such feckless idiots that a buffoon, a pedlar of indulgences, a mule with bells on its collar, or a fiddler at a crossroad will draw a greater crowd than a good preacher of the Gospel.

The people so pestered him, in fact, that he was compelled to take a rest on the towers of Notre-Dame; and when from there he saw so many, pressing all around him, he said in a clear voice:

'I think these clodhoppers want me to pay for my kind reception and offer them a *solatium*. They are quite justified, and I am going to give them some wine, to buy my welcome. But only in sport, *par ris*.'

Then, with a smile, he undid his magnificent codpiece and, bringing out his john-thomas, pissed on them so fiercely that he drowned two hundred and sixty thousand, four hundred and eighteen persons, not counting the women and small children.

A number of them, however, were quick enough on their feet to escape this piss-flood; and when they reached the top of the hill above the University, sweating, coughing, spitting, and out of breath, they began to swear and curse, some in a fury and others in sport (*par ris*). 'Carymary, Carymara! [1] My holy tart, we've been drenched in sport! We've been drenched *par ris*.'

1. A cabalistic spell.

Hence it was that the city was ever afterwards called Paris. Formerly it had been named *Leucetia*, as Strabo tells us in his fourth book; which in Greek signifies *white place*. This was on account of the white thighs of the ladies of that city. And since at this re-christening all the spectators swore, each by the saints of his own parish, the Parisians, who are made up of all nations and all sorts, have proved by nature both good swearers and good men of law, also somewhat overbearing. For which reason Joaninus de Baranco in *libro de copiositate reverentiarum*,[1] considers that they derive their name of Parrhesians from the Greek, in which language the word signifies bold of speech.

After this exploit Gargantua examined the great bells that hung in those towers, and played a harmonious peal on them. As he did so it struck him that they would serve very well for cow-bells to hang on the collar of his mare, which he had decided to send back to his father, loaded with Brie cheese and fresh herrings. So he took them straight off to his lodgings.

There passed in the meantime a Master-mendicant of the Order of St Anthony, on his begging quest for pig-meat; and he tried to sneak the bells, so that in future he might be heard from afar off, and the very hams tremble in the salting-pans. But he left them out of sheer honesty, not because they were too hot, but because they were a little too heavy for him to carry. This was not the Master at Bourg, who is too good a friend of mine for that.

The whole population was in an uproar, a state of things to which, as you know, Parisians are so prone that foreigners marvel at the patience of France's kings in not suppressing them, as in strict justice they might, considering the troubles that daily arise from their turbulence. I wish to God I knew the den in which these factions and plots are concocted, and I would report them to the guilds of my parish! You may be sure that the place where the people assembled, all befooled and alarmed, was the Hôtel de Nesle, at that time the seat of Lutetia's oracle, which it is no longer; and before that court the case of the stolen bells was pleaded, and the inconvenience of their loss deplored.

After a thorough argument *pro et contra*, it was decided by a simple syllogism that the oldest and most authoritative member of the faculty

1. Book on the multitude of Oaths.

should be sent to Gargantua to point out to him the terrible inconvenience caused by the loss of those bells; and despite the objections of
certain faculty members who claimed that this task could more fitly be
performed by an orator than by a sophist, our Master, Janotus de
Bragmardo, was chosen to carry it out.

CHAPTER 18: *How Janotus de Bragmardo was sent to recover the
great Bells from Gargantua*

WITH his hair cropped like a Caesar, and his doctor's hood swathed
round him like a toga, having first protected his stomach with bakehouse victuals, and holy water from the cellar, Master Janotus pro-
ceeded to Gargantua's lodging, driving three red-nosed calves or
beadles before him, and dragging five or six artless Masters of Art behind him, thoroughly bedraggled with mud.

At the door they were received by Ponocrates, who was terrified by
their strange clothes and who, thinking that they were some crazy
mummers, asked one of the artless Masters in the company what this
mummery meant. The reply he received was that they wanted the
bells restored to them.

As soon as he heard this, Ponocrates ran to tell Gargantua the news,
so that his pupil should have an answer ready for them and decide
immediately on a plan. On learning what had happened, Gargantua
called aside his tutor Ponocrates, his steward Philotomie, his squire
Gymnaste, and Eudemon, and held a summary conference with them
on the subject of what to say and what to do. They were all of the
opinion that the deputation should be taken to the buttery and there
made to drink like fish. And for fear that the old wheezer might prove
vainglorious if the bells were restored at his request, whilst he was
tippling they sent for the City Provost, the Rector of the Faculty, and
the Vicar of the Church to whom they had decided to deliver up the
bells before the sophist expounded his commission. After this they
would listen to his harangue in the company of those dignitaries. And
so it was. Shortly after their arrival the sophist was shown into the hall,
where they were assembled, and with a wheezing cough began the
following address:

CHAPTER 19: *The Harangue delivered by Master Janotus de Bragmardo to Gargantua for the recovery of the Bells*

'AHEM, hm, hm! G'day, sir, and g'day to *vobis*, gentleman. It would only be right if you were to give us back our bells, for we are greatly in need of them. H'm, h'm, hasch! Often in the past we have refused good money for them from the people of London in Cahors, and also from the people of Bordeaux in Brie, who wanted to buy them for the substantific quality of the elementary complexion which is inherent in the terrestriality of their quidditive nature, in order to extraneize the hailstorms and whirlwinds from our vines – not really from ours, though, but from some close by. For if we lose our drink we lose everything, rights and dues.

'If you restore them to us at my request, I shall gain six strings of sausages and a good pair of breeches, which will do my legs a great deal of good, or I shall be much deceived. Ho, by God, *Domine*, a pair of breeches is a good thing, *et vir sapiens non abhorrebit eam.*[1] Ha, ha, not everyone has a pair of breeches who wants one; I know that well from my own case. Consider, *Domine*; I have been eighteen days matagrabolizing this fine harangue; *Reddite quae sunt Caesaris Caesari, et quae sunt Dei Deo. Ibi jacet lepus.*[2]

'By my faith, *Domine*, if you want to sup with me, *in camera*, ods body, *charitatis, nos faciemus bonum cherubin. Ego occidi unum porcum, et ego habet bon vino.*[3] And from good wine you cannot make bad Latin.

'Well now, *de parte Dei, date nobis clochas nostras.*[4] Wait, in the name of the Faculty I'll give you a *Sermones de Utino*, so that, *utinam* you shall give us our bells. *Vultis etiam pardonos? Per diem, vos habebitis et nihil payabitis.*[5]

'Oh, sir *Domine, clochidonnaminor nobis!* indeed, *est bonum urbis.*[6] Everybody uses them. If they suit your mare they also suit our faculty, *qae comparata est jumentis insipientibus et similis facta est eis, psalmo nescio*

1. And a wise man will not dislike them.
2. Render unto Caesar the things that are Caesar's and unto God the things that are God's. That's the point.
3. In the reception hall we will make good cheer-ubim. I have killed a pig and I has good wino.
4. In God's name, give us back our bells.
5. Will you buy pardons? 'Struth, you shall have them and pay nothing.
6. They are the property of the city.

quo.[1] And yet I'd got the proper quotation in my notebook, *et est unum bonum Achilles*.[2] Hm, hm, ahem, hasch!

'See now, I prove to you that you ought to give them to me. *Ego sic argumentor :*[3]

'*Omnis clocha clochabilis, in clocherio clochando clochans clochative clochare facit clochabiliter clochantes. Parisius habet clochas. Ergo gluc.*[4]

'Ha, ha, that's well put, that is! It's in the third mood of the first figure of the syllogism, in *Darii* or somewhere. 'Pon my soul, I can remember a time when I could play the devil's tricks at argument, but at present my mind is just wandering, and from now on I want nothing but good wine, a good bed, my back to the fire, my belly to the table, and a good deep dish.

'Hey, *Domine*, I beg of you, *in nomine Patris et Filii et Spiritus Sancti*,[5] amen, to return us our bells, and God preserve you from sickness and Our Lady from health, *qui vivit et regnat per omnia secula seculorum*,[6] amen. Hm, hasch, ehasch, grenhenhasch!

'*Verum enim vero quando quidem, dubio procul, edepol, quoniam, ita certe, meus deus fidus*,[7] a city without bells is like a blind man without a stick, an ass without a crupper, and a cow without a cow-bell. Until you restore them to us we shall not cease to cry out after you like a blind man who has lost his stick, to bray after you like an ass without a crupper, to low after you like a cow without its cow-bell.

A certain Latinizing person living near the Hospital once said, citing the authority of a certain Taponus – no, I'm wrong. It was Pontanus, a secular poet – that he wished they were made of feathers and that the clapper was a fox's tail, because they engendered the colic in the bowels of his brains when he was composing his carminiform lines. But, ding-dong, bing-bang, clitter-clatter, he was declared a heretic; we make them quick as lightning. And the statement says no more. *Valete et plaudite. Calepinus recensui.*[8]

1. Which is like the beasts that perish. From what psalm it comes I don't know. (It is from Psalm 49.)
2. That is an unanswerable argument.   3. This is how I argue.
4. A gibberish of mock Latin on the subject of the bells, ending with a formal conclusion.   5. In the name of the Father, the Son, and the Holy Ghost.
6. Who lives and reigns, world without end.
7. An odd collection of tags.
8. Three alternate conclusions: the first legal, the second (Farewell and applaud) from Latin comedy, and the third, that of a copyist at the end of a manuscript.

CHAPTER 20: *How the Sophist carried off his Cloth, and how he fought a Lawsuit against the other Masters*

No sooner had the sophist concluded than Ponocrates and Eudemon burst out laughing so heartily that they very nearly gave up the ghost, exactly like Crassus when he saw a jackass eating thistles, and like Philemon, who died of laughing when he saw an ass eating some figs which had been prepared for his own dinner. Then Master Janotus began to laugh with them, and they laughed one against another till the tears came into their eyes from the violent concussion of the brain-substance, from which were expressed those lachrymal humidities which flowed down along the optic nerve. In this they represented Democritus heraclitizing and Heraclitus democratizing.

When their laughter had quite died down, Gargantua consulted with his people as to what was to be done. Ponocrates' opinion of the matter was that they should make this fine orator drink again, and that, since he had so amused them and made them laugh more than ever the actor Songecreux did, he should be given the ten strings of sausages mentioned in his jolly harangue, together with a pair of breeches, three hundred half-cords of firewood, twenty-five hogs-heads of wine, a bed with a triple mattress of goose-down, and a very capacious, deep dish; which he had said were necessary for his old age.

All this was done according to plan, except that Gargantua, doubt-ing whether they could immediately find breeches to suit his legs; doubting also what fashion would be most comfortable for the orator — whether the Martingale, which is in the form of a drawbridge at the backside for greater ease in shitting; or the Mariner's, for the better gratification of the kidneys; or the Swiss, to keep the lower belly warm; or the cod's tail, to avoid overheating the loins – had him given ten and a half yards of black cloth, and four of white for the lining. The wood was carried by the porters; the Masters of Arts carried the sausages and dishes; and Master Janotus himself decided to carry the cloth.

But one of the said masters, Master Jousse Bandouille by name, pointed out to him that this was neither seemly nor suitable to his degree, and that he ought to hand it to someone else.

'Ha,' said Janotus. 'Blockhead, blockhead; you're not concluding *in modo et figura.* That shows how much the suppositions and the *parva logicalia* are worth. *Pannus pro quo supponit?*'

'*Confuse,*' said Bandouille, '*et distributive.*'

'I am not asking you, blockhead,' said Janotus, '*quo modo supponit,* but *pro quo,* that is, blockhead, *pro tibiis meis.* And that is what I shall wear it for, *egomet, sicut suppositum portat adpositum.*' [1]

So he carried it off stealthily, as Patelin did his cloth. But the joke of it was when the old wheezer, before a full assembly held at the Mathurins, confidently demanded his breeches and sausages. For they were peremptorily refused him, on the score that he had already received them from Gargantua, according to their information on the subject. He pointed out that this had been a free gift on Gargantua's part, given out of sheer liberality, and that they were not thereby released from their promises. Notwithstanding this, he received the answer that he ought in reason to be contented, and that he would not receive a scrap more.

'Reason!' exclaimed Janotus; 'we use none of that here. You wretched, worthless traitors, there isn't a more depraved bunch than you on the whole face of the earth, as well I know. Don't try a false limp in front of a cripple; I've had a share in your villainies. God's spleen! I'll inform the king of the manifold abuses that are planned and carried out by you, with your own hands. The leprosy strike me if he doesn't have you all burnt alive as buggers, traitors, heretics and seducers, enemies of God and all virtue.'

At these words they framed a charge against him; and he, in his turn, served them a summons. In the end the case was adjourned by the court – it is before them still – and at that point the Masters made a vow not to clean off their dirt, and Master Janotus and his supporters vowed not to wipe their noses, until a definite judgement should be delivered.

True to their vows they have remained dirty and snotty to this day. For the court has not yet fully sifted all the documents; and the judgement will be given at the next Greek Kalends, that is to say never, be-

1. You are not concluding in due form, says Janotus, and catechizes Bandouille concerning the ownership of the cloth. Bandouille quibbles and supposes the question to relate to details concerning the cloth's nature, which Bandouille considers to be merely a matter of hearsay. Janotus insists that he is asking what the cloth is for, states that it is for his legs and that he is going to wear it himself, 'as the supposition carries the supplementaries'.

cause as you know, they can outdo Nature and violate their own articles. For the articles of Paris proclaim that God alone can perform actions without end, and that Nature makes nothing immortal, for she puts a term and period to all things by her produced; seeing that *omnia orta cadunt*, &c.[1] But these swallowers of the morning mist[2] make the suits pending before them both infinite and immortal; and by so doing have recalled and confirmed the saying of Chilon the Lacedaemonian, consecrated at Delphi, that misery is the companion of lawsuits, and that those who plead in them are wretched creatures, since they come to the end of their lives long before they attain the rights they lay claim to.

CHAPTER 21: *Gargantua's Studies, according to the Directions of his Tutors, the Sophists*

THE first days having been spent in this way and the bells restored to their place, the citizens of Paris, in acknowledgement of this courtesy, offered to maintain and feed Gargantua's mare for as long as he wished – an offer which he gladly accepted. So they sent her to graze in the Forest of Bière. I believe that she is no longer there.

After this Gargantua was anxious to put himself at Ponocrates' disposal in the matter of his studies. But for a beginning, his tutor ordered him to go on in his usual way, so that he might find out how it was that his former instructors had spent so long in making him so foolish, simple, and ignorant.

So Gargantua arranged his time in such a way that he generally woke between eight and nine, whether it was light or not; for these had been the orders of his former governors, who had cited the words of David: *Vanum est vobis ante lucem surgere*.[3] Then he turned and stretched and wallowed in his bed for some time, the better to rouse his animal spirits, and dressed according to the season. What he liked to wear was a great long gown of coarse frieze furred with foxskins. After this he combed his hair in the handsome fashion, that is to say with four fingers and a thumb. For his tutors said that to comb or

1. All things that rise, set.
2. Judges, who have the reputation of getting up early to catch the big fees.
3. It is vain for you to rise up early (Psalm cxxvii, Vulgate 126).

wash or clean oneself in any other way was to lose time in this world.

Then he shat, pissed, spewed, belched, farted, yawned, spat, coughed, hiccuped, sneezed, blew his nose like an archdeacon, and breakfasted, to protect himself from the dew and the bad air, on fine fried tripes, good rashers grilled on the coals, delicate hams, tasty goat stews, and plenty of early morning soup.[1]

Ponocrates protested that he ought not to eat so soon after getting out of bed without having first taken some exercise. But Gargantua replied: 'What, haven't I taken enough exercise? I rolled myself over seven or eight times before I got up. Isn't that enough? Pope Alexander adopted that habit on the advice of his Jewish physician, and lived till his dying day in despite of his enemies. My first masters have accustomed me to it. They said that breakfast is good for the memory; therefore they took their first drink then. I find that it does me a lot of good, and makes me enjoy my dinner better. Master Tubal told me – and he took first place as Licentiate in Paris – that all the advantage doesn't lie in running fast, but in starting early. So the total health of the human race consists in not gulping it down like ducks, but rather in drinking early. *Unde versus* – hence you find:

> Early to rise brings little wealth;
> But early drinking's good for the health.

After having taken a thorough breakfast, he went to church, and they carried in for him, in a great basket, a huge slippered breviary weighing, what with grease, clasps, and parchment, eleven hundred and six pounds. There he heard twenty-six or thirty Masses. In the meantime his orison-reader would arrive, muffled in his cloak like a hoopoe, and with his breath well disinfected by copious vine-syrup. With him Gargantua mumbled all the litanies, and fingered them over so carefully that not a single grain fell to the ground.

As he left church they brought him on an ox-wagon a heap of rosaries from Saint-Claude, each bead as big as a hatblock, and as he walked through the cloisters, galleries, or garden he told more of them than sixteen hermits.

Then he studied for a miserable half-hour, his eyes fixed on his book, but – as the comic poet says – his soul was in the kitchen. So,

1. The soups drunk in monasteries at the hour of Prime (6 a.m.).

after pissing a good pot-full, he next sat down to table; and, being of a phlegmatic nature, began his meal with some dozens of hams, smoked ox-tongues, botargos, sausages, and other advance-couriers of wine. Meanwhile his servants threw into his mouth, one after another, full bucketfuls of mustard, without stopping. Then he drank a monstrous gulp of white wine to relieve his kidneys; and after that ate, according to the season, meats agreeable to his appetite. He left off eating when his belly was tight.

For drinking he had neither end nor rule. For he said that the ends and limits of drinking were when the cork-sole of the drinker's shoe swelled up half a foot as he drank.

CHAPTER 22: *Gargantua's Games*

THEN, having sluggishly mumbled over some scraps of grace, Gargantua rinsed his hands in fresh wine, picked his teeth with a pig's trotter, and chatted gaily with his people. After which a green cloth was laid, and a stock of cards, of dice, and of games-boards were laid out. There he played

at Flushes	at Next Man Speak
at Primero	at Teetotum
at Grand Slam	at Marriage
at Little Slam	at Pair-royal
at Trumps	at Opinion
at Prick and Spare Not	at *Follow-my-leader*
at Hundred-up	at Sequences
at Penny-points	at Sheep and Wolves
at Old-maid	at Tarot
at Cheat	at The Loser Wins
at Ten-and-pass	at Gulls
at Thirty-one	at Torture
at Fair and Straight	at Snorer
at Three-hundred	at Hazard
at Beggar-my-neighbour	at Honours
at Odd Man Out	at Morra
at Turn the Card	at Chess
at Poor Jack	at Fox and Geese
at Lansquenet	at Squares
at Cuckold	at Pick-a-back

at Blanks
at Speculation
at Three Dice
at Tables
at Nick-nock
at Lurch
at Queen's Game
at Sbaraligno
at Backgammon
at Long Tables
at Fall-down
at S'welp me God
at Needs Must
at Draughts
at Sucks-to-you
at Primus Secundus
at Hit-the-blade
at The Keys
at Chuck-penny
at Odds or Evens
at Heads or Tails
at Pebbles
at Toss-pin
at Billiards
at Slipper-boxing
at The Owl
at Coddling the Hare
at *One More Pull*
at Skirmish
at Trudgepig
at Magpies
at The Horn
at The Shrovetide Ox
at The Madge-owlet
at Pinch without Laughing
at Prick-pin
at The Unshoeing of the Ass
at The Cocksess
at Hide-and-seek
at *I Sit Down*
at Shit-in-his-beard
at Buskins
at *Draw the Spit*
at *Chuck-him-out*

at *Uncle, Lend me your Sack*
at The Ramscod Ball
at *Out goes He*
at Marseilles Figs
at The Fly
at Bowman-shot
at Throw-it-up
at Pick-up
at Nine-holes
at Oat-selling
at Blow the Coal
at Marry Again
at Live Judge and Dead Judge
at Unoven the Iron
at The False Clown
at Nine Stones
at The Hunchback Courtier
at Find your Saint
at Hinch-pinch
at Stand-on-your-head
at The May-Queen
at The Breton Jig
at Whirligig
at The Sow
at Belly-to-belly
at The Dales
at Push-pin
at Quoits
at Pig-in-the-middle
at *Blow-it-out*
at Nine-pins
at Knock 'em Out
at Flatbowl
at Round-we-go
at Pick-a-back to Rome
at Bumbatch-touch
at Sly Jack
at Short Bowls
at Shuttlecock
at Dogs' Ears
at Smash-the-pot
at My Desire
at Twirly-whirly
at Rush-bundles

at Short Staff
at Spin Round
at Shut-your-eyes
at Spur-away
at Blanks
at Hunt-him-out
at The Iron Mask
at Triangles
at All in a Line
at The Cherry-pit
at The Humming-top
at The Whip-top
at The Peg-top
at The Hobgoblin
at Scare
at Old Hockey
at Fast and Loose
at Fat-arse
at Cock-horse
at *St Cosmo, I come to adore you*
at Brown Beetle
at *I Catch you Napping*
at *Fair and softly Lent Goes By*
at The Forked Oak
at Leap-frog
at The Wolf's Tail
at Nose to Breech
at *Willie, give me my Lance*
at See-saw
at Shocks of Corn
at Little Bowls
at Fly Away, Jack
at *Tit-tat-to*
at Cut-him-short
at Nine Hands
at Harry Racket
at The Bridge is Down
at Bridled Nick
at The Bull's-eye
at Battledore
at Blind-man's Buff
at Bob Cherry
at The Toad
at Cricket

at Pestle and Mortar
at Cup-and-ball
at Queens
at Trades
at Heads and Points
at Dot and Carry One
at Foul Death
at Fillips
at *I Wash your Cap, Madam*
at The Boulting-cloth
at Sowing the Oats
at Greedy-guts
at Windmills
at *Defendo*
at Pirouettes
at Drawbridges
at The Ploughman
at The Madge-owlet
at Angry Broomsticks
at The Dead Beast
at *Climb, Climb the Ladder*
at The Dead Pig
at The Salt-doup
at The Bird has Flown
at Barley-break
at Faggots
at Jump the Bush
at Andy-pandy
at Highwaymen
at Hawk's Nest
at Forward Hey
at Figs
at The Salvo of Farts
at Mustard-pounder
at First Home
at The Relapse
at Feathered Darts
at Duck your Head
at The Crane-dance
at Slash-and-cut
at Tweak-nose
at Larks
at Flip-finger

After he had thus enjoyed his games, and thoroughly sifted, win-nowed, and dispensed his time, the moment came to take a little drink – that was eleven quarts a head – and immediately afterwards to re-cline; that is, to stretch and sleep for two or three hours on a handsome seat or a good large bed, without an ill thought or an ill word. Then, when he was woken up, Gargantua shook his ears a little; and in the meantime they brought him fresh wine. Whereupon he drank better than ever.

Ponocrates used to remonstrate with him that it was a bad habit to drink like this after sleeping.

'It is,' said Gargantua, 'the true life according to the Holy Fathers. For naturally I sleep salt, and my sleep has been the equivalent of so much ham.'

Then he began to study a little, and it was Paternosters to the fore. So, to polish them off in better form, he mounted an old mule which had served nine kings; and thus, mumbling with his lips and nodding his head, he rode off to see some rabbits netted.

On his return he went to the kitchen to see what roast was on the spit. He supped very well, I promise you, cheerfully inviting some boozers from among his neighbours; and as they drank they told stories old and new. Among others he had as his servants the Lords du Fou, de Gourville, de Grignault, and de Marigny.

After supper they brought in the fair wooden Gospels, that is to say a number of games-boards, also the pleasant *Flush*, and *One, two, three,* or *Hazards* to shorten the time; or else they went to see the local girls, and held little feasts with them, and collations and post-collations. Then Gargantua slept without unbridling till eight o'clock next morning.

CHAPTER 23: *How Gargantua was so disciplined by Ponocrates that he did not waste an Hour of the Day*

WHEN Ponocrates saw Gargantua's vicious manner of living, he de-cided to educate him differently. But for the first days he bore with him, knowing that Nature cannot without great violence endure sud-den changes. Therefore, to make a better beginning of his task, he entreated a learned physician of that time, Master Theodore by name, to consider if it would be possible to set Gargantua on a better road, Theodore purged the youth in due form with black hellebore, and with this drug cured his brain of its corrupt and perverse habits. By this means also Ponocrates made him forget all that he had learnt from his old tutors, as Timotheus did for his pupils who had been trained under other musicians. The better to do this, Ponocrates introduced him into the society of the learned men of the region, in emulation of whom his wit increased, as did his desire to change his form of study and to show his worth; and after that the tutor subjected his pupil to such a discipline that he did not waste an hour of the day, but spent his entire time on literature and sound learning.

Gargantua now woke about four o'clock in the morning and, whilst he was being rubbed down, had some chapter of Holy Writ read to him loudly and clearly, with a pronunciation befitting the matter; and this was the business of a young page called Anagnostes, a native of Basché. Moved by the subject and argument of that lesson, he often gave himself up to worship and adoration, to prayers and entreaties, addressed to the good God whose majesty and marvellous wisdom had been exemplified in that reading. Then he went into some private place to make excretion of his natural waste-products, and there his tutor repeated what had been read, explaining to him the more obscure and difficult points. On their way back they considered the face of the sky, whether it was as they had observed it the night before, and into what sign the sun, and also the moon, were entering for that day.

This done, Gargantua was dressed, combed, curled, trimmed, and perfumed, and meanwhile the previous day's lessons were repeated to him. Next, he himself said them by heart, and upon them grounded some practical examples touching the state of man. This they sometimes continued for as long as two or three hours, but generally stopped as soon as he was fully dressed. Then for three full hours he was read to.

When this was done they went out, still discussing the subjects of the reading, and walked over to the sign of the Hound or to the meadows, where they played ball or tennis or the triangle game, gaily exercising their bodies as they had previously exercised their minds. Their sports were entirely unconstrained. For they gave up the game whenever they pleased, and usually stopped when their whole bodies

were sweating, or when they were otherwise tired. Then they were
well dried and rubbed down, changed their shirts, and sauntered off to
see if dinner was ready; and whilst they were waiting there they clearly and eloquently recited some sentences remembered from their lesson. In the meantime my lord Appetite came in, and when the happy
moment arrived they sat down at table.

At the beginning of the meal there was a reading of some pleasant
tale of the great deeds of old, which lasted till Gargantua had taken
his wine. Then, if it seemed good, the reading was continued. Otherwise, they began to converse gaily together, speaking in the first place
of the virtues, properties, efficacy, and nature of whatever was served
to them at table: of the bread, the wine, the water, the salt, the meats,
fish, fruit, herbs, and roots, and of their dressing. From this talk Gargantua learned in a very short time all the relevant passages in Pliny,
Athenaeus, Dioscorides, Julius Pollux, Galen, Porphyrius, Oppian,
Polybius, Heliodorus, Aristotle, Aelian, and others. As they held these
conversations they often had the afore-mentioned books brought to
table, to make sure of their quotations; and so well and completely
did Gargantua retain in his memory what had been said that there was
not a physician then living who knew half as much of this as he.

Afterwards they discussed the lessons read in the morning; and as
they concluded their meal with a confection of quinces, he picked his
teeth with a mastic branch, and washed his hands and eyes with good
fresh water. Then they gave thanks to God by reciting some lovely
canticles, composed in praise of the Divine bounty and munificence.
After this cards were brought in, not to play with, but so that he
might learn a thousand little tricks and new inventions, all based on
arithmetic. In this way he came to love this science of numbers, and
every day, after dinner and supper, whiled away the time with it as
pleasantly as formerly he had done with dice and cards; and so he
came to know the theory and practice of arithmetic so well that Tun-
stal, the Englishman who had written so copiously on the subject,
confessed that really, in comparison with Gargantua, all that he knew
of it was so much nonsense. And Gargantua did not only become
skilled in that branch, but also in such other mathematical sciences as
geometry, astronomy, and music. For while they waited for his meal
to be prepared and digested they made a thousand pretty instruments
and geometrical figures, and also practised the astronomical canons.

After this they amused themselves by singing music in four or five parts or on a set theme, to their throats' content. With regard to musical instruments, he learnt to play the lute, the spinet, the harp, the German flute, the nine-holed flute, the viol, and the trombone. After spending an hour in this way, his digestion being complete, he got rid of his natural excrements, and then returned to his principal study for three hours or more, during which time he repeated the morning's reading, went on with the book in hand, and also practised writing, drawing, and shaping the Gothic and Roman letters.

This done, they left their lodging in the company of a young gentleman of Touraine, named Squire Gymnaste, who taught Gargantua the art of horsemanship; and after changing his clothes, the pupil mounted in turn a charger, a cob, a jennet, a barb, and a light horse, and made each run a hundred courses, clear the ditch, leap over the barrier, and turn sharp round to the right and to the left. He did not break his lance. For it is the greatest nonsense in the world to say: 'I broke ten lances at tilt or in battle' – a carpenter could do it easily – but 'it is a glorious and praiseworthy thing with one lance to have broken ten of your enemies'. So with his lance steel-tipped, tough, and strong, he would break down a door, pierce a harness, root up a tree, spike a ring, or carry off a knight's saddle, coat of mail, and gauntlets; and all this he did armed from head to foot.

As for riding to the sound of trumpets and chirruping to encourage his horse, he had no master; the vaulter of Ferrara was a mere ape by comparison. He was singularly skilled also at leaping rapidly from one horse to another without touching the ground – these horses were called *desultories* – at getting up from either side, lance in hand and without stirrups, and at guiding his horse wherever he would without a bridle. For such feats are helpful to military discipline.

Another day he practised with the battle-axe, which he wielded so well, so lustily repeating his cutting strokes, so dexterously swinging it round his head, that he was passed as a knight-at-arms in the field and at all trials. Then he brandished the pike, played with the two-handed sword, the thrusting sword, the Spanish rapier, the dagger, and the poniard, in armour or without, with a buckler, a rolled cape, or a handguard.

He would hunt the stag, the roebuck, the bear, the boar, the hare, the partridge, the pheasant, and the bustard. He would play with the great ball, and make it fly into the air either with his foot or his fist. He wrestled, ran, and jumped, not at three steps and a leap, not with a hop or with the German action – for, as Gymnaste said, such leaps are useless and serve no purpose in war – but with one bound he would clear a ditch, sail over a hedge, or get six foot up a wall, and in this way climb into a window a lance-length high.

He would swim in deep water on his belly, on his back, on his side, with his whole body, or only with his legs, or with one hand in the air holding a book. Indeed, he would cross the whole breadth of the Seine without wetting that book, dragging his cloak in his teeth, as Julius Caesar did. Then with one hand he would powerfully lift himself into a boat, from there dive head foremost back into the water, sound the depths, explore the hollows of the rocks, and plunge into the gulfs and abysses. Then he would turn the boat, steer it, row it quickly, slowly, with the stream, against the current, check it in full course, guide it with one hand while flourishing a great oar with the other, hoist the sail, climb the mast by the shrouds, run along the spars, fix the compass, pull the bowlines to catch the wind, and wrench at the helm.

Coming out of the water, he sturdily scaled the mountain-side and came down as easily; he climbed trees like a cat, jumped from one to another like a squirrel, and tore down great branches like another Milo. With two stout poniards, as sharp as tried bodkins, he would run up the wall of a house like a rat, and then drop down from the top to the bottom with his limbs in such a posture that he suffered no hurt from the fall. He threw the dart, the bar, the stone, the javelin, the boar-spear, and the halbert; drew a bow to the full, bent by main force great rack-bent cross-bows, lifted an arquebus to his eye to aim it, planted the cannon, shot at the butts, at the popinjay, riding uphill, riding downhill, frontways, sideways, and behind him, like the Parthians. They tied a cable for him to the top of some high tower, with the end hanging to the ground, up which he climbed hand over hand, and then came down so firmly and sturdily that no one could have done better on a level plain. They put up a great pole for him, supported by two trees; and from this he would hang by his hands, moving up and down along it without touching anything with his feet, so fast that you could not catch up with him if you ran at full speed. And to exercise his chest and lungs, he would shout like all the devils. I heard him once calling Eudemon from the Porte St Victor to Mont-martre; never had Stentor such a voice at the battle of Troy.

Then, for the strengthening of his sinews, they made him two great sows of lead, each weighing eight hundred and seventy tons, which he called his dumb-bells. These he lifted in either hand, and raised in the air above his head, where he held them without moving for three-quarters of an hour and more, an inimitable feat of strength. He fought at the barriers with the strongest, and when the tussle came, his foot-hold was so firm that he would let the toughest of them try to move him, as Milo did of old; and in imitation of that champion he would hold a pomegranate in his hand and give it to whoever could get it from him.

After these pastimes and after being rubbed, washed, and refreshed by a change of clothes, he returned quietly; and as they walked through the meadows, or other grassy places, they examined the trees and the plants, comparing them with the descriptions in the books of such ancients as Dioscorides, Marinus, Pliny, Nicander, Macer, and Galen; and they brought back whole handfuls to the house. These were in charge of a young page called Rhizotome, who also looked after the mattocks, picks, grubbing-hooks, spades, pruning-knives, and other necessary implements for efficient gardening.

Once back at the house, while supper was being prepared, they re-peated some passages from what had been read, before sitting down to table. And notice here that Gargantua's dinner was sober and frugal, for he only ate enough to stay the gnawings of his stomach. But his supper was copious and large, for then he took all that he needed to stay and nourish himself. This is the proper regimen prescribed by the art of good, sound medicine, although a rabble of foolish physicians, worn out by the wrangling of the sophists, advise the contrary. Dur-ing this meal the dinner-time lesson was continued for as long as seemed right, the rest of the time being spent in good, learned, and profitable conversation. After grace had been said, they began to sing melodiously, to play on tuneful instruments, or to indulge in those pleasant games played with cards, dice, or cups; and there they stayed, making good cheer and amusing themselves sometimes till bedtime. But sometimes they went to seek the society of scholars or of men who had visited foreign lands.

When it was quite dark, they went before retiring to the most open side of the house, to view the face of the sky, and there took note of the comets, if there were any, also of the figures, situations, aspects, oppositions, and conjunctions of the stars. After which Gargantua briefly ran over with his tutor, in the manner of the Pythagoreans, all that he had read, seen, learnt, done, and heard in the course of the whole day. And so they prayed to God the Creator, worshipping Him, reaffirming their faith in Him, glorifying Him for His immense goodness, rendering thanks to Him for all the past, and recommending themselves to His divine clemency for all the future. This done, they went to their rest.

CHAPTER 24: *How Gargantua spent his Time in rainy Weather*

IF the weather chanced to be rainy and inclement, all the time before dinner was spent in the customary way, except that Gargantua had a fine, clear fire lighted to correct the distempers of the air. But after dinner, instead of taking exercise, they stayed under cover and, as a therapeutic measure, amused themselves by trussing hay, cutting and sawing wood, and threshing sheaves of corn in the barn. Then they studied the arts of painting and sculpture, or revived the ancient game of Greek dice, as described by Leonicus and as now practised by our good friend Lascaris; and while they played this game they recalled to mind those passages from ancient authors in which mention is made of it, or some metaphor drawn from it.

Alternatively, they went either to see the drawing of metals or the casting of cannon, or paid visits to jewellers, goldsmiths, and cutters of precious stones; or to alchemists and coiners; or to tapestry-workers, weavers, velvet-workers, watchmakers, looking-glass makers, printers, musical instrument makers, dyers, and other craftsmen of that sort; and everywhere, as they treated to wine, they learned and considered the processes and inventions of each trade. They went also to hear public lectures, the solemn statements, repetitions, declamations, and pleadings of the noble advocates, and the harangues of the Gospel-preachers. Gargantua walked through the halls and places appointed for fencing, and there practised against the masters with all weapons, conclusively proving to them that he knew as much as they did, or more. Also, instead of herborizing, they visited the druggists' shops, the herbalists, and the apothecaries, and carefully examined the fruit, roots, leaves, gums, seeds, and foreign ointments, also the way in which they were adulterated. They went to see the jugglers, conjurers, and sellers of quack remedies, and noted their antics, their tricks, their somersaults, and their smooth words, attending especially to those from Chauny in Picardy, for they are great babblers by nature, and fine reciters of tall stories on the subject of green monkeys.

When they got home for supper they ate more soberly than on other days, of more desiccative and extenuating dishes, as a method of correcting the humid inclemency of the air, communicated to the body by necessary proximity, and so that they might receive no harm from not having taken their usual exercise.

In this way Gargantua was tutored, and he kept to this course from day to day, profiting as you understand a young man can at his age, if he is sensible and takes such exercise continuously: a course of things which, though it seemed difficult at first, became so sweet, easy, and pleasant as it went on that it was more like a king's recreation than a student's plan of study.

Nevertheless, to give him a rest from this severe strain on his spirits, Ponocrates picked one very clear and serene day in every month, on which they left the city early, and went either to Gentilly, to Boulogne, to Montrouge, to the bridge at Charenton, to Vanves, or to Saint-Cloud; and there they spent the whole day enjoying themselves in every way they could imagine; bantering, making merry, drinking healths, playing, singing, dancing, sporting in some fine meadow, robbing sparrows' nests, taking quails, or fishing for frogs and crawfish.

But although the day was spent without books or reading, it was not profitless. For in that fine meadow they would repeat by heart a few pleasant lines of Virgil's *Georgics*, of Hesiod, or of Politian's *Husbandry*, and quote some neat Latin epigrams which they would turn into French rondeaux and ballades. While they were feasting, too, they would separate the wine from the water, according to Cato's instructions, in his *De re rust.*, and also to Pliny's, with a cup of ivy-root. Then they would wash the wine in a full basin of water; draw it out again with a funnel; make the water go from one glass to another; and construct several little *automatic machines*, that is to say machines that moved by themselves.

CHAPTER 25: *How a great Quarrel arose between the Cake-bakers of Lerné and the people of Grandgousier's country, which led to great Wars*

At that time, which was the vintage season at the beginning of autumn, the shepherds of the country were employed in guarding the vines to prevent the starlings from eating the grapes; and they were thus occupied at a moment when the bakers of Lerné were passing the great crossroad, taking ten or twelve loads of cakes to the town. Now the said shepherds courteously requested the bakers to sell them some of their cakes for cash at the market price. For note that grapes and fresh cake for breakfast is a dish for the gods, especially pineau-grapes, fig-grapes, muscatels, great black grapes, and purgative grapes for those whose bowels are constipated. For these make them squirt the length of a hunting-spear; and often when a man means to fart he shits himself; from which these grapes get the name of *wet-farters*.

The cake-bakers, however, were not at all inclined to accede to this request and, what is worse, they heaped insults on the shepherds, calling them babblers, snaggle-teeth, crazy carrot-heads, scabs, shit-a-beds, boors, sly cheats, lazy louts, fancy fellows, drunkards, braggarts, good-for-nothings, dunderheads, nut-shellers, beggars, sneak-thieves, mincing milksops, apers of their betters, idlers, half-wits, gapers, hovel-dwellers, poor fish, cacklers, conceited monkeys, teeth-clatterers, dung-drovers, shitten shepherds, and other such abusive epithets. They added that these dainty cakes were not for their eating, and that they must be satisfied with black bread and wholemeal loaves.

To which insults one of the shepherds, Forgier by name, a distinguished young man of very respectable appearance, replied quietly:

'Since when have you sprouted horns that you've grown so fresh? Bless my soul, you used to let us have them willingly enough, and now – if you please – you refuse. That's not the behaviour of honest neighbours. We never treat you like this when you come to buy our good corn, to make your cakes and scones with. What is more, we should have given you some of our grapes into the bargain. But, by God, you may come to be sorry for this one day, when there is something you want from us. Then we'll serve you as you serve us, and you'll remember this.'

Then Marquet, the grand mace-bearer of the cake-bakers' guild, re-plied: 'Your crest's very high this morning, my fine cock. You must have eaten too much millet last night. But come here, just come here, and I'll give you some of my cakes!'

Then in all simplicity Forgier went over to him, taking a shilling from his leather purse and thinking that Marquet was really going to hand him over some cakes. But the mace-bearer slashed him across the legs with his whip so hard that the weals showed, and began to run away. At this Forgier shouted 'Murder! Help!' at the top of his voice, and threw a great cudgel at him, which he carried under his arm. This struck Marquet on the coronal suture of his head, over the temporal artery on the right side; and he dropped from his mare, to all appear-ances more dead than alive.

Meanwhile the small farmers, who were shelling nuts near by, rushed up with their long poles and thrashed these cake-bakers like so much green rye. The shepherds and shepherdesses too, hearing For-gier shout, came up with their slings and sticks, and pursued them with great volleys of stones, which fell as thick as hail. Finally they caught the bakers up and took from them about four or five dozen cakes, for which they paid them the usual price, however, giving them a hundred walnuts and three baskets of white grapes into the bargain. Then the bakers helped Marquet, who had a nasty wound, on to his mare, and they returned to Lerné, turning off the Parilly road, with fierce and ugly threats against the drovers, shepherds, and small farmers of Seuilly and Cinais.

When they had gone, the shepherds and shepherdesses made a good feast of the cakes and fine grapes, and sported gaily to the pleasant sound of the bagpipe, scoffing at those grand, vainglorious cake-bakers, who had struck bad luck that morning, through not crossing themselves with the right hand when they got up. And they neatly dressed Forgier's legs with big common grapes, so that they soon healed.

CHAPTER 26: *How the Inhabitants of Lerné, at the command of their King Picrochole, made an unexpected attack on Grandgousier's Shepherds*

ON their return to Lerné the cake-bakers neither ate nor drank, but went straight to the Capitol, and there made their complaint before their King Picrochole, the third of that name, displaying their broken bread-baskets, their crumpled caps, their torn coats, their cakeless bags and, worse than that, the sorely wounded Marquet. All this damage, they declared, had been done by Grandgousier's shepherds and small-farmers, near the great highway beyond Seuilly.

The King promptly flew into a furious rage and, without any further question of why or how, called out his vassals great and small, commanding every one, under pain of the halter, to assemble armed in the great square in front of the castle at the hour of midday; and for the furtherance of this design he had the drum beaten all round the town. He himself, while his dinner was being prepared, went to see his artillery limbered up, his ensign and standard displayed, and his wagons loaded with store of ammunition both for the field and the belly. While he dined he made out the commissions; and by his edict Lord Hairychest was appointed to the vanguard, in which were numbered sixteen thousand and fourteen arquebusiers and thirty-five thousand and eleven free-booting volunteers. The artillery was put in charge of Blow-trumpet, the Grand Master of the Horse; and it was made up of nine hundred and fourteen great bronze pieces, including cannon, double-cannon, basilisks, serpentines, culverins, bombards, falcons, passevolans, spiroles, and other pieces. The rearguard was put in charge of Duke Rakepenny, and in the main body rode the King and the princes of his realm.

When they were thus hastily equipped but before setting out on the road, they sent forward three hundred light horsemen under the command of Captain Swillwind to reconnoitre the territory and see if there was any ambush in the countryside. But after a diligent search they found all the land around peaceful and quiet, and no gathering of people anywhere; upon the receipt of which news Picrochole ordered everyone to advance speedily under his colours.

Thereupon in rash and disorderly fashion they took to the fields pell-mell, wasting and destroying wherever they passed, sparing neither poor nor rich, sacred place nor profane. They drove off oxen, cows, bulls, calves, heifers, ewes, rams, she-goats, hens, capons, chickens, goslings, ganders, geese, hogs, sows, and little pigs; knocking down the nuts, stripping the vines, carrying off the vine-stocks, and shaking down all the fruit from the trees. The destruction they did was unparalleled, and they encountered no resistance. Everyone begged for mercy, and implored to be treated with more humanity, considering the fact that they had always been good and friendly neighbours, and that they had never committed any excess or outrage against the people of Lerné, to deserve this sudden harshness, for which, indeed, God would punish the perpetrators. But the only reply that the men of Lerné made to these remonstrances was that they would teach them to eat cakes.

CHAPTER 27: *How a Monk of Seuilly saved the Abbey-close from being sacked by the Enemy*

So they went on, wasting, pillaging, and stealing till they arrived at Seuilly, where they robbed men and women alike and took everything they could; nothing was too hot or too heavy for them. Although there was plague in almost every house, they broke into all of them and plundered everything inside; and none of them caught any infection, which is a most wonderful thing. For the priests, curates, preachers, physicians, surgeons, and apothecaries who went to visit, dress, heal, preach to, and admonish the sick had all died of the infection. Yet these robbing and murdering devils never took any harm. What is the reason for that, gentlemen? Consider the problem, I beg of you.

When the town was thus pillaged they went to the abbey in a horrible tumult, but they found it well bolted and barred. So the main body of their army marched on towards the ford of Vède, except for seven companies of foot and two hundred knights with their retainers, who remained there and broke down the walls of the close in order to ravage the vineyard. The poor devils of monks did not know which of their saints to turn to. Whatever the risk, they had the bell tolled for a meeting of the chapter, at which it was decided to march in a stately procession, rendered more effective by grand chants and litanies *contra hostium insidias*, and fine responses *pro pace*.[1]

There was in the abbey at that time a cloister monk, named Friar John of the Hashes, a young, gallant, sprightly, jovial, resourceful, bold, adventurous, resolute, tall, and thin fellow with a great gaping mouth and a fine outstanding nose. He was grand mumbler of matins, dispatcher of masses, and polisher off of vigils, and, to put it briefly, a true monk if ever there has been one since the monking world monked its first monkery; and moreover in the matter of his breviary he was a clerk to his very teeth.

Now when this monk heard the noise that the enemy were making in the close of their vineyard, he came out to see what they were doing; and finding them to be picking the grapes of their close, on which their provision for the whole year depended, he returned to the choir of the church, where the rest of the monks, gaping like so many stuffed pigs, were singing: *Ini nim, pe, ne, ne, ne, ne, ne, ne, mum, num, ini, i, mi, i, mi, co, o, ne, no, ne, no no, no, rum, ne, num, num.*[2]

'That's shitten well sung!' he cried when he saw them. 'But, for God's sake, why don't you sing: "Baskets farewell; the harvest's done"? The devil take me if they aren't in our close, and so thoroughly cutting both vines and grapes that, God's body, there'll be nothing but gleanings there for the next four years. Tell me, by St James's belly, what shall we drink in all that time? What'll there be for us poor devils? Lord God, *da mihi potum.*'[3]

Then said the Prior of the convent: 'What does this drunkard want here? Let him be taken to the punishment cell for disturbing the divine service!'

'But,' said the monk, 'what about the wine service? Let's see that isn't disturbed. For you yourself, my lord Prior, like to drink of the best, and so does every decent fellow. Indeed, no man of honour hates a good wine; which is a monkish saying. But these responses you're singing here are very much out of season, by God. Now tell me, why are our services short at the harvest-tide and the vintage, and during Advent too, and all the winter? The late Friar Mace Pelosse, of blessed

---

1. Against the snares of the enemy *and* for peace.
2. Fear not the enemy's attack (*Impetum inimicorum ne timueritis*): one of the October responses.
3. Give me a drink.

memory, a true zealot for our faith – devil take me if he wasn't – told me the reason, as I remember. It was that we might press and make the wine properly at the vintage, and in winter drink it down. So listen to me, all you who love wine; and follow me too, in God's name. For I tell you boldly, may St Anthony's fire burn me if anyone tastes the grape who hasn't fought for the vine. Church property it is, by God, and hands off it! Devil take it, St Thomas of Canterbury was willing to die for the Church's goods, and if I were to die for them, shouldn't I be a Saint as well? But I shan't die, for all that. It's I that will be the death of others.'

As he said this he threw off his heavy monk's cloak and seized the staff of his cross, which was made of the heart of a sorb-apple tree. It was as long as a lance, a full hand's grip round, and decorated in places with lily flowers, which were almost all rubbed away. Thus he went out in a fine cassock, with his frock slung over his shoulder, and rushed so lustily on the enemy, who were gathering grapes in the vineyard without order or ensign, trumpet or drum. For the standard-bearers and ensigns had put down their standards and ensigns beside the walls, the drummers had knocked in one side of their drums to fill them with grapes, the trumpeters were loaded with the fruit, and everyone was in disorder. He rushed, as I said, so fiercely on them, without a word of warning, that he bowled them over like hogs, striking right and left in the old fencing fashion.

He beat out the brains of some, broke the arms and legs of others, disjointed the neck-bones, demolished the kidneys, slit the noses, blackened the eyes, smashed the jaws, knocked the teeth down the throats, shattered the shoulder blades, crushed the shins, dislocated the thigh-bones, and cracked the fore-arms of yet others. If one of them tried to hide among the thickest vines, he bruised the whole ridge of his back and broke the base of his spine like a dog's. If one of them tried to save himself by flight, he knocked his head into pieces along the lambdoidal suture. If one of them climbed into a tree, thinking he would be safe there, Friar John impaled him up the arse with his staff. If any one of his old acquaintance cried out: 'Ha, Friar John, my friend, Friar John, I surrender!' he replied: 'You can't help it. But you'll surrender your soul to all the devils as well.' And he gave the fellow a sudden thumping.

If any man was seized with such a spirit of rashness as to try to face up to him, then he showed his muscular strength by running him through the chest by way of the mediastine to the heart. In the case of others, thrusting under the hollow of their short ribs, he turned their stomachs over, so that they died immediately. Others he smote so fiercely through the navel that he made their bowels gush out. Others he struck on the ballocks and pierced their bum-gut. It was, believe me, the most hideous spectacle that ever was seen.

Some invoked St Barbara, others St George, others St Hands-off, others Our Lady of Cunault, of Loretto, of Good Tidings, of Lenou, of Rivière. Some called on St James, others on the Holy Shroud of Chambéry – but it was burnt three months later so completely that they could not save a single thread – others on the Shroud of Cadouin, others on St John of Angély, others on St Eutropius of Saintes, St Maximus of Chinon, St Martin of Candes, St Cloud of Cinais, the relics of Javarzay, and a thousand other pleasant little saints.

Some died without a word, others spoke without dying; some died as they spoke, others spoke as they died, and others cried aloud: 'Confession! Confession! *Confiteor! Miserere! In manus!*'[1]

Such was the shouting of the wounded that the Prior of the abbey came out with all his monks; and when they saw these poor creatures tumbled there among the vines and mortally wounded, they confessed some of them. But whilst the priests amused themselves by taking confessions, the little monklings ran to the place where Friar John stood, and asked him how they could help him.

His reply was that they should slit the throats of those lying on the ground. So, leaving their great cloaks on the nearest fence, they began to cut the throats of those whom he had already battered, and to dispatch them. Can you guess with what instruments? With fine *whittles*, which are the little jack-knives with which the small children of our country shell walnuts.

Meanwhile, still wielding the staff of his cross, Friar John reached the breach which the enemy had made, while some of the little monks carried off the ensigns and standards to their cells, to cut them into garters. But when those who had made their confession tried to get out through this breach, the monk rained blows upon them, crying: 'These men are shriven and repentant, and have earned their pardons. They'll go right to paradise, as straight as a sickle or the road to Faye.'

1. I confess. Have mercy upon me. Into [thy] hands.

Thus, by his prowess, all that part of the army that had got into the close was discomfited, to the number of thirteen thousand, six hundred and twenty-two, not counting the women and small children – as is always understood. For never did Maugis the Hermit – of whom it is written in the Deeds of the Four Sons of Aymon – wield his pilgrim's staff so valiantly against the Saracens as this monk swung the staff of his cross in his encounter with the enemy.

CHAPTER 28: *How Picrochole stormed La Roche-Clermault, and of the reluctance and aversion with which Grandgousier made war*

WHILST the monk was skirmishing, as we have related, against those who had broken into the close, Picrochole with his people crossed the ford of Vède with all speed and attacked La Roche-Clermault, where he met with no resistance at all. Then because night had now fallen he decided to quarter himself and his men in that town, and there cool his stinging fury.

In the morning he stormed the bulwarks and the castle, which he then thoroughly repaired and stored with all necessary provisions, intending to retreat there if he were attacked from elsewhere. For the place was strong, both naturally and by fortification, on account both of its outlook and its situation.

So let us leave them there and return to our good Gargantua, who is in Paris, most intent on the pursuit of learning and athletic exercises, and to that good old man Grandgousier, his father, who is warming his codpiece after supper by a fine, large, clear fire and, while his chestnuts are roasting, is writing on the hearth with a stick charred at one end, which is used for poking the fire, as he tells his wife and family grand stories of the olden times.

It was at such an hour that one of the shepherds who had been guarding the vines, Pillot by name, presented himself before him and gave a full account of the outrages and robberies being committed by Picrochole, King of Lerné, in his lands and domains; how he had pillaged, wasted, and sacked the whole countryside, except the close of Seuilly which Friar John of the Hashes had saved, to his great honour;

and how the said King was at that time in La Roche-Clermault, and was most busily entrenching himself and his men in the place.

'Alas, alas!' cried Grandgousier. 'What is this, good people? Am I dreaming, or is what they tell me true? Picrochole, my old and perpetual friend, united to me by blood and by alliance, has he come to attack me? Who is inciting him? Who is urging him on? Who is leading him? Who has advised him to do this? Oh! Oh! Oh! Oh! Oh! My God, my Saviour, help me, inspire me, counsel me what I should do! I protest, I swear before thee – so mayest thou show me favour! – that never have I done him an ill turn, nor harmed his people, nor committed robbery on his lands. On the contrary, I have assisted him with men, money, favour, and counsel on every occasion when I found him in need of them. It must be the evil spirit that has prompted him to outrage me now. Lord God, Thou knowest my courage, for from thee nothing can lie concealed. If the fact is that he has gone mad and thou hast entrusted me with the restoration of his wits, give me power and wisdom to bring him back to the yoke of thy holy will by good sound discipline.

'Oh! Oh! Oh! My good people, my friends and my loyal servants, shall I have to call on you to aid me? Alas, all that my old age called for was repose. All my life I have sought peace above all things. But now I plainly see that I shall have to load my weak, tired shoulders with armour, and take the lance and the mace in my trembling hand, to help and protect my poor subjects. Justice demands it. For by their labour I am supported, by their sweat I am fed, I and my wife and family. Nevertheless I will not embark upon war till I have tried every art and means of peace. On that I am resolved.'

Thereupon he ordered his council to be convoked, and set the matter before them just as it was. Their decision was that some prudent man should be sent to Picrochole, to find out why he had so suddenly broken the peace and invaded lands to which he had absolutely no claim. Further, that Gargantua and his people should be sent for, to preserve the country and defend it in its present need. These conclusions were approved by Grandgousier, and he commanded that they should be carried into effect. He sent his Basque servant immediately to bring Gargantua back in all haste, and he wrote to his son as follows:

CHAPTER 29: *The Tenour of the Letter sent by Grandgousier to Gargantua*

THE fervency of your studies would have compelled me to leave you for a long time to philosophic repose, had not the presumption of our friends and former allies broken in upon the security of my old age. But since such is my fatal destiny that I am disturbed by those in whom I most trusted, I am bound to recall you to the rescue of the people and possessions for whom and which you are by natural right responsible.

For just as arms are powerless abroad unless there is good counsel at home, so study is vain and counsel useless unless at due season it is valorously applied and carried out.

My intention is not to provoke, but to appease; not to attack, but to defend; not to conquer, but to guard my loyal subjects and hereditary lands, which Picrochole has invaded in an unfriendly manner, without reason or excuse, and where day by day he pursues his furious enterprise with excesses intolerable to free-born men.

I have made it my duty to moderate his tyrannical violence, and offered him everything that I thought might give him satisfaction. Several times I have sent him friendly messages inquiring in what way, by whom, and how he felt himself wronged. But I have had no answer from him except wilful defiance, and the statement that he alleged no claim to my lands except his own good pleasure. From this I recognized that God Almighty has abandoned him to the guidance of his own free will and understanding, which cannot but be evil unless it be continually prompted by divine grace; and that He has entrusted me with the duty of recalling him to his obedience and bringing him to his senses by painful experience.

Therefore, my well-beloved son, return here with all speed as soon as you can after reading this letter, to aid not so much myself – which in any case you are bound by duty to do – as your people whom, in all reason, you should save and protect. Our measures will be carried out with the least possible bloodshed. If it is possible, we shall by subtler expedients, by tricks and stratagems of war, save all souls and send them to their homes rejoicing.

The peace of Christ our Redeemer be with you, my dearest son. Give my greetings to Ponocrates, Gymnaste, and Eudemon.

The twentieth of September.

Your father, GRANDGOUSIER

CHAPTER 30: *How Ulrich Gallet was sent to Picrochole*

AFTER dictating and signing this letter, Grandgousier ordered Ulrich Gallet, his Master of Requests, a wise and discreet man whose merit and sound advice he had tested in various matters of contention, to go to Picrochole and explain their resolutions to him.

Within an hour the excellent Gallet set out, and when he had crossed the ford he asked the miller for news of Picrochole. The reply which he got was that the King's soldiers had left the miller neither cock nor hen, and that they had shut themselves up in La Roche-Clermault. He advised Gallet to proceed no further, for fear of the scouts, for they were extremely ferocious; which Gallet readily believed, and lodged that night with the miller.

Next morning he advanced with a trumpeter to the gate of the castle and requested the guards to bring him before the King, that he might tell him something to his advantage. But when his message was reported to Picrochole, he refused absolutely to have the gates opened for him, but himself went out on the bulwarks and cried to the ambassador: 'What is your news? What do you want to say?'

Then the ambassador began to speak as follows:

CHAPTER 31: *Gallet's Speech to Picrochole*

'No juster cause of grief can arise among men than when they receive hurt and damage from that source to which they might rightly look for favour and good will. Indeed not without cause, though without reason, many who have sustained this misfortune have considered their indignity more unbearable than the loss of their own lives, and in cases where they have not been able to set things right by force or other means, have deprived themselves of this light.

'It is no wonder, therefore, if King Grandgousier, my master, is full of high displeasure and greatly perturbed in his mind by your furious and hostile attack. It would be a wonder indeed if he were not stirred by the unparalleled excesses committed by you and your soldiers upon his lands and his subjects, who have been treated with every kind of inhumanity. This in itself is so very grievous to him, on account of the cordial affection that he has always felt for his people, that it could not be more so to any mortal man. Yet it is beyond human computation more grievous to him that these wrongs and offences have been committed by you and yours. For from of old and since time immemorial you and your forefathers have maintained a friendship for him and all his ancestors, which has been, on both sides, inviolably kept, guarded, and preserved as a sacred bond up to the present day; so much so that not only he and his people, but the barbarous nations, Poitevins, Bretons, Manceaux, and those who dwell beyond the Canary Islands and Isabella, have thought it as easy to pull down the firmament and raise the abyss above the clouds as to sever the alliance between you, which in their enterprises they have so much dreaded that they have never dared to provoke, annoy, or injure one party for fear of the other.

'What is more, this sacred friendship has so filled the world's ears that there are few peoples to-day living anywhere in the continent or the isles of the ocean who have not ambitiously aspired to be admitted into it, on terms to be laid down by yourselves; valuing a confederation with you as highly as their own lands and dominions. Therefore it is that from time immemorial there has been no prince or league so proud and savage that they have dared to attack, I do not say your lands, but those of your confederates; and if by some rash counsel they have attempted any rash design against them, on hearing the name and title of your alliance they have immediately desisted from their enterprises.

'What fury is it, then, that stirs you now to break all alliance, tread all friendship underfoot, transgress all right, and make hostile incursion on to these lands, without having been in any way injured, annoyed, or provoked by him or his? Where is faith? Where is law? Where is reason? Where is humanity? Where is the fear of God? Do you think that these wrongs are concealed from the eternal spirits and from Almighty God, who is the just rewarder of all our undertakings? If you think so you are deceived, for all things will come before his judgement. Is it the fatal destinies or the influence of the stars that desire to put an end to your ease and repose? For all things have their term and period, and when they have reached their highest point they are in a trice tumbled down, since they cannot long remain at such an eminence. Such is the end of those who cannot by reason and temperance moderate their fortunes and prosperity.

'But if it was thus fated and ordained that your fortune and comfort should now reach their end, was it necessary that this should come through the troubling of my King, by whom you were set up? If your house was doomed to fall, was it needful that in its ruin it should fall on the hearth of him who embellished it? This thing is so far beyond the bounds of reason, so repugnant to common sense, as to be scarcely conceivable to human understanding; and it will remain incredible to strangers until the undoubted evidence of its effects convinces them that nothing is holy or sacred to those who have emancipated themselves from God and reason to follow their own perverse desires.

'If any wrong had been done by us to your subjects or domains, if any favour had been shown by us to those who wish you ill, if we had not aided you in your affairs, if your name and fame had been damaged by us or – to put it more truly – if the spirit of slander, striving to induce you to evil, had by deceitful appearances and fallacious visions put it into your head that we had acted towards you in any way unworthy of our ancient friendship, you should first have inquired into the truth of the matter and then have given us warning. We should then have acted so completely to your satisfaction that you would have had occasion to be pleased. But, in the name of God Almighty, what is this enterprise of yours? Do you wish, like a perfidious tyrant, to pillage and lay waste my master's kingdom? Have you found him so sluggish and stupid as to be unwilling, so lacking in men, money, counsel, and military skill as to be unable to resist your iniquitous assaults?

'Depart from here immediately, and during the course of tomorrow retire within your own territory, committing no disorder or violence on the way; and in addition you shall pay a thousand gold besants for the damage you have done in these lands. Half you must pay to-morrow, and half on the forthcoming Ides of May, leaving us in the meantime as hostages the Dukes of Treadmill, Lowbuttock, and Chuckout, together with the Prince of Itchskin and Viscount Scavenger.'

CHAPTER 32: *How Grandgousier, in order to buy Peace, had the Cakes returned*

WITH that the excellent Gallet concluded. But all the answer that Picrochole gave to his whole discourse was: 'Come and fetch them. Come and fetch them. They've a good ballocky pestle, and a mortar here, and they'll knead some cakes for you.'

So the ambassador returned to Grandgousier, whom he found on his knees, bareheaded, prostrate in a little corner of his chamber, praying God to moderate Picrochole's anger and to bring him to reason, without the need of force.

When the King saw that the good man had returned, he asked: 'Ah, my friend, my friend, what news do you bring me?'

'Order is overthrown,' said Gallet. 'That man is out of his mind. God has forsaken him.'

'But tell me, my friend,' said Grandgousier. 'What excuse does he give for this outrage?'

'He has given me no excuse at all,' replied Gallet. 'Only in his fury he said something to me about cakes. I wonder if some insult has been offered to his cake-bakers.'

'I will get to the bottom of this,' said Grandgousier, 'before making any further decisions as to what shall be done.'

Then he ordered inquiries to be made into this matter, and found it true that some cakes had been forcibly taken from Picrochole's people, also that Marquet had been cudgelled over the head, yet that everything had been duly paid for and that the said Marquet had previously slashed Forgier with his whip about the legs. It seemed, therefore, to all Grandgousier's council that the King must defend himself with all his strength.

Nevertheless Grandgousier said: 'Since it is only a matter of a few cakes I will try to satisfy him. For I very much dislike making war.'

Then he inquired how many cakes had been taken, and when he heard four or five dozen, commanded that five cart-loads should be made up that very night, and that one of them, loaded with cakes made with fresh butter, good yolk of egg, fine saffron, and choice spices, should be bestowed upon Marquet, also that as compensation he should be given seven hundred thousand and three philip-staters, to pay the barbers who had tended him. In addition Grandgousier granted him the farm of La Pomardière as a freehold for him and his heirs in perpetuity. To arrange and carry out all this, he sent Gallet, who on his way made his men gather, near the Willow-wood, quantities of boughs, reeds, and catkins, which he made his carters use as decoration for themselves and their carts. He himself carried one bough in his hand, intending in this way to show that all they wanted was peace, and that they had come to buy it.

When they arrived at the gate they asked to speak with Picrochole on behalf of Grandgousier. But he would not allow them entrance on any terms, nor go to speak with them. He informed them that he was prevented, but that they could say what they wished to Captain Touchspigot, who was planting a piece of ordnance on the walls.

Then said the good man to the captain: 'My Lord, to remove every cause for argument, and clear away every excuse for your not returning to your former alliance with us, we return you forthwith the cakes which are the subject of dispute. Five dozen our people took, and they were very well paid for. But we are such lovers of peace that we return you five cartloads, of which this one shall be for Marquet, who has the greatest grievance. Furthermore, to satisfy him entirely, here are seven hundred thousand and three philip-staters which I deliver to him; and for the damages he might claim, I deliver to him the farm of La Pomardière as a freehold for him and his heirs in perpetuity, to be held in fee-simple. See, here is the deed of conveyance. Now, for God's sake, let us henceforth live in peace. Withdraw cheerfully into your own lands, giving up this place, in which you have no right whatever, as you will yourselves admit. Then let us be friends as before.'

Touchspigot related all this to Picrochole, and exacerbated his spirit by saying: 'These clods are in a fine funk. By God, Grandgousier's shitting himself, the miserable boozer! He is not a fighting man. He is better at emptying flagons. My advice is that we keep these cakes and the money and, what is more, fortify ourselves here with all speed and follow up our fortune. Do they think they have some poor fool to deal with, whom they can stuff with their cakes? This is how it is. You've treated them too well in the past. You've been too familiar with them, and that has made them despise you.

> Lick a villain and he'll beat you;
> Beat a villain and he'll lick you.

'Yes, yes, yes,' said Picrochole. 'By St James, we'll give it to them! Do as you've proposed.'

'There is one thing I'd like to warn you of,' said Touchspigot. 'We're pretty badly victualled here, we're most meagerly provided with stomach-fodder. If Grandgousier were to besiege us, I should go immediately and have all my teeth drawn bar three, and I'd have the same thing done to each of your soldiers. Even with three teeth we shall make an uncomfortably big hole in our provisions.'

'We shall have only too many provisions,' said Picrochole. 'Are we here to eat or to fight?'

'To fight, of course,' said Touchspigot. 'But full belly and the dance is merry, and where hunger reigns no strength obtains.'

'That's enough chatter,' said Picrochole. 'Lay hold of what they have brought.'

Then they seized the money and the cakes, the oxen and the carts, and sent the men off without a word except that they were not to come so near again for a reason that would be given them next day.

So, with nothing achieved, they went back to Grandgousier and told him their story, adding that there was no hope of bringing Picrochole to terms except by sharp and vigorous war.

CHAPTER 33: *How certain of Picrochole's Advisers, by their headstrong Counsel, put him in extreme Peril*

THE cakes having been unloaded, there appeared before Picrochole the Duke of Chuckout, Earl Swashbuckler, and Captain Dungby, who said to him:

'Sire, to-day we make you the happiest and most chivalrous prince that ever was since the death of Alexander of Macedon.'

'Cover yourselves, put on your hats,' said Picrochole.

'We thank you,' they said. 'Sire, we offer you our humble duty. This is the plan. You will leave here some captain in garrison with a small company of men to hold the place, which seems to us fairly strong both by nature and by the ramparts of your devising. You will divide your army into two parts, as you well know how to do. One division will go and fall on this Grandgousier and his men; and they will easily overthrow him at the first attack. There you will gain money by the pile, for the scoundrel has enough and to spare; scoundrel we call him because no noble prince ever has a penny. To hoard a treasure is the mark of a scoundrel.

'Meanwhile the other division will make for Aunis, Saintonge, Angoumois, and Gascony, also for Périgord, Médoc, and the Landes. Cities, castles, and fortresses will fall to them without resistance. At Bayonne, Saint-Jean-de-Luz, and Fuenterabia you will seize all the shipping; and, coasting towards Galicia and Portugal, you will pillage every seaboard town as far as Lisbon, where you will get all the reinforcements necessary for a conqueror. Spain will surrender, by God, for the Spaniards are a lazy bunch! You will cross the Straits of Seville, and there you will erect two columns, grander than the Columns of Hercules, as a perpetual memorial to your name. This strait shall be called the Picrocholine Sea. Then, when you have passed the Picrocholine Sea, Barbarossa himself will yield himself as your slave' ...

'I shall grant him free pardon,' said Picrochole.

'That is,' said they, 'provided that he accepts baptism. Then you will storm the kingdoms of Tunis, Hippo, Algiers, Bône, Cyrene, and in fact all Barbary. Advancing further, you will lay your hands upon Majorca, Minorca, Sardinia, Corsica, and other islands of the Ligurian and Balearic seas. Coasting to the left, you will subdue all Gallia Narbonensis, Provence, and the Allobrogians, Genoa, Florence, and Lucca, and it'll be all up with Rome. Poor Master Pope is already dying of fear.'

'I'll never kiss his slipper, I promise you,' said Picrochole.

'With Italy taken, there is Naples, Calabria, Apulia, and Sicily all to be sacked, and Malta too. I only hope those jolly knights, once of Rhodes, will resist you, so that we can see what they're made of.'

'I should like to go to Loretto,' said Picrochole.

'No; impossible!' they said. 'That will be on your return. From there we will take Crete, Cyprus, Rhodes, and the Cyclades, and attack the Morea. It's ours. By St Trinian, may the Lord preserve Jerusalem! For the Sultan's power is not comparable with yours!'

'Then,' said Picrochole, 'I'll have Solomon's temple rebuilt.'

'Not yet,' they said. 'Wait a little. You must never be too precipitate in your decisions. Do you know what Octavian Augustus said?

Festina lente.[1] It will be better for you first to conquer Asia Minor, Caria, Lycia, Pamphilia, Cicilia, Lydia, Phrygia, Mysia, Bithynia, Charazia, Adalia, Samagaria, Castamena, Luga, and Sebaste, all as far as the Euphrates.'

'Shall we see Babylon and Mount Sinai?' asked Picrochole.

'There is no need to do so for the present,' they replied. 'Isn't it sufficient of a trail to have crossed the Hyrcanian Sea, ridden through the two Armenias and the three Arabias?'

'Lord Almighty,' exclaimed Picrochole. 'We're as good as dead! Poor creatures that we are!'

'Why?' they asked.

'What shall we drink in those deserts? For Julian Augustus and all his host died there of thirst, so they say.'

'We have already attended to all that,' they answered. 'In the Syrian Sea you have nine thousand and fourteen large ships, loaded with the best wines in the world, which have come into Jaffa. In that port are twenty-two hundred thousand camels and sixteen hundred elephants, which you have taken at one hunting near Sigeilmes, when you invaded Libya, and in addition you have captured the whole Mecca caravan. Didn't they provide you with a sufficiency of wine?'

'Yes,' said he, 'but we didn't drink it fresh.'

'Ye Gods and little fishes!' they cried. 'A mighty man, a conqueror, a claimant and aspirant to universal empire cannot always idle at his ease. God be praised that you have come, you and your men, safe and sound to the banks of the Tigris!'

'But,' he asked, 'what was that part of our army doing meanwhile, which overthrew that bibulous clown Grandgousier?'

'They're not idling,' they replied. 'We shall meet them soon. They have taken Brittany for you, Normandy, Flanders, Hainault, Brabant, Artois, Holland, and Zealand. They have crossed the Rhine over the bellies of the Swiss and Landsknechts, and a portion of them has subdued Luxemburg, Lorraine, Champagne, and Savoy as far as Lyons, at which place they have found your garrisons returning from their naval victories in the Mediterranean. They have reassembled in Bohemia, after having ransacked Swabia, Württemberg, Bavaria, Austria, Moravia, and Styria. Then, all together, they have made a fierce attack on Lübeck, Norway, Sweden, Riga, Dacia, Gothland,

1. More haste, less speed.

Greenland, and the Easterlings as far as the Arctic Sea and, crossing Sarmatia, they have conquered and mastered Prussia, Poland, Lithuania, Russia, Wallachia, Transylvania and Hungary, Bulgaria and Turkey, and are now at Constantinople.'

'Let's go,' said Picrochole, 'and join them as soon as possible. For I should like to be Emperor of Trebizond as well. Shan't we kill all these dogs of Turks and Mohammedans?'

'What the devil else shall we do with them?' they asked. 'And we'll give their goods and lands to those who have served you faithfully.'

'Reason demands it,' said Picrochole. 'It's only just. To you I give Carmania, Syria, and all Palestine.'

'Ah, sire,' they said. 'That is good of you. Many thanks. God grant that you may always prosper.'

Among those present was an old nobleman named Ecephron, a hardened warrior who had stood the test of many dangerous situations; and when he heard this speech he said: 'I am very much afraid that all this enterprise will be like the farce of the pitcher of milk, with which a shoemaker made his fortune, in his day-dreams. But when the pitcher was broken he hadn't enough to buy a dinner. What are you after with these fine conquests of yours? What will be the end of all these labours and journeyings?'

'The end will be,' said Picrochole, 'that when we are back we shall rest at our ease.'

Then said Ecephron: 'But suppose that you should never return from there, for the journey is long and perilous. Wouldn't it be better for us to take our ease now, and not run into all these dangers?'

'Oh,' said Swashbuckler, 'here's a fine dreamer, by God! Let's go and hide then in the chimney corner, and pass our lives there with the ladies, and spend our time threading beads or spinning like Sardanapalus. The man who ventures nothing wins neither horse nor mule, as Solomon said.'

'The man who ventures too much loses both horse and mule, as Malcon answered,' replied Eciphron.

'Enough!' said Picrochole. 'Let's go on. I fear nothing except these devilish legions of Grandgousier's. Supposing that while we are in Mesopotamia they were to strike at our rear, what remedy should we have?'

'A very good one,' said Dungby. 'A nice little order that you will send to the Muscovites will immediately put into the field for you four hundred and fifty thousand picked fighters. Oh, if you make me your lieutenant I'll kill a comb for a pedlar.[1] I bite, I charge, I strike, I seize, I slay, I stop at nothing.'

'On, on,' said Picrochole, 'let everything be got ready. Let him that loves me follow.'

CHAPTER 34: *How Gargantua left the city of Paris to save his Country, and how Gymnaste met the Enemy*

AT this same hour Gargantua, who had left Paris immediately after reading his father's letter, had already crossed the Nuns Bridge, riding on his white mare; and with him were Ponocrates, Gymnaste, and Eudemon, who had taken post-horses to follow him. The rest of his train came on by even stages, bringing all his books and philosophical equipment.

When he arrived at Parilly he was informed by the farmer Gouguet that Picrochole had fortified himself at La Roche-Clermault, that he had sent Captain Tripet with a huge army to attack the Wood of Vède and Vaugaudry; that they made a clean sweep of every hen as far as the winepress at Billard, and that it was strange, almost incredible indeed, what outrages they were committing about the country. This account of things so alarmed Gargantua that he did not know what to do or say. But Ponocrates suggested that they should go to the lord of La Vauguyon, who had always been their friend and ally, since they would get better advice from him on the whole business. This they immediately did, and found him firmly disposed to help them. His advice was that Gargantua should send one of his men to reconnoitre the country and find out in what condition the enemy were, so that they might advance to La Roche-Clermault with plans formed in accordance with the actual situation. Gymnaste volunteered to go alone. But it was decided that it would be better for him to take with him someone who knew the roads and by-ways and rivers of the district.

So he set out with Prelinguand, Vauguyon's squire, and without

1. Another saying reversed. To kill a pedlar for a comb, is to take a man's life for a trifle.

raising an alarm scouted in all directions. Meanwhile Gargantua refreshed himself and took a little food with his men; and he ordered
that his mare should be given a *picotin* of oats: that is to say seventy-
four quarters, three bushels.

Gymnaste and his companion rode on until they met the enemy, all
scattered and in disorder, pillaging and plundering everything they
could; and at their first sight of him in the far distance, they ran up
in a crowd to rob him.

Upon this he shouted out to them: 'Sirs, I'm a poor devil. Have
mercy on me, I pray you. I have just one crown left, and we'll spend
it on drink. For it is *aurum potabile*[1] and this horse here shall be sold to
buy my welcome. After that, enlist me as one of your men. For there
was never a better hand at catching, larding, roasting and dressing
and, by God, at dismembering and gobbling a hen than I, your
humble servant. And now, to buy my welcome, I drink to all good
fellows.'

Then he undid his leather bottle, and without sticking his nose into
it took a handsome gulp. The rogues looked at him, opening their
mouths a good foot wide and putting out their tongues like greyhounds, in the hope of drinking after him. But at this point Tripet,
their captain, came up to see what was the matter.

To him Gymnaste offered his bottle, saying: 'Here, Captain, take
a good swig of this. I've made a proof of it. It's wine of La Faye-
Monjault.'

'What!' exclaimed Tripet. 'This johnny's taking a rise out of us.
Who are you?'

'I'm a poor devil,' answered Gymnaste.

'Ha!' said Tripet. 'Since you're a poor devil it's only right you
should go on your way. For a poor devil can go free anywhere, without paying tax or toll. But it's not usual for poor devils to be so well
mounted. Therefore, Master Devil, get down and let me have your
horse. And if he doesn't carry me well, Master Devil, you shall. For I
like the idea of being carried off by a devil like you.'

1. Potable gold: a medieval panacea.

CHAPTER 35: *How Gymnaste neatly killed Captain Tripet and others of Picrochole's men*

WHEN they heard him say this, some of them began to be afraid, and crossed themselves with all the hands on their bodies, thinking that this was a devil in disguise. One of them, indeed, Good John, Captain of the Free-Molesmen, pulled his prayer-book out of his codpiece and cried aloud:

'*Agios ho theos*.[1] If you are on God's side speak. If you're one of the other faction, get you gone!' But he did not go away. Several of the band heard this, however, and departed from the company; all of which Gymnaste noticed and reflected on.

It was for that reason that he pretended to dismount. But having poised himself on the mounting side, he nimbly performed the stirrup-trick, with his short sword at his thigh and, passing beneath his horse, sprang into the air, alighting with both feet on the saddle and his back to the horse's head. 'My case goes backwards,' said he.

Then, in that posture, he twirled round on one foot in the leftward direction and succeeding in recovering his proper position exactly.

Then said Tripet: 'I won't do that at this moment, and for a good reason.'

'Bah,' said Gymnaste. 'I missed. Now I'll do the leap in reverse.'

Then with great strength and agility he twirled round in the same manner as before, but to the right. When he had done this he put his right thumb on the pommel of the saddle and raised his whole body in the air, resting his entire weight on the nerve and muscle of that thumb, and so turned himself round three times. On the fourth, reversing his whole body without touching anything, he sprang between his horse's ears, keeping the whole of his body rigid in the air on his left thumb; and in this posture he turned a complete circle. Then, clapping the palm of his right hand on the middle of his saddle, he swung himself so far as to alight on the crupper, where the ladies ride. This done, he quite easily passed his right leg over the saddle, and got into the position to ride on the crupper.

'But,' he said, 'it would be better for me to get between the pommels.'

1. Holy is God (from the Liturgy of the Passion).

So, supporting himself by pressing his two thumbs on the crupper before him, he turned a back-somersault in the air and landed firmly seated between the pommels. Then he somersaulted the whole of his body into the air, and so came down with his feet together between the pommels, and there twirled round more than a hundred times, with his arms extended crosswise; and as he did so he cried in a loud voice: 'I rage, devils, I rage, I rage! Hold me, devils, hold me, hold me!'

Whilst he swung round like this, the rogues said to one another in great amazement: 'Mother of God, this is a hobgoblin or a devil in disguise. *Ab hoste maligno libera nos, Domine.*[1] And they departed in headlong flight, glancing behind them like a dog running off with a hen.

Then, seeing his advantage, Gymnaste got down from his horse, drew his sword, and charged at the proudest of them, striking mighty blows and overthrowing them in great heaps, wounded, damaged, and bruised. They offered no resistance, for they thought that he was a devil, and starving, not only on account of his marvellous vaulting feats, but also because of the conversation Tripet had held with him, when he had called him *poor devil.* Only Tripet treacherously tried to split his skull with his short, two-edged broad-sword. But Gymnaste was well armoured, and felt no more of this stroke than the weight of the blow. However he swung quickly round and struck a flying thrust at the said Tripet. Then, as the captain covered the upper part of his body, Gymnaste with one blow sliced him through the stomach, colon, and half the liver, so that he fell to the ground; and as he fell he threw up more than four pot-fulls of soup and, mingled with the soup, his soul.

This done, Gymnaste withdrew, being of the opinion that strokes of luck should never be pressed too far, and that all knights should treat their good fortune with moderation, neither harassing nor torturing it. Mounting his horse, therefore, he gave him the spur and rode straight along the way to La Vauguyon, and Prelinguand with him.

1. From the evil enemy, deliver us, O Lord!

CHAPTER 36: *How Gargantua demolished the Castle at the Ford of Vède and how they passed the Ford*

THE moment he arrived Gymnaste recounted the condition in which he had found the enemy and the stratagem he had used, single-handed, against their whole band. He declared that they were nothing but marauders, pillagers, and brigands, ignorant of all military discipline, and that Gargantua and his followers should advance boldly, for it would be easy for them to knock the enemy down like cattle.

Then Gargantua mounted his great mare and, with the company already described, went on his way, in the course of which he found a huge, tall tree – which was commonly called St Martin's Tree, because it had grown from a pilgrim's staff once planted by St Martin. 'This is just what I needed,' he said. 'This tree will serve me for a pilgrim's staff and a lance.' And he easily rooted it up out of the ground, stripped off its branches, and trimmed it to his liking.

Meanwhile his mare pissed to relieve her belly, but so abundantly that she made a flood twenty-one miles wide, and all her piss drained down to the Ford of Vède, so swelling the stream along its course that the whole of that enemy band was hideously drowned, except for some who had taken the road towards the slopes on the left.

When Gargantua came to the region of the Wood of Vède, he was informed by Eudemon that inside the castle were some remnants of the enemy; and to make sure of this Gargantua shouted at the top of his voice: 'Are you there, or are you not? If you are there, get out. But if you are not, I have nothing to say.'

But a ruffian of a gunner who was on the parapet fired a cannon-shot at him, which hit him violently on the right temple. Yet for all this he did him no more harm than if he had thrown a plum at him.

'What is that?' asked Gargantua. 'Do you throw grape pips at us here? You shall pay dearly for your vintage.' For he really thought that the shot was a grape pip.

Those who were in the castle, amusing themselves at Little Slam, heard the noise and ran out on to the towers and battlements, from which they fired more than nine thousand and twenty-five falconet and arquebus shots, all aimed at his head; and so thick did they fall round him that he cried:

'Ponocrates, my friend, these flies here are blinding me. Give me a branch of one of those willows to drive them off.' For he thought that the lead shot and cannon-balls were horse-flies.

Ponocrates informed him that they were not flies, but artillery shot, fired at him from the castle. So he charged with his great tree against it, and with mighty blows threw down the towers and fortifications, laying it all level with the ground. In this way those inside were all crushed and smashed to pieces.

Then, setting out from there, Gargantua and his men came to the mill-bridge and found all the ford so thick with dead bodies that they had choked the mill-stream; these were the men who had perished in the mare's urinary flood. So here they came to a stop, and considered how they could cross, seeing the obstruction caused by those corpses.

But Gymnaste said: 'If the devils have crossed over there I shall cross easily enough.'

'The devils,' explained Eudemon, 'have crossed to carry off the damned souls.'

'By St Trinian,' cried Ponocrates, 'it follows sure enough, then, that Gymnaste will get across.'

'Yes, indeed,' said Gymnaste, 'or I shall stick halfway.'

And spurring on his horse, he leapt straight over, without the beast taking the least fright at the corpses. For his master had accustomed him, by Aelian's method, to fear neither dead bodies nor souls – not by killing men, as Diomedes killed the Thracians and Ulysses threw the corpses of his enemies at his horse's feet, according to Homer's story, but by putting a dummy amongst his straw, and making the beast tread on it when he gave him his oats.

The three others followed him without accident, excepting Eudemon, whose horse plunged his right leg knee-deep into the belly of a great, fat ruffian, who was lying there on his back, drowned. He could not get it out, and there he stayed stuck, till Gargantua pushed the rest of the ruffian's guts down in the water with his staff, while the horse pulled out his leg. And that horse – by a miracle of veterinary science – was cured of a ring-bone which he had on that leg, through contact with that great oaf's guts.

CHAPTER 37: *How Gargantua, in combing his Head, made the Cannon-balls fall out of his Hair*

ONCE clear of the banks of the Vède, in a very short while they came to Grandgousier's castle, where that King was most eagerly awaiting them; and on Gargantua's arrival they entertained him enthusiastically. Never was seen a more joyful company. *Supplementum Supplementi Chronicorum*[1] says that Gargamelle died of joy. For my part, I know nothing about it, and I care precious little about her or any other woman.

The truth was that while changing his clothes and passing a comb through his hair (which comb was a hundred canes long, and set with great elephants' tusks entire) at each combing he brought down more than seven cannon-balls, which had stayed in his hair from the destruction of the castle at the wood of Vède.

When his father Grandgousier saw these he thought that they were lice, and said: 'Come now, my dear son, have you brought us sparrow-hawks from Montaigu college?[2] I didn't mean you to reside at that place.'

To which Ponocrates replied: 'My lord, do not imagine that I placed him in that verminous college that goes by the name of Montaigu. Considering the enormous cruelties and villainy I've seen there, I would rather have put him among the beggars in the Holy Innocents' graveyard. For galley-slaves among the Moors and the Tartars, and murderers in felons' prisons, and certainly the dogs in your house, are better treated than the poor wretches in that place. If I were king in Paris, devil take me if I wouldn't set fire to it, and leave the Principal and supervisors to be burnt to death for suffering such inhumanity to be perpetrated before their eyes.'

Then, picking up one of the shot, he said: 'These are cannon-balls, which were shot at your son Gargantua just now by your treacherous enemies, as he was passing by the Wood of Vède. But they have been thoroughly paid back. They all perished to a man in the ruins of the castle, as the Philistines did by Samson's ruse, and just like the men

1. The Supplement to the Supplement of the Chronicles.
2. A University residence in Paris, attacked both by Erasmus and Rabelais for its filth.

who were overwhelmed by the Tower of Siloam, according to Luke xiii. My counsel is that we should pursue the rest while Fortune is in our favour. For Chance wears all her locks in front, and once she has passed you by, you cannot recall her. For the back of her head is bald, and she never turns back.'

'But this is certainly not the time,' said Grandgousier. 'I want to give you a feast this evening and to offer you a good welcome.'

This said, they made supper ready and, on top of the usual fare, there were roasted sixteen oxen, three heifers, thirty-two calves, sixty-three suckling kids, ninety-five sheep, three hundred suckling pigs in wine sauce, eleven score partridges, seven hundred woodcock, four hundred capons from Loudun and Cornouaille, six thousand pullets and as many pigeons, six hundred guinea-fowls, fourteen hundred leverets, three hundred and three bustards and seventeen hundred capon chicks.

Game they could not get so quickly, except eleven wild boars sent by the abbot of Turpenay, and eighteen fallow deer presented by the lord of Grandmont, together with seven score pheasants, sent by the lord of Essars, and some dozens of ring-doves, water-hens, teal, bitterns, curlews, plovers, heath-cock, briganders, sea-ducks, young lapwings, sheldrakes, shovelers, herons, hernshaws, coots, criels, storks, little bustards, orange flamingoes (which are called *phoenicopters*), landrails, and turkey hens, together with plenty of dumplings and quantities of soups.

There was an abundance of food there, and no mistake; and it was decently served by Slapsauce, Hotch-potch, and Pinch-the-grape, Grandgousier's cooks, while Janot, Micquel, and Scour-glass took good care of the drinks.

CHAPTER 38 : *How Gargantua ate six Pilgrims in a Salad*

THE story requires us to relate the adventures of six pilgrims, on their way from Saint-Sebastien, near Nantes. To find themselves shelter for that night, they had hidden themselves, out of fear of the enemy, among the pea-straw in the garden, between the cabbages and the lettuces. Now Gargantua found himself rather thirsty, and asked if there were any lettuces to be had to make a salad; and hearing that some of

the finest and largest in the country grew there, as big as plum or walnut trees, he decided to go to the garden himself, and brought away
as many as he fancied in his hand. With them he picked up the six pilgrims, who were so terrified that they had not the courage to speak or
cough.

As Gargantua was giving his lettuces a preliminary washing at the
fountain, the pilgrims said to one another in a whisper: 'What's to be
done? We shall drown here among the lettuces. Shall we speak? But
if we speak he will kill us as spies.' And as they were thus deliberating,
Gargantua put them with his lettuces into a dish belonging to the
house, which was as large as the tun of Cîteaux, and ate them with oil,
vinegar, and salt as an appetizer before his supper, stuffing into his
mouth at the same time five of the pilgrims.

The sixth was in the dish, hidden under a lettuce except for his pilgrim's staff, which was sticking out, and which Grandgousier saw.
Whereupon he exclaimed: 'That's a snail's horn, I think. Don't eat it.'
'Why?' asked Gargantua. 'They're good all this month.' And pulling at the staff, he picked up the pilgrim with it, making a good meal
of him. Then he took a huge gulp of strong white wine, and they
waited for the supper to be brought in.

The pilgrims, thus devoured, kept themselves out of the way of his
molars as best they could, and felt as if they had been put into the
lowest dungeon of some prison. When Gargantua took his great gulp,
indeed, they expected to drown in his mouth. The torrent of wine
almost carried them down into the abyss of his stomach. However,
leaping on their staffs, like pilgrims to St Michael's Mount, they got
into shelter behind his teeth. But unfortunately one of them, testing
the ground with his staff to see whether they were in safety, struck
roughly into the hole of a decayed tooth, hitting the mandibular
nerve. This gave Gargantua very great pain, and he began to cry out
in sudden rage. Then, to ease his pain, he sent for his toothpick, and
probing towards the young walnut-tree, dislodged the noble pilgrims
from their nest.

He caught one by the legs, another by the shoulders, another by the
pouch, another by the scarf, and the poor wretch who had probed
him with his staff he hooked up by the codpiece; which was, however, a great stroke of luck for him, for it broke an ulcerous lump
which had been torturing him ever since they had passed Ancenis.

So the dislodged pilgrims fled across the plantation at a lively trot, and Gargantua's pain died down, just at the moment when he was called by Eudemon to supper, for everything was ready.

'I'll go and piss away my misfortune, then,' he answered.

So copiously did he piss indeed that his urine cut the pilgrims' road, and they were compelled to cross the great canal. Passing from there by the bank of La Touche along the open road, they all fell, except Fournillier, into a trap that had been laid for catching wolves in a net, from which they escaped by the resourcefulness of the said Fournillier, who cut all the meshes and ropes. When they had escaped from there, they lay for the rest of the night in a lodging near Le Couldray, and there they were comforted for their misfortunes by the good words of one of their company named Wearybones, who pointed out to them that this adventure had been predicted by David in the Psalms. *Cum exurgerent homines in nos, forte vivos deglutissent nos,* when we were eaten in a salad with a grain of salt; *cum irasceretur furor eorum in nos, forsitan aqua absorbuisset nos,* when he drank down the great gulp; *torrentem pertransivit anima nostra,* when we crossed the great canal; *forsitan pertransisset anima nostra aquam intolerabilem,* with his urine, with which he cut our road. *Benedictus Dominus, qui non dedit nos in captionem dentibus eorum. Anima nostra, sicut passer, erepta est de laqueo venantium,* when we fell into the trap; *laqueus contritus est* by Fournillier, *et nos liberati sumus. Adjutorium nostrum,* &c.'[1]

CHAPTER 39: *How the Monk was feasted by Gargantua, and of the fine Discourse he delivered during Supper*

WHEN Gargantua was at table, and the first part of the good things had been consumed, Grandgousier began to recount the origins and cause of the war being waged between him and Picrochole; and when he came to the point of narrating how Friar John of the Hashes had triumphed at the defence of the abbey-close, he commended his prowess as above that of Camillus, Scipio, Pompey, Caesar, and Themistocles.

Then Gargantua desired that the friar should be sent for at once, so

1. This is the 124th Psalm [Vulg. 123rd] less its first verse, with a free interpretation, after the manner of the more ignorant priesthood.

that he might be consulted on what was next to be done. At their request the major-domo went to fetch him, and brought him back merrily with the staff of his cross on Grandgousier's mule; and when he arrived he was greeted with a thousand caresses, a thousand embraces, a thousand good-days:

'Ha, Friar John, my friend, Friar John, my fine cousin, Friar John, devil take you! Let me hug you round the neck, my friend.'

'Let me take you in my arms!'

'Come let me grip you, my ballocky boy, till I break your back.'

And what a joker Friar John was! Never was a man so charming or so gracious.

'Come, come,' said Gargantua, 'take a stool here beside me, at this end.'

'Most willingly,' said the monk, 'since it is your pleasure. Page, some water! Pour it out, my boy, pour it out. It will refresh my liver. Give it here, and let me gargle.'

'*Deposita cappa*,' said Gymnaste, 'off with this habit.'

'Ho, by God,' said the monk, 'my dear sir, there's a chapter *in statutis Ordinis* – in the Statutes of my Order – that would object to that.'

'A turd!' said Gymnaste. 'A turd for your chapter. That frock weighs down both your shoulders. Take it off.'

'My friend,' said the monk, 'let me wear it. For, by God, it only makes me drink the better. It jollifies my whole body. If I take it off, my friends the pages will cut it up into garters, which was what happened to me once at Coulaines. And I shall have no appetite into the bargain. But if I sit down to table in this habit I shall drink, by God I shall, both to you and to your horse – with all my heart. God save the company! I had supped; but I shan't eat any the less for that. I have a paved stomach as hollow as St Benedict's tun, and always gaping like a lawyer's purse. Of every fish except the tench – take the wing of a partridge or a nun's thigh. Isn't it a jolly death, to die with a stiff johnthomas? Our Prior's very fond of white capon meat.'

'In that,' said Gymnaste, 'he's unlike a fox. They never eat the white meat of the hens, pullets, and capons they carry off.'

'Why?' asked the monk.

'Because,' said Gymnaste, 'they have no cooks to cook it, and if it isn't properly cooked it stays red and not white. The redness of meat is a sign that it is not properly cooked, except for lobsters and cray-fish, which are cardinalized in the cooking.'

'Holy God's day, as Bayard would say,' answered the monk. 'The hospitaller of our abbey has his head underdone, then, for his eyes are as red as an alder-wood bowl. This leveret's thigh is good for the gout. Talking of trowels – why is it that a young lady's thighs are always cool?'

'That problem,' said Gargantua, 'is neither in Aristotle, nor in Alexander of Aphrodisias, nor in Plutarch.'

'It is for three causes,' said the monk, 'which make a place naturally cool: in the first place, because the water runs all down it; secondly, because it is shady, obscure, and dark, a place never lit by the sun; and thirdly, because it is continually fanned by winds from the northern hole, the smock, and also the codpiece. And heartily too! Page, let's get tippling! ... Gulp, gulp, gulp. ... How good God is to give us this good drink! ... I swear to the Almighty that if I had lived in the time of Jesus Christ, I should have taken good care that the Jews didn't take him in the garden of Olivet. What's more, the devil fail me if I should have failed to hamstring those gentlemenly Apostles, who ran away like such cowards after eating a grand supper, and left their good Master in the lurch! I hate a man worse than poison who runs away when he ought to wield a bold knife. Oh, why can't I be king of France for eighty – or for a hundred years? I'd clip the ears and the ballocks of those dogs who fled from Pavia! May they catch the ague! Why couldn't they have died there, instead of leaving their good prince in that plight? Isn't it better and more honourable to die fighting valiantly than to save your life by villainous flight? ... We shan't eat many goslings this year. ... Ho, my friend, pass me some of that pig. ... Diabolo! There's no more grape-juice: *germinavit radix Jesse.*[1] May I die the death, but I'm perishing of thirst. ... This wine is not a bad one. What wine did you drink in Paris? The devil take me if I didn't once keep open house there, for more than six months, to all comers! ... Did you know Friar Claude from the Hault-Barrois? Oh, what a fine companion he was! But what fly has stung him? He has been doing nothing but study since I don't know when. For my part, I do no studying. In our abbey we never study, for fear of the mumps. Our late abbot used to say that it's a monstrous thing to see a learned

1. There came forth a shoot out of the stem of Jesse.

monk. By God, my noble friend, *magis magnos clericos non sunt magis magnos sapientes.*[1] ... You never saw so many hares as there are this year. I haven't been able to get hold of a goshawk or a tassel-gentle anywhere on earth. My lord de la Bellonière did promise me a lanner-hawk, but he wrote to me a little while ago that the beast had gone short of breath. The partridges will eat our corn in the ear this year. I don't enjoy fowling with a net; it always makes me catch cold. If I'm not running and bustling about I'm never happy. It's true that when I jump hedges and bushes, my habit leaves some of its wool behind. I've got hold of a splendid greyhound. Devil seize me if a hare escapes him. A lackey was taking him to my lord de Maulevrier, and I pinched him. Was I wrong?'

'No, Friar John,' said Gymnaste. 'Oh no, by all the devils you weren't!'

'Here's a health to such devils,' cried the monk, 'and long life to them! By the power of God, what would that lame fellow have done with him? He's better pleased, by God, when they give him a good yoke of oxen!'

'What, do you swear, Friar John?' cried Ponocrates.

'It's only to embellish my language,' answered the monk. 'It's rhetorical colouring, Ciceronian.'

CHAPTER 40: *Why Monks are shunned by the world, and why some have bigger Noses than others*

'By my faith as a Christian,' said Eudemon, 'this monk's an astoundingly good fellow. He's an entertainment to every one of us. Now tell me why men won't allow monks in any good company? Why are they called spoil-sports and driven off, much as bees drive the drones from around their hives? – *"Ignavum fucos pecus a presepibus arcent,"*[2] as Virgil puts it.'

To which Gargantua replied: 'It's the absolute truth that the frock and the cowl draw on themselves the opprobrium, insults, and curses of the world, just as the wind called Caecias attracts the clouds. The conclusive reason is that they eat the world's excrement, that is to say,

1. The greatest clerics are not the most learned.
2. The cowardly swarm drive the drones from the hives.

sins; and as eaters of excrement they are cast into their privies – their convents and abbeys that is – which are cut off from all civil intercourse, as are the privies of a house. If you can understand why a monkey is always teased and mocked by the family, then you will realize why monks are rejected by all, old and young alike. A monkey doesn't guard a house, like a dog; he doesn't draw the plough, like an ox; he produces no milk or wool, like a sheep; he doesn't carry burdens, like a horse. All that he does is to beshit and ruin everything, which is the reason why he gets mockery and beatings from everyone. Similarly a monk – I mean one of these lazy monks – doesn't till the fields like a peasant, nor guard the country like a soldier, nor cure the sick like a physician, nor preach and instruct the world like a good gospeller and preceptor, nor carry commodities and things that the public need like a merchant. That is the reason why everyone hoots at them and abhors them.'

'Yes,' said Grandgousier, 'but they pray to God for us.'

'Nothing of the sort,' replied Gargantua. 'The fact is that they disturb their whole neighbourhood with the clanking of their bells.'

'Yes indeed,' said the monk. 'A Mass, a Matins, or a Vespers well rung is half sung.'

'They mumble through ever so many miracle stories and psalms which they don't in the least understand. They count over a number of Paternosters interlarded with long Ave-Marias, without understanding them or giving them so much as a thought; and that I call not prayer, but mockery of God. Still, may the Lord come to their aid if they do pray for us, and not through fear of losing their fresh bread and fat soups. All true Christians, of all degrees, in all places and at all times, pray to God, and the Holy Spirit prays and intercedes for them, and God receives them into his grace. Now our good Friar John is a true good Christian. Therefore everyone desires his company. He's no bigot, he's no wastrel; he is honest, gay, and resolute, and a good companion; he works, he labours, he defends the oppressed, he comforts the afflicted, he aids the suffering, and he saves the close of his abbey.'

'I do a great deal more than that,' said the monk. 'For whilst we're dispatching our Matins and Masses for the dead in the choir I make cross-bow strings, I polish bolts and quarrels, I manufacture snares and nets to catch rabbits. I'm never idle. But ho, ho there! Drink! Bring us some drink! Bring in the fruit. These are chestnuts from the wood of Estrocs. With good fresh wine they'll set you farting. You're not frisked up here yet. By God, I drink at every ford, like a proctor's horse.'

'Friar John,' said Gymnaste, 'wipe off that drip that's hanging on your nose.'

'Ha, ha!' said the monk, 'am I not in danger of drowning, seeing that I'm in water up to the nose? No, no, *quare*? *Quia*.[1]

> It goes not in as water, though as water it may come out,
> For it's properly corrected with grape-juice antidote.

O my friend, anyone who had winter boots of such leather could boldly preach to the oysters, for they would never let water.'

'Why is it,' asked Gargantua, 'that Friar John has such a handsome nose?'

'Because,' replied Grandgousier, 'God wished it so, and he makes us in such shape and to such end as pleases his divine will, even as a potter fashions his pots.'

'Because,' said Ponocrates, 'he was one of the first at Nose-fair. He chose one of the finest and biggest.'

'Stuff and nonsense,' said the monk. 'According to true monastic reasoning it was because my nurse had soft breasts: when she suckled me my nose sank in, as if into butter, and there it swelled and grew like dough in the kneading-trough. Hard breasts in nurses make children snub-nosed. But come, come! *Ad formam nasi cognoscitur, ad te levavi.*[2] I never eat sweets. ... Page, some drink, and bring some more toast!'

CHAPTER 41: *How the Monk made Gargantua sleep, and of his Hours and Breviaries*

SUPPER over, they discussed the business in hand, and it was decided that about midnight they should go out skirmishing to discover what precautions and watch the enemy kept; and that in the meantime they

---

1. Why? Because.
2. A garbled psalm: By the shape of his nose he is known,
   I have lifted up [mine eyes] to thee.

should rest a little, in order to be the fresher for their foray. But Gargantua could not sleep whichever way he turned. Whereupon the monk said to him: 'I never sleep really comfortably, except when I am at a sermon, or at my prayers. Let's begin, I beg of you, you and I, the seven penitential psalms, and see if you won't soon be asleep.'

The idea greatly pleased Gargantua and, beginning with the first psalm, when they came to the *Beati quorum* they both fell asleep. But the monk never failed to wake up before midnight, so used was he to the hour of claustral Matins; and when he woke up he roused all the rest by loudly singing the song:

> Ho, Regnault, wake, awake!
> O, Regnault, wake!

When they were all awake he said: 'Gentlemen, they say that Matins generally begin with a cough, and supper with drinking. Let us act the other way round. Let's begin our Matins now with a drink, and this evening, when supper comes in, we'll cough as hard as we can.'

'To drink so soon after sleeping,' said Gargantua at this, 'is to behave contrary to the rules of medicine. We ought first to clear the stomach of superfluities and excrements.'

'The prescription's good,' replied the monk. 'A hundred devils leap on my body if there aren't more old drunkards than old physicians. I have come to an agreement with my appetite to this effect, that it always goes to bed when I do, and in return I always take good care of it during the day; also it gets up with me. You take as much trouble with your droppings as you like, I'm going to attend to my purge.'

'What purge do you mean?' asked Gargantua.

'My breviary,' said the monk. 'For just as falconers, before they feed their hawks, make them seize on a hen's leg to purge their brains of vapours, and give them an appetite, so by taking up this jolly breviary of mine in the mornings, I scour my lungs through, and here I am ready to drink.'

'According to what rite do you recite this fine Book of Hours of yours?' asked Gargantua.

'According to the rite of When-and-where: with three psalms and three lessons, or with nothing at all for those who want nothing. I never subject myself to hours; hours were made for man, and not man for hours. Therefore I make mine in the fashion of stirrup-leathers. I shorten them or lengthen them when I see fit; *brevis oratio penetrat celos, longa potatio evacuat cyphos.*[1] Where is that written?'

'By my faith,' said Ponocrates, 'I don't know, my pillicock, but you're worth more than gold.'

'In that,' said the monk, 'I resemble you. But *venite, apotemus.*'[2]

Then they cooked an abundance of rashers on the coals and some early morning soup, and the monk drank as he would, some keeping him company and some leaving the stuff alone. After that each began to arm and equip himself, and they forced the monk to do the same, although he wanted no other protection but his habit over his stomach and the staff of his cross in his hand. Nevertheless at their wish he was encased in armour from head to foot and mounted on a fine Neapolitan charger, with a stout short-sword at his side. With him rode Gargantua, Ponocrates, Gymnaste, Eudemon, and twenty-five of the most adventurous of Grandgousier's house, all armed at proof, with lances in their hands, and mounted like St George, each with an arquebusier following him.

CHAPTER 42: *How the Monk encouraged his Companions, and how he hanged on a Tree*

THUS the noble champions set out on their adventure, resolutely seeking what enterprise they should pursue and what guard against when the day of the great and terrible battle should come.

And the monk encouraged them, saying: 'My children, have neither fear nor doubts. I will conduct you safely. May God and St Benedict be with us! If I had strength equal to my courage, by God I'd pluck 'em for you like a duck! I'm afraid of nothing except artillery. Yet I know a prayer, taught me by the sub-sacristan of our abbey, which safeguards a man against all fiery mouths. But it will do me no good because I have no faith in it. Nevertheless the staff of my cross will play Old Harry with them. And if one of you does a bolt, the devil may take me if I don't make him a monk instead of me, and tie my frock round his neck, by God. It carries a cure for cowardice in men. Have you never heard of my lord of Meurles' greyhound, which

1. A short prayer pierces heaven, a long drink clears out the hump.
2. Come, let us take liquor.

was no good in the field? My lord put a frock round his neck and, by the living God, not a hare or a fox ever escaped him and, what's more, he covered all the bitches in the country, though up to then he'd been weak in the back and *de frigidis et maleficiatis*.'[1]

As he spoke these heated words, the monk passed beneath a walnut-tree, on the way to the Willow-wood, and spitted the vizor of his helmet on the broken end of a great bough. Nothwithstanding this, he spurred his horse fiercely. The beast, being skittish under the spur, made a bound forward, and the monk, trying to disengage his vizor from the hook, let go the reins and hung on to the branch with his hand, while his horse slipped from under him. In this way he was left suspended in the walnut tree, crying 'Help!' and 'Murder!', and swearing also that there was treason afoot.

Eudemon was the first to perceive him, and he called out to Gargantua: 'Sire, come and see Absalom hanging!' But when Gargantua rode up, he looked closely at the monk's countenance and at the way he was hanging. Then he said to Eudemon: 'You're a bit out when you compare him to Absalom. Absalom hung by the hair. But the monk, being cropped, is hanging by the ears.'

'Help me,' cried the monk, 'in the name of the devil! Do you think this is the moment for chatter? You remind me of the Decretalist preachers, who say that if anyone sees his neighbour in peril of death he must, under pain of three-pronged excommunication, admonish him to make confession and put himself in a state of grace, before coming to his aid. When I see anyone in future, who has fallen into the river and is just going to drown, instead of going after him and lending him a hand, I'll read him a fine, long sermon *de contemptu mundi et fuga seculi*,[2] and when he's stark dead I'll go and fish him out.'

'Don't you stir, my dear fellow,' said Gymnaste. 'I'll come and help you, for you're a pretty little *monachus*.

> Monachus in claustro
> Non valet ova duo;
> Sed, quando est extra,
> Bene valet triginta.[3]

1. Concerning the cold and those made impotent through sorcery.
2. On contempt for the world and the avoidance of secular things.
3. A monk in his cloister is not worth two eggs. But when he is outside he is worth a good thirty.

I've seen more than five hundred hanged men, but I never saw one who hung more gracefully. If I hung as gracefully I'd willingly stay there for the whole of my life.'

'Will you soon have finished preaching?' asked the monk. 'Help me in God's name, since you won't for the other Power's sake. But by the habit I wear you'll repent of this, *tempore et loco prelibatis.*'[1]

Then Gymnaste dismounted and, climbing the tree, lifted the monk up by the armpits with one hand, while with the other he unhooked his vizor from the broken branch. Then he dropped him to the ground and himself followed after.

Once on the ground, the monk took off all his armour and, picking up the staff of his cross, remounted his horse, which Eudemon had stopped from running away. And so they went merrily on, keeping to the road to the Willow-wood.

CHAPTER 43: *How Picrochole's Scouts were met by Gargantua; and how the Monk killed Captain Drawforth, and was then captured by the Enemy*

WHEN Picrochole heard the tale of those who had escaped from the rout when Tripet was detriped, he flew into a great fury at the news that the devils had attacked his men; and he held a council all that night, at which Hasticalf and Touchspigot affirmed that he had enough power to defeat all the devils in hell, if they should come. This Picrochole did not entirely believe nor entirely disbelieve.

So, to reconnoitre the country, he sent out, under the command of Count Fireahead, sixteen hundred knights, all mounted on light horses in skirmishing order, all thoroughly sprinkled with holy water, and each having as a mark of identification a stole slung round him, against all hazards, in case they should meet the devils. Then, by virtue of this Gregorian water and of the stoles together, they would make them vanish and disappear.

They advanced, therefore, to the neighbourhood of La Vauguyon and the Hospital, but never found anyone to speak to. So they returned by the upper road, and in a shepherd's cottage near Le Couldray found the five pilgrims. After binding and blindfolding them as if

1. In the right time and place.

they were spies, they took them off, despite all their protests, con-jurations, and entreaties.

When they had come down from there towards Seuilly they were heard by Gargantua, who said to his men: 'Comrades, here is an en-counter for us. They are ten times as many as we are. Shall we charge them?'

'What the devil else should we do?' asked the monk. 'Do you reckon men by numbers, and not by their valour and courage?' Then he cried: 'Charge, devils, charge!'

Hearing this, the enemy thought that these were real devils, and so began to fly headlong, with the exception of Fireahead, who couched his lance and struck the monk with all his might in the middle of the chest. But when it met the horrific frock, its steel point buckled. It was like striking an anvil with a small candle. Whereupon the monk gave him such a fierce thwack with the staff of his cross between the neck and the shoulders, on the acromion bone, that he stunned him, deprived him of all motion and feeling, and tumbled him at the feet of his horse. Then, seeing the stole that he wore slung around him, the monk said to Gargantua: 'These men are no more than priests; which is only the first stage towards a monk. But, by St John, I'm a monk complete; I'll kill 'em for you like flies.'

Then the great galloper ran after them till he caught the hindmost, and beat them down like rye, striking right and left at random; and at that moment Gymnaste inquired of Gargantua if they ought to pur-sue them. 'On no account,' replied Gargantua. 'For according to true military practice you must never drive your enemy into the straits of despair, because such a plight multiplies his strength and increases his courage; which was cast down and failing before. There is no better aid to safety for men who are beaten and dismayed than to have no hope of safety whatever. How many victories have the conquered wrested from the hands of the victors when the latter have not been satisfied with moderation, but have attempted to make a complete massacre and totally to destroy their enemy, without leaving so much as one alive to convey the news! Always leave every door and road open to your enemies. Make them a bridge of silver, in fact, to help them get away.'

'Yes,' said Gymnaste, 'but they've captured the monk.'

'Have they got the monk?' asked Gargantua. 'Then upon my

honour they'll suffer for it! But to provide against all chances, let us not retire yet. Let us wait here quietly. For I think that by now I understand our enemies' tactics pretty well. They are guided by luck, not by judgement.'

While they were thus waiting beneath the walnut trees, the monk had gone on in pursuit, charging all those whom he met, and giving no quarter to any until he met a horseman who was carrying one of the poor pilgrims behind him. And there, as he was about to strip him, the pilgrim cried out: 'Ah, my lord Prior, my friend, my lord Prior, save me, I beg of you!'

When they heard these words the enemy turned back and, seeing that it was only the monk who was making all this trouble, they loaded him with blows, as men load an ass with wood. But he felt nothing of all this, especially when they hit his frock, so tough was his skin. Then they put him under a guard of two archers and, turning round, saw no one opposing them, which made them think that Gargantua and his troop had fled. So they ran to the walnuts as hard as they could to find them, and left the monk behind, alone with his guard of two archers.

Gargantua heard the noise and the neighing of the horses, and said to his men: 'Comrades, I hear our enemy approaching. I can see some of them already rushing against us in a bunch. Let us close up here, and hold the road in good formation. By this means we shall be able to withstand them to their loss and our honour.'

CHAPTER 44: *How the Monk got rid of his Guards, and how Picrochole's Scouts were defeated*

SEEING them thus depart in disorder, the monk guessed that they were going to charge on Gargantua and his men; and he was strangely sad that he could not come to their assistance. Then he examined the faces of his two archers, who were longing to run after the band in the hopes of looting something, and were watching the valley into which their comrades were dropping. And the monk reasoned to himself further, saying: 'These men are most inexpert in the practice of war. They haven't asked for my parole and they haven't taken my sword.'

Immediately on this, he drew the said sword and with it struck the archer who guarded him on the right, entirely severing the jugular veins and sphagitid arteries of his neck together with his uvula as far as the two glands; and as he withdrew the blade he laid open his spinal marrow between the second and third vertebrae; upon which the archer fell down dead. Then, turning his horse to the left, the monk charged his other guard, who, seeing that his companion was dead and that the monk had the better of him, cried aloud: 'Oh, my lord Prior, I surrender! My lord Prior, my good friend, my lord Prior!'

And the monk cried out after him: 'My lord Posterior, my friend! My lord Posterior, you're going to catch it on your posterior.'

'Oh, my lord Prior,' cried the archer, 'my dear lord Prior, may God make you an abbot!'

'By the habit that I wear,' replied the monk, 'I'll make you a cardinal here and now. Do you hold churchmen to ransom? You shall receive a red hat at my hands this very moment.'

And the archer cried: 'My lord Prior, my lord Prior, My lord Abbot to-be, my lord Cardinal, my lord Everything! Oh, oh, hey, no, my lord Prior, my dear kind lord, my noble Prior, I surrender to you!'

'And I surrender you to all the devils,' said the monk.

Then at one blow he sliced his head, cutting his skull over the temple-bone and taking off the two parietal bones and the sagittal suture, together with a great part of the frontal bone; and in doing this he cut through the two membranes and made a deep opening in the posterior lobes of his brain. So his cranium remained hanging on his shoulders by the skin of his pericranium, falling backwards like a doctor's cap, black outside and red within. And he fell to the ground stark dead.

After this feat, the monk spurred his horse and followed the direction which the enemy had taken. But they had met Gargantua and his companions on the high road, and were so diminished in numbers from the enormous slaughter wrought upon them by Gargantua with his great tree, and by Gymnaste, Ponocrates, Eudemon, and the others, that they began to retire in haste, in a complete fright and as troubled in their wits and understanding as if they had seen death's very shape and semblance before their eyes.

And as you see an ass with a Junonian gadfly on his rump or a common fly stinging him, running in every direction, following no track or road, tumbling his load on the ground, snapping his reins and bridle, without so much as a moment's breath or rest – and nobody can tell what has upset him, for nothing can be seen to be touching him – so these men fled, utterly out of their senses and without any idea why they were flying. For they were pursued by no more than a panic terror which they had hatched in their own souls.

Seeing that they had no thought except of taking to their heels, the monk dismounted from his horse, climbed a great rock beside the way, and struck at the fugitives with his stout short-sword, making great sweeps with his arm and neither stinting nor sparing; and so many did he kill and bring to the ground that his sword broke in two. Then he decided that he had killed and massacred enough, and that the rest should be left to escape and carry the news. Therefore he seized hold of a battle-axe belonging to one of those who lay there dead and climbed back on to the rock, where he amused himself by watching the enemy fly and stumble over the corpses. Nevertheless he made them all lay down their pikes, swords, lances, and arquebuses; and he made those who carried the trussed-up pilgrims dismount and deliver their horses to these same pilgrims, whom he kept with him under the shelter of the hedge, together with Touchspigot, whom he held as his prisoner.

CHAPTER 45: *How the Monk brought in the Pilgrims, and how Gargantua welcomed them*

THIS skirmish over, Gargantua retired with his men, except the monk; and at daybreak they went to Grandgousier, who was in bed, praying to God for their safety and victory. And when he saw them all safe and sound, he embraced them with hearty affection and asked for news of the monk. But Gargantua replied that without doubt their enemy held the monk prisoner.

'Then,' said Grandgousier, 'they are out of luck' – which was only too true. But this is the origin of the saying 'to wish the monk on somebody'.[1]

Then he ordered a very good breakfast to be prepared, to refresh them; and when it was ready Gargantua was called. But he was so

1. See note to Chapter 12.

upset that the monk had not turned up that he would neither drink nor eat. Suddenly, however, Friar John arrived, and from the gate of the outer court bawled out: 'Fresh wine, some fresh wine, Gymnaste my friend!'

Then Gymnaste went out and saw that it was Friar John bringing in the five pilgrims and Touchspigot as his prisoner. Whereupon Gargantua went outside, and they made him the best possible welcome, bringing him to Grandgousier, who inquired about his whole adventure. The monk told him everything: how he had been captured, how he had got rid of the archers, about the slaughter he had made on the road, and how he had rescued the pilgrims and brought in Captain Touchspigot. Then they fell to banqueting joyfully all together.

Meanwhile Grandgousier questioned the pilgrims, asking them of what country they were, where they had come from, and where they were going; and Wearybones answered for them all: 'My lord, I'm from Saint-Genou in Berry, this fellow is from Palluau, this one from Onzay, this one from Argy, and this one here from Villebrenin. We have come from Saint-Sebastien near Nantes, and we are returning by our usual short stages.'

'Yes,' said Gargantua, 'but what was your purpose in going to Saint-Sebastien?'

'We went,' said Wearybones, 'to offer up our vows to that saint against the plague.'

'Oh,' said Grandgousier, 'you poor creatures. Do you imagine that the plague comes from Saint Sebastian?'

'Yes, of course,' replied Wearybones, 'our preachers assure us that it does.'

'Indeed?' said Grandgousier. 'Do the false prophets tell you such lies, then? Do they blaspheme God's holy saints in this fashion, making them seem like devils who do men nothing but harm? It is like Homer's story that the plague was introduced into the Grecian army by Apollo, and the poets' invention of a whole host of Anti-joves and other maleficent gods. There was a canting liar preaching at Cinais to the same tune, that St Anthony sent fire into men's legs, and St Eutropius sent the dropsy, and St Gildas sent madness, and St Genou the gout. But I made such an example of him, although he called me a heretic, that not a single hypocrite of that kidney has ventured to enter my territories to this day. I'm surprised that your king allows them to preach such scandalous doctrine in his kingdom. Why, they deserve worse punishment than those practitioners of magical arts and suchlike who, they say, actually did bring the plague into this country. Pestilence only kills the body, but these impostors poison the soul.'

As he was speaking these words, the monk entered most briskly and asked them: 'Where do you come from, you poor wretches?'

'From Saint-Genou,' they said.

'And how is that great boozer Abbot Tranchelion?' asked the monk. 'And the monks, what cheer are they keeping? God's body, they'll be having a fine fling at your wives while you're out on your pilgrimage!'

'H'm, h'm!' exclaimed Wearybones. 'I'm not afraid about mine. For anyone who has seen her by day won't break his neck to go and visit her by night.'

'You've spoken out of your turn!' said the monk. 'She may be as plain as Proserpine. But, by God, she'll be turned over, seeing that there are monks about. For a good workman finds a use for all timber alike. Pox take me if you don't find them considerably plumper when you get back, for even the shadow of an abbey-steeple is fruitful.'

'It's like the Nile water in Egypt, if you believe Strabo,' said Gargantua, 'and Pliny, in the third chapter of his seventh book. Why, their crumbs, their clothes, or their bodies will serve to get a woman with child.'

Then said Grandgousier: 'Go your ways, poor men, in the name of God the creator. May he be a perpetual guide to you, and don't be so ready to undertake these idle, useless journeys in future. Look after your families, work, each man at his vocation, instruct your children, and live as the good apostle St Paul directs you. If you do so you'll have God's protection, the angels and saints will be with you, and no plague or evil will bring you harm.'

Then Gargantua led them into the hall to take their meal. But the pilgrims could not stop sighing. 'Oh, how happy is the country,' they said to him, 'that has such a man for its lord! We have been more edified and instructed by his conversation than by all the sermons that were ever preached to us in our town.'

'That,' said Gargantua, 'is what Plato says, in the fifth book of his *Republic*, where he says that states will only be happy when the kings shall be philosophers and the philosophers kings.'

Then he made them fill their wallets with food, and their flasks with wine; and to each of them he gave a horse to help him on the rest of his journey, also some Charles-crowns for provisions.

CHAPTER 46: *On Grandgousier's humane treatment of his Prisoner Touchspigot*

TOUCHSPIGOT was presented to Grandgousier and questioned about Picrochole's expedition, about the state of his affairs and his aim in starting up this disorderly riot. And Touchspigot answered that the King's aim and purpose was to conquer the whole country, if he could, because of the injury done to his cake-bakers.

'That's a big undertaking,' said Grandgousier. 'He who grasps at too much grips almost nothing. The time is past for the conquering of kingdoms, to the hurt of his Christian neighbour and brother. This emulation of the ancient Herculeses, Alexanders, Hannibals, Scipios, Caesars, and suchlike, is contrary to Gospel teaching, by which we are enjoined each to guard, protect, rule, and administer his own lands and territories, and not to make hostile attacks on those of others. What the Saracens and Barbarians of old called deeds of prowess we now call robbery and wickedness. He would have done better to stay in his own domains, governing them like a king, than to make trouble in mine, by pillaging them like an enemy. If he had ruled his own wisely he would have increased them, but by robbing me he will be destroyed. Go your ways, in God's name, and follow noble aims. Remonstrate with your king when you see him to be in error, and never give him counsel with an eye to your private profit. For when the State comes to grief private interests fail with it. As for your ransom, I freely renounce it, and I will have your arms and horse restored to you.

'Such is the proper conduct between neighbours and old friends, seeing that this difference of ours is not, properly speaking, a war. Plato, indeed, in the fifth book of his *Republic*, wished it to be called no war but a sedition when the Greeks took up arms, one against another. If by misfortune such things should happen, he says, all moderation should be shown. However, if you do call it war, it is only skin-deep; it has not entered into the secret places of our hearts.

For none of us has been wronged in his honour, and the sum total of it is only a question of redressing some fault committed by our people – I mean both yours and ours. You acted upon this incident, but you should have let it pass. For these quarrelsome people were beneath your notice, especially since I had offered them satisfaction commensurate with the wrong. God will be a just assessor of our differences, and I pray Him rather to remove me by death and let my goods perish before my eyes, than to suffer any offence from me and mine.'

When he had concluded these words, he called the monk and asked him before them all: 'Friar John, my dear friend, is it you that took prisoner Captain Touchspigot, here present?'

'Sire,' said the monk, 'he is present, and he is of age and discretion, but I would rather you learnt it from his lips than by any words of mine.'

Then said Touchspigot: 'My lord, it is indeed he that took me, and I freely acknowledge myself his prisoner.'

'Have you asked a ransom for him?' Grandgousier inquired of the monk.

'No,' replied Friar John. 'I have no interest in ransoms.'

'How much would you take for his capture?' asked Grandgousier.

'Nothing, nothing,' replied the monk, 'I'm not interested, not in the least.'

Then Grandgousier commanded that fifteen thousand five hundred pounds should be paid to the monk in Touchspigot's presence as a reward for his capture; which was done. Meanwhile they made a little feast for the said Touchspigot, and Grandgousier asked him whether he would rather stay with him or to return to his king.

Touchspigot replied that he would follow Grandgousier's advice in the matter.

'In that case,' said Grandgousier, 'return to your king and God be with you.'

Then he gave him a fine Vienne sword in a gold scabbard decorated with beautiful scrolls of goldsmith's work, and a golden collar weighing one thousand three hundred and fifty pounds, inset with precious stones to the value of a hundred and sixty thousand ducats, and ten thousand crowns in addition as an honourable gift. After this conversation Touchspigot mounted his horse; and Gargantua gave him an escort of thirty men-at-arms and a hundred and twenty archers under Gymnaste's command, to take him safely to the gates of La Roche-Clermault, if need be.

When he had departed, the monk returned the fifteen thousand five hundred pounds he had received to Grandgousier, saying: 'Sire, this is not the time for you to make such presents. Wait till the end of the war. No one knows what accidents may occur in the meantime, and the strength of a war waged without monetary reserves is as fleeting as a breath. Silver is the sinews of battle.'

'Well,' said Grandgousier, 'when it's over I will give you an honourable and sufficient reward, and the same to all those who shall have served me faithfully.'

CHAPTER 47: *How Grandgousier sent for his Legions, how Touchspigot killed Hasticalf and how he was afterwards killed at Picrochole's Orders*

IN these same days the men of Bossé, Marché Vieux, Bourg Saint-Jacques, Trainneau, Parilly, Roches Saint-Paul, Vaubreton, Pautille, Bréhémont, Pont-de-Clam, Cravant, Grandmont, Bourdes, La Villaumaire, Huymes, Sergé, Ussé, Saint-Louant, Panzoust, Coldreaux, Verron, Coulaines, Chouze, Varennes, Bourgueil, the Isle Bouchart, Croulay, Narsy, Cande, Montsoreau, and other neighbouring places, sent ambassadors to Grandgousier to tell him that they were aware of the wrongs which Picrochole was doing him, and that on account of their old alliance they offered him all their power, both in men and money and in other munitions of war.

The total money raised by their joint agreements amounted to a hundred and thirty-four million and two and a half gold crowns. The forces consisted of fifteen thousand men-at-arms, thirty-two thousand light horse, eighty-nine thousand arquebusiers, a hundred and forty thousand volunteers, eleven thousand two hundred cannon, double-cannon, basilisks and spiroles, and with them were forty-seven thousand pioneers: the whole paid and supplied for six months and four days.

This offer Gargantua did not entirely accept or refuse; but thanking them warmly, he said that he would settle this war by such tactics that there would be no need to call out so many decent men. He merely dispatched an officer to bring up in proper order his legions, which he commonly kept in garrison at La Devinière, Chaviny, Gravot, and Les Quinquenais, amounting to the number of two thousand five hundred men-at-arms, sixty-six thousand foot-soldiers, and twenty-six thousand arquebusiers, with two hundred large pieces of artillery, twenty-two thousand pioneers, and six thousand light horse; all in companies, and duly provided with their paymasters, quartermasters, farriers, armourers, and other necessary members of a fighting column. All were so well trained also in the military art, so well armed, so quick to pick out and follow their standards, so prompt to hear and obey their captains, such nimble runners, so fierce in a charge, so cautious in risky enterprises, that they seemed more like a concert of musical instruments or a perfect clockwork mechanism than an army or a squadron of horse.

When Touchspigot arrived he presented himself before Picrochole and gave him a long account of what he had done and seen; and this he concluded by forcefully recommending that an agreement be made with Grandgousier, whom he had found the most honest man in the world. It was neither right nor reasonable, he added, thus to molest their neighbours, from whom they had never received anything but good treatment; and, so far as the main point was concerned, he assured the King that they would never conclude this enterprise without sustaining great damage and mischief. For Picrochole's power was not so great that Grandgousier could not easily destroy it.

He had hardly finished his speech, however, when Hasticalf cried out loud: 'I pity the prince who is served by men like this, men so easily corrupted as I perceive Touchspigot to be. For his heart is so changed, as I see, that he would willingly have joined our enemies to fight against us and betray us if they had been willing to keep him. But as everyone praises and values virtue, friends and enemies alike, so wickedness is quickly known and suspected; and though our enemies will take advantage of it, still they abominate traitors and evil-doers.'

At these words Touchspigot lost patience, drew his sword and ran Hasticalf through a little above the left breast; from which thrust he immediately died. Then, drawing his sword out of the body, Touchspigot boldly proclaimed: 'So perish every man who slanders a loyal servant!'

But Picrochole flew into a sudden fury. Catching sight of the sword and its richly chased scabbard, he cried: 'Did they give you this weapon on purpose that you should maliciously slay my very good friend Hasticalf here in my presence?'

Whereupon he commanded his archers to hack Touchspigot to pieces; which was instantly done, and so savagely that the whole chamber floor was covered with blood. Then he ordered that Hasticalf's body should be honourably buried, and Touchspigot's thrown over the walls into the ditch.

The news of this bloodshed travelled round the army, and some of the soldiers began to murmur against Picrochole, to such an extent that Winepincher said to him: 'My lord, I do not know what the outcome of this enterprise will be. But I notice that your men are not too resolute of heart. They consider that we are badly off for victuals here, and already much reduced in numbers from our two or three sallies. Furthermore, the enemy is receiving considerable reinforcements. Once we are besieged I do not see any prospect but our total defeat.'

'Stuff and nonsense,' cried Picrochole. 'You are like the eels of Melun. You cry out before you're skinned. Just wait till they come.'

CHAPTER 48: *How Gargantua attacked Picrochole in La Roche-Clermault, and defeated the said Picrochole's Army*

GARGANTUA had entire charge of his forces. Grandgousier remained in his castle, and inspired them with fine words, promising to give rich rewards to those who should perform mighty deeds.

Then the army came to the ford of Vède, and by hastily improvised boats and bridges crossed over without a halt. Viewing from there the situation of the town, which was in a high and commanding position, Gargantua deliberated overnight on what was to be done.

Gymnaste, however, said to him: 'My lord, the nature and temperament of the French is such that they are worth nothing except at the first assault. Then they are fiercer than devils, but if they delay they are worse than women. My advice is that this very moment, as soon as your men have taken breath and a little food, you should order the attack.'

His advice found favour, and Gargantua drew out his army into the open plain, posting his reserves on the hillside flank. Meanwhile the monk, taking with him six companies of foot-soldiers and two hundred men-at-arms, most expeditiously crossed the marsh and advanced above Le Puy as far as the main Loudun road.

All this time the assault continued, and Picrochole's men were uncertain whether it would be better to come out and meet them, or to remain quiet in the town. But the King rushed madly out with a troop of men-at-arms of his guard, and was there received by a salvo of great cannon shot which hailed down on the hillsides, from which the Gargantuans retired into the valley to give the artillery better range. Against this the men in the town put up the best defence they could, but their shots passed over and away without wounding anyone.

Some of Picrochole's band who were spared by the artillery rushed fiercely on our men, but gained little advantage, for our ranks were opened to receive them, and they were thrown to the ground. In view of this, they attempted to retire. But in the meantime the monk had cut off their retreat. Whereupon they took to their heels in undisciplined rout. Some of our men wanted to pursue them. But the monk held them back, fearing that in following the fugitives they might fall into disorder, and that at this point the men from the town might set upon them. But after waiting a short while and no one coming out to meet him, he sent Duke Phrontiste with a message for Gargantua to advance and seize the hill on the left, thereby cutting off Picrochole's retreat through the gate on that side.

This Gargantua did most expeditiously, sending there four legions of Sebaste's force. But quickly though they gained the hilltop they met there, face to face, Picrochole and the men who had scattered with him. There they charged them fiercely, but suffered severe casualties, nevertheless, from the archery and artillery of the soldiers on the walls. Seeing this, Gargantua went with a strong party to their relief, and opened fire with his artillery on this part of the walls, so powerfully that all the forces in the town were drawn to that point.

When the monk saw the side that he was besieging stripped of men and guards, he courageously advanced on the fortress and succeeded with some of his men in gaining a foothold, being of the opinion that more fear and terror are struck by men coming fresh into a battle than by those already fighting in it with all their might. All the same, he raised no alarm whatever until all his men were on the walls, with the exception of two hundred men-at-arms, whom he left outside in case of emergency. Then they gave a terrifying shout, he and his men together, and killed the unresisting guards of that gate, which they opened to the men-at-arms. After this, in high courage, they ran, all together, to the East gate, where the turmoil was, and coming up from the rear, defeated the whole enemy force.

When the besieged saw on every side that the Gargantuans had gained the town, they threw themselves on the monk's mercy; and he, after making them give up their arms and weapons, told them to retire and shut themselves in the churches. Then, seizing all the staffs of the crosses and putting guards on the doors to prevent their coming out, he threw open the East gate and sallied forth to Gargantua's assistance.

But Picrochole thought that this was help coming to him from the town, and foolhardily took greater risks than ever, until the moment when Gargantua shouted: 'Friar John, my friend, Friar John, welcome! You've come at a good moment!'

Upon this Picrochole and his men recognized that all was lost, and took to flight on every side. Gargantua followed them to near Vaugaudry, killing and massacring, and then sounded the retreat.

CHAPTER 49: *How Picrochole was overtaken by Misfortune in his Flight, and what Gargantua did after the Battle*

IN his despair Picrochole fled towards the Isle Bouchart, and on the road to Rivière his horse stumbled and fell; which so infuriated him that in his anger he slew the beast with his sword. Then, finding no one to remount him, he tried to take a miller's ass that was near by. But the millers rained blows upon him, stripped him of his clothes, and gave him a wretched smock to cover him. So the poor angry wretch went off, and as he crossed the water at Port Huaux, where he related his misfortunes, he was promised by an old witch that his kingdom would be restored to him at the coming of the Cocklicranes. No one knows what has become of him since then. All the same I have been told that at present he is a miserable porter at Lyons, furious as ever, and always inquiring of strangers about the coming of the

Cocklicranes, in the certain hope that he will be restored to his kingdom at their coming, as the old witch prophesied.

After their return Gargantua first called a roll of his men, and discovered that there had been few casualties in the battle – in fact only some foot-soldiers of Captain Tolmere's company, and Ponocrates, who had received an arquebus shot in his doublet. Then he had refreshment brought for them, each in his company, and gave orders to his paymasters that the cost of this repast should be refunded to them, and that no outrage whatever should be committed in the town, seeing that it was his. And after their repast they were to parade in the square before the castle, where they would receive six months' pay. All this was done.

Then he had all that remained of Picrochole's followers called before him in the same square, and to them he spoke as follows, in the presence of his princes and captains:

CHAPTER 50: *Gargantua's Address to the Vanquished*

'OUR fathers, grandfathers, and ancestors from time immemorial have been of such nature and disposition that as a memorial to the victories and triumphs they have won in the battles they have fought, they have preferred to erect monuments in the hearts of the vanquished by a display of clemency, than to raise trophies in the form of architecture in the lands they have conquered. For they have valued the lively gratitude of men, won by their liberality, more highly than mute inscriptions on arches, columns, and pyramids, which are subject to the injuries of climate and all men's spite.

'You may very well remember the clemency they showed towards the Bretons on the day of Saint-Aubin-du-Cormier and at the dismantling of Parthenay. You have heard – and as you heard admired – of the generous treatment they extended to the barbarians of Spagnola, who had pillaged, depopulated, and sacked the maritime borders of Olonne and Thalmondais.

'This whole hemisphere has resounded with praise and congratulations extended by yourselves and your fathers when Alpharbal, king of Canaria, not satisfied with his own fortune, made a furious assault upon the land of Aunix, practising piracy among all the Armorican islands and down the neighbouring coasts. He was taken and defeated in fair naval battle by my father – God preserve and protect him! – But what did we see? Whereas other kings and emperors, even such as call themselves *Catholic*, would have miserably ill-treated him, harshly imprisoned him, and asked a prohibitive ransom for him, my father treated him courteously and kindly, lodged him near to himself, in his own palace, and with incredible generosity sent him back under safe conduct, loaded with gifts, loaded with favours, loaded with every evidence of friendship. And what was the result? When he got back to his country he summoned all the princes and estates of his kingdom, explained to them the humanity he had met with in us, desiring them to deliberate on this, and consider how to show the world an example of gracious honour to match the example we had shown of honourable graciousness. Whereupon it was unanimously decreed that an offer should be made to us of their entire lands, dominions, and kingdom, to be disposed of according to our discretion.

'So Alpharbal immediately returned in person with nine thousand and thirty-eight large ships of freight, bearing the treasures not only of his house and the royal line, but of almost his entire country. For as he was embarking, to set sail with a west-north-east wind, everyone in the crowd threw on board gold, silver, rings, jewels, spices, drugs and aromatic perfumes, parrots, pelicans, apes, civet-cats, spotted weasels, and porcupines. If anyone did not throw in anything rare that he possessed he was accounted no good mother's son.

'When Alpharbal arrived he wished to kiss my aforesaid father's feet; but this act was considered unworthy and was not permitted. So they exchanged the embrace of allies. The king then offered his presents, which were not accepted, being excessive by far. Then he yielded himself voluntarily as servant and vassal, himself and his posterity; and this gesture was not accepted, since it did not seem an equitable one. By virtue of his estates' decree, he then surrendered his lands and kingdoms, proffering the title and conveyance, signed, sealed, and ratified by all those whose concern it was; but this was refused outright and the documents thrown in the fire.

'The end of it was that my said father began pitifully to lament and to weep copious tears, when he considered the frank generosity and the simplicity of the Canarians. Carefully choosing his words, he made a speech conceived to minimize the favour he had shown them, saying that the good turn he had done them was not worth a button, and that if he had treated them with any kindness, this was no more than he was by duty bound to do. But Alpharbal only insisted the harder.

'What, then, was the outcome? Whereas for his ransom, levied at the highest rate, we might by some exercise of tyranny have exacted two million crowns and kept his eldest children as hostages, they had voluntarily made themselves perpetual tributaries and undertaken to deliver to us each year two million crowns of twenty-four carat gold. These were paid to us here in the first year; in the second they paid of their own freewill two million three hundred thousand crowns; in the third, two million six hundred thousand; in the fourth, three millions; and each year they so increase their payment out of sheer good will that we shall soon be compelled to forbid their bringing us any more. Such is the nature of gratitude. Time, which gnaws and fritters all things away, only augments and increases the value of benefits. For one good turn freely done to an intelligent man grows continuously by his generous thoughts and remembrances.

'Being unwilling therefore in any way to fall short of the hereditary graciousness of my parents, I now absolve and deliver you, and make you as free and independent as before. Moreover, as you go out through the gate every one of you shall be given three months' pay, so that you may return to your homes and families; and you shall be safely escorted by six hundred men-at-arms and eight thousand foot under the command of my squire Alexander, so that you shall not be molested by the peasants. God be with you!

'I am sorry with all my heart that Picrochole is not here. For I would have given him to understand that this war was not waged at my wish, or in the hope of augmenting my possessions or fame. But since he is lost, and no one knows how or where he has vanished, it is my desire that his kingdom shall devolve in its entirety on his son; and because he is too young, being not yet five years old, he shall be guided and instructed by the ancient princes and learned men of the kingdom; and inasmuch as a kingdom thus desolate would easily be ruined, were not some check put on the covetousness and avarice of its administrators, I ordain and will that Ponocrates shall be supervisor over all his governors, with all requisite authority, and that he attend constantly to the child until he finds him fit and able to act and rule for himself.

'I hold that a too feeble and spineless readiness to pardon male-factors is the cause of their lightly doing wrong again, in the pernicious expectation of being pardoned. I bear in mind that Moses, the meekest man that was in his time on earth, sharply punished the mutineers and rebels among the Children of Israel. I remember also that Julius Caesar, who was so gracious a commander that according to Cicero the ability to save and pardon every man was to him the height of good fortune, and the will to do so something to be counted among his supreme virtues, nevertheless in certain instances rigorously punished the promoters of rebellion.

'Following these examples, I desire you to give up to me before you depart: first, that swaggering fellow Marquet, who by his vain presumption has been the origin and fomentor of this war; secondly, his companions the cake-bakers, who neglected to correct his headstrong folly; and lastly, all Picrochole's advisers, officers, and servants, who have incited, encouraged, or counselled him to cross his frontiers for the purpose of troubling us.'

CHAPTER 51: *How the victorious Gargantuans were rewarded after the Battle*

AFTER Gargantua had delivered this speech, the mutineers he had named were handed over to him, with the exception of Swashbuckler, Dungby, and Chuckout, who had fled six hours before the battle, the first in one bound as far as the Col d'Agnello, the second to the Vire valley, and the third to Logrono, without looking back or taking breath on the way. Also missing were two cake-bakers who had been killed in the battle. But the only punishment that Gargantua inflicted on them was to order them to pull at the presses in his printing-house, which he had recently installed.

Then he had those who had died there honourably buried in the Walnut-tree valley and in Burn-hag field, and he had the wounded dressed and treated in his great *Nosocomion*, or hospital. Afterwards he ascertained what damage had been done to the town and its inhabitants, and had them reimbursed for all their losses, on their sworn declaration. He had a strong fort built there also, which he garrisoned with a guard of his people, so that he could be defended better in the future against sudden uprisings.

On his departure he graciously thanked all the soldiers of his legions who had been present at this victory, and sent them to winter in their posts and garrisons, excepting some of the Decumane legion, whom he had witnessed performing feats in the field, and the captains of the companies, all of whom he took with him to Grandgousier.

When he saw them coming, the good man's joy was such as to defy description. He immediately made them the most magnificent, the most sumptuous and delicious feast that had been seen since the days of King Ahasuerus. As they rose from table he distributed amongst them all the ornaments of his sideboard, which weighed eighteen hundred thousand and fourteen besants of gold, and consisted of great ancient vessels, huge pots, large basins, big bowls, cups, goblets, candlesticks, baskets, sauce-boats, flower-vases, sweet-dishes, and other such plate, all of solid gold, besides the precious stones, enamelling, and workmanship, which, by common estimation, exceeded the worth of their material. Furthermore, he had twelve hundred thousand crowns in cash counted out from his coffers, for each one, and in addition gave to each in perpetuity – unless he should die without heirs – such of his castles and land adjoining as they should find most convenient: to Ponocrates he gave La Roche-Clermault; to Gymnaste, Le Couldray; to Eudemon, Montpensier; Le Rivau to Tolmere; to Ithybole, Montsoreau; to Acamas, Cande; Varennes to Chironacte; Gravot to Sebaste; Les Quinquenais to Alexander; Ligré to Sophrone, and so on with his other places.

CHAPTER 52: *How Gargantua had the Abbey of Thélème built for the Monk*

THERE only remained the monk to be provided for, and Gargantua wanted to make him abbot of Seuilly, but he refused the post. He next proposed to give him the abbey of Bourgueil or of Saint-Florant, whichever would suit him better, or both, if he fancied them. But the monk answered categorically that he wanted neither charge nor government of monks.

'For how should I be able to govern others,' he said, 'when I don't know how to govern myself? If it seems to you that I have done you, and may in the future do you welcome service, give me leave to found an abbey after my own devices.'

This request pleased Gargantua, and he offered him all his land of Thélème, beside the River Loire, to within six miles of the great forest of Port-Huault. The monk then requested Gargantua to institute his religious order in an exactly contrary way to all others.

'First of all, then,' said Gargantua, 'you mustn't build walls round it. For all other abbeys have lofty walls (murs).'

'Yes,' said the monk, 'and not without reason. Where there's a *mur* before and a *mur* behind, there are plenty of murmurs, envy, and mutual conspiracy.'

Moreover, seeing that in certain monasteries in this world it is the custom that if any woman enters – I speak of chaste and honest women – they wash the place where she trod, it was ordained that if any monk or nun happened to enter here, the spot where he or she had stood should be scrupulously washed likewise. And because in the religious foundations of this world everything is encompassed, limited, and regulated by hours, it was decreed that there should be no clock or dial at all, but that affairs should be conducted according to chance and opportunity. For Gargantua said that the greatest waste of time he knew was the counting of hours – what good does it do? – and the greatest nonsense in the world was to regulate one's life by the sound of a bell, instead of by the promptings of reason and good sense. Item, because at that time they put no women into religious houses unless they were one-eyed, lame, hunchbacked, ugly, malformed, lunatic, half-witted, bewitched, and blemished, or men that were not sickly, low-born, stupid, or a burden on their family ....'

'By the way,' said the monk, 'if a woman is neither fair nor good, what can you do with her?'

'Make her a nun,' said Gargantua.

'Yes,' said the monk, 'and a sempstress of shirts.'

It was decreed that here no women should be admitted unless they were beautiful, well-built, and sweet-natured, nor any men who were not handsome, well-built, and of pleasant nature also.

Item, because men never entered nunneries except secretly and by stealth, it was decreed that here there should be no women when there were no men, and no men when there were no women.

Item, because both men and women, once accepted into a monastic order, after their novitiate year, were compelled and bound to remain for ever, so long as they lived, it was decreed that both men and women, once accepted, could depart from there whenever they pleased, without let or hindrance.

Item, because ordinarily monks and nuns made three vows, that is of chastity, poverty, and obedience, it was decreed that there anyone could be regularly married, could become rich, and could live at liberty.

With regard to the lawful age of entry, women were to be received at from ten to fifteen, and men at from twelve to eighteen.

CHAPTER 53: *How the Thélèmites' Abbey was built and endowed*

FOR the building and furnishing of the abbey Gargantua had counted out in ready money two million seven hundred thousand, eight hundred and thirty-one fine gold Agnus Dei crowns; and for every year until the work was completed he assigned out of his income from the River Dive, one million, six hundred and sixty-nine thousand Sun crowns, and an equal number stamped with the sign of Pleiades. While for its foundation and upkeep he granted in perpetuity two million three hundred and sixty-nine thousand rose nobles as a free-hold endowment, exempt from all burdens and services, and payable every year at the abbey gate; and this he confirmed in due letters-patent.

The building was hexagonal in shape and so planned that at each angle was built a large circular tower, sixty yards in diameter; and all were alike in size and architecture. The River Loire ran along its north side, and on its bank was placed one of the towers, named Arctic, and facing to the east was another named Calaer; the next in order was Anatole, after that came Mesembrine, then Hesperie, and lastly Cryere.[1] Between each tower was a space of three hundred and twelve yards. The whole was built in six storeys, including the underground cellars. The second was vaulted to the shape of a high arch, and the rest of the ceilings were of Flanders plaster in circular patterns. The

1. These names are derived from the Greek and signify Northern, Airy, Eastern, Southern, Western, and Glacial.

roof was covered in fine slates with a lead coping, which bore figures of grotesques and small animals, gilded and in great variety, and with gutters projecting from the walls between the casements, painted in gold-and-blue diagonals to the ground, where they flowed into great pipes, which all led into the river below the house.

The said building was a hundred times more magnificent than Bonnivet or Chambord or Chantilly. For it contained nine thousand, three hundred and thirty-two apartments, each one provided with an inner chamber, a closet, wardrobe, and chapel, and each one giving on a great hall. Between each tower, in the middle of the said main building, was an internal winding stair, the steps of which were, some of porphyry, some of Numidian marble, and some of serpentine, but all twenty-two feet broad, three inches thick, and twelve in number between each landing. On each landing there was a fine old-fashioned double-arcade through which the light was admitted, and through it one entered a lattice-windowed closet of the breadth of the stairway. The steps went on to the roof and there ended in a pavilion. By this same stair there was an entrance on each side into a great hall, and from the halls into the apartments.

From the Arctic tower to the Cryere tower ran the fine great libraries of Greek, Latin, Hebrew, French, Italian, and Spanish books, divided storey by storey according to their languages.

In the centre was a marvellous winding staircase, the entrance to which was on the outside of the building through an arch thirty-six feet wide; and this was built of such size and symmetry that six men-at-arms with lance in rest could ride abreast up to the top of the whole building.

Between the Anatole tower and the Mesembrine tower were fine wide galleries, all painted with ancient feats of arms, histories, and views of the world; and in the middle was a similar ascent and gate to the one described on the river side. Above this gate was written in large Gothic letters the following inscription:

CHAPTER 54: *The Inscription set above the great Gate of Thélème*

ENTER not here, vile hypocrites and bigots,
Pious old apes, and puffed-up snivellers,
Wry-necked creatures sawnier than the Goths,
Or Ostrogoths, precursors of Gog and Magog,
Woe-begone scoundrels, mock-godly sandal-wearers,
Beggars in blankets, flagellating canters,
Hooted at, pot-bellied, stirrers up of troubles,
Get along elsewhere to sell your dirty swindles.

    Your hideous deceits
    Would fill my fields and streets
    With villainy
    And with their falsity
    Would untune my song's notes,
    Your hideous deceits.

Enter not here, lawyers insatiable,
Ushers, lawyers' clerks, devourers of the people,
Holders of office, scribes, and pharisees,
Ancient judges who tie up good citizens
Like stray dogs with cord on their necks,
Your reward is earned now, and it is the gibbet.
So go and bray there. Here is done no violence,
Such as in your courts sets men fighting lawsuits.

    Lawsuits and wrangling
    Set us not jangling;
    We come here for pleasure.
    But may your leisure
    Be filled up with tangling
    Lawsuits and wrangling.

Enter not here, miserly usurers,
Gluttons and lechers, everlasting gatherers,
Tricksters and swindlers, mean pettifoggers,
Hunchbacked and snub-nosed, who in your lockers
Never have enough of gold coin and silver.
However much you pocket you're never satisfied.
You pile up still more, you mean-featured dastards,
May cruel death for this spoil your faces.

> Most hideous of faces,
> Take them and their grimaces,
> Shave them elsewhere, for here
> They're out of place, I fear.
> Shift them to other places,
> Most hideous of faces.

Enter not here, you rambling mastiff curs,
Morning nor evening, jealous, old and spiteful,
Nor you either, seditious mutineers,
Spirits, goblins, and fond husbands' familiars,
Greeks or Latins, more to be feared than wolves,
Nor you with your sores, gnawed to the bone by pox,
Take your ulcers elsewhere and show them to others,
Scabby from head to toe and brimful of dishonour,

> Grace, honour, praise, and light
> Are here our sole delight;
> Of them we make our song.
> Our limbs are sound and strong.
> This blessing fills us quite,
> Grace, honour, praise, and light.

Enter in here, and you shall be most welcome,
And having come, stay noble gentlemen!
Here is the place where income comes in well,
And having come affords good entertainment
For great and small, though thousands of them come.
Be then my cronies, my especial favourites,
Merry and nimble, jolly, gay, and sprightly,
And, in a word, the best of good companions.

> All worthy gentlemen,
> Keen witted and serene,
> From every coarseness free,
> Here find civility,
> Among your hosts will reign,
> All worthy gentlemen.

Enter in here, you who preach with vigour
Christ's Holy Gospel, never mind who scoffs,
Here you will find a refuge and a tower
Against the foeman's error, the picked arguments,

Which falsely seek to spread about their poison.
Enter, here let us found a faith profound,
And then let us confound by speech and writing,
All that are the foemen of the Holy Writ.

> Our Holy Writ and Word
> For ever shall be heard
> In this most holy spot.
> Each wears it on his heart,
> Each wears it as a sword,
> Our Holy Writ and Word.

Enter in here, you ladies of high lineage,
Here be frank and fearless, enter gaily in,
Flowers of all beauty, with heaven in your faces,
Upright in bearing, modest in behaviour,
Here you will find the dwelling-place of honour.
That noble gentleman who of this place was donor,
And gives rewards, has destined it for you.
He has provided gold sufficient for its upkeep.

> Gold freely given,
> A man's freely shriven,
> In exchange for awards.
> For it brings rewards
> To all mortal men,
> Gold freely given.

CHAPTER 55: *Concerning the Establishment of the Thélèmites' House*

IN the middle of the first court was a magnificent fountain of fine alabaster, on the top of which were the three Graces with horns of abundance, spouting water from their breasts, mouths, ears, eyes, and other physical orifices. The rooms of the building above this first court stood upon stout pillars of chalcedony and porphyry, with magnificent old-fashioned arches between; and inside were fine, long, spacious galleries, decorated with paintings, with horns of stags, unicorns, rhinoceroses, and hippopotami, with elephants' tusks and with other remarkable objects. The ladies' lodging stretched from the

Arctic tower to the Mesembrine gate, the men occupying the rest. In front of this ladies' lodging, to provide them with entertainment, there was outside, between the first two towers, the tilt-yard, the riding ring, the theatre, and the swimming-bath with excellent baths on three levels, well provided with all necessary accommodation and with a store of myrrh-water.

Beside the river were the handsome pleasure-gardens, in the middle of which was a neat maze. Between the two other towers were the tennis and ballon-courts. On the side of the Cryere tower was the orchard, well stocked with all fruit trees planted in the pattern of the quincunx; and at the end of it was the great park, which teemed with all kinds of wild game. Between the third pair of towers were the butts for arquebus, bow, and cross-bow; the offices were in a single-storey building outside the Hesperie tower; the stables were beyond the offices; and in front of them was the falconry, managed by falconers most expert in their art, and annually stocked by Candians, Venetians, and Sarmatians with all manner of birds, the finest of their breed: eagles, gerfalcons, goshawks, great falcons, lanners, falcons, sparrow-hawks, merlins, and others, so well trained and tamed that when they flew from the castle to disport themselves over the fields, they would capture all the game they met. The hunting stables were a little further off, in the direction of the park.

Every hall, room, and closet was hung with various tapestry, according to the season of the year. All the floors were covered with green cloth. The beds were embroidered. In each retiring room was a crystal mirror, set in a fine gold frame embellished all round with pearls, and it was large enough to give a true reflection of the whole figure.

At the outer doors of the halls in the ladies' lodgings were the perfumers and barbers, through whose hands the men passed on their visits to the ladies. These attendants also provided the ladies' rooms each morning with rose-water, orange-water, and myrtle-water, and brought for each lady a precious casket, which breathed of every aromatic scent.

CHAPTER 56: *How the Monks and Nuns of Thélème were dressed*

THE ladies, at the foundation of this order, dressed according to their own taste and pleasure. Afterwards, of their own free will, they reformed themselves in the following fashion: they wore scarlet or pink stockings, which they drew exactly three inches above the knee and which were bordered with fine embroidery or slashing. Their garters were of the colour of their bracelets, and were tied above and below the knee. Their shoes, sandals, and slippers were of crimson, red, or violet velvet, and jagged in points like lobsters' beards. Over their smocks they wore a corset of pure silk camblet; and over this a farthingale of white, red, brown, grey, or some other colour, on top of which was a silver taffeta skirt embroidered with gold thread and close-patterned needlework; or according to a lady's taste and the temperature of the season, this skirt might be of satin, damask, or velvet, and orange, brown, green, ash-grey, blue, bright yellow, crimson, or white cloth, gold-thread work, or embroidery, as suited each feast-day. Their gowns, according to the season, were of cloth of gold fringed with silver, of red satin embroidered with gold-thread-work, of white, blue, black, brown, taffeta, silken serge, silk camblet, velvet, cloth of silver, cloth of gold, gold thread, velvet, or satin picked out with gold in various patterns.

On some summer days, instead of gowns they wore beautiful light capes of the materials mentioned, or sleeveless Moorish cloaks of violet velvet with gold fringe over silver thread, or corded with gold and studded at the seams with little Indian pearls: and always a fine plume of feathers, matching the colour of their cuffs and spangled with little embroidered motifs in gold. In winter, on the other hand, they wore taffeta gowns of the colours already named, trimmed with the fur of spotted lynxes, black weasels, Calabrian martens, sables, and other costly furs.

Their beads, rings, neck-chains, and collars were of precious stones: carbuncles, rubies, spider rubies, diamonds, sapphires, emeralds, turquoises, garnets, agates, beryls, pearls, and magnificent margarites. Their head-dresses conformed to the season; in winter they followed the French fashion, in spring the Spanish, and in summer the Italian, except on feast days and Sundays, when they wore the French head-dress, which is more dignified and more befitting to matronly modesty.

The men were dressed in their fashions, with stockings on their legs of light wool or serge-cloth, scarlet, pink, black, or white. Their trunkhose were of velvet of the same colour, or of one almost matching, and were embroidered or pointed to their taste. Their doublets were of cloth of gold or silver, velvet, satin, damask, or taffeta of the same colour, cut, embroidered, and trimmed to perfection. Their points were of silk of the same colour, with tags of well-burnished gold. Their mantles and cloaks were of cloth of gold, gold tissue, cloth of silver, or velvet picked out according to their fancy. Their gowns were as costly as those of the ladies. Their belts were of silk, of the same colour as their doublets. Each wore a fine sword at his side, with a hilt of gold and a velvet scabbard of the colour of his hose, tipped with chased gold; also a dagger was to match. Their caps were of black velvet decorated with many rings and gold buttons, and with white plumes above them, neatly divided by gold spangles, at the end of which fine rubies, emeralds, etc. hung on wires.

But such was the sympathy between the men and the women, that each day they were dressed in like apparel, and to ensure that this should be so, certain gentlemen were appointed to tell the men each morning what colours the ladies intended to wear that day. For everything followed the ladies' decision.

Do not suppose, however, that any time was wasted by either men or women over these handsome clothes and rich accoutrements. For the masters of the wardrobe had all the clothing so neatly laid out each morning, and the chambermaids were so skilful, that in a minute they were all ready and dressed from head to foot. And in order that they might have these accoutrements close at hand, around the Thélème wood was a great block of houses, a mile and a half long, very smart and well arranged, in which lived the goldsmiths, jewellers, embroiderers, tailors, wire-workers, velvet-weavers, tapestry makers, and upholsterers; and there each man worked at his trade, and all of them for the aforesaid monks and nuns.

They were provided with supplies and material by the lord Nausiclete, who brought seven ships to them each year from the Perlas and Cannibal Islands, loaded with gold ingots, raw silk, pearls, and precious stones. And if any pearls began to look old and lose their natural whiteness, they restored them by their art, which was to give them to certain fine cocks, as castings are given to falcons.

CHAPTER 57: *The Rules according to which the Thélèmites lived*

ALL their life was regulated not by laws, statutes, or rules, but according to their free will and pleasure. They rose from bed when they pleased, and drank, ate, worked, and slept when the fancy seized them. Nobody woke them; nobody compelled them either to eat or to drink, or to do anything else whatever. So it was that Gargantua had established it. In their rules there was only one clause:

DO WHAT YOU WILL

because people who are free, well-born, well-bred, and easy in honest company have a natural spur and instinct which drives them to virtuous deeds and deflects them from vice; and this they called honour. When these same men are depressed and enslaved by vile constraint and subjection, they use this noble quality which once impelled them freely towards virtue, to throw off and break this yoke of slavery. For we always strive after things forbidden and covet what is denied us.

Making use of this liberty, they most laudably rivalled one another in all of them doing what they saw pleased one. If some man or woman said, 'Let us drink', they all drank; if he or she said, 'Let us play', they all played; if it was 'Let us go and amuse ourselves in the fields', everyone went there. If it were for hawking or hunting, the ladies, mounted on fine mares, with their grand palfreys following, each carried on their daintily gloved wrists a sparrow-hawk, a lanneret, or a merlin, the men carrying the other birds.

So nobly were they instructed that there was not a man or woman among them who could not read, write, sing, play musical instruments, speak five or six languages, and compose in them both verse and prose. Never were seen such worthy knights, so valiant, so nimble both on foot and horse; knights more vigorous, more agile, handier with all weapons than they were. Never were seen ladies so good-looking, so dainty, less tiresome, more skilled with the fingers and the needle, and in every free and honest womanly pursuit than they were.

For that reason, when the time came that anyone in that abbey, either at his parents' request or for any other reason, wished to leave it, he took with him one of the ladies, the one who had accepted him as her admirer, and they were married to one another; and if at Thélème they had lived in devotion and friendship, they lived in still greater devotion and friendship when they were married. Indeed, they loved one another to the end of their days as much as they had done on their wedding day.

I must not forget to write down for you a riddle which was found in digging the foundations of the abbey, engraved on a great bronze plate. It ran as follows:

CHAPTER 58: *A Prophetic Riddle*

POOR mortals who good fortune do desire,
Cheer up your hearts, to what I say give ear.
If it be lawful firmly to believe
That by the bodies in the firmament
The human spirit can alone attain
To prophecy of things that are to come,
Or if we may with aid of help divine
Obtain the knowledge of our future fate,
So as to judge by certain argument
The course and destiny of years remote,
I here divulge to any who will hear
That this next winter without more delay,
Or even sooner, in this present place
There will emerge a certain sort of men,
Weary of rest and tired of staying quiet,
Who will go boldly round by light of day,
Suborning men of every walk in life
To difference and factions, party-strife.
And those who listen and believe their words,
At whatsoever cost or consequence
They'll bring to public and quite open feud,
Friend against friend and kinsman against kin.
The headstrong son will not fear a reproach
For taking part against his very father;
And even great men, come of noble line,
Will find themselves attacked by their own vassals;

Honour and reverence will lack their due,
Order and sense of rank will be forgotten.
For men will say that each one in his turn
Should rise to heights and then return below;
And on this point will be so many quarrels,
So many discords, so much to and fro,
That history, mighty wonders though it tells,
Has no record of like disturbances.
Then shall there many valiant men be seen,
Pricked onward by the spur of their hot youth,
Too trusting of the flames of their desire,
To live a while and then die in their prime.
And none shall ever quit this enterprise
Once he has pledged his bounding courage to it
Till he has filled, by clamour and disputes,
The sky with noise, the earth with trampling feet.
Then faithless men will have authority
As great as have the champions of the truth;
For all shall follow the will and beliefs
Of the ignorant and stupid multitude,
The dullest of whom shall be held as judge.
O hideous and most destructive Flood!
Noah's flood I call on, and I have the right,
For this great turmoil's reign will never pass,
Nor shall earth ever be delivered from it,
Until the waters shall burst headlong forth
Of a sudden, and the hardened combatants
Be caught and drenched, those who are fighting hardest.
And this is just, because their violent hearts,
Intent upon this struggle, will have spared
Not even the unoffending herds of cattle,
But of their sinews and entrails unclean
Will make a sacrifice, not to the Gods
But to the common use of mortal men.
So I leave you to consider how
The Universe can be restored to rights
And what repose from this profound turmoil
This round machine, the mighty globe, shall find.

The happiest those who value her the most,
And best abstain from damage and destruction,
Attempting in whatever ways they can
To master her and hold her prisoner.
In such a place that she, poor ruined globe,
Shall turn for help only to Him that made her,
And, as the ugliest outcome of her troubles,
The clear sun, before sinking in the West,
Shall spread a darkness over her, more deep
Than the eclipse or normal night-time's blackness,
Whence at a stroke she'll lose her liberty
And all the grace and brightness of high heaven,
Or, at the least, shall henceforth be deserted.
But ere this ruin and destruction she
Will long ago have shown for all to see
An earthquake of more violence and vastness
Than Etna once was so much shaken by,
When she was hurled upon the son of Titan;
Nor should we think that tremor was more sudden
That Ischia made that moment when Typhoeus
Let loose his rage and out into the sea
Hurled the high mountains that were pressing on him.
Thus, in a little time, she'll be reduced
To sad condition and endure such change
That even those that shall have ruled upon her
Will leave their places vacant for successors.
Then shall the good and happy times be near
To put an end to all this long ordeal.
For the great waters of which we have told
Will make each think it time now to retreat.
Nevertheless, before this parting comes
There shall be seen most clearly in the air
The rigorous heat of a great flame, intent
On quelling both the flood and enterprise.
And when these dire events are done, remains
To see the elect most joyfully refreshed
With every good thing and celestial manna,
And as an honest recompense rewarded

With riches; while the others, at the last,
Will be stripped bare. So reason has it that,
These labours once concluded, at this point
Each man shall have what's due to him by fate.
Such was the bargain. How praiseworthy he
Who shall have persevered even to the end!

The reading of this inscription concluded, Gargantua heaved a deep sigh, and said to those with him: 'This is not the first time that men called to the Gospel faith are persecuted. But happy indeed is he who is not offended and shall always aim at the mark or target that God, by His dear Son, has set up for us, and shall not be distracted or lured aside by his carnal affections.'

'What is the meaning and significance of the riddle according to your understanding?' asked the monk.

'What?' replied Gargantua. 'Why, the continuance and steadfastness of Divine Truth.'

'By St Goderan!' exclaimed the monk. 'That is not my explanation. The style is like Merlin the Prophet. You can read all the allegorical and serious meanings into it that you like, and dream on about it, you and all the world, as much as ever you will. For my part, I don't think there is any other sense concealed in it than the description of a game of tennis wrapped up in strange language. The suborners of men are those who make up the matches, who are usually friends; and after two sets are played, the one who was serving goes out of play and the other comes in. People believe the first man who says whether the ball passed over or under the cord. The waters are the sweat; the racket strings are made of the guts of sheep or goats; the round machine is the pellet or tennis-ball. After the game they refresh themselves before a clear fire and change their shirts, and they are glad to feast, but gladdest of all are the winners. And here's good cheer!'

[THE SECOND BOOK]

PANTAGRUEL

KING OF THE DIPSODES
GIVEN IN HIS TRUE CHARACTER
TOGETHER WITH HIS TERRIBLE DEEDS AND
ACTS OF PROWESS
COMPOSED BY
THE LATE M. ALCOFRIBAS
ABSTRACTOR OF THE QUINTESSENCE

DIZAIN BY MASTER HUGUES SALEL

TO THE AUTHOR OF THIS BOOK

If for combining profit with delight
An author wins great popular renown,
You shall be praised, of that be certain quite;
I know it well; in this small book alone,
Your understanding in its jolly tone
Has drawn so well what useful is to us
That I can see a new Democritus
Mocking the deeds done in the life of man.
Go on; and if not meritorious
In earthly view, be praised in Heaven's domain.

THE AUTHOR'S PROLOGUE

MOST illustrious and most valorous champions, noblemen, and others, who gladly devote yourselves to all gentle and honest pursuits, you have recently seen, read, and come to know The Great and Inestimable Chronicles of the enormous Giant Gargantua, and as true believers have nobly believed them; and you have often amused yourselves in the company of ladies and maidens, by telling them fine long stories from that book, when you were short of other conversation; for which you are deserving of great praise and to be eternally remembered.

So far as I am concerned, I would have every man put aside his proper business, take no care for his trade, and forget his own affairs, in order to devote himself entirely to this book. I would have him allow no distraction or hindrance from elsewhere to trouble his mind, until he knows it by heart; so that if the art of printing happened to die out, or all books should come to perish, everyone should be able, in time to come, to teach it thoroughly to his children, and to transmit it to his successors and survivors, as if from hand to hand, like some religious Cabala. For there is more profit in it than may be imagined by a rabble of scabby swaggerers, who understand far less of these jolly little productions than Raclet does of the Institutes.

I have known high and mighty noblemen in great numbers, hunters of great game or hawkers after ducks, who if the game happened not to be caught where it was expected, or the hawk saw her prey gaining on her by power of wing and began to hover, grew most annoyed, as you know well enough. But their refuge and comfort, and their method of avoiding a chill was to re-read the inestimable deeds of the said Gargantua. There are others in the world – these are no fairy-tales – who, when greatly afflicted with toothache, after expending all their substance on doctors without any result, have found no readier remedy than to put the said Chronicles between two fine linen sheets, well warmed, and apply them to the seat of the pain, dusting them first with a little dry-dung powder.

But what shall I say of the poor victims of pox and gout? Oh, how often we have seen them at a moment when they were well anointed and thoroughly greased, with their faces shining like a larder lock plate, and their teeth rattling like the keys on the manual of an organ or a spinet when it is being played, and their gullets foaming like a wild boar which the hounds have driven into the toils. And what were they doing then? Their one consolation was to have some pages of this book read to them. And some of them we have *seen who would have given themselves to a hundred barrels-full of old devils if they had not felt a perceptible alleviation of their pain from the reading of the said book, while they were being kept in the sweat-room, exactly as women do in the pangs of childbirth when the Life of St Margaret is read to them.*

Is that nothing? Find me a book in any language, on any subject or science whatever, which has such virtues, properties, and prerogatives, and I will pay you a quart of tripe. No, gentlemen, no. It is peerless, incomparable, and beyond comparison. This I maintain to any point short of the stake; and those who would maintain otherwise let them be reckoned deceivers, predestination-men, impostors, and seducers.

It is very true that one finds in some books of luxuriant growth certain occult properties; and among these are counted Toss-pint, Orlando Furioso, Robert the Devil, Fierabras, William the Fearless, Huon of Bordeaux, Mandeville, *and* Matabrune; *but they are not comparable to the book of which we speak. The world has thoroughly acknowledged by infallible experience the great returns and benefits proceeding from this* Gargantuine Chronicle. *For more copies of it have been sold by the printers in two months than there will be of the Bible in nine years.*

Wishing therefore still further to increase your entertainment, I, your humble slave, offer you now another book of the same stamp, though one a little more reasonable and credible than the last. But do not suppose – unless you wish to be wilfully deceived – that I speak of it as the Jews do of the Law. I was not born under that planet, nor have I ever come to lie, or to affirm a thing to be true which was not. I speak of it as a lusty Onocrotary – no, I mean Crotonotary of martyred lovers and Crocquenotary of love. Quod vidimus testamur.[1] *It tells of the horrific feats and deeds of Pantagruel, whom I have served for wages since I grew out of my page-hood till to-day, when by his leave I have come to visit my pastures and discover if any of my kindred survives there.*

Therefore, to make an end of my prologue, I offer myself, body and soul, tripe and bowels, to a hundred thousand basket-loads of fine devils in case I lie in so much as a single word in the whole of this History. And, similarly, may St Anthony's fire burn you, the epilepsy throw you, the thunder-stroke and leg-ulcers rack you, dysentery seize you, and may the erysipelas, with

1. We testify to what we have seen (a quotation from the Book of Revelations). The previous word-play marks an oblique reference to the Protonotary or Chancellor of the Roman Court, and to the onocrotary or pelican.

its tiny cowhair rash, and quicksilver's pain on top, through your arse-hole enter up, and like Sodom and Gomorrah may you dissolve into sulphur, fire, and the bottomless pit, in case you do not firmly believe everything that I tell you in this present Chronicle!

CHAPTER 1: *Of the Origin and Antiquity of the great Pantagruel*

IT will be no idle or unprofitable matter, seeing that we have leisure, to remind you of the fount and origin from which the good Pantagruel was born to us. For I observe that all good historiographers have thus dealt with their Chronicles, not only the Arabs, Barbarians, and Romans, but also the gentile Greeks, who were everlasting boozers. It is fitting that you should note, therefore, that at the beginning of the world – I am speaking of a distant date, more than forty times forty nights ago, to count by the method of the ancient Druids – a little after Abel was killed by his brother Cain, the earth, being soaked in the blood of the righteous, was that day so very fertile in all those fruits that from her loins she bears for us, and especially in medlars, that from time immemorial it has been called the year of the great medlars, for three of them went to a bushel.

In that year the Kalends were fixed by the Greek date-books, the month of March was outside Lent, and mid-August fell in May. In the month of October, I believe, or perhaps in September – if I am not mistaken, and I want to take particular care not to be – came the week so famous in our annals, that is called the Week of Three Thursdays. For it had three of them on account of the irregular bissextiles, since the sun strayed a little to the left *as we forgive our debtors*, and the moon veered more than ten feet from her course, and the movement of trepidation in the firmament, which is called Aplanos, was clearly observed. For the middle Pleiad left her companions and declined towards the Equinoctial, and the star called Spica left the constellation of the Virgin and moved away towards the Scales; which are very alarming happenings, and so hard and difficult that the astrologers cannot get their teeth into them. Their teeth would have been pretty long, indeed, if they could have reached as far as that!

Account it a fact that everybody gladly ate those medlars, for they were pleasant to the eyes and a delight to the taste. But just as Noah, that holy man to whom we are so much obliged and indebted for his having planted us the vine, from which comes that ambrosial, delicious, precious, celestial, joyous, and deific liquor which is called *drink*, made a mistake in drinking it, since he did not know its great virtue and power, so the men and women of that time ate this fine, big fruit with great delight.

But because of that a variety of accidents befell them. All of them were afflicted with a most horrible swelling on the body, but not all in the same place. For some swelled in the belly, and their bellies became round, like great tuns, whence comes the phrase *ventrem omnipotentem*.[1] They were all honest men and good jokers, and of their stock was born St Fatpaunch and Shrove Tuesday.

Others swelled at the shoulders and became so humpbacked that they were called Montifers, that is *hill-carriers*; and you will still see them about the world, of different sexes and rank. From this stock came Aesop, whose excellent deeds and sayings you have in writing.

Others grew in the length of that member which is called Nature's labourer, so that it grew marvellously long, big, stout, fat, lusty, and proud, after the ancient fashion, so much so that men made use of it as a belt, twisting it four or five times round the body. But if it happened to be in good fettle and sailing before the wind, you would have said when you saw them that such men had their lances couched for jousting at the quintain. Of these the stock is extinct, so the ladies say. For they are continually lamenting that

There are no more of those stout, &c.

You know the rest of the song.

Others grew so enormously in the matter of ballocks that three comfortably filled a hogshead. From them are descended the balls of Lorraine, which never stay in a codpiece, but always fall to the bottom of the breeches.

Others grew long in the leg, and when you saw them you would have taken them for cranes or flamingoes, or perhaps for people walking on stilts, and little schoolboys call them in Latin Iambics.[2] In others, the nose grew so much that it looked like the spout of a retort, striped all over and starred with little pustules, pullulating, purpled, pimpled, enamelled, studded, and embroidered gules, as you have seen in the cases of Canon Bellybag and of Clubfoot, the Angers physician. Of this stock were a few who loved barley-water, but they were all devoted to the septembral juice. From them Naso and Ovid derived

1. Almighty belly, a play on *patrem omnipotentem* (Father Almighty).
2. *Iambics*, a pun on *jambes* (legs).

their origins, also all those of whom it is written: *Ne reminiscaris*.[1]

In others the ears grew, till they were so great that out of one of them you could have made a doublet, a pair of breeches, and a jacket, and have covered yourself with the other as with a Spanish cape; and it is said that in Bourbonnais the race still persists, whence comes the term Bourbon ears.

Others grew in the length of their bodies, from whom came the giants, and from them Pantagruel. The first was Chalbroth, who begat Sarabroth, who begat Faribroth, who begat Hurtali – who was a greater consumer of soups and reigned in the time of the Flood – who begat Nimrod, who begat Atlas – who with his shoulders kept the heavens from falling – who begat Goliath, who begat Eryx – who was the inventor of the game of thimble-rigging – who begat Titus, who begat Eryon, who begat Polyphemus, who begat Cacus, who begat Etion – who was the first to get the pox through not having drunk fresh in summer – who begat Enceladus, who begat Ceus, who begat Typhoeus, who begat Aloeus, who begat Otus, who begat Aegeon, who begat Briareus – who had a hundred hands – who begat Porphirio, who begat Adamastor, who begat Antaeus, who begat Agatho, who begat Porus – against whom Alexander the Great fought – who begat Aranthas, who begat Gabbara – who was the first inventor of drinking healths – who begat Goliath of Secundilla, who begat Offot – who had a terribly fine nose through drinking from the cask – who begat Artachaeus, who begat Oromedon, who begat Gemmagog – who was the inventor of pointed shoes – who begat Sisyphus, who begat the Titans, from whom sprang Hercules, who begat Enac – who was very expert in taking little worms out of the hands – who begat Fierabras – who was beaten by Oliver, peer of France and companion of Roland – who begat Morgan – who was the first in this world to play at dice with his spectacles – who begat Fracassus, of whom Merlin Coccai has written, from whom sprang Ferragus, who begat Happemousche – who was the first inventor of smoking ox-tongues over the fire, for until then people salted them as they do hams – who begat Bolivorax, who begat Longys, who begat Gayoffe – whose balls were of poplar and his tool of sorb-apple wood – who begat Maschefain, who begat Bruslefer, who begat Engolevent, who begat Galahad, the inventor of flagons, who begat Mirelangault, who begat Galaffre,

1. Do not remember (my sins).

who begat Falourdin, who begat Roboastre, who begat Sortibrant of Coimbra, who begat Brulant of Mommiré, who begat Bruyer – who was beaten by Ogier the Dane, peer of France – who begat Maubrun, who begat Foutasnon, who begat Hacquelebac, who begat Vit-de-grain, who begat Grandgousier, who begat Gargantua, who begat the noble Pantagruel, my master.

I know very well that in reading this passage, you will feel in your hearts a very reasonable doubt and ask how it is possible that this should be so, seeing that at the time of the Flood the whole world perished except Noah and seven persons with him in the Ark, amongst whom the said Hurtali is not included. No doubt the question is well put and quite justified. But unless my wits are ill-caulked my reply will satisfy you. Since I was not alive in that age, and so cannot tell you anything of my own invention, I will cite the authority of the Massoretes, good ballocky fellows and fine Hebraic bagpipers, who affirm that in fact Hurtali was not in Noah's Ark. Indeed, he could not get in, for he was too big. But he sat astride of it, with one foot on each side, as small children do on hobby-horses, or as the great Bull of Berne, who was killed at Marignan, riding astride on a great stone-hurling cannon, which is undoubtedly a beast, of a fine, jolly pace.

In this fashion, by God's aid, he saved the said Ark from danger. For he kept it balanced with his legs, and with one foot turned it whichever way he wished, as one does a ship with the tiller. The people inside sent him up abundant victuals through a chimney, to reward him for the service he was doing them; and sometimes they chatted together, as Icaromenippus did with Jupiter, according to Lucian's account.

Have you thoroughly understood all this? Then drink a good draught without water. For if you do not believe it – 'Indeed I don't!' said she.

CHAPTER 2: *Of the Nativity of the most redoubted Pantagruel*

GARGANTUA at the age of four hundred, four score, and forty-four years begat his son Pantagruel upon his wife Badebec, daughter of the king of the Amaurots in Utopia, who died in childbirth; for he was so amazingly large and so heavy that he could not come into the world without suffocating his mother.

But in order fully to understand the cause and reason of the name which was given to him at baptism, you will note that in that year there was so great a drought throughout all the land of Africa, that thirty-six months, three weeks, four days, thirteen hours, and somewhat more passed without rain, and with the sun's heat so torrid that the whole earth was parched by it. Indeed the heat was no more violent in the days of Elijah than it was then. For there was not a tree in the land that had either leaf or flower. The grass lost its green; the rivers drained away; the springs ran dry; the poor fish, abandoned by their own element, strayed and cried on the ground most horribly; the birds fell from the air through lack of dew; the wolves, foxes, stags, boars, deer, hares, rabbits, weasels, martens, badgers, and other animals were to be found dead in the fields, with their throats gaping. As for men, their case was most piteous. You would have seen them lolling out their tongues like greyhounds that have run for six hours; many threw themselves into wells; others crept into a cow's belly, to be in the shade, and these Homer calls *Alibantes*. The whole country was at a standstill. It was pitiable to see the pains that mortals took to save themselves from this dreadful plight. It was hard work to keep the holy water in the churches from being exhausted. But they so organized it, by the advice of My Lords the Cardinals and the Holy Father, that no one dared to take more than one dip. Yet when anyone entered the church you might have seen scores of poor thirsty souls coming up behind him, and him distributing it to anyone who had his mouth wide open to catch a drop of it, like the wicked rich man,[1] in order that nothing should be lost. Oh, how fortunate in that year was the man who had a cool and well furnished cellar!

The Philosopher relates, in debating the question why the waters of the sea are salt, that at the time when Phoebus handed over the driving of his light-giving chariot to his son Phaeton, the said Phaeton, unskilled in the art and not knowing how to follow the ecliptic line between the two tropics of the sun's orbit, strayed from his track and approached so near to the earth that he dried up all the lands beneath him, scorching a large portion of the sky which the philosophers call *Via lactea*,[2] and simpletons call St James's Path, although the more highfalutin' poets say that it is the region where Juno's milk fell when

1. A reference to the story of Dives – the rich man.   (Luke 16, 19-25).
2. The Milky Way.

she suckled Hercules. That was the time when the earth was so heated that it burst into a great sweat, which caused it to sweat out the whole sea, which for that reason is salt, for all sweat is salt; which you will admit to be true if you taste your own, or that of pox-patients when they make them sweat. It is all one to me.

An almost similar case occurred in that year. For one Friday, when everyone was at devotions, and they were making a fine procession with all manner of litanies and grand sermons, calling on God Almighty to deign with his eye of mercy to look down on them in their great distress, great drops of water were plainly seen to break out of the earth, as when someone bursts into a copious sweat. And the poor people began to rejoice, as if this had been something to their profit. For some said that there was not a drop of moisture in the air from which they could expect rain, and that the earth was making up for this lack. Other learned people said that it was rain from the Antipodes, about which Seneca tells in the fourth book of his *Questiones naturales*, in speaking of the origin and source of the River Nile. But they were mistaken. For after the procession, when each one wanted to gather up some of this dew and drink it by the bowlful, they found that it was only brine, saltier and far nastier than sea-water.

And because Pantagruel was born on that very day, his father gave him the name he did: for *Panta* in Greek is equivalent to *all*, and *Gruel*, in the Hagarene language, is as much as to say *thirsty*; by this meaning to infer that at the hour of the child's nativity the world was all thirsty, and also seeing, in a spirit of prophecy, that one day his son would be ruler over the thirsty, as was demonstrated to him at that very hour by another sign even more convincing. For when the child's mother Badebec was being delivered of him and the midwives were waiting to receive him, there came first out of her womb sixty-eight muleteers, each pulling by the collar a mule heavily laden with salt; after which came out nine dromedaries loaded with hams and smoked ox-tongues, seven camels loaded with salted eels; and then twenty-four cartloads of leeks, garlics, and onions: all of which greatly alarmed the said midwives.

But some of them said: 'Here is fine fare. We were only drinking slackly, not like Saxons. This is bound to be a good sign. These are spurs to wine.' And whilst they were gossiping amongst themselves about such little matters, out came Pantagruel, as shaggy as a bear.

Whereupon one of them said in a spirit of prophecy: 'He is born with all his hair. He will perform wonders; and if he lives he'll reach a ripe age.'

CHAPTER 3: *Of the Mourning Gargantua made for the Death of his Wife Badebec*

WHEN Pantagruel was born no one could have been more astonished and perplexed than his father Gargantua. For, seeing on the one side his wife Badebec newly dead, and on the other his son Pantagruel newly born, and so big and handsome, he did not know what to say or do. His mind was troubled with the doubt whether he ought to weep in mourning for his wife, or laugh out of delight at his son. On either side he found sophistical arguments which took his breath away. For he framed them very well *in modo et figura*,[1] but he could not resolve them. And consequently he remained trapped, like a mouse caught in pitch, or a kite taken in a noose.

'Shall I weep?' said he. 'Yes. Why then? Because my wife who was so good is dead. She was the most this, and the most that, that ever was in the world. I shall never see her again, and I shall never find one like her. This is a loss beyond all calculation! O my God, what have I done to thee that thou shouldst punish me so? Why didst Thou not send death to me before sending it to her? For to live without her is no more than a lingering death. Ah, Badebec, my sweet, my darling, my little coney – hers was a good three acres and two roods in size for all that – my tenderling, my codpiece, my shoe, my slipper, never shall I see you again. Oh, poor Pantagruel, you have lost your good mother, your sweet nurse, your beloved lady. Ah, false death, how unkind you are to me, how cruel you are to me, to wrench from me her whose rightful due was immortality!'

And as he spoke he bellowed like a cow. But when Pantagruel came into his mind, he suddenly began laughing like a calf. 'Ho, my little son,' he cried, 'my ballocklet, my footkin, how pretty you are! How grateful I am to God for having given me such a fine son, such a jolly little fellow, so smiling and gay! Ho, ho, ho, ho! How glad I am. Let's drink, ho, and banish all melancholy! Bring some of the best. Rinse

1. By the method and figure of the syllogism.

the glasses. Lay the cloth. Drive out those dogs. Blow up that fire. Light that candle. Shut that door. Cut up this toast for soup. Send these poor people away, and give them that they want. Take my gown, and let me strip to my doublet the better to entertain my company.'

As he said this he heard the litanies and dirges of the priests who were carrying his wife to the grave. So he broke off his talk, and was suddenly carried off in another direction, saying: 'Lord God, must I turn sad again? It grieves me. I am no longer young. I am growing old. The weather is dangerous. I might catch some fever, and then I should be done for. By my faith as a nobleman, it's better to weep less and drink more. My wife is dead. Well, in God's name – *da jurandi*[1] – I shan't bring her back to life by my tears. She is well off. She is in Paradise at least, if in no better place. She's praying to God for us, she's very happy, she's not worrying any more about our miseries and calamities. The same fate hangs over our heads! God care for those who remain alive! I must think of finding another.'

'But this is what you must do,' said he to the midwives, the wise women. 'But where are they? Good creatures, I cannot see you anywhere – Go to her burial, and in the meantime I'll rock my son here. For I feel very unwell, and might be in danger of falling sick. But drink a good draught beforehand. You'll find yourselves the better for it, believe me, on my honour.'

In obedience to his orders, they went to the funeral service and burial, and poor Gargantua remained at home, during which time he composed an epitaph to be engraved as follows:

> DEAD IS THE NOBLE BADEBEC
> WHO HAD A FACE LIKE A REBEC;
> A SPANISH BODY AND A BELLY
> LIKE A SWISS FRAU; SHE DIED, I TELL YE
> IN CHILD-BED. PRAY TO GOD THAT HER
> HE PARDON WHEREIN SHE DID ERR.
> HERE LIES HER BODY, WHICH DID LIVE
> FREE FROM ALL VICE, AS I BELIEVE,
> AND DID DECEASE, POOR SIMPLE BRIDE,
> THE YEAR AND DAY ON WHICH SHE DIED.

1. *Da jurandi* [*veniam*]. Pardon my swearing.

CHAPTER 4: *Of Pantagruel's Childhood*

I FIND from the old historiographers and poets that many were born into this world in very strange manners, which would take too long to recount. Read the seventh book of Pliny, if you have the leisure. Yet never did you hear of so marvellous a birth as Pantagruel's, for it was almost beyond belief how he grew in body and strength in so short a time. What Hercules did was as nothing, when in his cradle he killed two serpents, for those serpents were only small and weak. But Pantagruel, while still in the cradle, did quite astounding things. I will omit to relate here how, at each of his meals, he swigged off the milk of four thousand six hundred cows; and how all the saucepan makers of Saumur in Anjou, of Villedieu in Normandy, and of Bramont in Lorraine were employed in making him a saucepan to boil his soup in; and how they gave him this soup in a great drinking-trough, which is to this day at Bourges, near the palace. But his teeth were already so well grown and strong that he broke a great piece out of this trough, as can well be seen.

One day, in the early morning, when they wanted him to suck one of his cows – for he never had any other wet-nurses, so the history tells us – he got one of his arms free from the bands that held him in the cradle, and he ups with the cow, gripping her under the ham. Then he ate her two udders and half of her paunch, together with the liver and kidneys, and would have devoured her entire, had she not bellowed horribly, as if the wolves had caught her by the legs. At this noise people rushed up, and got her out of Pantagruel's grasp. But they could not prevent the ham's remaining in his hands; and this he ate right off, as if it were a sausage. Indeed when they tried to get the bone from him, he bolted it down as a cormorant would a little fish, and afterwards began to say: 'Good, good, good.' For he was not able to speak well yet, but wished them to understand that he had found it very good, and would like nothing better than the same again. When they saw this his attendants tied him down with stout cables, like those that are made at Tain for the salt traffic to Lyons; or like those of the great ship *Françoise* which lies at Havre-de-Grace in Normandy.

But at a certain time when a great bear which his father kept escaped and came to lick his face – for his nurses had not properly wiped his mouth – he freed himself from those cables as easily as did Samson from the Philistines and, seizing Master Bear, tore him to pieces like a chicken. He made a nice tit-bit of him for that meal. Whereupon, for fear that he might hurt himself, Gargantua had four great iron chains made to bind him, and buttresses firmly fixed to his cradle. Of these chains you have one at La Rochelle, which is drawn up at night between the two great towers of the harbour; another is at Lyons; another at Angers, and the fourth was carried off by the devils to bind Lucifer, who was breaking loose at the time because of a colic that tormented him horribly, as a result of his eating the fricasseed soul of a sergeant for his breakfast. So you can well believe Nicolas de Lyra's comment on that passage in the Psalms, where it is written: *Et Og regem Basan*, to the effect that the same Og, while still small, was so strong and vigorous that he had to be bound to his cradle with iron chains. So Pantagruel remained quiet and peaceable; for he could not break those chains so easily, especially as he had no room in his cradle to swing his arms.

But this is what happened on one great festival day, when his father Gargantua was giving a grand banquet to all the princes of his court. I believe that all his court officers were so busily occupied with the preparation of this banquet that no one bothered about poor Pantagruel, and he was left neglected. What did he do? Listen, my good people, to what he did. He tried to break the chains of his cradle with his arms; but they were too strong and he could not. Then he banged so hard with his feet that he broke the end of his cradle, even though it was made of a beam five foot square; and as soon as he had got his feet outside he slid down as well as he could until his feet touched the ground. Then with great strength he raised himself up, carrying his cradle thus tied on his back, just like a tortoise climbing up a wall; and to look at him, he seemed like a great five-hundred-ton carrack on its end. In this condition he went into the hall where they were banqueting, so boldly that he greatly alarmed the company. Since he had his arms bound inside, however, he could not take anything to eat, but with a great effort bent down to pick up a snack with his tongue. When his father saw this he realized that they had left him without anything to eat, and ordered that he should be loosed from those chains. This was the advice of the princes and lords assembled; and in addition, Gargantua's physicians observed that if he were kept in his cradle like this, he would be subject to gravel all his life. When he was released they made him sit up, and he ate very heartily. Then he broke that cradle of his into more than five hundred thousand pieces with a blow of his fist, which he struck at the middle of it in his rage, swearing that he would never go back into it.

CHAPTER 5: *The youthful Deeds of the noble Pantagruel*

So Pantagruel grew from day to day, and visibly progressed, which rejoiced his father's natural affections. While he was quite small Gargantua had a cross-bow made for him, to shoot at little birds, and this is now known as the great bow of Chantelle.

Then he sent him to school, to learn and to make profitable use of his youth. So he went to Poitiers to study, and did well there. Moreover, seeing that the scholars of that place were sometimes at leisure and did not know how to amuse themselves, he took pity on them, and one day took from a rocky place called Passelourdin a huge rock fifty foot square and ten foot thick. This he quite easily set up on four pillars in the middle of a field, so that these scholars could enjoy themselves by climbing on it and there banqueting with plenty of flagons, hams, and pies, and could carve their names on it with a knife. This is known to-day as the Upright Stone, and in memory of this exploit no one is now entered in the matriculation book of the said University of Poitiers until he has drunk in the Caballine fountain of Croustelle, passed at Passelourdin, and climbed on to the Upright Stone.

Afterwards, when he read the great chronicles of his ancestors, he found that Geoffrey of Lusignan, called Geoffrey of the Long Tooth, grandfather of the cousin-by-marriage of the eldest sister of the aunt of the son-in-law of the uncle of the daughter-in-law of his stepmother, was buried at Maillezais, and he took french leave one day to pay him a visit, as a decent man should. He left Poitiers with some of his companions. They passed through Ligugé, where they visited the noble Abbot Ardillon, through Sansay, Celles, Colognes, and Fontenay-le-Comte, where they called on the learned Tiraqueau; and from there came to Maillezais, where Pantagruel visited the tomb of the said Geoffrey of the Long Tooth, of whom he felt considerable fear when he saw his portrait. For he is represented there as a man in a rage, drawing his great scimitar half out of its scabbard.

When Pantagruel asked the reason for this, the canons of the place told him that there was none except *Pictoribus atque poetis*, &c; that is to say that poets and painters have the licence to describe what they will, according to their fancy. But he was not satisfied with that answer and said: 'He has not been painted like that for no reason. I suspect that at his death some wrong was done him, which he requires his relatives to revenge. I will inquire more deeply into this, and will do what is reasonable.'

Then he did not return to Poitiers, but decided to visit the other Universities of France. So, going on to La Rochelle, he took ship and came to Bordeaux, in which place he found nothing much to amuse him except the lightermen playing at sheep and wolves on the quay. From there he went to Toulouse, where he learned to dance very well and to play with the two-handed sword, as is the custom of the students of that university. But he did not stay there long when he saw that they had their professors burnt alive like red-herrings. 'God forbid that I should die that death,' he cried, 'for I am sufficiently dry by nature without being heated any further'.

Then he came to Montpellier, where he found very good Mirevaux wines and jolly company; and he thought of setting himself to the study of medicine, but decided that the profession was far too wearying, besides being melancholy, and that physicians smelt of the suppository, like old devils. He made up his mind, therefore, to study the law. But, seeing that there were only one bald-headed and three patchy legists in that place, he departed; and on his way he built the Pont-du-Gard and the amphitheatre at Nîmes in less than three hours, which really sounds more like divine handiwork than human; and so he came to Avignon, and had not been there three days before he was in love. For the women there love to play the two-backed beast, because it is Papal territory.

On observing this, his tutor Epistemon removed him from there, and took him to Valence in Dauphiné, where he found that there was not much amusement and that the town hooligans beat up the students, which annoyed him. One fine Sunday, indeed, when everyone was at the public dance, and a student wanted to join in, these hooligans would not allow him. Seeing this, Pantagruel pursued them with a rain of blows as far as the banks of the Rhone, and would have made them all drown, had they not hidden underground like moles a good mile and a half under the water. The hole is still to be seen there. After this he went off, and with three steps and a jump came to Angers, where he found himself very comfortable and would have stayed for some time if the plague had not driven him away.

So he came to Bourges, where he studied for a considerable time, and did very well in the Faculty of Law. Sometimes he said that the law-books seemed to him like a fine cloth-of-gold robe, marvellously grand and costly but trimmed with dung. 'For', he said, 'there are no books in the world so fine, so ornate, and so elegant as the texts of the Pandects. But the trimming of them – that is to say Accursius's gloss – is so foul, stinking and infamous that it is no better than filth and villainy.'

When he left Bourges he came to Orléans and there found a lot of lumpish scholars who made him a great welcome on his arrival; and in a short time he learnt to play tennis with them, so well that he became a champion. For the students of that place are great practitioners of the game; and sometimes they took him to the islands also, to amuse himself at ninepins. But as for breaking his head with overmuch study, he would not do that at all, for fear of spoiling his sight; especially as one of the professors often said in his lectures that there is nothing so bad for the sight as disease of the eyes. And one day when a scholar of his acquaintance, who hardly had more knowledge than the rest of the brood, but on the other hand was very good at dancing and tennis, took his licentiate in law, Pantagruel composed this blazon and device for the licentiates of that university:

> A tennis ball in the cod-placket,
> In the hand a tennis-racket,
> Skill at the slow dance to trip it,
> And there's the Licentiate hooded.

CHAPTER 6: *How Pantagruel met a Limousin who murdered the French Language*

ONE day, I do not know when, Pantagruel was walking with his friends after supper near the gate on to the Paris road, when he met a pretty spruce young scholar coming along the way, of whom, after they had exchanged greetings, he asked: 'Where are you coming from at this hour, my friend?'

'From the alme, inclite, and celebrated academy that is vocitated Lutetia,' replied the scholar.

'What does that mean?' Pantagruel asked one of his people.

'It means from Paris,' he answered.

'So you come from Paris,' said Pantagruel. 'And how do you spend your time, you gentlemen students at this same Paris?'

'We transfretate the Sequana at the dilucule and crepuscule; we deambulate through the compites and quadrives of the urb; we despumate the Latin verbocination and, as verisimile amorabunds, we captate the benevolence of the omnijugal, omniform, and omnigenous feminine sex. At certain intervals we invisitate the lupanars, and in venerean ecstasy we inculcate our veretres into the penitissim recesses of the pudenda of these amicabilissime meretricules. Then we cauponizate, in the meritory taverns of the Pineapple, the Castle, the Magdalen, and the Slipper, goodly vervecine spatules, perforaminated with petrosil. And if by fort fortune there is rarity or penury of pecune in our marsupies, and they are exhausted of ferruginous metal, for the scot we dimit our codices and vestments oppignerated, prestolating the tabellaries to come from the penates and patriotic lares.'

At which Pantagruel exclaimed: 'What devilish language is this? By God, you must be a heretic.'

'No, signor,' answered the scholar. 'For libentissimily, as soon as there illucesces any minutule slither of day, I demigrate into one of these excellently architected minsters; and there irrorating myself in fine lustral water, mumble a snatch of some missic precation of our sacrificules and, submirmillating my horary precules, I illave and absterge my anima from its nocturnal inquinaments. I revere the Olimpicoles. I latrially venerate the supernal astripotent. I dilect and redame my proximes. I observe the decalogical precepts, and according to the facultatule of my vires, do not discede from it by the latitude of an unguicule. It is veriform, nevertheless, since Mammon does not supergurgitate a drop in my locules, that I am a little rare and neglectful in supererogating the eleemosynes to those indigents who hostially solicit their stipe.'

'A turd, a turd!' exclaimed Pantagruel. 'What does this fool mean? I believe he is coining some new devilish language for us here, and throwing an enchanter's spell on us.'

'My lord, there's no doubt about it,' replied one of his followers.

'This fellow's trying to imitate the Parisians' language. But all he is doing is murdering Latin. He thinks he is pindarizing, and imagines he's a great orator in French because he disdains the common use of speech.'

'Is that true?' asked Pantagruel.

'My lord, sir,' answered the scholar. 'My genius is not aptly nate, as this flatigious nebulon asserts, to excoriate the cuticle of our vernacular Gallic, but vice-versally I gnave opere, and by sail and oar I enite to locuplete it from the latinicome redundance.'

'By God,' cried Pantagruel, 'I'll teach you to speak. But before I do so, tell me one thing. Where do you come from?'

To which the scholar replied: 'The primaeval origin of my aves and ataves was indigenous to the Lemovic regions, where requiesces the corpus of the hagiotate Saint Martial.'

'I understand you all right,' said Pantagruel. 'What it comes to is that you're a Limousin, and here you want to play the Parisian. Well, come on, then, and I'll give you a combing.' Then he took him by the throat and continued: 'You murder Latin, by Saint John, I'll make you skin the fox. I'll skin you alive.'

Then the poor Limousin began to plead: 'Haw, guid master! Haw, lordie! Help me, St Marshaw. Ho, let me alane, for Gaud's sake, and dinna hairm me!'

Whereupon Pantagruel replied: 'Now you're speaking naturally,' and released him. But the poor Limousin beshat all his breeches, which were cut codtail fashion and not full-bottomed.

At which Pantagruel exclaimed: 'By St Alipentine, what a sweet scent! Devil take this turnip-eater, how he stinks!' And he let him go.

But this gave the Limousin such a lifelong terror and such a thirst that he would often swear Pantagruel held him by the throat; and after some years he died a Roland's death, this being a divine vengeance and proving the truth of the Philosopher Aulus Gellius's observation, that we ought to speak the language in common use, and of Octavian Augustus's maxim, that we should shun obsolete words as carefully as ships' pilots avoid the rocks at sea.

CHAPTER 7: *How Pantagruel came to Paris, and of the fine Books in the Library of Saint Victor's*

AFTER Pantagruel had made thorough studies at Orléans, he decided to visit the great university of Paris. But before his departure he was informed that there was an enormous great bell at Saint Aignan in this same Orléans, which had been lying on the ground for the past two hundred and fourteen years. It was so huge that they could not even raise it from the earth by any device, although they had attempted all the methods suggested by Vitruvius, in his *Architecture*, by Albertus, in his *Art of Building*, by Euclides, Theon, Archimedes, and Hero on *Engines*. None of them were any good.

Condescending willingly, therefore, to the humble request of the citizens and inhabitants of that place, Pantagruel made up his mind to transport it to the tower intended for it. So he went to the place where it lay, and picked it up from the ground with his little finger, as easily as if it were a hawk's bell. But before carrying it to the bell-tower, he decided to play a serenade round the town, and to sound it in all the streets, while carrying it in his hand. This gave everyone great pleasure, but it led to one very great inconvenience. For as he thus carried it and rang it through every street, all the good wine in Orléans turned and was spoilt. Which the people did not notice till the following night, when they all found themselves so thirsty from drinking these sour wines that they did nothing but spit, as white as Maltese cotton. And they said: 'We've caught the Pantagruel, and have salt in our throats.'

When he had performed this feat Pantagruel went to Paris with his party; and at his entry everyone came out to see him. For, as you know, the people of Paris are foolish by nature, in every note of the scale. They gazed at him with great astonishment, and not without considerable fear that he might carry the Palace away into some remote country, as his father had carried off the bells of Notre-Dame, to tie on his mare's neck. But after he had been there for some time, and had made a thorough study of the seven liberal arts, Pantagruel said that it was a good city to live in, but not to die in, because the beggars at St Innocent's used to warm their rumps on the bones of the dead.

He found the Library of St Victor most magnificent, especially for certain books which he discovered in it, of which the catalogue follows, and *primo*:

Bigua salutis (The Props of Salvation).

Bragueta juris (The Codpiece of the Law).

Pantofla decretorum (The Slipper of the Decretals).

Malogranatum vitiorum (The Pomegranate of Vice).

The Thread-ball of Theology.

The Long Broom of Preachers, composed by Turlupin.

The Elephantine Testicle of the Valiant.

The Henbane of the Bishops.

Marmotretus, de babouynis et cingis, cum commento Dorbellis (Marmotretus on Baboons and Monkeys, with commentary by des Orbeaux).

Decretum universitatis Parisiensis super gorgiasitate muliercularum ad placitum (Decree of the University of Paris on the Gorgiosity of pretty Women, for pleasure).

The Apparition of St Geltrude to a Nun of Poissy in labour.

Ars honeste petandi in societate, by M. Ortuinum (The Art of farting decently in public, by Hardouin de Graetz).

The Mustard-pot of tardy Penitence.

The Garters, alias the Boots of Patience.

Formicarium artium (The Ant-heap of the magic Arts).

De brodiorum usu, et honestate Chopinandi, per Silvestrem prieratem, Jacopinum (The Use of Soups and the Propriety of Hobnobbing, by Sylvester of Priero, Jacobin).

The Cuckold at Court.

The Frail of the Notaries.

The Marriage-packet.

The Crucible of Contemplation.

The Nonsense of the Law.

The Goad of Wine.

The Spur of Cheese.

Decrotatorum scholarium (On the Foulness of Scholars).

Tartaretus, de modo cacandi (Tartaret, on methods of Shitting).

The Fanfares of Rome.

Bricot, *de differentiis soupparum* (On the Varieties of Soups).

The Tail-piece of Discipline.

The Old Shoe of Humility.

The Tripe-pod of Big Thoughts.

The Kettle of Magnanimity.

The Puzzlements of Confessors.

The Vicars' Raps over the Knuckles.

Reverendi patris fratris Lubini, provincialis Bavardie, de croquendis lardonibus libri tres (The most reverend father Gobble, Provincial of Babbleland, on Bacon-eating – three volumes).

Pasquilli, doctoris marmorei, de Capreolis cum chardoneta comedendis, tempore papali ab Ecclesia interdicto (Pasquin, the marble doctor, that it is permissible to eat kid with artichokes, in the Papal Lent decreed by the Church).

The Invention of the Holy Cross, for six actors, performed by the Clerks of Sharp-practice.

The Spectacles of the Romeward-bound.

Majoris, de Modo faciendi boudinos (Mayr, On the Art of making Puddings).

The Prelates' Bagpipe.

Beda, *de Optimitate triparum* (Beda, on the Excellence of the Belly).

The Advocates' Suit for the Reformation of their Refreshers.

The Furred Cap of the Attorneys.

Of Peas and Bacon, *cum commento.*

The Ash-Wednesday cake of Indulgences.

Praeclarissimi juris utriusque doctoris Maistre Pilloti Raquedenari, de bobelidandis glossae Accursiane Baguenaudis repetitio enucidiluculi- dissima (A most lucidly unravelled treatise on pricking the Blad- ders of the Glosses of Accursius, by the most illustrious Doctor of Laws, Master Catchpenny, the Pilferer).

Stratagemata Francarchieri de Bagnolet (The Tricks of the Free- archer de Bagnolet).

De usu et utilitate escorchandi equos et equas, authore M. Nostro de Que- becu (On the Use and Practice of flaying Horses and Mares, by Master de Chêne).

Franctopinus, *De re militari, cum figuris Tevoti* (On the Military Art, with illustrations by Tevot).

The Clownishness of Little Priests.

M. N. Rostocostojambedanesse, *de Moustarda post prandium servienda, lib. quatuordecim, apostilati per M. Vaurillonis* (On the Serving of Mustard after Meals, fourteen volumes, collected by M. Vaurillon).

The Wedding-fees due to Procurators.

Jabolenus, *De cosmographis purgatorii* (On the Geography of Purgatory).

Questio subtilissima, utrum Chimera, in vacuo bombinans, possit comedere secundas intentiones, et fuit debatuta per decem hebdomadas in concilio Constantiensi (The most subtle question whether a Chimaera, bombinating in the Void, can be nourished on secondary intentions: one which was debated for ten weeks before the Council of Constance).

The Voracity of Advocates.

Barbouillamenta Scoti (The Scrawlings of Scotus).

The Cardinals' Bat.

De calcaribus removendis decades undecim, per M. Albericum de Rosata (On the Removal of Spurs, eleven decades by Alberic de Rosata).

Ejusdem, *De castrametandis crinibus lib. tres* (By the same, On the Need for Garrisons in the Hair. Three volumes).

The Entry of Anthoine de Leive into the Scorched Land.

Marforii bacalarii cubentis Rome, de pelendisque mascarendisque Cardinalium mulis (Marforio, Bachelor of the See of Rome, On the skinning and scorching of the Cardinals' mules).

Protest by the same, against those who say that the Pope's mule only eats at his hours.

Prognosticatio que incipit, Silvi Triquebille, balata per M. N. Songecrusyon (The Prophecy which begins, *Sylvi Triquebille*, a ballad by M. N. Songecreux).

Boudarini episcopi, de emulgentiarum profcctibus enneades novem, cum privilegio papali ad triennium, et postea non (Bishop Boudarin, Nine Enneads on the Efficacy of Emulgences, with papal sanction for three years and no more).

The Maidens' Shittery.

The Bald Arse of Widows.

The Monks' Hood.

The Mumblings of the Coelestine Fathers.

The Toll of the Belly-beggars.

The Teeth-chatter of the Oafs.

The Theologians' Rat-trap.

The Master of Arts' Ambuscade.

The Scullions of Occam, with a single tonsure.

*Magistri N. Fripesaulcetis, De grabellationibus horarum canonicorum lib.
quadraginta* (Master N. Lickthedish, On the scrupulous Examination of the Canonical Hours, forty volumes).

Cullebutatorium confratriarum, incerto authore (The Overthrow of the
Friaries, author unknown).

The Gluttons' Cavity.

The Body-odours of the Spaniards, supercockcrowed by Brother
Inigo (de Loyola).

The Poor Wretches' Worm-powder.

Poiltronismus rerum Italicarum, authore Magistro Bruslefer (The Pol-
troonery of Things Italian, by Master Brûlefer).

R. Lullius, de Batisfolagiis principum (On the Foolish Pursuits of
Princes).

Callibistratorium caffardiae, actore M. Jacobo Hocstratem hereticometra
(The Calibration of Hypocrisy by Jacob Hochstraten, gauger of
heretics).

*Chaultcouillonis, de magistro nostrandorum magistro nostratorumque
beuvetis, lib. octo galantissimi* (Hotball, on the drinking shops of
our Doctors-to-be and To-be-doctors, eight most sportive
books).

The Insertions of bullists, copyists, writers, epitomizers, notaries,
and reporters, compiled by Regis.

Perpetual Almanac for the Gouty and Poxy.

Maneries ramonandi fournellos, par M. Eccium (The Manner of Sweeping Flues, by Master Eck).

The Merchant's Packing-thread.

The Comforts of the Monastic Life.

The Omnium-gatherum of Bigots.

The History of the Hauntings.

The Scoundrelism of the Old Soldiers.

The Knavish Tricks of Ecclesiastical Judges.

The Gold-beater's skin of Tax-collectors.

Badinatorium Sophistarum (The Tomfooleries of the Sophists).

Antipericatametanaparbeugedamphicribrationes   merdicantium
(The Greek prepositions discussed by the Turdicants).

The Ramblings of Ballad-makers.

The Bellows of the Alchemists.

The Hey-presto of the Begging Friars, pocket-walleted by Friar Graspit.

The Shackles of Religion.

The Lecher's Lattice.

The Elbow-rest of Old Age.

The Muzzle of Nobility.

The Ape's Paternoster.

The Handcuffs of Devotion.

The Long Face of Ember-week.

The Magistrate's cap of Political Life.

The Hermit's Fly-flap.

The Penitent's Hood.

The Backgammon of the Knocking Friars.

Lourdaudus, De vita et honestate braguardorum (Blockhead, On the Life and Morals of Braggarts).

Lyripipii Sorbonici Moralisationes, per M. Lupoldum (Moralizings on a long-tailed graduate's Hood, by Master Lupoldus).

Travellers' Knick-knacks.

The Tipplings of the Bishops *ex-potibus.*

Tarrabaleationes doctorum Coloniensium adversus Reuchlin (The Attacks of the Cologne Scholars upon Reuchlin).

The Cymbals of the Ladies.

The Shitters' Martingale.

Virevoustatorum nacquettorum, per F. Pedebillitis (The Teetotum of the Tennis Markers, by Friar Whirligig).

The Heavy Shoes of a Stout Heart.

Mummery of the Spooks and Fairies

Gerson, De Auferibilitate pape ab Ecclesia (On the Power of the Church to depose a Pope).

The List of Candidates and Graduates.

Jo. Dytebrodii, De terribilitate excommunicationum libellus acephalos (Little book, without a head-piece, on the Terror of Excommunication).

Ingeniositas invocandi diabolos et diabolas, per M. Guingolfum (The Method of Invoking Demons, male and female, by Master Gingulf).

The Hotch-potch of Perpetual Beggars.

The Morris-dance of the Heretics.

The Old Wives' Tales of Gaietanus.

Moillegroin doctoris cherubici, de origine patepelutarum et torticollorum ritibus, lib. septem (The Cherubic Doctor Moillegrain, On the Origin of the Hairy-handed and Wrynecked Cheats, seven volumes).

Sixty-nine Fat Breviaries.

The Nightmare of the Five Orders of Mendicants.

The Skin of the Heretics, extracted from the Yellow Boot, incornifistibulated in the *Summa angelica* (The Writings of Aquinas).

The Brooder on Cases of Conscience.

The Fat Paunch of the Presidents.

Sutoris, adversus quemdam qui vocaverat eum fripponatorem, et quod fripponatores non sunt damnati ab Ecclesia (Pierre Couturier, against one who called him a rascal, and to prove that rascals are not condemned by the Church).

Cacatorium medicorum (The Doctors' Purge).

The Chimney-Sweep of Astrology.

Campi clysteriorum per S.C. (The Use of Suppositories, by Symphorien Champier).

The Wind-dispeller of the Apothecaries.

The Kiss-my-arse of Surgery.

Justinianus, *De Cagotis tollendis* (On the Education of Canters).

Antidotarium animae (The Antidote-book of the Soul).

Merlinus Coccaius, *de Patria diabolorum* (On the Country of the Devils).

Of these some are already published and others are now being printed in the noble city of Tübingen.

CHAPTER 8: *How Pantagruel, when at Paris, received a Letter from his Father Gargantua, together with a copy of the same*

As you may well suppose, Pantagruel studied very hard. For he had a double-sized intelligence and a memory equal in capacity to the measure of twelve skins and twelve casks of oil. But while he was staying in Paris, he one day received a letter from his father which read as follows:

Most dear Son,

Among the gifts, graces, and prerogatives with which the Sovereign Creator, God Almighty, endowed and embellished human nature in the beginning, one seems to me to stand alone, and to excel all others; that is the one by which we can, in this mortal state, acquire a kind of immortality and, in the course of this transitory life, perpetuate our name and seed; which we do by lineage sprung from us in lawful marriage. By this means there is in some sort restored to us what was taken from us by the sin of our first parents, who were told that, because they had not been obedient to the commandment of God the Creator, they would die, and that by death would be brought to nothing that magnificent form in which man has been created.

But by this method of seminal propagation, there remains in the children what has perished in the parents, and in the grandchildren what has perished in the children, and so on in succession till the hour of the Last Judgement, when Jesus Christ shall peacefully have rendered up to God His Kingdom, released from all danger and contamination of sin. Then all generations and corruptions shall cease, and the elements shall be free from their continuous transformations, since peace, so long desired, will then be perfect and complete, and all things will be brought to their end and period.

Not without just and equitable cause, therefore, do I offer thanks to God, my Preserver, for permitting me to see my grey-haired age blossom afresh in your youth. When, at the will of Him who rules and governs all things, my soul shall leave this mortal habitation, I shall not now account myself to be absolutely dying, but to be passing from one place to another, since in you, and by you, I shall remain in visible form here in this world, visiting and conversing with men of honour and my friends as I used to do. Which conversation of mine has been, thanks to God's aid and grace, although not free from sin, I confess – for we all sin, and continually pray to God to wipe out our sins – at least without evil intention.

If the qualities of my soul did not abide in you as does my visible form, men would not consider you the guardian and treasure-house of the immortality of our name; in which case my pleasure would be small, considering that the lesser part of me, which is my body, would persist, and the better part, which is the soul, and by which our name continues to be blessed among men, would be bastardized and degenerate. This I say not out of any distrust of your virtue, which I have already tried and approved, but in order to encourage you more strongly to proceed from good to better. For what I write to you at present is not so much in order that you may live in this virtuous manner as that you may rejoice in so living and in so having lived, and may strengthen yourself in the like resolution for the future, for the furtherance and perfection of these ends I have, as you will easily remember, spared no expense. Indeed, I have helped you towards them as if I treasured nothing else in this world but to see you, in my lifetime, a perfect model of virtue, honour, and valour, and a paragon of liberal and high-minded learning. I might seem to have desired nothing but to leave you, after my death, as a mirror representing the person of me your father, and if not as excellent and in every way as I wish you, at least desirous of being so.

But although my late father Grandgousier, of blessed memory, devoted all his endeavours to my advancement in all perfection and political knowledge, and although my labour and study were proportionate to – no, even surpassed – his desire; still, as you may well understand, the times were not as fit and favourable for learning as they are to-day, and I had no supply of tutors such as you have. Indeed the times were still dark, and mankind was perpetually reminded of the miseries and disasters wrought by those Goths who had destroyed all sound scholarship. But, thanks be to God, learning has been restored in my age to its former dignity and enlightenment. Indeed I see such improvements that nowadays I should have difficulty in getting a place among little schoolboys, in the lowest class, I who in my youth was reputed, with some justification, to be the most learned man of the century. Which I do not say out of vain boastfulness, although I might commendably do so in writing to you, – for which you have the authority of Marcus Tullius in his work on Old Age, and Plutarch's statement in his book entitled: How a Man may praise himself without Reproach – but in order to inspire you to aim still higher.

Now every method of teaching has been restored, and the study of languages has been revived: of Greek, without which it is disgraceful for a man to call himself a scholar, and of Hebrew, Chaldean, and Latin. The elegant and accurate art of printing, which is now in use, was invented in my time, by divine inspiration; as, by contrast, artillery was inspired by diabolical suggestion. The whole world is full of learned men, of very erudite tutors, and of most extensive libraries, and it is my opinion that neither in the time of Plato, of Cicero, nor of Papinian were there such facilities for study as one finds to-day. No one, in future, will risk appearing in public or in any company, who is not well polished in Minerva's workshop. I find robbers, hangmen, freebooters, and grooms nowadays more learned than the doctors and preachers were in my time.

Why, the very women and girls aspire to the glory and reach out for the celestial manna of sound learning. So much so that at my present age I have been compelled to learn Greek, which I had not despised like Cato, but which I had not the leisure to learn in my youth. Indeed I find great delight in reading the Morals of Plutarch, Plato's magnificent Dialogues, the Monuments of Pausanias, and the Antiquities of Athenaeus, while I wait for the hour when it will please God, my Creator, to call me and bid me leave this earth.

Therefore, my son, I beg you to devote your youth to the firm pursuit of your studies and to the attainment of virtue. You are in Paris. There you will find many praiseworthy examples to follow. You have Epistemon for your tutor, and he can give you living instruction by word of mouth. It is my earnest wish that you shall become a perfect master of languages. First of Greek, as Quintilian advises; secondly, of Latin; and then of Hebrew, on account of the Holy Scriptures; also of Chaldean and Arabic, for the same reason; and I would have you model your Greek style on Plato's and your Latin on that of Cicero. Keep your memory well stocked with every tale from history, and here you will find help in the Cosmographes of the historians. Of the liberal arts, geometry, arithmetic, and music, I gave you some smattering when you were still small, at the age of five or six. Go on and learn the rest, also the rules of astronomy. But leave divinatory astrology and Lully's art alone, I beg of you, for they are frauds and vanities. Of Civil Law I would have you learn the best texts by heart, and relate them to the art of philosophy. And as for the knowledge of Nature's works, I should like you to give careful attention to that too; so that there may be no sea, river, or spring of which you do not know the fish. All the birds of the air, all the trees, shrubs, and bushes of the forest, all the herbs of the field, all the metals deep in the bowels of the earth, the precious stones of the whole East and the South – let none of them be unknown to you.

Then scrupulously peruse, the books of the Greek, Arabian, and Latin doctors once more, not omitting the Talmudists and Cabalists, and by frequent dissections gain a perfect knowledge of that other world which is man. At some hours of the day also, begin to examine the Holy Scriptures. First the New Testament and the Epistles of the Apostles in Greek; and then the Old Testament, in Hebrew. In short, let me find you a veritable abyss of knowledge. For, later, when you have grown into a man, you will have to leave this quiet and repose of study, to learn chivalry and warfare, to defend my house, and to help our friends in every emergency against the attacks of evildoers.

Furthermore, I wish you shortly to show how much you have profited by your studies, which you cannot do better than by publicly defending a thesis in every art against all persons whatsoever, and by keeping the company of learned men, who are as common in Paris as elsewhere.

But because, according to the wise Solomon, Wisdom enters not into the malicious heart, and knowledge without conscience is but the ruin of the soul, it befits you to serve, love, and fear God, to put all your thoughts and hopes in Him, and by faith grounded in charity to be so conjoined with Him that you may never be severed from Him by sin. Be suspicious of the world's deceits and set not your heart on vanity; for this life is transitory, but the word of God remains eternal. Be helpful to all your neighbours, and love them as yourself. Respect your tutors, avoid the company of those whom you would not care to resemble, and do not omit to make use of those graces which God has bestowed on you. Then, when you see that you have acquired all the knowledge to be gained in those parts, return to me, so that I may see you and give you my blessing before I die.

My son, the peace and grace of Our Lord be with you. Amen.

From Utopia, this seventeenth day of the month of March,

Your father, GARGANTUA

After receiving and reading this letter, Pantagruel took fresh courage and was inspired to make greater advances than ever. Indeed, if you had seen him studying and measured the progress he made, you would have said that his spirit among the books was like fire among the heather, so indefatigable and ardent was it.

CHAPTER 9: *How Pantagruel found Panurge, whom he loved all his life*

ONE day when Pantagruel was walking outside the city towards the Abbey of Saint-Antoine, arguing and philosophizing with his people and some other students, he met a man of handsome build, elegant in all his features, but pitifully wounded in various places, and in so sorry a state that he looked as if he had escaped from the dogs, or to be more accurate, like some apple-picker from the Perche country.

When he caught sight of this fellow from the distance, Pantagruel said to his companions: 'Do you see that man coming along the road from the Charenton bridge? On my faith, he is only poor in fortune. His physiognomy tells me for certain that he comes of some rich and noble stock. It must be the misfortunes which always befall the adventurous that have reduced him to his present ragged and penurious state.' Then, when the fellow had come right up to them, Pantagruel asked him: 'My friend, stay here a little, I beg you, and be so kind as to answer certain questions that I shall ask you. You will not repent it, I assure you. For I have a very great desire to give you all the aid in my power in the calamity in which I find you. In fact, I feel great pity for you. Therefore, my friend, tell me who you are, where you come from, where you are going, what you are looking for, and what is your name.'

The fellow answered him in the German tongue:

'*Junker, Gott geb euch Glück unnd hail. Zuvor, lieber juncker, ich las euch wissen, das da ihr mich von fragt, ist ein arm unnd erbarmglich ding, unnd wer vil darvon zu sagen, welches euch verdruslich zu hœren, unnd mir zu erzelen wer, vievol, die Poeten unnd Orators vorzeiten haben gesagt in iren Sprüchen und Sententzen, das die Gedechtnus des Ellends unnd Azmuot vorlangst erlitten ist ain grosser Lust.*'[1]

To this Pantagruel replied: 'My friend, I don't understand a word of this gibberish. If you want to be understood you must speak another language.'

Upon which the fellow replied:

'*Al harildim gotfano dech min brin alabo dordin falbroth ringuam albaras. Nin porth zadilkin almucathim milko prim al elmin enthoth dal heben ensouim: kuth im al dim alkatim nim broth dechoth porth min michas im endoth, pruch dal maisoulum hol moth dansririm lupaldas im voldemoth. Nin hur diavolth mnarbothim dal gousch pal frapin duch im scoth pruch galeth dal chinon, min foulthrich al conin butathen doth dal prim.*'[2]

'Do you understand any of that?' Pantagruel asked the company;

1. Young sir, may God give you fortune and prosperity. My dear young sir, let me tell you first, that the story you ask me to tell you is a sad and pitiable one. It is a subject on which there would be much to say that would be tiresome for you to hear and for me to relate, although the poets and orators of the old times affirmed in their sayings and their maxims that the memory of pain and poverty is a great joy.

2. This is complete nonsense except for a distorted place name or two.

and Epistemon replied: 'I think that it is the language of the Antipodes. The devil himself couldn't get his teeth into it.'

Then said Pantagruel: 'My friend, I don't know whether the walls can understand you. But not one of us can make out a syllable.'

Then said the fellow:

'Signor mio, voi vedete per essempio che la cornamusa non suona mai s'ela non a il ventre pieno; cosi io parimente non vi saprei contare le mie fortune, se prima il tribulato ventre non a la solita refectione, al quale è adviso che le mani et il dent habbiano perso il loro ordine naturale et del tuto annichillati.'[1]

To which Epistemon replied: 'No better than the last.'

Then said Panurge in English: Lord, if you be so vertuous of intelligence, as you be naturally releaved to the body, you should have pity of me: for nature hath made us equal, but fortune hath some exalted, and others depreit: non ye less is vertue often deprived, and the vertuous man despised: for before the last end iss none good.

'Obscurer than ever,' replied Pantagruel.

Upon which Panurge said:

'Jona andie, guassa goussyetan behar da er remedio beharde versela ysser landa. Anbates oyto y es nausu eyn essassu gour ray proposian ordine den. Nonyssena bayta facheria egabeb genherassy badia sadassu nouraa ssia. Aran Hondouan gualde cydassu nay dassuna. Estou ossyc eguinan soury hin er darstura eguy harm. Genicoa plasar vadu.'[2]

'Are you there?' asked Epistemon. 'I'm not.'

Upon which Carpalim exclaimed: 'Saint Trinian, d'ye hail from Scotland, or have I mishaird you?'

Then Panurge replied:

'Prug frest frins sorgdmand strochdt drhds pag brlelang Gravot Chavigny

1. (Italian.) Example will show you that the bagpipe can never sound except with a full paunch. In the same way, I cannot tell you my adventures unless my rumbling belly receives its customary nourishment, for lack of which my hands and teeth have lost their usual function and are totally annihilated.

2. (Basque.) Great Lord, for all evils there must be a remedy; to do the right things, that is the difficulty. I have implored you again and again! Reduce our conversation to some sort of order. That will come, without trouble, if you will give me my bellyful. Afterwards, ask me whatever you like. But I pray God you won't fail to provide enough for two.

Pomardière rusth pkalhdracg Devinière près Nays. Bouille Kalmuch monach drupp delmeupplist rincq dlrndodelb up drent loch minc stz rinquald de vin ders cordelis but jocststzampenards.'[1]

And Epistemon replied: 'Are you speaking a human Christian language, my friend, or are you raving? But I know, it's Lantern-language.'

Panurge's reply was:

'Heere, ie en spreeke anders geen taele, dan kersten taele: my dunct nochtans, al en seg ie u niet een woordt mynen nood verklaart ghenonch wat ie beglere; gheest my wyt bermherticheyt yet waer un ie ghevoed magh zunch.'[2]

To which Pantagruel answered: 'And that's no better.'

Then said Panurge:

'Seignor, de tanto hablar yo soy cansado. Por que suplico a Vuestra Reverencia que mire a los preceptos evangelicos, para que ellos movant Vuestra Reverencia a lo que es de consciencia; y si ellos non bastarent para mover Vuestra Reverencia a piedad, yo supplico que mire a la piedad natural, la qual yo creo que le movra como es de razon, y con esto non digo mas.'[3]

To which Pantagruel replied: 'Really, my friend, I haven't the least doubt that you can talk several languages. But tell us what you want in some language that we can understand.'

Then the fellow said:

'Myn Herre, endog, jey med inghen tunge ta lede, lygeson bocon, oeg uskuulig creatner! Myne Kleebon och my ne legoms magerhed udviser allique klalig huuad tyng meg meest behoff girered somder sandeligh mad och drycke; hvuarpor forbarme teg omsyder offuermeg; oc befarlat gyffuc meg

1. This again is nonsense, interspersed with occasional place names.
2. (Dutch.) Sir, I am not speaking an unchristian language. But I think, all the same, that without my speaking a single word my tatters must reveal to you what I want. Be kind enough to give me something to restore me.
3. (Spanish.) Sir, I am tired from so much talking. So I beg your Reverence to remember the Gospel injunctions. Let them move you, sir, to act with a conscience; and if they are not enough to move your Reverence to pity, I beg you to resort to your natural pity, which I believe will move you, as it should; and with that I say no more.

nogueth; aff hvylket ieg kand styre myne groeendes magher lygeruff son man Cerbero en soppe forsetthr. Soa shal tuloeffue lenge och lycksaligth.' [1]

'I believe that the Goths spoke like that,' said Eusthenes, 'and if God wished us to speak through our backsides we should speak like that too.'

Then said the fellow:

'Adoni, scholom lecha: im ischar harob hal habdeca, bemeherah thithen il kikar lehem, chancatbub: Laah al Adonia chonenral.' [2]

To which Epistemon replied: 'This time I did understand him. That was the Hebrew language most beautifully pronounced.'

Then said the fellow:

'Despota tinyn panagathe, diati sy mi uc arto dotis? horas gar limo analiscomenon eme athlios. Ce en to metaxy eme uc eleis udamos, zetis de par emu ha u chre, ce homos philologi pantes homologusi tote logus te ker-hemata peritta hyparchin, opote pragma asto pasi delon esti. Entha gar anan-kei monon logi isin, hina pragmata (hon peri amphisbetumen) me phosphoros epiphenete.' [3]

'Why!' exclaimed Pantagruel's lackey Carpalim. 'It's Greek, I understood him. But how is that? Have you lived in Greece?'

And the fellow replied:

'Agonou dont oussys vou denaguez algarou, nou den farou zamist vou mariston ulbrou, fousquez vou brol tam bredaguezmoupreton den goul houst, daguez daguez nou croupys fost bardou noflist nou grou. Agou paston tol

1. (Danish.) Sir, Even supposing that, like some small child or a wild animal, I did not speak any language, my clothes and the thinness of my body would show you clearly what I need, that is to say food and drink. Take pity on me, therefore, and get them to give me something to tame my crying stomach, as men throw a sop to Cerberus. So you will live happily and long.

2. (Hebrew.) Sir, peace be with you. If you wish to do your servant a favour, give me a crumb of bread immediately. For it is written: He that hath pity on the poor lendeth to the Lord.

3. (Greek.) Excellent master, why do you not give me some bread? You see me miserably perishing from hunger, and yet you have no pity on me, and ask me improper questions. All lovers of learning are agreed, however, that speeches and words are superfluous when the facts are evident to all. Speeches are only necessary when the facts under discussion are not completely clear.

nalprissys hourtou los ecbatonous, prou dhouquys brol panygou den bascrou nou dous cagnous goulfren goul oust troppassou.[1]

'I seem to understand,' said Pantagruel. 'For either it is the language of my native Utopia, or else it has a very similar sound.'

But just as he was going to begin some observations the fellow said:

'Jam toties vos, per sacra, perque deos deasque omnis, obtestatus sum, ut, si qua vos pietas permovet, egestatem meam solaremini, nec hilum proficio clamans et ejulans. Sinite, quaeso, sinite, viri, impii, quo me fata vocant abire, nec ultra vanis vestris interpellationibus obtundatis, memores veteris illius adagii, quo venter famelicus auriculis carere dicitur.'[2]

'Really, my friend,' asked Pantagruel, 'don't you know how to speak French?'

'Yes, very well, my lord,' replied the fellow. 'Heaven be praised, it's my natural mother-tongue. For I was born and brought up as a child in Touraine, which is the garden of France.'

'Then,' said Pantagruel, 'tell us what your name is and where you come from. I've taken such a liking to it, I swear, that if I have my way you'll never stir from my side. Indeed you and I will make such another pair of friends as Aeneas and Achates.'

'My lord,' said the fellow, 'my true and proper baptismal name is Panurge, and just now I have come from Turkey, where I was taken prisoner during the ill-fated attack on Mytilene. I'll gladly tell you my story. For I have had adventures more marvellous than Ulysses. But since it is your wish to keep me with you – and I gladly accept your offer, and swear that I'll never leave you even if you go down to the devils in hell – we shall have leisure enough to speak of them at some more convenient time. For at this present moment I feel an urgent necessity to feed. Whetted teeth, empty belly, dry throat, clamorous appetite, all are bent on it. If you will only set me to work it'll be a treat for you to see me stuff myself. In Heaven's name, order me some food.'

1. An invented language.
2. (Latin.) I have implored you so often, by all that is sacred, by every god and goddess, that if you are susceptible to pity, you may relieve my extreme want, but all my crying and imploring does not benefit me a jot. Let me, I beg of you – let me go, most pitiless of men, where the fates call me, and bother me no more with your vain questions. Only remember the old adage that an empty stomach has no ears.

Then Pantagruel commanded that Panurge should be taken to his lodging, and that plenty of victuals should be put before him, which was done; and the fellow ate heartily that evening. Then he went to bed at roosting time, and slept till dinner time next day, when he had only three steps and a jump to make from bed to table.

CHAPTER 10: *How Pantagruel made a fair Judgement in a Controversy which was strangely difficult and obscure, and of the Admiration which this very fair Judgement inspired*

WITH his father's letter and admonitions well in mind, Pantagruel decided one day to test his learning. Accordingly at all the crossways of the city he put up propositions to the number of nine thousand, seven hundred and sixty-four, on all subjects, touching in them on the most debated points in every science. And first of all in the Rue du Feurre,[1] he contended against all the professors, students in arts and orators, and turned them all upside down. Then in the Sorbonne he argued with the theologians for the space of six weeks, from four in the morning till six at night, except for a two-hour interval to take his refreshment and repast. And here were present the majority of the lords of the court, the masters of requests, presidents, councillors, treasury-men, secretaries, advocates, and others, together with the sheriffs of that city, the physicians, and the canon-lawyers. And note that the greater part of these took the bit between their teeth. But notwithstanding their ergos and sophistries, he made fools of them all, and conclusively proved to them that they were just calves in petticoats.

At this all the world began to be loud with talk of his amazing knowledge, even to the old women, laundresses, go-betweens, roast-meat sellers, penknife-merchants, and others, who called out 'That's he!' when he passed through the streets. At this he was as delighted as was Demosthenes, the prince of Greek orators, when a bent old woman pointed her finger at him and said: 'That is the man!'

Now at this very time there was a suit pending in the court between two great lords, Lord Kissmyarse, the plaintiff, on the one hand, and Lord Suckfizzle, the defendant, on the other; and their difference was

1. Straw-litter Street.

on such rare and difficult points of law that the court of parliament understood it no better than double-Dutch. So by the king's command there were assembled four of the most learned and fattest from all the *parlements* of France – including the Great Council – and all the principal professors of the universities, not only of France, but also of England and Italy; men such as Jason, Philippus Decius, Petrus de Petronibus, and a rabble of other old Rabanists.[1] But, after remaining in session for the space of forty-six weeks, they had been unable to get their teeth into it, or to gain a clear enough understanding of the case to settle any aspect of it whatever; which so upset them that they most villainously beshat themselves for shame.

But one of them, named Du Douhet, the most learned, the most expert, and the shrewdest of them all, said to them one day when they were philogrobolized in the brain: 'Gentlemen, we have been here for a long time now without doing anything but waste time, and we can find neither shore nor bottom to this abysmal matter. The more we study it, the less we understand it, which is a great shame and a burden on our consciences; and it is my opinion that we shall emerge from all this in disgrace. For in our discussions we are doing nothing but wander. But here is an idea that occurs to me. You must have heard of that great personage, Master Pantagruel by name, who has proved himself learned above the capacities of the present age, in the public disputes which he has maintained against all comers. It is my opinion that we ought to call him in, and confer with him on this matter. For no one will ever get to the bottom of this if he does not.'

All the councillors and doctors readily agreed to this. So they sent for Pantagruel immediately, and begged him kindly to investigate the case, to sift it thoroughly, and to draw them up a report on it, in due legal form and at his own discretion; and they delivered over to him the brief-sacks, deeds, and documents, which were nearly enough to load four great jackasses.

But Pantagruel said to them: 'Gentlemen, are the two lords who are fighting this suit still alive?' To which came the answer, 'Yes'. 'Then what the devil's the use of all this accumulation of papers and transcripts you are giving me? Isn't it better to hear their dispute from

1. A name derived from the monk Rabanus, who composed a version of the Cabala in Latin verse.

their own lips than to read all this monkey-business here? It will be nothing but trickery, and devilish dodges out of Cepola's book, and twistings and perversions of the law. I am sure that you, and all those through whose hands the suit has passed, have worked in all you could *pro et contra* by now, and that even if their dispute was clear and easy to decide at first you have obscured it with stupid and illogical arguments and inept opinions from Accursius, Baldus, Bartolus, de Castro, de Imola, Hippolytus, Panormitanus, Bertachin, Alexander, Curtius, and all those other old mastiffs. They never understood the simplest law in the Pandects. They were just so many blockheads who did not even know the first thing you need for a legal understanding. They had no knowledge of Latin or Greek – you can be certain of that – but only of the Gothic and Barbarian tongues. Yet, in the first place, law derives from the Greeks, a fact for which you have the testimony of Ulpian, in the final book of his Origin of the Law, and all the laws are full of Greek words and sentences; also secondly, a digest has been made of them in Latin, the most elegant and ornate writing in all the Latin tongue – and I will not willingly make an exception for Sallust, or Varro, or Cicero, or Seneca, or Titus Livius, or Quintilian. How then could those old dodderers have understood the text of the laws, since they had never seen a good book in the Latin tongue, as is manifestly clear from their style, which is the style of a chimney-sweep, or a cook, or a scullion, but not that of a jurisconsult?

'What is more, the laws are based on essential philosophy both moral and natural. How can these fools understand them then, when they have studied less philosophy, by God, than my mule? As for humane learning and knowledge of antiquities and history, they know about as much of that as a toad has feathers. But the laws are full of it, and they cannot be understood without it, as one day I shall demonstrate at greater length and in writing.

'Therefore, if you wish me to take cognizance of this suit, first do me the favour of having all these papers burnt, and secondly, let the two gentlemen come before me in person. Then, when I have heard them, I will give you my opinion of the case without any sort of disguise or dissimulation.'

Some of the lawyers made objections, since, as you know, there are more fools than wise men in all societies, and the larger party always gains the upper hand, as Titus Livius says, when speaking of the

Carthaginians. But the aforementioned Du Douhet manfully opposed them, contending that Pantagruel was right, and that these records, questionnaires, replies, discrediting of witnesses, rehabilitations of witnesses, and other such hellish practices were nothing but perversions of the law and means of prolonging the suit. They would all go to the devil, he said, if they did not change their course, and proceed according to Evangelical and philosophical equity.

In short, all the papers were burnt, and the two gentlemen were summoned in person. Upon which Pantagruel inquired:

'Are you the two who have this great difference between you?'

'Yes, my lord,' they answered.

'Which of you is the plaintiff?'

'I am,' said the lord Kissmyarse.

'Now, my friend, tell me your whole complaint, point by point, and stick to the truth. For, so help me God, if you tell so much as one word of a lie I'll strike your head from off your shoulders, just to show you that when it is a question of justice and judgements, nothing must be said that is not the absolute truth. So take good care not to add or subtract a jot or a tittle in telling me your case. Proceed.'

CHAPTER 11: *How the Lords Kissmyarse and Suckfizzle pleaded before Pantagruel without Advocates*

THEN Kissmyarse began to the following effect:

'My lord, it is true that a good woman of my household was carrying eggs to sell in the market. ...'

'Cover your head, Kissmyarse,' said Pantagruel.

'Many thanks, my lord,' said the lord Kissmyarse. 'But to the matter in hand. There passed between the two tropics the sum of threepence towards the zenith and a halfpenny, for as much as the Rhiphean mountains had that year been most sterile in tricksters, owing to a sedition of Babblers stirred up between the Jabberers and the Accursians to aid the rebellion of the Swiss, who had collected to the number of the bum-bees to go to the distribution of presents on the first hole of the year, when they hand soup to the oxen, and the key of the charcoal to the maids so that they may give the oats to the dogs.

'All night they did nothing but keep their hands on the pot, and dispatch bulls on foot and bulls on horse-back to hold back the boats. For the tailors wanted to make out of the stolen shreds a blow-pipe to cover the Ocean sea, which was pregnant at the time with a potful of cabbage, according to the opinion of the hay-trussers. But the physicians said that from her urine they could detect no evident sign, in the pace of the bustard, of axes eaten with mustard, except that the gentlemen of the court were giving the pox an order in B flat to stop going about gathering silk-worms, because the clods had already made a good beginning at dancing a jig to a diapason, with one foot in the fire and their head in the middle, as good old Ragot used to say.

'Ah, gentlemen, God moderates all things to his pleasure, and against Fortune, the perverse creature, a carter broke his whip through his nose. It was on the return from La Bicoque, when Master Antitus of Cressplots was given his degree in all dullness, as the canon-lawyers say: *Beati Dunces, quoniam ipsi stumblaverunt*. But the reason why Lent is so high, by St Fiacre of Brie, is only because Pentecost never comes but to my cost. But, lawks a mercy, you will find a little rain lays a great wind, seeing that the sergeant put the bull's-eye at the butts so high for me that the clerk did not orbicularly lick his fingers, which are feathered like ganders; and we plainly see that everyone holds himself to blame, unless he has ocularly looked at himself in perspective towards the fireplace, at the spot where hangs the ensign of the wine with forty hoops, which are necessary for twenty stockings with a five-year respite. At least, he who would not fly the bird before the cheesecakes should say so, for the memory is often lost when a man puts on his stockings inside out. Well, God preserve you from harm, Thibault Mitaine!'

'Softly, my friend, softly,' said Pantagruel at this point. 'Don't be in a hurry, and don't speak in temper. I understand the case. Go on.'

'Now, my lord,' said Kissmyarse, 'this said good woman, saying her *Gaudes* and her *Audi noses*, could not protect herself from a treacherous backblow, ascending by the powers and privileges of the university, except by warming herself well with an angular pan, covering it with a seven of diamonds, and then landing a flying thrust as near as possible to the place where they sell the old rags that the Flemish painters use when they want to shoe the grasshoppers properly; and I very much wonder why the world does not lay, seeing that it is so good at hatching.'

Here the lord of Suckfizzle tried to interrupt and say something. But Pantagruel cut him short.

'By St Anthony's belly,' he exclaimed. 'Is it your place to speak without being told to? Here I am sweating from my efforts to understand the matter of your dispute, and you come and disturb me. Peace, in the devil's name, peace! You shall speak your belly-full when this man has finished.'

'Go on,' he said to Kissmyarse, 'and don't hurry yourself.'

'Seeing then,' said Kissmyarse, 'that the pragmatic sanction made thereof no mention, and that the Pope gave every man leave to fart at his ease if the blankets were not streaked, whatever poverty there was in the world, and provided no one crossed himself with the ribald crew, the rainbow, freshly sharpened at Milan to hatch larks, agreed that the good woman should tread down the heels of the sufferers from sciatica, on the complaint of the ballocky little fishes, who were then needed to understand the construction of old boots.

'However Jan Calf, her cousin Gervais, stirred up by a log from the pile, advised her on no account to take the risk of seconding the brim-ballatory lye, without first dipping the paper in alum, and then spinning the teetotum. For

Non de ponte vadit, qui cum sapientia cadit[1]

seeing that the masters of accounts did not agree in reckoning the number of German flutes, out of which they had made *The Spectacles of Princes*, lately printed at Antwerp.

And there, gentlemen, is what makes a bad return, and I believe the other party in this, *in sacer verbo dotis*.[2] For, wishing to conform to the king's pleasure, I had armed myself from head to foot in belly timber, to go and see how my grape-gatherers had slashed their tall bonnets, the better to play the lecher. For the time was a little dangerous for coming from the fair, and so several free-archers had been turned away from the parade, notwithstanding the fact that the chimneys were high enough, according to the proposition of the windgalls and malanders, friend Baudichon.

'So in this way it was a great year for copper-beetles throughout

1. He does not travel from the bridge who falls with care (a proverb jumbled up).
2. On the word of a priest. Here again the words are mixed up.

the whole land of Artois, which was no small profit for the faggot-carrying gentry, when they ate, without unsheathing, cocklicranes with unbuttoned stomachs. And it is my wish that everyone had as fine a voice; they would play much better tennis for it, and those little tricks they perform to etymologize the pattens would descend more easily into the Seine, to serve for ever at the Miller's Bridge, as once was decreed by the King of Canaria, and the order is still in the Record office here.

'Therefore, my lord, I request your lordship that a judgement should be made and proclaimed in this case, conforming to reason, with costs, damages, and interest.'

Then Pantagruel asked: 'My friend, do you wish to say anything more?'

'No, my lord,' replied Kissmyarse. 'For I've said the whole lesson from beginning to end, and I haven't varied from it in any way, upon my honour.'

'You then,' said Pantagruel, 'my lord of Suckfizzle, say what you wish and be brief, without, however, omitting anything that will serve your purpose.'

CHAPTER 12: *How the Lord of Suckfizzle pleaded before Pantagruel*

THEN my lord Suckfizzle began as follows:

'My lord and gentlemen, if the iniquity of men were as easily seen in categorical judgement as one detects flies in milk, the world – by the four oxen! – would not be so rat-eaten as it is, and there would be many ears on earth that have been too disgracefully nibbled away. For, although everything that the opposing party has said is of down, quite true, as to the letter and history of the *factum*, nevertheless, gentlemen, the subtleties, the trickeries, the little catches are hidden under the rose pot.

'Ought I to endure their coming at the very moment when I am eating my soup with the best, without an evil thought or an evil word, to rack and trouble my brain, playing the old dance at me and singing:

> He that with his soup will drink
> When he is dead shall see no wink?

And, Holy Mother, how many captains have we seen, on the open battlefield – when they were given hunks of the holy bread of the Fraternity the more honestly to nod their heads – play the lute, crack with their bums and give little platform leaps!

'But now the world is all out of joint from the tufts of Leicester fleeces: one becomes debauched, the other five, four, and two; and if the court does not impose some order, it will be as bad gleaning this year as ever it was, or else it will make goblets. If a poor old body goes to the stoves to light up his muzzle with cowdung or to buy winter boots, and the sergeants passing by, or perhaps the watchmen, receive the decoction of an enema or the fecal matter of a *garde-robe* on their noisy jaws, ought one on that account to clip testers and fricassee crowns – the wooden ones?

'Sometimes we think one thing, but God does the other; and when the sun is set all beasts are in the shadow. I do not want to be believed on this point if I do not prove it bravely by people of daylight. In the year thirty-six I had bought a docked German horse, tall and short, of fairly good wool and dyed in the grain, as the goldsmiths assured me; though the notary put in an *et cetera*. I am no scholar to catch the moon in my teeth; but in the butter-pot where they sealed the volcanic instruments, the rumour was that the salt beef made one find the wine at midnight without a candle, even if it were hidden at the bottom of a collier's sack, caparisoned and saddled with the head-piece and thigh-pieces necessary for thoroughly frying sauciness; I mean a sheep's head. And that is just what it says in the proverb, that it is good to see black cows in burnt wood, when one enjoys one's love. I had a consultation on this matter with the gentlemen clerks, and for resolution they concluded *in frisesomorum*[1] that there is nothing like mowing in summer in a cellar well supplied with paper and ink, pens, and a penknife from Lyons on the Rhone, balderdam balderdash. For the moment a coat of armour smells of garlic, the rust eats at his liver, and then one does nothing but fiddle at a wryneck, smelling of after-dinner sleep; and that is what makes the salt so dear.

'My lords, do not believe that at the time when the said good woman caught the spoon-bill with birdlime the better to make the younger son's portion for the record of the sergeant, and when the sheep's pudding took detours round the usurer's purses, there was

1. By the fifth figure of the syllogism.

nothing better to preserve us from the cannibals than to take a rope of onions tied up with three hundred turnips, and a little calf's chaldron of the best alloy the alchemists have, and to thoroughly befoul and calcine his slippers, muff-in, muff-out, with a good cudgel sauce and to hide in some little mole's earth, saving the bacon rashers. But if the dice will never give you anything else but bad throws, two threes at the great end, watch that ace and put the dame on the corner of the bed. Tousle her, toureloura la la, and drink to the dregs, *depiscando grenouillibus*,[1] with fine cothurnian gaiters. This will be for the little cooped goslings, which amuse themselves at the game of blow-it-out, while waiting for the heating of the metal and the beating of the wax at the babbling of healths.

'It is quite true that the four oxen in question had rather short memories. Nevertheless, since they knew the scale, they feared neither cormorant nor savoy duck; and the good people of my land had good hope by that, saying: "These children will become great in algorism; this shall be a precept in law for us." We cannot fail to take the wolf. Let us make our hedges above the windmill of which the opposite party has spoken. But the great devil was envious and put the Germans behind, who played the devil at tippling: "*Herr, trink, trink!*" with the double thrown on the point. For there is no probability in the saying, *in Paris on the Petit Pont, hens on straw*, even if they were as high-crested as fen-whoops, unless they truly sacrificed the little tufts to the red colour newly set on the letters uncial and cursive, it is all one to me, provided the head-band of the book does not breed worms. And suppose the case that at the coupling of the hounds the puppies had put on airs before the notary had made his return by cabalistic art, it does not follow – saving the better judgement of the court – that six acres of meadowland of generous measure will make three butts of fine ink without paying ready money, considering that at King Charles's funeral one got in open market a fleece for two or so, I swear on my oath, of wool.

'And I see ordinarily in all good bagpipes that when one goes luring birds, making three turns of a broom about the chimney-piece and putting one's name on record, all one does is to bend the bow backwards and blow one's rear horn, if it happens to be too hot, and then skedaddle.

1. In despite of the frogs.

> The letters seen, incontinent
> The cows were straightway backwards sent

'And a similar order was given on St Martin's Day in the year seventeen because of the bad government of Louzefougerouse, of which may it please the court to take notice.

'I do not say indeed that one may not, in equity and with just title, dispossess those who drink of the holy water, as one does with a weaver's shuttle, of which one makes suppositories for those who will not resign except on terms of fair pay and fair play.

'*Tunc*, gentlemen, *quid juris pro minoribus?*[1] For the common custom of the Salic Law is such that the first fire-brand who flays and dishorns the cow, and blows his nose in a full concert of instruments, without sol-faing the cobbler's stitches, should in time of nightmare sublimate the penury of his member with moss gathered when men catch cold at midnight Mass, to give the strappado to these white wines of Anjou, which trip a man, neck to neck, in the Breton manner.

'Concluding as above, with costs, damages, and interest.'

After the Lord of Suckfizzle had ended, Pantagruel said to the Lord of Kissmyarse: 'My friend, do you want to make any reply?' To which Kissmyarse replied: 'No, my lord, for I have told nothing but the truth; and, for God's sake, let us make an end of our differences, since it is at great expense that we are here.'

CHAPTER 13: *How Pantagruel delivered Judgement on the Differences between these two Gentlemen*

THEN Pantagruel arose, assembled all the presidents, counsellors, and doctors there present and said to them: 'Well now, Gentlemen, you have heard, *vivae vocis oraculo*,[2] the question that is in dispute. How does it look to you?'

And they replied: 'We have heard it indeed, but devil a bit of the case have we understood. We pray you therefore, unanimously, and beseech you in courtesy to be so kind as to give sentence as you see fit, and *ex nunc prout ex tunc*[3] we will accept it and ratify it with our full agreement.'

1. Then ... what law for minors?   2. By actual word of mouth.
3. Both prospectively and retrospectively.

'Very well, gentlemen,' said Pantagruel, 'since you wish it, I will do so. But I do not find the case as difficult as you do. Your paragraph *Cato*, the law *Frater*, the law *Gallus*, the law *Quinque pedum*, the law *Vinum*, the law *Si dominus*, the law *Mater*, the law *Mulier bona*, the law *Si quis*, the law *Pomponius*, the law *Fundi*, the law *Emptor*, the law *Praetor*, the law *Venditor*, and plenty of others are, in my opinion, much more difficult.'

After saying this, he walked once or twice up and down the hall, thinking very deeply, as could be imagined. He groaned like an ass that is girthed too tight, considering that he must do right to each one without bias or favouritism. Then he returned to his seat and began to pronounce the judgement that follows:

'Having seen, heard, and thoroughly considered the differences between my Lords of Kissmyarse and of Suckfizzle, the court declares that, in view of the quaking of the bat, declining bravely from the summer solstice to woo the trifles which have checkmated the pawn through the wicked vexations of the light-shunners that are in the meridian of Rome, of an ape on horseback bending a crossbow backwards – the plaintiff had due cause to caulk the vessel which the old woman was blowing up, with one foot shod and the other naked, reimbursing him low and stiff in his conscience with as many bladdernuts as there is hair on eighteen cows, and as many for the embroiderer.

'Likewise, he is declared innocent of the privileged case of the foul bums, which it was thought he would have incurred, since he could not shit merrily, by the decision of a pair of gloves perfumed with farts, at the walnut taper, as is usual in his country of Mirebalais, letting go the bowline with bronze bullets. Whereupon the stableboys, in protest, made pies of his interquilted pulse from the Loire, together with hawk-bells made of Hungarian point, which his brother-in-law carried as a record in an adjacent basket, embroidered gules with three worn-out chevrons, of woven-work, at the corner doghole, from which they shoot at the vermiform popinjay with the feather-flap.

'But inasmuch as he charges the defendant that he was a botcher, a cheese-eater, and a caulker of mummy-flesh, which has been found untrue in the sifting, as the said defendant has well argued, the court condemns him to pay three glassfuls of curds, cemented, prelorelitanted, and codpieced according to the custom of the country, to the said defendant, payable at mid-August in May.

'But the said defendant shall be bound to furnish hay and stubble for stopping the prickles of his throat, confused with gobbets of meat well examined in slices. And let them be friends once more, without costs and with good reason.'

After this sentence had been pronounced, the two parties departed, each satisfied with the decision, which was an almost incredible thing. For it had not happened since the great rains, nor will it happen again for thirteen jubilees, that two parties, contending in judgement on opposite sides, should be equally content with a definitive decision.

As for the counsellors and other doctors who were there present, they remained in a swoon of ecstasy for quite three hours, all entranced with admiration for Pantagruel's superhuman wisdom, which they clearly perceived in the decision of this most difficult and thorny case. And they would have remained in that state till now, had not a quantity of vinegar and rose-water been brought to restore them to their ordinary sense and understanding. For which God be praised in all ways.

CHAPTER 14: *Panurge's account of the way in which he escaped from the Turks*

PANTAGRUEL'S judgement was immediately known and acknowledged by all the world, and printed in quantity, and stored up in the palace archives, as a result of which people began to say: 'Solomon, who by guesswork restored the child to its mother, never performed such a masterpiece of wisdom as the good Pantagruel has done. We are fortunate to have him in our country.'

And indeed they wanted to make him Master of Requests and President of the Court. But he refused all their offers with gracious thanks.

'For there is,' he said, 'too much servility in such offices, and it is only with the greatest difficulty that those who hold them can be saved, seeing the corruption of men; and I think that if the vacant places among the angels are not filled by some other sort of people, we shall not have the Last Judgement for thirty-seven jubilees, and Cusanus's conjectures will be proved wrong. I give you notice of this in good time. But if you have any hogsheads of good wine I will accept the present willingly.'

This they heartily gave him, sending him of the best in the city, and he drank pretty well. But poor Panurge drank it up valiantly. For he was as thin as a red herring, and walked gingerly like a lean cat. In fact, someone rebuked him when he was out of breath from drinking a great bowlful of red wine, saying: 'Gently, my friend, gently. You're swilling it like a madman.'

'Go to Hell!' replied Panurge. 'You haven't got one of your namby-pamby Paris drinkers here, who never put down more than a chaffinch, and only take a beakful when they are tapped on the tail like sparrows. If I could mount up, comrade, as well as I can swallow down, I should be with Empedocles already, above the sphere of the Moon. But I don't know what the devil you are talking about. This wine is very good and most delicious, but the more I drink of it the thirstier I am. I believe that the shadow of my lord Pantagruel makes men thirsty, as the moon breeds catarrhs.'

At this all the company began to laugh. Upon which Pantagruel demanded: 'Panurge, what have you got to laugh about?'

'My lord,' he replied, 'I was telling them how very unfortunate these devilish Turks are not to drink a drop of wine. If there were no other evil in Mahomet's Koran, I still wouldn't put myself under its law, not for a moment.'

'Now tell me how you escaped from their hands,' said Pantagruel.

'By the Lord, sir,' said Panurge, 'I won't tell you a single untrue word. The rascally Turks had put me on a spit, all larded like a rabbit. For I was so thin that my flesh would have been very poor meat any other way, and at this point they were having me roasted alive. Now, as they were roasting me I commended myself to the Divine Mercy, keeping the good St Laurence in my mind and still trusting in God that he would deliver me from this torment: which came to pass in a very strange fashion. For as I was most fervently commending myself to Him, crying: "Lord God, help me! Lord God, save me! Lord God, release me of this torment which these treacherous dogs are inflicting on me for holding fast to Thy law!" the turnspit fell asleep, by the will of God – or else by the virtue of some good Mercury, who cunningly put Argus to sleep, with all his hundred eyes.

'When I realized that he had stopped turning me on the spit, I looked at him and saw that he was asleep. Then with my teeth I picked up a firebrand by the end that was not burnt, and threw it into my roaster's lap; and I threw another, as best I could, under a camp bed, which stood near the fireplace, and on which was the straw mattress of my friend, Master Turnspit.

'Immediately the fire caught the straw, and from the straw caught the bed, and from the bed the floor, which was made of pine-planks, laid in squares, like the bottoms of lamps. But the good thing was that the fire I had thrown into my rascally roaster's lap burnt his whole groin and began to catch his ballocks; and his sense of smell was not so bad that he did not perceive it sooner than daylight. Then, jumping up as frightened as a goat, he shouted out of the window at the top of his voice: "*Dal baroth, dal baroth!*", which is as much as to say "Fire, fire!", and came straight at me, to throw me right into the flames. Indeed, he had already cut the cords with which they had tied my hands and was cutting the bonds from my legs. But the master of the house had heard the cry of fire and smelt the smoke from the street, where he was walking with some other pashas and musaffiz, and he ran as hard as he could to bring help and save his baggage. The moment he arrived he drew out the spit on which I was trussed, and struck my roaster stone dead with a wound from which he died on the spot – for lack of treatment or for some other reason. For he ran him through with the spit, a little above the navel towards his right side, and pierced the third lobe of his liver. The blow, striking upwards, penetrated his diaphragm; and, transfixing his pericardium, the spit came out through the upper part of his shoulders, between the vertebrae and the left shoulder-blade.

'It is true that as he drew the spit out of my body I fell down near the andirons, and the fall hurt me a little. But it was not much, for the bacon-slices took the shock. Then, when my pasha saw that the situation was desperate, that there was no chance of saving his house from burning, and that all his goods were lost, he offered his soul to all the devils, naming Grilgoth, Astaroth, Rappallus, and Gribouillis, each nine times.

'At the sight of this I felt more than fivepennyworth of fear, thinking in my terror: The devils will come this very moment to carry off this fool! And won't they be just the people to carry me off too? I'm half roasted already. My bacon-slices will be my undoing. For these devils here are fond of bacon, for which you have the authority of the philosopher Iamblichus and of Murmault in his apology, *De Bossutis et contrefactis pro Magistros nostros*.[1] But I made the sign of the Cross, crying: *Agyos athanatos, ho Theos!*[2] and not one of them came.

'When he discovered this, my rascally pasha tried to kill himself with my spit, and to drive it through his heart. In fact he put it against his chest. But it would not go in, for it was not pointed enough. He forced it as hard as he could, but to no effect.

'Then I went up to him and said: "Messer Bugrino, you are wasting your time here. You will never kill yourself like that. But very likely you will do yourself some hurt, from which you will suffer all your life at the hands of the barber-surgeons. If you like, however, I will kill you here outright in such a way that you will feel nothing. You may trust me, for I have killed many others who were very satisfied with my handiwork."

' "Ah, my friend," he said, "I beg you to do so, and for the deed I give you my purse. Wait, here it is. There are six hundred seraphs in it, and some perfect diamonds and rubies." '

'And where are they?' asked Epistemon.

'By St John,' said Panurge. 'They are far enough off by now if they are still moving: "But where are the snows of yesteryear?" which was the great preoccupation of the Parisian poet Villon.'

'Conclude,' said Pantagruel, 'I beg of you, and let us know how you dressed your pasha.'

'By my faith as an honest man,' said Panurge, 'I won't tell you so much as a word of a lie. I tied him up with a wretched strip of linen that I found there half burnt, and secured his hands and feet roughly with my cords, so well that he could not have struggled. Then I passed my spit through his throat and slung him up, hanging the spit on to two great hooks which were used to support halberds. Then, kindling a fair fire under him, I warmed Milord up, as they dry red herrings over the fireplace. After which, taking his purse and a little javelin which hung on the hooks, I went off at a good pace. And God knows I smelt like a shoulder of mutton!

'When I came down into the street I found that everyone had run out to the fire with quantities of water, to put it out. And when they

1. About hunchbacks and impostors, for our Masters.
2. God is holy and immortal (from the Liturgy of the Passion).

saw me like this, half roasted, they naturally took pity on me and threw all their water over me, which was the jolliest refreshment, and did me a great deal of good. Then they gave me a little food. But I hardly ate, for they offered me nothing but water to drink, as is their custom.

'They did me no other harm, except a villainous little Turk, with a hump on his chest, who was stealthily eating my bacon, when I gave him such a sound rap on the knuckles with my whole javelin that he did not come back for more; and a young Corinthian harlot, who had brought me a pot of round mirobolan plums, conserved in their manner, who looked at my poor fly-bitten devil, which was just as it had been taken from the fire, for it then hung down no further than my knees. But note that this roasting cured me completely of a sciatica to which I had been subject for more than seven years, on the side on which my roaster had let me burn when he fell asleep.

'Now while they were amusing themselves with me the fire succeeded – never mind how – in catching more than two thousand houses. In the end one of them noticed it and cried out: "By the belly of Mahomet, the whole town's burning, while we stay here amusing ourselves." So each one went off to his own place.

'For my part, I made my way towards the gate; and when I was on a little hillock near it I turned back, like Lot's wife, and saw the whole town burning. At which I was so glad that I almost shat myself for joy. But God soundly punished me for it.'

'How?' asked Pantagruel.

'As I was gazing in great delight on this beautiful fire,' answered Panurge, 'joking to myself and saying: Ah, poor fleas, ah, poor mice, you'll have a bad winter, the fire's in your bedstraw! there came out more than six – yes, more than thirteen hundred and eleven – dogs, great and small, rushing all together from the town to escape the fire. The moment they appeared, they ran right at me, catching the odour of my wretched, half-roasted flesh, and they would have eaten me on the spot if my good angel had not given me a fine inspiration, and taught me a very opportune remedy against toothache.'

'And for what reason,' asked Pantagruel, 'were you afraid of toothache? Weren't you cured of your sciatic chill?'

'By the palms on Sunday!' exclaimed Panurge. 'Can teeth give you any greater pain than when the dogs have you by the legs? But suddenly I remembered my bacon-slices and threw them into the midst of the animals. Then they started fighting with each other with all their teeth as to which should get the bacon. So they left me, and I left them too, worrying one another. In that way I escaped, lively and gay – and long live roasting!'

CHAPTER 15: *How Panurge demonstrated a very new way of building the Walls of Paris*

ONE day, to refresh himself from his studies, Pantagruel was walking towards the Saint-Marceau suburb, wishing to visit the Gobelin pleasure-house; and with him was Panurge, carrying as always a flask under his gown, together with a piece of ham. For without this he never went out; he said that it was his bodyguard. He carried no other sword, and when Pantagruel wanted to give him one, he answered that it would heat his spleen.

'Yes,' said Epistemon. 'But if you were attacked, how would you defend yourself?'

'With stout blows from my leggings,' he replied, 'supposing that thrusts were forbidden.'

On their return Panurge considered the walls of Paris, and said to Pantagruel in derision: 'Oh, how strong they are! They're just the thing for keeping goslings in a coop. By my beard, they are pretty poor defences for a city like this. Why a cow could knock down more than twelve foot of them with a single fart.'

'Oh, my friend,' said Pantagruel, 'do you know Agesilaus's reply, when he was asked why the great city of Lacedaemon was not walled? Well, he pointed to the inhabitants and citizens of the town, who were such experts in military discipline, so strong and so well armed. "These," he said, "are the city walls," signifying thereby that there are no walls save of bone, and that towns and cities could have no surer and stronger fortification than the virtue of their citizens and inhabitants. Similarly, this city is so strong from the multitude of warlike people in it that they do not trouble to make any other walls. Besides, if any one wanted to wall it round like Strasbourg, Orléans, or Ferrara, it would be impossible; the cost and charges would be excessive.'

'Yes,' said Panurge; 'still it is good to have an appearance of stone when one is invaded by the enemy, if it is only so that one can ask: "Who is there, down below?" As for the enormous cost that you say would be incurred if they wanted to wall it, if the gentlemen of the city will give me a good mug of wine, I will teach them a very new method by which they will be able to build cheaply.'

'How?' asked Pantagruel.

'Don't say a word about it,' said Panurge, 'and I'll tell you.

'I notice that in this country the thing-o'-my-bobs of the ladies are cheaper than the stone. The walls ought to be built of them, arranged in good architectural symmetry with the biggest in front; and then sloping downwards, like the back of an ass. The middle-sized ones should be arranged next, and the little ones last of all. This done, there must be a fine little interlacing of them, in diamond points, as in the great tower of Bourges, with an equal number of stiff what-d'you-call-'ems, such as dwell in the claustral codpieces. What devil would be able to overthrow walls like that? There is no metal like that for resisting blows. So much so that if cannon-balls came to rub themselves against them you would immediately see a distillation of that blessed fruit of the great pox, as small as rain, but devilish dry. What is more the lightning would never strike them. And why? They are all blessed or consecrated. I can only see one drawback.'

'Ho, ho, ha, ha, ha!' exclaimed Pantagruel, 'and what is that?'

'The flies are marvellously fond of them. They would quickly gather round and leave their excretions there, and then all the work would be spoilt. But there's a way of remedying that. They must be swatted with fine fox-tails, or good large ass-pizzles from Provence. And on that subject I should like to tell you, as we go to supper, a fine example set down by Friar Lubin, in his book *De compotationibus mendicantium*.[1]

'In the time when animals spoke – which is not more than three days ago – a poor lion, walking in the forest of Bièvre and reciting his private devotions, passed beneath a tree which a poor charcoal-burner had climbed to cut wood. Now when the man saw the lion, he flung his hatchet at him and severely wounded him in one leg. The lion ran limping about all over the forest to find help, until he met a carpenter, who kindly looked at his wound, cleaned it as best he could, and

1. On the convivial drinking of beggars.

dressed it with moss, telling him that he must wipe the place well and not let the flies make their muck in it while he went to find some yarrow.

'After receiving this attention, the lion went for a stroll in the forest, where at that moment the most ancient of hags was gathering woods into bundles. Now when she saw the lion approaching she tumbled over backwards in such a way that the wind blew up her dress, petticoat, and smock above her shoulders. At this sight the lion ran up out of pity to see if she had done herself any harm; and when he looked at her what-d'ye-call-it, he said: "Oh, my poor woman, who gave you that wound?"

'And as he spoke he saw a fox, whom he called to him, saying: "Come here, brother fox! Here, here, you are needed."

'And when the fox came up he explained: "Look, brother, look, my friend! Someone has given this old woman a dreadful wound here, between her legs. There's a manifest cleavage in the flesh. Look how big the wound is; from the backside to the navel, it measures four, no fully five and a half breadths of the hand. It must have been a hatchet blow, and I suspect that it is an old wound. You must keep the flies off it, so wipe it well, I beg of you, inside and out. You have a good long tail; wipe it, my friend, wipe it, I implore you, and in the meantime I'll go and find some moss to put in it. For so we ought to succour and help one another. Wipe it hard, like this, my friend. Wipe it well. For this wound ought to be wiped often. Otherwise the creature will be uncomfortable. Now wipe it well, my little fellow, wipe away! God has provided you with a tail, a long one and correspondingly thick. Wipe hard, and don't get tired. A good wiper who wipes continuously, and keeps wiping with his wiper will never be visited by flies. Wipe away, my dear fellow. Wipe, my little darling, I won't be away a moment."

'Then he went to find a supply of moss, and when he was a little way off he shouted out to the fox: "Go on wiping properly, and don't be sparing of your wiping, my dear fellow. I'll have you made paid wiper to Don Pedro of Castile. Just wipe and wipe, and nothing more."

'The poor fox wiped very well, this way and that, up and down. But the naughty old woman pooped and blew, and stank like a hundred devils. The poor fox was very uncomfortable, for he did not know which way to turn to avoid the perfume of the creature's farts; and as he turned he saw that in her backside there was yet another hole, not as big as the one he was wiping, from which this stinking and infected breeze was escaping.

'Finally the lion returned, bringing with him more than eighteen packfuls of moss, which he began to stuff into the wound with a stick that he had brought; and he had already got sixteen and a half packs in when he exclaimed in amazement: "This wound's devilish deep. It would take two cartloads and more."

'At which the fox remarked: "Oh, brother lion, my dear friend, don't put all the moss in there, I beg of you. Keep a little bit back. For there is still another little hole underneath that stinks like five hundred devils. I'm quite poisoned with the smell, it's so filthy."

'Now that is the way in which these walls should be kept free of flies, and some people must be paid wages for wiping them.'

Then Pantagruel asked: 'How do you know that the private parts of women are so cheap? There are many modest and chaste women, indeed there are many virgins in the city.'

'*Et ubi prenus?*'[1] asked Panurge. 'I will tell you my opinion on this point, and that on certain and assured knowledge. I won't make a boast of having stuffed four hundred and seventeen of them since I have been in this town – and that's only nine days. But this morning I met a good fellow carrying two little girls, two or three years old at the most, in a saddle-bag like Aesop's, one before and one behind. He begged an alms of me, but I answered him that I had many more ballocks than pence. After that I asked him: "My good man, are those two girls virgins?" "Brother," he answered, "I've been carrying them like this for two years. As for the one in front, I never take my eyes off her, and in my opinion she is a virgin; but I wouldn't put my finger in the flames for it, all the same. As for the one who rides behind, I really can't say."

'Truly,' said Pantagruel, 'you're a jolly companion. I should like to put you in my livery.'

And he had him smartly dressed, after the prevailing fashion, except that Panurge insisted on having the codpiece of his breeches cut three foot long and square, not round. This was done, and it made him a

1. Where are we to find them? (Dog-Latin.)

most noteworthy sight. He often said, indeed, that the world had not yet discovered what profit and use there is in wearing great codpieces. But time, he continued, would teach them one day, since all things are the inventions of time.

'God preserve the man,' he used to say, 'whose long codpiece has saved his life! God preserve the man whose long codpiece has been worth a hundred and sixty thousand and nine crowns to him in a single day! God preserve the man who by his long codpiece has saved a whole city from dying of hunger! And, by God, I'll make a book on the Utility of Long Codpieces when I have more leisure.'

In fact he composed a fine great book with illustrations; but it is not printed yet, so far as I know.

CHAPTER 16: *Panurge's Character and Qualities*

PANURGE was of middling stature, neither too big nor too small, and his nose was somewhat aquiline, the shape of a razor handle. At that time he was thirty-five or thereabouts, and about as fit for gilding as a lead dagger. He was a very proper-looking fellow, but for the fact that he was a bit of a lecher and naturally subject to a malady that was called at that time 'the lack of money, pain incomparable'. However, he had sixty-three ways of finding it at a pinch, the commonest and most honest of which was by means of cunningly perpetrated larceny. He was a mischievous rogue, a cheat, a boozer, a roysterer, and a vagabond if ever there was one in Paris, but otherwise the best fellow in the world; and he was always perpetrating some trick against the sergeants and the watch.

At one time he collected three or four good yokels, made them drink like Templars all the evening, and afterwards took them under the walls of Sainte-Geneviève, or to a spot near the College of Navarre just when the watch was coming up that way – and to discover the moment, he rested his sword on the pavement and put his ear to it. For when he heard his sword quiver it was an infallible sign that the watch was at hand. At that moment, then, he and his companions took a dung-cart and pushed it off, so that it rushed with all its force down the hill and knocked all the watch over like so many pigs. Then he and his yokels ran away in the other direction. For in less than two days he knew all the streets, lanes, and alleys in Paris as well as he knew his grace.

At another time he laid a train of gunpowder at a good place which the said watch was bound to pass. Then, at the hour when they were due, he set fire to it, and was highly delighted by the graceful way in which they took to their heels when they thought that St. Anthony's fire had got them by the legs.

As for the poor masters of art and the theologians, he persecuted them most of all. When he saw any of them in the street, he never failed to play them some trick. Sometimes he would put dung in their graduate hoods, sometimes he would tie little fox-tails or hare's-ears behind them, and at other times he would do them some other mischief.

One day, when all the theologians were summoned to meet in the Rue du Feurre, he made a mud pie composed of garlic, galbanum, asafoetida, and castoreum in quantity and of turds that were still warm. This he steeped in the runnings from sores. Then, very early in the morning, he smeared and anointed the pavement, so that the devil himself could not have endured it. Three or four of them brought up the complete contents of their stomachs, there before everyone, as if they had flayed the fox; ten or twelve of them died of the plague, fourteen caught leprosy; eighteen got the gout, and more than twenty-seven contracted pox; but he did not care a fig.

He generally carried a whip under his gown, with which he mercilessly beat any page he found carrying wine to his master, just to hurry him along. In his cloak he had more than twenty-six pockets, small and great, which were always full. In one was a little lead dice and a small knife as sharp as a furrier's needle, with which he cut purses; in another was some grape-juice, which he threw into the eyes of anyone whom he met; in another were burrs flighted with little goose or capon's feathers, which he threw at the good men's gowns and bonnets; and often he made them fine horns, which they wore all about the city, sometimes indeed for the whole of their lives. For the women also he sometimes made horns in the shape of a male member, and planted them on the backs of their hoods.

In another he carried a quantity of small cones filled with fleas and lice, which he borrowed from the beggars of St Innocent's. These he tossed with little reeds or writing quills on to the collars of the sweetest young ladies he could find, and especially in church: for he never sat up in the choir, but always stayed in the nave among the women, at mass and at vespers as well as at the sermon..

In another pocket he kept a large supply of hooks and buckles, with which he would often fasten men and women together, in places where they were crowded close. And he especially chose those who were wearing thin taffeta gowns, so that when they tried to get apart they tore all their clothes.

In another pocket he kept a tinder-box, with tinder, matches, and flint, and all the other tackle necessary for his purpose; and in yet another two or three burning glasses, with which he sometimes made men and women quite mad, and put them out of countenance in church. For he said that there was only a very little difference between a woman *folle à la messe* and *molle à la fesse*.[1]

In another pocket he had a collection of needles and thread, with which he performed a thousand little devilments. On one occasion, at the entrance from the Palace into the Great Hall, he met a grey friar who was about to say mass to the councillors, and helped him to dress and robe himself. But, in apparelling him, he sewed his alb on to his cloak and shirt, and then, when the gentlemen of the court took their seats to hear the mass, he retired. But when it came to the *Ite, missa est* and the poor friar tried to take off his alb, he took his gown and his shirt off with it, since they were thoroughly well sewn together, and so stripped himself to the shoulders, displaying his what-you-may-call-it to all the world; and certainly it was no small one. And the friar went on tugging, and went on uncovering himself further until one of the gentlemen of the court said: 'Tell me, is it this holy father's wish to make us the offering of his arse to kiss? May it be kissed by Saint Anthony's fire!' And from that time it was ordained that the poor fathers should never disrobe in public, but always in their vestry, especially when women were at Mass, for fear they might arouse in them the sin of desire.

People asked why it is that friars have such long tools, and the said Panurge solved the problem very neatly by saying: 'What makes asses' ears so long is because their dams do not put bonnets on their heads, as De Alliaco says in his *Suppositions*. By parallel reasoning, what makes the tools of the poor blessed fathers so long is that they

1. Mad at mass and pliant in the buttock.

do not wear bottomed breeches, and their poor member stretches freely, without let or hindrance, and so it goes waggling down to their knees, like a woman's string of beads. But the reason why they have it correspondingly stout is because as it waggles the humours of the body descend into the said member. For according to the lawmen, agitation and continual motion are the cause of attraction.'

Item, he had another pocket full of itching powder, which he threw down the backs of those women whom he saw carrying their heads highest, and so made some of them strip before all the world; and others dance like a cock on hot cinders, or a drumstick on a drum; and still others run about the streets, and he after them. And he would offer to hold his cloak at the back of those who stripped, like a courteous and good-mannered gentleman.

Item, in another pocket he had a little flask full of old oil, and when he saw a man or woman in any sort of finery, he would smear oil on them and spoil all the nicest parts of their clothes. He would pretend to stroke them, saying as he did so: 'That's fine cloth. That's a good satin. That's a nice taffeta, madam. God grant you the dearest desire of your noble heart. You have a new robe, a new friend. May God permit you to live long in the enjoyment of it!' As he said this he would put his hand on the collar, and from his touch the nasty stain would remain for ever,

> In such deep characters of blame
> On soul, on body, and on fame,
> That the devil could not remove the same,

and finally he would say: 'Mind that you don't fall, Madam. For there's a filthy great hole in front of you.'

Another pocket he had full of euphorbium very finely powdered, and in it he put a fine, beautifully worked handkerchief, which he had stolen from a pretty laundress of the Palace, while picking a louse from her breast, which he had put there himself, of course. Then, when he was in the company of some fine ladies, he would introduce the subject of linen and put his hand into their bosoms, asking: 'Now is this Flemish work or from Hainault?' Next he would pull out his handkerchief and say: 'Look, just look at this. Here's fine work for you. It's from Spunkignan or Spunkarabia.' And he would shake it vigorously under their noses, causing them to sneeze for four hours on end. All the time he would fart like a horse, and they would say with a laugh!

'How you do fart, Panurge.' 'Oh dear, no, Madam,' he would reply, 'I'm merely tuning myself to the counterpoint of the music you are making with your nose.'

In another pocket he had a pick-lock, a lever, a hook, and some other instruments, with which there was no door or strong-box that he could not prise open. He had another full of little cups, with which he played very cunningly. For he was born with fingers as pliant as Minerva's or Arachne's, and had once been a seller of quack remedies. Indeed, when he changed a tester or any other piece of money, the changer would have to have been sharper than Master Fly to prevent Panurge from conjuring away five or six small coins each time, visibly, openly, and manifestly, without making any wound or lesion of which the changer would have felt so much as the breath.

CHAPTER 17: *How Panurge gained the Pardons and married the old Women, and of the Lawsuits he had in Paris*

ONE day I found Panurge somewhat woe-begone and taciturn, and I very much suspected that he had not a penny. I said to him therefore: 'Panurge, as I can read from your countenance, you are sick, and I understand your disease. You have a flux of the purse. But don't worry, I have still "six sous and a half that father and mother never saw", and they shan't fail you in your need, any more than the pox.'

'A fart for your money,' he replied. 'I shall have only too much one day. For I have a philosopher's stone that draws me money out of purses as the magnet attracts iron. But will you come and buy pardons?' he asked.

'Faith,' I replied, 'I am no great man for pardons in this world of ours, and I don't know whether I shall be in the next. But let's go in, in God's name. There's only a penny in it, more or less.'

'Well, lend me the penny, then, at interest,' said he.

'Not a bit of it,' I replied. 'But I'll give it to you with all my heart.'

'*Grates vobis dominos*,'[1] said he.

So we went, beginning at St Gervais, and I bought pardons at the first box only, for in such matters I am easily satisfied. Then I made my small petitions and said the St Bridget prayers. But he bought at

1. The formula of a gabbled grace.

all the boxes, and each time he gave money to the collector. From there we went on to Notre-Dame, to St Jean, to St Anthoine, and to the other churches where there was a fund of pardons. For my part I bought no more. But, as for him, he kissed the relics at all the boxes, and gave at each one. In fact when we got back he took me to drink at the Castle Inn and showed me ten or twelve of his little pockets full of money.

Upon this I blessed myself, making the sign of the Cross, and asked him: 'Where have you got so much money from, and in so short a time?' To which he answered that he had taken it out of the offertory plates. 'For when I gave them the first penny,' he said, 'I put it in so deftly that it looked like a large silver coin. So, with one hand I took out a dozen pence – or perhaps a dozen threepenny bits – or sixpences, they must have been – and, three or four dozen of the same with the other; and so on in all the churches we visited.'

'Come now,' said I. 'You're damning yourself like the serpent. You've been thieving and committing sacrilege.'

'Oh yes,' said he, 'it looks like that to you. But it doesn't look like that to me. For really the pardoners give it to me when they offer me the relics to kiss and pronounce the words: "Centuplum accipies",[1] which is as much as to say that that for one penny I am to take a hundred. For accipies is said after the manner of the Hebrews, who use the future tense instead of the imperative, as you have it in the Law, where it reads Diliges Dominum,[2] for dilige.[3] So when the bearer of pardons said to me: "Centuplum accipies" he meant centuplum accipe.[4] For so Rabbi Kimy and Rabbi Ben Ezra explain it, and all the Massoretes and ibi Bartolus as well. What is more, Pope Sixtus gave me fifteen hundred francs of income from his domain and ecclesiastical treasure, for having cured him of a cankerous sore, which so tortured him he was afraid he would be lame for the whole of his life. So, since he is not lame, I take my payment into my own hands, out of the said ecclesiastical treasure. Ho, my friend,' said he, 'if you knew how I feathered my nest from the Crusade you would be astounded indeed. It was worth more than six thousand florins to me.'

'And where the devil have they gone?' I asked. 'For you haven't half of one left.'

1. You will receive a hundredfold. 2. You will love the Lord.
3. Love. 4. Receive a hundredfold.

'Gone where they came from,' he replied. 'They did no more than change owners. But I used at least three thousand of them in making marriages, not of young girls, for they find only too many husbands, but of sempiternal old bodies without a tooth in their heads. For I thought: these good creatures here have employed their time very well in their youth, playing the close-buttock game with stern hoisted for all comers, until no one has wanted them any more. But, by God, I'll have them shake the sheets once again before they die. For this reason I gave one a hundred florins, another a hundred and twenty, another three hundred, according to their degree of infamy, repul-siveness, and hideousness. For the more horrible and detestable they were, the more they would have to give; otherwise the devil himself would not have rogered them.

'Immediately after that I went to some great fat faggot-bearer, and made the match myself. But before I showed him the old woman, I showed him the money and said: 'Here's something for you, my friend, if you'll do a bout of lechery.' At this the poor devil would frisk up like an old mule. So I had a good banquet and the best of drink prepared for them, with plenty of spices to put the old women in rut and on heat. To cut the story short, they sweated at it, like all good souls. Only in the case of the most horribly ugly and ill-favoured women I had a sack put over their faces. In addition I have lost a great deal in lawsuits.'

'And what lawsuits can you have had?' I asked. 'You have neither land nor houses.'

'My friend,' he said. 'By the instigation of the devil from hell, the ladies of this town discovered a kind of neckerchief or gorget worn high on the neck, which concealed their breasts so completely that a man could no longer put his hand under them. For they made the thing open behind, and it was entirely closed in front, much to the displeasure of their poor, doleful, and pensive lovers. One fine Tues-day I presented a petition to the Court, opening a suit against these fine gentlewomen and setting forth the great injury caused to me thereby, at the same time protesting that, by the same argument, I would have the codpiece of my trousers sewn on behind, unless the Court made an order in my favour. To sum things up, the ladies formed a syndicate, showed their grounds of defence, and engaged lawyers to defend their case. But I pursued the matter so vigorously that it was decreed by sentence of the Court that these high gorgets should be worn no longer, unless slightly open at the front. But it cost me a great deal.

'I had another suit, a filthy, dirty one, against Sam Cesspool and his assistants, that they should no longer read the *Puncheon-pipe* and the *Fourth Book of Smells* at night, but in full light of day, and that in the Schools of Peurre, before all the rest of the sophists. But in this suit I was condemned to pay costs, on account of some formality in the return of the sergeant's writ.

'On another occasion I laid a complaint before the court against the mules of the presidents, counsellors, and others, to the effect that when they were left to champ their bits in the lower court of the Palace, the counsellors ought to make them handsome bibs, so that they should not spoil the pavement with their spittle, and that the Palace pages should consequently be able to play on it with fair dice, or at S'welp-me-God, in comfort, without staining the knees of their breeches. Here I got a favourable judgement; but it cost me a pretty penny. Now at this point you must reckon up how much I spend on the little banquets I give to the Palace pages every day or two.'

'And for what purpose?' I asked.

'My friend,' he said, 'you have no fun at all in this world. But I have more than the King, and if you will join up with me, we'll play the devil together.'

'No, no,' I answered, 'by St Adauras, you'll be hanged one of these days.'

'And you,' he said, 'one of these days you'll be buried. And which is the more honourable, the earth or the air? Ho, you dull beast, wasn't Jesus Christ hung up in the air? But, by the way, while these pages are banqueting I look after the mules; and I'll cut the stirrup girths of one on the mounting side, so that it only hangs by a thread. Then when some bloated counsellor or other has taken his swing to get up, he'll fall as flat as a hog before everybody, and provide more than a hundred francs' worth of laughter. But I have a bigger laugh still, because when they get back home they have Master Page beaten like green rye. So I don't complain of what it costs me to banquet them.'

To sum it up, he had, as I have already said, sixty-three ways of recovering money. But he had two hundred and fourteen ways of spending it, excluding the replenishments required just under his nose.

CHAPTER 18: *How a great English Scholar attempted to argue against Pantagruel and was worsted by Panurge*

IN these same days, a learned man named Thaumaste, hearing the fame and renown of Pantagruel's incomparable learning, came from the land of England with the sole intention of seeing this same Pantagruel, and knowing him, and testing whether his knowledge was as great as it was reported. So, when he arrived in Paris, he went to the house of the said Pantagruel, who was lodging in the Hôtel Saint Denis, and was at the time walking in the garden with Panurge, philosophizing after the manner of the Peripatetics. At his first entrance Thaumaste quite started with fear, when he saw how tall and stout Pantagruel was. Then he saluted him courteously, as is the fashion, and said:

'How true is the saying of Plato, Prince of Philosophers, that if the image of science and learning were corporal and visible to the eyes of men, it would arouse admiration from the whole world. For the mere report of it, scattered on the air, should it be received by the studious and by its lovers, who are called Philosophers, will not suffer them to sleep or rest at their ease, but spurs and inflames them to run to the place and see the person in whom this science is said to have set up her temple and to reveal her oracles.

'Of this we had manifest proof in the case of the Queen of Sheba, who came from the most distant East, from the Persian Sea, to behold the order of the wise Solomon's house and to hear his wisdom; in the case of Anacharsis, who from Scythia went to Athens to see Solon; in the case of Pythagoras, who visited the soothsayers of Memphis; in the case of Plato, who sought out the Egyptian magi and Archytas of Tarentum; in the case of Apollonius of Tyana, who went as far as Mount Caucasus, passing by the Scythians, the Massagetae, and the Indians, who navigated the great river Physon as far as the Brahman country, to see Hiarchus, and who travelled in Babylonia, Chaldea, Media, Assyria, Parthia, Syria, Phoenicia, Arabia, Palestine, and Alexandria as far as Ethiopia, to see the Gymnosophists. We have a similar example in Titus Livius, to see and hear whom several studious persons came to Rome from the utmost borders of France and Spain.

'I dare not count myself in the number and rank of such perfect men; but I certainly wish to be accounted a scholar, and a lover not only of learning but of learned men. In fact, hearing the report of your most inestimable scholarship, I have left country, family, and home, and have transported myself here, counting as nothing the length of the journey, the weariness of the sea, and the strangeness of the land, only to see you and to confer with you on some passages of philosophy, of geomancy, and of the Cabala, on which I am in doubt and cannot satisfy my mind. If you can explain these to me I will be your slave from now on, I and all my posterity. For I have no other gift which I should esteem sufficient to reward you. These questions I will reduce to writing, and communicate to-morrow to all the learned men of the city, so that we may publicly argue them in their presence. But this is the manner in which I propose that we shall dispute.

'I do not want to argue *pro* and *contra*, as do the stupid sophists of this city and elsewhere. Likewise, I do not wish to dispute in the academic manner by declamation, nor yet by numbers, as Pythagoras did, and as Pico Mirandola wished to do at Rome. I desire to dispute by signs only, without speech. For these matters are so difficult that human words would not be adequate to expound them to my satisfaction. May it please your Magnificence, therefore, to be present there – that is to say in the great Hall of Navarre – at seven o'clock in the morning.'

When he had concluded this speech Pantagruel courteously replied: 'Sir, of the graces which God has given me there is none that I would refuse to communicate to anyone, to the extent of my powers. For all good comes from Him, and it is His pleasure that it should be increased when we find ourselves among men worthy and suitable to receive this heavenly manna of honest learning. And since I clearly see that at the present time you hold first rank among that number, I proclaim to you that at all hours you will find me ready to comply with each one of your requests, according to my small ability, although I should really learn from you rather than you from me. But, as you have proposed, we will discuss your problems together, and will seek a resolution for them, even to the bottom of that inexhaustible well in which, as, Heraclitus said, Truth lies hidden. And I highly commend the manner of arguing that you have proposed, that is to say by signs and without speaking. For in that way you and I will understand one another, and will not be disturbed by that applause in which the doltish sophists indulge during a dispute, when one party has the better of the argument. So to-morrow I shall not fail to appear at the place and hour which you have appointed. But I beg of you that there shall be neither strife nor wrangling between us, and that we shall seek neither honour nor the applause of men, but the truth only.'

To which Thaumaste replied: 'Sir, may God maintain you in his grace. I thank you that your high magnificence has so greatly condescended to my poor baseness. So, God keep you till to-morrow.'

'God keep you,' replied Pantagruel.

Gentlemen, you who read these present writings, consider that never were men more elevated and transported than those two were all through that night, Thaumaste no less than Pantagruel. For this same Thaumaste said to the keeper of the Hostel of Cluny, in which he was lodged, that never in all his life had he found himself so thirsty as he then did.

'I feel,' he said, 'as if Pantagruel held me by the throat. Order us some drink, I beg of you, and see also that we have some fresh water, so that I may gargle my throat.'

On the other side, Pantagruel got into a high state of excitement, and did nothing all night long but brood on Bede's book *De Numeris et Signis*,[1] on Plotinus *De Inenarrabilibus*,[2] on Proclus *De Magia*,[3] on Artemidorus's books, *Peri onirocriticon*,[4] on Anaxagoras *Peri Semion*,[5] on Ynarius *Peri Aphaton*,[6] on the books of Philistion, on Hipponax *Peri Anecphoneton*,[7] and a host of others, until Panurge said to him:

'My lord, leave all these thoughts and go to bed. For I feel you to be so troubled in your spirits that you may soon fall into some quotidian fever from this excess of thinking. First drink some twenty-five or thirty good draughts, and then retire and sleep at your ease. For in the morning I will answer and argue against Master Englishman, and if I don't reduce him to speechlessness, then abuse me as you will.'

'Yes, Panurge, my friend,' replied Pantagruel. 'But how will you satisfy him? He is marvellously learned.'

'Perfectly well,' replied Panurge. 'Let's say no more about it, I beg of you. Just leave it to me. Is there any man as learned as the devils are?'

1. On Numbers and Signs.   2. On Things Indescribable.
3. On Magic.   4. On the Meaning of Dreams.
5. On Signs.   6. On Unspeakable Things.
7. On Things Better not Discussed.

'No, indeed,' said Pantagruel, 'except by special grace of God.'

'Nevertheless,' answered Panurge, 'I have many times argued against them, made fools of them, and turned them upside down. So you need have no doubts about this vainglorious Englishman. I'll make him shit vinegar to-morrow, before the whole world.'

So Panurge spent the night tippling with the pages and played away all the points of his breeches at *Primus-secundus* and push-pin. But when the appointed hour came, he led his master Pantagruel to the agreed spot and, believe me, there was no one in Paris, great or small, who did not come there, thinking to himself: 'This devil of a Pantagruel who has got the better of all these tricksy, callow sophists will be paid out this time. For this Englishman is another Devil of Vauvert. We shall see who gets the best of this.'

So everybody was assembled and Thaumaste was waiting for them. Then, when Pantagruel and Panurge came into the hall, all the scholars, bachelors, and benchers began to clap their hands, as their silly custom is.

But Pantagruel shouted out in a voice as loud as the report of a double cannon: 'Peace, in the devil's name, peace! By God, you rogues, if you disturb me here with your noise I'll cut off the heads of every one of you.'

These words struck them all as scared as ducks. They would not have dared to cough, not even if they had swallowed fifteen pounds of feathers; and they were so afflicted with thirst by this voice alone that their tongues hung half a foot out of their mouths. It was as if Pantagruel had salted their throats.

Then Panurge began to speak, saying to the Englishman: 'Sir, have you come here contentiously to dispute on these propositions you have set out, or merely to learn and know the truth concerning these matters?'

To this Thaumaste replied: 'Sir, no other cause brings me here but my desire to learn and know things that I have been uncertain about for the whole of my life. For I have never found a book or a man to offer me a satisfactory answer to the problems which I have put forward. As for disputing contentiously, I do not wish to do so; that is too base a practice. I leave it to those rascally sophists, who never seek the truth in their disputations, but only contradiction and debate.'

'Then,' said Panurge, 'if I, who am a minor disciple of my master

Pantagruel, content and satisfy you in all and every respect, it would be shameful, would it not, to worry my said master with this matter. It would be better, therefore, if he were to preside and to judge our speeches. He would also satisfy you, of course, should it seem to you that I fall short of your scholarly expectations.'

'Indeed,' said Thaumaste, 'that is a very good idea.'

'Then begin.'

Now note that Panurge had tied on to the end of his long codpiece a fine silken tuft, red, white, green, and blue, and inside he had hidden a beautiful orange.

CHAPTER 19: *How Panurge confounded the Englishman who argued by Signs*

THEN, with everyone attending and listening in perfect silence, the Englishman raised his two hands separately high in the air, clenching all the tips of his fingers in the form that is known in the language of Chinon as the hen's arse, and struck the nails of one against the other four times. Then he opened them and struck the one with the flat of the other, making a sharp noise. Next, clenching them again, as before, he struck twice more and, after opening them, yet another four times. Then he joined them afresh and laid them one beside the other, as if offering up devout prayers to God.

Suddenly Panurge lifted his right hand in the air, and placed his thumb inside his right nostril, holding his four fingers stretched out and arranged in their natural order, parallel to the tip of his nose, shutting his left eye entirely and winking with the right, at the same time deeply depressing his eyebrows and lids. Then he raised his left hand, widely stretching and extending his four fingers and elevating the thumb, and held it in a line directly continuous with that of the right, the distance between the two being two and a quarter feet. This done, he lowered both hands towards the ground in this same attitude, and finally held them half way up, as if aimed straight at the Englishman's nose.

'And if Mercury ...' said the Englishman.

Upon which Panurge interrupted him by saying: 'You have spoken, mask.'

Then the Englishman made this sign: he raised his left hand, wide
open, high into the air, then closed the four fingers into his fist and
placed his extended thumb on the tip of his nose. Next he suddenly
lifted his right hand, wide open, and lowered it, still open, joining his
thumb to the place closed by the little finger of his left hand. After this,
he waggled the four fingers of that hand slowly in the air. Then, in
reverse, he did with the right what he had done with the left, and with
the left what he had done with the right.

Not at all astonished by this, Panurge raised his thrice mighty codpiece into the air with his left hand, and with his right drew from it a
piece of white ox-rib and two pieces of wood of the same shape, one
of black ebony, the other of red brasil-wood, which he placed sym-
metrically between the fingers of that hand. These he struck together,
making the sort of noise that the lepers of Brittany make with their
clappers – but it sounded better and more harmonious. At the same
time, with his tongue contracted in his mouth, he hummed joyously,
all the while looking at the Englishman. By which sign the theologians, doctors, and surgeons imagined Panurge to infer that the
Englishman was a leper. But the counsellors, lawyers, and canon-
lawyers thought that in so doing he wished also to imply that some
kind of human felicity lay in the leprous state, as Our Lord once
affirmed.

The Englishman was not alarmed by this and, raising both his hands
aloft, held them in such a way as to close his three master fingers in his
fist and poke his thumbs between his index and middle fingers, with
his little fingers extended at full length. In this attitude he presented
them towards Panurge, then put them together in such a way that the
right thumb touched the left, and the left little finger touched the
right.

Whereupon Panurge silently raised his hands and made this sign:
He put the nail of his left-hand forefinger on to that of the thumb,
making as it were a ring in the space between them and clenched all
the fingers of his right into his fist except the fore-finger, which he
repeatedly thrust in and drew out of the space between the two others
of his before-mentioned left hand. Then he stretched the fore and
middle fingers of his right, keeping them as far apart as possible, and
pointing them at Thaumaste. Next he put the thumb of his left hand
to the corner of his left eye, extending his whole hand like the wing of

a bird or the fins of a fish, and flapping it very daintily this way and that, afterwards repeating the action with his right at the corner of his right eye.

Thaumaste began to tremble and grow pale, and made him this sign: With the middle finger of his right hand he struck the muscle of the palm beneath the thumb, then put the forefinger of his right hand into a ring formed with his left; only, unlike Panurge, he put it in from below, not from above.

Then Panurge struck one hand against the other and blew in his palm. After which he once more thrust the forefinger of his right hand into the ring made by his left, pushing it in and drawing it out several times. Then he stuck out his chin and looked intently at Thaumaste. By which the spectators, who understood nothing of these signs, realized that he was silently asking Thaumaste: 'What do you mean by that?'

Thaumaste now began to sweat great drops, and had all the appearance of a man rapt in high contemplation. Then he got an idea, and put all the nails of his left hand against those of his right, opening his fingers in a semi-circular fashion, and raised his hands as high as he could in this attitude.

Upon this Panurge suddenly put the thumb of his right hand beneath his jaw, and the forefinger of that hand in the ring of the left; and at this point made a most melodious noise with his teeth, gnashing his lower jaw against the upper.

Thaumaste got up in great alarm, but as he did so let a great baker's fart – for the bran followed it – pissed very strong vinegar, and stank like all the devils. Upon which the spectators began to hold their noses, since he was shitting himself with anguish. Then he raised his right hand, clenching it in such a fashion as to bring the ends of all his fingers together, and placed his left hand quite flat upon his chest.

Upon this Panurge drew out his long codpiece with its tuft and extended it two foot and a quarter, holding it aloft with his left hand; and with his right, he took out his orange and threw it seven times into the air. The eighth time he covered it with his right fist, holding it quite calmly aloft. Then he began to shake his fine codpiece, displaying it before Thaumaste.

After this, Thaumaste began to puff up both his cheeks like a bagpiper, and blew as if he were blowing up a pig's bladder. Whereupon

Panurge put one finger of his right hand up his arse-hole, and sucked in air with his mouth as a man does when eating oysters in the shell or supping broth. This done, he slightly opened his mouth and struck it with the flat of his right hand, making a great deep noise, which seemed to come from the surface of the diaphragm by way of the trachean artery; and this he did sixteen times. But Thaumaste kept on puffing like a goose.

Then Panurge put the forefinger of his right hand into his mouth, sucking it very hard with his cheek-muscles. Next he drew it out and, as he did so, made a great noise, as when little boys fire turnip pellets out of guns made of elderwood; and this he did nine times. Whereat Thaumaste cried out: 'Ha, gentlemen, the great secret! He has put his hand in up to the elbow,' and drew out a dagger which he wore, holding it point downwards.

At that Panurge took his long codpiece and shook it as hard as he could against his thighs. Then he put both his hands, clenched like a cockscomb, on top of his head, sticking out his tongue as far as he could, and rolling his eyes in his head like a dying nanny-goat.

'Ha, I understand,' said Thaumaste, 'but what?' and as he did so made this sign: He put the handle of his dagger against his chest, and placed the flat of his hand upon the point, slightly revolving the tips of his fingers.

Upon this Panurge bent his head towards the left and put his little finger in his right ear, pointing his thumb upwards. Then he crossed both his arms on his chest, coughing five times, and on the fifth cough struck his right foot on the ground. He next raised his left arm and, closing all his fingers into his fist, held his thumb against his forehead, striking his right hand six times against his chest.

But Thaumaste did not seem to be content with this. He put the thumb of his left hand to the tip of his nose, closing the rest of the same hand. Whereupon Panurge placed his two forefingers at each corner of his mouth, drawing it back as wide as he could and showing all his teeth. Then, with his thumbs, he drew down his eyelids very low, making rather an ugly grimace, or so it seemed to the spectators.

CHAPTER 20: *Thaumaste speaks of the Virtues and Knowledge of Panurge*

THEREUPON Thaumaste got up and, lifting his cap from his head, thanked the said Panurge politely. Then, in a loud voice, he said to all the spectators:

'Gentlemen, at this moment I may well pronounce the words of the Gospel: *Et ecce plus quam Salomon hic.*[1] You have here in your presence an incomparable treasure. I mean my lord Pantagruel, whose renown has brought me here from the farthest corner of England to confer with him on certain insoluble problems of magic, alchemy, the Cabala, geomancy, and astrology, also of philosophy, all of which had been long in my mind. But now I protest that Fame seems to have a grudge against him. For she does not report the thousandth part of his talents. You have seen how his mere pupil has satisfied me and told me more even than I asked of him. Furthermore, he has stated for me, and at the same time resolved, certain other knotty points of inestimable importance; and in so doing he has, as I can assure you, opened to me the true and encyclopaedic well and abyss of learning. Yes, and by a manner of argument in which I did not expect to find a man who could attain even to the first degree. I refer, of course, to our disputations by signs, in which we did not speak so much as one word, or even half a word. But I will, in due course, commit to writing both our conversation and our conclusions, so that no one may think that these have been fooleries; and I will have it all printed so that everyone may learn from him as I have done. You will then have a good idea of what the master could have said, when you read of the pupil's valiant performance. For *non est discipulus super magistrum.*[2] The Lord be praised at all events, and I thank you most humbly for the honour you have done us on this occasion. God reward you for it eternally!'

Pantagruel offered a like tender of thanks to the whole company and, as he left the hall, he took Thaumaste with him to dinner. Believe me, they drank with unbuttoned bellies – for at that time men buttoned up their bellies, as they do their collars at present – until they did not know whether they were coming or going.

1. Behold, a greater than Solomon is here.
2. The disciple is not above his master.

Blessed Mother, how they pulled at the goat's skin! How the flagons went round, and how they called for them! 'Give it here!' 'Page, some wine!' 'Reach it here, in the devil's name, reach it here!' There was not anyone who did not drink twenty-five or thirty pipes, and you know how! *Sicut terra sine aqua*,[1] for the weather was warm; and what is more they were thirsty.

As for the significance of the propositions set out by Thaumaste, and the meaning of the signs which they used in argument, I would have expounded them to you, but I am told that Thaumaste has made a great book of them, printed in London, in which he explains everything without exception. Therefore I refrain for the present.

CHAPTER 21: *How Panurge fell in love with a great Parisian Lady*

PANURGE began to gain a reputation in the city of Paris by this disputation in which he beat the Englishman, and from that time he made great use of his codpiece; which he caused to be decorated with embroidery in the Romanesque style. The world was loud in his praise. Indeed, a song was made about him, which the children sang when gathering mustard, and he was welcome in all companies of ladies and gentlewomen. He finally became so presumptuous, in fact, that he set out to conquer one of the great ladies of the city.

So, omitting the mass of long prologues and protestations habitually made by doleful and contemplative lent-lovers who never tamper with the flesh, he said to her one day: 'Madam, it would be most beneficial to the whole state, delightful for you, and an honour to your progeny, as it is a necessity to me, that you should be covered and breed from me. You must believe what I say, for experience will prove me right.'

At these words the lady pushed him back more than three hundred miles, and said: 'What right have you, you miserable idiot, to make such proposals to me? Whom do you think you are talking to? Go away, and never come near me again! But for one small thing, I'd have your arms and legs cut off.'

'Well,' he said, 'it would be all the same to me to have my arms and

1. Like a land without water.

legs cut off, provided you and I had a bout of fun together, at the up-and-down game. For' (showing his long codpiece) 'here's Master John Thursday, who will play you a jig that you'll feel in the very marrow of your bones. He's a sprightly fellow, and he is so good at finding all the cracks and quirks and special spots in the carnal trap that after him there is no need of a broom.'

To which the lady replied: 'Go away, you wretch, go away! If you say one word more, I'll call the people and have you beaten on the spot.'

'Ho,' said he, 'you're not as bad as you say, or I am very much deceived by your face. For sooner shall the earth ascend into the heavens, the high heavens descend into the abyss, and the whole order of nature be perverted, than there could be one drop of gall or malice in such beauty and grace as yours. It's a true saying that hardly ever

> Does one see a woman fair
> Who's not difficult as well

But that is said of mere common beauties. Your beauty is so transcendent, however, so singular, and so celestial that I believe Nature has made you for her paragon, so that we may understand how much she can do if she chooses to employ her full powers and her entire wisdom. There is nothing in you that is not honey, that is not sugar, that is not heavenly manna. It is to you that Paris should have awarded the golden apple, not to Venus, oh dear no; nor to Juno, nor to Minerva. For there was never such magnificence in Juno, such wisdom in Minerva, or such grace in Venus, as there is in you. O ye celestial gods and goddesses, how happy will be the man to whom you grant the favour of embracing this woman, of kissing her, and rubbing his bacon with her. By God, I shall be that man, as well I see, for already she loves me entirely; I am sure of it. I was predestined for this by the fairies. Therefore, to spare time, let's to and fro and at it.'

And he would have embraced her, had she not struggled to get to the window and call on the neighbours for help.

At this Panurge departed hurriedly, saying to her as he ran out: 'Wait for me here, madam. I'll go and fetch them for you. Don't trouble yourself.'

Next day he was at the church at the hour when she went to Mass, and in the porch he offered her the holy water, making a deep bow before her. After this he knelt close beside her most familiarly and said: 'Madam, I must tell you that I am so amorous of you that I can neither piss nor shit for love. I don't know what you think. But if some harm were to befall me, it would be a very dreadful thing!'

'Go away,' she said, 'go away. That is no affair of mine. Leave me alone to say my prayers.'

'But,' he said, 'what does *A Beaumont le Vicomte* remind you of?'

'I have no idea,' she replied.

'Of, "*A beau cont le vit monte*".[1] But as for that, pray God to grant me what your noble heart desires, and be so kind as to give me those beads.'

'Take them,' she said, 'and don't bother me any more.'

As she spoke she tried to take off her rosary, which was of lemon-wood, with large gold beads at intervals of ten. But Panurge promptly drew out one of his knives, cut them neatly, and took them off to the pawnshop, saying to her as he went: 'Would you like my knife?'

'No, no,' said she.

'All the same,' he replied, 'it's very much at your service, body and goods, tripe and bowels.'

However, the lady was not very pleased about her beads, for they helped to keep her in countenance in church. 'This fine babbler,' she thought to herself, 'is a giddy fool from some strange country. I shall never get my rosary back. What will my husband say to that? He will be cross with me. But I'll tell him that some thief cut it off me in church, which he will easily believe, when he sees the end of the ribbon on my girdle.'

After dinner Panurge went to see her, carrying in his sleeve a great purse full of palace-tokens and counters, and he began by saying: 'Which of us two loves the other best, you me, or I you?'

To which she replied: 'For my part, I do not hate you. For, as God commands us to, I love all the world.'

'But to the point,' he replied. 'Aren't you in love with me?'

'I have already told you very many times,' she answered, 'not to use such words to me. If you speak to me like that again I'll show you that I'm not the woman to be addressed in this indecent way. Get out of here, and give me back my rosary, in case my husband asks me for it.'

'What, madam,' said he, 'your rosary? I'll do no such thing, I swear. But I'll willingly give you a new one. Now which would you like?

1. A most indelicate pun, quite untranslatable.

One of well-enamelled gold in the shape of great round knobs, or of true love-knots, or all solid like great ingots? Or would you prefer one of ebony, or of large jacinths, or of great cut garnets, with every tenth stone a fine turquoise or a magnificent sapphire or a spider-ruby, and with the biggest beads of diamonds with twenty-eight facets? But no, no, that's too poor. I know of a beautiful rosary of fine emeralds, with every tenth bead of rounded amber, and at the clasp a Persian pearl as a big as an orange, and it costs no more than twenty-five thousand ducats. I should like to make you a present of that. I have enough ready money.'

And as he spoke he made his counters jingle, as if they were Sun-crowns.

'Would you like a piece of violet-crimson velvet, dyed in the grain, or a piece of embroidered satin, or of crimson perhaps? Would you like chains, gold ornaments, headbands, rings? You have only to say yes. Up to fifty thousand ducats; it is nothing to me.'

By virtue of these words he made her mouth water. Nevertheless she replied: 'I thank you, no. I want nothing to do with you.'

'By God,' said he, 'I certainly want something to do with you, though. But it is something that will cost you nothing, and you won't be the worse off for it. Look,' said he, pointing to his long codpiece. 'Here's Master John Owl, who wants a nest.'

At this he tried to embrace her. But she began to shout, although not very loud. Whereupon Panurge put off his disguise, and said to her: 'So you won't let me do a little business, then? A turd for you! You have no title to such a favour, nor to such an honour. But, by God, I'll make the dogs ride you.'

And with this he ran away fast for fear of a beating, of which he was afraid by nature.

CHAPTER 22: *How Panurge played a Trick on the Parisian Lady which was not at all to her advantage*

Now you must know that the next day was the great feast of Corpus Christi, on which all women wear their best clothes; and for that occasion this lady was dressed in a very fine gown of crimson satin, and a very costly white velvet bodice.

On the vigil of that day, Panurge hunted in all directions for a hot sheep-dog bitch; and when he had secured her with his belt, he took her to his room and fed her very well on that day and all the next night. In the morning he killed her and removed that part which the Greek necromancers know. This he cut into the smallest possible pieces, which he took away well wrapped up. Then he went to the church where the lady must go to follow the procession, as is the custom on this festival; and when she came in, he gave her the holy water, bowing to her most courteously. A little while later, after she had said her prayer, he sat down beside her on the same bench, and gave her this rondel, written out and running as follows:

> Just for this once, when I declared my mind,
> And you, most lovely dame, proved so unkind
> And sent me packing hopeless of return,
> Who never any wrong to you had done
> In word or deed, in slander or in slight,
> Since you disliked my suit, I think you might
> Have said to me, without wound or offence:
> 'My friend, be kind enough to go from hence
>   Just for this once.'
> I wrong you not if I my thoughts reveal,
> Saying how the beauty that your clothes conceal
> Is like a spark that sets afire my heart.
> I only ask that you then, for your part,
> Will be a saddle and will let me ride,
>   Just for this once.

And as she was opening this paper to see what was in it, Panurge deftly sprinkled the drug that he was carrying on to various parts of her, chiefly on the pleats of her sleeves and her dress.

Then he said to her: 'Madam, poor lovers are not always at peace. For myself, I hope that the sleepless nights, the evils and despites which I suffer from the love of you will earn me a deduction of so much pain in purgatory. But at least pray God to give me patience in my suffering.'

Panurge had no sooner spoken than all the dogs in the church ran up to the lady, attracted by the smell of the drug he had sprinkled on her. Small and great, big and little, all came, lifting their legs, smelling her and pissing all over her. It was the most dreadful thing in the world.

244 RABELAIS · BOOK TWO · CHAPTER 22

Panurge made a show of driving them off, then took leave of her and retired into a chapel to see the fun. For these beastly dogs pissed over all her clothes, a great greyhound wetting her on the head, others on her sleeves, others on her backside; and the little ones pissed on her shoes; so that all the women who were thereabouts had great difficulty in saving her.

At this Panurge burst out laughing, and said to some of the gentlemen of the city: 'I think that woman's on heat, or else she has recently been covered by a greyhound.'

And when he saw all the dogs snarling around her as they do round a hot bitch, he went off to fetch Pantagruel. Everywhere on the way when he saw a dog, he gave it a kick and said: 'Aren't you going to join your mates at the wedding? Get on, get on, devil take you! Get along with you now!'

Then, having got to their lodgings, he said to Pantagruel: 'Master, I beg of you, come and see all the dogs, come and see all the dogs of this land, flocking round a lady. She is the most beautiful lady in the town, and they want to roger her.'

Pantagruel very gladly accepted this invitation and went to see the show, which he found very fine and original. But the best of it all was the procession, in which more than six hundred thousand and fourteen dogs were seen all around her, bothering her greatly, and everywhere she passed fresh hosts of dogs followed her trail, pissing in the road where her gown had touched it.

Everyone stopped to see the show, gazing with admiration at the dogs, who leapt as high as her neck and spoiled all her fine clothes. For this she could find no other remedy but to retire into her mansion. So she ran to hide, with the dogs after her and all the chambermaids laughing. But once she was inside and the door closed behind her, all the dogs ran up from two miles around, and pissed so hard against the gate of the house, that they made a stream with their urine big enough for the ducks to swim in. And it is this stream which now passes by Saint Victor, in which Madame Gobelin dyes her scarlet, thanks to the specific virtue of those piss-hounds, as our Master Dungpowder once proclaimed in a public sermon. So, God help you, a mill could have ground corn by it; but not so much as do the mills of Bazacle at Toulouse.

CHAPTER 23: *How Pantagruel left Paris, on hearing that the Dipsodes were invading the Country of the Amaurots; and the reason why Leagues are so short in France*

A LITTLE later Pantagruel heard news that his father had been translated into Fairyland by Morgan, as were Ogier and Arthur of old; also that, the rumour of his translation having spread, the Dipsodes had crossed their frontiers, devastated a great tract of Utopia, and were just then besieging the great city of the Amaurots. So he left Paris without taking leave of anyone since the matter was urgent, and he made for Rouen.

Now as they were travelling Pantagruel observed that leagues in France are extremely short, compared with those of any other country, and asked Panurge the cause and reason. Whereupon Panurge told him a story that Marotus du Lac, a monk, relates in the *Deeds of the Kings of Canaria*. The land was not measured of old, he tells us by leagues, Roman miles, stades, and parasangs, until King Pharamond made those divisions, which he did in the following manner. He chose in Paris a hundred fine, gallant young fellows, and a hundred pretty Picardy girls, and had them well entertained and feasted for a week. Then he called them before him, gave each man his girl and plenty of money for his expenses, and commanded each to go to a different place, in one direction or another; and at every spot where they turned their girls on their backs they were to set up a stone – and that should be a league.

So the fellows set out joyfully, and as they were fresh and well rested, they took their pleasure at the end of every field, which is why leagues in France are so short. But when they had gone a long distance, and were then as weary as poor devils, with no more oil in their lamps, they did not play the ram so often, and were quite content (I am speaking of the men) with one poor, wretched bout a day. And that is what makes the leagues in Brittany, the Landes, Germany, and other more distant countries so long. Others give other reasons, but I think this one the best; and Pantagruel gladly accepted it.

Leaving Rouen, they came to Honfleur, where they embarked: Pantagruel, Panurge, Epistemon, Eusthenes, and Carpalim. And as they were waiting there for a favourable wind, and caulking their ship, Pantagruel received from a Parisian lady, whom he had kept as his mistress for some time, a letter addressed in the following manner:

To the best beloved of the Fair and the least faithful of the brave, P.N.T.G.R.L.

CHAPTER 24: *A Letter brought to Pantagruel from a Lady of Paris, and the explanation of a Motto on a gold Ring*

WHEN Pantagruel had read the address he was greatly astonished, and asked the messenger for the name of the lady who had sent it. Then he opened the envelope and found no writing inside it, only a gold ring with a flat-cut diamond. So he called Panurge and explained matters to him. Whereupon Panurge said that the leaf of paper was written on, but in such a subtle way that no one could see the writing. Therefore, to bring it out, he put the letter before the fire, to see if it was not written with sal-ammoniac soaked in water. Then he put it in water to see if it was not written with tithymal juice. After that he held it up in front of a candle, to see if it was not written with the juice of white onions. Then he rubbed a part of it with walnut oil, to see if it was not written with fig-wood ash. Then he rubbed a part of it with the milk of a woman suckling her first-born daughter, to see if it was not written with bull-frog's blood. Then he rubbed a corner with the ashes of a swallow's nest, to see if it was written in the dew that is found in the winter-cherry. Then he rubbed another corner with ear-wax, to see if it was written in raven's gall. Then he soaked it in vinegar, to see if it was written in castor-oil. Then he anointed it with bat's grease, to see if it was written in whale sperm, which is called ambergris. Then he put it quite gently into a basin of fresh water, and drew it out quickly, to see if it was written in feather-alum. And seeing that he could discover nothing, he called the messenger and asked him: 'Fellow, did not the lady who sent you here give you a stick to bring?' For he thought that she had used the subtle trick that Aulus Gellius records. But the messenger answered: 'No, sir.'

Then Panurge wanted to have the man's hair shaved off to see if the lady had had the message she wanted to send written on his shaven head. But seeing that his hair was very long he desisted, considering that it could not have grown to that length in so little time.

Then he said to Pantagruel: 'Master, by the Wonders of God, I don't know what to say or do about this. To find out whether anything is written here I have used a fair proportion of the ideas of Messer Francesco di Nianto the Tuscan, who has written on the subject of reading invisible writing. I have also tried those of Zoroaster, *Peri grammaton acriton,*[1] and of Calphurnius Bassus, *De litteris illegibilibus.*[2] But I can see nothing there, and I believe that there is nothing but the ring. Now let's look at that.'

And when they examined it, they found written inside in Hebrew: LAMAH HAZABTHANI. So they called Epistemon, and asked him what it meant; and he replied that this was the Hebrew for, *Why hast thou forsaken me?*

Then suddenly Panurge gave his reply: 'I understand the case. Do you see this diamond? It's a false one. So this is the explanation of the lady's message. "Say, false lover, why have you abandoned me?"'

Pantagruel understood this explanation at once, and remembered that, on departing, he had not bidden the lady farewell. This depressed him, and he would gladly have returned to Paris to make his peace with her. But Epistemon reminded him of Aeneas's conduct towards Dido, and of Heraclides of Tarentum's saying that when the ship is at anchor and the case is urgent it is better to cut the cable than to waste time untying it. He advised his master, therefore, to put aside all other thoughts in order to assist the city of his birth, which was in danger.

Indeed, an hour later the wind arose, which is called the north-northwest, to which they set their full sails, and took to the open sea; and in a few days, passing Porto Santo and Madeira, they landed on the Canary Islands. Leaving there, they passed by Cape Blanco, Senegal, Cape Verde, Gambia, Sagres, Melli, and the Cape of Good Hope, and disembarked in the kingdom of Melinda. Setting out from that place with a northerly wind and passing by Meden, Uti, Udem Gelasim, and the Fairy Isle, and along the coast of the kingdom of Achoria, they finally arrived at the port of Utopia, a little more than nine miles away from the city of the Amaurots

When they had refreshed themselves a little on land, Pantagruel said: 'My lads, the city is not far from here. But before marching further, it would be as well to consider a plan, so that we may not be

1. On writing hard to make out.   2. On illegible writing.

like the Athenians, who never took counsel till everything was over. Are you resolved to live and die with me?'

'Yes, my lord,' they all replied. 'You may be as sure of us as of your own fingers.'

'Then,' said he, 'there is only one point on which my mind is in doubt and suspense. I do not know the disposition or numbers of the enemy that are besieging this town. If I knew that, I should go forward with the greatest confidence. Therefore let us consult together as to the means of finding out.'

Whereat they all said at once: 'Let us go there and see. You may wait for us here. On this very day we will bring you reliable information.'

'I,' said Panurge, 'undertake to get into their camp through the midst of their guards and of their watch, to banquet with them and lecher at their expense without being noticed by anyone, to inspect their artillery, to visit the tents of all their captains, and to lounge past their companies without ever being detected. The devil himself would never deceive me, for I am of the race of Zopyrus.'

'I,' said Epistemon, 'know all the tricks and exploits of the brave captains and champions of olden times, and all the ruses and devices of military science. I will go, and even if I am unmasked and discovered I will escape, making them at the same time believe any story about you I please. For I am of the race of Sinon.'

'I,' said Eusthenes, 'will get in across their trenches, despite the watch and all the guards. For I'll tread over their bellies, and break their arms and legs, even if they are as strong as the devil. For I am of the line of Hercules.'

'I,' said Carpalim, 'will get in, if the birds can get in. For my frame is so nimble that I shall leap over their trenches, and run right through their camp before they notice me. I fear neither shot, arrow, nor the swiftest horse. Even from the Pegasus of Perseus or from Pacolet I shall escape safe and sound. I'll undertake to walk upon the ears of corn or the grasses of the fields, without their bending under me. For I am of the race of Camilla the Amazon.'

CHAPTER 25: *How Pantagruel's Companions, Panurge, Carpalim, Eusthenes, and Epistemon, most cunningly discomfited six hundred and sixty Knights*

JUST as he was saying this, they spied six hundred and sixty knights, well mounted on light horses, coming up to see what ship it was that had newly arrived in the harbour, and galloping all out to capture them if they could.

Then said Pantagruel: 'My lads, retire into the ship. For here are some of our enemies riding up. But I'll knock them down for you on the spot, like so many cattle, and I would do the same to ten times as many. So retire and enjoy the spectacle.'

'No, my Lord,' replied Panurge. 'It wouldn't be right for you to do this. On the contrary, you must retire into the ship, you and the rest, and I will discomfit them here, I alone. But we must not delay. Forward, my men!'

'That's right, my Lord,' said the others. 'Please retire yourself, and we'll help Panurge here. You will see that we know our trade.'

'I am quite content,' answered Pantagruel. 'But should you prove the weaker party, I shall not fail you.'

Then Panurge took two great cables from the ship, tied them to the capstan, which was on the deck, and threw them ashore. With them he made two large loops, an outer one, at some distance, and another inside it. Upon which he said to Epistemon: 'Go aboard the ship, and when I signal you, turn the capstan on deck with all your might, drawing in these two ropes.'

Next he said to Eusthenes and Carpalim: 'Wait here, my lads, and submit yourselves freely to the enemy. Do what they command, and pretend to surrender. But take care not to enter within the circle of these ropes. Keep always outside.'

He went immediately aboard, took a truss of straw and a barrel of gunpowder, spread them round the circle of the ropes, and kept close with a firebrand in his hand.

Suddenly the knights rode up in great strength, the foremost charging right up to the ship; and because the bank was slippery, they fell together with their horses, forty-four of them in all. Upon the sight of which, the rest advanced, thinking that their comrades had met with resistance when they arrived.

Panurge, however, said to the fallen men: 'Sirs, I think that you have hurt yourselves. Forgive us, nevertheless. Yet it is not our fault, but the slipperiness of the sea-water, which is always dangerous. We submit ourselves to your will.'

His two companions said the same, and so did Epistemon, who was on the deck. Panurge meanwhile went further off and, observing that while the enemy were all within the circle of the ropes his two companions had got outside, to make way for all those knights who were crowding up to see the ship and its crew, he cried out to Epistemon: 'Haul in! Haul in!'

Then Epistemon began to wind the capstan, and the two ropes got entangled among the horses' legs, throwing them down quite easily together with their riders. But at this the knights drew their swords and would have cut the invaders down. But Panurge laid fire to the powder-train, and set them burning like souls in hell. Not a horse or a man escaped except one rider on a Turkish mount, who got away by flight. But when Carpalim noticed him, he ran after him with such speed and agility that he caught him in less than a hundred yards, leapt on the crupper of his horse, grasped him from behind, and dragged him to the ship.

With the enemy thus defeated, Pantagruel was in high spirits, and most extravagantly praised the resourcefulness of his companions. He had refreshment brought and a feast spread for them on the shore with great jollity; and he made them drink too, with their bellies to the ground, and their prisoner as well, in all friendliness, except that the poor devil was not sure whether Pantagruel was not going to devour him whole; which he might have done, so wide was his throat, as easily as a grain of forage, and the poor fellow, once in his mouth, would not have amounted to more than a grain of millet in an ass's throat.

CHAPTER 26: *How Pantagruel and his Companions were tired of eating Salt Meat, and how Carpalim went hunting after Venison*

As they were thus feasting, Carpalim exclaimed: 'By St Quenet's belly, shall we never taste venison? This salt meat gives me a desperate thirst. I will go and fetch you a thigh of one of those horses we set light to; it will be well enough roasted.'

Just as he was getting up to do this, he noticed a fine great roebuck on the edge of the wood, which had come out of the thicket on seeing Panurge's fire, as I suppose.

Carpalim immediately ran after him with such speed that he seemed like a great bolt shot from a cross-bow. He caught him in a moment and, as he ran plucked down with his hands out of the air

> Four great bustards,
> Seven bitterns,
> Twenty-six grey partridges,
> Thirty-two red ones,
> Sixteen pheasants,
> Nine woodcocks,
> Nineteen herons,
> Thirty-two wood-pigeons.

And with his feet he killed ten or twelve leverets and rabbits, which were already past their pagehood, also

> Eighteen rails, running in couples,
> Fifteen young boars,
> Two badgers,
> Three large foxes.

So striking the buck with his sword over the head, he killed it; and as he brought it back he picked up his leverets, rails, and young boars. Then from as far off as his voice could be heard, he called out: 'Panurge, my friend, some vinegar, some vinegar!'

Whereupon the good Pantagruel thought that he was fainting and ordered that vinegar should be brought to him. But Panurge saw quite well that there was leveret in the bag. Indeed, he pointed out to the noble Pantagruel that Carpalim was carrying a fine roebuck on his shoulders and that his whole belt was studded with leverets.

Immediately, Epistemon made nine fine wooden spits in the ancient fashion, and in the names of the nine Muses; Eusthenes helped in the skinning, and Panurge placed two of the knights' saddles in such a position that they served for andirons. So they made their prisoner their turnspit, and at the fire in which the knights were burning they set their venison to roast. Afterwards they made good cheer with plenty of vinegar. The devil take any man who held back! It was glorious to see them stuff themselves.

Then said Pantagruel: 'I wish to God you had each a pair of hawk's bells on your chins, and that I had the great chimes of Rennes, Poitiers, Tours, and Cambrai on mine. What a peal we would make with the mumbling of our lips!'

'But,' said Panurge, 'it would be better if we were to give some thought to our business, and to how we are to overcome our enemy.'

'That's good advice,' said Pantagruel, and, turning to their prisoner, he asked: 'Now tell us the truth, my friend, and don't utter a single lie unless you want to be flayed alive. For I am the man who eats little children. Relate to us in full the disposition, number, and strength of their army.'

'My lord,' replied the prisoner, 'I'll tell you the truth. In the army there are three hundred giants, all armed with freestone, amazingly big, yet not quite as big as you, except one, who is their chief and is called Werewolf. He wears a complete armour of Cyclopean anvils. There are also sixty-three thousand foot, all in hobgoblin-skin armour, strong and courageous men; eleven thousand four hundred men-at-arms; three thousand six hundred double cannons, and siege artillery without number; ninety-four thousand pioneers; a hundred and fifty thousand whores, as fair as goddesses. …'

'They're for me,' exclaimed Panurge.

'Of whom some are Amazons, others are from Lyons, others from Paris, from Touraine, Anjou, Poitou, Normandy, and Germany. There are some, in fact, from all lands and of all languages.'

'Indeed,' said Pantagruel. 'But is the king there?'

'Yes, sire,' replied the prisoner. 'He is there in person, and we call him Anarch, King of the Dipsodes, which is as much as to say the thirsty ones. You never saw people so thirsty, or who drink with a better will. His tent is guarded by the giants.'

'That's enough,' said Pantagruel. 'Up, my lads! Are you resolved to go there with me?'

To which Panurge replied: 'God damn any man who deserts you! I've been thinking of a way of laying them out for you as dead as pigs, so that not so much as a leg of one escapes. But I am rather bothered about one point.'

'And what is that?' asked Pantagruel.

'It's how I can manage to roger all those whores there this afternoon; "so that there remain not one that I in common form don't drum."'

'Ha, ha, ha!' laughed Pantagruel.

'By the devil in person!' exclaimed Carpalim. 'But I'll stuff some of them too, I swear!'

'And I too,' said Eusthenes. 'I've never had a stand since we left Rouen, at least not so much of one that my needle went up to ten or eleven o'clock. So now it's as hard and strong as a thousand devils.'

'Indeed you shall have some of the fattest and those in best condition,' said Panurge.

'What,' cried Epistemon. 'Is all the world to ride and I to lead the the ass? Devil take the man who does that! We'll observe the right of war: *Qui potest capere capiat.*'[1]

'No, no,' said Panurge, 'you tie your ass to a stump and ride like the rest.'

And the good Pantagruel laughed at all this. 'You're reckoning without your host,' he said after a moment, 'I'm very much afraid that before night falls I may see you in such a state that you'll have no great desire to stand up. You are more likely to be battered down with great blows of the pike and lance.'

'Basta,' said Epistemon. 'I'll hand them over to you, to be roast or boiled, to be fricasseed or put into pasties. They are not so great in number as the army that Xerxes led. For he had three hundred thousand fighting men, if you believe Herodotus and Pompeius Trogus, but Themistocles with a few soldiers overthrew them all the same. Don't worry about them, I implore you.'

'A turd for them, a turd!' exclaimed Panurge. 'My codpiece alone will sweep all the men down, and St Shakehole that lies inside will brush out all the women.'

'Up then, my lads,' said Pantagruel. 'Let's set out on our march.'

1. A reference to Matt. xix, 12. But here it means, let him take who can.

CHAPTER 27: *How Pantagruel set up a Trophy in memory of their Prowess, and Panurge another in memory of the Leverets; and how Pantagruel with his Farts begot little men, and with his Poops little women; and how Panurge broke a great Staff over two Glasses*

'BEFORE we depart,' said Pantagruel, 'I should like to erect in this place a handsome trophy, to commemorate the prowess that you have just displayed.'

Then all together, with great joy and singing country snatches, they set up a huge trunk, and hung upon it a knight's saddle, a horse's head-stall, harness bosses, stirrup-leathers, spurs, a coat of chain-mail, a tempered steel corselet, a battle-axe, a knight's sword, a gauntlet, a mace, gussets, greaves, and a gorget, with all the other requisite decorations of a triumphal arch or trophy.

Then, as an eternal memorial, Pantagruel wrote the following victor's legend:

> Here was displayed the valour bright
> Of four knights, worthy men of brawn,
> Who with no armour but their wit
> (Like Fabius and the Scipios twain)
> Six hundred and sixty lice did burn
> Like chaff, all hefty rogues and coarse,
> By this learn, king, duke, rook, and pawn,
> That trickery's worth more than force.
> > For victory,
> > Says History,
> > Doth only lie
> > With that domain
> > In which doth reign
> > The Lord on high.
> So not to strong or great 'tis given,
> But those He loves, so we believe,
> Those who place faith and hope in Heaven,
> Fame, gain and glory do receive.

Whilst Pantagruel was writing these verses Panurge fixed upon a great stake the horns of the roebuck and its skin and right forefoot; then the ears of three leverets, the chine of a rabbit, the chaps of a hare, the wings of two bitterns, the claws of four wood-pigeons, a vinegar cruet, a horn in which they had put the salt, their wooden spit, a larding-spit, a crazy kettle full of holes, a bowl in which they had made the sauce, an earthern salt-cellar, and a Beauvais goblet. And in imitation of Pantagruel's verses and trophy he wrote the following:

> 'Twas here that squatted in delight
> Four merry boozers on the lawn,
> Feasting and pledging Bacchus' might,
> Drinking their fill like carp at dawn.
> Here Master Leveret came to mourn
> The loss of chaps and chine, perforce,
> With vinegar and salt chased down,
> Scorpions they carried in their stores.
> > The Inventory
> > Defensory
> > Against the heat,
> > Is drinking just
> > The best, which must
> > De swallowed neat.
> To vinegar must thought be given
> Since hare without it makes you grieve,
> For vinegar's its soul and leaven,
> A lack that nothing can retrieve.

Then said Pantagruel: 'Come, my lads, we have brooded here too long on our victuals. It is no easy thing, as we know, for great feasters to perform great deeds of arms. But there is no shade like that of banners, there is no smoke like that of horses, nor clattering like that of armour.'

At this Epistemon began to smile and said: 'There is no shade like that of kitchens, no smoke like pie-smoke, and no clattering like that of cups.' To which Panurge answered: 'There is no shade like that of curtains, no smoke like steaming breasts, and no clattering like the sound of ballocks.'

Then, getting up, he gave a fart, a leap, and a whistle, and joyously cried aloud: 'Long live Pantagruel!'

At this sight, Pantagruel tried to do the same. But with the fart he blew the earth trembled for twenty-seven miles round, and with the fetid air of it he engendered more than fifty-three thousand little men, misshapen dwarfs; and with a poop, which he made, he engendered as many little bowed women, such as you see in various places, and who never grow, except downwards like cows' tails, or in circumference, like Limousin turnips.

'What now,' exclaimed Panurge. 'Are your farts so fruitful? By God, here are fine clumpish men, fine stinking women. Only let them be married together, and they'll breed horse-flies.'

So Pantagruel did, and called them pygmies. He sent them to live on an island close by, where they have since multiplied mightily. But the cranes make continual war on them, and they put up a courageous defence. For these little stumps of men (whom in Scotland they call dandiprats) most readily lose their tempers; the physical reason for which is that they keep their bowels close to their hearts.

At that same time Panurge took two glasses that were there, both of a size, and filled them with as much water as they would hold. He put one of them on one stool, and the other on another, placing them five foot apart. Then he took the shaft of a spear, five foot and a half long, and placed it on top of the two glasses, so that the two ends of the staff just touched the edges. This done, he took a great stake, and said to Pantagruel and the others:

'Gentlemen, I will show you how easily we shall gain the victory over our enemies. For just as I shall snap this shaft here on top of the glasses without in any way breaking or cracking them, and – what is more – without spilling a single drop of the water in them, even so shall we break the heads of our Dipsodes, without one of us being wounded and without any loss of our possessions. But in case you think there is any magic in this,' said he, turning to Eusthenes, 'take this stake and strike the spear with all your strength in the middle.'

This Eusthenes did, and the shaft broke quite cleanly in two, without a drop of water spilling from the glasses. Then said Panurge: 'I know plenty of other tricks like that. But come, let us march confidently forward.'

CHAPTER 28: *How Pantagruel won a very strange Victory over the Dipsodes and the Giants*

AFTER all this talk Pantagruel called their prisoner and sent him away, saying: 'Go off to your king in his camp, and take him news of what you have seen. Tell him to make up his mind to give me a feast to-morrow, at about noon. For as soon as my galleys have arrived – which will be to-morrow at the latest – I will prove to him, with eighteen hundred thousand fighting men and seven thousand giants, all greater than I who stand before you, that he has acted both foolishly and unreasonably in thus invading my country.' This was a trick of Pantagruel's, to pretend that he had an army on the sea.

But the prisoner replied that he gave himself up to Pantagruel as a slave, and that he was satisfied never to return to his people, but instead to fight for Pantagruel against them. Indeed, he begged him in God's name to grant him this favour. However, Pantagruel would not consent, but commanded him to depart speedily and go as he had been ordered. And he gave him a box full of euphorbium and spurge-laurel grains steeped in brandy, made up into pastilles. This he commanded the prisoner to carry to his king and to say that if he could eat an ounce of it without drinking, he need not be afraid to put up a resistance.

Then the prisoner begged him with clasped hands to take pity on him on the day of battle. Upon which Pantagruel said to him: 'After you have reported everything to your king, place all your hope in God, and He will not abandon you. For my part, though I am mighty, as you can see, and have countless men-at-arms, nevertheless I put no trust in my own strength or my endeavours. All my confidence is in God, my protector, who never abandons those who have placed their hope and reliance in Him.'

After this the prisoner requested him to be moderate in the matter of his ransom. To which Pantagruel replied that his purpose was not to plunder men or hold them to ransom, but to enrich them and set them at complete liberty. 'Depart,' said he, 'in the peace of the living God, and never keep bad company or you may meet with trouble.'

When the prisoner had gone, Pantagruel said to his men: 'My lads, I have given this prisoner to understand that we have an army on the sea and, at the same time, that we shall not attack them until tomorrow at about midday. My intention was to make them expect a great landing of men, so that they should be busy to-night setting things in order and building up their defences. My plan is, however, for us to attack them about the hour of their first sleep.'

Let us leave Pantagruel here with his apostles, and speak of King Anarch and his army.

When the prisoner had arrived he went straight to the king and told him how a great giant had come, named Pantagruel, who had dis-comfited all the six hundred and fifty-nine knights and caused them to be cruelly roasted, and how he was the only man to escape and bring the news. Further, that he had been charged by the said giant to tell him to have dinner prepared for him next day at noon, for he intended to attack at that hour.

Then he gave the king the box containing the pastilles. But as soon as King Anarch had swallowed down one spoonful, he was seized with such a burning in the throat and with such an ulceration of the uvula that his tongue peeled; and try what remedies they would, he found no relief except in continuous drinking. For the moment he took the wineglass from his lips, his tongue was on fire. Therefore they did nothing but pour wine down his throat with a funnel.

When they saw this, his captains, pashas, and bodyguards tasted these drugs to see if they were, in fact, so thirst-making; and they were taken in the same way as their king. Indeed, they all lifted the flagon to such effect that the rumour went right through the camp that the prisoner had returned, that they were to be attacked next day, and that the king and his captains together with the bodyguard were already preparing for that event, and this by drinking full draughts. As a consequence, each man in the army began to tipple, to ply the pot and swill it down. In fact, they drank so much and so much that they fell asleep like hogs, in disorderly fashion, all about the camp.

Now let us return to the good Pantagruel, and tell what part he played in this business. Setting out from the site of the trophy, he took the mast of their ship in his hand, like a pilgrim's staff, and put into the mast-hatch two hundred and thirty-seven puncheons of white Anjou wine, out of the stock which he had brought from Rouen. He then tied the ship to his belt, filled it up with salt, and carried it there as easily as German mercenaries' women carry their little loot-baskets. So he went on his way with his comrades.

But when he was near the enemy's camp, Panurge said to him: 'My lord, do you want to do the sensible thing? Then get this white wine of Anjou out of the mast-hatch, and let us drink it here Breton-fashion.'

This Pantagruel willingly condescended to do, and they drank so clean that there was not a drop of the two hundred and thirty-seven puncheons left, except one leather bottle of Tours manufacture, which Panurge filled for himself – for he called it his Vade mecum – also some miserable dregs for their vinegar.

When they had thoroughly pulled at the goat's skin, Panurge gave Pantagruel some devilish drug to eat, composed of lithontripon, nephrocatharticon, quince jellied with cantharides, and other kinds of diuretics. Upon which Pantagruel said to Carpalim:

'Get into the city by scrambling over the wall like a rat, as you well know how to. Tell them to charge out at once, and set about the enemy as briskly as they can. Then, when you have done that, come down, carrying a lighted torch, and with it set fire to all the tents and pavilions in their quarters. After that shout as loudly as you can in your mightiest voice, and clear out of the camp.'

'Yes,' said Carpalim. 'But wouldn't it be a good thing if I were to spike all their artillery?'

'No, no,' said Pantagruel. 'Just set fire to their powder.'

In obedience to this, Carpalim immediately set out, and did as Pantagruel had instructed him. So all the combatants who were there rushed out of the town. And when he had set fire to the tents and pavilions, Carpalim passed lightly through the enemy without their noticing anything, so deeply were they sleeping and snoring. So he came to the place where their artillery was, and set fire to their munitions. But this was the dangerous stroke. For the fire was so quick that it almost seized on poor Carpalim; and had it not been for his marvellous speed, he would have been fried like a pig. But he rushed out so quickly that a bolt from a cross-bow could not fly faster; and when he was over the trenches he gave such a terrifying shout that it sounded as if all the devils were loose. At this sound the enemy woke up, but in what state you can guess. As dazed as monks at the first peal of Matins, which is called in the district of Luçon rub-ballock.

Meanwhile Pantagruel began to scatter the salt which he had in the ship, and because they were sleeping with their mouths gaping open, he filled their whole gullets with it, so that the poor wretches coughed like foxes, crying: 'Ha, Pantagruel, Pantagruel, you're adding heat to the firebrand that's in us!' Suddenly, because of the drugs that Panurge had given him, Pantagruel felt a desire to piss; and he pissed over the camp, so well and copiously that he drowned them all, and there was a special flood for thirty miles round. In fact, history avers that if his father's great mare had been there and had pissed likewise there would have been a vaster flood than Deucalion's. For she never pissed once that she did not make a river greater than the Rhone or the Danube.

Seeing this, those who had come out of the city said: 'They have all been cruelly slaughtered. Look at the stream of blood.' For they mistakenly imagined that Pantagruel's urine was the blood of their enemies, since they only saw it by the glow of the burning pavilions and a slight glimmer from the moon.

When the enemy had awoken, seeing on one side the fire in their camp, on the other the inundation and deluge of urine, they did not know what to say or think. Some said that it was the end of the world and the last judgement, which is to be consummated by fire; others that the gods of the sea – Neptune, Proteus, the Tritons and others – were attacking them, and that in fact it was salt and sea-water.

Oh, who will now have skill to relate how Pantagruel bore himself against the three hundred giants? O my Muse, my Calliope, my Thalia, inspire me at this hour! Restore to me my spirits! For here is that bridge where asses stumble, here is the pitfall, here the supreme difficulty. How shall I have power to describe the dreadful battle which then took place? Would to God I had a bottle of the best wine ever drunk by those who shall read this most authentic history!

CHAPTER 29: *How Pantagruel defeated the three hundred Giants armoured with Freestone, and Werewolf, their Captain*

SEEING that their whole camp was drowned, the giants carried their King Anarch off on their shoulders, as best they could, out of the fort, as Aeneas did his father Anchises from the burning of Troy. And at the sight of them Panurge said to Pantagruel:

'My lord, look at the giants coming out there. Lay into them with your mast gallantly, in the old fencing fashion. For this is the moment to show yourself a valiant man; and we, on our side, won't fail you. Bold's the word, and I'll kill plenty of them for you. Why not? David killed Goliath easily enough. Then this great lecher Eusthenes, who is as strong as four oxen, won't spare himself. Take courage, strike out right and left, point and edge.'

'Courage,' exclaimed Pantagruel. 'Well, I've more than fifty francs' worth of that. But come now, Hercules never dared to take on two at a time.'

'That's a fine turd to drop under my nose,' said Panurge. 'Do you compare yourself to Hercules? By God, you have more strength in your teeth and more sense (scents) in your bum than ever Hercules had in his whole body and soul. A man's worth as much as he thinks he is.'

As they were holding this conversation, up came Werewolf with all his giants; and, seeing Pantagruel quite alone, he was seized with such temerity and presumption as to hope to kill the poor good man. So he said to his fellow giants: 'By Mahoun, if any of you lecherous peasants attempts to fight against these, I will put you to a cruel death. I wish to be left to fight them alone. You shall have the amusement, in the meantime, of watching us.'

Thereupon all the giants retired with their king a little way off, where the flagons were; and with them Panurge and his companions, the former of whom, imitating a man who has had the pox, twisted his gullet, contorted his fingers, and said to them in a hoarse voice: 'I swear to God, my friends, it's not we who make war. Give us something to eat with you while our masters fight.' Which the king and the giants readily agreed to do, inviting them to share their feast, during which Panurge told them the fabulous story of Turpin, the miracles of St Nicholas, and the tale of the Stork.

Werewolf then faced up to Pantagruel with a club of solid steel weighing nine hundred and seventy tons, one hundredweight. It was of Chalybean steel, and at the tip were thirteen diamond studs, the smallest of which was as big as the largest bell in Notre-Dame at Paris – or smaller, perhaps, by the thickness of a nail, or at most, to be quite truthful, by the blunt edge of one of those knives that they call earcutters, but not a bit more than that either at front or back – and it was so enchanted that it would never break. On the contrary, everything that he touched with it shattered immediately.

So therefore, as he most arrogantly approached, Pantagruel turned his eyes to Heaven, recommending himself most heartily to God, and making a vow as follows: 'O Lord God! Thou hast been my protector and my saviour. Thou seest the distress in which I now am. Nothing has led me here but that natural zeal which thou hast conferred upon men, that they may keep and defend themselves, their wives and children, their country and family, in cases not involving thine own proper cause, which is the Faith. For in such matters thou wishest for no ally but the Catholic Confession and the Keeping of thy Word, and hast forbidden us all arms and defences. For thou art the Almighty, who in thine own affairs, and where thine own cause is called into question, can defend thyself a great deal better than man can conceive. Thou who hast thousands and thousands of hundreds of millions of legions of angels, the least of whom can slay all mankind, and turn the heavens and earth upside down at his pleasure, as was clearly proved of old upon the army of Sennacherib. But if it should please thee at this hour to come to my aid, since in thee alone is my whole trust and hope, I vow unto thee that in every land where I may have power and authority, in this country of Utopia as elsewhere, I will cause thy Holy Gospel to be preached purely, simply, and in its entirety, so that the abuses of that rabble of popelings and false prophets who have by human imaginations and depraved inventions poisoned the whole world shall be exterminated from about me.'

Then a voice was heard from Heaven, saying: '*Hoc fac et vinces*'; that is to say: Do this and you shall win.

Thereupon Pantagruel, seeing Werewolf advancing with open mouth, went boldly against him, shouting at the top of his voice: 'Die, villain. You shall die!', his intention being to frighten him with this horrible cry, according to the practice of the Lacedaemonians. Then from the ship, which he carried on his belt, he threw at him eighteen kegs and one bushel of salt, with which he filled his mouth and throat, his nose and eyes.

Thus provoked, Werewolf aimed a blow at him with his club, meaning to dash in his brains. But Pantagruel was nimble, and had always a quick foot and a keen eye. So he took one step backwards with his left foot. But he could not prevent the blow from falling on the ship, which broke into four thousand and eighty-six pieces, and spilled the rest of the salt on the ground. In view of this, Pantagruel gallantly put forth his strength and, following the science of battle-axe play, dealt him a great thrust with the big end of his mast, above the breast. Then, whipping his weapon to the left, he hit him between the neck and the shoulders. After this, putting out his right foot, he gave him a stab in the ballocks with the upper end of his mast, of which he smashed the top, spilling the three or four puncheons of wine that remained. Whereupon Werewolf thought that he had pierced his bladder, and that the wine was his urine gushing out.

Not content with this, Pantagruel intended to redouble the blow as he disengaged. But, raising his club, Werewolf advanced against him, and prepared to bring it down on Pantagruel with all his might. Indeed, he attacked so violently that if God had not come to the good Pantagruel's aid, he would have been cut open from the top of his head to the base of his spleen. But, thanks to Pantagruel's speed and agility, the blow glanced off to the right, and the club went more than seventy-three feet into the ground, cutting through a huge rock, from which it struck more than nine thousand and six barrel-loads of flame.

Seeing Werewolf engaged in pulling out his same club, which was stuck in the ground, deep in the cleft of the rock, Pantagruel ran at him, intending to strike his head right off. But, by ill-luck, his mast brushed against the handle of Werewolf's club, which was – as we have already said – enchanted; and as a result the mast broke off, three fingers' breadth from the shaft. At this Pantagruel was struck with utter amazement, and shouted: 'Ho, Panurge, where are you?' On hearing his cry, Panurge said to the king and the giants: 'By God, they'll hurt one another, if someone doesn't part them.' But the giants were as happy as if they were at a wedding. Then Carpalim tried to get up and help his master. But one of the giants exclaimed: 'By Gobbler, the nephew of Mahoun, if you stir from here I'll shove you up the bottom of my breeches, like a suppository. For I'm very constipated in the guts, and can scarcely do a crap without grinding my teeth.'

Then Pantagruel, thus bereft of his staff, retrieved the end of his mast, and struck right and left at the giant. But he did him no more harm than you would by flipping your thumb on a blacksmith's anvil. All this time Werewolf was pulling his club out of the ground. Indeed he had already got it out and was preparing to strike Pantagruel with it. But Pantagruel, who was quick in his movements, avoided all his blows, until the moment when, seeing Werewolf threatening him, and crying: 'Villain, I will now chop you into mince-meat. Never again shall you give poor men a thirst,' he kicked him so hard in the belly that he pitched him backwards, with his legs in the air, and dragged him like this, if you please, flaying his bum, for more than an arrow's flight.

Then, spitting blood from his mouth, Werewolf cried: 'Mahoun!

Mahoun! Mahoun!' And at this cry, all the giants rose up to help him. But Panurge said to them: 'Sirs, don't venture in. For, believe me, our master's mad. He's striking out at random, and not looking where his blows fall. He will do you a mischief.' But the giants took no notice of him, seeing that Pantagruel was without his staff.

When Pantagruel saw them approaching, he took Werewolf by both his feet, and raised his body aloft in the air like a pike. Then, it being armoured with anvils, he struck out with it at those giants, who were armoured with freestone, and knocked them down as a mason does stone chips, so that not one of them stood up to him that he did not fling to the ground. Moreover, with the smashing of their stony armour, he made such a horrible clatter, that I was reminded of the time when the great Butter Tower, which once crowned St Stephen's at Bourges, melted in the sun.

Panurge, with Carpalim and Eusthenes, in the meanwhile, cut the throats of all those that were knocked to the ground. You may be perfectly sure that not one escaped. To look at Pantagruel, he seemed like a mower with his scythe – which was Werewolf – cutting down the grass of a meadow – that is the giants. But in this fencing-bout Werewolf lost his head. This was at the point when Pantagruel felled one whose name was Puddingthief, and who was armed cap-a-pie with gritstone, a splinter of which cut right through Epistemon's neck. The greater part of the others were lightly armoured, some with tufa, and others with slate.

Finally, when he saw that they were all dead, Pantagruel threw Werewolf's body as hard as he could on to the city; and it fell like a frog on its belly in the main square of the said city, killing in its fall a singed tom-cat, a wet she-cat, a small bustard, and a bridled goose.

CHAPTER 30: *How Epistemon, who had his Chop headed off, was skilfully healed by Panurge, and some news from the Devils and the Damned*

THIS gigantic discomfiture achieved, Pantagruel retired to the place of the flagons, and called for Panurge and the rest, who all came to him safe and sound, except Eusthenes, whom one of the giants had slightly scratched on the face whilst he was cutting off his head, and

Epistemon, who did not appear at all. Pantagruel was so grieved by this that he longed to kill himself. But Panurge said to him: 'Courage, sir, wait a moment, and we'll look for him among the dead. Then we'll see the truth of the matter.' So as they were searching they found him stone dead, and his head between his arms, all bloody.

Then Eusthenes cried out: 'O wicked death, you have bereft us of the most perfect of men!' At which cry Pantagruel arose with the greatest lamentation that ever was in the world, and said to Panurge: 'Ho, my friend, the augury of your two glasses and the spear-shaft was only too deceptive!' But Panurge answered: 'Don't weep, my lads, not so much as a single tear. He is still quite warm. I'll heal him for you, and he'll be as sound as ever he was.'

Saying this, he took the head and held it over his codpiece, all warm, so that the air should not get to it. Meanwhile, Eusthenes and Carpalim carried the body to the place where they had feasted, not in the hope that he would ever be restored, but so that Pantagruel might see him. Panurge comforted them, nevertheless, saying: 'If I don't heal him, I'm willing to lose my head – which is a fool's wager. – Now stop these tears, and help me.'

Then he thoroughly cleansed the neck with pure white wine, and afterwards the head, and dusted them with dry-dung powder, which he always carried in one of his pockets. Next he greased both with I know not what ointment, and fitted them exactly, vein to vein, nerve to nerve, vertebra to vertebra, so that Epistemon should not be wry-necked – for such people he mortally hated. – This done, he made fifteen or sixteen stitches with a needle all round, so that the head should not fall off again. Then he anointed it with a little of an ointment that he called resuscitative.

Suddenly Epistemon began to breathe, then to open his eyes, then to yawn, then to sneeze, and then he blew a great household fart. Upon which Panurge said: 'Now he is certainly healed', and gave him a glass of strong, rough white wine to drink, together with some sugared toast steeped in wine. In this manner Epistemon was skilfully healed, except that he was hoarse for more than three weeks, and had a dry cough, which he could only get rid of by constant drinking.

And now he began to speak, saying that he had seen the devils, and held intimate conversation with Lucifer, and feasted both in hell and in the Elysian Fields. He swore to them all that the devils were good fellows; and, as for the damned, he said that he was quite sorry that Panurge had called him back to life so promptly. 'For,' said he, 'I was taking a singular pleasure in seeing them.'

'What?' exclaimed Pantagruel.

'They don't treat them as badly as you'd think,' said Epistemon. 'But their way of life is most strangely altered. For I saw Alexander the Great darning breeches for a miserable livelihood.

Xerxes was hawking mustard,
Romulus sold taxed salt,
Numa sold nails,
Tarquin was a miser,
Piso, a peasant,
Sulla, a ferryman,
Cyrus was a cowherd,
Themistocles, a glazier,
Epaminondas, a mirror-maker,
Brutus and Cassius, land-surveyors,
Demosthenes, a vine-dresser,
Cicero, a blacksmith's bellows-man,
Fabius, a threader of rosaries,
Aeneas, a miller,
Achilles had ringworm,
Agamemnon licked the dishes,
Ulysses was a mower,
Nestor, a snatch-thief,
Darius, a cleaner of cesspools,
Ancus Martius, a caulker of ships,
Camillus, a shoemaker,
Marcellus, a bean-sheller,
Drusus, an almond-breaker,
Scipio Africanus hawked lye in a clog,
Hasdrubal was a lantern-maker,
Hannibal, a poulterer,
Priam sold old rags,
Lancelot of the Lake was a flayer of dead horses.

'All the knights of the Round Table were poor starvelings, who tugged an oar on the Rivers Cocytus, Phlegethon, Styx, Acheron, and Lethe, whenever my lords the devils wanted to sport on the water, being just like Lyons boatmen or the gondoliers at Venice. But for every time they crossed they were only paid a flick of the nose, and a bit of mouldy bread in the evening.

Trajan was a fisher of frogs,
Antoninus, a lackey,
Commodus made jet trinkets,
Pertinax was a walnut-peeler,
Lucullus, a turnspit,
Justinian a toymaker,
Hector was a sauce-taster,
Paris was a poor ragged fellow,
Achilles, a hay-trusser,
Cambyses, a muleteer,
Artaxerxes, a pot-scraper,
Nero was a fiddler, and Fierabras his serving-man; but he played his master a thousand tricks, made him eat brown bread and drink sour wine, but himself ate and drank of the best.
Julius Caesar and Pompey were ship-caulkers,
Valentine and Orson stoked the stoves of hell and were mask-snatchers,
Giglain and Gawain were poor swineherds,
Geoffrey of the Long Tooth was a match-seller,
Godfrey of Bouillon, a masker.
Jason was a beadle,
Don Pedro of Castille, a hawker of indulgences,
Morgan, a brewer of beer,
Huon of Bordeaux was a hooper of barrels,
Pyrrhus, a kitchen-scullion,
Antiochus was a chimney-sweep,
Romulus was a patcher of old shoes,
Octavian, a parchment-scraper,
Nerva, a scullion,
Pope Julius, a crier of little pies; but he had left off wearing his great, buggerly beard,
John of Paris was a greaser of boots,
Arthur of Brittany, a cap-cleaner,
Pierceforest, a faggot-porter,
Pope Boniface VIII was a skimmer of pots,

Pope Nicholas III was a paper-maker,
Pope Alexander was a rat-catcher,
Pope Sixtus was an anointer of pox sores.'

'What!' exclaimed Pantagruel, 'are there people with the pox down there?'

'Certainly,' said Epistemon; 'I never saw so many. There are more than a hundred million of them. For, believe me, everyone who hasn't had the pox in this world gets it in the next.'

'God Almighty,' cried Panurge. 'Then I'm quit of it. For I've been as far as the Hole of Gibraltar, and stopped the Pillars of Hercules and brought down some of the ripest fruit!'

'Ogier the Dane was a furbisher of armour,
King Tigranes was a tiler,
Galen Restored, a mole-catcher,
The four sons of Aymon, tooth-extractors,
Pope Calixtus was a cunt-shaver,
Pope Urban, a bacon-chewer,
Melusina was a scullery-maid,
Matabrune, a washerwoman,
Cleopatra, an onion-hawker,
Helen, a placer of chambermaids,
Semiramis, a delouser of beggars,
Dido sold mushrooms,
Penthesilea hawked cress,
Lucretia was a sick-nurse,
Hortensia, a yarn spinner,
Livia, a scraper of verdigris.

Thus did those who had been great lords in this world here gain their poor, miserable, scurvy livelihood down there. On the other hand, the philosophers and those who had been penurious in this world, had their turn at being great lords down below.

'I saw Epictetus, gaily dressed in the French fashion, in a beautiful arbour, frolicking, drinking, dancing, and making all sorts of good cheer, with a number of maidens; and beside him was a pile of gold crown-pieces. Above the trellis these words were written, as his motto:

To drink and dance, to sport and play,
And drink wine, red and white,
With nothing more to do each day
And crowns to count each night.

'When he saw me he courteously invited me to drink with him,
which I gladly did, and we tossed it down like theologians. Meanwhile Cyrus came up to beg a farthing of him, for Mercury's sake, to
buy a few onions for his supper. "No, no," said Epictetus, "I don't
give farthings. Here, you rogue, here's a crown for you, and behave
yourself." Cyrus was very pleased to have struck such booty. But the
other rascally kings down there – Alexander, for instance, and Darius
and others – robbed him that night.

'I saw Patelin, Rhadamanthus's treasurer, bargaining for the little
pies that Pope Julius was hawking. "How much a dozen?" he asked
him. "Threepence," said the Pope. "No," said Patelin. "Three blows
of the cudgel. Give them here, you rogue. Give them here, and go and
fetch some more." And the poor Pope went off weeping, and when
he came to his master the pieman, he told him that he had been robbed
of his pies. Then the pieman whipped him with an eel-skin, so soundly
that his skin would have been worth nothing to make bagpipes
with.

'I saw Master John Lemaire impersonating the Pope, and making
all the poor popes and kings of the underworld kiss his feet. Puffing
himself up, he gave them all his blessing, saying: "Buy pardons, you
rascals, buy pardons. They're very cheap. I absolve you from bread
and soup, and exempt you from ever being good for anything." Then
he called Caillette and Triboulet, saying: "My lords Cardinals, dispatch their bulls for them, one blow of the stick for each, on the
rump." And this was immediately administered.

'I saw Master François Villon asking Xerxes: "How much a pot
of mustard?" "A farthing," said Xerxes. To which the said Villon
replied: "The quartan ague seize you, wretch! Five times the quantity
is only worth half a farthing. You're overcharging us for victuals
down here, aren't you?" Then he pissed into his tub, as mustard-
makers do in Paris.

'I saw the mercenary archer of Baignolet, who was an inquisitor of
heretics. He found Pierceforest pissing against a wall, on which was
painted St Anthony's Fire. He declared him a heretic, and would have

had him burnt alive, had it not been for Morgan, who for his *solatium* and other small fees gave him nine barrels of beer.'

'Now,' said Pantagruel, 'keep us these fine stories for another time. Only tell us how usurers are treated down there.' 'I saw them,' said Epistemon, 'all busy looking for rusty pins and old nails in the gutters of the streets, as you see rascals doing in this world. But a hundred-weight of such old iron is worth no more than a scrap of bread there; and yet there's a very poor supply of it. So the poor misers sometimes go for more than three weeks without eating a crumb or a morsel, and working day and night in anticipation of the fair to come. But they are so accursedly active that they think nothing of all this labour and misery, provided that by the end of the year they have gained a wretched pittance.'

'Come,' said Pantagruel, 'let's have a bit of feasting, and let's drink I beg of you, my lads. It's a good drinking season all this month.'

Then they brought out flagons in piles, and made grand cheer with the camp stores. But poor King Anarch could not make merry. Whereupon Panurge said: 'To what trade shall we put our lord the King here, so that he shall be thoroughly skilled in his art when he goes down there to all the devils?'

'Really,' said Pantagruel, 'that's a good question of yours. Here, do what you like with him. I make you a present of him.'

'Many thanks,' replied Panurge. 'The present's not one to be refused, and I take it kindly from you.'

CHAPTER 31: *How Pantagruel entered the City of the Amaurots; and how Panurge found a Wife for King Anarch, and made him a crier of Green Sauce*

AFTER this marvellous victory Pantagruel sent Carpalim into the Amaurots' city, to proclaim that King Anarch was taken and the enemy utterly defeated. When they heard this news, all the city's inhabitants came out to meet him, in good order; and in great triumphal pomp they most joyfully led him through the gate. Then huge bonfires were lit all about the city, and fine round tables, loaded with plenty of food, were set up in the streets. It was the Golden Age renewed, such good cheer did they make in that place.

But, after assembling all the Senate, Pantagruel said: 'Gentlemen, we must strike whilst the iron is hot. So, before we take further relaxation, it is my wish that we go and capture the whole kingdom of the Dipsodes by storm. Therefore let those who will come with me get ready to-morrow, after drinking, for then I shall begin my march. Not that I need more men to help me conquer it, since I have as good as captured it already. But I see that this city is so full of inhabitants that they can't turn round in the streets. So I shall take them as colonists into Dipsodia, and give them the whole land, which is finer, healthier, more fruitful, and more pleasant than any country in the world, as many of you know who have been there in the past. Let each one of you who wishes to come, be ready as I have said.'

This recommendation and decision was proclaimed all over the city, and next day there appeared in the square before the palace people to the number of eighteen hundred and fifty-six thousand and eleven, not counting the women and small children. So they began to march straight into Dipsodia, in such good order that they were like the Children of Israel when they departed from Egypt to cross the Red Sea.

But before following up this enterprise I want to tell you how Panurge treated his prisoner King Anarch. He remembered what Epistemon had said about the way that kings and rich men of this world are treated in the Elysian Fields, and how they earn their bread there in base and foul occupations. Therefore, one day, he dressed his king in a dainty little canvas doublet, all jagged and slashed like an Albanian's head-dress, and in fine sailor's trousers, though without shoes – for, said he, they would spoil his eye-sight – and in a little blue bonnet, with a great capon's feather – No, I'm wrong. I think there were two feathers in it – and in a fine blue and green (pers et vert) belt; a livery which Panurge said suited him well, seeing that he had been a perverse fellow all his life.

In this condition he led him before Pantagruel, and said to him: 'Do you know this clod?' 'No, indeed,' answered Pantagruel. 'It's His peerless Highness the King. I want to make an honest man of him. But these accursed kings are absolute dolts. They know nothing, and they're good for nothing except harming their poor subjects, and troubling the whole world with wars, for their wicked and detestable pleasure. I mean to put him to a trade, and make him a hawker of

green sauce. Now you, start crying, "D'you want any green sauce" '—
and the poor devil began his cry.

'That's too low,' interrupted Panurge, and took him by the ear,
saying: 'Sing higher in the scale of G. Like this, devil! You've a good
voice. It was your greatest stroke of luck when you stopped being a
king.'

And Pantagruel enjoyed everything. For I am bold enough to say
that he was the best little fellow that ever was for many a yard around.
So Anarch became a good crier of green sauce. Two days afterwards
Panurge married him to an old whore, and himself gave the wedding
feast with fine sheep's heads, rich slices of roast pork with mustard,
and excellent tripe with garlic: of which he sent five mule-loads to
Pantagruel, who ate them all, so tasty did he find them; and he drank
good perry and sorb-apple cider. Now, to give them a dance Panurge
hired a blind man, who made them music on his fiddle, and after
dinner he led them to the palace, to show them to Pantagruel, saying
to him as he pointed to the bride: 'There's no fear of her farting.'
'Why?' asked Pantagruel. 'Because she's well slit,' replied Panurge.
'What riddle is this?' asked Pantagruel. 'Don't you see?' replied
Panurge. 'Well, if the chestnuts you roast at the fire aren't slit, they
crack like mad. So to prevent their cracking you slit them. Well, this
bride is well split underneath. Therefore she won't fart.'

Pantagruel gave them a little lodge near the lower street, and a stone
mortar to pound their sauce on. In this manner they set up their little
household; and he was as pretty a crier of green sauce as ever was seen
in Utopia. But I have been told since that his wife pounds him like
plaster; and the poor fool dares not defend himself, he is so simple.

CHAPTER 32: *How Pantagruel covered a whole Army with his
Tongue, and what the Author saw in his Mouth*

So when Pantagruel with all his company entered the land of the
Dipsodes everyone was delighted, and immediately surrendered to
him. Of their own free will they brought him the keys of all the towns
where he went; except the Almyrods, who tried to hold out against
him, and replied to his heralds that they would not surrender except
on good terms.

'What,' exclaimed Pantagruel, 'do they ask for better terms than hand on pot and glass in fist? Come, let's put them to the sack.' Then all lined up in their ranks, as if resolved to deliver an attack. But on the way, as they were passing over a great plain, they were overtaken by a huge storm of rain. Whereupon they began to shiver and bunch close together. When he saw this, Pantagruel sent them a message by his captains that it was nothing. For he could see above the clouds that it would be no more than a little dew. But anyhow, they must put themselves in good order, and he would cover them. So they drew themselves up in good order, and close together; and Pantagruel, putting his tongue only half out, covered them as a hen does her chickens.

Meanwhile I, who am telling you this most authentic tale, had hidden myself under a burdock leaf, which was quite as wide as the arch of the Bridge of Monstrible. But when I saw them so well protected I went off to shelter with them. This I could not do, there were so many of them. For, as the saying goes, At the yard's end there's no cloth left. So I clambered on his tongue as best I could, and travelled for quite six miles over it before I came to his mouth. But, oh ye gods and goddesses, what did I see there? Jupiter confound me with his three-forked lightning if I lie. I walked over it as one does in Santa Sophia at Constantinople, and there I saw huge rocks like the Dental Mountains – I think they must have been his teeth – and large meadows, wide forests and great, strong cities, every bit as large as Lyons or Poitiers. The first man I met was a good fellow planting cabbages, and in my amazement I asked him: 'What are you doing here, my friend?' 'I'm planting cabbages,' he said. 'But how and what for?' I asked. 'Ah, sir,' said he: 'not everyone can have his ballocks as heavy as a mortar, and we can't all be rich. I earn my living this way, and take them to sell in the market, in the city, which is further in here.' 'Jesus!' I said. 'Is there a new world here?' 'Of course,' said he. 'But it isn't in the least new. They do say, indeed, that outside there is a new earth, where they have both Sun and Moon, and that it's packed full of fine things. But this one here is the older.' 'Oh yes,' said I. 'But, my friend, what's the name of this town where you take your cabbages to sell?' 'It's called Gullettown,' said he, 'and they're Christians there, excellent people who'll give you a good welcome.' To be brief, I decided to go there.

Now on the road I met a fellow who was setting nets for pigeons, and I asked him: 'My friend, where do these pigeons of yours come from?' 'Sir,' said he, 'they come from the other world.' Then it occurred to me that when Pantagruel yawned the pigeons flew into his mouth in great flocks, thinking it was a dovecot.

After that I went into the town, which I found a fine one, very strong and in a good climate. But at the gate the keepers asked me for my bill of health, at which I was greatly astonished and asked them: 'Sirs, is there risk of the plague here?' 'Oh, my lord,' said they. 'They die so fast not far away that the cart's always running about the streets.' 'Good God,' said I, 'and where?' They answered me that it was in Larynx and Pharynx, which are two large cities like Rouen and Nantes, rich places with a great trade. And the cause of the plague was a stinking and infectious exhalation, which had recently been rising from the abyss, and of which more than twenty-two hundred and sixty thousand and sixteen people had died in the last eight days. Then I considered and calculated, and decided that it was a rank breath which had been coming from Pantagruel's stomach, since he ate so much garlic sauce, as has been mentioned above.

Departing from there, I passed between the rocks, which were his teeth, and went so far as to climb one. And there I found the most beautiful spots in the whole world, fine great tennis-courts, magnificent galleries, beautiful meadows, plenty of vines, and an abundance of summer-houses in the Italian fashion, scattered through fields full of delights. And there I stayed for quite four months, and never enjoyed myself as much as I did then.

After that I went down by the back teeth and arrived at the lips. But on the way I was robbed by brigands in a great forest, which lies in the region of the ears. I found a little village on the way down – I have forgotten its name – where I was better entertained than ever, and earned a little money to live on. Do you know how? By sleeping. For there they hire men by the day as sleepers, and you earn five or six halfpence a time. But those who snore very loud are paid a good seven and a half. I informed the senators there how I had been robbed on the way down, and they told me that the people on that side were evil-livers and robbers by nature. Which taught me that just as we have countries Cismontane and Ultramontane, so they have them Cisdentine and Ultradentine. But it is a great deal better on the first-named side, and the air is purer.

There I began to think how true the saying is that one half of the world doesn't know how the other half lives, seeing that no one had ever written about those countries, in which there are more than twenty-five inhabited kingdoms, not counting the deserts and a broad arm of the sea. But I have made up a great book entitled the *History of the Gorgians*. For that is what I have called them, since they live in my master Pantagruel's gorge.

In the end I decided to return and, passing by his beard, jumped on to his shoulders, from which I slid down to the ground and fell in front of him.

When he noticed me, he asked: 'Where have you come from, Alco-fribas?' 'From your throat, my lord,' I replied. 'And since when were you there?' said he. 'Since the time when you went against the Almy-rods,' said I. 'That's more than six months ago,' said he. 'And what did you live on? What did you drink?' 'My lord,' I replied, 'the same fare as you. I took toll of the tastiest morsels that went down your throat.' 'Indeed,' said he, 'and where did you shit?' 'In your throat, my lord,' said I. 'Ha, ha. You're a fine fellow,' said he. 'We have, by God's help, conquered the whole country of the Dipsodes. I confer on you the Wardenship of Salmagundia.' 'Many thanks, my lord,' said I. 'You reward me beyond my deserts.'

CHAPTER 33: *How Pantagruel fell ill, and the Method of his Cure*

A SHORT time after this the good Pantagruel fell ill, and was so afflicted in his stomach that he could neither eat nor drink. Also, since misfortunes never come singly, he was taken with a hot-piss, which pained him more than you might imagine. But his doctors came to his aid, and most successfully. For with plenty of lenitive and diuretic drugs they made him piss his complaint away. But his piss was so hot that it has not grown cold since that day, and you will find some of it in different places, in France, according to where it flowed. These are called hot baths, as at Cauterets, at Limons, at Dax, at Balaruc, at Néris, at Bourbon-Lancy and elsewhere; and in Italy at Monte Grotto, at Abano, at San Pietro Montagnone, at Sant' Elena Battaglia, at Casanova, at San Bartolommeo, at La Porretta, in the province of Bologna, and in a thousand other places.

And I am greatly astonished at the crowd of foolish philosophers and doctors who waste time disputing where the heat of these waters comes from, whether it is because of the borax, or the sulphur, or the alum, or the saltpetre which the minerals contain. For they are only rambling, and they would do better to go and rub their rumps against a thistle than waste their time like this, disputing about something they do not know the origin of. For the answer is easy, and there is no need to make further inquiry. These baths are hot because they arose from a hot piss by the good Pantagruel.

Now to tell you how he was cured of his principal ailment, I will record here how he took as a laxative, four hundredweight of scammony from Colophon, a hundred and thirty-eight cart-loads of cassia, and eleven thousand nine hundred pounds of rhubarb, not to count other messes.

You must understand that, on the advice of his physicians, it was decided that what caused him his stomach-ache should be removed. Therefore they made seventeen great copper balls, larger than the one on Virgil's needle at Rome, and so contrived that they opened in the middle and closed with a spring. Into one of them climbed one of his men, carrying a lantern with a lighted wick; and Pantagruel swallowed him in this way like a little pill. Into five others went other stout fellows, each carrying a pick at his neck; into three more went three peasants, each carrying at his neck a shovel, and into seven others went seven faggot-porters, each with a basket on his shoulders. And thus they were all swallowed as pills.

When they were in the stomach each released his spring, and they came out of their cabins, the man who carried the lantern first. Thereupon they tumbled more than half a league into a horrible gulf, fouler and more stinking than Mephitis, or the marsh of Camarina, or the fetid Sorbonian lake of which Strabo writes; and had it not been that they were well protected in the heart, stomach, and wine-pot (which is called the cranium), they would have been suffocated and destroyed by these abominable vapours. Oh what a perfume, what effluvia to soil the dainty masks of young and elegant maidens!

Afterwards, by groping and sniffing, they drew near to the fecal matter and the corrupted humours; and finally they found a mound of ordure. Then the pioneers picked at it to break it down, and the others piled it into their baskets with their shovels. Then, when it was all cleared away, each one retired into his ball. This done, Pantagruel forced himself to vomit, and easily threw them up; they were no more considerable in his throat than a gurk in yours. Then they came out of their pills most joyfully – I was reminded of the Greeks emerging from the Trojan Horse – and in this way Pantagruel was cured, and restored to his former good health.

And of these brazen pills you have one at Orléans, on the steeple of the Church of the Holy Cross.

CHAPTER 34: *The Conclusion of the Present Book, and the Author's Excuse*

Now, Gentlemen, you have heard a beginning of the horrific history of my lord and master, Pantagruel, and here I will make an end of this present book. For I have a slight headache, and I clearly see that the registers of my brain are somewhat confused by this new September wine. You will have the rest of the story at the very next Frankfort book-fair, when you will learn how Panurge was married, and cuckolded within a month of his wedding; how Pantagruel found the Philosopher's Stone, together with the manner of his finding it and using it; also how he crossed the Caspian Mountains, how he sailed across the Atlantic Sea, how he defeated the cannibals and conquered the Perlas Islands; how he married the daughter of the King of India, Prester John; how he fought against the devils, set five chambers of hell on fire, sacked the great black hall, threw Proserpine into the flames, and broke four of Lucifer's teeth, also one horn on his rump; and how he visited the regions of the moon, to find out whether that orb would not be whole but for the fact that women have three-quarters of it in their heads; together with a thousand other little jests, all of them true. These are fine matters. So good-night, gentlemen. *Perdonate mi,*[1] and do not dwell so much on my faults as not to give good thought to your own.

If you say to me: 'It does not seem very wise of you to have written down all this gay and empty balderdash for us,' I would reply that you do not show yourselves much wiser by taking pleasure in the reading of it. Still, if you read it as I wrote it, for mere amusement,

1. Pardon me. (Italian.)

we are both more deserving of forgiveness than that great rabble of false-cenobites, hooded cheats, sluggards, hypocrites, canters, thumpers, monks in boots, and other such sects of people, who have disguised themselves like maskers, to deceive the world. For while they give the common folk to understand that they are only occupied in contemplation and devotions, in fasts and the mortification of the flesh, except in so far as it is necessary to sustain and nourish their slight and frail human natures, in reality they live very well – God knows how well!

Et Curios simulant, sed bacchanalia vivunt
They pretend to be as austere as Curius, but live in bacchic riot

as you may read, written in great characters, illuminated on their red noses and their protuberant bellies, except at such times as they perfume themselves with sulphur. As for their studies, they are entirely devoted to the reading of the Pantagrueline books, not so much for a merry pastime, but for the purpose of doing someone a wicked mischief, by means of articulating, monarticulating, wry-neckifying, buttocking, ballocking, and diabolicating – that is to say calumniating him. In this they resemble those village ragamuffins who snuffle and rake through little children's shit when cherries are in season, black and white, in order to find the stones and sell them to the druggists, who make them into pomander oil.

Fly from these men, abhor them, and hate them as much as I do, and I swear to you that you will find yourselves the better for it. If you want to be good Pantagruelists, moreover – that is to say to live in peace, joy, and health, always making good cheer – never trust in men who peer from under a cowl.

End of the Chronicles of Pantagruel, King of the Dipsodes,
drawn in their natural colours, with his terrible
deeds and exploits, composed by the
late MASTER ALCOFRIBAS,
abstractor of the quint-
essence

THE THIRD BOOK

OF THE HEROIC DEEDS AND SAYINGS OF

THE GOOD PANTAGRUEL

COMPOSED BY

François Rabelais
DOCTOR OF MEDICINE

REVISED AND CORRECTED BY THE AUTHOR TO
COMPLY WITH FORMER CRITICISMS

*The aforesaid author beseeches his kindly readers
to reserve their laughter till the
Seventy-eighth Book*

FRANÇOIS RABELAIS

TO THE SPIRIT OF THE QUEEN OF NAVARRE

Abstracted soul, ravished in ecstasy,
Returned now to thy home, the Firmament,
Leaving thy body, formed in harmony,
Thy host and servant, once obedient
To thy commands in this life transient,
Wouldst thou not care to quit, just fleetingly,
Thy heavenly mansion and perpetual,
And here below for the third time to see
The jovial deeds of good Pantagruel?

PROLOGUE OF THE AUTHOR

MASTER FRANÇOIS RABELAIS
TO THE THIRD BOOK OF THE HEROIC DEEDS AND
SAYINGS OF THE GOOD PANTAGRUEL

GOOD people, most illustrious boozers, and you thrice precious and gouty sirs, did you ever see Diogenes, the cynic philosopher? If you did see him, then your vision was as keen as ever; or I am devoid of all intelligence and logic. It is a fine sight to see the glint of wine and twinkling gold – of the sun, I mean. I call the man born blind as my witness, that renowned figure in Holy Scriptures who, when Almighty God, whose words are instantaneously transformed into deeds, gave him the choice of any wish in the world, asked only for the gift of sight.

Now you are not young; and so you are equipped to philosophize – vinously and not vainly, and therefore metaphysically – and so to be raised at once to the Bacchic Council, where by tasting you may test the substance, colour, odour, excellence, eminence, property, faculty, virtues, effect, and value of the said blessed and coveted liquor.

If you have not seen Diogenes – and I should not take much persuading that you have not – you have at least heard some talk of him. For the whole sky and the air have rung with his fame, and his name has remained memorable and famous till this day. Besides, you are all descended from the blood of Phrygia – or I am much mistaken – and if you have not as many crowns as Midas had, you have something else which he had, something which the ancient Persians valued most highly in their spies and which the Emperor Antoninus required his servants to possess: a something from which the basilisk of Rohan, in after times, derived its surname of Fine Ears.

If you have never heard of Diogenes, I will tell you a story about him presently, while we start on the wine – Drink up, my boys – and I start my argument. Now listen to me! But first let me inform you – in case, in your simplicity, you are deceived, like so many infidels – that in his day he was a rare philosopher and the cheerfullest among a thousand. If he had certain imperfections, so have you, so have we all, for none but God is perfect. Nevertheless Alexander the Great, though he had Aristotle for his tutor and servant, held him in such esteem that if he had not been Alexander he would have wished to be Diogenes of Sinope.

When Philip, King of Macedon, undertook the siege and destruction of Corinth, the Corinthians were warned by their spies of the grand array and the huge forces that he was leading against them. So they were all, not unreasonably, afraid, and neglected no precautions. Each man scrupulously performed his tasks and duties, in the hopes of beating off this hostile attack and protecting the city. Some brought movables, cattle, corn, wine, fruit, victuals, and all necessary supplies out of the fields and into the fortress. Others repaired the walls, erected bastions, squared ravelins, dug ditches, repaired countermines, improvised parapets, constructed platforms, emptied gun-pits, repaired outer ramparts, built look-out points, re-dug counterscarps, cemented curtain walls, set up sniping posts, sloped parapets, mortised barbicans, strengthened battlements, fitted fresh chains to the portcullises – both Greek and Saracenic – posted sentries, and sent out patrols. Everyone was on the watch, everyone took his part. Some polished corselets, varnished back and breast-plates, cleaned housings, front-stalls, habergeons, jackets of mail, sallets, beavers, knights' head-pieces, double-pikes, closed helmets, morions, coats of mail, chain armour, arm-pieces, thigh-pieces, gussets, gorgets, arm- and thigh-plates, breast-pieces, scale-armour, hawberks, shields, bucklers, leggings, greaves, foot-pieces, and spurs. Others prepared bows, slings, arbalests, sling-shot, catapults, fire-arrows, grenades, fire-pots, balls and brands, ballistas, scorpions, and other hideous engines of war, calculated to destroy the enemy's siege-towers. They sharpened scythes, pikes, claws, halberds, brown-bills, long hooks, lances, Turkish spears, tridents, partisans, clubs, battle-axes, darts, dartlets, javelins, great javelins, and boar-spears. They put an edge on scimitars, cutlasses, curved blades, spears, sabres, short swords, tucks, stilettos, stabbing-swords, daggers, mandousians, poniards, knives, blades, and barbs. Every man practised with his weapon, every man scoured the rust from his hanger. Even the oldest and most prudish of the women furbished up her harness; for, as you know, Corinthian women of old had plenty of courage in battle.

Now when Diogenes saw them all so warm at work and himself assigned no duties by the magistrates, he watched their behaviour for some days in complete silence. Then, as if spurred by the martial spirit, he slung his cloak across his chest, rolled his sleeves up to his elbows, trussed himself up like an apple-gatherer, handed his wallet to an old comrade of his, together with his books and double-sided scrolls, and made off out of the town towards Cranium, which is a jutting hill not far from Corinth, and a fine look-out place. Thither he rolled his earthen tub, which served him as a shelter against the

PROLOGUE OF THE AUTHOR

inclemencies of the weather; and putting out all his strength, in a tremendous outburst of spirits, he twirled it, whirled it, scrambled it, bungled it, frisked it, jumbled it, tumbled it, wheedled it, scratched it, stroked it, churned it, beat it, bumped it, banged it, battered it, up-ended it, tempered it, tapped it, stamped it, stopped it, unstopped it, shifted it, shook it, thumped it, pummelled it, waggled it, hurled it, teased it, staggered it, tottered it, raised it, rinsed it, nailed it, tethered it, veered it, steered it, stuffed it, bustled it, lifted it, soiled it, tackled it, shackled it, mocked it, spiked it, patted it, plaited it, fondled it, fumbled it, dashed it, splashed it, crashed it, slashed it, planed it, charmed it, armed it, speared it, harnessed it, pennoned it, caparisoned it, rolled it from top to bottom of the hill, and precipitated it from the Cranium. Then he rolled it uphill again, as Sisyphus did his stone, so violently that he almost knocked the bottom out of it.

At the sight of this activity one of his friends asked him what moved him thus to torment his body, his spirit, and his tub. To which the philosopher replied that, not being entrusted with any other duties by the State, he was giving his tub a thrashing in order not to seem the one lazy idler among a people so feverishly busy. In the same way, although I have nothing to fear, I am still not unperturbed at finding myself counted unworthy of employment, whereas throughout the whole of this most noble kingdom of France, on both sides of the Alps, I see everyone to-day busily and earnestly working, some at the fortification and defence of their country, some in repelling the enemy, and some in attacking them: and all this under such excellent direction, so admirably ordered and with such a clear view to future advantages — for the frontiers of France will soon be magnificently extended, and our people rest in peace and security. I can almost subscribe, therefore, to the opinion of the excellent Heraclitus, to the effect that war is the father of all good things. Indeed, I believe that war is called Bellum *(a fine thing) in Latin, not out of antithesis, as certain botchers of old Latin tags have believed, because they saw but little beauty in war, but positively and literally, because in war every kind of beauty and virtue shines out, every kind of evil and ugliness is abolished. I will give you another proof. That wise and pacific king, Solomon, knew no better way of expressing the ineffable perfection of divine wisdom than by comparing it to an army with banners.*

I have been considered too weak and impotent to be enrolled in our country's attacking force, and have not been employed by its other, defensive army, even as a carrier of hods, a bender of rods, or a cutter of sods — I should not have cared which. But I have felt it to be most disgraceful to stand idly watch-

ing all these valorous, eloquent, and warlike persons who are performing their noble interlude and tragi-comedy before the watching eyes of all Europe. I have been ashamed not to exert myself, not to contribute that nothing, which is all that I have left, my all. For I think that little glory accrues to those who only employ their eyes in this exploit, but are sparing of their strength, conceal their crowns, and hide their small-change, scratch their heads with one finger like bored sluggards, gape at flies like the parson's calves, prick up their ears like asses in Arcady to the tune of the music, and silently show by their countenances that they approve of the performance.

Having made my choice, having made up my mind, I decided that I should perform no useless or tiresome role if I were to tumble my Diogenic tub, which is all that is left to me from the shipwreck of my past in the Straits of Misfortune. Now, how do you advise me to set about my tub-rumbling? By the Virgin who ups her skirts, I do not yet know. Wait a little, till I've swallowed a draught from this bottle. It is my true and only Helicon, my one Pegasus spring, my sole enthusiasm. As I drink I here deliberate, discourse, resolve, and conclude. After the epilogue I laugh, write, compose, and drink again. Ennius wrote as he drank, drank as he wrote. Aeschylus, if you put any trust in Plutarch's Symposiacs, used to drink as he composed, to compose as he drank. Homer never wrote on an empty stomach, Cato never wrote except after drinking. So do not say that I am not following the example of good and praiseworthy men. It is fine fresh stuff, as you might say, entering into its second, or rarified state. God, the good lord Sabaoth – that is to say, the Lord of Hosts – be eternally praised for it! So if at the same time the rest of you will take one large or two little gulps under your hoods, I can see no objection, providing that you give God a pinch of thanks for it.

So since this is my lot or my destiny – for it is not granted to everyone to go and live in Corinth – I am resolved to serve both attackers and defenders. For I will not stand by as a useless idler. Amongst the diggers, pioneers, and engineers, I will do what Neptune and Apollo did under Laomedon in Troy, what Renaud of Montauban did in his latter days. I will help the masons, I will set the pot boiling for them, and when the meal is finished I will measure the musings of the bemused with the music of my little pipe. Even so did Amphion found, build, and complete the great and celebrated city of Thebes, to the sound of his lyre.

For the benefit of the warriors I am about to rebroach my cask, the contents of which you would have sufficiently appreciated from my two earlier volumes if they had not been adulterated and spoiled by dishonest printers. I am about to draw for them, out of the product of our after-dinner entertainments, a gallant third draught – and later a jovial fourth – of Pantagrueline Sentences. You have licence from me to call them Diogenical. So, though I cannot be their companion in arms, they shall have me as their faithful steward, cheering them to the best of my small powers on their return from the fray, and as the eulogist, the indefatigable eulogist, of their brave and glorious feats of arms. I shall not fail in this, by God's flower of patience, unless Mars fails in Lent; and he will take good care not to do that, the lecher.

At this point I remember reading how one day Ptolemy, the son of Lagus, in the crowded theatre, among other spoils and booty from his conquests, presented the Egyptians with a completely black Bactrian camel, and a slave parti-coloured in such a way that one portion of his body was black and the other white. He was not, by the way, divided horizontally at the diaphragm, like that female votary of the Indian Venus, who was seen by the philosopher of Tyana somewhere between the Hydaspes and Mount Caucasus, but perpendicularly. Such phenomena had never yet been seen in Egypt, and Ptolemy hoped that by offering the people these rarities he would increase their love for himself. But what was the result? At the appearance of the camel they were all frightened and indignant; at the sight of the parti-coloured man, some mocked and others were shocked by what they considered a loathsome monster, created by an error of Nature. In short, his hopes of pleasing his Egyptians, and in this way increasing their natural affection for him, slipped through his fingers. He discovered that they took more pleasure and delight in the handsome, the elegant, and the perfect than in ridiculous and monstrous objects. After this he had a very poor opinion of the slave and the camel; so poor indeed that soon afterwards, owing to neglect and lack of common sustenance, they exchanged life for death.

This example sets me wavering between hope and fear, uncertain whether I may not meet with an unpleasant reception instead of the appreciation I expect; whether my treasure may not be coals, and I may not throw a blank instead of the double-six. Instead of doing them a service I may offend them; instead of amusing them annoy them, instead of pleasing them displease them. Mine may be the fate of Euclio's cock, so celebrated by Plautus in his Pot, by Ausonius in his Gryphus, and elsewhere: the creature that discovered the treasure with his scratching and had his throat cut for his pains. Would it not be distressing if that were to happen to me? Such a thing has happened before; it could easily happen again. But I swear by Hercules that it will not!

For in every soldier I detect that specific trait and individual quality which our ancestors used to call Pantagruelism; which assures me that they will never take in bad part anything that they know to spring from a good, honest, and loyal heart. I have so often seen them take the will for the payment, and be content with it, when that was all the debtor had.

With this point settled, I return to my cask. Up, lads, and to the wine! Gulp it down, my boys, in brimming cups. Or, if you do not like it, leave it alone. I am not one of your tiresome Germans, who make their comrades drink – and what's worse, to carouse and trink allaus – by brute force and violence. Every honest boozer, every decent gouty gentleman, everyone who is dry, may come to this barrel of mine, but need drink only if he wishes. If they wish, and the wine is to the taste of their worshipful worships, let them drink frankly, freely, and boldly without stint or payment. Such is my statute; and have no fear that the wine will give out, as it did at the marriage at Cana in Galilee. As much as you draw out at the tap, I will pour in at the bung. In this way the cask will remain inexhaustible, endowed with a living spring and a perpetual flow. So my liquor shall be like that within the cup of Tantalus, which the Brahmin sages represented figuratively; like the mountain of salt in Iberia, so celebrated by Cato; like the sacred golden bough, dedicated to the goddess of the underworld, so celebrated by Virgil. It is a true cornucopia of ridicule and fun; and if at times it seems to you to be emptied to the lees, still it will not be dry. As in Pandora's jug, good hope lies at the bottom, not despair, as in the Danaids' tub.

Take good note of what I have said, and of what manner of people I invite. For to avoid any deception I will imitate Lucilius. He stated that he wrote only for his Tarentines and Calabrians, and I proclaim that I have broached my cask only for you sound fellows, drinkers of prime vintage and sufferers from gout in your own right. Those great legal bribemongers who rise with the mists to catch the early fee will find enough game in their brief-bags, enough business in their own privies. Let them smell round it if they like, this is no booty for them. As for those high-hatted pettifoggers who are always on the look-out for mistakes, do not mention them to me, I beg of you, by the reverence you bear to the four buttocks that engendered you and the life-giving peg which at that moment united them. As for the breed of pious hypocrites, do not speak to me of them either, though they are all outrageous drinkers, all scurvy and poxy, all possessed of an inexhaustible thirst and insatiable powers of mastication. And why not? Because they are not of good, but of evil – and of that evil from which we daily pray God to deliver us –

even though sometimes they pretend to be poor in spirit. Never did an old ape make pretty faces. Down, curs! Out of my way! Out of my sunlight! Cowls, to the devil with you! So you have come here, wagging your tails, to sniff at my wine, and piss on my barrel, have you? See, here is the stick that Diogenes willed should be placed near him after his death, to drive off and break the backs of all such graveyard ghouls and Cerberian hell-hounds.

Get packing, you hypocrites! To your sheep, you dogs! Clear out of here, you canting cheats! To the devil with you! What, are you still there? I'll renounce my share in Papimania if I can get my teeth into you. Gzz, gzzz, gzzzz! Off with you! Off with you! Are they not gone yet? May you never manage a shit without being lashed with stirrup leathers, may you never squeeze out a piddle without being strappadoed, and may your body never be warmed except by a good hiding!

CHAPTER I: *How Pantagruel transported a Colony of Utopians into Dipsodia*

AFTER having completely conquered the land of Dipsodia, Pantagruel transported there a colony of Utopians to the number of 9876543210 men, not counting the women and small children. These included artisans of all trades and professors of all the liberal sciences, and were intended to restore the people, and cultivate and improve that country, which had till then been thinly inhabited and largely a desert. His principal reason for this colonization was not the over-population of Utopia, though the Utopians bred like rabbits. You know that well enough. There is no need to explain how their organs of reproduction were so fertile and their women's wombs so ample, greedy, retentive, and architecturally cellulated that at the end of every ninth month seven children, at the least, male and female, were born to each marriage – and in this they were like the Children of Israel in Egypt, if de Lyra was not delirious when he wrote his commentary. Nor was his principal reason the fertility of the soil, the wholesomeness of the air, and the amenities of the land of Dipsodia. His purpose was simply to keep the Dipsodians to their duty and obedience by this importation of his ancient and loyal subjects, who from time immemorial had known, acknowledged, and owned no other lord, nor served any but him; who from the time of their birth and entry into this world had imbibed the sweetness and mildness of his rule with their mother's milk, and were reared and nourished in it. This gave him an assured hope that they would sooner renounce the life of the body than swerve from the exclusive and primitive obedience naturally due to their prince, never mind to what place they might be scattered or removed. It made him confident that not only would they and the successive generations born of their blood remain thus submissive, but that they would also keep the peoples newly joined to his empire similarly loyal and obedient. So, indeed, it turned out, and he was not at all disappointed in his plan. For if the Utopians had been loyal and dutiful before their transportation, the Dipsodes, after a few days of their society, were even more so, thanks to some kind of enthusiasm common to all human beings at the beginning of enterprises which are to their liking. Their only complaint was – as they called all the heavens and guardians of the spheres to witness – that the good Pantagruel's renown had not come to their ears before.

So here, my dear boozers, please take note, that the way of preserving and retaining newly conquered countries is not – as has been the erroneous opinion of certain tyrannical spirits, to their own hurt and dishonour – to pillage, distress, torment, ruin, and persecute the people, ruling them with a rod of iron; in fact to devour and consume them after the fashion of that wicked king whom Homer calls the Demovore, that is to say Devourer of his People. In this connexion I will not quote you examples from the ancient histories, but will merely remind you of what your fathers have seen – and yourselves too, if you are not too young. Newly conquered peoples have to be suckled, cradled, and dandled, like new-born children. Like freshly planted trees, they have to be propped, supported, and protected from all disasters, damage, and calamities. Like men recovering from a long and severe illness and returning to convalescence, they must be indulged, pampered, and restored to life. In this way they will eventually be convinced that there is no king or prince in the world whom they would less desire to have for an enemy, whom they would rather have for a friend. Thus Osiris, the great king of the Egyptians, subdued the whole earth not so much by force of arms, as by easing the peoples of their burdens, by instructing them in the good and healthy life, by suitable laws, by graciousness, and by favours. Therefore he was called by mankind the great king Euergetes – that is to say the benefactor – this in fulfilment of Jupiter's prophecy, given to a woman named Pamyla.

Indeed, Hesiod in his hierarchy places the good demons – call them angels or geniuses, if you will – as mediators, half-way between gods and men, superior to mankind but inferior to the gods; and because the riches and favours of heaven come to us from their hands because they are continually doing us good and always preserving us from harm, he says that they are in the position of kings; since always to do good, and never evil, is an act exclusively royal.

Just such another was that Emperor of the Universe, Alexander of Macedon. In just such a way did Hercules gain possession of the whole continent, by relieving mankind of monsters, oppressions, exactions, and tyrannies, by governing them with kindness, by providing them with equity and justice, by instituting kindly government and laws suitable to the condition of each country, by supplying men with what they lacked, by removing what was superfluous and pardoning all the past, with a perpetual oblivion for previous offences. Another example is the Athenians' amnesty, after the tyrants were exterminated by the prowess and energy of Thrasybulus. This was later cited by Cicero at Rome, and imitated under the emperor Aurelian.

These are the love-philtres, charms, and incitements by which a man peacefully retains what he has painfully acquired. The conqueror cannot reign more happily, be he king, prince, or philosopher, than by making justice second his valour. His valour has been shown in his victory and conquest; his justice will appear in his giving of laws, publishing of edicts, establishing of religions, and doing right to everyone – all this with the goodwill and affection of his people. As the noble poet Maro said of Octavian Caesar:

> The conqueror who won with the goodwill
> Of those he conquered, made his laws prevail.

That is why Homer, in his *Iliad*, calls the good princes and great kings Κοσμήτορας Λαῶν, that is to say Adorners of the People.

Such was the reflection of Numa Pompilius, second king of the Romans, a just politician and philosopher, when he ordained that nothing that had suffered death should be sacrificed to the god Terminus on the day of his festival, called the Terminales. By this he taught us in his own way that the boundaries, frontiers, and dependencies of kingdoms should be kept guarded in peace, amity, and gentleness, without the staining of hands in pillage and blood. Whoever acts otherwise will not only lose what he has gained, but also incur the disgraceful reputation of having acquired it by wicked and unjust means, since all that he has won has fallen to pieces in his hands. For ill-acquired gains split violently apart; and even if he has enjoyed the peaceful enjoyment of his conquests for the whole of his life, should they fall apart in the hands of his heirs the same reproach will fall on him after his death. The ignominy of an unjust conqueror will hang about his money. For, as the common proverb runs: Ill-gotten gains die with the grandson.

Take note also, under this head, you who enjoy gout by right of descent, how in this way Pantagruel made two angels out of one, which is the opposite idea to Charlemagne's, who out of one devil made two, when he transplanted the Saxons into Flanders and the Flemings into Saxony. For being unable to keep the Saxons, whom he had added to his empire, in subjection, or to prevent their breaking into rebellion at any such moment as he was drawn away into Spain or some other distant territory, he transplanted them into his own country which gave him natural obedience, into Flanders, that is; and transplanted the Hainaulters and Flemings, his natural subjects, into Saxony, not doubting their loyalty even when settled in a strange land. But, as it turned out, the Saxons maintained their rebellion and were as obstinate as ever, and the Flemings dwelling in Saxony imbibed the manners and aped the perversities of the Saxons.

CHAPTER 2: *How Panurge was made Warden of Salmagundia in Dipsodia, and ate his Wheat in the Blade*

IN giving orders for the government of all Dipsodia, Pantagruel assigned the Wardenship of Salmagundia to Panurge. This office was worth 6789106789 gold reals in fixed revenue, not counting the variable income from cockchafers and snails, which amounted, taking the good years with the bad, to from 2435768 to 2435769 Agnus Dei crowns of France. On occasions it amounted to 1234554321 seraphs, when it was a good year for snails and cockchafers were in request. But that was not every year; and the new warden managed his affairs so well and prudently that in less than a fortnight he had squandered the whole income of his wardenship, both fixed and variable, for the next three years. He did not squander it, properly speaking, in such enterprises as founding monasteries, erecting churches, building colleges and hospitals, or throwing his bacon to the dogs. But he spent it on a thousand little banquets and jolly feasts, open to all comers, especially to all who were good company, all young girls and pretty wenches; on felling his timber and burning the great trunks to sell the ashes; on taking money in advance, buying dear, selling cheap, and eating his wheat in the blade.

When Pantagruel heard this news he was not in any way indignant, angry, or perturbed. For, as I have already told you, and I tell you once more, he was the best little great good fellow that ever wore a sword. He took everything in good part, put favourable interpretation on every act, never tormented himself, and was never scandalized. Indeed he would have strayed many miles from the divine Palace of Reason, if he had been in any way grieved or afflicted. For all the wealth that the sky covers and earth contains in all its dimensions – height, depth, length, and breadth – is not worth so much that we should upset our affections, or trouble our sense and spirits for it.

He merely took Panurge aside, and mildly pointed out to him that if he wished to live in this style and not alter his way of house-keeping, it would be impossible, or at least very difficult, ever to make him rich.

'Rich?' replied Panurge. 'Had you set your heart on that? Did you really mean to make me rich in *this* world? Set your heart on a merry life, in the name of God and all good men! Don't allow any other care or thought into the sacrosanct domicile of your celestial brain. Never trouble its serenity with any clouds of thought, with their borders of pain and vexation. So long as you're alive, and jolly, sprightly and merry, I shall be more than rich. All the world cries: "Thrift! thrift!" But some who talk of thrift know nothing at all about it. They ought to consult me. And now I should like to inform you that what you call a vice in me I have imitated from the University and High Court of Paris: places in which you will find the true source and living image of Pantheology – and of all justice too. Anyone who doubts this, anyone who does not firmly believe it, is a heretic. Why, in one day they consume their bishop, or the revenue of his see – it's all one – for a whole year, even sometimes for two. That is on the day of his installation, and he has no chance of avoiding it unless he wishes to be stoned on the spot.

'My behaviour has also been based on the four cardinal virtues: on *Prudence*, in taking money in advance, for one never knows who will die or kick the bucket. Who can tell whether the world will last another three years? And supposing it were to last longer, is any man such a fool as to dare promise himself three years of life?

> Man never found the deities so kindly
> As to assure him that he'd live to-morrow.

'On *Justice commutative*, in buying dear – I mean on credit – and selling cheap – that is for cash. What does Cato say on this point in his Book of Husbandry? The father of a family, he says, must be a perpetual seller. In this way he will unfailingly become rich in the end, always supposing that his stock lasts.

'On *Justice distributive*, by feasting good – note, good – and charming companions, whom Fortune has thrown like Ulysses on the rock of good appetite, without providing them with the victuals, and also good – note good – young wenches – note young; for according to the maxim of Hippocrates, youth is impatient of hunger, especially when it is vigorous, lively, brisk, stirring, and volatile. These wenches willingly and gladly give good men pleasure, and they are so Platonic and Ciceronian that they consider themselves born into this world not for themselves alone, but that their country may have one share of their persons, and their men friends another. On *Fortitude*, in felling the great trees, like a second Milo, demolishing the dark forests, the haunts of wolves, wild boar and foxes, the dens of brigands and murderers, the lurking-places of assassins, the workshops of forgers, the retreats of heretics; levelling them to make great clearings and pleasant heaths, playing old harry with the timber and preparing the seats for the Eve of Judgement. On *Temperance*, by eating my wheat in the blade like a hermit, living on salads and roots, freeing myself from sensual appetites, and so saving something for the cripples and distressed. In doing this I save the expense of hoers, who cost money; of reapers, who drink lustily and drink neat; of gleaners, who must have their cakes; of threshers, who, on the authority of Virgil's Thestylis, never leave garlic, onion, or shallot in the gardens; of millers, who are generally thieves, and of bakers, who are little better. Is that a small saving? Besides this, there is the damage done by the field-mice, the wastage in the barns, and the destruction by mites and weevils. From wheat in the blade you make a fine green sauce, simple to mix and easy to digest, which rejoices the brain, exhilarates the animal spirits, delights the sight, induces the appetite, pleases the taste, fortifies the heart, tickles the tongue, clarifies the complexion, strengthens the muscles, tempers the blood, eases the diaphragm, refreshes the liver, unblocks the spleen, comforts the kidneys, relaxes the vertebrae, empties the ureters, dilates the spermatic glands, tautens the testicle-strings, purges the bladder, swells the genitals, straightens the foreskin, hardens the ballock, and rectifies the member: giving you a

good belly, and good belching, farting – both noisy and silent – shitting, pissing, sneezing, crying, coughing, spitting, vomiting, yawning, snotting, breathing, inhaling, exhaling, snoring, sweating, and
erections of the john-thomas; also countless other rare advantages.'

'I understand perfectly,' said Pantagruel. 'You mean to infer that
mean-spirited persons have not the skill to spend much in a short
time. You are not the original inventor of that heresy. Nero subscribed to it, and admired his uncle Caius Caligula above all human
beings, for his marvellous ingenuity in spending in a few days the
whole substance and patrimony left to him by Tiberius. But instead
of keeping and observing the alimentary and sumptuary laws of the
Romans: viz. the *lex Orchia, Fannia, Didia, Licinia Cornelia, Lepidiana*,
and *Antia*, and that of the Corinthians, by which all men were rigorously forbidden to spend more in a year than the amount of their annual
income, you have made the sacrifice for the road, which was to the
Romans what that of the Paschal lamb was to the Jews. For it entailed
eating all that was eatable and throwing the rest in the fire, reserving
nothing for the morrow. I can say this of you fairly, as Cato did of
Albidius, who after having most extravagantly eaten all that he possessed, until he had nothing left but a house, set fire to that, in order
that he might truly say *consummatum est* – which is what Thomas
Aquinas said when he had eaten the whole of his lamprey. But let
that pass.'

CHAPTER 3: *Panurge's praise of Debtors and Borrowers*

'BUT,' asked Pantagruel, 'when will you be out of debt?'

'At the Greek Kalends,' replied Panurge, 'when all the world will
be content, and you will be your own heir. God forbid that I should
be debt-free. For then I shouldn't find anyone to lend me a penny. A
man who leaves no leaven overnight will never raise dough in the
morning. Always owe something to someone. Then there will be
prayers continually offered up to God to grant you a long and happy
life. Through fear of losing his money, your creditor will always
speak well of you in all company. He will always gain new creditors
for you, so that by borrowing from them you may pay him, and fill
his ditch with other men's soil. When, by the Druidical law of ancient
Gaul, slaves, servants, and attendants were burnt alive at the funerals

of their lords and masters, had they not fine reason to fear the deaths of these same lords and masters, since they must needs die with them? Did they not continuously pray their great god Mercury, and Dis, the father of wealth, to preserve their health for long years? Were they not careful to serve and look after them well? For together they could live, at least till death.

'Believe me, your creditors will pray God for your life and fear your death even more fervently and devotedly, since they are fonder of the open palm than of the whole right arm, and love pennies better than their lives. Remember the usurers of Landerousse, who hanged themselves not long ago when they saw the prices of wine and corn falling and the good times returning.'

As Pantagruel gave no answer, Panurge continued, 'Lord bless me, now I come to think of it, when you twit me with my debts and creditors you're challenging my trump card. Why, by that achievement alone I thought I had earned respect, reverence, and awe. For – notwithstanding the universal opinion of philosophers, who say that out of nothing nothing is made – although I possessed nothing and had no prime substance, in this I was a maker and creator.

'And what had I created? So many good, fine creditors. Creditors are fine, good creatures – and I'll maintain that to everything short of the stake. The man who lends nothing is an ugly, wicked creature, created by the great ugly devil of hell. And what had I made? Debts. Rare and excellent things! Debts, I say, exceeding in number the syllables resulting from the combination of all the consonants with the vowels; a number once computed by the noble Xenocrates. If you judge of the perfection of debtors by the multitude of their creditors, you will not be far out in your practical arithmetic.

'Don't you suppose I'm pleased when, every morning, I see these debtors around me so humble, serviceable, and profuse in their bows? And when I notice that if I show a pleasanter face and a warmer welcome to one than to another, the fellow imagines he will be the first to get a settlement, that his payment will be first in date, and deduces from my smile that he will be paid cash? Then I seem to be playing God in the Saumur Passion-play, in the company of his angels and cherubim. These are my fawners, my parasites, my saluters, my sayers of "Good day", my perpetual speechifiers.

'I truly used to think that debts were the material of that hill of heroic virtues described by Hesiod, on which I hold the first degree of my licentiate, and towards which all human beings seem to aim and aspire, but which few climb owing to the difficulty of the path. For I see the whole world to-day in a fervent desire and vehement hunger to make fresh debts and creditors.

'All the same, not everyone is a debtor who wishes to be; not everyone who wishes makes creditors. And you want to deprive me of this sovereign felicity? You ask me when I shall be out of debt?

'But worse still, I give myself to the good saint, St Babolin, if I haven't all my life looked upon debts as the connecting link between Earth and Heaven, the unique mainstay of the human race; one, I believe, without which all mankind would speedily perish. I looked upon them as, perhaps, that great soul of the Universe which, according to the Academics, gives all things life.

'In proof of this, calmly call up before your mind the idea and shape of some world. Take, if you will, the thirtieth of those imagined by the philosopher Metrodorus, or the seventy-eighth of Petron – in which there is no debtor or creditor. A world without debts! There among the planets there will be no regular tracks; all will be in disorder. Not recognizing his debt to Saturn, Jupiter will dispossess him of his sphere, and with his Homeric chain hold all Intelligences, Gods, Heavens, Demons, Geniuses, Heroes, Devils, Earth, Sea, and all the elements in suspense. Saturn will ally himself to Mars, and they will put this whole world into confusion. Mercury will refuse to subject himself to the others; he will cease to be their Camillus, as he was called in the Etruscan tongue. For he will be in no way their debtor. Venus will not be venerated, for she will have lent nothing. The moon will remain bloody and dark. For why should the Sun impart his light to her? He will be in no way bound to. The Sun will not throw light on the Earth. The Stars will not send down their good influences. For the Earth will have given up lending them nourishment in the form of those vapours and exhalations, by which – as Heraclitus said, the Stoics proved, and Cicero maintained – the Stars are fed. Amongst the Elements there will be no combinations, alternations, or transmutations of any kind. For one will not feel obliged by another, which has lent it nothing. Earth then will not be made into Water; Water will not be transmuted into Air; from Air no Fire will be made; Fire will not warm Earth. Earth will produce nothing but monsters, Titans, Aloids, and Giants; rain will not rain on it; light will not light it; the wind will not blow on it, and it will have no summer or autumn. Lucifer will break his bonds and, issuing from the depths of hell with the Furies, fiends, and horned devils, will try to dislodge the gods of all nations, major and minor alike, from the heavens.

'This world in which nothing is lent will be no better than a dog-fight, a more disorderly wrangle than the election of a Rector in Paris, an interlude more confused than the devils' play at the Mysteries of Doué. Among men, one will not save the other; it will be lost labour to cry, "Help!" "Fire!" "Water!" "Murder!" No one will go to help. Why? Because he has lent nothing; no one owes him anything. No one has any interest in his fire, in his shipwreck, in his ruin, in his death. Not only has he not lent anything till then, but he would not have lent anything afterwards.

'In short Faith, Hope, and Charity will be banished from that world, for men are born to aid and succour one another. In their place will come Mistrust, Contempt, and Rancour, with a cohort of all the evils, all the curses, and all the miseries. You will think, rightly enough, that Pandora has spilt her jug on it. Men will be wolves to men, were-wolves and hobgoblins, like Lycaon, Bellerophon, and Nebucha-dnezzar of old. They will be brigands, assassins, poisoners, evil-doers, evil-thinkers, evil-wishers, bearing hate, each against all, like Ishmael, like Metabus, like Timon of Athens, who for that reason was called the Misanthrope. Wherefore it would be easier for Nature to keep fish in the air or to graze stags at the bottom of the ocean, than to nourish this rascally rabble that does not lend. I thoroughly hate them all, on my oath I do.

'And if on the model of this peevish and perverse world which lends nothing, you imagine the other little world, which is man, there you will find a terrible confusion. The head will refuse to lend the sight of his eyes to guide the feet and hands; the feet will not agree to carry it, and the hands will cease to work for it. The heart will grow tired of continually beating for the benefit of the pulses in the limbs, and will lend them no more help. The lungs will not oblige it with their bellows. The liver will not send it blood for its nourish-ment. The bladder will not care to be in debt to the kidneys – and the urine will be stopped. When the brain considers this unnatural state of things, it will fall into a daze, and give no feeling to the nerves, no movement to the muscles. In brief, in this disorganized world, which will owe nothing, lend nothing, and borrow nothing, you will see a more pernicious conspiracy than Aesop imagined in his *Apology*. The man will perish, no doubt; and not only perish but perish soon, even if he be Aesculapius himself. The body will rot immediately; and the soul in indignation will take its flight to all the devils, following my money.'

CHAPTER 4: *The Continuation of Panurge's speech in praise of Lenders and Debtors*

'ON the other hand, imagine to yourself another world in which everyone lends and everyone owes, where all are debtors and all are lenders. Oh, what a harmony there will be in the regular motions of the heavens! I believe that I can hear them just as clearly as Plato did. What sympathy there will be between the elements! Oh, how Nature will delight in her works and productions! Ceres will be loaded with corn; Bacchus with wines; Flora with flowers; Pomona with fruit; Juno in her serene air, herself serene, salubrious, and delightful. I am lost in this contemplation.

'Among mankind peace, love, affection, fidelity, repose, banquets, joy, gladness, gold, silver, small change, chains, rings, and merchandise will pass from hand to hand. No lawsuits, no war, no strife; no one there will be a usurer, nor a glutton, nor a miser, nor a refuser. Dear God, will it not be the age of gold, the reign of Saturn, the true image of the Olympic regions, in which all other virtues are suspended, and Charity alone rules, governs, dominates, and triumphs? All men will be good, all will be just. Oh, happy world! Oh, happy people in that world, three times and four times blest! I really feel as if I were there. I swear to you by God's truth, that if this world, this blessed world, which lends to everyone and refuses no one, had only a Pope with his troops of Cardinals and members of his holy College, in a few years you would see the saints there thicker on the ground and working more wonders, with more services, more vows, more banners, and more wax-candles, than there are in all the nine bishoprics of Britanny, excepting only Saint Ives.

'Please remember that when the noble Patelin wanted to deify the

father of William Jousseaulme and by divine praises to extol him to
the third heaven, all that he said was:

> ... Yes, and he lent
> His wares to those who wanted them.

What a fine saying!

'Now on this model imagine our microcosm, our little world that
is, which is man, with all his limbs lending, borrowing, and owing –
that is to say, in his natural state. For Nature has created man for no
other purpose but to lend and borrow. The harmony of the heavens
is not greater than his shall be under good government. The intention
of the builder of this microcosm is that it shall house the soul, which
he has put in as a guest, and shall also support life. Life consists of
blood. Blood is the seat of the soul. Therefore there is only one task
entrusted to this microcosm, that is continuously to forge blood. At
the forge all the members play their different parts; and their hierarchy is such that one borrows incessantly from another, one lends to
another, one is another's debtor. The material ore suitable to be transmuted into blood is provided by Nature; it is bread and wine, and
these two provide every kind of nourishment. Hence it is that the
Gothic word *companage* can cover all the rest. To find, prepare, and
cook this nourishment, the hands work; the feet move and transport
the whole mechanism; the eyes act as guides; the appetite, in the
orifice of the stomach, by means of a little sour black humour, which
comes to it from the spleen, gives warning to shut in the food. The
tongue makes a test of it; the teeth chew it; the stomach receives it,
digests it, and chylifies it. The mesaraic veins suck out of it what is
good and suitable, leaving the excrements, which are voided by an
expulsive mechanism along special conduits, and conduct it to the
liver; which transmutes it once more, and turns it into blood.

'Think now what joy there must be among these officers at the
sight of this golden stream, which is their sole restorative. The Alchemists can know none greater, when after long toil, great trouble,
and heavy expense they see the metals transmuted in their furnaces.

'Then each member prepares itself and strives anew to purify and
refine this treasure. The kidneys, by the renal conduits, draw off that
liquid which you call urine, and pass it down through the ureters.
Below is its proper receptacle, the bladder, which in due course

empties it out. The spleen draws off the earthy part and the lees, which you call melancholy. The bile duct extracts the superfluous choler. Then the blood is transported for further refinement to another workshop, that is the heart, which by its diastolic and systolic movements so subtilizes and fires it that it is perfected in the right ventricle, and sent through the veins to all the members. All the members – the feet, the hands, the eyes, and all the rest – absorb it, and take nourishment from it, each in its own way. Thus they become debtors who previously were lenders. In the left ventricle the heart so subtilizes it that it is called spiritual, and then sends it to all the members through its arteries to heat and ventilate the rest of the blood in the veins. The lungs never cease to refresh it with their lappets and bellows and in return for this service the heart gives them of its best blood through the pulmonary artery. In the end it is so refined in the *miraculous network*, that it later becomes the material of the animal spirits, which endow us with imagination, reason, judgement, resolution, deliberation, ratiocination, and memory.

'God's my life, I drown, I perish, I lose my way when I begin to consider the profound abyss of this world of lenders and owers. It is, believe me, a divine thing to lend, a heroic virtue to owe. Yet this is not all. This borrowing, owing, lending world is so good that when this act of feeding is over, it immediately thinks of lending to those who are not yet born, by that loan perpetuating itself, if it can, and multiplying itself by means of its own replicas; that is children. For this purpose each member cuts off and pares away some of the most precious of its nourishment, and sends it below, where Nature has prepared fitting vessels and receptacles for it, through which it descends to the genitories by long and circuitous windings. There it receives proper form and finds fitting places, in man and woman alike, for the conservation and perpetuation of the human race. This is all done by loans and debts, one to another; whence it is called the debt of marriage. Penalties are inflicted by Nature on those who refuse to pay, in the form of grievous vexation of the limbs and disturbance of the senses. But the reward assigned to the lender is pleasure, joy, and sensual delight.'

CHAPTER 5: *Pantagruel's detestation of Debtors and Borrowers*

'I UNDERSTAND,' answered Pantagruel. 'You seem to me good at argument and an enthusiast for your cause. But if you preach and sermonize from now till Whitsun, you'll be astonished to find me finally unconvinced. With all your fine talk you will never make me a debtor. Owe no man anything, says the holy Apostle, save love and mutual delight. You provide me with fine illustrations and figures, which please me greatly. But let me tell you that if one of your shameless swaggerers and tiresome borrowers were to make a second visit to a city that knew his habits, you would find the citizens more worried and alarmed by his entrance than if the plague had come in person, dressed up as the Tyanian philosopher saw it at Ephesus. I don't think the Persians were wrong either when they reckoned lying to be the second vice; to owe being the first. For debts and lies are generally involved together.

'I do not want to infer, nevertheless, that one must never owe, and never lend. No man is so rich that he does not sometimes owe money. No man is so poor that sometimes one may not borrow from him. But the occasion must only be such as that described by Plato in his *Laws*, when he says that no one must let his neighbours draw water at his well unless they have first dug on their own soil so deep as to find that kind of earth that is called Ceramite – that is potter's clay – and yet have found no spring or water channel. For owing to its texture, which is oily, strong, smooth, and dense, this clay holds the moisture, and does not easily allow escape or evaporation. It is a great disgrace, therefore, always and in all places, to borrow from everybody rather than to work and earn; and, in my opinion, one should only lend when a person has worked, but has not been able to earn by his labours, or when he has suddenly sustained an unexpected loss of his goods. However, let us leave this subject, But henceforth do not have recourse to creditors. From past owings I absolve you.'

'The least I can do in this matter,' said Panurge, 'is to thank you. And if thanks should be proportionate to the benefactor's affection I must thank you infinitely and everlastingly. For the love that, of your grace, you bear me, is beyond the hazard of computation; it is infinite and everlasting. But if I take the calibre of the benefits and the recipient's pleasure as my standard, my thanks won't be so very great. You do me many favours, far more than my own merits or my services to you deserve – that I am bound to confess – but in the present case you have not done as much as you think.

'What pains me, what gripes and itches me is to think what sort of figure I shall cut in future, now that I am out of debt. I shall be pretty awkward, believe me, for the first few months, seeing that I haven't been brought up to this state of things, and I'm not used to it. Indeed, it frightens me very much. What's more, from now on not a fart will blow off in all Salmigundia that isn't aimed at my nose. For every farter in the whole world says as he farts: "Now we're quits!" My life will soon be over, I can foresee that. I leave you the making of my epitaph. For I shall die pickled in farts; and if some day the ordinary medicaments fail to restore her blowing power to some good woman in the last agony of a windy colic, the mummy oil from my wretched befarted body will serve the physicians as a quick remedy. After the smallest dose imaginable, they'll fart more than they expect.

'That is why I implore you to leave me some hundred or so debts, as Milles d'Illiers, Bishop of Chartres, begged King Louis the Eleventh to leave him a few lawsuits, to keep his hand in, when the King offered him a complete immunity. I would rather give them all my revenue from snails together with my income from cockchafers, though I'll surrender no part of my capital.' 'Let us leave this subject,' said Pantagruel, 'this is the second time I have suggested it.'

CHAPTER 6: *Why newly married Men were exempted from going to the Wars*

'By the way,' asked Panurge, 'by what law was it ordained and established that the planters of new vineyards, builders of new houses, and the newly married should be exempted from going to the wars for the first year?'

'By the law of Moses,' replied Pantagruel.

'Why the newly married?' asked Panurge. 'As for planters of vineyards, I'm too old to bother about them; I leave the vinedressers to look after themselves. As for your grand builders up of dead stones, there is nothing written about them in my book of life. I only build up live stones, by which I mean men.'

'According to my judgement,' replied Pantagruel, 'the purpose of the law was that for the first year they should enjoy all the pleasures to the full, have time to produce progeny, and provide themselves with heirs. Then, even if in the second year they were killed in the war, their name and coat of arms would be perpetuated by their children. Another purpose was to make certain whether their wives were barren or fruitful – for the trial of one year seemed to them enough, seeing the ripe age at which they used then to marry. This made a second marriage easier to arrange after the decease of the first husband: the fertile being wedded to men who wished to multiply and have issue; the barren to those who did not desire family and would accept wives for their virtues, learning, and charm, solely for the sake of domestic comfort and good housekeeping.'

'The preachers of Varennes,' said Panurge, 'decry second marriages. They call them foolish and dishonourable.'

'Yes, they're about as fond of them as of a good quartan ague,' answered Pantagruel.

'I agree,' said Panurge, 'and so does Father Trumpery. When he was preaching a sermon at Parilly against second marriages he swore that the swiftest devil in hell could fly off with him if he wouldn't prefer to take a hundred virgins' maidenheads than to roger one widow.'

'I find your argument good and well founded. But what would you say if this exemption were granted them only because, in the course of this same first year, they had done such valiant field-work on their newly possessed loves – as was only right and proper – and so exhausted their spermatic vessels that they were left quite ragged and unmanned, all weak and drooping? For then, when the day of battle came, they would be more likely to dive in among the baggage like ducks, than to stand among the combatants, among the brave champions, there where Enyo stirs the fray and sword rings on sword. Under Mars's banner they wouldn't strike one worth-while blow. For their great blows would have been struck behind the curtains of his sweetheart Venus.

'In proof of this, I can quote you an old custom, surviving to-day among other relics of antiquity. Remember, how in all good houses, after a certain number of days, they sent newly married men to see an uncle, so as to get them away from their wives and give them a temporary rest, during which time they can replenish themselves in order to fight better on their return. Very often, in fact, they have no uncle or aunt at all. In the same way King Crackard after the battle of Cornabons did not, properly speaking, discharge us – Pothunter and myself I mean – but sent us to take a rest in our own houses. He's still looking for his. My grandfather's godmother used to tell me, when I was little, that

> Paternosters and prayers are for those
> Who know how to remember their sound.
> One piper going to the wars
> Is better than two homeward bound.

'What confirms me in this opinion is that vine planters seldom ate the grapes or drank the wine of their labours during the first year, and builders, for the first year, did not inhabit their newly made houses, for fear of suffocation: a fact that is noted by the learned Galen in his second book, *On Difficulties of Breathing*. I did not ask this question without most consequent cause and most resonant reasons, so don't be displeased, sir.'

CHAPTER 7: *Panurge has a Flea in his Ear, and gives up wearing his magnificent Codpiece*

THE next day Panurge had his right ear pierced in the Jewish fashion, and put in a little gold ring of inlaid work, in the bezel of which was set a flea. I should not like you to remain in doubt on any point, for it is a fine thing to be well informed in every particular. So I will tell you that the flea was black, and the cost of it, carefully checked by his Exchequer, amounted quarterly to only little more than the marriage of a Hyrcanian tigress, or as you might say 600,000 maravedis. He was bothered by this excessive expenditure, now that he was out of debt. But afterwards he fed it, like any tyrant or lawyer, on the sweat and blood of his subjects.

He took five yards of coarse brown cloth, which he wore draped around him like a long coat. He left off his breeches, and he tied a pair of spectacles to his cap. In this condition he presented himself before Pantagruel, who found the disguise strange, especially as he missed that fine and magnificent codpiece on which Panurge had once relied, as on a holy anchor, as his last resort in all the shipwrecks of adversity. Somewhat mystified, therefore, the good Pantagruel questioned him, asking what this new transformation might signify. 'I have the flea in my ear,' replied Panurge, 'I have a mind to marry.'

'Good luck to you,' said Pantagruel. 'I am delighted with the news, though really I wouldn't reckon on it. I wouldn't pledge my oath it'll come off. It isn't the habit of lovers to have their trousers tumbling down like this and their shirts hanging out over their breechless knees, or to wear brown serge, a most unusual colour for the robes of persons of honour and quality. If certain adherents to particular heresies and sects have dressed themselves like this in the past I will not blame them or pass any adverse judgement on them, though many have imputed this habit to quackery, imposture, and an affectation of superiority over the common herd. Everyone is full of his own ideas, especially on external, peripheral, and indifferent matters, that are neither good nor bad in themselves because they do not proceed from our hearts and minds, which are the factory of all good and all evil: good if the feelings are good and controlled by the righteous spirit; evil, if the feelings are wickedly depraved by the spirit of evil. It is only the novelty and this contempt for common fashion that I dislike.'

'The colour,' replied Panurge, 'is suitable, suitable for my office. Henceforth I mean to have an office, and to look closely into my affairs. Since I am now out of debt, I shall be as disagreeable as any man you have ever seen, if God doesn't help me to be patient. Look at my spectacles. If you saw me from a distance, I expect you would say "Here's Father Jean Bourgeois," and you would not be far out. Next year I really believe I shall preach a new Crusade. God keep my pill-grims safe in my ball-bag! Do you see this brown serge? Believe me, there's an occult quality about it, that's known to very few. I only put it on this morning, but already I'm raging, itching, and crackling to be married and to work at my wife like a brown devil, without fear of a beating. Oh what a great householder I'll be! After my death they'll have me burnt on a noble pyre, so as to keep my ashes as a memory and a relic of the perfect householder. God's truth, my treasurer had better not play at cooking the accounts on this brown cloth of mine,[1] or the blows will soon begin to rain down on him.

1. This brown cloth was used to cover exchequer tables. There are a number of puns on this point which cannot be brought over into English.

'Look at me both before and behind. It is in the shape of a toga, the ancient apparel of the Romans in times of peace. I took the pattern from Trajan's column at Rome, also from the triumphal arch of Septimius Severus. I'm tired of wars, tired of military cloaks and padded jerkins. My shoulders are quite worn out by the weight of harness. Let there be an end of armour! Let togas reign, at least for all this next year, if I marry – as you explained to me yesterday when you talked about the Mosaic law.

'As for breeches, my great-aunt Laurence told me long ago that they were made only for the codpiece. I believe it, by the same argument as that jolly fellow Galen uses, when he says in his ninth book *On the Use of our Limbs*, that the head was made for the eyes. For Nature could have placed our heads on our knees or on our elbows. But since she required the eyes to see things from afar, she fixed them in the head, as it were on a pole, at the highest part of the body. In just the same way we see lighthouses and high towers erected above seaports, so that the lantern may be seen from far off.

'Now because I should like for some space of time, a year at least, to take a respite from the profession of arms – I mean because I should like to marry – I no longer wear a codpiece, and consequently I no longer wear breeches. For the codpiece is the first piece of harness in the arming of a warrior, and I maintain even to the stake – though stopping short of actual burning, you understand – that the Turks are not properly armed, seeing that the wearing of codpieces is a thing forbidden by their law.'

CHAPTER 8: *To prove that the Codpiece is the principal piece in a Warrior's Armour*

'WOULD you maintain,' asked Pantagruel, 'that the codpiece is the principal piece of military harness? That is a very new and paradoxical doctrine. For we say that a man's arming begins with his spurs.'

'I maintain it,' replied Panurge, 'and not wrongfully do I maintain it. Consider Nature. She wishes the plants, trees, shrubs, herbs, and zoophytes, which she has created, to be perpetuated and to last into all successive ages, without the species ever dying out, although the individuals perish. She has cunningly armed their germs and seeds, therefore, in which lies this same perpetuity. She has provided and covered them, with admirable ingenuity, with husks, sheaths, caps, kernels, small cups, shells, ears, down, bark, and prickly hulls, which are to them like fine, strong natural codpieces. This is clearly exemplified in peas, beans, haricots, walnuts, white apricots, cotton-plants, sorb-apples, corn, poppies, lemons, chestnuts, and all plants generally in which, quite obviously, the germ and seed is better covered, protected, and armoured than any other part. Now Nature did not provide in this way for the survival of the human race. She created man naked, tender, and fragile, without arms offensive or defensive, in a state of innocence, the first Golden Age. She created man as an animate being, not a plant; as an animate being, I say, born for the miraculous enjoyment of all fruits and vegetable plants, an animate being born for pacific domination over all the beasts.

'When evil began to multiply among men, with the coming of the Iron Age and the Reign of Jupiter, the earth began to produce among the vegetables, nettles, thistles, thorns, and other such kinds of rebels against man. Furthermore, by a decree of fate, nearly all the animals broke free from him, and tacitly conspired together to serve him no longer, to obey him no longer, in so far as they could resist him, but to harm him to the extent of their faculties and power.

'Man, therefore, wishing to maintain his original enjoyment and continue in his former dominion, not being able, moreover, conveniently to do without the services of several animals, was compelled for the first time to arm himself.'

'By the holy goose of Guenet,' exclaimed Pantagruel, 'you've become a great slipperslopper – I should say philosopher – since the last rains.'

'Consider,' Panurge went on, 'how Nature inspired him to arm himself, and what part of the body he first began to armour. It was, as God's my life, his ballocks,

> And when Master Priapus was done
> He did not ask for the same again.

'Such is the testimony of that Hebrew captain and philosopher Moses, who affirms that man armed himself with a brave and gallant codpiece, made after a mighty fine invention from the leaves of a fig-tree, which are simple and altogether suitable in toughness, delicacy of shape, curliness, smoothness, size, colour, smell, virtues, and faculties for covering and arming the ballocks. I make an exception, of course, of those tremendous Lorraine ballocks, which fall at a gallop to the bottom of the breeches, cannot bear to dwell in a high codpiece, and are altogether monstrous; as witness Viardière, the noble Valentine, whom I discovered one May Day at Nancy scrubbing his, which he had spread out on a table like a Spanish cloak, in order to make himself more captivating.

'So henceforth let no one who doesn't want to make a gaff say to a militiaman as he sees him off to the war:

Stevie, look after the pot of wine,

meaning, of course, his head. Instead he must say

Stevie, look after the pot of milk,

that is to say his testicles, in the name of all the devils in hell. When a man loses his head, only the individual perishes; but if the balls were lost, the whole human race would die out. It was this that moved the gallant Galen in his first book, *On the Sperm*, to conclude boldly that it would be better – that is to say less bad – to have no heart than to have no genitories. For in the testicles, as in a sacred repository, lies the germ which preserves the whole human stock. Indeed, I should not ask as much as a hundred francs to believe that these were the very stones with which Deucalion and Pyrrha restored the race of man, when it was destroyed by the deluge of which the poets tell. It was this that moved the valiant Justinian, in his fourth book *On Putting up with Bigots*, to place the *summum bonum in braguibus et braguetis*.[1]

'It was for this and other reasons, that once when the Lord of Merville was trying on a new suit of armour, in order to follow his king to the war – for he could not use his old half-rusty suit any more because for some years the skin of his stomach had stood rather far away from his kidneys – his wife observed in a contemplative spirit that he attached very little value to the common store and staff of their marriage, seeing that he only armed it with links of mail. She advised him to protect and parapet it well with a great jousting helmet, which was

1. The supreme virtue in breeches and codpieces.

lying idle in his closet. Of this lady the following verses were written in the third book of *The Maidens' Shittery*:

> She saw her husband fully armed
> But for his codpiece, going to war.
> She said, 'My dear, in case you're harmed,
> Arm that as well, that is most dear.'
> Should she be blamed for this warning?
> I say, 'Oh no'. Think of her fear
> That she might lose that little thing
> That stirred – and that she held so dear.

'So recover from your astonishment at this new rig-out of mine, sir.'

CHAPTER 9: *How Panurge consulted Pantagruel as to whether he should marry*

As Pantagruel did not reply, Panurge continued with a deep sigh: 'My lord, you have heard my intention, which is to marry, unless by bad luck all holes have been closed, stopped, and secured. I beg you, by the love you have so long borne me, to give me your advice on this subject.'

'Well,' replied Pantagruel, 'since you have cast the dice once and for all, and have decreed and taken a firm resolution in the matter, there's no need for further talk. All that remains is to put your resolution into effect.'

'Yes,' said Panurge, 'but I shouldn't want to put it into effect without your counsel and good advice.'

'I advise you to do it,' said Pantagruel, 'I counsel you to marry.'

'But,' said Panurge, 'if you knew that it was better for me to stay as I am, and not undertake anything new, I would much rather not marry.'

'Then don't marry,' answered Pantagruel.

'But,' said Panurge, 'would you want me to remain single like this for the whole of my life, without conjugal company? You know that it is written, *Vae soli*.[1] A man on his own has never the comforts that you see married people have.'

1. Woe to him that is alone.

'For God's sake marry then,' replied Pantagruel.

'But if,' said Pantagruel, 'my wife were to make me a cuckold – and you know this is a great year for cuckolds – that would be enough to make me fly off the hinges of patience. I like cuckolds all right. They seem good fellows to me, and I like visiting their houses. But I'd rather die than be one of them. That's a point that pricks me hard.'

'It points then against your marrying,' replied Pantagruel. 'For Seneca's maxim, What you have done to another, be sure another will do to you, applies without exceptions.'

'Do you say without exceptions?' asked Panurge.

'Without exceptions. He says it,' replied Pantagruel.

'Ho, ho,' said Panurge, 'that's the devil! But I suppose he means either in this world or in the next. Still, you see, since I can't do without a woman, any more than a blind man can do without a stick – for the old john-thomas has to be kept occupied, otherwise I couldn't live – wouldn't it be better for me to ally myself with some honourable and virtuous woman rather than change from day to day like this, in continual danger of getting a beating or, even worse, the pox. For I have never had to do with an honest wife, I mean no disrespect to the husbands.'

'Get married then, for God's sake,' replied Pantagruel.

'But,' said Panurge, 'what if by God's will I happened to marry some honest woman and she were to beat me? Unless I were a perfect little Job, that would drive me stark mad. For these very virtuous women, I've been told, usually have bad tempers. That's why they keep good vinegar in their cupboards. But if she got violent I'd go one better. I'd so beat and bang her giblets – her arms and legs and lungs and liver and spleen, I mean. I'd so mangle and tatter her clothes with the banging I'd give her that the great Devil himself would come to Hell's door to wait for her accursed soul. But I could do without that sort of shindy for this year. Indeed I'd be glad never to run into one at all.'

'Have nothing to do with marrying, then,' replied Pantagruel.

'But,' said Panurge, 'being in the state that I am, free of debt and unmarried – mark what I say, out of debt and bad luck to it! For if I were heavily in debt, my creditors would be only too careful of my paternity. But being out of debt and unmarried, I haven't anyone who would fuss over me, or feel the sort of love for me that they say conjugal love is. And if I happened to fall ill, I should not be at all well looked after. The Wise Man says, *Where there is no woman* – I understand by that a mother of family, bound in lawful wedlock – *the sick man is in a bad way*. I have seen clear instances of it in the case of popes, legates, cardinals, bishops, abbots, priors, priests, and monks. You shall never find me in that state.'

'Then for God's sake marry,' replied Pantagruel.

'But if,' said Panurge, 'I were ill and incapable of my husbandly duties, my wife might be impatient of my sickness and give herself to another man. Then not only wouldn't she help me in my need, but she'd laugh at my misfortune, and – what's worse – she'd rob me, as I've often seen it happen. That would put the finishing touch to my misery, and send me running about the fields in my night-shirt.'

'Don't run into marriage, then,' replied Pantagruel.

'But,' said Panurge, 'there's no other way of getting legitimate sons and daughters, by whom I can hope to perpetuate my name and armorial bearings, and to whom I can leave my inheritances and acquisitions – and I shall get some fine ones too, one of these days, without a doubt, and what's more I shall be a great dealer in mortgages. For I want children that I can be happy with when otherwise I should be glum. There would be the same love between me and my children as I see every day there is between your benign and gracious father and yourself, and as there is between all worthy people in the privacy of their own homes. Being free from debt and unmarried, being perhaps vexed and angry. ... But instead of comforting me, I think you're laughing at my troubles.'

'Get married, then, for God's sake,' replied Pantagruel.

CHAPTER 10: *Pantagruel points out to Panurge the difficulty of offering Advice about Marriage, and something is said of the Homeric and Virgilian Lotteries*

'Your advice, if I may be allowed to say so,' said Panurge, 'seems like Ricochet's song to me. It's nothing but taunts and jokes and contradictory repetitions. One of them cancels out the other, and I don't know which to go by.'

'But there are so many ifs and buts about your propositions too,' replied Pantagruel, 'that I can't base anything on them or come to any conclusions. Aren't you certain of your own wishes? That's the principal point; all the rest is fortuitous and depends on the disposition of the heavenly fates. We see a good number of people so lucky in this respect that their marriage seems a shining reflection, a very embodiment of the joys of paradise. Others are so unlucky that the devils who tempt the hermits in the deserts of the Thebaid and Montserrat are not more miserable. The only thing, then, is to put things to the chance, with blindfolded eyes, bowing your head, kissing the earth, and, for the rest, entrusting yourself to God, seeing that you have made up your mind to go in for it. That is the only thing I can tell you for certain.

'But here is something that you can do if you think fit. Bring me the works of Virgil. If you open it three times at random, and on the page that your finger strikes read the lines whose number we have agreed on, then we can explore your future as a husband. Many a man has learnt his fate by the Homeric Lots, witness Socrates in prison who, hearing this line concerning Achilles recited from the ninth *Iliad*:

Ἤματί κεν τριτάτῳ Φθίην ἐρίβωλον ἱκοίμην.

I shall arrive and with no long delay
In fair and fertile Phthia, the third day

foresaw that he would die on the third day following, and assured Aeschines of the fact. This is recorded by Plato in the *Crito*, by Cicero in his first *Book on Divination*, and by Diogenes Laertius. Witness also Opilius Macrinus, who wished to know whether he would be Emperor of Rome, and drew as a lot this sentence from the eighth *Iliad*.

ὦ γέρον ἦ μάλα δή σε νέοι τείρουσι μαχηταί,
σὴ δὲ βίη λέλυται, χαλεπὸν δέ σε γῆρας ὀπάζει.

Old man, these youthful warriors press you hard,
Your vigour's spent, and grievous age o'erwhelms you.

In fact he was already old, and after ruling the Empire for only a year and two months, was dispossessed and slain by the young and powerful Heliogabalus. Witness also Brutus, who wished to learn the outcome of the battle of Pharsalia, in which he was killed and drew this verse, spoken of Patroclus in the sixteenth *Iliad*:

ἀλλά με μοῖρ' ὀλοὴ καὶ Λητοῦς ἔκτανεν υἱός,

By treacherous fate and Leto's son I'm slain,

That is to say, by Apollo, whose name was the watchword on the day of that battle.

Many notable events and matters of great importance were ascertained and foretold, in the olden days, by the Virgilian Lots also, even including the succession to the Roman Empire, as in the case of Alexander Severus, who, on consulting the lotteries, lighted on the following verse: from the sixth *Aeneid*:

> *Tu regere imperio populos, Romane, memento*

> Know, Roman that thy business is to reign

And a few years later he was actually and in fact made Emperor of Rome. The Roman Emperor Hadrian also, when he was in some doubt and perplexity as to what the Emperor Trajan thought of him and whether he loved him, consulted the Virgilian lots, and came upon these lines, from the sixth *Aeneid*:

> *Quis procul ille autem ramis insignis olivae*
> *Sacra ferens? Nosco crines, incanaque menta*
> *Regis Romani.*

> But who is he, conspicuous from afar,
> With olive boughs, that doth his offering bear?
> By the white hair and beard I know him plain,
> The Roman king.

After this he was adopted by Trajan, and succeeded him as Emperor. Claudius the Second, that much-belauded Emperor of Rome, also resorted to these lots and drew the following verse from the sixth *Aeneid*:

> *Tertia dum Latio regnantem viderit aestas*

> Whilst the third summer saw him reign a king
> In Latium.

In fact he only reigned two years. Again he consulted the lots about his brother Quintilius, whom he wished to take as co-Emperor, and drew this verse from the sixth *Aeneid*.

> *Ostendent terris hunc tantum fata*
>
> > whom fate just let us see
> > And would no longer suffer him to be.

Which proved correct, for he was killed seventeen days after taking over the administration of the Empire. The same lot fell to the Emperor Gordian the younger; and to Clodius Albinus, when he was anxious to hear good news of the future, came these lines from the sixth *Aeneid*:

> *Hic rem Romanam magno turbante tumultu*
> *Sistet eques*, etc.
>
> > The Romans boiling with tumultuous rage,
> > This warrior shall the dangerous storm assuage;
> > With victories he the Carthaginian mauls,
> > And with strong hand shall crush the rebel Gauls.

Also when Divus Claudius, the Emperor before Aurelian, was eagerly inquiring after the fate of his posterity, the following lot was drawn, from the first *Aeneid*:

> *His ego nec metas rerum, nec tempora pono.*
>
> > No bounds are to be set, no limits here.

Indeed he had a long line of successors. And when Master Pierre Amy experimented, in order to know if he would escape from the hobgoblins'[1] plots, he drew this verse from the third *Aeneid*:

> *Heu fuge crudeles terras, fuge littus avarum*
>
> > Ah flee the bloody land, the wicked shore.

And so he escaped from their hands, safe and sound. There are thousands of others, whose adventures it would be too tedious to relate, yet all of which fell out according to the prophecies read from verses drawn in this way, by the lots. I do not wish to infer, however, that this lottery is universally infallible. For I should not like you to be deluded.'

---

1. The hobgoblins, as in other passages, are the ignorant and bigoted Franciscans.

CHAPTER 11: *Pantagruel points out that Divination by Dice is unlawful*

'It would be sooner decided and done with,' said Panurge, 'with three good dice.'

'No,' replied Pantagruel, 'that method is deceptive, unlawful, and utterly scandalous. Never rely on it. That accursed book, the *Game of Dice*, was concocted by our old enemy, the Eternal Calumniator, long, long ago, near Boura in Achaea. He led many a simple soul into error in ancient times before the statue of the Bouraic Hercules. He enticed many and many a man into his snares, and still does so to-day, in many places. You know that my father Gargantua has forbidden this book throughout his dominions, and has had it burnt with all its types and engravings. Indeed he has completely exterminated, suppressed, and abolished it, as a most dangerous plague.

'What I have said to you of dice, I say also of the double-cubes: an equally deceitful form of divination. Do not bring forward as an argument against me the fortunate throw of double-cubes made by Tiberius in the fountain of Aponus, at the oracle of Geryon. These are hooks by which the Calumniator draws simple souls to their eternal perdition. Nevertheless, in order to satisfy you, I am quite agreeable for you to throw three dice on this table. Then, according to the score that you throw, we will pick the line on the page of the book where you open it. Have you any dice here in your purse?'

'A whole bag full,' answered Panurge. 'They're my green sprig, my safeguard against the devil, as recommended by Merlin Coccaius, in his second book, *About the Country of the Devils*. The devil would catch me napping if he caught me without dice.'

The dice were produced and thrown, and showed five, six, and five. 'That,' said Panurge, 'is sixteen. Let us take the sixteenth line on the page. The number pleases me. I think that our luck will be good. I'll go charging against all the devils of hell, like a bowl against a set of nine-pins, or a cannon-ball through a battalion of foot-soldiers, and let the devils look out for themselves, if I don't work on my future wife just that number of times on my wedding night.'

'I have no doubt that you will,' replied Pantagruel. 'There was no need to come out with such a thundering affirmation. The first time you'll serve a fault, which will count fifteen; and as you come down from roost you'll amend it. That'll make exactly sixteen.'

'Do you understand it like that?' asked Panurge. 'Never was a solecism committed by that valiant champion who stands sentinel for me just under my belly. Have you ever found me in the brotherhood of defaulters? Never, never, never till the last game. I perform like a holy father, like a father confessor, without fault. I appeal to the players.'

As soon as he had spoken these words, the works of Virgil were brought in. But before opening them, Panurge said to Pantagruel: 'My heart's flapping in my breast like a glove. Just feel how the pulse in my left arm's beating. You would imagine from its fevered rapidity that I was being mauled by the examiners of the Sorbonne. Don't you think that before proceeding further we ought to invoke Hercules and the Tenite goddesses, who are said to preside over the Chamber of Lots?'

'Neither Hercules nor the goddesses,' replied Pantagruel. 'Just open the book with your finger.'

CHAPTER 12: *Pantagruel inquires of the Virgilian Lottery how Panurge's marriage will turn out*

THEN Panurge opened the book and found the following verse on line sixteen:

Nec Deus hunc mensa, Dea nec dignata cubili est

The god him from his table banishéd,
Nor would the goddess have him in her bed.

'That,' said Pantagruel, 'is not in your favour. It signifies that your wife will be a whore, and consequently you'll be a cuckold. The goddess whose opposition you will meet is Minerva, a very fierce virgin, a most powerful and fire-eating goddess, an enemy of cuckolds, fancy-boys, and adulterers, a foe to lewd women who do not keep their promised vows to their husbands and are free with themselves to others. The god is Jupiter, who thunders and flashes lightning from the heavens. And you will note that, according to the doctrine of the ancient Etruscans, the *manubies* – for that is what they called the hurling of the Vulcanian thunderbolts – is reserved for her alone – an instance of this you'll find in her burning of the ships of Ajax Oileus – and for Jupiter, who bore her from his head. The rest of the Olympian gods are not permitted to hurl the thunder, and are therefore not so much dreaded by humankind. I will tell you more, and you may take it as drawn from divine mythology. When the giants made war upon the gods, the gods at first despised such enemies, and said that there was not one of them who was a match even for their pages. But when they saw Mount Pelion piled upon Mount Ossa by these giants' labours, and Mount Olympus beginning to shake as they prepared to place it on the other two, they were all afraid. Then Jupiter held a general council, at which all the gods decided that they must put up a valiant defence. And since they had several times seen battles lost through the interference of women among the soldiers, it was decreed that for the time being the whole crew of goddesses should be banished from the heavens into Egypt and the borders of the Nile, disguised as weasels, pole-cats, bats, shrewmice, and such-like. Only Minerva was kept back to throw the thunder with Jupiter, she being a goddess both of learning and war, of counsel and execution, a goddess born armed, a goddess dreaded in heaven, in the air, in the sea, and on earth.'

'By the belly of St Buff,' exclaimed Panurge. 'Could I, then, be that Vulcan the poet speaks about? No, I'm not lame, nor a coiner of false money, nor a blacksmith, as he was. Perhaps my wife will be as beautiful and attractive as his Venus, but she won't be such a whore; and I won't be a cuckold like him. The wretched cripple had himself declared a cuckold by judgement given in full assembly of the gods.

' So now listen to the other side. This augury denotes that my wife will be modest, chaste, and faithful, not up in arms, or rebellious, or headstrong and head-born like Pallas. And this fine ram Jupiter won't be my rival; he won't dip his bread in my soup, even though we sit together at table. Consider his exploits and gallant deeds. He was always the stoutest wencher and most infamous friar – I should say whoremonger – that ever was; always as lecherous as a boar – indeed he was fostered by a sow on Dicte in Crete, if Agathocles the Babylonian is not a liar. He was as randy as a goat – which is why others say that he was suckled by the she-goat Amalthea. By the powers of Acheron, he played the ram one day to a third part of the world, animals and men, river and mountains; I am thinking of Europa. For that rammish feat the people of Ammon had him represented as a ram ramming, a horned ram. But I know the way to protect myself against this horned fellow. Believe me, he'll find me no foolish Amphitryon, no silly Argus with his hundred pairs of spectacles, no cowardly Acrisius, no fantastic Lycus of Thebes, no dreamy Agenor nor phlegmatic Asopus, no hairy-footed Lycaon, no misshapen Corytus of Tuscany, no Atlas with a strong back. He can transform himself hundreds and hundreds of times, into a swan, a bull, a satyr, a shower of gold, or a cuckoo, as he did when he took the maidenhead of his sister Juno; into an eagle, a ram, or a pigeon, as he did when he was in love with the virgin Phthia, who lived at Aegium; into fire, into a serpent, or even into a flea, into Epicurean atoms or, *magistronostrally*, into the thought of a thought, but I'll catch him by the neck. And d'you know what I'll do to him? God's truth, I'll do to him what Saturn did to his father Caelus – Seneca said it before me and Lactantius confirmed it – what Rhea did to Atys. I'll cut off his ballocks flush with his bum; there won't be a shred left. For that reason he'll never be Pope, for *testiculos non habet.*'

'That'll do, my lad. That'll do,' said Pantagruel. 'Open the book a second time.'

This time he met with the following verse:

> *Membra quatit, gelidusque coit formidine sanguis.*
>
> Fright shakes his limbs, with fear his blood turns cold.

'That signifies,' said Pantagruel, 'that she'll beat you, back and belly.'

'On the contrary,' said Panurge, 'the prognostication applies to me, and says that I shall maul her like a tiger if she annoys me. Martin Wagstaff will do the job; and if I have no staff the devil devour me if I don't eat her up alive, as Cambles, King of the Lydians, ate his Queen.'

'You're very brave,' said Pantagruel. 'Hercules himself wouldn't take you on in your present fury. But they say that Poor Jack is worth two, and Hercules never dared fight alone against two.'

'And am I Poor Jack?' asked Panurge.

'Oh no, no,' answered Pantagruel. 'I was thinking of the games of lurch and backgammon.'

On his third attempt Panurge drew the verse:

Foemineo praedae et spoliorum ardebat amore.

She burnt with all a woman's love for spoils
And booty ...

'That signifies,' said Pantagruel, 'that she'll rob you. I can see your fate perfectly from these three draws. You'll be cuckolded, you'll be beaten, and you'll be robbed.'

'On the contrary,' replied Panurge, 'this verse signifies that she'll love me with a perfect love. The satirist didn't lie when he said that a woman burning with love supreme sometimes takes pleasure in stealing from her lover. And what, I ask you? A glove or a clasp, to make him search for it. Some trivial thing, nothing of importance. In the same way, these little arguments, these wranglings that arise at times between lovers, are just fresheners and spurs to love. Don't we sometimes see cutlers, for example, hammer their whetstones, the better to sharpen their tools on them? For that reason I take these three omens as most definitely favourable to me. If not, I appeal.'

'One can never appeal,' said Pantagruel, 'from what is decreed by lot and fortune, as our ancient jurisconsults attest, and as is stated by Baldus in his last chapter, *On the Laws*. The reason is that Fortune recognizes no superior to whom one can appeal from her and her decrees; and in this case the ward cannot be restored to his full rights, as is plainly declared in *L. Ait praetor* § *ult. ff. de minor.*'[1]

CHAPTER 13: *Pantagruel advises Panurge to test the future Happiness or Unhappiness of his Marriage by Dreams*

'Now since we don't agree in the interpretation of the Virgilian Lottery, let us try another form of divination.'

'Which one?' asked Panurge.

'A good, old, and genuine institution,' replied Pantagruel, 'divination by dreams. For when we dream under the conditions described by Hippocrates in his *Dream Book*, by Plato, Plotinus, Iamblichus, Synesius, Xenophon, Galen, Plutarch, Artemidorus, Daldianus, Herophilus, Q. Calaber, Theocritus, Pliny, Athenaeus, and others, the soul

1. Laws from the Digest, concerning Inheritance and Wardship.

often foresees future events. There is no need to prove it to you at greater length. You'll be convinced by a common example. Think how once well-washed, well-fed, and well-suckled children are sleeping soundly, their nurses go off to enjoy a bit of freedom, feeling at that time licensed to do as they like. For they have no need to stay around the cradle. In the same way, once our body is sleeping and the digestion is everywhere complete, nōthing more being necessary till it awakes, the soul enjoys itself and revisits its own country, which is the heavens. There it receives intimations of its first and divine origins. There it contemplates that infinite, intellectual sphere, the centre of which is at all points in the Universe and the circumference nowhere – which sphere, according to the doctrine of Hermes Trismegistus, is God. Nothing new befalls the soul, nothing in the past escapes it, it suffers no diminution. To it, all time is present. It notes not only events in this lower world of motion, but also future happenings; and when it reports them to the body and, through the body's senses and organs communicates them to its friends, it is called vaticinal and prophetic. It is true that it does not report them as straightforwardly as it saw them, being prevented by the imperfection and frailty of the bodily senses; even as the moon, receiving her light from the sun, does not communicate it to us as clearly, purely, vividly, and ardently as she received it. Therefore these somnial vaticinations require an interpreter, a skilful, wise, and industrious, expert, rational, and absolute Oneirocritic and Oneiropolist, for so the Greeks called them.

'That is why Heraclitus said that dreams did not reveal anything to us, nor conceal anything from us, but that they gave us a sign and indication of things to come, fortunate or unfortunate for ourselves, or for others. Holy Scripture testifies to this, and profane history confirms it by relating a thousand instances in which events have occurred in fulfilment of a dream, sometimes to the dreamer, sometimes to someone else. The Atlanteans and those living on the island of Thasos are lacking in this faculty. For in those countries no one has ever dreamed. Cleon of Daulia, Thrasymedes, and, in our own time, the learned Frenchman Villanovanus were also among those who did not dream.

'To-morrow, therefore, at the hour when jocund dawn shall with her rosy fingers drive away the darkness of the night, give yourself up to sound dreaming. Till then put aside all human affections: love, hatred, hope, and fear. For as of old the great seer Proteus, while disguised and transformed into fire, water, a tiger, a dragon, and other strange shapes, could not foretell events to come and, therefore, in order to foretell them had to be restored to his own native shape, so man cannot receive the divine art of prophecy except when that part of him which is most divine – to wit his *Nous* or *Mens*[1] – is quiet, tranquil, peaceable, and neither occupied nor distracted by extraneous passions or affections.'

'I'm willing,' said Panurge. 'Should I take a small or a large supper this evening? If I don't eat a good, large supper I never sleep really well. My sleep is disturbed all night, and my dreams are as empty as my belly is at the time.'

'No supper at all would be best,' said Pantagruel, 'considering your good state and healthy constitution. An ancient prophet, called Amphiaraus, insisted that those who received his oracles in dreams should eat nothing all that day, and drink no wine for three days previously. But we will not resort to so extreme and rigorous a regimen. I well believe that a man full of meat and overstuffed would have difficulty in gaining knowledge of spiritual matters. But I do not agree with those who believe that they can enter into deeper contemplation of celestial things after long and obstinate fasting. You may easily remember how my father Gargantua, whom I mention in all honour, has often told us that the writings of the fasting hermits are as flat, meagre, and sourspittled as were their bodies when they composed them; and that it is difficult to keep the spirits sound and serene while the body is in a state of inanition, seeing that philosophers and doctors affirm that the animal spirits spring up, are born, and are active in the arterial blood, purified and refined to a pure state in that *miraculous network* which lies beneath the ventricles of the brain. He gives us an example of a philosopher who thought he was in solitude, and that, having departed from the crowd, he could now theorize, reason, and write; and yet all the time around him dogs were barking, wolves howling, lions roaring, horses neighing, elephants trumpeting, serpents hissing, asses braying, grasshoppers chirping, and turtle-doves cooing. In fact he was in more turmoil than if he had been at the fair of Fontenay or of Niort. For hunger racked his body, and to remedy hunger the stomach barks, the sight grows dim, the veins suck up the very substance of the fleshy limbs and draw down the roaming spirit. The spirit then

1. The spiritual mind.

neglects to look after its nourisher and natural host, the body; as when a hawk upon the fist, striving to fly up into the air, is suddenly pulled downwards by the leash. And on this point he also quoted to us the authority of Homer, father of all philosophy, who said that the Greeks did not put an end to their mourning for Patroclus, the great friend of Achilles, till the moment when hunger declared itself, and their bellies protested that they would provide no more tears. For in their bodies, exhausted by their long fast, nothing was left to weep or cry with.

'Mediocrity is in all cases meritorious, and here you shall observe it. You will eat at supper not beans, not hare, or any other flesh, nor squid – which is called polypus – nor cabbage, nor any other food which might trouble and darken your animal spirits. For as the mirror cannot reflect the images of the things presented and exposed before it if its polish is obscured by breath or misty weather, so the spirit does not receive the shapes for divination by dreams if the body is disquieted and troubled by the vapours and fumes of meats previously eaten; and this on account of the indissoluble sympathy between the body and soul. You can eat some good Sabine and Bergamo pears, one Ribstone pippin, some plums from Tours, and a few cherries from my own orchard. Then you need not fear that your dreams will prove doubt-ful, fallacious, or suspicious, as some of the Peripatetics have declared them to be in autumn; that is when men feed more generously on fruit than at the other seasons. This same idea is stated in mystical form by the ancient prophets and poets, who say that empty and fallacious dreams lie hidden under the leaves that have fallen to the ground, because it is in autumn that the leaves fall from the trees. But really the natural heat which abounds in fresh fruit, and which on account of its volatility easily evaporates into the animal parts – as we see in new wine – has died out and dissolved long ago. As for drink, you shall have pure water from my fountain.'

'The conditions are rather hard for me,' said Panurge. 'I agree, all the same. It's dear, but it's worth it! I do stipulate, however, that we have breakfast early to-morrow, immediately after this dreaming business. Furthermore, I commend myself to Homer's two gates, to Morpheus, to Icelos, to Phantasos, and Phobetor. If they help me in my need, I'll build them a jolly altar all made of the finest down. If I were in Laconia, in the temple of Ino, between Oetylus and Thalames, she would resolve my problem for me in my sleep with sound, jovial dreams.'

'But wouldn't it be a good thing,' he asked Pantagruel a little later, 'if I were to put a few sprigs of laurel under my pillow?'

'There is no need for that now,' replied Pantagruel. 'It's a super-stition, and all that has been written about it by Serapion Ascalonites, Antiphon, Philochorus, Artemon, and Fulgentius Planciades is just so much nonsense. I would say the same about the left shoulder of the crocodile and the chameleon, but for my respect for old Democritus; and the same about the Bactrians' stone called Eumetrides; the same about the horn of Ammon – which is the name given by the Ethio-pians to a precious stone of a gold colour and in the shape of a ram's horn like the horn of Jupiter Ammon; and they say that the dreams of those who wear it are as true and infallible as the divine oracles. This is not much unlike what Homer and Virgil write of as the two gates of sleep, to which you just commended yourself. One is of ivory, and through it come confused, fallacious, and uncertain dreams; just as through ivory, however thin it is, no one can possibly see, since its density and opacity prevent the penetration of the visual spirits and the reception of the visible emanations. The other is of horn, and through it come certain, true, and infallible dreams, just as through horn all objects are clearly and distinctly visible.'

'Do you wish to infer,' asked Friar John, 'that the dreams of horned cuckolds, such as Panurge will be, with God's help and his wife's, are always true and infallible?'

CHAPTER 14: *Panurge's Dream and its Interpretation*

AT seven o'clock the following morning Panurge appeared before Pantagruel, in whose room were Epistemon, Friar John of the Hashes, Ponocrates, Eudemon, Carpalim, and others, to whom Pantagruel said as Panurge entered: 'Behold, the dreamer cometh.'

'Those words,' said Epistemon, 'were very costly in olden times. The sons of Jacob paid very dearly for them.'

'I've done well at Billy's in the land of Nod,' said Panurge at this. 'I've dreamed good and plenty, but I don't understand a word of it all, except that I had a young and charming wife, a perfect beauty, who treated me kindly, and made as much fuss of me as if I were her darling fancy-boy. Nobody could have been happier or gayer than I was. She flattered me, tickled me, tapped me, stroked me, kissed me, and cuddled me, and for a joke she made two pretty little horns to go above my forehead. I pointed out to her, jokingly too, that it was under my eyes that she ought to put them, so that I could see better what I wanted to butt. Then Momus would find no fault with her. He would not find anything to grumble about, the way he did about the position of the ox's horns. But the crazy girl took no notice of my remonstrance. She just pushed them a bit further in; and this did not hurt me in the least – which is a most remarkable thing. A little later I seemed to have been turned into a little drum, and she into an owl. At this point my sleep was broken, and I woke up with a start, quite vexed, and puzzled, and angry. Now there's a fine dishful of dreams, and I hope you enjoy yourself with them. Explain them to me, if you please, to the best of your understanding. And now let's go to breakfast, Carpalim.'

'It is clear to me,' said Pantagruel, 'if I have any skill in the art of divination by dreams, that your wife will not actually plant horns on your forehead, as the Satyrs wear them. But she will not keep faith or conjugal loyalty with you. She will give herself to other men and make you a cuckold. This point is clearly set out by Artemidorus, as I understand it. Also there will be no actual metamorphosis into a small drum in your case. But she'll beat you like a small drum at a wedding. Nor will she be turned into an owl. But she'll rob you, as is the nature of the owl. See now how your dreams conform to the Virgilian Lottery: you'll be cuckolded, you'll be beaten, and you'll be robbed.'

Then Friar John cried out and said: 'By God, he's speaking the truth. You'll be a cuckold, and a proper one, I promise you. You'll have a fine pair of horns. Ha, ha, ha! Our master de Cornibus, God help you! Preach us two words of a sermon, and I'll collect alms about the parish.'

'On the contrary,' said Panurge, 'my dream prognosticates that in my marriage I shall receive good things, planted with the horn of abundance. You assert that they will be Satyr's horns. *Amen, amen, fiat, fiatur! ad differentiam papae.*[1] Then I shall always have a stiff and tireless

1. Panurge is burlesquing the Papal form of assent: 'So be it till the Pope says no'.

john-thomas, as the Satyrs have; and that's a gift which all desire but
which heaven grants to few. Consequently I shall never be a cuckold.
For the lack of this stiffness is the operative defect, the sole cause that
makes husbands cuckolds. What is it that causes rogues to beg? It's
because they haven't enough at home to fill their sacks. What makes
the wolf leave the forest? Shortage of meat. What makes women
whores? You understand me, I'm sure. I appeal to the worshipful
clerics, presidents of courts, counsellors, lawyers, procurers, and other
commentators on the venerable script *De frigidis et maleficiatis*.[1] Pardon me if I misunderstand you. But you seem to me patently to err
in making horns the equivalent of cuckoldry. Diana wears them on her
head in the shape of a fair crescent. Is she a cuckold for that? How the
devil could she be a cuckold, since she was never married? Talk sense,
if you please, or she may make you horns of the kind she made for
Actaeon. The good Bacchus wears horns, also Pan, Jupiter Ammon,
and many others. Are they cuckolds? Can Juno be a whore? For that
would follow by the figure of speech called *metalepsis*, just as calling a
child a bastard or foundling in the presence of its father and mother
amounts plainly and tacitly to calling the father a cuckold and his wife
a whore. But let us speak less bawdily. The horns my wife made for
me are horns of abundance, and abundance of all goods. I'll stake my
oath on it. As for the rest, I shall be as jolly as a little drum at a wedding, always booming and echoing, always rumbling and thundering.
Believe me, this is where my luck will come in. My wife will be as
neat and dainty as a pretty little owl

>   Who doesn't believe what I tell
>   May go to the gibbet of Hell.
>   Noel, Noel, Noel.

'I note the last point that you mentioned,' said Pantagruel, 'and I
compare it with the first. At the beginning you were totally immersed
in the delights of your dream. But at the end you woke up with a
start, quite vexed, and puzzled and angry.'

'Of course,' interrupted Panurge. 'For I hadn't had any dinner at
all.'

'Everything will go to ruin,' continued Pantagruel. 'I foresee it.
Be quite certain that all sleep which ends with a start, and leaves the

1. About the frigid and those rendered impotent by spells.

sleeper vexed and angry, either signifies evil or portends evil. *Signifies evil:* that is to say a cacoethetic, malignant, pestilent, hidden disease lurking in the centre of the body, which in sleep – which always strengthens the powers of incubation, according to medical theory – would begin to declare itself and move towards the surface. At this unhappy stirring the sleeper's rest would be broken and the first organ of feeling be warned to sympathize and provide help, according to those proverbs that speak of stirring a hornets' nest, prodding La Camarina, or waking a sleeping cat. *Portends evil:* that is to say when the soul, by her activity in the matter of divination by dreams, gives us to understand that some misfortune is destined and prepared, and that it will shortly take place. As an instance, there is Hecuba's dream and terrible awakening; and there is the dream of Eurydice, Orpheus' wife; at the end of which, as Ennius declares, they each woke up with a frightened start. Hecuba, on waking, saw her husband Priam and her children murdered, and her country destroyed; and Eurydice, not long after her dream, perished miserably. Again there is Aeneas, who dreamt that he was talking to the dead Hector and suddenly woke up in a fright; and it was on that very night that Troy was sacked and burnt. On another occasion he dreamt that he saw his Penates and domestic gods, and awoke terrified, to encounter next day a terrible storm at sea. And there is Turnus, who on being incited by a fantastic vision of the infernal Fury to start a war against Aeneas, woke up angry and, later, after a series of disasters, was slain by this same Aeneas. There are thousands more instances. And when I tell you of Aeneas, note that Fabius Pictor says of him that he did nothing, embarked on no enterprise – and indeed that nothing ever happened to him – which he had not previously known and foreseen by divination of dreams.

'For these events there is no lack of reason. For if sleep and rest are the gift and special favour of the Gods, as the philosophers maintain and the poet attests when he says:

> Then came the hour when sleep, the Heavens' gift,
> Comes graciously to greet weary mankind,

such a gift cannot end in anger and irritation without some great misfortune being portended. Otherwise rest would not be rest and a gift would not be a gift, since it would not come from the gods, our friends, but from the devils, our enemies. Remember the common proverb:[1] ἐχθρῶν ἄδωρα δῶρα.

Suppose the master of the house, sitting at his rich table, with a good appetite and just beginning his meal, should be seen suddenly to jump up in alarm? Anyone who did not know the cause might well be astonished. Why did he do it? He had heard his servants cry "Fire", his maids cry "Thief", his children cry "Murder". He was compelled to leave the table, to run up and bring help, to give orders. Indeed, I remember that the Cabalists and Massoretes, interpreters of Holy Writ, in explaining how one can make sure of the genuineness of an angelic apparition – for often Satan's angels take the form of angels of light – say that the difference between the two lies in this: that when the good and consoling angel appears to man, he alarms him at first, but comforts him in the end, and leaves him happy and contented; whereas the wicked and corrupting angel rejoices a man at the beginning, but in the end leaves him troubled, angry, and perplexed.

CHAPTER 15: *Panurge's Excuse, and the Explanation of the Monastic Cabala in the matter of Salt Beef*

'THE Lord preserve those who see but do not hear!' said Panurge. 'I can see you very well, but I can't hear you at all, and I don't know what you're saying. The hungry stomach has no ears. I'm raging from a wild fury of hunger, I swear I am. I have been through a little too much, and it'll take more than Master Hocuspocus to set me off dreaming again this year. To miss my supper entirely, devil take it! That's a pox of a business! Come, Friar John, to breakfast. When I've well and truly breakfasted, and my stomach is well and truly lined and foddered, at a pinch and in case of necessity I'll do without my dinner. But to miss my supper! That's a pox of a business! Why, it's an error, a scandal in nature. Nature made the day for exercise, for work, and for each man to occupy himself in his business; and to help us do this more deftly, she provides us with a candle, the clear and joyful light of the sun. In the evening she begins to withdraw it from us, as much as to say to us: "You are good honest children. That's enough work.

1. The presents of enemies are not presents.

Night is coming, and now you ought to cease from your labours and take some refreshment. What you need is good bread, good wine, and good meat. After that you should enjoy yourselves a bit, then lie down and rest, so as to be as fresh and joyful for your next day's labours." That is the way falconers work. When they have fed their birds, they don't make them fly with their gorges full, but let them digest on the perch. This was very well understood by that good Pope who first instituted fasts. He ordered that the fast should be kept till the hour of Nones, and that for the rest of the day a man should be free to feed. In the olden days few dined at noon except, you might say, the monks and canons, who really have no other occupation. Every day is a feast day for them. They carefully observe the monkish proverb, *de Missa ad mensem*.[1] It has never been their practice to wait for the coming of the Abbot before getting down to their victuals. Of course, so long as they are eating, they have always been willing to wait for him as long as he liked, but not otherwise or under any other conditions. In the olden days everybody supped, except a few dozy fools; which is why supper is called *coena*, which means that it is common to all. You know that all right, Brother John. Come, my friend, let's have none of this devilish hanging about, but come along! My stomach's barking like a dog that's raging with hunger. Let's throw plenty of sops into his throat to keep him quiet, as the Sibyl did to Cerberus. You like your snacks at ungodly hours. But I prefer hare soup, accompanied by a good slice of the ploughman salted in nine lessons.'

'I understand you,' replied Friar John. 'That metaphor is drawn from the stock-pot of the cloister. The ploughman is the ox that labours or has laboured; in nine lessons, that is to say, cooked to a turn. For the Good Fathers of religion, by a certain cabalistic institution of the ancients, unwritten but passed from hand to hand, used in my time, on getting up for Matins, to go through certain important preliminaries before entering the church. They shat in the shitteries, pissed in the pisseries, spat in the spitteries, coughed melodiously in the cougheries, and dreamed in the dreameries, so that they might bring nothing unclean to the Divine service. Once they had done all this, they used to move devotedly to the Holy Chapel – for that in their jargon was the name they gave to the convent kitchen – and they

1. From Mass to table.

devotedly saw to it that from that moment the beef was on the fire for the breakfast of the holy friars, brethren in Our Lord. Often they lit the fire under the pot themselves.

By that rule, when Matins had nine lessons they had to get up earlier; and so their appetite and thirst increased as they bayed their chant, more than when Matins were pared down to one or three lessons only. The earlier they arose, by the said cabala, the earlier the beef was on the fire; the longer it was on, the better it was stewed; the better it was stewed the tenderer it was, the less it wore down the teeth, the more it delighted the palate, the less it weighed on the stomach, and the better it nourished the good monks; which was the sole purpose and prime aim of the founders, who remembered that far from eating to live, monks live to eat, having no other possession in this world but their lives. Let us go, Panurge.'

'Now,' said Panurge, 'I've understood you, my velvety ball-bag, my cloistral and cabalistic and ballocky friend. I give up my share in the capital. The principal, interest, and charges I forego, and content myself only with the costs, since you have so eloquently expounded this remarkable chapter of the Cabala culinary and monastic. Come, Carpalim. Brother John, my dear fellow, let's go. Good day to you all, my dear lords. I have dreamt enough for a drink. Let us go.'

Panurge had not spoken his last word when Epistemon cried out loudly: 'It's a most common and ordinary thing among men to realize, foresee, understand, and predict other men's misfortunes. But, oh what a rarity it is to realize, foresee, understand, and predict one's own! How wisely Aesop set this out in his *Fables*, when he said that every man born into this world carries a wallet round his neck, in the front pocket of which are the faults and misfortunes of others, which are always before his eyes and in his mind, while in the pocket that hangs behind him are his own faults and misfortunes, which are never seen or realized except by those on whom the heavenly constellations smile.'

CHAPTER 16: *Pantagruel advises Panurge to consult a Sibyl of Panzoust*

A SHORT time afterwards, Pantagruel sent for Panurge and said to him: 'The love that I bear you, which has deepened with the long course of time, prompts me to think of your welfare and advantage. Listen to what I have thought. I have heard that at Panzoust, near Le Croulay, there is a very famous sibyl, who predicts all future events. Take Epistemon for company, go into her presence, and hear what she has to say to you.'

'But perhaps,' said Epistemon, 'she is a Canidia, a Sagana, a pythoness, and sorceress. What gives me that idea is that the place has a bad name for sorceresses. There are said to be more there than ever there were in Thessaly. I shouldn't like to go there at all. The thing is wrong and it's forbidden by the law of Moses.'

'We are not Jews,' said Pantagruel, 'and it is neither verified nor admitted that she is a sorceress. Postpone the sifting and winnowing of these matters till your return. How do we know that she isn't an eleventh sibyl, a second Cassandra? And even if she is no sibyl and does not deserve the name of sibyl, what harm do you incur, Panurge, by consulting her in your perplexity, especially when you consider that she has the reputation for more wisdom and more understanding than is usual in her country or among her sex? What harm is there in gaining knowledge every single day, even from a sot, a pot, a fool, a stool, or an old slipper? You remember how Alexander the Great, after gaining his victory over King Darius at Arbela, once when surrounded by his princelings, refused to listen and afterwards vainly repented of his refusal, thousands and thousands of times. He was the victor in Persia, but so far away from his hereditary kingdom of Macedonia that to his great distress he could not devise any means of getting news from home, both because of the enormous distance between the countries, and because of the impediment of broad rivers, the obstacles provided by deserts and the barriers of mountain ranges. Whilst he was brooding perplexedly on these troubles, which were not small ones, for his native kingdom might have been occupied, and a new king and new conquerors have been in possession long before he could have had warning to prevent it – whilst he was brooding, as

I said, there appeared before him a man from Sidonia, an experienced and intelligent merchant, but poor enough otherwise and unimpressive to look at, who announced and insisted that he had discovered a way by which Alexander's country could be informed of his Indian victories, and he could have news of conditions in Macedonia and Egypt in less than five days. But Alexander considered this claim so impossibly ridiculous that he would not even listen to the merchant or give him an audience. What would it have cost him to hear the man and examine his claim? What harm or damage could he have incurred in ascertaining what the way was, what the proposition was that the man wanted to explain to him? There must be some reason why Nature has made our ears open, and placed no door or cover over them, as she has done over our eyes, our tongue, and the other openings in our bodies. Her purpose is, I believe, that all day and all night we shall continually be able to hear, and through our hearing perpetually to learn. For our hearing is the most educable of all our senses. Now that merchant might have been an angel, that is to say a messenger sent from God, as Raphael was sent to Tobias. But Alexander was too ready to despise him, and regretted it for a very long time.'

'You are right,' said Epistemon. 'But you'll never persuade me that it is a very profitable thing to take counsel and advice from a woman, and from such a woman in such a country.'

'I'm very lucky in women's counsel,' said Panurge, 'and especially when they're old women. Thanks to their advice, I always produce an extra evacuation or two of the bowels. They're real pointer dogs, my friend, real manuals of the law. They're right to call them sage women. But it's my general custom to call them *presage* women. Sage they are, because they're extremely handy at finding things out. But I say *presage*, because they foresee by divination and infallibly foretell all things to come. Sometimes I call them not harlots but harbingers, as the Romans called Juno. For we always get salutary and useful warnings from them. On this point you should refer to Pythagoras, Socrates, Empedocles, and our master Ortuinus. Moreover, I have the very highest opinion of the ancient custom of the Germans, who set the counsel of old women at a price above that of the Temple weights, and greatly revered it. Thanks to the advice and answers they received, they met with success and prosperity, in due proportion to

the wisdom with which they followed their guidance – as witness old
Aurinia, and good mother Velleda, in the days of Vespasian. Old age
in women, I assure you, is always productive of sublime – I mean
sibylline – qualities. May God help us, may the power of God aid us,
and let us go. Let us go. Good-bye, Friar John. I entrust my codpiece
to you.'

'Very well,' said Epistemon. 'I'll follow you. But I give you warning that if I hear she resorts to lotteries or spells for her answers, I shall
leave you at the door. You shall have no further company from me.'

CHAPTER 17: *Panurge speaks to the Sibyl of Panzoust*

THEIR journey took three days; and on the third, the prophetess's
dwelling was pointed out to them. It was on the brow of a mountain,
beneath a great broad chestnut tree, and they had no difficulty in
entering her straw-thatched cottage, which was badly built, badly
furnished, and filled with smoke.

'No matter,' said Epistemon, 'Heraclitus, a great Scotist and obscure philosopher, showed no astonishment on entering a house like
this, but explained to his followers and disciples that the gods resided
there just as much in palaces full of delights. I believe that the cottage
of the famous Hecale, in which she feasted the young Theseus, was
like this; and like this too was the cottage of Hireus or Eunopion,
which Jupiter, Neptune, and Mercury were not ashamed to enter, all
together, and to take a meal and lodge there too; and to pay for their
lodging they forged Orion, from their piss-pot.'

They found the old woman in the chimney corner.

'She is a real sibyl,' cried Epistemon, 'faithful to the living image
of the one Homer described, when he compared Ulysses to a sibyl.'

The old woman was grim to look at, ill-dressed, ill-nourished,
toothless, bleary-eyed, hunchbacked, snotty, and feeble. She was making a soup out of some green cabbage, a rind of yellow bacon, and an
old marrow bone.

'Odd's my life!' exclaimed Epistemon, 'we've gone wrong badly.
We shall never get an answer out of her, because we haven't brought
the golden bough.'

'I've provided for that,' replied Panurge. 'I've got it here in my bag, in the shape of a golden ring and some fine, sparkling Charles crowns.'

Having said this, Panurge gravely saluted her, and presented her with six smoked ox-tongues, a large butter-pot full of dumplings, a long bottle complete with beverage, and a ramscod purse full of newly minted Charles crowns. Lastly, with a deep bow, he put on her ring-finger a very fine gold ring, in which was a Beuxe toadstone, magnificently set. Then in a few brief words he explained to her the purpose of his coming, begging her courteously to give him her advice and tell him what good fortune would come of his marriage enterprise.

The old hag remained silent for some time, deep in thought, and grinning like a dog. Then she sat down on the bottom of a tub, took three old spindles in her hands, turned and twisted them in her fingers in various ways, and felt their points, keeping the sharpest in her hand and throwing the two others under a millet-mortar. After that she took the reels of her spindle and turned them nine times, lifting her hands off them at the ninth turn, but watching their movement and waiting till they were perfectly still. Then I saw her take off one of her clogs – we call them *sabots* – put her apron over her head, as priests do their amice when about to sing the Mass, and tie it under her throat with an ancient piece of striped and spotted cloth. Then all muffled up, she took a long swig from the bottle, extracted three crowns from the ramscod purse, put them in three walnut shells, and placed them on the bottom of a pot of feathers. Next she swept her broom three times across the hearth and threw half a faggot of briar and a branch of dry laurel on the fire, watching them burn in silence, and noticing that in burning they made no crackling or noise of any kind.

Then she gave a horrible cry, muttering some barbarous words with strange endings, which caused Panurge to say to Epistemon: 'By all the powers, I'm trembling. I believe I'm bewitched. She doesn't talk Christian. Just look, she seems to me quite three foot taller than she was when she put her apron over her head. What does this waggling of the cheeks mean? What's the significance of this shoulder shrugging? Why does she mumble with her lips like an ape shelling shrimps? I've got a singing in my ears. I seem to hear Proserpine crying. The devils will soon break loose on this spot. Oh, the ugly beasts! Let us run away! Holy snakes, I'm dying of fear. I don't like these devils. They worry me and they're most unpleasant. Let's run away. Good-bye, madam, thank you very much for your kindness. I won't marry at all. I renounce the idea from this moment. It shall be in the future as it was in the past.'

With this he started to scamper out of the room. But the old hag was before him, still holding her spindle, and went out into a back-yard beside her house, in which was a sycamore tree. She shook this tree three times, and on the eight leaves which fell she summarily wrote some brief lines with her spindle. Then she threw them into the air and said: 'Go and look for them if you like; find them if you can. The fatal destiny of your marriage is written upon them.'

After saying this, she retired into her den. But on the doorstep she hitched up her gown, petticoat, and smock to her armpits, and showed them her arse. 'Odds tripe and onions,' cried Panurge as he saw it, 'look, there's the sibyl's cavern.'

Quickly she barred the door, and was seen no more. They, however, ran after the leaves and picked them up, though it cost them great efforts. For the wind had scattered them among the bushes of the valley. Then, when they had arranged them in order, they found the following sentence in rhymes:

> Of fame you're shelled
> So, even so,
> And she with child,
> Of you, oh no.
> Your good end
> Suck she will
> And flay you, friend,
> But not all.

CHAPTER 18: *Pantagruel and Panurge find different explanations for the Verses of the Sibyl of Panzoust*

WHEN they had collected the leaves, Epistemon and Panurge re-turned to Pantagruel's court, partly glad and partly vexed; glad at their return, but vexed by the labours of the road, which they found rugged, stony, and ill-made. They presented a full report of their journey to Pantagruel, together with a description of the sibyl, and then handed him the sycamore leaves, showing him the short lines of writing.

When Pantagruel had read them all, he said to Panurge with a sigh: 'You've done very well. The sibyl's prophecy clearly confirms what was already stated by the Virgilian Lottery and also by your own dreams; that is, that you will be disgraced by your wife, that she'll make you a cuckold by giving herself to another and becoming pregnant by another; that she'll rob you of some good part of your possessions, and that she'll beat you, flaying and bruising some part of your body.'

'You understand as much about the exposition of modern prophecies,' replied Panurge, 'as a sow does of spiced lozenges. Don't be ruffled by what I say, but I feel rather cross. The truth is quite the opposite. Now listen patiently. What the old woman means is that just as the bean isn't seen if it isn't shelled, so my virtue and perfections will never be famous unless I marry. How many times have I heard you say that judgeship and office reveal a man, and bring to light what he has in his paunch? That is to say that people only know for certain what a man is and what he is worth, when he is called to the management of affairs. Before that – that is to say when a man is a private citizen – no one knows for certain what he is. Would you maintain the contrary, that a good man's honour and renown depend on the rump of a whore? The second article says: my wife will be with child – here, you see, is the first joy of marriage – but not of me. God save me, I can believe that! It'll be a pretty little boy that she'll be big with. I love him already most heartily; in fact I'm quite silly about him. He'll be my little calf-skin. There'll be no vexation in life, no trouble so great or so tiresome that I shan't throw it off the moment I see him and hear him prattle his childish prattle. Blessings on the old woman! I should like, really I should, to settle a good pension on her, in Salmigundia – not one of your pensions that's like a flighty bachelor of art, but a fixed one, as dependable as a grand professor in his chair. But to take the other view, would you have my wife carry me in her belly, and conceive me? And bring me into the world? Would you have people say, "Panurge is a second Bacchus. He has been born twice. He is René (born again), as Proteus was, once of Thetis, and a second time of the philosopher Apollonius's mother; and as the two Palici were, beside the river Simethus, in Sicily. His wife carried him in her womb. In him is repeated the ancient *palin-tocia* of the Megareans, and the *palingenesia* of Democritus." What utter nonsense! Don't speak to me of it again.

'The third article says: my wife will suck my good end. I am quite agreeable. Of course you understand that this is the single-ended staff which hangs between my legs. I shall always keep it succulent and well supplied. She won't suck it in vain, I promise you. There will always be a little bit there, or rather more. Now you expound this line allegorically, and interpret it to mean larceny and theft. I commend the exposition, the allegory pleases me, but not in your sense. It may be the sincere affection you feel for me that makes you see difficulties and reverses ahead. For the learned tell us that love is a strangely fearful thing, and that true love is never free from fear. But I really believe you to understand in your heart that theft, in this passage as in so many others of the Latin and ancient writers, signifies the sweet fruit of passing love; which Venus would have us pluck secretly and stealthily. Why so, I ask you? Because the little deed, performed on the spur of the moment between closed doors, on the staircase behind the hangings, or on the sly on an untied bundle of firewood, is more pleasing to the Cyprian goddess – and I say this without prejudice to higher authority – than when done in full daylight after the Cynics' fashion, or under a precious canopy, behind gold-embroidered curtains, perfunctorily and at long intervals, with a crimson silk fly-flap and a plume of Indian feathers to chase the flies from round about while the female is picking her teeth with a bit of straw that she will, in the meantime, have pulled out of the bottom of the mattress. Would you maintain, on the other hand, that by sucking me as one sucks oysters from their shells, or as the women of Cilicia – as Dioscorides tells us – suck the scarlet grain from the oak, she will be robbing me? A robber doesn't suck, but grabs. He doesn't swallow, but packs up, spirits away, and hey-presto it's gone.

'The fourth article says my wife will flay me, but not all. Oh, what a lovely line! And you interpret it to mean blows and bruises. That's prettily to the point, God bless you! But raise your spirits, I beg of you, from earthly thoughts to the high contemplation of Nature's marvels. Admit and take the blame for the errors you have committed in perversely expounding the prophetic words of the divine sibyl. Putting – but not admitting or conceding – the case that my wife, at the instigation of our hellish enemy, should wish and attempt to play me a mean trick, to defame me, to make me a downright cuckold, to rob me and do me violence, still she would never be successful in her attempt. The reason which moves me to say this is based on my final point, which is drawn from the arcana of monastic pantheology. Brother Arthur Rumper told it me once, and it was on a Monday morning, as we were sharing a bushel of trotter-pies, and it was raining, as I remember. God give him good weather!

'At the creation of the world, or a little after, the women conspired together to flay the men alive, for trying to lord it over them everywhere. And this resolution was formed, confirmed and sworn to by them, by the holy blood of St Bridget. But, oh, the vain endeavours of women! Oh, the great frailty of the female sex! They began to flay the man, or peel him, as Catullus puts it, by the part that gives them most delight, to wit the nervous and hollow member. That was more than six thousand years ago, and yet up to the present they have only peeled its tip. For which reason, in pure despite, the Jews themselves snip it and cut it back in circumcision, preferring to be called clipyards and circumcised infidels, rather than be flayed by woman like the other peoples. My wife, not wishing to betray this common enterprise, will flay it for me, if it is not done already. I consent to that most willingly, but not to *all*, I assure you, my noble king.'

'You give no explanation of the laurel branch,' said Epistemon, 'that burnt without any noise or crackling while we looked on and she watched it, and exclaimed over it with hideous and frightening cries. That, you know, is a bad omen and a most fearful portent, as is attested by Propertius, Tibullus, Porphyry the subtle philosopher, Eustathius on Homer's *Iliad*, and others.'

'Really,' replied Panurge, 'you do drive some queer calves to market. As poets they were fools, and as philosophers, dreamers; as full of fine folly as their philosophy was.'

CHAPTER 19: *Pantagruel speaks in praise of Dumb men's Counsel*

AFTER this reply Pantagruel remained for some time silent, and seemed to be in deep thought. Then he said to Panurge: 'You're misled by the evil spirit; but listen. I have read that in the old days the truest and surest oracles were not those delivered in writing or offered by word of mouth. Very often even those who were reckoned subtle and ingenious have been mistaken in them, both because of the ambiguities, equivocations, and obscurities in the words, and because of the brevity of the sentences. For which reason Apollo, the god of prophecy, was surnamed Lôxias – the Indirect. Those oracles that were declared by gestures and signs were looked upon as the truest and most dependable. This was the opinion of Heraclitus; this was the manner of Jupiter's prophecies at Ammon, and in this way Apollo prophesied among the Assyrians. Which is why they depicted him with a long beard and clothed, like an old person of sound judgement, not naked, young, and beardless as the Greeks drew him. Let us use this method, and by signs, without resorting to speech, take counsel of some dumb person.'

'I agree,' replied Pantagruel.

'But,' said Pantagruel, 'it would be as well if this dumb person had been deaf from birth, and were dumb for this reason. For there is no dumb man so simple as one who has never had his hearing.'

'What do you mean by that?' asked Panurge in reply. 'If it were true that no man ever spoke who had never heard speech, I would lead you by logical inference to a most absurd and paradoxical conclusion. But let it pass. You don't believe, then, what Herodotus wrote about the two children kept shut in a cottage by the command of Psammetichus, king of Egypt, and brought up in complete silence, who after a certain time pronounced the word *becus*, which in Phrygian means bread?'

'Not in the very least,' replied Pantagruel. 'It's nonsense to say that we have a natural language; languages arise from arbitrary conventions and the needs of peoples. Words, as the dialecticians say, have meanings not by nature, but at choice. I don't make this statement without backing. For Bartolus, in his first book, *On the Purpose of Language*, recounts that in his time there was in Gubbio a certain

Messer Nello de Gabrielis, who happened to have been born deaf. Nevertheless he understood every Italian, however cryptically he expressed himself, merely by the sight of his gestures and the movements of his lips. I have read also, in a learned and eloquent writer, the story of Tiridates, the king of Armenia in Nero's time. He visited Rome, and was received with honour and solemnity and magnificent pomp, since they wanted to retain his eternal friendship for the Senate and the Roman people; and there was nothing of importance in the city which was not shown and pointed out to him. On his departure the Emperor gave him exceedingly large presents and, in addition, allowed him to choose the thing in Rome that most pleased him, promising on his oath not to refuse him, whatever he might desire. All that he asked for was a certain comic actor, whom he had seen in the theatre, where he had perfectly understood his meaning by his signs and gestures, although he had not understood what he said. The reason he gave was that there were under his rule people of different languages, to converse with whom he required several interpreters; but this man would be enough by himself; for he was so good at expressing himself by gestures that he seemed to speak with his fingers.

'Therefore you must choose a dumb person who is deaf from birth, so that his gestures and signs may be naturally prophetic, not feigned, artificial, or affected. But it still remains undecided whether you wish to take this counsel from a man or a woman.'

'I should like to take it from a woman,' said Panurge, 'if I didn't fear two things: one is that whatever women see, they immediately connect in the privacy of their own minds with the entry of the sacred Ithyphallus. Whatever gestures or signs one may make, however one may behave in their sight and presence, they always refer everything to the act of androgynation. So we should be deceived. For this woman would take all our signs for signs concupiscent. Do you remember what happened in Rome two hundred and sixty years after the foundation of the city? A young Roman gentleman, meeting on Mount Caelion a Latin lady named Verona, who was deaf and dumb from birth, asked her with Italian gesticulations but in ignorance of her deafness, what senators she had met on her way up. Not hearing what he said, she imagined him to be suggesting what was in her own thoughts, and what a young man naturally asks of a woman. Therefore by signs – which in love-making are incomparably more delightful, efficacious, and precious than words – she drew him into her house, and indicated to him that she was fond of the game. Finally, without uttering a word with their lips, they played some fine music with their thighs.

'The second thing that I fear is that she might make no response to our signs, but promptly fall on her back, as in act consenting to our tacit demands. Or if she did make any signs to us in response to our propositions, they might be so senseless and stupid that we should ourselves realize her thoughts to be concupiscent. You remember what happened at Brignolles. How sister Fatbum the nun was got with child by that lecherous young monk Stiffcock, and how, when her pregnancy was discovered, she was cited by the abbess in full chapter and accused of incest. She defended herself by pleading that it had not been done with her consent, but that she had been overborne and raped by Brother Stiffcock. The abbess cut her short, crying: "You wicked creature, it was in the dormitory. Why didn't you shout out? We would all have come to your help." But the nun answered that she dared not shout in the dormitory because the dormitory is a place of perpetual silence. "But, you abandoned wretch," cried the abbess, "why didn't you make a sign to the sisters next to you in the room?" "I did signal to them with my bottom, which was the best I could do," said Fatbum, "but no one helped me." "But why didn't you come and tell me immediately, you hussy," demanded the abbess, "and make a proper accusation against him? I should have done so, if the thing had happened to me, in order to prove my innocence." "You see," answered Fatbum, "after it happened I was afraid of remaining in a state of sin and damnation, in case I was overtaken by sudden death. So I confessed to him before he went out of the room; and he enjoined me as a penitence not to tell anyone, and not ever to reveal it. It would have been too huge a sin, too great an abomination in the sight of God and his angels, to break the seals of confession. It might perhaps have caused the whole abbey to be burnt by fire from heaven, and all of us to fall into the pit with Dathan and Abiram." '

'You won't make me laugh with that,' said Pantagruel. 'I am perfectly aware that the whole of monkdom is less afraid of transgressing God's commandments than of infringing their own provincial statutes. So let it be a man. Goatsnose seems a suitable choice to me. He is deaf and dumb from birth.'

CHAPTER 20: *Goatsnose answers Panurge by Signs*

GOATSNOSE was sent for and arrived the next day. On his arrival Panurge gave him a fat calf, half a hog, two puncheons of wine, a load of wheat, and thirty francs in small change. Then he led him before Pantagruel and, in the presence of the gentlemen of the bedchamber, he made him this sign: he took a longish yawn, and as he yawned he made, outside his mouth, with the thumb of his right hand, the figure of the Greek letter known as Tau, which he frequently repeated. Then he raised his eyes to heaven and rolled them in his head like a nanny-goat in an abortion, coughing as he did so and heaving a deep sigh. This done, he pointed to his lack of a codpiece, and beneath his shirt he took his prodding-tool in his fist and made it clatter melodiously between his thighs. He then bowed, bending his left knee, and remained with both his arms folded on his chest, one over the other.

Goatsnose looked at him curiously, then raised his left hand in the air, keeping all the fingers clenched except the thumb and the index finger, the two nails of which he softly laid together.

'I understand what he means by that sign,' said Pantagruel. 'He means marriage. According to the theory of the Pythagoreans, that sign denotes marriage, and the number thirty as well. You will be married.'

'Thank you very much,' said Panurge, turning to Goatsnose. 'Thank you, my little major-domo, my galley-master, my nigger-driver, my constable, my sergeant of police.'

Then Goatsnose raised his aforesaid left hand higher in the air than ever, extending all its five fingers and stretching them as wide as he could.

'Now,' said Pantagruel, 'he is informing us more positively, by giving us the sign of the quinary number. That means that you will certainly be married, and not only affianced, espoused, and married, but that, furthermore, you will cohabit and get well on with the job. Pythagoras called the quinary number the nuptial number, which indicates a wedding and the consummation of a marriage, being composed of the triad, which is the first odd and superfluous number, and of the dyad, which is the first even number. This signifies the male and female in copulation. Indeed at Rome, in the olden times, they would light five wax candles on a wedding day; and it was not permissible to light more, even at the marriage of the wealthiest, or fewer, even at the marriage of the very poorest. Moreover, in the olden days the pagans used to implore the assistance of five deities, or one god for five good offices, on behalf of those about to be married: of Jupiter, the nuptial god; of Juno, who presided over the feast; of Venus the fair; of Pitho, the goddess of persuasion and eloquence, and of Diana, who presided over childbirth.'

'Oh, the gentle Goatsnose!' cried Panurge. 'I shall give him a farm near Sinais, and a windmill in Mirebalais.'

Hereupon the dumb man sneezed with a signal vehemence that shook his whole body, and turned to the left.

'By the power of the wooden ox,' cried Pantagruel, 'what's that? It's not a good sign. It denotes that your marriage will be inauspicious and unhappy. Sneezing, according to the doctrine of Terpsion, denotes the presence of the Socratic daemon. A sneeze to the right signifies that a man may do whatever, and go wherever, he proposes with boldness and assurance. Everything will be good and fortunate from beginning to end. But a sneeze to the left means the contrary.'

'You always see things at their worst,' said Panurge. 'You are for ever upsetting everything, like the slave Davus. I don't believe a word of it. I never met that old wretch Terpsion yet when he wasn't cheating.'

'Cicero says something about it in his second book of *Divinations*, all the same,' said Pantagruel.

Then he turned towards Goatsnose and made him this sign: he rolled up his eyelids, swivelled his jaws from left to right, and stuck his tongue half-way out of his mouth. This done, he opened the fingers of his left hand, with the exception of the middle one, which he kept perpendicularly on his palm, and placed it in this attitude where his codpiece should have been; keeping his right hand clenched except for the thumb, which he stuck straight back under his right armpit and settled above his arse in the place which the Arabs call *al katim*.[1] Then he quickly changed hands, holding his right in the attitude of his left and putting it in the position where his codpiece should have been, and in place of his right, he clenched his left, and placed it on

1. The sacrum.

the *al katim*. This changing of hands he repeated nine times. On the ninth he restored his eyelids to their natural position, and did the same to his jaws and his tongue. Then he squinted at Goatsnose, shaking his chops, as apes do when they are happy, and as rabbits do when eating oats in the sheaf.

Thereupon Goatsnose raised his right hand in the air, wide open, putting the thumb up to the third joint between the third joints of the middle and the ring finger, which he clenched rather lightly round his thumb, drawing the other joints of these fingers into his fist and stretching his index and little fingers out straight. Then he placed his hand, thus clenched, on Panurge's navel, continually moving the aforesaid thumb, and supporting this hand on his index and little fingers, as on a pair of legs. In this posture he made his hand climb up Panurge's belly, stomach, chest, and neck, in succession, to his chin, and put his aforesaid waggling thumb in Panurge's mouth. Then he rubbed his nose with it, and, climbing further, up to his eyes, made a show of putting them out with his thumb. This finally annoyed Panurge, who tried to withdraw and shake the dumb man off. But Goatsnose went on touching him with his waggling thumb, first on his eyes, then on his forehead, and then just underneath his cap.

Finally Panurge cried out: 'By God, Master Fool, you'll get a beating if you don't leave me alone. Don't you go on annoying me, or my foot will pummel your rascally face till you look as if you were wearing a mask.'

'He's deaf,' said Friar John. 'He can't hear what you say, old cock. Give him the sign to show you mean a bang on the nose.'

'What the devil does Master Quack think he's up to?' cried Panurge. 'He's nearly poached my eyes in melted butter. By God – if I may be forgiven – I'll give you a fine feast of punches, with double-raps on the nose between the courses.' With this he let Goatsnose go, blowing him a salvo of farts.

When the dumb man saw Panurge about to go, he got in front of him, held him back by force, and made him the following sign. He dropped his right arm to its full extent towards his knee, clenching all his fingers together, and poking his thumb between his middle and index fingers. Then he rubbed the inside of the elbow of that right arm with his left hand and, little by little, as he rubbed it, he raised that arm in the air to the level of the elbow and higher. Then he suddenly dropped it to its former position, raising it and dropping it at intervals, and all the time exhibiting it to Panurge.

In an absolute fury, Panurge raised his fist to give the dumb man a punch. But out of respect for Pantagruel's presence, he restrained himself. Then said Pantagruel: 'If the signs annoy you, you will be very much more annoyed by their fulfilment. For all the prophecies agree. The dumb man is demonstrating and foretelling that you will be married, cuckolded, beaten, and robbed.'

'The marriage I admit,' said Panurge. 'The rest I deny, and I beg you to be so kind as to believe me when I say that no man was ever so lucky in his wife and his horses as I am predestined to be.'

CHAPTER 21: *Panurge takes Counsel with an old French poet called Raminagrobis*

'I NEVER expected to meet a man who stuck to his own ideas as obstinately as you do,' said Pantagruel. 'All the same, I think we should leave no stone unturned to resolve these doubts of yours. Listen to my idea. Swans, which are birds sacred to Apollo, never sing except when about to die. This is especially true on the Meander, a river in Phrygia – which I mention because Aelian and Alexander Myndius write that they have seen several die elsewhere, but never heard one sing at its death. A swan's song, therefore, is a certain presage of its approaching death, and it never dies unless previously it has sung. In the same way poets, who are also under the protection of Apollo, upon the approach of death generally become prophets and sing by Apollonine inspiration, foretelling things which are to come. I have often heard it said, besides, that any old man, when decrepit and near his end, can easily divine future events. In fact, I remember Aristophanes, in one of his comedies, calling all old people sibyls. For just as when we are on a jetty and see the sailors and passengers afar off in their ships on the open sea, we merely watch them in silence and pray fervently for their happy landing; but when they come near to harbour we greet them by words and gestures, and congratulate them on having reached a safe haven and come amongst us; so also angels, heroes, and good spirits – according to the doctrine of the Platonists – when they see human beings draw near to death, as into the surest and safest of harbours, the harbour of quiet and rest, out of the troubles and worries of this earth, greet them, comfort them, speak with them, and even then begin to teach them the art of divination. I will not quote you the ancient examples of Isaac to Jacob, of Hector to Patroclus, of Hector to Achilles, of Polymnestor to Agamemnon and Hecuba, of the Rhodian celebrated by Posidonius, of Calanus the Indian to Alexander the Great, of Orodes to Mezentius, and others. I will call to your mind only that learned and valiant knight Guillaume du Bellay, once Lord of Langley, who died on Mont Tarare on the tenth of January, in the critical year of his life, in our computation the year 1543 by the Roman reckoning. The three or four hours before his decease he spent predicting to us in vigorous language, with a calm and tranquil mind, events that we have since witnessed in part and in part still expect to happen. At the actual time, however, these prophecies seemed to us somewhat unlikely and strange, since there appeared to us to be no cause or present sign which heralded what he predicted. Now we have here, near La Ville-au-Maire, one who is both old and a poet – Raminagrobis I mean, who married the great sow for his second wife, who bore him the fair Syphilis. I have heard that he is *in articulo*, and at the point of death. Go and visit him, and hear his song. It may be that you'll hear what you desire from him, and that through him Apollo will resolve your doubts.'

'I'm willing,' said Panurge. 'Let's go to him, Epistemon, as fast as we can, for fear that death may forestall us. Will you come, Brother John?'

'I'm willing,' replied Friar John, 'perfectly willing, for love of you, old cock. For I love you with all my liver.'

They set out immediately, and when they arrived at the poetic abode they found the good old man in his death-agony, but cheerful in his looks, with a bright face and a shining eye. On saluting him, Panurge put on the ring-finger of his left hand, as a free gift, a golden ring in the bezel of which was a fine, large oriental sapphire. Then, in imitation of Socrates, he offered him a beautiful white cock which, when placed on his bed, immediately raised its head, flapped its wings with delight, and crowed loud and lustily. After this Panurge courteously asked the dying poet to give and expound his judgement on the problem of the proposed marriage.

The good old man ordered ink, pen, and paper to be brought to him; which was promptly done. Then he wrote as follows:

> Take her, take her not,
> If you take her, good enough.
> If you take her not, in truth
> All is to perfection wrought.
> Gallop, but a gentle pace.
> Back, go on and win the race
> > Take her, &c.
> Fast, but eat a double feast,
> What was re-made, that unmake.
> What was unmade, that re-make.
> Wish her life and wish her death
> > Take her, &c.

This he handed to them and said: 'Go, my children, under the protection of the great God of heaven, and bother me no more about this matter or about anything else. I have to-day, which is the last both of May and of me, with great labour and difficulty, driven out of my house a pack of ugly, unclean, pestilential beasts. Some were black, some piebald, some dun, some white, some ash-grey, and some speckled. They wouldn't leave me to die in peace, but by fraudulent prickings, harpyish clutchings, and waspish importunities, all forged in the smithy of I know not what insatiable greed, called me out of the sweet dream in which I was reposing. For just then I was contemplating and seeing, yes even touching and tasting, the blessings and happiness that the good God has prepared for His faithful and elect, in the other life and the immortal state. Refrain from imitating them, do not be like them. Bother me no more, and leave me in silence, I implore you.'

CHAPTER 22: *Panurge defends the Order of Friars Mendicant*

As he came out of Raminagrobis's room, Panurge said, as if thoroughly scared: 'By the power of God, I believe he's a heretic. Devil take me if he is not. He slanders the good mendicant fathers, Franciscan and Dominican, who are the two hemispheres of Christendom, on whose gyrognomic circumbilivaginations, as on two celivagous counterpendulums, the whole antonomatic matagrobolism of the

Roman Church homocentrically revolves, when it feels itself obfusticulated by any heretical or erroneous clap-trap. But what in the name of all the devils have these poor devils of Capuchins and Friars Minim done to him? Aren't they afflicted enough already, the miserable sods? Aren't they already sufficiently fumed and perfumed with misery and disaster, the poor wretched offscourings of Ichthiophagia?[1] On your oath, Brother John, is he in a state of salvation? He's damned like a serpent, I swear he is, and he's on his way to thirty thousand basketfuls of devils. To slander those good and valiant pillars of the Church! Do you call that poetic frenzy? I can't feel happy about him; he is a gross sinner and a blasphemer against the faith. I am greatly scandalized.'

'I don't give a damn,' said Friar John. 'They slander everybody, and if everybody slanders them I can't pretend to be worried. Let's see what he has written.'

Panurge read the good old man's writing with attention: 'He's rambling, the poor boozer,' he said. 'But forgive him, all the same. He must be near his end. Let's go and write his epitaph. The answer he gives us leaves me just about as wise as we were before we put the bread in the oven. Listen to me, Epistemon, old paunch. Don't you find him a bit too downright in his answers? He is, by God, a sophist, subtle, argumentative, and clever. I bet he's an apostate. By the belly of an ox, he takes good care not to make any mistake in his words. He only answers in disjunctives. He can't fail to tell the truth, since for such statements to be true it's enough that one half's true. Oh, what a prattling cheat! By St Lago of Bressuire, there are still some of that breed left, are there?'

'The great prophet Tiresias began with a warning of that kind before all his divinations,' put in Epistemon. 'He said plainly to those who came to consult him: "What I tell you either will take place or it will not." That is the method of all prudent prognosticators.'

'Juno poked out both his eyes all the same,' said Panurge.

'Yes,' replied Epistemon, 'but that was out of spite because he had given a better opinion than she had on a certain question propounded by Jupiter.'

'But,' said Panurge, 'what devil possesses this Master Raminagrobis that he should, without purpose reason or excuse, so malign the poor blessed fathers, Dominicans, Minorites, and Minims? I'm

1. The country of fish-eaters: a reference to the Friday fast.

greatly shocked by it, really I am. Indeed, I can't keep quiet on the subject. He has grievously sinned, and his soul will go bounding off to thirty thousand pannier-loads of devils.'

'I don't understand you at all,' answered Epistemon. 'You shock me yourself, and greatly, by perversely interpreting what the good poet said about beasts black, dun, etcetera, as said about the mendicant friars. He does not, in my judgement, intend any such sophistical and fantastic allegory. He is speaking simply and straightforwardly of fleas, lice, food-worms, flies, gnats, and other such beasts; of which some are black, others dun, others grey, others leathery and tawny, but all tiresome, bothersome, and troublesome, not only to the sick but to strong and healthy men as well. It may be that he has ascarides, lumbrics, and tapeworms in his body. Perhaps he suffers – as is the common and usual thing in Egypt and the countries along the Red Sea – some pricking in his arms and legs from those speckled flesh-worms that the Arabs call 'veins of Medina'. You are to blame for reading any other explanation into his words. You wrong the good poet by detraction, and the said friars by the imputation of baseness. In one's neighbour's case one should always interpret everything in a good sense.'

'You teach your grandmother!' exclaimed Panurge. 'He's a heretic, by God! A full-blown heretic I say, a scabby heretic, a heretic as fit for the fire as any little clockmaker. His soul will be sliding off shortly to thirty thousand cartloads of devils. And do you know where? God's truth, my friend, right under Proserpina's close-stool, in the very infernal pot into which she drops the fecal produce of her suppositories, on the left hand side of the great cauldron, within six yards of Lucifer's claws, on the way to the black chamber of Demogorgon. Ho, the villain!'

CHAPTER 23: *Panurge speaks in favour of returning to Ramina-grobis*

'LET us return,' said Panurge, without stopping, 'and warn him to think of his salvation. Let us go to him in God's name and for God's sake. It will be a work of charity we shall be performing. If he is to lose his body and life, at least let him not damn his soul. We will

induce him to repent of his sin, to implore pardon of the most holy
fathers, absent as well as present. What's more, we'll put it in writing,
so that they don't declare him a damned heretic, when he's dead, as
the hobgoblins did in the case of the provost's wife at Orléans. He
shall make them satisfaction for the insult by leaving bequests for
extra snacks, and the recitation of obits, masses, and anniversaries, all
to be enjoyed by the good holy fathers throughout the convents of
this province. We will also provide that on the anniversary of his decease they shall all be served with fivefold rations for ever, and that
the big leather bottle, full of the best, shall pass from rank to rank
down their tables, for the idling brothers, the lay-brothers, and the
gorging-brothers as well as for the priests and clerks; for the novices
as well as for the professed. In that way he will be quite sure to win
God's pardon. But, ha, ha, no. What am I saying? I'm rambling and
I'm raving. Devil take me if I go. By the power of God, the room's
full of devils already. I can hear them now tearing at one another and
battling most devilishly as to who shall gulp down the Raminagro-
bidic soul, as to who shall carry it first to Master Lucifer, hot from the
spit. Come away! I'm not going there. The devil take me if I go there.
Who knows if they mightn't try a *qui pro quo* and instead of Raminagrobis, hook poor Panurge, now that he's free of his debts? Many
times they've just failed to catch me when I lived under the bankrupt's
saffron sign and owed all round. Come away! I'm not going there.
Struth, I'm half dead of the very fever of fear. To find oneself among
hungry devils! Among factious devils! Among devils at work! Come
away! I bet you that the same fear will prevent them all – Dominican,
Franciscan, Carmelite, Capuchin, Theatine, and Minim, from reading
his burial service. And very wise of them too! The more so since he
has left them nothing in his will. Devil take me if I go. It's his own
damage if he's damned. Why did he malign the good fathers of religion? Why did he chase them out of his room at the very hour when
he was in most need of their aid, of their devout prayers and their holy
admonitions? Why didn't he bequeath in his will at least some scraps,
some stuffing, some belly-lining, for the poor folk who possess nothing but their lives in this world? Let anyone go there who will. The
devil take me if I go. If I did go the devil would carry me off. The pox
on him! Come away. Brother John, would you like thirty thousand
cartloads of devils to carry you off this instant? If so, you must do

three things. First, give me your purse, for the cross is an enemy to charms, and the same thing would happen to you as happened not long ago to John Dodin, the exciseman at Coudray, at the ford of Vède, when the soldiers broke the planks.

'The rascal met Friar Adam Screwball, a strict Franciscan from Mirebeau, on the bank, and promised him a new frock, if he would carry him pick-a-back on his shoulders over the water. For the monk was a powerful scoundrel. The deal was made, Friar Screwball trussed himself up to the ballocks, and lifted the said petitioner Dodin on to his back, like a pretty little St Christopher. In this way he carried him gaily, as Aeneas carried his father Anchises out of the fires of Troy, singing a grand *Ave maris stella*. When they came to the deepest part of the ford, above the mill-wheel, the monk asked him if he had any money on him. Dodin replied that he had a whole bagful, and that he had no need to doubt his promise of a new frock. "What," exclaimed Brother Screwball, "you know very well that by an express regulation of our order, we are rigorously forbidden to carry money on us. You're a miserable fellow indeed for making me sin in this way. Why didn't you leave your purse with the miller? You'll be punished immediately for this, without fail, and if ever I can get you before our chapter at Mirebeau, you'll get the Miserere right down to the *vitulos*."[1] Then suddenly he throws down his burden and chucks Dodin headlong into the deep water.

'Take warning by this, Brother John, my sweet friend. If you want the devils to carry you off in comfort in the first place hand me your purse. Carry no cross upon you. The danger of that is plain enough. If you have any money stamped with the cross, they'll throw you down on some rocks, as eagles drop tortoises to break their shells, as witness the bald head of the poet Aeschylus – and you'd be badly hurt, my friend, and I should be very sorry for it – or they might drop you into some sea or other, I don't know where, but somewhere far away – as happened to Icarus – and afterwards it will be called the Hashmanian Sea.

'Secondly, see that you're out of debt. For the devils are very fond of men with no debts. I know that very well from experience. The wretches never stop courting and making up to me, which they used

1. The last word of the penitential psalm which was recited during a scourging.

not to do when I lived under the saffron sign and still had all my debts. The soul of a man in debt is all feverish and wretched. It's no meat for devils.

'Thirdly, go back to Raminagrobis in your grand frock and your hood, and if thirty thousand boatloads of devils don't carry you off, thus qualified, I'll pay for your drink and firewood. And if for safety's sake you want company, don't come for me. Oh dear, no! I give you fair warning of that. Come away, I'm not going there. The devil take me if I go!'

'I shouldn't mind about it,' replied Friar John, 'not so much as some people suppose, if I had my cutlass in my fist.'

'You've hit the nail on the head,' said Panurge. 'You speak like a subtle doctor of pigosophy. At the time when I was studying at the school of Toledo, the reverend father in devilry Picatris, Rector of the Diabological Faculty, told us that devils naturally fear the brightness of swords, as they do the light of the sun. In fact when Hercules paid his visit to all the devils in hell, he did not terrify them so much, having only his lion's skin and his club, as Aeneas did later, covered in shining armour, with his cutlass in his belt well furbished and cleaned of rust, thanks to the help and advice of the sibyl of Cumae. That was perhaps the reason why when the great John James Trivulzi was dying at Chastres, he asked for his sword and died with his naked blade in his hand, laying about him all round his bed, like a valiant and chivalrous man. By that sword-play he put to flight all the devils who were waiting to waylay him on his passage to death. When one asks the Massoretes and Cabalists why devils never enter the Earthly Paradise, the only reason they give is that at the gate is a Cherub, holding a naked sword in his hand. But, to speak accurately, according to the diabolology of Toledo, I must admit that devils cannot really die by sword-strokes. I maintain, nevertheless, according to the same diabolology, that they can suffer dissolution of continuity. It is as if you were to cut across a flame of burning fire or a thick dark smoke with your cutlass. They shriek most devilishly when they feel this dissolution, which to them is devilish painful.

'When you see the shock of two armies charging, do you think, Ballockasso, that the mighty and horrible noise you hear comes from human shouts, from the clashing of harness, from the jingling of trappings, from the slashing of maces, from the clashing of pikes, from the drums and trumpets, from the neighing of horses, and from the thunder of muskets and cannons? There is something in all that of course, I must confess. But the most terrifying and loudest din of all comes from the howlings and lamentations of the devils, crowding in disorder to wait for the poor souls of the wounded, who receive un-expected sword-strokes and suffer dissolution in the continuity of their aerial and invisible substances, in much the same way as lackeys, gob-bling down bacon-slices from the spit, get a rap over the knuckles from Greasyfist the cook. That makes them scream and howl like devils, just as when Mars was wounded by Diomedes before Troy, he cried out, according to Homer, more loudly and in more fearful alarm than ten thousand men could have done, all screaming to-gether. But what am I talking about? We were speaking of furbished arms and bright swords. But your cutlass is in a very different con-dition. For by discontinuance of office and lack of exercise it's rustier, I swear, than the lock of an old meat-safe. So you've got a clear choice before you. Either clean it well and smartly or, if you keep it rusty as it is, don't go back to Raminagrobis's house. I'm not going there my-self. Devil take me if I do.'

CHAPTER 24: *Panurge consults Epistemon*

As they were leaving La Ville-au-Maire and returning to Pantagruel, Panurge addressed Epistemon on the road: 'My dear companion and old friend,' said he, 'you see what a confusion my mind is in. You know so many good remedies. Could you not help me?'

Epistemon began by pointing out to Panurge that everyone was talking and joking about his strange disguise. He urged him, therefore, to take a little hellebore to purge him of his errant humour, and then to resume his ordinary clothes.

'My dear friend Epistemon,' said Panurge, 'I have a fancy to marry. But I am afraid of being a cuckold and of being unlucky in my choice. Therefore I have made a vow to St Francis the Younger – who is a great favourite at Plessis-les-Tours and much invoked by all the women there, since he was the original founder of the *Good Men*, and they naturally long for one of them. I've sworn to wear spectacles in my cap and no codpiece on my breeches until my mind is resolved and my doubts are set at rest.'

'That's a fine and splendid vow indeed,' laughed Epistemon. 'I'm really astounded that you don't pull yourself together and call your wildly wandering wits back to their proper state of tranquillity. As I listen to you, I'm reminded of the long-haired Argives' vow, when they lost their battle against the Lacedaemonians in the quarrel about Thyrea and swore not to wear hair on their heads till they had recovered their honour and their land. You remind me, too, of that cheerful Spaniard Michael Doris, who swore never to take a piece of his thigh-armour off until ... But it is really difficult to decide which of the two better deserves to wear the green-and-yellow cap with hare's ears: the glorious champion aforesaid, or Enguerrant, who gives such a long, painful, and tedious account of the incident, and entirely forgets the art of writing history, as set out by the philosopher of Samosata. For as one reads his long narrative one supposes that this is the prelude and beginning of some great war or notable national upheaval. But at the end of the story one just laughs at the fatuous champion and his English challenger, and at the scribbler Enguerrant into the bargain, who drivels worse than a mustard-pot. It is all as comical as Horace's mountain, that cried out and groaned so much, like a woman in labour. At its cries and lamentations all the neighbours ran up, expecting to see some marvellous and monstrous childbirth; but all that she produced in the end was a little mouse.'

'It'll take more than your mouse to make me laugh,' exclaimed Panurge. 'It's the halt mocking the lame. I shall do as my vow impels me. Long ago we swore faith and friendship together by Jupiter Philios, you and I. Now give me your advice. Ought I to marry or not?'

'Indeed the case is full of hazards,' replied Epistemon. 'I feel far too inadequate to give a decision. If the dictum of old Hippocrates of Lango, that judgement is difficult, was true in the art of medicine, it is most true in this case. I have certainly one or two ideas in my mind that might give us a solution of your perplexity. But they do not satisfy me entirely. Some Platonists declare that anyone who can see his guardian spirit can read his destiny. But I don't very well understand their teaching, and I don't think that you ought to go by it. It is full of mistakes. I have seen it tried in the case of a studious and curious gentleman in the land of East Anglia. So much for the first point. But there's another. If there were still authority in the oracles of Jupiter in Ammon, of Apollo in Lebadia, Delphi, Delos, Cyrrha, Patara, Tegyra, Praeneste, Lycia, and Colophon; at the Castalian Spring, near Antioch in Syria, and among the Brachidae; in those of Bacchus in Dodona; of Mercury at Phares, near Patras; of Apis in Egypt; of Serapis at Canopus; of Faunus in Maenalia and at Albunea; near Tivoli; of Tiresias at Orchomenus; of Mopsus in Cilicia; of Orpheus in Lesbos and of Trophonius in Leucadia, I should advise you – or perhaps I shouldn't – to go there and hear what their opinion might be of your affair. But, as you know, they've all been struck dumber than fish by the coming of our Saviour and King. Since then all oracles and all prophecies have ceased; as, on the coming of the clear sun's light, all spectres, lamias, ghosts, werewolves, hobgoblins, and spirits of darkness vanish. Moreover, even if they were still working, I should not advise you to trust their replies too readily. Too many people have been deceived by them. Besides, I remember reading that Agrippina charged the fair Lollia with having interrogated the oracle of Apollo Clarius to learn if she would marry the Emperor Claudius; for which reason she was first banished and afterwards ignominiously put to death.'

'Let's do better, then,' said Panurge. 'The Ogygian Islands are not far from the port of Saint Malo. Let us first speak to our king and then make a voyage there. In that one of the four which has the most westerly aspect, they say – I have read it in good and ancient authors – there live soothsayers, diviners, and prophets. There, as it's reported, lies Saturn bound to the hollow of a rock with fine golden chains, fed on divine ambrosia and nectar, which are daily brought to him out of the skies by I don't know what kind of birds. It may be they are the same ravens who fed St Paul, the first hermit, in the desert. He plainly predicts, it is rumoured, to anyone who wants to know it, his lot, his destiny, and what is going to happen to him. For there is nothing that the Fates spin, nothing that Jupiter plans or thinks of, that the good father does not know in his sleep. It would be a great saving of labour for us, if we were to hear something from him about this difficult business of mine.'

'That's too obvious an imposture,' said Epistemon, 'too fabulous a fable. I won't go.'

CHAPTER 25: *Panurge consults Herr Trippa*

'BUT listen to me,' Epistemon went on; 'here's something you can do, even before we return to our king, if you'll take my advice. Here, near the Isle Bouchart, lives Herr Trippa; and he, as you know, predicts all future events by the arts of astrology, geomancy, cheiromancy, metopomancy, and other sciences of that kidney. Let us consult him about your business.'

'I know nothing about any of that,' replied Panurge. 'But I do know that while he was talking to the great king one day about celestial and transcendental matters, the court lacqueys were screwing his wife to their hearts' content on the stairs between the doors, and she was a pretty good-looking wench. There he was, peering into every ethereal and terrestrial concern without his glasses, discoursing of all events past and present and predicting the entire future. But one thing he entirely failed to see, and that was the jig his wife was dancing on the stairs. He never even heard about it. But still, let's go to him, since you wish to. One can't learn too much.'

The next day they came to Herr Trippa's abode, and Panurge presented him with a wolfskin gown, a great short-sword, finely gilt, with a velvet scabbard, and fifty freshly minted angels. Then he held a friendly discussion with him about his business.

Immediately on his arrival Herr Trippa looked him in the face and said: 'You have the physiognomy and metaposcopy of a cuckold, of a notorious and infamous cuckold, I say.' Next, after considering Panurge's right hand all over, he said: 'This broken line that I see here just above the *Mons Jovis*, was never on anybody's hand that wasn't a cuckold.'

Then with a stylus he hastily pricked a certain number of odd points, joined them together by geomancy, and said: 'Truth itself is no truer, and certainty couldn't be more certain than that you'll be a cuckold very soon after your marriage.' After this he asked Panurge for the horoscope of his nativity; and when Panurge gave it to him, he promptly drew his heavenly house complete. Having considered its position and the aspects in their triplicities, he heaved a great sigh and said: 'I had already clearly foretold that you will be a cuckold. You couldn't fail to be one. But here I have abundant confirmation.

What is more you'll be beaten by your wife and she'll rob you. For I find the seventh house malignant in all its aspects, and exposed to the assaults of all the signs bearing horns, such as Aries, Taurus, Capricorn, and others. In the fourth I find Jupiter in decline, and a tetragonal aspect of Saturn, associated with Mercury. You'll be soundly peppered with the pox into the bargain, my good man.'

'Shall I indeed?' answered Panurge, 'and may you catch a sound quartan ague, you old fool, you foul doddering old idiot. When all the cuckolds come together you'll carry the flag. Tell me, how did I get fleshworm between these two fingers?'

As he said this he pointed his first and middle finger straight at Herr Trippa, open in the form of a pair of horns, closing the rest into his fist, saying to Epistemon at the same time :'Here you have the original of Martial's Ollus, who devoted his whole attention to watching and listening to the ills and miseries of others, whilst his wife kept a bawdy gambling-house. As for this fellow, he's a lousier beggar than ever Irus was. Yet he's more boastful, overbearing, and intolerable than seven devils. In one word, he's πτωχαλαζών,[1] as the ancients rightly called such worthless rabble. Come, let's leave this raving fool, this violent idiot, to drivel his bellyful with his familiar devils. But I should take some convincing that the devils would be willing to serve such a scoundrel. He doesn't know the first point of philosophy, which is: *Know thyself.* He's so proud of seeing the mote in another's eye that he doesn't see a great beam poking out both his own. He's the sort of busybody that Plutarch describes. He's another Lamia, who had keener eyes than a lynx in strangers' houses, in public, and out of doors, but was blinder than a mole in her own. She saw nothing at home. For when she came in from outside into the privacy of her own room, she took her eyes out of her head, they being as easy to remove as spectacles, and hid them in a wooden shoe, which hung behind the door.'

At these words Herr Trippa picked up a tamarisk branch.

'That's the thing,' said Epistemon; 'Nicander calls it the divining tree.'

'Would you like a fuller knowledge of the truth,' asked Herr Trippa, 'by pyromancy, by aeromancy – much esteemed by Aristophanes in his *Clouds* – by hydromancy, or by lecanomancy, which

1. A boastful beggar.

was most celebrated of old amongst the Assyrians and attempted by Hermolaus Barbarus? In a basin full of water I'll show you your future wife being rogered by two rustics.'

'When you poke your nose up my arse,' said Panurge, 'don't forget to take off your spectacles.'

'I can do it by catoptromancy,' continued Herr Trippa, 'by means of which Didius Julianus, Emperor of Rome, foresaw all that was to come to him. You'll need no spectacles. You'll see her being poked in a mirror, as clearly as if I were to show her to you in the fountain of Minerva's temple, near Patras. Or by coscinomancy, which was once religiously practised among the ceremonies of the Romans. Let's have a sieve and tongs, and you shall see devils. By alphitomancy, described by Theocritus in his *Pharmaceutria*, and by aleuromancy, mixing wheat with flour. By astragalomancy. I have the pictures here ready. By tyromancy. I have a Bréhémont cheese handy. By gyromancy. I'll twist you round and round in circles, and you'll fall to the left every time, I promise you. By sternomancy. And your chest's no beauty, as it is, I swear. By libanomancy. All you need is a little incense. By gastromancy, which was for long employed by the lady Jacoba Rhodogina, the ventriloquist, in Ferrara. By cephalonomancy, which the Germans used to practise, roasting an ass's head on burning coals. By ceromancy, in which by melting wax in water you'll see the figure of your wife and her belly-drummers. By capnomancy. We'll put poppy seeds and sesame on burning coals – a very pleasant method! By axinomancy. All you have to bring me is a hatchet and some jade, which we'll put on the embers. That was a fine use of it that Homer made against Penelope's suitors! By onymancy. Let us have oil and wax. By tephramancy. You'll see ashes exposed to the air, which will show your wife in a fine state. By botanomancy. I have some sage here for the purpose. By sycomancy. On the divine art of using fig leaves! By ichthyomancy, once both praised and frequently practised by Tiresias and Polydamas, and formerly practised with equal success in Dina's pond, in the wood sacred to Apollo, in the land of the Lycians. By choeromancy. Bring us a herd of swine, and you shall have the bladder. By cleromancy, as sure as they find the bean in the cake on the night before Epiphany. By anthropomancy, which was employed by Heliogabalus, Emperor of Rome. This isn't a pleasant practice, but you'll stand it well enough, since you're fated

to be a cuckold. By sibilline stichomancy. By onomatomancy; what's
your name?'

'Chewturd,' answered Panurge.

'Or perhaps by alectryomancy. I'll draw a pretty circle here, and
while you look on and consider I'll divide it into twenty-four equal
portions. On each I'll put a letter of the alphabet, and on each letter
I'll place a grain of wheat. Then I'll let a fine virgin cock loose among
them. You'll see him eat the grains lying on the letters C.O.Q.U.S.E.R.A.[1]
I promise you that. It's just as prophetical as it was in the Emperor
Valens' time. When he wanted to know the name of his successor,
the fatidic and alectryomantic cock ate the grains on the letters
Θ.Ε.Ο.Δ.[2]

'Would you like to know the answer by the arts aruspicine or
extispicine? By auguries taken from the flight of birds, from the
croaks of birds of omen, or from the dance of the gobbling ducks?'

'By the art crappisine,' replied Panurge.

'Or perhaps by necromancy. I'll quickly have someone raised from
the devil for you, someone who died a short time ago, as Apollonius
of Tyana did for Achilles, and as the Witch of Endor did in the presence of Saul. He shall tell us the whole business, just as the dead man
who was called up by Erictho predicted to Pompey the whole course
and issue of the battle of Pharsalia. Or if you are afraid of the dead, as
all cuckolds naturally are, I will just employ sciomancy.'

'Go to the devil, you raving lunatic,' cried Panurge. 'Get yourself
buggered by an Albanian, and earn yourself one of their pointed hats.
Why the devil don't you tell me to hold an emerald or a hyena-stone
under my tongue? Or to collect a store of lapwings' tongues or of
green frogs' hearts? Or to eat the heart and liver of some dragon, so
that I may hear my destiny from the voice of the swan and the song of
the birds, as the Arabs did of old in the land of Mesopotamia? Thirty
devils take the horned cuckold! To the devil with the heretic, the sor-
cerer, the wizard of Antichrist! Let's return to the king. I'm sure he'll
be displeased with us if ever he hears that we've entered the den of
this long-robed devil. I'm sorry I came, and I'd gladly give a hundred
nobles and fourteen commoners on condition that the man who used
to blow into the bottom of my breeches could light up that fellow's

1. Will be a cuckold.
2. The first letters of the name Theodosius.

moustaches with his spittle. Good God, he's positively stunk me out
with his vexations and his devilishness, with his charms and his sorcery. The devil fly away with him! Say amen, and let's go and drink.
I shan't be merry for two days, no, not for four.'

CHAPTER 26: *Panurge consults Friar John of the Hashes*

PANURGE was peeved by Herr Trippa's talk, and after they had
passed the small town of Huymes, he turned to Friar John, stuttering
and scratching his left ear.

'Cheer me up a little, old cock,' he said. 'I feel quite down in the
dumps from that benighted idiot's claptrap. Listen, my dainty ballock
ball-bag:

stumpy b.	interlined b.	encircled b.
lumpy b.	sworn b.	stuffed b.
dumpy b.	bourgeois b.	swollen b.
plaited b.	scarlet-died b.	polished b.
leaded b.	enticing b.	brightening b.
milky b.	furious b.	flashing b.
silky b.	pitched b.	lively b.
caulked b.	overcoated b.	positive b.
veined b.	posted b.	gerundive b.
mastered b.	long-hooded b.	genitive b.
plastered b.	desired b.	active b.
grotesque b.	varnished b.	gigantic b.
Arabesque b.	ebony b.	vital b.
reinforced b.	brazil-wood b.	oval b.
hare-on-the-spit-like	boxwood b.	magistral b.
b.	organized b.	cloistral b.
ancient b.	Latin b.	monkish b.
confident b.	mounted b.	virile b.
provident b.	hooked up b.	subtle b.
calendered b.	thrusting b.	respectful b.
embroidered b.	headlong b.	abandoned b.
diapered b.	raving b.	easeful b.
tinned b.	unnatural b.	audacious b.
hammered b.	piled up b.	massive b.

lascivious **b.**

handy b.

greedy b.

absolute b.

resolute b.

valiant b.

round-topped b.

double-topped b.

courteous b.

Turkish b.

fertile b.

brilliant b.

whistling b.

currying b.

high-born b.

urgent b.

common b.

glistening b.

suitable b.

brisk b.

prompt b.

nimble b.

fortunate b.

bawling b.

fatted b.

usual b.

well-formed b.

exquisite b.

requisite b.

droll b.

backside b.

hotprick b.

seamed b.

Guelph b.

Orsini b.

sorted b.

smartened b.

household b.

patronymical b.

pretty b.

waspish b.

alidadic b.

amalgamic b.

algebraic b.

robust b.

attractive b.

hungry b.

insuperable b.

succourable b.

agreeable b.

redoubtable b.

terrible b.

affable b.

profitable b.

memorable b.

notable b.

palpable b.

muscular b.

armable b.

subsidiary b.

tragic b.

satyric b.

transpontine b.

repercussive b.

digestive b.

convulsive **b.**

incarnative b.

restorative b.

sigillative b.

masculine b.

reddening b.

curvetting b.

leaping b.

healthy b.

lightning b.

thundering b.

sparkling b.

hammering b.

ramming b.

slamming b.

aromatizing b.

ringing b.

diaspermatizing b.

mincing b.

snoring b.

lecherous b.

pilfering b.

cheerful b.

nodding b.

spurring b.

shielding b.

aborted b.

shalloted b.

reprimanded b.

rummaging b.

fumbling b.

tumbling b.

'Oh my arquebussing ball-bag, my waggling ball-bag, my dear friend, brother John, I have the greatest reverence for you, and I've kept you till last as the choicest morsel. Give me your advice, I implore you. Should I marry or not?'

Friar John answered him with a light heart: 'Marry in the devil's name, and ring out a double peal on your balls. I say as quickly as you can, and I mean it. Call the banns and make the bed creak this very evening. What are you saving yourself for, in God's name? Don't you know that the end of the world's drawing near? We're two poles and three feet closer to it than we were the day before yesterday. Antichrist's already born, so I've been told. True he's only scratching his nurse and his governesses at present. He hasn't shown his treasures yet, for he's still small. *Crescite. Nos qui vivimus, multiplicamini*,[1] as it's written. That's stuff from the Breviary – so long as a sack of corn is not worth three farthings, you know, and a puncheon of wine six pence. Surely you don't want to be found with full ballocks on the Judgement Day, *dum venerit judicare*.'[2]

'You have a very clear and serene mind, brother John, my dear old cock,' replied Panurge, 'and you speak to the point. That was the prayer that Leander of Abydos in Asia addressed to Neptune and all the sea-gods as he swam the Hellespont to visit his mistress Hero, at Sestos in Europe,

> If on my way you keep me sound,
> Who cares if I sink homeward bound?

He did not want to die with his balls full. I'm quite determined that henceforth throughout my land of Salmigundia, whenever a criminal is sentenced to judicial execution, for a day or two before he shall be allowed to poke like a pelican, until his spermatic vessels are so drained that there isn't enough in them to write the letter Y. Such precious stuff should not be foolishly wasted. Besides, he might beget a boy, and then he'd die without regret, leaving a man for a man.'

CHAPTER 27: *Friar John gives Panurge some cheerful Advice*

'By St Rigomer, Panurge, my dear friend,' said Friar John, 'I'm not advising you to do anything that I wouldn't do myself in your place. Only take care and precautions to carry on and continue your work. If ever you let up you're lost, my poor fellow. You'll be in the same trouble as nurses get into. If they stop suckling they lose their

---

1. Increase – (meaning) we who live – and multiply.
2. When he shall come to judge.

milk. If you don't give your john-thomas continuous exercise, it'll lose its milk and only be good for a pisser. In the same way your balls will be of no use to you except to fill your bag. I give you warning of that, my friend. I have seen it happen in the cases of several who couldn't when they would, because they hadn't when they could. Thus by lack of usage, as the clerks say, all privileges are lost. Therefore, my son, keep all this low, mean troglodyte, codpiece-dwelling population in a state of perpetual labour; see to it that they don't live like gentlemen, on their rents and in idleness.'

'Good lord, no,' replied Panurge. 'I'll believe you, brother John, my own left ballock. You go straight to the point. Without exceptions and circumlocutions, you've honestly dispelled every fear that might have held me back. So may heaven grant you always to work stiff and low. Well, on your word I'll get married. Nothing will go wrong. I'll always have pretty waiting-maids when you come to see me, and you shall be protector of their sisterhood. So much for the first part of the sermon.'

'Listen,' said Friar John, 'to the oracle of the bells of Varennes. What do they say?'

'I can hear them,' answered Panurge. 'By my thirst, their sound is more fateful than the clanging of Jupiter's cauldrons at Dodona. Listen: *Take a wife, take a wife; marry, get married. If you get married, get married, get married, all will be well with you, well, very well*. I promise you I'll get married; all the elements invite me to. Let these words be to you as a wall of bronze. As for the second point, you seem slightly to doubt, even to mistrust, my powers of paternity, as though I were no favourite with the stiff garden-god. I beg you to do me the favour of believing that I can command his services, that he is most docile, obliging, willing, and obedient in all places and under all circumstances. I've only to let go his leash – his buckle, I mean – and show him the prey at close quarters, saying: "Forward, my lad!", and even if my future wife should be as ravenous for bedtime sports as was Messalina, or the Marchioness of Winchester in England, I beg you to believe me that I've sufficient supplies to satisfy her. I am not unaware that Solomon says – and he spoke on the subject as a clerk and a learned man – also that since his time Aristotle has declared – that the nature of women is in itself insatiable. But I should like it to be known that I have an indefatigable instrument of the same calibre. Don't quote me the fabulous example of those fornicating paragons Hercules, Proculus, Caesar, and Mahomet, who boasts in his Koran that he has the strength of sixty strong men in his genitals. He lied, the lecher. And don't tell me about that Indian that Theophrastus, Pliny, and Athenaeus make such a fuss about, who with the aid of a certain drug performed more than seventy times in a day. I don't believe a word of it. The figure is imaginary, and I wouldn't like you to believe it either, if you please. But I beg you to believe – and it's the cold sober truth – that my pioneer of nature, the sacred Ithyphallus, Mister Thingumajig of Tiddly-push is the *primo del mondo*.[1] Listen to this, old cock. Did you ever see the frock of the monk of Castres? When it was put in any house, whether it was seen or whether it was hidden, suddenly, by its terrible power, all the dwellers and inhabitants in the place went on heat, animals and humans, men and women, even to the cats and rats. I swear to you that sometimes I've felt a certain force in my codpiece even more terrific than that. I won't speak to you of house or cottage, church or market, but once when I came in to the spectators' enclosure, as they were acting the passion-play at Saint-Maixent, I suddenly saw everyone, players and audience alike, overpowered by its occult properties. They were seized with such a terrific temptation that there wasn't an angel or a man, or a devil, male or female, that didn't want to play the two-backed beast. The prompter put down his copy; the man who played St Michael climbed down by the wings; the devils came out of their hell and pulled all the pretty girls in; even Lucifer broke his chain. Seeing the disorder, I finally disenclosed myself from the enclosure, following the example of Cato the Censor who, when he saw the festival of Flora disturbed by his presence, withdrew from the audience.'

CHAPTER 28: *Friar John comforts Panurge about the doubtful matter of his Cuckoldry*

'I UNDERSTAND you,' said Friar John, 'but time saps all things. There is no marble or porphyry that isn't subject to old age and decay. If you haven't come to it now, I shall hear you confess in a few years' time that many men's balls hang down through lack of a bag to hold them.

1. The world-champion.

I can see the hair on your head turning grey already. Your beard looks to me like a map of the world with its mixture of greys and whites, of reds and blacks. Look here. See this is Asia; here are the Tigris and Euphrates. There's Africa. Here are the Mountains of the Moon. Do you see the Nile marshes? On this side is Europe. Do you see Thélème? This quite white tuft here is the Hyperborean Mountains. By my thirst, dear friend, when the snows are on the mountains – the head and the chin, I mean – there's no great heat in the valleys of the cod-piece.'

'By the blisters on your heels,' answered Panurge, 'you don't understand plain logic. When the snow's on the mountains there is thunder, lightning, thunderbolts, whirlwinds, avalanches, tempests, and all the devils in the valleys. Do you want a proof? Then go to Switzerland, and look at the lake of Wunderberlich, twelve miles from Berne, in the direction of Sion. You mock me for my greying hair, but you don't consider that my nature is like the leeks, which we find white on top when its tail's green, straight, and vigorous. It's true that I see in myself a certain sign indicative of old age – of green old age, I mean. Don't tell anyone; it shall remain a secret between us two. It is that I find wine better and more pleasing to my palate than I used to; that I'm more afraid of meeting with bad wine than I was. Notice that this argues a touch of the setting sun, and signifies that noon is past. But what of that? I'm good company still, as good or better than ever. That's not what I fear, the devil take me. It's not there that the shoe pinches. What I fear is that during some long absence of our king Pantagruel, whom I'm compelled to accompany even if he goes to all the devils, my wife may make me a cuckold. That's the long and the short of it. For everyone I've consulted in the matter threatens me with that fate. They all swear that I'm predestined to it by heaven.'

'Not everyone's a cuckold who wants to be,' answered Friar John. 'If you're a cuckold, *ergo* your wife will be beautiful; *ergo* you'll be well treated by her; *ergo* you'll have plenty of friends; *ergo* you'll be saved. These are monkish reasonings. This is what we monks call logic. You'll be worth all the more, you sinner. You'll never have been so comfortable. You'll find just as much left for you. Your substance will grow even greater. Besides, if it's predestined to be so, would you oppose your fate? Tell me that, you faded ball-bag, jaded ball-bag.

musty ball-bag
mouldy b.
mildewed b.
dangling b.
chilled b.
swallowed b.
cowardly b.
cowed b.
broken-down b.
broken-backed b.
incongruous b.
defective b.
threadbare b.
buggered b.
prostrated b.
beshitten b.
squatting b.
wheedled b.
skimmed b.
squeezed b.
suppressed b.
dispirited b.
recalcitrant b.
putative b.
exhausted b.
worm-eaten b.
wasted b.
wheezing b.
frozen b.
luckless b.
wretched b.
spoilt b.
rotten b.
corky b.
squashed b.
transparent b.
squeezed-out b.
disgusted b.

burst b.
chewed b.
scattered b.
shalloted b.
gleaned b.
mitred b.
reprimanded b.
censured b.
churned b.
cheated b.
tickled b.
pustuled b.
mudded b.
bespattered b.
emptied b.
wrinkled b.
chagrined b.
pale b.
unhafted b.
blunted b.
wormy b.
ragged b.
funking b.
foundered b.
malandered b.
damaged b.
gelded b.
emasculated b.
eunuchized b.
battered b.
incised b.
twisted b.
speckled b.
mangy b.
quarrelsome b.
varicose b.
gangrenous b.
maggoty b.

tottering b.
limping b.
ragged b.
trifling b.
stamped out b.
adulterated b.
conceited b.
queer b.
hairy b.
coddled b.
trepanned b.
whoring b.
swarthy b.
unravelled b.
unmanned b.
ass-faced b.
thumbed-over b.
floured b.
pickled b.
atrophied b.
extirpated b.
eviscerated b.
constipated b.
misted b.
hailed-on b.
elided b.
slapped b.
cupped b.
buffeted b.
slashed b.
pinked b.
face-slapped b.
plucked b.
scarfaced b.
blighted b.
eructed b.
panting b.
skunkish b.

thrashed b.	soaked b.	declining b.
beaten b.	mannered b.	horning b.
beery b.	paralytic b.	solecizing b.
chapped b.	antedated b.	appealing b.
fistular b	degraded b.	thin b.
scrupulous b.	crippled b.	striped b.
langourous b.	numbed b.	assassinated b.
sealed b.	confused b.	patched b.
criminal b.	batlike b.	robbed b.
rancid b.	disagreeable b.	starved b.
feverish b.	farting b.	listless b.
diminutive b.	overwhelmed b.	done for b.
worn-out b.	weather-beaten b.	doughy b.
tinkling b.	sanded b.	annulled b.
abashed b.	torn b.	gaping b.
gormandizing b.	sorry b.	crumpled b.
brooding b.	stunned b.	unloaded b.
rusty b.		

'The devil take my ballocks, Panurge, my friend. Since it's predestined so, do you want to make the planets go backwards, to upset all the celestial spheres, to accuse the motive intelligences of error, to blunt the spindles, to argue with the spindle-heads, to slander the bobbins, to discredit the reels, to condemn the spun thread, and unwind the skeins of the Fates? A quartan ague take you, old ball-bag. You would be doing worse damage than the giants. Come here, old cock, and tell me. Would you rather be jealous without reason or a cuckold without knowing it?'

'I shouldn't like to be either,' replied Panurge. 'But once I'm warned of it I'll put things right, if there are any cudgels left in the world. But Lord bless me, brother John, the best thing I can do is not to marry at all. Listen to what the bells say now that we've come nearer to them: *Don't marry, don't marry, don't, don't, don't, don't. If you get married – Don't marry, don't marry, don't, don't, don't, don't – you'll soon be sorry, be sorry, be sorry: a cuckold you'll be.* By the great wrath of God I'm beginning to lose my temper. Don't those brains of yours, underneath your cowl, know any remedy against this? Has Nature so impoverished humankind that a married man can't pass through this world without falling into the perilous abysses of cuckoldry?'

'I'll teach you one expedient,' said Friar John, 'which will prevent your wife from ever making you a cuckold without your knowledge and consent.'

'I beg you to, my downy cock,' said Panurge. 'Tell it to me now, my friend.'

'Take the ring of Hans Carvel,' said Friar John, 'jeweller to the king of Melinda. Hans Carvel was a learned, skilled, serious, and worthy man, a man of sound sense and judgement, courteous and charitable, an alms-giver and a philosopher. He was merry also, and a good companion and a wit, if ever there was one, but a little pot-bellied, with a slight waggle of the head and rather unwieldy in his body. In his old age he married the daughter of the bailiff in chancery, who was young, pretty, frisky, flirtatious, oncoming, and a good deal too charming to his neighbours and his servants. And so it came about at the end of a few weeks that he became as jealous as a tiger; and grew suspicious that she was getting her buttocks bumped elsewhere. To obviate this, he filled her ears with fine stories about the miseries arising from adultery; often read her the *Legend of Chaste Women*; preached modesty to her; gave her a book in praise of conjugal fidelity, which also long and loudly decried the sins of licentious wives; and presented her with a fine necklace all encrusted with eastern sapphires. Notwithstanding this he found her still so headstrong and so merry with her neighbours that he grew more and more jealous. One night, in particular, as he lay beside her in this state, he dreamt that he talked to the devil and told him his grievances. The devil comforted him, and put a ring on his middle finger, saying: "I will give you this ring. Whilst you wear it on your finger your wife will not be carnally known by any man without your knowledge and consent." "Many thanks, Master Devil," said Hans Carvel; "I renounce Mahomet, if ever anyone gets it off." The devil vanished, and Hans Carvel awoke quite delighted to find that he had his finger in his wife's what's-its-name. I forgot to mention that when his wife felt it she drew back her bottom, as much as to say: "Oh, no, that's not the right thing to put in there"; and then it seemed to Hans Carvel that someone was trying to rob him of his ring. Isn't that an infallible remedy? Follow his example, then. And, if you take my advice, you'll always keep your wife's ring on your finger.'

Here they came to the end of their conversation and their journey.

CHAPTER 29: *How Pantagruel summoned a meeting of a Theo-*
logian, a Doctor, a Lawyer, and a Philosopher, to consider
Panurge's Perplexity

ON their arrival at the palace, they gave Pantagruel an account of
their journey, and showed him Raminagrobis's writings. After reading them and re-reading them, Pantagruel said: 'I've never seen an
answer that pleased me better. His meaning is, concisely, that in the
matter of marriage everyone should be his own judge and take counsel with himself. That has always been my opinion, and I told you as
much the first time you spoke to me on the subject. But you, as I remember, tacitly scorned my advice. I see that you are misled by
philauty – by self-love, that is. Let us change our line of action. Now
listen. Whatever we are and whatever we possess consists of three
things, our soul, our body, and our goods. For the respective conservation of each of these three, three classes of persons are to-day ordained:
theologians for the soul, physicians for the body, and lawyers for the
goods. My advice is that we invite here to dinner for next Sunday a
theologian, a physician, and a lawyer. We will then confer with them
together about your perplexity.'

'By St Picault,' answered Panurge, 'that won't be any good. I
can see that very well already. You yourself know how out of joint
the world is. We put our souls into the keeping of theologians, who
are for the most part heretics; our bodies into that of physicians, who
all loathe medicaments and never take medicine; and our goods into
that of lawyers, who never go to law with one another.'

'You speak like a courtier,' said Pantagruel. 'But I dispute your first
point, seeing that the principal – indeed the sole – activities of good
theologians are devoted to extirpating by words, deeds, and writing
all errors and heresies. So far are they from being tainted by them that
they expend their whole energies in implanting deep in the hearts of
men the true and living Catholic faith. Your second point I commend.
For good physicians so carefully observe the prophylactic and con-
servative rules of health in their own persons that they need never resort to its therapeutic and curative measures, which require the use of
medicaments. Your third point I concede. For good lawyers are so
busy with their pleadings and rulings in other men's cases that they

have neither time nor leisure to attend to their own. Nevertheless, next Sunday let us have our father Hippothadeus as our theologian, our master Rondibilis as our physician, and for our lawyer our friend Bridlegoose. But I am of the opinion that we should resort to the Pythagorean tetrad and have, in addition, as our fourth and extra our trusty friend, the philosopher Wordspinner. I stress this because your perfect philosopher – one such as Wordspinner – gives positive answers to all questions laid before him. Give orders, Carpalim, that we have all four of them next Sunday to dinner.'

'I don't think you could have chosen better in the whole country,' said Epistemon. 'I am not thinking only of each one's perfections in his own province, which are beyond every hazard of judgement, but over and above that because Rondibilis is married and formerly wasn't, Hippothadeus formerly wasn't and isn't still, Bridlegoose has been and isn't now, and Wordspinner is and was once before. I will relieve Carpalim of one of his tasks. I will, if you agree, go and invite Bridlegoose, who is an old acquaintance of mine. I have to speak to him about the profit and advancement of an honest and learned son of his, who is studying at Toulouse under the tutelage of the most learned and virtuous Boissoné.'

'Just as you like,' said Pantagruel, 'and find out if I can do anything for the advancement of the son and the dignity of the Master Boissoné, whom I love and respect as one of the ablest men in his profession to-day. I will most willingly do him a service.'

CHAPTER 30: *Hippothadeus the Theologian gives Panurge advice on the subject of his Marriage*

DINNER was no sooner ready on the following Sunday than the guests arrived, with the exception of Bridlegoose, deputy governor of Fonsbeton. When the dessert was brought in Panurge said with a deep bow: 'Gentlemen, it is only a question of one word. Should I marry or not? If you can't relieve me of my doubt, then it's insoluble, like one of the *Insolubilia*[1] in Pierre d'Ailly's book. For you're all picked, chosen, and sieved, each one in his respective profession, like so many fine peas on a sifter.'

1. The Insoluble Problems.

At Pantagruel's invitation Father Hippothadeus began, amidst bows from all the company, and he replied with incredible modesty: 'My friend, you ask us for advice. But first you should so consult with yourself. Do you feel in your body the importunate pricking of the flesh?'

'Most strongly,' replied Panurge, 'if it does not offend you, Father.'

'It doesn't, my friend,' said Hippothadeus. 'But in this trouble have you God's gift and special grace of continence?'

'Gracious me, no,' replied Panurge.

'Then marry, my friend,' said Hippothadeus. 'For it is far better to marry than to burn in the fire of concupiscence.'

'That's what I call talking,' cried Panurge, 'boldly and without circumbilivaginating about the bush. Thank you very much, my noble Father. I'll get married without fail, and very soon. I invite you to my wedding. By the hen's blood, we'll make good cheer. You shall wear my colours, and we'll eat goose. But, oxbodykins, it shan't be of my wife's roasting. Also I shall ask you to lead off the first dance of the bridesmaids, if you'll do me the gracious favour of undertaking such a thing. But there's still one little scruple to be overcome. Little, do I say? Why, less than nothing. Are you sure I shan't be a cuckold?'

'Quite, my friend,' replied Hippothadeus, 'if it please God.'

'Oh, the Lord help us!' exclaimed Panurge. 'Where are you driving me to, good people? To the conditionals, which in argument admit of all contradictions and impossibilities. If my transalpine mule should fly, my transalpine mule would have wings. If God pleases I shan't be a cuckold, and if God pleases I shall. Gracious, if it were a proviso that I could prevent, I shouldn't despair at all. But you refer me to God's privy council, to the court of his petty pleas. Which way do we Frenchmen take to go there? I think it would be best for you not to come to my wedding, worthy Father. The noise and bustle of the wedding guests would break your train of thought. You like rest, silence, and solitude. I really don't believe you'll come. And then you're a poor dancer, and you would be too bashful to lead off the first dance. I'll send you some pork rissoles up to your room, and the wedding favours too. You'll drink to our health, if you will.'

'My friend,' said Hippothadeus, 'take my words in good part, I beg of you. Am I doing you any wrong when I say to you, if it please

God? Were those bad words? Is that a blasphemous or scandalous proviso? Does it not do honour to the Lord, our creator, protector, and preserver? Does it not recognize him as the sole giver of all good? Does it not declare that we all depend on his goodness? That without him we are nothing; that we are worth nothing and can do nothing if his holy grace is not infused into us? Does it not put a canonical qualification on all our enterprises, and refer everything that we propose to the dispositions of the divine will on earth as in Heaven? Is it not the true sanctification of his blessed name? My friend, if God pleases you won't be a cuckold. If you wish to know his pleasure on this point, there is no need to despair, as if it were some abstruse thing for the understanding of which it would be necessary to consult his privy council and travel to the court of his most holy pleas. The good God has done us the favour of revealing, announcing, declaring, and openly stating his pleasure to us in the Holy Scriptures. You will find there that you will never be a cuckold, that is to say that your wife will never be a lewd woman, if you take the daughter of honest parents who has been brought up in virtue and honesty, who has only haunted and frequented the company of moral people, who loves to please God by faith and the observance of his holy commandments, who fears to offend him and lose his favour through faithlessness and the transgression of his divine law, by which adultery is sternly forbidden. For a woman is commanded to cleave to her husband alone, to cherish him, serve him, and love him entirely next to God. To reinforce these commands, you, on your side, will maintain her in conjugal affection, continue in your integrity, show her a good example, and live modestly, chastely, and virtuously at home, as you would have her do, on her side. For as the mirror that is considered good and perfect is not the one most profusely decorated with gilding and precious stones, but the one that truly reflects the objects set before it, so the most estimable of wives is not one who is rich, beautiful, well-dressed, and of noble extraction, but one who with God's help strives hardest to keep herself in good grace and to conform to her husband's way of life. Consider that the moon does not take her light from Mercury or Jupiter or Mars, or any other planet or star that may be in the sky. She receives none but from the sun, her husband, and from him receives no more than he gives her by his aspect and radiations. So you will be to your wife a pattern and example of virtue and goodness, and you will continually implore the grace of God to protect you both.'

'You would have me, then, marry the virtuous woman described by Solomon?' said Panurge, twisting the ends of his moustache. 'But she's dead, without a shadow of doubt. I never saw her that I know of, the Lord forgive me! Many thanks all the same, Father. Eat this piece of marzipan; it will help you with your digestion. Then drink a cup of red hippocras; it is healthy and good for the stomach. Let us proceed.'

CHAPTER 31: *How Rondibilis the Physician advised Panurge*

'THE first word,' continued Panurge, 'spoken by the man who was gelding the brown monks at Saussignac after he had dealt with Friar Hotear, was, "Next, please." That's what I say. Next, please. Now, my lord and master Rondibilis, pray polish off my question. Ought I to marry or not?'

'By the ambling of my mule,' answered Rondibilis, 'I don't know what answer to give to that question. You say that you feel in you the pricking stings of sensuality. I find in our theory of medicine – and we base our belief on the decisions of the ancient Platonists – that carnal concupiscence is restrained by five means. By wine ...'

'I can believe you,' said Friar John. 'When I'm properly drunk I want to do nothing but sleep.'

'I mean,' said Rondibilis, 'by wine taken immoderately. For from intemperance in wine there comes to the human body a chilling of the blood, a slackening of the sinews, a dissipation of the generative seed, a dulling of the senses, and an impairment of the movements, all of which are hindrances to the act of generation. Indeed, you see Bacchus, the drunkards' god, portrayed beardless and in woman's dress, as if completely effeminate and a gelded eunuch. It is different with wine taken in moderation. The ancient proverb demonstrates this when it says that Venus catches cold when not accompanied by Ceres and Bacchus; and it was the opinion of the ancients according to Diodorus Siculus's account, and particularly of the Lampsacenes, as Pausanias affirms, that Master Priapus was the son of Bacchus and Venus.

'Secondly, by certain drugs and plants, which render a man frigid, put him under a spell, and make him incapable of the act of generation. Among these are the water-lily, cow-parsley, amerine, willow, hemp-seed, honeysuckle, tamarisk, agnus-castus, mandrake, hemlock, the small orchid, hippopotamus skin, and others; which, when absorbed by the human body, both by reason of their elementary virtues and of their specific properties, freeze and mortify the prolific germ, or dissipate the spirits which should conduct it to the place appointed by nature, or block the passages and conduits by which it might have been discharged; just as, on the contrary, we have other drugs that heat, excite, and energize a man for the act of Venus.'

'I've no need of them, thank God,' said Panurge. 'What about you, master? But don't be offended. I didn't say that out of any ill-will I feel towards you.'

'Thirdly,' said Rondibilis, 'by assiduous toil. For in this way the body becomes so weakened that the blood, which is dispersed throughout it for the nourishment of each of the members, has neither time, leisure, nor power to make this seminal secretion, which is the surplus product from the third process of digestion. Nature under such circumstances reserves this product for herself, as being much more important for the conservation of the individual than for the multiplication of the human race and species. So it is that Diana is called chaste, since she continually labours at the chase; and so of old were camps called *castra*, since athletes and soldiers continually laboured there. So also Hippocrates writes, in his book, *On Airs, Waters, and Places*, of some people in Scythia who were in his time more impotent than eunuchs in the sports of Venus because they were continually on horseback and at work. On the other hand, the philosophers tell us that idleness is the mother of incontinence. When Ovid was asked the reason why Aegisthus became an adulterer, he merely replied that it was because he was indolent, and that if idleness were driven from the world, Cupid's arts would soon perish; his bow, his quiver, and his arrows would be a useless burden to him, and he would never wound anyone with them. For he is by no means a good enough archer to hit cranes flying through the air, or stags leaping from the thicket – as the Parthians did. That is to say that he could not hit human beings toiling and moiling; he must have them sitting or lying, quiet and at their ease. In fact, when Theophrastus was sometimes asked what kind of beast or thing he supposed the act of love to be, he replied that it was a passion of the idle spirits. Diogenes likewise said that lechery is the occupation of people not otherwise occupied. For this reason when Canachus of Sicyon, the sculptor, wished to convey that idleness, sloth, and inertia were the promoters of lust, he made his statue of Venus not standing, as all his predecessors had done, but sitting.

'Fourthly, by fervent study. For by this means the spirits are so dissolved that not enough is left to impel this generative secretion to its destined place, and so to inflate the cavernous nerve whose office it is to ejaculate it for the propagation of humankind. To prove this to yourself, contemplate the form of a man intent on some study. You will see all the arteries of his brain stretched like the string of a crossbow, to furnish him readily with sufficient spirits to fill the ventricles of the common intelligence, of imagination and apprehension, of ratiocination and determination, of memory and remembrance, and to run lightly from one to the other by the channels that are revealed by anatomy at the end of the *miraculous network*. This is the terminal point of the arteries, which take their rise from the left ventricle of the heart and, in their long convolutions, refine the vital spirits into animal spirits. So in such a studious person you will see all the natural faculties suspended, all the external senses blocked. In short, you will judge him not to be living in himself but to be ecstatically transported out of himself. For philosophy is nothing else but the contemplation of death. Possibly that is why Democritus blinded himself, preferring the loss of his sight to the reduction of his contemplations, which he felt to be interrupted by the straying of his eyes. That is why Pallas, the goddess of wisdom and protectress of scholars, is said to be a virgin; that is why the Muses are virgins; that is why the Graces remain perpetually chaste. And I remember having read that Cupid, when sometimes asked by his mother Venus why he did not attack the Muses, used to reply that he found them so beautiful, so pure, so modest, bashful, and continually occupied – one in the contemplation of the stars, another in the calculation of numbers, another in the measurement of geometrical bodies, another in rhetorical invention, another in poetical composition, another in the arrangement of music – that when he drew near them he unstrung his bow, closed his quiver, and put out his torch, since they made him shy and afraid of injuring them. Then he would take the bandage from his eyes to look them more openly in the face, and to hear their pleasing songs and poetic odes. In this he took the greatest pleasure in the world; so much so that often he felt himself quite transported by their beauties and fine graces and fell asleep to the tune of their music, so far was he from wishing to attack them or distract them from their studies. Under this head I include what Hippocrates wrote in the aforesaid book on the subject of the Scythians, also in his book entitled *On the Subject of Breeding*, in which he said that all men are incapable of generation who have once had their parotid arteries cut – these are beside the ears – for the reason already explained when I was speaking of the dissolution of the spirits and of the spiritual blood, of which the arteries are the receptacles. He maintains further that a great part of the material of reproduction springs from the brain and the spinal column.

'Fifthly, by the venereal act .... '

'I was waiting for that,' said Panurge. 'That's the one for me. Anyone's welcome to the rest.'

'It is,' said Friar John, 'what Brother Scyllino, Prior of St Victor, near Marseilles, calls mortification of the flesh. And I am of the opinion, as was the hermit of Saint Radegonde above Chinon, that the hermits of the Thebaid could not more properly mortify their bodies, subdue their villainous lust, and crush the rebellion of the flesh than by doing it twenty-five or thirty times a day.'

'I see Panurge,' continued Rondibilis, 'well proportioned in his limbs, of a well-balanced temperament, constitutionally sound, of proper age, at the right moment for marriage, and reasonably inclined towards it. If he meets a woman of similar temperament, they will engender together children worthy of some Transpontine monarchy. So the sooner it takes place the better, if he wishes to see his children provided for.'

'Worthy master,' said Panurge, 'I shall marry, have no doubt of that – and very soon. During your learned speech this flea that I have in my ear has been tickling me more than ever it did. I invite you to the feast. We'll make good cheer, and more than that, I promise you. You will bring your wife, if you please – with her neighbours, that's understood. And there shall be good sport all round!'

CHAPTER 32: *Rondibilis declared that Cuckoldry is one of the natural Attributes of Marriage*

'THERE remains,' said Panurge, 'one small point to clear up. You have at some time seen on the banner of Rome, S.P.Q.R., *Si peu que rien*; almost nothing, that is. Shan't I be a cuckold?'

'By the harbour of refuge!' exclaimed Rondibilis, 'what are you asking me? If you'll be a cuckold? My friend, I am married, and you'll be married shortly. Just write this phrase on your brain with an iron pen, that every married man is in danger of being a cuckold. Cuckoldry is one of the natural attributes of marriage. The shadow doesn't follow the body more naturally than cuckoldry follows married people. When you hear these three words spoken of a man, "He is married", if you add that therefore he has been, or will be, or may be a cuckold, you won't be accounted an unskilled reader of natural consequences.'

'By the bowels of all the devils,' shouted Panurge, 'what are you saying to me?'

'My friend,' replied Rondibilis, 'once when Hippocrates was travelling from Lango to Polystylo, to visit Democritus, the philosopher, he wrote a letter to his old friend Dionysius, begging him during his absence to take his wife to the house of her parents – who were honest people of good reputation – since he did not wish her to remain alone at home. Even so, he asked his friend to watch carefully over her and spy out where she went with her mother, and who visited her at her parents' house. "Not that I distrust her virtue and modesty," he wrote, "which I have tested and proved in the past, but she is a woman. That's all." The nature of women, my friend, is depicted for us by the moon, in this respect among others: that they conceal themselves, restrain themselves, and dissemble in the sight and presence of their husbands. When these are absent, they take their advantage, give themselves a good time, roam, gad about, lay aside their pretences, and come into the open; just as the moon, when in conjunction with the sun, does not appear in the heavens or on earth, but when most distant from the sun shines in her plenitude and appears full, notably in the night-time. Thus all women are just women. When I say women, I speak of a sex so frail, so variable, so easily moved, so inconstant and imperfect that, in constructing woman, Nature seems to me – to speak of her with all honour and reverence – to have lapsed badly from the intelligence she showed in the creation and shaping of all other things. Having reflected on the matter over a hundred – no five hundred – times, I do not know what other conclusion to come to except that when she shaped woman she had far more thought for the social delectation of man and the perpetuation of the human race than for the perfection of the individual female. Indeed, Plato does not know in what way to class them, whether as reasoning animals or brute beasts. For Nature has placed in a secret and interior place in their bodies an animal, an organ that is not present in men; and here there are sometimes engendered certain salty, nitrous, caustic, sharp, biting, stabbing, and bitterly irritating humours, by the pricking and painful itching of which – for this organ is all nerves and sensitive feelings – their whole body is shaken, all their senses transported, all their passions indulged, and all their thoughts confused. So that if Nature had not sprinkled their foreheads with a little shame you would see them more insanely chasing the codpiece than ever the Proetides did, or the Mimallonides, or the Bacchic Thyiades on the day of their Bacchanals. For this terrible animal has a close connexion with all the principal parts of the body, as is evident in anatomy. I call it an animal in adherence to the doctrine both of the Academies and the Peripatetics. For if self-motion is a sure indication that a thing has life, as Aristotle writes, and if everything that moves of itself is to be styled animal, Plato has every right to call it an animal, since he recognizes in it its own proper motions of suffocation, precipitation, corrugation, and indignation; motions so violent that often they deprive a woman of all other sense and movement. It is as if she were in a faint, a swoon, an epilepsy, an apoplexy, or true simulation of death. What is more, we find in it a manifest discrimination in scents. Women feel it turn from bad smells and follow what is fragrant. I know that Cl. Galen endeavours to prove that these are not its own proper movements, but accidental, and that others of his school labour to demonstrate that it possesses no sensible discrimination in smells but merely a variable response, depending on the diversity of odoriferous substances. But if you studiously examine their propositions and arguments, and weigh them in the balance of Critolaus, you will find that in this matter and many others they have spoken out of sheer frivolity and from a wish to criticize their elders rather than out of any affection for the truth. I will not go any further in this disputation. I will only say that no small praise is due to those honest women who have lived chaste and blameless lives and have had the strength to make this unbridled animal submit to reason. And here I will end, although I would add that once this animal is satiated – if it can be satiated – by the nourishment that Nature has prepared for it in the man, all its particular motions are put to rest, all its appetites assuaged, and all its passions appeased. Do not be astonished, however, that we are in perpetual danger of becoming cuckolds, we who have not always the wherewithal to pay and satisfy it to the full.'

'Ye gods and little fishes,' exclaimed Panurge, 'don't you know any remedy for this with all your art?'

'Why of course I do, my friend,' replied Rondibilis, 'and a very good one, of which I make use. It is to be found in the writings of a celebrated author, who died eighteen hundred years ago.'

'God's truth,' said Panurge, 'you're a worthy man, and I love you with all my heart. Eat a little of this quince cheese; quinces are good for closing the orifice of the ventricle, on account of some astringent quality that is in them; and they are helpful in the initial digestion too. But come! I'm speaking Latin before clerks. Wait while I give you something to drink from this Nestorian bowl. Would you like another draught of white hippocras? Don't be afraid of the quinsy, no. There's no squinancy in it, or ginger, or cardamum-seed. There's nothing but choice sifted cinnamon and the best refined sugar, with good white wine from Le Devinière, grown in the vineyard of the great sorb-apple, above the rooky walnut tree.'

CHAPTER 33: *Rondibilis's Remedy for Cuckoldry*

'AT the time when Jupiter set up the Olympic household and made the calendar of all his gods and goddesses,' said Rondibilis, 'having established for each the day and season of his festival, assigned places for their oracles and pilgrimages, and ordained their sacrifices ... .'

'Didn't he do like Tinteville, Bishop of Auxerre?' asked Panurge. 'That noble prelate loved good wine, as every worthy man does. Therefore he had a special regard and care for the vine, Bacchus's own grandfather. It happened that for several years he saw the vine-shoot lamentably ravaged by frosts, cold drizzles, icy mists, hoar-frost, chills, hailstorms, and disasters occurring on the feasts of St George, St Mark, St Vitalis, St Eutropius, and St Philip, on Holy Cross Day, Ascension Day, and other days, which fall at the time when the sun passes beneath the sign of Taurus. So he came to the conclusion that the forementioned saints were St Hailers, St Freezers, and St Spoilers of the vine-buds. Therefore he decided to transfer their feasts into the winter, between Christmas and Typhany – which was the name he gave to the mother of the Three Kings – granting them licence, in all honour and reverence, to hail and freeze then as much as they liked. For then the frost would not be in the least harmful, but clearly profitable to the vine-bud. Into their places he decided to transfer the feasts of St Christopher, St John the Decollated, St Mary Magdalene, St Anne, St Dominic, and St Laurence, and to put mid-August in May. For on these festivals so far is there from being any danger of frost that there is no trades-man then so much in request as your maker of cool drinks, binder of leaf-fans, decorator of arbours, and cooler of wine.'

'Jupiter,' said Rondibilis, 'forgot the poor devil cuckoldry, who wasn't present at the time. He was in Paris, at the law-courts, plead-ing some paltry case for one of his tenants and vassals. A few days afterwards, however, he heard of the trick that had been played on him, threw up his brief out of sudden anxiety that he might be ex-cluded from the household, and appeared in person before the great Jupiter, pleading his previous merits and the good and useful services he had rendered him in the past, and requesting not to be left without a festival, without sacrifices, and without honour. Jupiter excused him-self by pointing out that all his offices were filled and that his house-hold was complete. Nevertheless he was so pestered by Master Cuckoldry that in the end he put him into his household and on his list, and appointed for him on earth honours, sacrifices, and a festival. His festival was fixed – since there was no empty and vacant date in the whole calendar – on the same day as the goddess Jealousy's, and was to be celebrated jointly with hers. His dominion was to be over married men, especially over those with beautiful wives. His sacri-fices were to be suspicion, mistrust, frowning moods, watchfulness, searching, and spying of husbands over their wives. Every married

man was rigorously commanded to revere and honour him, to celebrate his festival with double rites, and to make him the aforesaid
sacrifices, under pain and penalty to those who did not pay him his
due, that he would never take any notice of them, never enter their
houses, and never frequent their company, however much they might
invoke him. He would, on the other hand, leave them eternally to rot
on their own, with their wives and without any rival whatsoever, and
would eternally avoid them as sacrilegious heretics, as is the practice
of the other gods towards those who do not pay them due honour;
of Bacchus towards vine-dressers, Ceres towards farmers, Pomona towards fruit-growers, Neptune towards sailors, Vulcan towards black-
smiths, and so on. Together with this warning, on the other hand,
went an infallible promise that to those who should duly make a holiday of his feast, ceasing from all work, and neglecting their own affairs
in order jealously to spy on their wives, lock them up and ill-treat
them, as the order for his sacrifices prescribes, he would show continual favour, loving them, associating with them, and frequenting
their houses night and day. Never would they be free from his presence. I have finished.'

'Ha, ha, ha,' exclaimed Carpalim with a laugh, 'this is a subtler
remedy than Hans Carvel's ring. Devil take me if I don't believe in it.
The nature of women is just like that. Lightning does not strike or
scorch anything but hard, solid, resistant substances. It does not stop
for soft, hollow, yielding things. It will melt a steel sword without
damaging its velvet sheath. It will consume the bones of the body
without attacking the flesh that covers them. In the same way women
never bend their stubborn, subtle, and contrary minds except towards
what they know is prohibited and forbidden them.'

'To be sure,' said Hippothadeus, 'some of our doctors say that the
first woman in the world, whom the Hebrews call Eve, would
scarcely have yielded to the temptation to eat the fruit of all knowledge if it had not been forbidden. In proof of this, just consider how
the crafty tempter reminded her with his first words that the deed was
prohibited, as if he meant to infer: "It's forbidden to you. Therefore
you must eat of it, or you would be no woman."'

CHAPTER 34: *How Women generally long for Forbidden Things*

'AT the time when I kept a brothel at Orléans,' said Carpalim, 'I had
no more powerful trick of rhetoric, no more persuasive argument
with which to draw the ladies into the toils and attract them to the
game of love than to point out to them forcibly, openly, and with
feigned disapproval, how jealous their husbands were on their account. This was no invention of mine. It's written of in books, and
we have rules and examples, explanations and daily experiences of it.
Once they get that belief into their heads, they will make their husbands cuckolds, infallibly, by God – but I won't swear – even if they
have to act like Semiramis, Pasiphae, Egesta, or the women of Mendes
island, in Egypt that Herodotus and Strabo tell us about – and other
such whores.'

'I've been told a tale on that subject,' said Ponocrates, 'and I believe
that it is a true one, when Pope John XXII was passing Fontevrault he
was asked by the abbess and a few modest nuns to grant them a dispensation allowing them to confess to one another. Their plea was
that women of religion have a few small secret imperfections, which
it is unbearably shameful for them to reveal to male confessors, but
which they could more easily and freely admit to one another, under
the confessional seal. "There's no favour that I wouldn't willingly
grant you," said the Pope, "but I can see a difficulty here –. A confession, as you know, has to be kept secret, and you women would not
be likely to keep quiet about anything that you heard." "We are very
good at keeping quiet," said they, "we're a good deal better at it than
men are." That same day the holy Father left a box in their keeping,
which contained a small linnet. This he gently entreated them to put
in some safe and secret place, promising on his Papal oath to grant
them their request if they would keep it safely concealed. At the same
time, he rigorously enjoined them on no account to open it, under
pain of ecclesiastical censure and eternal excommunication. No sooner
had he pronounced his prohibition than their minds were all in a turmoil of impatience to see what was inside, and they could hardly wait
for him to be out of their gates before getting busy with it. The Pope
was not more than three yards from the abbey when the good ladies
all rushed in a crowd to open the forbidden box and see what was in-

side. Next day the Pope visited them, for the purpose – as they supposed – of granting them their indulgence. But before beginning his
speech he ordered his box to be brought to him. It was duly brought;
but the little bird was no longer in it. Whereupon he pointed out that
they would find it too hard to keep confessions to themselves, since
they had not, even for so short a time, kept their fingers off the box
which had been so strictly entrusted to them.'

'My worthy master,' proclaimed Pantagruel, 'you are heartily
welcome. I have greatly enjoyed listening to you, praise be to God
for all good things. I hadn't seen anything of you since you acted at
Montpellier with our old friends, Anthony Saporta, Guy Bougier,
Balthasar Noyer, Tolet, John Quentin, François Robinet, John Per-
drier, and François Rabelais, in the moral comedy of *The Man who
Married a Dumb Wife* ... .'

'I was there too,' said Epistemon. 'The good husband wanted her
to speak and, thanks to the art of the physician and the surgeon, who
cut a string that she had under her tongue, she did speak. But once she
had her speech back she spoke such a lot that her husband returned
to the physician for a cure to make her quiet. The physician replied
that medically it was possible to make a woman speak, but that there
was no medical way of making one silent. The only defence against
this interminable female chattering, he said, was deafness in the husband. By the use of some charm or another, the poor wretch lost his
hearing; and when his wife saw that he was deaf, and that she was
talking to no purpose, since he could not hear her, she went raving
mad. Then, when the physician asked for his fee, the husband made
out that he was too deaf to understand what was wanted. So the
physician threw some powder or another on his back, which drove
him out of his wits, too. Then the half-witted husband and the raving
wife joined forces and gave the doctor and the surgeon such a battering that they left them half-dead. I've never laughed as much as I did
at that farce.'

'Let's return to our muttons,' said Panurge. 'Translated from gibberish into French, your speech means that I ought boldly to get married and not worry about being made a cuckold. There wouldn't be
many trumps in that hand of cards. What's more, Master Doctor,
something tells me that on my wedding day you'll be detained elsewhere by your patients and won't be able to attend. I excuse you.

Stercus et urina Medici sunt prandia prima,
Ex aliis paleas, ex istis collige grana.[1]

'You're misquoting,' said Rondibilis, 'the second verse goes

Nobis sunt signa, vobis sunt prandia digna.'[2]

'If my wife were ill ...'

'I would, before proceeding further, examine her water,' said Rondibilis, 'feel her pulse, and look at the state of her lower belly and umbilical parts, as Hippocrates ordains in his second book of *Aphorisms*, No. 35.'

'No, no,' said Panurge; 'that's not to the point. That's for us lawyers who have the rule *De ventre inspiciendo*.[3] I'll prepare a rhubarb suppository for her myself. Please don't neglect your more urgent business elsewhere. I'll send you some rissoles to your house, and you shall always be our friend.'

Then he went up to him and, without saying a word, put four rose nobles in his hand. Rondibilis took them most eagerly, but said with a start, as if offended: 'He, he, he, my dear sir, it really wasn't necessary. Thank you all the same. From wicked people I never take anything. From honest people I never refuse anything. I am always at your service.'

'So long as I pay you,' said Panurge.

'That's understood,' replied Rondibilis.

CHAPTER 35: *How the Philosopher Wordspinner handles the difficulty of Marriage*

AFTER this conversation, Pantagruel said to Wordspinner, the philosopher: 'My trusty friend, the torch now passes into your hands. It's now your turn to reply. Should Panurge marry or not?'

'Both,' replied Wordspinner.

'What are you saying to me?' asked Panurge.

'What you heard,' replied Wordspinner.

'What did I hear?' demanded Panurge.

1. Excrement and urine are fine meals for a doctor. From the one he gathers chaff and grain from the other.
2. To us they are signs, to you they are sound meat.
3. About the inspection of the belly.

'What I said,' replied Wordspinner.

'Ha, ha, ha,' laughed Panurge. 'Is that where we've got to? I pass. All the same, ought I to marry or not?'

'Neither,' replied Wordspinner.

'Devil take me,' exclaimed Panurge, 'if my wits aren't softening. And may he carry me off if I understand you. Wait, I'll put my spectacles over this left ear of mine, so as to hear you better.'

At this moment Pantagruel saw at the door of the hall Gargantua's little dog, which he had called Kyne, after Tobit's dog in the Bible. So he said to the assembled company: 'Our king is not far away. Let us stand up.' And no sooner had he spoken than Gargantua entered the banqueting hall. Everyone then arose to make him a bow, and after graciously saluting the company Gargantua said: 'My good friends, you will do me the favour, I beg of you, not to leave your seats or interrupt your discussion. Bring me a chair up to this end of the table, and give me something to drink to the health of the company. You are all very welcome. Now tell me, what was it that you were discussing?'

Pantagruel replied that at the bringing in of the dessert, Panurge had posed a problem, to wit whether he should marry or not, that Father Hippothadeus and Master Rondibilis had already delivered their answers, that just as he had entered the hall the loyal Wordspinner was replying, and that the first time Panurge had asked him: 'Ought I to marry or not?' he had answered. 'Both together,' and the second time he had said, 'Neither, nor.'

'Now Panurge is protesting against these conflicting and contradictory answers,' he concluded, 'and objects that he can't understand a word of them.'

'I believe that I understand, though,' said Gargantua. 'This answer is like the one given by an ancient philosopher, when asked whether he had a certain woman, whose name they gave him as his wife. "I have her," he answered, "but she hasn't got me. I possess her, but I'm not possessed by her."'

'A similar answer was made by a Spartan servant girl,' said Pantagruel, 'when she was asked whether she had ever had intercourse with a man. She answered, "Never," but that occasionally men had had intercourse with her.'

'So,' said Rondibilis, 'let us put it as neuter in medicine and a mean in philosophy: going to both extremes and avoiding both extremes, and by division of time, swinging now to one extreme, now to the other.'

'The Holy Apostle seems to me to have put it more plainly,' said Hippothadeus, 'when he said: "Let those that are married be as if they were not married; those who have wives be as if they had no wives."'

'I interpret having and not having a wife in this way,' said Pantagruel, 'that to have a wife is to have her for the purpose for which Nature created her, that is for the aid, pleasure, and society of man. Not to have her means not to be tied to her apron-strings; not for her sake to debase the unique and supreme love that a man owes to God; not to neglect the duties that a man owes to his country, the community, and his friends; not to abandon his studies and his business in order to be continuously waiting on his wife. Taking having and not having a wife in this way I see no conflict or contradiction in terms.'

CHAPTER 36: *Continuation of the Replies of Wordspinner, the Ephectic and Pyrrhonian Philosopher*

'You talk like a book,' replied Panurge. 'But I feel as if I were at the bottom of the dark well where Heraclitus says truth is hidden. I can't see a thing, I hear nothing, I feel my senses all numbed, and I very much wonder whether I'm not bewitched. But I'll change my style of speaking. Don't stir, my trusty friend. Don't rake your money in. Let's change the stakes and speak without disjunctives. These ill-joined parts of speech confuse you, as I see. Now proceed. In God's name, shall I marry?'

WORDSPINNER. It seems likely.

PANURGE. And if I don't marry?

W. I can see no objection to that.

P. You can see none at all?

W. None, or my eyes deceive me.

P. I can see more than five hundred.

W. Enumerate them.

P. I was only speaking roughly, using a fixed number for an uncertain one, and taking the determinate for the indeterminate. What I meant was *plenty*.

w. I'm listening.

p. I can't do without a wife. By all the devils, I can't.

w. Away with the foul beasts!

p. Well, by God, if you like! For my Salmigundians say that to sleep alone or without a wife is a brutish life, and Dido said as much in her lamentation.

w. I'm at your service.

p. Odsbodikins, I'm grateful to you. Now, shall I get married?

w. Possibly.

p. Shall I do well by it?

w. According to the circumstances.

p. Then if the circumstances are favourable, as I hope, shall I be happy?

w. Fairly.

p. Let's turn it the other way, against the grain. What if I meet with bad circumstances?

w. Don't blame me.

p. But advise me, please. What shall I do?

w. Whatever you like.

p. That's hocus-pocus!

w. None of your invocations, I beg of you.

p. Very well, in God's name be it! All I want is for you to advise me. What do you advise me to do?

w. Nothing.

p. Shall I marry?

w. I wasn't there.

p. Then perhaps I shan't marry?

w. I can't do anything about it.

p. If I'm not married, then I shall never be a cuckold?

w. So I've always supposed.

p. Let's put the case that I'm married.

w. Where shall we put it?

p. I mean, let's take the case that I'm married.

w. I can't. I'm otherwise engaged.

p. This is a stinker! Lord, if only I dared have a quiet little swear it'd relieve me greatly! Come now, patience! ... And if I'm married shall I be a cuckold?

w. One would say so.

P. But if my wife is chaste and modest, then I shan't be a cuckold?

W. You seem to me to speak correctly.

P. Listen.

W. As much as you like.

P. Will she be chaste and modest? There's only that point to settle.

W. I doubt it.

P. You never saw her?

W. Not to my knowledge.

P. Why then do you doubt a thing you don't know?

W. For reasons.

P. But if you knew her?

W. The doubts would be graver.

P. Page, my sweet page, here's my cap. I give it to you, less my spectacles. Go down into the courtyard and swear for me, just for half an hour. I'll swear for you whenever you like. ... But who'll make me a cuckold?

W. Somebody.

P. Odsbellykins, I'll give him a hiding, that Master Somebody.

W. So you say.

P. May the devil, who has no white in his eye, fly away with me, if I don't lock my wife in a chastity belt when I leave my seraglio.

W. Moderate your language.

P. It's 'well shitten well sung', all this speechifying. Let's come to some conclusion.

W. I've no objection.

P. Wait. Since I can't draw blood from you in this quarter, I'll try another vein. Are you married or are you not?

W. Neither the one nor the other, and both together.

P. God help us! I'm sweating with exhaustion, od's my life! I feel my digestion blocked. All my phrenes, metaphrenes, and diaphragms are strung up and waiting to incornifistibulate the words of your answer into the gamebag of my understanding.

W. I'm not preventing you.

P. Gee up, old friend. Now, are you married?

W. I am of that opinion.

P. And you were so once before?

W. It is possible.

P. Did you come off well the first time?

w. It's not impossible.

p. How are you getting on this second time?

w. As my fated destiny decrees.

p. But tell me, honestly, are you getting on well?

w. It is conceivable.

p. Come now, in Heaven's name! By the burden of Saint Christopher, I'd as soon undertake to get a fart out of a dead donkey as an answer out of you. Still, I'll catch you this time. Trusty friend, let's shame the devil in hell and confess the truth. Were you ever a cuckold? I mean *you* that are here, I don't mean the *you* downstairs by the tennis-court.

w. Not unless it was predestined.

p. God's flesh, I give it up! God's blood, I throw in my hand! God's body, I abjure! He's slipping out of my grasp.

At these words Gargantua got up and said: 'Good God be praised in all things! So far as I can see, the world's got into a fine old mess since first I began to watch it. Now we've come to this, have we? So the most learned and cautious philosophers have all joined the thinking establishment of the Pyrrhonians, Aporrhetics, Sceptics, and Ephectics, have they? Good God be praised! Truly, from now on it will be easier to seize lions by the mane, horses by the hair, oxen by the horns, wild oxen by the muzzle, wolves by the tail, goats by the beard, and birds by the claws, than to catch philosophers of this kind by the words they speak. Farewell, my dear friends!'

After pronouncing this speech he withdrew from the company, and Pantagruel and the others wished to follow him. But he would not allow them to.

Once Gargantua had left the hall Pantagruel said to the guests: 'Plato's Timaeus counted his guests at the beginning of the feast. We, on the other hand, will count ours at the end. One, two, three. Where's the fourth? Wasn't it our friend Bridlegoose?'

Epistemon replied that he had been to his house to invite him, but had not found him at home. An usher of the high court of Mirelinguais in Mirelingues had come to find him, and to cite him to appear in person and state his grounds to the senators for some decision that he had pronounced. Therefore he had departed on the preceding day, to put in an appearance at the time appointed, in order not to fall into default or contumacy.

'I should like to know what it is,' said Pantagruel. 'He has been the district judge at Fonsbeton for more than forty years; and during that time he has given more than four thousand final sentences. In three thousand two hundred and nine of these cases which he has decided, an appeal has been made by the losing parties to the supreme court of the Mirelinguais assembly in Mirelingues, by decree of which they have all been ratified, approved, and confirmed, and the appeals dismissed and quashed. If now in his old age he has been cited to appear in person, after performing his duties blamelessly throughout the past, some disaster must certainly have occurred. I should like to help him in every way I equitably can. The world has grown so wicked to-day, as well I know, that honest justice stands in great need of support. I'm resolved to appear there immediately, for fear that some accident may occur.'

After this the tables were removed, and Pantagruel gave his guests precious and honourable presents of rings, jewels, and plate, both of gold and of silver. Then, after thanking them most cordially, he retired to his room.

CHAPTER 37: *Pantagruel persuades Panurge to take counsel of a Fool*

As Pantagruel was retiring, he saw Panurge from the gallery in a state of deep reverie, mumbling and nodding his head.

'You look like a mouse caught in a trap,' he said; 'the harder it tries to free itself from the pitch the faster it gets stuck. It is the same with you. All your efforts to escape from the noose of your perplexity only leave you more firmly caught than before. I know of only one remedy. Listen. I've often heard the vulgar proverb quoted, that a fool may well give lessons to a wise man. Now since you're not fully satisfied by the answers of the wise, take counsel of some fool. You may get more agreeable advice in that way, and be better contented. You know how many princes, kings, and republics have been saved, how many battles won, how many perplexities resolved, by the advice, counsel, and predictions of fools. There is no need to refresh your memory now with instances. You will accept this argument: As you call a man worldly wise who looks carefully after his private and domestic affairs, who is vigilant and watchful in the management of his household, whose mind never wanders, who never misses any opportunity of acquiring and amassing property, even though he may be a fool in the estimation of the celestial spirits; so in order to be wise in their eyes – wise, I mean, in knowing, and foreknowing by divine inspiration, and fit to receive the gift of divination – a man must forget himself, rise above himself, rid his senses of all earthly affection, purge his spirit of all human solicitude, and view everything with unconcern: all of which are commonly supposed to be symptoms of folly. Hence it was that the great prophet Faunus, the son of Picus, King of the Latins, was styled *Fatuus* by the common herd. Hence it is that when the strolling players distribute their parts, the role of fool and jester is always played by the most skilful and perfect actor in the company. Hence it is, so astrologers assert, that the same horoscope may preside over the births of a king and a fool. They give the example of Aeneas and Choroebus – whom Euphorion declares to have been a fool – for they were born under the same influences. I shall not be wandering from the point if I tell you a remark of Giovanni Andreas on the subject of a clause in a certain papal decree addressed to the mayor and citizens of La Rochelle, and Panormitanus's subsequent comment on the same clause. I will quote Barbatias as well on the subject of the *Pandects*, and the most recent pronouncement of Jason in his *Consilia* on Seigny John, a famous fool of Paris and grandfather of Caillette. The case is this: In Paris, among the cook-shops by the Petit-Châtelet, a porter was standing in front of a roast-meat stall eating his bread in the steam from the meat, and finding it, thus flavoured, very tasty. The cook let this pass, but finally, after the porter had gobbled his last crust, he seized him by the collar and demanded payment for the steam from his roast. The porter answered that he had done no damage to his meat, had taken nothing of his, and was not his debtor in any way. The steam in question was escaping outside, and so, in any case, was being lost. No one in Paris had ever heard of the smoke from a roast being sold in the streets. The cook replied that it wasn't his business to nourish porters on the steam from his meat, and swore that if he wasn't paid he'd confiscate the porter's pack-hooks. The porter drew his cudgel and prepared to defend himself. The altercation grew warm. Gaping Parisians assembled from all quarters to watch the quarrel and, fortunately, among them was Seigny John, the town fool.

'When he saw him, the cook asked the porter: "Are you willing to accept the noble Seigny John's decision in our dispute?" "Yes, by the goose's blood, I am," replied the porter.

'Then, after hearing their arguments, Seigny John ordered the porter to take a piece of silver out of his belt; and the porter thrust an old coin of Philip's reign into his hand. Seigny John took it and put it on his left shoulder, as though to feel if it were full weight. Then he rang it on the palm of his left hand, as if to see that it was a good alloy. Next he held it close up to his right eye, as if to make sure that it was well minted. All this took place in complete silence on the part of the gaping mob, while the cook watched in confidence, the porter in despair. Finally the fool rang the coin several times on the stall. Then, with presidential majesty, grasping his bauble as if it were a sceptre, and pulling over his head his ape's fur hood with its paper ears ridged like organ pipes, after two or three sound preliminary coughs he announced in a loud voice: "The court declares that the porter who ate his bread in the steam of a roast has civilly paid the cook with the chink of his money. The court orders that each shall retire to his eachery, without costs. The case is settled." This decision of the Parisian fool seemed so equitable, so admirable even, to the aforesaid doctors that they doubt whether a more judicial sentence would have been given if the case had been tried before the High Court of that city, or before the Rota of Rome, or indeed before the Areopagites ... Consider, therefore, whether you won't consult a fool.'

CHAPTER 38: *How Pantagruel and Panurge proclaimed the virtues of Triboulet*

'UPON my soul,' replied Panurge, 'I will. I seem to feel my bowels loosening. A moment ago they were all tight and constipated. But just as we have chosen the fine cream of wisdom to advise us, so I should like someone who is a fool of the first water to preside over our new deliberations.'

'Triboulet seems sufficient of a fool to me,' said Pantagruel.

'A proper and total fool,' replied Panurge.

PANTAGRUEL	PANURGE
A fatal fool.	A high-toned fool.
A natural fool.	A B sharp and B flat fool.
A celestial fool.	A terrestrial fool.
A jovial fool.	A jolly, mocking fool.
A mercurial fool.	A merry, sportive fool.
A lunatical fool.	A fool with pompoms.
An erratic fool.	A fool with tassels.
An eccentric fool.	A fool with bells.
An aetherial and Junonian fool.	A laughing Venerian fool.
An arctic fool.	A fool from the bottom of the
A heroic fool.	barrel.
A genial fool.	A fool of the first pressing.
A predestined fool.	A fool of the first broaching.
An Augustan fool.	A fool in fermentation.
A Caesarine fool.	A popular fool.
An imperial fool.	A so-and-so fool.
A royal fool.	A fool graduated in folly.
A patriarchal fool.	A fool dining-companion.
A fool by birth.	A fool with first class honours.
A loyal fool.	A train-bearing fool.
A ducal fool.	A fool by supererogation.
A banner-bearing fool.	A fool collateral.
A seigneurial fool.	A fool *a latere*, deteriorated.
A palatine fool.	A fool caught in the nest.
A principal fool.	A migratory fool.
A praetorian fool.	A half-fledged fool.
A total fool.	A haggard-hawk fool.
An elected fool.	A gentle-hawk fool.
A court fool.	A speckled fool.
A fool chief-centurion.	A pilfering fool.
A triumphant fool.	A fool of the second plumage.
A vulgar fool.	A wild fool.
A domestic fool.	A rambling fool.
An exemplary fool.	A fool punched on the chin.
A rare and peregrine fool.	A puffed-up fool.
An aulic fool.	A fool prouder than a peacock.
A civil fool.	A corollary fool.

PANTAGRUEL	PANURGE
A familiar fool.	An eastern fool.
A famous fool.	A fool supreme.
A favourite fool.	An original fool.
A Latin fool.	A papal fool.
An ordinary fool.	A consistorial fool.
A much feared fool.	A conclavist fool.
A transcendent fool.	A bullist fool.
A sovereign fool.	A synodal fool.
A special fool.	An episcopal fool.
A metaphysical fool.	A doctoral fool.
An ecstatic fool.	A monkly fool.
A categorical fool.	A fiscal fool.
A predictable fool.	An extravagant fool.
A decumanal fool.	A bonnetted fool.
An obliging fool.	A fool with a simple tonsure.
A fool in prospect.	A crimson fool.
A fool in algorism.	A fool dyed in the grain.
An algebraical fool.	A citizen fool.
A cabalistic fool.	A feather-duster fool.
A talmudic fool.	A fool for mockery.
An algamalic fool.	A modal fool.
A compendious fool.	An abstract fool.
An abbreviated fool.	An almanac-making fool.
A hyperbolical fool.	A heteroclite fool.
An antonomatic fool.	A summist fool.
An allegorical fool.	An abbreviating fool.
A tropological fool.	A morris-dancing fool.
A pleonasmic fool.	A well-sealed fool.
A capital fool.	A mandatory fool.
A cerebral fool.	A hooded fool.
A cordial fool.	A titulary fool.
An intestinal fool.	A sly fool.
A hepatic fool.	A repulsive fool.
A splenetic fool.	A well-tooled fool.
A windy fool.	A clutch-loose fool.
A legitimate fool.	A big-ballocked fool.
A fool in the azimuth.	A pedantic fool.

PANTAGRUEL	PANURGE
A fool in the almicantarath.	A winded fool.
A well-proportioned fool.	A culinary fool.
An architraval fool.	A fool of high growth.
A fool on a pedestal.	An andiron fool.
A paragon of a fool.	A miserable fool.
A cheerful fool.	A rheumatic fool.
A solemn fool.	A bragging fool.
An annual fool.	A twenty-four carat fool.
A festival fool.	A motley fool.
An amusing fool.	An asymmetrical fool.
A village fool.	A fool in a martingale.
A humorous fool.	A fool with a stick.
A privileged fool.	A fool with a bauble.
A rustic fool.	A fool of high price.
An ordinary fool.	A fool broad in the beam.
An ever-ready fool.	A stumbling fool.
A fool in diapason.	A superannuated fool.
A resolute fool.	A clownish fool.
A hieroglyphical fool.	A full-busted fool.
An authentic fool.	A pompous fool.
A fool of value.	A gorgeous fool.
A precious fool.	An uninterrupted fool.
A fanatical fool.	A riddling fool.
A fantastic fool.	A formal fool.
A lymphatic fool.	A hooded fool.
A panic fool.	A redoubled fool.
A distilled fool.	A damascene fool.
An even tempered fool.	A variegated fool.
	An ass-faced fool.
	A baritone fool.
	A spotted fool.
	A bullet-proof fool.

PANTAGRUEL. For the same good reason that the Quirinalia in Rome were called All Fools' Day, we might justly inaugurate the Tribouletinalia in France.

PANURGE. If all fools wore cruppers, he'd have his rump well galled.

PANTAGRUEL. If he were the god Fatuus we've spoken of, the husband of the goddess Fatua, his father would be Bonadies and his
mother Bonadea.

PANURGE. If all fools ambled, he'd pass them by a good yard,
although he's got bow-legs. Let's go to him without wasting time.
We shall get a fine answer from him, I'm certain.

'I mean to attend Bridlegoose's trial,' said Pantagruel. 'But while
I'm on my way to Mirelingues, which is on the other side of the
Loire, I'll send Carpalim to bring Triboulet here from Blois.'

So Carpalim was dispatched, and Pantagruel, accompanied by his
servants, Panurge, Epistemon, Ponocrates, Friar John, Gymnaste,
Rhizotome, and the rest, took the road for Mirelingues.

CHAPTER 39: *How Pantagruel was present at the Trial of Judge
Bridlegoose who decided Cases by the Fall of the Dice*

ON the next day, at the appointed hour, when Pantagruel arrived at
Mirelingues, the president, senators, and counsellors begged him to
enter with them and hear their judgement on Bridlegoose's defence
of a certain sentence which he had pronounced against Toucheronde,
the tax-assessor, and which seemed most inequitable to the centum-
viral court. Pantagruel willingly accepted their invitation. He found
Bridlegoose seated in the middle of the judicial enclosure, and offering
no other reason or excuse except that he was now old, and that his
sight was not as good as it had been. He further pleaded several of the
misfortunes and calamities concomitant upon old age, as recorded by
Archid. D. lxxxvj c. tanta.[1] By reason of these infirmities, he said, he
had not been able to make out the score on the dice as he had done in
the past, whence it might have arisen that, as Isaac when old and dim-
sighted took Jacob for Esau, so in deciding the case in question he
might have taken a four for a five, particularly as on that occasion he
had used very small dice. He pleaded further that by provision of
equity the imperfections of nature ought never to be accounted a
crime, as is clear from *ff. De re milit. l. qui cum uno; ff. De reg. jur. l.*

---

1. Most of the citations in this and the following chapters are of passages in
the Roman code and the Digest. But as this is a satire against legal pedantry,
it would be absurd to produce a footnote on each one.

fere; *ff. De edil. ed. per totum*; *ff. de term. mod. l. Divus Adrianus resolut. per Lud. Ro. in l. si vero*; and *ff. solu. matr.* Anyone who took the opposite view, therefore, would be accusing not the man but Nature, as is evident in *l. maximum vitium. C. De lib. praeter.*

'What dice do you mean, my friend?' inquired Blowbroth, grand president of this court.

'The dice of judgement,' replied Bridlegoose, 'those *alea judiciorum* of which it is written in *Doct.* 26 *quaest. ij. cap. Sors*; *l. nec emptio. ff. De contrahend. empt. l. quod. debetur*; *ff. De pecul. et ibi Barthol.*; the same dice as you gentlemen use in this supreme court of yours, as do all other judges in deciding their cases, according to the comments of D. Hen. Ferrandat, *et not. gl. in c. fin. De sortil. et l. sed cum ambo*; and *ff. De jud.*, where the learned doctors remark that chance is a very good, honest, useful, and necessary element in the settling of suits and contentions. This has been even more clearly stated by Bald., Bart., and Alex. *C. communia De leg. Si duo.*'

'And how do you work it, my friend?' asked Blowbroth.

'I will reply briefly,' answered Bridlegoose, 'according to the provisions of the law *ampliorem*, § *in refutatoriis, C. De appella.* and to what is said *Gl. l. j. ff. quod met. cau. Gaudent brevitate moderni.*[1] I do like the rest of you, gentlemen, I follow the customs of the judicature, to which our laws command us always to defer: *ut not. Extra De consuet. c. ex literis, et ibi Innoc.* First I thoroughly view and review, read and re-read, thumb over and peruse, the bills of complaint, sub poenas, appearances, reports, investigations, preliminary proceedings, statements, allegations, interrogatories, rebuttals, written testimonies, protests, complaints, objections, cross-examinations, confrontations, and face-to-facing of witnesses, demands, letters dimissory, royal missives, warrants, demurrers, anticipatories, injunctions, returns of injunctions, appeals, final judgements, citations of argument, decrees, adjournments for appeal, acknowledgements, executions, and other such drugs and spiceries on one side, and on the other, as a good judge is bound to do, in order to conform to *no. Spec. De ordinario* § *iij, et tit. De offic. omn. jud.* § *fin. et de rescriptis praesenta.* § *j.* I then place on the end of the table in my chamber all the defendant's bags of documents, and give him the first throw, as the rest of you gentlemen do. This is enjoined by *l. Favorabiliores ff. De reg. jur., et in c. cum sunt eod tit. lib. vj*,

1. Moderns rejoice in brevity.

which says: *Cum sunt partium jura obscura, reo favendum est potius quam actori*.[1] This done, I put down the plaintiff's bags of documents as you other gentlemen do, at the other end, *visum visu* – face to face. For *opposita juxta se posita magis elucescunt*,[2] as is noted in *l. j. § Videamus ff. de his qui sunt sui vel alie. jur. et in l. munerum. j. mixta ff. de muner. et honor*. Then likewise, and turn for turn, I throw for him too.'

'But, my friend,' demanded Blowbroth, 'in what way do you determine the degree of obscurity of the claims put forward by the litigants?'

'As you other gentlemen do,' replied Bridlegoose, 'that is to say by the number of bags brought in by either party. And then I use my little dice, as you other gentlemen do, to conform to the law, *semper in stipulationibus, ff. De reg. juris*, and the law in capitals versified *que; eod. tit.*

> *Semper in obscuris quod minimum est sequimur*.[3]

which was also adopted by canon law in *c. in obscuris. eod. tit. lib. vj.* Of course I have large dice as well, fine and most proper ones, that I use, as you other gentlemen do, when the matter is more fluid; that is to say when there are less bundles.'

'And after that,' asked Blowbroth, 'how do you pronounce judgement, my friend?'

'As you other gentlemen do,' replied Bridlegoose, 'I pronounce in favour of the party to whom fate first awards a good throw of the judiciary, tribunian, and praetorial dice. So our laws ordain, *ff. qui pot. in pig. l. potior. leg. creditor. C. De consul. l. j. Et de reg. jur. in vj. Qui prior est tempore, potior est jure*.'[4]

CHAPTER 40: *Bridlegoose explains his reasons for examining the Documents of the Cases which he has decided by the Throw of the Dice*

'YES, my friend,' said Blowbroth, 'but since you settle your judgements by chance and by the fall of the dice, why don't you put things to the hazard on the same day, at the precise hour when the

1. When the law is obscure, favour the defendant rather than the plaintiff.
2. Opposites, when confronted, shed greater light.
3. In difficult cases, always take the least consequential course.
4. The first comer has the best case in law.

parties at variance appear before you? Why all this further delay? What use do you make of the writs and documents in the litigants' bags?'

'The same use as you other gentlemen do,' answered Bridlegoose. 'They serve me for three exquisite, requisite, and authentic purposes. First for the sake of formality. For if form is not observed there is no validity in anything that is done, as is proved very well by *Spec. tit. De instr. edit. et tit. De rescript. praesent.* Besides which, as you know only too well, often in judicial proceedings the formalities destroy all materiality and substance. For, *forma mutata, mutatur substantia.*[1] *ff. ad exhib. l. Julianus; ff. ad leg. falcid. l. Si is qui quadringenta. Et extra. De deci. c. ad audientiam, et De celebrat. miss. c. in quadam.* Secondly, as with you other gentlemen, they give me honest and salutary exercise. The late Master Othoman Vadare, a great physician – as you would say, *C. De comit. et archi. lib. xij* – told me many times that lack of physical exercise is the sole cause of the poor health and short lives to which you gentlemen and all officers of the law are subject. Which was very well noted before him by Bartolus in *lib. j. C. De senten. quae pro eo quod.* For which reason, to us in our turn as to you gentlemen, *quia accessorium naturam sequitur principalis, De reg. jur. l. vj., et § cum principalis, et l. nihil dolo. ff. eod. titu. ff. De fidejusso l. fidejussor, et extra De offic. deleg. c j.,* are conceded certain honest and decent games for recreation, *ff. Do al. lus. et aleat. l. solent. et autent. ut omnes obediant, in princ. coll. 7, et ff. De praescript. verb. l. si gratuitam; et l. j. C. De spect. lib. xj.* And such is the opinion of D. Thomas, *in secunda secundae quaest. clxviii,* very appositely quoted by D. Alber. de Ros., who *fuit magnus practicus* and a solemn doctor, as Barbatia attests *in prin. consil.* The reason is set out *per gloss. in praemio. ff. § nc autem tertii.*

Interpone tuis interdum gaudia curis.[2]

'In fact, one day in the year 1489, having some monetary business in the court of their worships the judges of excise, and entering by the pecuniary permission of the usher – for, as you gentlemen know, *pecuniae obediunt omnia,*[3] as Baldus said in *l. Singularia ff. Si certum pet.; et Salic. in l. recepticia. C. De constit. pec.; et Card. in Clem. j. De baptis.,*

1. When the forms are changed the substance is changed.
2. Take a holiday every now and then between your studies.
3. All things obey money.

I found them all playing at fly, a healthy exercise before or after meals
– I don't care which. Provided *hic not.*,[1] that the game of fly is honest,
healthy, ancient, and lawful, *a Musco inventore de quo C. De petit.
haered. l. Si post motam. et Muscarii. j.*, those who play at fly are ex-
cusable by law *l. j. C. De excus. artif. Lib. x.* And on that occasion
Master Tielman Picquet was fly, and he was laughing at the way in
which all the gentlemen of the court were ruining their caps by swat-
ting him on the shoulders. He told them, all the same, that they
would have no excuse for this damage to their caps when they left
the courts and returned to their wives, by *c. j. extra. De praesumpt. et
ibi gl.* Now, *resolutorie loquendo*, I should say, as you other gentlemen
do, that there's no comparable exercise, no exercise more aromatizing
in all this litigious world, than the emptying of bags, the thumb-
ing of papers, the assessing of costs, the filling of baskets and the examination of suits, *ex Bart. et Jo. De Pra., in l. falsa. De condit. et
demon. ff.*

'Thirdly, like you other gentlemen, I consider that time ripens all
things; with time all things come to light; time is the father of truth,
gl. in l. j. C. De servit.; *Autent. de restit. et ea quae pa.*; *et Spec. tit. De
requis. cons.* That is why, like you other gentlemen, I suspend, delay,
and postpone judgement, so that the case, being well ventilated, sifted,
and debated, may in course of time come to its maturity, and so that
the decision by dice, afterwards ensuing, may be borne more patiently
by the losing party, as *not. gloss. ff. De excus. tut. l. Tria onera.*

Portatur leviter quod portat quisque libenter.[2]

If judgement were given when the case was raw, unripe, and in its
early stages, there would be a danger of the same trouble as physicians
say follows on the lancing of an abscess before it is ripe, or the purging
of some harmful humour from the human body before it has fully
matured. For, as it is written in *Autent. haec constit. in Inno. constit.
princ.*, and repeated, *gl. in c. Caeterum. extra De jura. calum.*

Quod medicamenta morbis exhibent, hoc jura negotiis.[3]

'Furthermore, Nature instructs us to pick and eat fruit when they

1. Here take note.
2. A load willingly borne is light to bear.
3. What medicine is to disease, the law is to business.

are ripe, *Instit. De re. div.* § *is ad quem*; *et ff. de act. empt. l. Julianus*; likewise to marry our daughters when they are nubile, *ff. De donat. inter vir. et uxor. l. cum hic status.* § *si quia sponsa, et* 27, *q.j.c. Sicut* says *gl.*

> *Jam matura thoris plenis adoleverat annis*
> *Virginitas.*[1]

Indeed not to do anything except in full maturity, *xxiij, q.ij.* § *ult.* and *xxxiij. d.c. ult.*'

CHAPTER 41: *Bridlegoose's Story of the Man who settled Cases*

'I REMEMBER in this connexion,' continued Bridlegoose, 'that at the time when I was studying law at Poitiers, under Professor Axiom, there was at Smarve, one Peter Nitwit, an honest man, a good farmer, a fair singer in the choir, a man of good reputation, and of the age of most of you gentlemen. He used to say that he had seen that grand old man, the Lateran Council in his broad red hat, together with his wife, the lady Pragmatic Sanction, with her broad blue satin ribbon and her great jet rosary. This good fellow used to settle more lawsuits than were ever tried in all the courts of Poitiers, in the session house of Montmorillon, and in the market hall of Parthenay-le-Vieux; which won him the respect of all the countryside. Every dissension, dispute, and quarrel in Chauvigny, Nouaillé, Croutelles, Esgne, Ligugé, La Motte, Lusignan, Vivonne, Meseaux, Étables, and the neighbouring places was settled on his rulings as if by a high court judge, although he was no judge, but just a simple fellow. *Arg. in l. sed si unius. ff. De jurejur. et de verb. obl. l. continuus.* There wasn't a hog killed in the whole neighbourhood that he didn't get part of the roasting meat and the sausages, and almost every day he was at some banquet, feast, wedding, christening, or churching, or at the tavern – to effect some settlement, you understand. For he never brought any parties to agree that he did not make them drink together, as a symbol of reconciliation, of perfect concord, and of happiness renewed; *ut not. per Doct. ff. De peric. et com. rei vend. l. j.* He had a son called Stevie Nitwit, a grand lad and a a good fellow, s'welp me God,

1. Virginity, now ripe with years, was ready for the marriage bed.

who also wanted to take a hand in the settling of disputes. For you know that

> *Saepe solet similis filius esse patri*
> *Et sequitur leviter filia matris iter.*[1]

ut ait gl. vi. qu. i. c. Si quis; gl. De cons. d.5.c.j. fi et est not. per Doct. C. De impu. et aliis et subst. l. ult. et l. legitimae; ff. De stat. hom. gl. in l. quod si nolit; ff. De aedil. ed. l. quis. C. ad leg. Jul. majes.: Excipio filios a moniali susceptos ex monacho, per gl. in c. impudicas, xxvij. q. j. And he took as his title, Lawsuit-settler out of Court. He was so watchful and active in his business, for *vigilantibus jura subveniunt, ex leg. pupillus. ff. quae in fraud. cred. et ibid. l. Non enim, et Inst. in prooemio,* that the moment he got wind, *ut ff. si quad. paup. fec. l. Agaso. gl. in verb. olfecit i. nasum ad culum posuit,*[2] and heard of any suit or dispute in that country he pushed his nose in to reconcile the parties. It is written

> *Qui non laborat non manige ducat*[3]

and *gl. ff. De damn. infect. l. quamvis,* says the same; as does *Currere* more than a trot *vetulam compellit egestas*[4] and *gl. De lib. agnos. l. Si quis. pro qua facit. l. si plures. C. De condit. incerti.* But he was so unfortunate in his business that he never reconciled a single dispute, not even the most trivial one. Instead of reconciling the parties, indeed, he merely exasperated and antagonized them. You know, gentlemen, that

> *Sermo datur cunctis, animi sapientia paucis*[5]

gloss. ff. De alie. ju. mut. caus. fa. l. ij. And the inn-keepers of Smarve said that, in his time, they had not sold as much wine of reconciliation – which was what they called the good wine of Ligugè – as they used to do in half an hour in the old man's time.

'Now he happened to complain of his bad luck to his father, attributing its causes to the perversity of the men of his day. He roundly argued that if the world had been as perverse, litigious, unrestrained,

1. The son generally takes after his father, and the daughter after her mother. An exception is made in the next clause for the children of monks and nuns.
2. This refers to a case of a groom whose horse sniffed at a mule in an inn-yard; in which *olfecit* was defined as *nose sniffing arse.*
3. If any do not work he shall not manage a household (a bad pun on II Thess. iii. 10).
4. Old age made the old hag run.
5. Everyone is gifted with speech, but few have wisdom of soul.

and irreconcilable in the olden times, he – his father – would never have won such honour nor the title of the "unfailing peacemaker" by which he had been known. In this Stevie was breaking the law which forbids children to reproach their own parents, *per gl. et Bart. L. iij. § Si quis ff. De condit. ob caus.; et Autent. de nup. § sed quod sancitum, coll. 4.*

'You must change your methods, Stevie, my son,' answered Peter. 'For

> When Lord Oportet[1] is the King
> This is the course for following.

gl. C. De appell. l. eos etiam. You're barking up the wrong tree. You never settle cases – and why? Because you catch hold of them at their beginnings, when they're still raw and unripe. I settle them all, – and why? Because I catch hold of them at the end, when they're nearly ripe and digested. You know the line,

> *Dulcior est fructus post multa pericula ductus*[2]

l. non moriturus. C. De contrah. et comit. stip. Don't you remember the common proverb that runs: He's a lucky doctor who's called in at the end of the illness? The illness, of course, had reached its crisis and was beginning to abate naturally without any intercession by the doctor. In the same way, my litigants were drifting unaided towards an end of their disputes, because their purses were empty. They were ceasing of themselves to prosecute and defend, for they had no coin in the kitty to prosecute or defend with,

> *Deficiente pecu, deficit omne, nia.*[3]

All they wanted was someone to act as sponsor and mediator, to make the first mention of a settlement, to save each party from the awful shame of having it said of him: "It was he that gave in first. He was the first to talk of an agreement. He got tired first. He hadn't got the better case, and he felt the shoe pinching." Then I find myself as welcome as peas and bacon. That's my happy moment, my moment of advantage, when my luck's in. And I tell you, Stevie my dear son, that by this method I could make peace – or at least a truce – between

1. Necessity.
2. A fruit is sweeter for having survived many dangers.
3. If money is lacking everything is lacking (somewhat garbled).

the Great King and the Venetians, between the Emperor and the Swiss, between the English and the Scots, or between the Pope and the people of Ferrara. Shall I be bolder? S'welp me God, I could make peace between the Turk and the Sophy, or between the Tartars and the Muscovites. Now listen carefully to me. I should catch them at the moment when both sides were tired of making war, when they had emptied their coffers, squeezed their subjects' purses dry, sold their estates, mortgaged their lands, and exhausted their stores and munitions. Then, by God or his holy mother, spite or no spite, they are compelled to take breath and curb their wicked ambitions. That is the lesson in *gl. xxxvii d. c. S. quando.*

Odero si potero; si non, invitus amabo.'[1]

CHAPTER 42: *How Lawsuits are born, and how they come to full Growth*

'THAT is why,' continued Bridlegoose, 'like you other gentlemen, I temporize, waiting for a lawsuit to mature and to attain full growth in all its limbs – in its bags and documents that is. *Arg. in l. si major. C. commu. divi.; et De cons. d. j. c Solennitates, et ibi gl.* A lawsuit, when newly born, seems to me, as it does to you other gentlemen, shapeless and imperfect, even as a bear at birth has neither feet, paws, skin, fur, nor head, but is merely a lump of raw and formless flesh. The she-bear, by dint of licking, perfects its limbs, *ut not. Doct. ff. ad leg. Aquil. l. ij in fi.* Thus, like you other gentlemen, I see lawsuits born shapeless and limbless in their origins. They have nothing but a document or two, and at that time they're ugly beasts. But once they're well packed, racked, and sacked, they can really be said to have shape and limbs. For *forma dat esse rei, l. Si is qui ff. ad. l. Falcid. in c. cum dilecta extra de rescript. Barbatia, Cons.* 12 *lib.* 11, and before that Bald. *in c. ulti. extra de consuet.; et l. Julianus. ff. ad exhib. et l. quaesitum. ff. De leg. iij.* The method is as set down in *gl. p. q. j., c. Paulus:*

Debile principium melior fortuna sequetur.[2]

Like you other gentlemen, so the sergeants, ushers, summoners,

---

1. I will hate if I can, but otherwise, reluctantly, I will love.
2. Better fortune follows poor beginnings.

pettifoggers, proctors, commissioners, advocates, examiners, scribes, notaries, registrars, and petty judges, *de quibus tit. est lib. iij. Cod.*, by sucking very hard and continuously at the parties' purses, provide their suits with head, feet claws, beak, teeth, hands, veins, arteries, nerves, muscles, and humours. These are the bags, *gl. De cons. d. 4, c. accepisti.*

> *Qualis vestis erit, talia corda gerit.*[1]

Hic not. that in this respect litigants are more fortunate than the ministers of justice, for,

> *Beatius est dare quam accipere*[2]

ff. comm. lib. iij. et extra, De celebra. Miss. c. cum Marthae, and 24 *q. j. c. Odi. gl.*

> *Affectum dantis pensat censura tonantis.*[3]

In this way they make the suit perfect, handsome, and shapely, as says the canonical gloss,

> *Accipe, sume, cape, sunt verba placentia Papae*[4]

which is more clearly stated by Alber. de Ros., *in verb. Roma.*:

> *Roma manus rodit, quas rodere non valet, odit.*
> *Dantes custodit, non dantes spernit et odit.*[5]

And what's the reason for that?

> *Ad praesens ova, cras pullis sunt meliora*[6]

ut est glos. in l. cum hi, ff. De transact. The drawback of the contrary is set out in *gloss. C. De allu. l. fi.*:

> *Cum labor in damno est, crescit mortalis egestas*[7]

The true derivation of the word Lawsuit is from the number of *law-sacks* that it requires for its *pursuit*, on which point we have such

1. Laces will be worn to suit the coat.
2. It is more blessed to give than to receive.
3. Jupiter in his judgement considers the disposition of the giver.
4. Take, accept, and receive are words that please the Pope.
5. Rome gnaws hands; those that it cannot gnaw it hates. It looks after givers, spurns and dislikes non-givers.
6. To-day's eggs are better than to-morrow's hens.
7. When work is wasted human need increases.

celestial maxims as: *Litigando jura crescunt, Litigando jus acquiritur.*[1]
*Item gl. in c. Illud ext., De praesump., et C. De prob., l. instrumenta, l.
non epistolis, l. non nudis.*

> *Et cum non prosunt singula, multa juvant.'*[2]

'Yes,' said Blowbroth, 'but how do you proceed in a criminal case,
when the party has been caught *flagrante crimine*?'

'As you other gentlemen do,' replied Bridlegoose. 'I permit, or
command, the plaintiff to take a good sound sleep as a preliminary
to the case, and then to appear before me, bringing me good and
attested evidence of his sleep, according to the gloss, 32 *q. vij. c. Si quis
cum.*

> *Quandoque bonus dormitat Homerus*[3]

'This act provides a new limb, and from that one springs another,
as link by link a coat of mail is made. Finally, by investigation, I find
the case well shaped and perfect in all its limbs. Then I have recourse
to my dice; and I don't intervene at this point without good reason
and valid precedents. I remember that in the camp at Stockholm a
Gascon named Gratianauld, a native of Saint-Sever, lost all his money
at play, to his very great fury – for, as you know, *pecunia est alter
sanguis,*[4] as Ant. de Butrio says, in *c. accedens. ij, extra ut lit. non contest.,*
and Bald. in *l. Si tuis. C. De op. li. per no. et l. advocati C. de advo. diu.
jud. Pecunia est vita hominis, et optimus fidejussor in necessitatibus.*[5] Now as
he came out of the gambling house, he shouted to his companions: "By
the bull's head, boys, may drink harden our livers! Now that I've lost
my two dozen bawbees, I'm in far better trim to punch you, clout you,
and kick you if anyone'll challenge me to a scrap." As nobody answered him, he went on to the camp of the heavy-weights, and repeated the same words, challenging them also to a fight. But these
great Frieslanders merely answered: "Der Guascongner thut schich
usz mitt eim iedem zu schlagen, aber er ist geneigter zu staelen;
darumb, lieben frauuen, hend serg zu inu inuerm hausraut."[6] And none
of their company offered to fight. So the Gascon went on to the camp

---

1. Laws grow by litigation, law is acquired by litigation.
2. When things fail singly they prevail in quantity.
3. Sometimes the good Homer nods.   4. Money is a second blood.
5. Money is a man's staff, and his best defender in need.
6. The Gascon behaves as if he wants to fight with everybody. But really he
is better at stealing. Therefore, dear ladies, look to the baggage.

of the French mercenaries, saying the same as before and gallantly offering them a fight with a number of gasconading flourishes. But no one answered him. Then the fellow lay down at the far end of the camp, near the tent of fat Christian, the Chevalier de Crissé, and went to sleep. At that moment a mercenary who had also lost all his money came out with his sword, firmly resolved to fight with the Gascon, seeing that he had lost too:

Ploratur lachrymis amissa pecunia veris[1]

as says the gloss *De poenitent., dist.* 3, *c. sunt plures.* So he searched for him right through the camp, and found him asleep. "Hi there," he shouted at him. "Hi there, by all the devils! Get up! I've lost all my money, just like you. Come, let's have a fight, my lad, let's have a good bang at one another. See, my sword's no longer than your rapier." But the Gascon answered him in a daze: "By St Arnault's head, who are you that wake me up? May the tavern-fever send you staggering! By St Sever, patron of Gascony, I was just having a good sleep when this scoundrel came and started pestering me!" The mercenary once more challenged him to fight, but the Gascon replied: "I'll skin you, you miserable devil, now that I've had a rest. But just come and have a little sleep like me first. Then we'll fight." Having forgotten his loss, he had lost his wish to fight: and in the end, instead of fighting and possibly killing one another, they went off to drink together, each pawning his sword for the cash. Sleep had performed this good deed, and calmed the burning fury of the two good champions. The golden phrase of Giovanni Andrea applies here, *in c. ult. De sent. et re judic. libro sexto*:

Sedendo et quiescendo fit anima prudens.'[2]

CHAPTER 43: *Pantagruel justifies Bridlegoose's Judgements by Dice*

WITH this Bridlegoose concluded his speech, and Blowbroth ordered him to withdraw from the judicial enclosure, which he did. Then Blowbroth addressed Pantagruel as follows: 'It is rightful, most august prince, not only on account of the obligation which this court

1. The loss of money is bewailed with real tears.
2. By leisure and quiet the soul becomes wise.

and the whole marquisate of Mirelingues feel towards you, but also in consideration of the sound sense, judicial discretion, and admirable learning that the good God, giver of all good things, has conferred upon you, that we place the decision in your hands. The case of Bridlegoose is most strange, most paradoxical, and entirely unprecedented. In your presence, in your sight, and your hearing, he has confessed to giving judgement by the throwing of dice. We beg you, therefore, to be so good as to give such sentence as shall seem just and equitable to you.'

To this Pantagruel replied: 'Gentlemen, my rank, as you well know, is not such that I profess to decide lawsuits. But since you are pleased to do me this honour, instead of performing the office of judge I will assume that of petitioner. I recognize in Bridlegoose several qualities which make him, in my opinion, deserving of pardon in this case under judgement. In the first place his old age, in the second his simplicity; both of which, as I need not remind you, speak in favour of a pardon and as an excuse for misdeeds, both in equity and according to our laws. Thirdly, I recognize another point, likewise grounded in equity, that is in Bridlegoose's favour; which is that this single fault ought to be effaced, extinguished, and swallowed up in the immeasurable ocean of just decisions which he has made in the past, also that in more than forty years no reprehensible act has been brought up against him. It is as if I were to throw a drop of sea-water into the river Loire; no one would notice it, no one would say that the river was brackish because of a single drop. I think too that I can perceive some touch of God's hand here, since, in his dispensation he has caused all Bridlegoose's previous decisions in cases of this kind to be upheld by this venerable and supreme court of yours. For God, as you know, often wishes his glory to be manifested in the confounding of the wise, the humbling of the mighty, and the raising up of the simple and humble. But all these points I will waive. I will merely beg you, not out of the obligation you profess towards my house – for which I am grateful – but because of the sincere affection which you have found us to bear you from time immemorial, on this and on the other side of the Loire, in the maintenance of your estates and dignity, to pardon him on this occasion, and this on two conditions: firstly that he satisfy – or give surety that he will satisfy – the party wronged by the sentence in question – for which satisfaction I will myself provide, and generously; secondly, that as assistant in his duties you will give him some younger, more learned, prudent, skilled, and virtuous counsellor, whose advice he shall henceforth take in performing his judicial functions. But in case you should wish entirely to relieve him of his office, I earnestly entreat you to confer his services upon me as a present and an unconditioned gift. I shall find places and duties enough in my kingdoms to employ him, and shall make very good use of him. In conclusion, I will pray the good God, creator, preserver, and giver of all good things, to keep you for ever in his holy grace.'

When he had spoken, Pantagruel bowed to the whole court and left the judicial enclosure. At the door he found Panurge, Epistemon, Friar John, and others, and there they mounted their horses, to return to Gargantua's. On the way Pantagruel told them, point by point, the story of Bridlegoose's judgement. Friar John said that he had known Peter Nitwit, in the time when he lived under the noble Abbot Ardillon at Fontaine-le-Comte. Gymnaste said that he was in the tent of fat Christian, the Chevalier de Crissé, when the Gascon gave his answer to the mercenary. Panurge said that he had some difficulty in believing that Bridlegoose's judgements by dice had been successful, particularly for so long a time. And Epistemon said to Pantagruel: 'A parallel case is related of a provost of Montlhéry. But what do you think of his luck in being successful with the dice for so many years? I should not be surprised at one or two judgements given like this at haphazard, especially in cases that were intricate, ambiguous, muddled and obscure. But ...'

CHAPTER 44: *Epistemon tells a strange story of the Perplexities of Human Judgement*

'THE controversy debated before Cneius Dolabella, proconsul in Asia,' continued Epistemon,[1] 'was equally difficult. This is the case: A woman of Smyrna had by her first husband a child named A.B.C. Her husband died and after a certain time she remarried; by her second husband she had a child named F.G. It happened – for, as you

1. In the later editions this speech is given to Pantagruel. But the book seems to read more smoothly if the whole story is given to Epistemon. I have altered the chapter heading accordingly.

know, step-fathers and step-mothers rarely feel any affection for the children of the late first husbands or wives – that this second husband and his son secretly, treacherously, and of malice aforethought, murdered A.B.C. When the wife discovered their treacherous crime she took the law into her own hands and killed the pair of them, thus avenging the murder of her elder son. She was then arrested by the constables and brought before Dolabella, and in his presence she confessed her crime without any dissimulation, merely pleading that it had been right and reasonable to kill them, and this was the state of the case.

He found the decision so difficult that he did not know to which side to incline. On the one side it was an execrable crime. A woman had killed her second husband and her second son. On the other hand, the reasons for the murder seemed to him so natural and to be, as it were, founded on natural law, seeing that together they had murdered her elder son – treacherously and of malice aforethought, without being insulted or wronged by him, but merely out of greed to possess the whole inheritance – that before deciding he sent to the Areopagites in Athens, to hear what their advice and verdict would be in the case. The Areopagites in reply requested him to send the disputing parties before them in a hundred years' time, to make a personal appearance, and to reply to certain questions not contained in the written record. The import of this was that the case seemed so perplexed and obscure to them that they did not know what to say, or what judgement to give. If a man had settled that case by a throw of the dice he wouldn't have been far wrong whichever way they had fallen; if it had gone against the woman, she would have deserved her punishment since she had herself taken the revenge which by right belonged to justice; if it had gone in the woman's favour, the terrible grief would have seemed an excuse for her deed. But that Bridlegoose should have been successful for so many years, that does astound me.'

'I couldn't give you a categorical explanation of that,' replied Pantagruel. 'That I must confess. At a guess, I should attribute the success of his judgements to a benevolent aspect of the heavens, and the favour of the guiding intelligences, who have taken into account Judge Bridlegoose's simplicity and plain kindness. For he doubted his own knowledge and capacity, knew the inconsistencies and contradictions of the laws, edicts, customs, and ordinances, and was aware of the deceptions of the eternal Calumniator, who often disguises himself as a messenger of light – deceptions practised through his ministers, the wicked advocates, counsellors, attorneys, and other such instruments. He turns black into white, and fantastically persuades both parties that they are in the right. For, as you know, there is no cause so bad that it doesn't find its advocate; and if that wasn't so there'd be no suits in the world. Being aware of all this, I say, Bridlegoose would commend himself to God, the just Judge, invoke the aid of the divine grace, and put himself under the guidance of the most Holy Spirit. Thus, avoiding the dangers and perplexities of a definite decision, he would by the throwing of dice discover the divine will and pleasure, which we call the final judgement. The said intelligences would then move and turn the dice to fall in favour of the party who, having a just case, would have a fair claim to see his rights maintained. Indeed, as the Talmudists say, there is nothing wrong in throwing the dice. On the contrary, when human beings are anxious and in doubt, only in this way can the divine will be manifested.

'I should not care to think or say, as certainly I do not believe, that those who give judgement in the Mirelinguian High Court in Mirelingues are so patently wicked and so abnormally corrupt that a case would not be worse decided – come what might – by the fall of dice than if it were to pass through their bloodstained and perversely influenced hands. This I say though I am well aware that their entire guidance in common law is derived from one Tribonian, a miscreant, an infidel, and a barbarian of such malice, perversity, greed, and wickedness that he used to sell laws, edicts, bills, constitutions, and ordinances for cash down to the highest bidder. That was how he shaped the legal hotch-potch which they use at present, out of tag ends and scraps, suppressing and abolishing all the rest – which amounted to the entire law – for fear that, if it had remained whole and the books of the ancient legal authorities expounding the Twelve Tables and the Edicts of the Praetors had been left open to view, his wickedness would have been exposed before the great world. Therefore it would often be better – that is to say less harm would come of it – if the parties at variance were to walk over spikes rather than to resort to his law for their answers and judgements. Indeed Cato, in his time, desired, and recommended that courts of law should be paved with spikes.'

CHAPTER 45: *How Panurge consulted Triboulet*

ON the sixth day following, Pantagruel returned at the same hour as Triboulet arrived by river from Blois. On his arrival Panurge gave him a pig's bladder well blown up and rattling with the dried peas inside, also a grandly gilt wooden sword, a small purse made of a tortoise shell, a wicker-covered bottle full of Breton wine, and a peck of hard, green apples.

'What,' said Carpalim, 'is he such an utter fool then?'

Triboulet slung the sword and the purse round his waist, took the bladder in his hand, ate some of the apples, and drank all the wine. Whereat Panurge gazed at him curiously and observed: 'I never yet saw a fool – and I've seen them to the tune of more than ten thousand francs – who didn't drink gladly and in long gulps.'

He then expounded his problem in rhetorical and elegant language. But before he had finished, Triboulet gave him a great punch between the shoulders, shoved the bottle into his hand, flipped his nose with the pig's bladder, and for all answer said to him with a violent wag of the head: 'By God, God, mad fool, beware of the monk! The hornpipe of Buzançais!'[1] When he had said this he retired from the company and played with his bladder, delighting in the melodious rattle of the peas. Afterwards it was impossible to get a word of any kind out of him. Indeed, when Panurge tried to interrogate him further, the fool drew his wooden sword and tried to strike him.

'We've been nicely caught,' said Panurge. 'That's a fine answer. He's a fool all right. There's no denying that. But the man who brought him to me is even more of a fool, and I am a perfect fool for explaining my thoughts to him.'

'That second remark is aimed point-blank at me,' said Carpalim.

'Without getting excited,' said Pantagruel, 'let's consider his words and gestures. I detected portentous mysteries in them. What's more, I'm not as astounded as I used to be that the Turks revere such fools as their Musaphis and prophets. Did you notice how his head shook and waggled before he opened his mouth to speak? By the teaching of the ancient philosophers, the ceremonies of the Magi, and the observations of the legal authorities, you may consider this movement to have

1. A town famous for the manufacture of bagpipes.

been caused by the invasion and inspiration of the prophetic spirit which shook it, by its sudden entrance into such weak and petty material. For you know that a small head cannot contain a large brain. It is in just that way that doctors say a trembling strikes the limbs of the human body; that is to say, partly from the weight and violent impact of the burden carried, partly from the virtual weakness of the carrying organ. A clear example of this can be found in the case of those who cannot carry a large beaker full of wine, on an empty stomach, without their hands trembling. The Pythian prophetess demonstrated this to us of old when, before giving her oracle, she shook her domestic laurel. Lampridius similarly records that, to win the reputation of a diviner, the Emperor Heliogabalus, on several of the festivals of his great idol, publicly shook his head in front of his fanatical eunuchs. Plautus too declares in his *Asinaria* that Saurias went about shaking his head, as if raving and out of his senses, and frightened everyone he met; and in another place, to explain why Charmides shook his head, he says that he was in an ecstasy. Catullus also tells in *Berecynthia and Atys* of a place where the Maenads, Bacchic woman, priestesses of Dionysus, and frenzied prophetesses who carried ivy-boughs, used to shake their heads; as the gelded Galli, priests of Cybele, did under similar circumstances, when holding their ceremonies. Whence it is, according to the ancient theologians, that the goddess derives her name; for κυβιστᾶν means to turn, twist, shake the head, and act as if wry-necked. Similarly, Titus Livius writes that at the Bacchanalia in Rome, because of a certain shaking and convulsion of the body which they affected, men and women seemed to be uttering prophecies. For the common voice both of philosophers and of public opinion held that the heavens never gave the gift of prophecy without frenzy and a shaking of the body, which did not only tremble and quiver on receiving it but also at the time of manifesting and declaring it. Indeed, when Julian, a famous legal authority, was asked on some occasion whether a slave should be reckoned sane who had, in the company of possessed and raving people, spoken and been known to prophesy, he replied that since he had not shaken his head, he should be considered sane.

'In a similar way, we see tutors and schoolmasters shake their pupils' heads, as one would a pot, by the handles, pinching and pulling them by the ears – which are, according to the teaching of the Egyptian sages, the organs consecrated to memory – in order to recall their thoughts to good philosophical discipline. For a schoolboy's mind often strays after strange fancies and, as it were, runs wild from unruly desires. Virgil acknowledged that this was true of himself when he told of his shaking by Apollo Cynthius.'

CHAPTER 46: *Pantagruel and Panurge interpret Triboulet's words in contradictory ways*

'He says that you're a fool, and what kind of a fool? A raging fool, for wanting in your old age to bind and subject yourself in marriage. "Beware of the monk!" he says to you. 'Pon my soul, you'll be cuckolded by some monk. I stake my honour on it, and I couldn't give you a greater pledge than that if I were sole and undisputed despot over Europe, Africa, and Asia. Note what importance I attach to our wisefool Triboulet. The other oracles and answers have stated that you will be a peaceable cuckold, but as yet they have not openly declared who it is that will make your wife an adulteress and you a cuckold. The noble Triboulet has told you. Your cuckolding will be infamous and a flagrant scandal. Alas, that your marriage bed should be defiled and contaminated by monkery. But he said more, that you will dance a hornpipe to the bagpipes of Buzançais, that is to say that you'll be well-horned, hornified, and cornuted. You'll make the same sort of mistake as he did when he begged King Louis the Twelfth to give his brother the salt-controllership of this same Buzançais, and referred to it as the Buzançais bagpipe. You'll imagine that you are marrying some decent honest woman, but in fact you'll be tying yourself up to some immodest creature, as full of the wind of pride, as shrill and unpleasant as these same bagpipes. Note further, that he flipped you on the nose with his bladder. That presages that you'll be beaten, mocked, and robbed, in the same way as you robbed the little boys of Vaubreton of their bladder.'

'Quite the contrary,' said Panurge. 'Not that I wish shamelessly to exempt myself from allegiance to the realm of folly. I am its vassal, and I belong to it; that I confess. Everyone is foolish, and it is quite right that the village of Foul in Lorraine is close to Toul, or, as you might say that *fool* and all almost rhyme. All are fools. Solomon says that the number of fools is infinite; nothing can be added to infinity. and nothing can be subtracted from it, as Aristotle proves. And I should be a raging fool if, being a fool, I did not consider myself one. That is exactly what makes the number of maniacs and madmen infinite. Avicenna says that there are infinite varieties of madness. But the rest of this fool's words and gestures are in my favour. He says to my wife: "Beware of the monk"; which is a pet monkey that she will keep as Catullus's Lesbia kept a sparrow. He'll chase the flies and spend his time as gaily as ever Domitian the fly-catcher did. What's more, he says that she'll be as pleasant and countrified as a jolly bagpipe at Saulieu or Buzançais. Triboulet the truthful perfectly understood my nature and my secret desires. For let me tell you, I much prefer gay, dishevelled shepherd-girls, whose thighs smell of wild thyme, to your great court ladies with their rich attire and their musky maljamin perfumes. The sound of the country bagpipe gives me more pleasure than the quaverings of lutes, rebecks, and court violins. He dealt me a clout on the old backbone. Let's take it as a kindness, and a remission of some of the pains of Purgatory. He didn't do it out of malice. He thought he was hitting a page. He is a good-natured fool and quite harmless, I promise you. It would be a sin to think badly of him. I pardon him with all my heart. He tweaked me on the nose too; that will signify some little fooleries my wife and I will get up to, as all newly married couples do.'

CHAPTER 47: *Pantagruel and Panurge resolve to visit the Oracle of the Holy Bottle*

'HERE's another point that you don't take into account; and yet it's the crux of the matter. He handed me the bottle. What does that signify? What's the meaning of that?'

'Perhaps it means that your wife will be a drunkard,' said Pantagruel.

'Quite the opposite,' replied Panurge, 'because it was empty. I swear to you by the backbone of St Fiacre of Brie, that our wise-fool, the unique and non-lunatical Triboulet, is referring me to the bottle. So I renew my former vow, and swear by the Styx and Acheron in your presence to wear spectacles on my cap and no codpiece on my breeches until I have the Holy Bottle's answer to my question. There is a discreet fellow and a friend of mine who knows the place, the land, and the country where this temple and oracle are. He will certainly lead us there safely. Let us go together, you and I. Don't dismiss me, I beg of you. I'll be an Achates to you, a Damon and a companion for the journey. I have long known you to be a lover of travelling, who is always anxious to see and to learn. We shall see some marvellous sights, believe me.'

'I'm perfectly willing,' replied Pantagruel, 'but before embarking on this long peregrination, with all its risks, with all its evident dangers ...'

'What dangers?' broke in Panurge, interrupting his speech. 'Dangers fly from me, wherever I may be, for twenty miles around; as when the prince comes the deputy resigns, when the sun comes the darkness vanishes, and as sickness flies at the approach of St Martin's body at Candes.'

'By the way,' said Pantagruel, 'there are various things we must do before we set out. The first is to send Triboulet back to Blois.' This was done immediately, and Pantagruel gave him a cloth of gold coat, beautifully embroidered. 'Secondly, we must obtain the advice and leave of the king, my father, and then we must find some sibyl for our guide and interpreter.'

Panurge replied that his friend Xenomanes would be guide enough. Besides, he intended to pass through Lanternland and there take some learned and serviceable Lanterness, who would be to them for this voyage what the sibyl was to Aeneas when he went down into the Elysian Fields. Carpalim, who was departing to escort Triboulet home, heard this speech and cried out: 'Hi, Panurge, Master Quit-of-your-debts, take my Lord Debt-puty from Calais with you, for he's a good *fellow*. And don't forget *our debtors*, our lanterns that is. Then you'll have a torch (*fallot*) and lanterns as well.'

'My prophecy is that we shan't engender melancholy on the way,' said Pantagruel. 'I can see that clearly already. Only I don't like not being able to talk good Lanternese.'

'I'll speak it for all of you,' replied Panurge. 'I understand it like a native. I'm as used to it as to the vernacular.

> Briszmarg d'algotbric nubstzne zos,
> Isquebfz prusq: alborz crinqs zacbac.
> Misbe dilbarlkz morp nipp stancz bos;
> Strombtz, Panrge walmap quost grufz bac.'[1]

'Now guess what that means, Epistemon.'

'Those are the names of devils errant, devils passant, and devils rampant,' answered Epistemon.

'That's good donkey truth, my fine friend,' said Panurge. 'It's the court language of Lanternland. On the way I'll make you a smart little dictionary of it, which won't last you much longer than a pair of new shoes. You'll have learnt it off before you see the sun rise the next day. What I said, translated from Lanternese into the vulgar tongue, goes like this:

> All miseries attended me whilst I
> A lover was. I had no good thereby.
> The married folk of better fortune tell;
> Panurge is one of them and knows it well.'

'All that remains, then,' said Pantagruel, 'is to hear the will of the king my father, and to obtain leave from him.'

CHAPTER 48: *Gargantua points out that it is not lawful for Children to marry without the knowledge and consent of their Fathers and Mothers*

As he entered the great hall of the castle, Pantagruel met the good Gargantua coming out from his council, and thereupon gave him a summary account of their adventures, outlined their new project, and begged for his leave and consent to carry it out. The excellent Gargantua was carrying two great bundles of petitions granted and requests to be considered, one in each hand; and these he gave over to Ulrich Gallet, his trusted Master of Petitions and Requests. Then he drew Pantagruel aside and, with a jollier face than usual, said: 'Praise be to God, my dearest son, for keeping you still in the path of virtue. I am most willing that you should make this journey. But I could also

1. This, like an earlier piece of Lanternese, in the first book, is pure nonsense but for the introduction of Panurge's name, misspelt.

wish that you felt the wish and urge to marry. I think that you are now approaching the right age for it. Panurge has taken some trouble to surmount the difficulties which might have stood in his way. Now tell me your views.'

'Most gracious father,' replied Pantagruel, 'till now I had not given the subject a thought. In this whole matter I have deferred to your desires and your paternal authority. I would rather lie stark dead at your feet and under your displeasure than be found living and married without your consent. That I swear to God. By no laws, sacred or profane and barbarous, that I have ever heard of have the children ever been free to marry, unless their fathers, mothers, and nearest relatives deign to desire and promote the match. No lawgiver has vested this right in the children. Every one of them has reserved it for the parents.'

'My very dear son,' said Gargantua, 'I take your word for that. Praise be to God that only good and praiseworthy thoughts come into your head, and that nothing has entered the dwelling-place of your spirit but liberal knowledge by way of the windows of your senses. For in my day there was found on the Continent a country in which lived certain image-bearing molecatchers, who were as hostile to marriage as the priests of Cybele in Phrygia – only they were not capons but the most lecherous and salacious of cocks – and they dictated laws to married folk on the subject of marriage. Really I don't know which is the more abominable, the tyrannical presumption of these dreaded molecatchers – who do not confine themselves within the bars of their mysterious temples but meddle with matters utterly foreign to their condition – or the superstitious stupidity of the married folk, who have sanctioned and obeyed such perfectly malicious and barbarous laws. For they do not see what is clearer than the morning star, that these connubial sanctions are entirely to the advantage of the Fraternity, and in no way for the good and profit of husbands and wives; which is sufficient reason to arouse suspicions of inquity and fraud. It would be no more presumptuous if the married were to set up laws for the Fraternity to govern their ceremonies and sacrifices, seeing that these image-bearers take tithe of their goods, and nibble at the profit earned by their labours and the sweat of their brows, to provide themselves with abundant food and ample leisure. Such laws would not, in my opinion, be as perverse and presumptuous as those which the married folk have received from the Fraternity. For, as you very well said, there never has been a law in the world that gave children permission to marry without their fathers' knowledge, will, and consent. Yet by the laws of which I am speaking there is no scoundrel, criminal, rogue, or gallows-bird, no stinking, lousy, leprous ruffian, no brigand, robber, or villain in their country, who may not snatch any maiden he chooses – never mind how noble, lovely, rich, modest, and bashful she may be – out of her father's house, out of her mother's arms, and in spite of all her relations, so long as this ruffian has entered into an agreement with some image-bearer, for a future division of the spoils. Could the Goths, the Scythians, or the Massagetae perform worse or crueller wrongs in an enemy town, captured after a long siege and a costly attack? So grieving fathers and mothers see some unknown stranger, some barbarian, some rotten, poxy, cadaverous, penurious, and miserable cur, pick up, and carry from home their most lovely, delicate, rich, and healthy daughters. They had tenderly schooled the girls in all the virtuous arts and brought them up in all modesty, hoping in due course to marry them to the sons of their neighbours and old friends, who had been brought up and schooled with the same care. They had looked forward to the birth of children from these happy marriages, who would inherit and preserve not only the morals of their fathers and mothers, but also their goods and lands. Can you imagine what a sad sight this is for them? Don't imagine that the sorrow of the Romans and their allies was greater when they heard of the death of Germanicus Drusus. Don't imagine that the anguish of the Lacedaemonians was more pitiable when they saw the Grecian Helen thievishly abducted from their land by the Trojan adulterer. Don't imagine that their grief and lamentations were any less than those of Ceres when her daughter Proserpine was ravished from her, of Isis at the loss of Osiris, of Venus at the death of Adonis, of Hercules at the bearing of Hylas, or of Hecuba at the abduction of Polyxena.

'The parents, nevertheless, are so afraid of the Devil and so riddled with superstition that they dare not object, since the molecatcher has been present and solemnized the marriage. So they stay at home, robbed of their beloved daughters, the father cursing the day and hour of his wedding, the mother wishing that she had miscarried instead of bearing a child whose fate has proved so luckless and sad: and both end their lives in tears and lamentation, when they might have expected to end them in joy, under their daughters' tender care.

'Others have been so driven out of their minds, have become so maniacal, that out of mourning and grief, they have drowned themselves, hanged themselves, or stabbed themselves, unable to bear their shame. But others have shown a more heroic spirit and, following the example of Jacob's sons when they avenged the rape of their sister Dina, have caught the ruffian together with his molecatcher, secretly persuading and corrupting their daughters, and have cut them to pieces on the spot, feloniously murdering them, and afterwards throwing their bodies into the fields for the wolves and crows. Such manly and chivalrous actions have set the molecatching mystagogues trembling and miserably lamenting. They have drawn up hideous protests, and most importunately summoned and implored the secular arm and the state judiciary, arrogantly demanding and claiming that exemplary punishment should be inflicted in cases of such gravity. But neither in natural equity, in common right, nor in any imperial law, has any clause, paragraph, point, or title been discovered, prescribing any penalty or torture for such an act. Such penalty would defy reason, and fly in the face of Nature. For there is no virtuous man in the world who would not, naturally and reasonably, be more perturbed by the news of his daughter's rape, shame, and dishonour than by her death. Now anyone finding a murderer in the act of homicide with malice aforethought upon the person of his daughter may reasonably, and naturally must, kill him on the spot, for which deed he will not be answerable at law. It is not surprising, therefore, if the father, when he finds the ruffian, at the instigation of the molecatcher, corrupting his daughter, and stealing her out of his house, even though she is a consenting party, is impelled to slay them ignominiously and throw their bodies to be torn by the wild beasts, as unworthy to receive the dear, desired, and final embrace of our kind and great mother earth; which we call burial.

'My dearest son, take care that such laws are not accepted in this kingdom after my death; so long as I am living and have breath in this body, I shall, with God's aid, take all proper precautions myself.

'Now since you refer the matter of your marriage to me, I am in favour of it, and will provide for it. Make preparations for this voyage of Panurge's. Take with you Epistemon, Friar John, and such others as you may choose. My treasury is entirely at your disposal. Take any ships you please from my arsenal at Thalassa, and any pilots, sailors, or interpreters you require. Set sail with the first favourable wind, in God's name and under Our Saviour's protection. During your absence I will set about choosing you a wife and preparing a feast. For I want yours to be a famous wedding, if ever there was one.'

CHAPTER 49: *How Pantagruel prepared to put to sea, and of the Herb called Pantagruelion*

PANTAGRUEL took leave of the good Gargantua, who offered up fervent prayers for the success of his son's voyage, and a few days later he arrived at the port of Thalassa, near Saint Malo, accompanied by Panurge, Epistemon, Friar John of the Hashes, Abbot of Thélème, and others of the royal house, notably by Xenomanes, the great traveller and journeyer by perilous ways, who had come at Panurge's command, since he had some small holding in the domain of Salmigundia. When they got there, Pantagruel equipped a fleet of vessels, equal in number to those which Ajax of Salamis once gathered to escort the Greeks to Troy. He collected sailors, pilots, boatswains, interpreters, craftsmen, and soldiers, also provisions, artillery, munitions, clothes, money, and other such goods as were needed for a long and perilous voyage. These he took on board, and amongst the cargo I noticed a great store of his herb Pantagruelion,[1] both in its raw green state and also prepared and manufactured.

The herb Pantagruelion has a small hardish, roundish root, ending in a blunt point, and does not strike more than a foot and a half into the ground. From the root grows a single round, umbelliferous stem, green on the outside, white within and hollow like the stems of Smyrnium, Olus atrum, beans, and gentian. It is woody, straight, friable, and slightly denticulated after the fashion of a lightly fluted column; and it is full of fibres, in which lie all the virtue of the herb, particularly in the part called *Mesa*, or middle, and in that called *Mylasea*. Its height is commonly from five to six feet. But sometimes it is taller than a lance; that is to say when it grows in a sweet, spongy, light soil, moist but not cold, like that of Olonne, and that of Rosea,

1. This will prove to be hemp.

near Praeneste in Sabine territory, and provided that it does not lack rain around the fishermen's festivals and the summer solstice. Then it grows higher than some trees, and so, on Theophrastus's authority, is called *dendromalache*, although the herb dies each year, and has not the root, trunk, peduncles, or permanent branches of a tree.

Great, strong branches issue from the stem. Its leaves are three times longer than they are wide. They are always green, slightly rough like alkanet; toughish, with sickle-shaped indentations all round, like betony; and terminating in points like a Macedonian pike or a surgeon's lancet. Their shape is not very different from that of ash or agrimony leaves; and it is so like hemp-agrimony that many herbalists have called it cultivated hemp-agrimony, and have called hemp-agrimony wild pantagruelion. The leaves sprout out all round the stalk at equal distances, to the number of five or seven at each level; and it is by a special favour of Nature that they are grouped in these two odd numbers, which are both divine and mysterious. Their scent is strong, and unpleasant to delicate nostrils.

The seeds form near the top of the stalk, and a little below. They are as numerous as those of any herb in existence, spherical, oblong, or rhomboid in shape, black, bright, or brown in colour, hardish, enclosed in a light husk, and much loved by all such singing birds as linnets, goldfinches, larks, canaries, yellowhammers, and others. But in man they destroy the generative seed if eaten often and in quantity; and although the Greeks of old used sometimes to make certain kinds of cakes, tarts, and fritters of them, which they ate after supper as a dainty and to enhance the taste of their wine, still they are difficult to digest, lie heavy on the stomach, make bad blood, and, by their excessive heat, harm the brain, filling the head with noxious and painful vapours. Just as in many plants there are two sexes, male and female – as we see in laurels, palms, oaks, yews, asphodels, mandragora, ferns, agarics, birthwort, cypress, turpentine, pennyroyal, peonies, and others – so in this herb there is a male, which has no flower but plenty of seeds, and a female, which is thick and has little whitish useless flowers, but no seed to speak of; and as in other plants of this kind, the female leaf is larger but less tough than the male, and does not grow as high.

This pantagruelion is sown at the first coming of the swallows, and pulled out of the ground when the cicadas begin to get hoarse.

CHAPTER 50: *How to prepare and apply the famous herb Panta-gruelion*

PANTAGRUELION is prepared at the autumn equinox in different ways according to the fancies of the people and to national preferences. Pantagruel's first instructions were to strip the stalk of its leaves and seeds; to soak it in still – not in running – water for five days, if the weather is fine and the water warm, and for nine to twelve if the weather is cloudy and the water cold; then to dry it in the sun, and afterwards in the shade, remove the outside, separate the fibres – in which, as has been said, lies all its use and value – from the woody part, which is useless except to make a fire blaze, as kindling, or for blowing up pigs' bladders to amuse children. Sometimes also gluttons will find a sly use for them, as syphons to suck up new wine through the bung-hole.

Some modern Pantagruelists, to avoid the manual labour entailed in making this separation, use certain pounding instruments, formed in the shape in which the angry Juno held the fingers of her hands together, to prevent the delivery of Alcmena, the mother of Hercules. With the aid of these they bruise and break up the woody part, making it useless, in order to recover the fibres. The only people who practise this process are those who defy the world's opinion, and in a manner considered paradoxical by philosophers earn their livings by walking backwards.[1] Those who want to make better and more valuable use of the fibre imitate the fabled pastime of the three sister Fates, the nocturnal recreation of the noble Circe, and the lengthy stratagem practised by Penelope to ward off her amorous suitors during the absence of her husband Ulysses. In this way it can be put to all its inestimable uses, of which I will tell you some only – for it would be impossible for me to reveal them all – if first I may explain to you the plant's name.

I find that plants are named in different ways. Some have taken their name from the man who first discovered them, recognized them, demonstrated them, cultivated them, domesticated them, and applied them to their uses; as dog's mercury from Mercury; panacea (all-

---

1. These are the ropemakers, who draw the fibre from a bag, and walk backwards as they plait the rope.

heal) from Panace, the daughter of Aesculapius; artemisia from Artemis, who is Diana; eupatoria from king Eupator; telephium from
Telephus; euphorbium from Euphorbus, king Juba's physician;
clymenos (honeysuckle) from Clymenus; alcibiadion from Alcibiades; gentian from Gentius, King of Slavonia. And so highly valued
of old was this prerogative of giving one's name to a newly discovered
plant that, just as there was a controversy between Neptune and Pallas
as to which should name the country discovered by them both jointly,
which was afterwards called Athens from Athena, that is to say
Minerva – even so did Lyncus, King of Scythia attempt treacherously
to murder the young Triptolemus, who was sent by Ceres to show
mankind wheat, which was till then unknown. For by the youth's
death Lyncus hoped to give the grain his own name and, to his
honour and immortal glory, to be called the discoverer of a food
both useful and necessary to the life of man. But, for his treachery, he
was transformed by Ceres into an ounce or lynx. Similarly, great and
long wars were waged of old between certain kings in and around
Cappadocia, their only difference being which of them should give
his name to a certain herb. Owing to their quarrel, the name it eventually received was *Polemonia*, since it was the cause of war.

Others have kept the names of the regions from which they were
once brought; Median apples – or lemons – for instance from Media
where they were first found; Punic apples – that is pomegranates –
which were brought from the Punic country, which is Carthage;
ligusticum – that is lovage – which came from Liguria, the coast of
Genoa; rhubarb, from the barbarian river called Rha, as Ammianus
testifies; also santonica, fenugreek, chestnuts, peaches, Sabine juniper,
and stoechas, which owe their name to my own islands of Hyères,
called in ancient days the Stoechades, also *spica celtica*, etcetera.

Others take their names by antiphrasis or irony; absinthe, for instance, because it is the contrary of *pynthe* – the Greek for beverage –
being unpleasant to drink; holosteon, which means all bone, because
there is no herb in all Nature more fragile and tender.

Others derive their names from their properties and uses, as aristolochia, which helps women in childbirth; lichen, which heals the skin
eruptions so called; mallow, which mollifies; callithricum, which
beautifies the hair, alyssum, ephemerum, bechium, nasturtium – or nosetwister, which is a breath-catching cress – pig-nut, henbane, and others.

Others derive their names from the admirable qualities discovered in them, as heliotrope, or *solsequium*, follower of the sun, which opens as the sun rises, climbs as it ascends, declines as the sun sinks, and closes as it disappears; adiantum, or waterless, since it never retains any moisture, although it grows near the water, and even though it be plunged in water for a considerable time; also hieracia, eryngion, etcetera.

Others get their names from men or women who have been transformed into them, as daphne, the laurel, from Daphne; the myrtle from Myrsine; pitys, the stonepine, from Pitys; cynara, which is the artichoke; narcissus; crocus, the saffron; smilax, etcetera.

Others from physical resemblance, as hippuris, or horse-tail, since it is like a horse's tail; alopecuros, which is like a fox's tail; psyllion, which is like a flea; delphinium, like a dolphin; bugloss, like an ox's tongue; iris, whose flowers are like a rainbow; myosotis, like a mouse's ear; coronopus, like a crow's foot, etcetera.

Reciprocally, some men have taken their names from plants; the Fabii from beans, the Pisones from peas, the Lentuli from lentils, and the Ciceros from chick-peas. And again from more exalted similarities come Venus' navel, venushair, Venus' basin, Jupiter's beard, Jupiter's eye. Mars's blood, Mercury's fingers, hermodactyls, etcetera.

Others, again, are named from their form, as trefoil, which has three leaves; pentaphyllon, which has five leaves; serpillum, which creeps along the ground; helxine or pellitory from its clinging properties; petasites or sunshades, and myrobolan plums, which the Arabs call *been*, for they are acorn-shaped and oleaginous.

CHAPTER 51: *Why the Plant is called Pantagruelion, also something about its marvellous properties*

THE plant Pantagruelion got its name in all these ways – always excepting the mythological one. For Heaven forbid that we should in any way resort to myth in this most truthful history. Pantagruel was its discoverer; I do not mean the discoverer of the plant, but of a certain application of it. Thus applied, it is more loathed and abhorred by robbers, and is their more unremitting enemy than are dodder and choke-weed to flax, than reed to ferns, than horse-tail to mowers, than broom-rape to chick-peas, than darnel to barley, than hatchet-weed to lentils, than antranium to beans, than tares to wheat, than ivy to walls; than the water-lily *Nymphaea heraclea* to lecherous monks; than the strap and the birch to the scholars of the College of Navarre; than the cabbage to the vine, garlic to magnetic iron, onion to the eyes, fern-seed to pregnant women, the seed of willow to immoral nuns, and the yew-tree's shade to those who sleep beneath it; than wolf's bane to panthers and wolves; than the smell of a fig tree to mad bulls, than hemlock to goslings, than purslane to the teeth, than oil to trees. For we have seen many robbers end their lives high and briefly because of its use, after the manner of Phyllis, Queen of the Thracians; of Bonosus, Emperor of Rome; of Amata, wife of King Latinus; of Iphis, Auctolia, Lycambes, Arachne, Phaedra, Leda, Achaeus, King of Lydia, and others, whose only complaint was that, without their being otherwise sick, the channels through which their witticisms came out and their dainty snacks went in were stopped by the herb Pantagruelion, more scurvily than ever they could have been by the dire spasms or the mortal quinsy.

Others we have heard, at the moment when Atropos was cutting their life-thread, woefully lamenting and complaining that Pantagruel had them by the throat. But, gracious me, it wasn't Pantagruel at all. He never broke anyone on the wheel. It was Pantagruelion, doing duty as a halter, and serving them as a cravat. Besides they were speaking incorrectly and committing a solecism, unless they could be excused on the plea that they were using the figure synecdoche, taking the inventor for the invention, as one uses Ceres for bread, and Bacchus for wine. I swear to you here, by the wit residing in that bottle, cooling there in the tub, that Pantagruel never took anyone by the throat, except such men as neglect to ward off an impending thirst.

Pantagruelion is also so called by similarity. For when he was born into the world Pantagruel was as tall as the herb in question; and it was easy to make this measurement since he was born in a time of drought when they gather the said herb, and when Icarus's dog, by barking at the sun, makes every man a troglodyte, forcing the whole world to live in caves and subterranean places.

Pantagruelion owes its name also to its virtues and peculiarities. For as Pantagruel has been the exemplar and paragon of perfect jollity – I don't suppose that any one of you boozers is in any doubt about that –

so in Pantagruelion I recognize so many virtues, so much vigour, so many perfections, so many admirable effects, that if its full worth had been known when, as the Prophet tells us, the trees elected a wooden king to reign over them and govern them, it would no doubt have gained the majority of their votes and suffrages. Shall I go further? If Oxylus, son of Oreius, had begotten it on his sister Hamadryas, he would have taken more delight in its worth alone than in his eight children, so celebrated by our mythologists, who have caused their names to be eternally remembered. The eldest, a daughter, was called the vine; the next, a son, was called the fig; the next, the walnut; the next, the oak; the next, the sorb-apple; the next, the mountain-ash; the next, the poplar; and the last, the elm, which was a great surgeon in its time.

I shall forbear to tell you how the juice of this herb, squeezed and dropped into the ears, kills every kind of vermin that may have bred there by putrefaction, and any other beast that may have got in. If you put some of this juice into a bucket of water, you will immediately see the water coagulate like curds, so great are its virtues; and this coagulated water is a prompt remedy for horses with colic and broken wind. Its root, boiled in water, softens hardened sinews, contracted joints, sclerotic gout, and gouty swellings. If you want quickly to heal a scald or a burn, apply some Pantagruelion raw; that is to say just as it comes out of the earth, without any preparation or treatment; and be sure to change it as soon as you see it drying on the wound.

Without it kitchens would be a disgrace, tables repellent, even though they were covered with every exquisite food, and beds pleasureless, though adorned with gold, silver, amber, ivory, and porphyry in abundance. Without it millers would not carry wheat to the mill, or carry flour away. Without it, how could advocates' pleadings be brought to the sessions hall? How could plaster be carried to the workshop without it? Without it, how could water be drawn from the well? What would scribes, copyists, secretaries, and writers do without it? Would not official documents and rent-rolls disappear? Would not the noble art of printing perish? What would window screens be made of? How would church bells be rung? It provides the adornment of the priests of Isis, the robes of the pastophores, and the coverings of all human beings in their first recumbent position. All the woolly trees of Northern India, all the cotton plants of Tylos on the Persian Gulf, of Arabia, and of Malta have not dressed so many people as this plant alone. It protects armies against cold and rain, much more effectively than did the skin tents of old. It protects theatres and amphitheatres against the heat; it is hung round woods and coppices for the pleasure of hunters; it is dropped into sweet water and sea-water for the profit of fishermen. It shapes and makes serviceable boots, high-boots, heavy boots, leggings, shoes, pumps, slippers, and nailed shoes. By it bows are strung, arbalests bent, and slings made. And as though it were a sacred plant, like verbena, and reverenced by the Manes and Lemurs, the bodies of men are never buried without it.

I will go further. By means of this herb, invisible substances are visibly stopped, caught, detained and, as it were, imprisoned; and by their capture and arrest great, heavy mill-wheels are lightly turned to the signal profit of humankind. It astounds me that the practicability of such a process was hidden for so many centuries from the ancient philosophers, considering the inestimable benefit it provides and the intolerable labours they had to perform in their mills through lack of it. By its powers of catching the waves of the air, vast merchant ships, huge cabined barges, mighty galleons, ships with a crew of a thousand or ten thousand men are launched from their moorings and driven forward at their pilots' will. By its help nations which Nature seemed to keep hidden, inaccessible, and unknown, have come to us, and we to them: something beyond the power of birds, however light of wing, and whatever freedom to swim down the air Nature may have given them. Ceylon has seen Lapland, Java has seen the Riphaean Mountains, Phebol shall see Thélème; the Icelanders and Greenlanders shall see the Euphrates. By its help Boreas has seen the mansion of Auster, Eurus has visited Zephyrus; and as a result, those celestial intelligences, the gods of the sea and land, have all taken fright. For they have seen the Arctic peoples, in full sight of the Antarctic peoples, by the aid of this blessed Pantagruelion, cross the Atlantic sea, pass the twin Tropics, go down beneath the torrid zone, measure the entire Zodiac, disport themselves below the Equinoctial Line, and hold both Poles in view on the level of their horizon. In a similar fright the gods of Olympus cried: 'By the power and uses of this herb of his, Pantagruel has given us something new to think about, which is costing us a worse headache than ever the Aloides did. He will shortly be married. His wife will bear him children. This is fated and we cannot prevent it. It has passed through the hands and over the spindles of the fatal sisters, the daughters of necessity. Perhaps his children will discover a plant of equal power, by whose aid mortals will be able to visit the sources of the hail, the flood-gates of the rain, and the smithy of the thunder; will be able to invade the regions of the moon, enter the territory of the celestial signs, and there take lodging, some at the Golden Eagle, others at the Ram, others at the Crown, others at the Harp, others at the Silver Lion; and sit down with us at table there, and marry our goddesses: which is their one means of rising to be gods.

In the end they decided to deliberate on a means of preventing this, and called a council.

CHAPTER 52: *How a certain kind of Pantagruelion cannot be consumed by Fire*

WHAT I have told you is great and wonderful. But if you have the courage to believe in yet one more divine property of this blessed Pantagruelion, I will tell you of that also. But I do not care whether you believe me or not. It is enough for me that I have told you the truth; and tell the truth I shall. But as a beginning, since this is a thorny and difficult subject to begin, I will ask you a question. 'If I had put two gills of wine and one of water in this bottle, thoroughly mixed together, how would you unmix them, so as to give me back the water alone, without wine, and the wine without water, in the same measure as I put them in?'

Put it another way, if your carriers and bargemen, bringing a certain number of tuns, pipes, and puncheons, of Graves, Orléans, Beaune, and Mirevaux wines, to stock your cellar, had broached and drunk half of them, filling them up with water, as Limousins do by the shoeful when they cart the wines of Argenton and Saint-Gaultier, how would you completely get rid of the water? How would you purify them? I know very well that you'll talk of an ivy funnel. That has been written about. It is good, and proved by countless experiments. You knew about it already. But people who did not know it, and never saw one, would not believe it possible. Let us go on.

If we were in the times of Sulla, Marius, Caesar, and other Roman commanders, or in the days of our ancient Druids who burned the bodies of their relatives and lords; and you wanted to drink the ashes of your wives or fathers in an infusion of some good white wine, as Artemisia drank the ashes of her husband Mausolus or, on the other hand, to keep them whole in some urn or reliquary, how would you preserve these ashes and separate them from the ashes of the logs and the funeral pyre? Tell me that. Crikey, you'd find that hard! But I'll quickly tell you how. Take as much of this divine Pantagruelion as you would need to cover the body of the deceased. Then, after carefully wrapping his body in it, and binding and sewing it with the same material throw it on as great and blazing a fire as you like. The fire will burn the body and bones through the Pantagruelion, and reduce them to ashes. The Pantagruelion will not only not be consumed or burnt, will not only not spill a single atom of the ashes enclosed in it, or let in a single atom of the ashes of the pyre, but when the flames have died down it will be taken out fairer, whiter, and cleaner than it was when you threw it in. For this reason it is called asbestos. You will find plenty of it in Carpasium and at Dia Syenes, quite cheap.

Oh, what a great and wonderful thing it is! Fire, which destroys, wastes, and consumes all things, only cleans, purifies, and whitens this Carpasian and asbestine Pantagruelion. If, like so many Jews and infidels, you refuse to believe this and ask for confirmation and the usual sign, take a fresh egg and bind it all round with this divine Pantagruelion. Thus wrapped, put it in as large and hot a brazier as you like. Leave it there as long as you like. Finally you will take the egg out roasted. It will be hard and burnt, but the holy Pantagruelion will be in no way changed. It will not have deteriorated or even be warm. You can make the experiment for less than fifty thousand Bordeaux crowns, or indeed for as little as the twelfth part of a farthing.

Now don't talk to me here about that paragon the salamander; that is a legend. I admit, of course, that a little fire of straw invigorates and delights the creature. But I assure you that in a great furnace it is choked and consumed like any other animal. We have seen the experiment. Galen confirmed it long ago, and demonstrated it, in his third book, *On the Humours*; and Dioscorides maintains the same in his second book. Do not talk to me about feather-alum either, or about that wooden tower in the Piraeus that L. Sulla could never set alight because Achelaus, governor of the town for King Mithridates, had coated it all over with alum. Don't quote to me that tree which Alexander Cornelius called *eones*, and said was like the mistletoe oak, and could not be consumed or damaged by fire or water, any more than could the oak's mistletoe; and which he also claimed had provided the wood of which that famous ship the Argo was built. Find someone else to believe those tales; I refuse.

Do not offer me the comparison either of that sort of tree – however wonderful it may be – that you find in the mountains of Briançon and Ambrun, which nourishes the good agaric on its roots, and with its trunk gives us a resin so excellent that Galen dares to proclaim it the equal of turpentine. On its delicate leaves it catches for us that sweet honey of heaven, which is called manna and, though gummy and oily, is indestructible by fire. In Greek and Latin you call the tree larix; the men of the Alps call it *melze*, the Paduans and Venetians call it *larege*, which gave its name to Larignum, the fortified tower in Piedmont which baffled Julius Caesar on his march back from Gaul. He had issued orders to all the landowners and inhabitants of the Alps and Piedmont to bring victuals and stores to the stations he had set up on the military road, for his army as it passed through. All obeyed him except those within the walls of Larignum who, trusting in the natural strength of their town, refused their contribution. To punish them for this refusal, he sent his army marching straight to their town. In front of the fortress gate was a tower built of great beams of larix, laid one on the other cross-wise, like a pile of timber, and rising so high that from the battlements they could easily beat off all attackers with stones and bars. When Caesar heard that the inhabitants had no better defence than stones and bars, and that they could scarcely hurl them as far as the approaches, he commanded his soldiers to throw great quantities of faggots all round and set them alight. This was immediately done. The faggots were kindled, and the flames were so great and high that they enveloped the whole castle. They supposed, therefore, that the tower would quickly be burned to the ground. But when the flames died down and the faggots were consumed, the tower appeared whole and entirely undamaged. When Caesar saw this he commanded a circuit of ditches and trenches to be built all round it, and out of stone shot. Then the people of Larignum surrendered on terms; and from their account Caesar learned the marvellous nature of that wood, which of itself produces neither fire, flame, nor charcoal. In this respect it would deserve to be ranked with the true Pantagruelion – the more so because Pantagruel ordered all the doors, gates, windows, gutters, weather-moulding, and facings of Thélème to be made of it, and also used it to cover the sterns, prows, galleys, decks, gangways, and fo'c'sles of his carracks, brigs, galleys, galleons, brigantines, light galleys, and other vessels in his arsenal at Thalassa – were it not for the fact that larix in a great fiery furnace consuming other kinds of wood, is finally consumed and destroyed in the same way as the stones in a limekiln. Whereas the asbestine Pantagruelion is renewed and cleansed by this treatment rather than consumed and changed. Therefore

> Arabians, Indians, and Sabaeans,
> Cease your praise, sing no more paeans
> To incense, myrrh or ebony.
> Come here a nobler plant to see.
> We'll give you seed to take away;
> And if it grow with you, then say
> A million prayers of thanks to Heaven;
> And swear the realm of France, that's given
> The sacred Pantagruelion's
> The happiest beneath the sun.

End of the Third Book of the Heroic Deeds
and Sayings of the good
Pantagruel

THE FOURTH BOOK

OF THE HEROIC DEEDS AND SAYINGS OF

THE NOBLE PANTAGRUEL

COMPOSED BY

François Rabelais
DOCTOR OF MEDICINE

To the Most Illustrious Prince and Most Reverend

LORD ODET

CARDINAL DE CHÂTILLON

YOU are well aware, most illustrious Prince, how many great personages have been, and daily are, pressing me, urging me, and begging me
for a continuation of the Pantagrueline fictions. They tell me that many
dispirited, sick, and otherwise moping and sadly persons have escaped
from their troubles for a cheerful hour or two, regained their spirits
and taken fresh consolation by reading them. My usual answer is that I
composed them for my own amusement, and have claimed no praise or
glory for them; that my sole aim and purpose in writing them down was
to give such little relief as I could to the sick and unhappy, in my absence, as I gladly do when with them in their moments of need, and
when my art and services are requested.

Sometimes I make them a long discourse, and tell them how Hippocrates, in several places especially in his sixth book *On Epidemics* –
describes the character of the doctor, his disciple. Soranus the Ephesian,
Oribasius, Cl. Galen, Hali Abbas, and other writers of equal consequence have described the ideal doctor's gestures, his bearing, his look,
his touch, his expression, his charm, his straightforwardness, his clear-
cut features, his dress, his beard, his hair, his hands, his mouth, and have
even described the nature of his nails. You might suppose that he was a
character about to play the lover or suitor in a famous comedy, or to
enter the lists to fight against some mighty enemy. In fact the art of
medicine is compared by Hippocrates to a fight, or to a play for three
performers, the patient, the doctor, and the disease; and sometimes as I
read that passage I am reminded of what Julia said to her father Augustus
Caesar.

One day she had appeared before him in a gorgeous, loose gown, the
immodesty of which had displeased him greatly, though he had not
uttered a word. Next day she changed into more modest apparel, and
appeared before him in the fashion then prevalent among the chaste
ladies of Rome. Now though he had not expressed his displeasure at

seeing her so immodestly dressed on the previous day, he could not conceal the delight he now felt at her change. 'How much more becoming your dress is to-day,' he said. 'Now you look more like a daughter of Augustus.' But she had her excuse ready. 'To-day I dressed for my father's eyes,' she answered. 'The gown I wore yesterday was to please my husband.'

The physician is in the same case. When disguised in looks and gait, especially when dressed in that rich and strange four-sleeved coat which was once the fashion – it was called the *philonium*, as Petrus Alexandrinus observes in his sixth book, *On Epidemics* – he could reply to those who found his disguise odd: 'I have put on these clothes not out of pomp and circumstance, but for the sake of the patient I am visiting. He is the one person I entirely wish to please. I should not care to offend or disappoint him in any way.'

Furthermore, when we read a certain passage in the aforementioned book of Father Hippocrates, the question over which we sweat, dispute, and rack our brains, is not whether the physician's visage depresses the patient, if he is frowning, sour, morose, severe, ill-humoured, discontented, cross, and glum; nor whether he cheers the patient if his expression is joyful, serene, gracious, frank, and pleasant. There is no doubt on that score. The real question is whether the patient's depression or cheerfulness arises from his apprehensions on reading these signs in his physician's face and from his consequent deductions of the probable course and issue of his disease; or whether it is caused by the transmission of the serene or gloomy, aerial or terrestrial, joyous or melancholy spirits from the doctor to the person of the sick man – as is the opinion of Plato and Averroes.

First and foremost, the aforesaid authors have given particular instructions to physicians as to the language, topics, argument, and conversation suitable to the patients to whose bedsides they have been called. Everything that is said must aim at one effect, must be directed to one end: to cheer the patient up, though without imperilling his soul, and in no way to depress him. In this connexion Herophilus attaches great blame to the physician Callianax, who on being asked by a patient, 'Shall I die?' shamelessly answered:

> Patroclus died, whom all allow
> By much a better man than you.

When another man asked him the state of his disease, putting his question in the words of the noble Patelin:

> Does not my water
> Tell you that I shall die?

this same doctor flippantly answered: 'No, you won't, provided of course that Latona, who bore the fair twins Phoebus and Diana, was your mother.' Cl. Galen also, in his fourth book of comments on the *Epidemics*, strongly censures Quintus, his instructor in medicine, for his reply to a certain Roman gentleman, a patient of his, who had said: 'You've had your lunch, doctor. Your breath smells of wine.' 'Yours,' answered Quintus, 'smells of fever. And which do you think is pleasanter to the nostrils? Which has the sweeter perfume, wine or fever?'

But I was so hideously and baselessly slandered by certain cannibals, misanthropists, and sour-pusses that I lost all patience and decided not to write another word. One of the lesser accusations that they made against me was that my books were crammed full of different heresies. Yet they could not point out a single one anywhere all the same. Gay fooling, offensive neither to God nor the King, is there in plenty. For that is the sole theme and subject of my books. But heresies there are none, except for those who make perverse interpretations and twist plain statements and common speech. Rather than even think some of the thoughts they have attributed to me, I would die a thousand deaths – if that were possible. To them bread seems to mean a stone, a fish to mean a snake, and an egg a scorpion. Sometimes when complaining of this in your presence I have said boldly that if I did not think myself a better Christian than they make me out to be, indeed if I detected any spark of heresy in my life, my writings, my words, or even in my thoughts, they would be spared from falling so lamentably into the snares of the spirit of calumny, that Διάβολος who uses them to accuse me of such crimes. For I would myself imitate the Phoenix, pile up the dry wood, light the fire, and burn myself to death.

You told me then that the late King Francis, of eternal memory, had been informed of these slanders against me, and that he had carefully listened to these books of mine, which had been read to him in the clear voice and with the perfect enunciation of this kingdom's most learned and loyal lector – I say *of mine* because certain false and infamous works have been maliciously attributed to me. But he had, as you told me, found no dubious passage: and felt nothing but loathing for a certain snake-swallower, who based charges of mortal heresy on an N which had appeared instead of an M[1] through the wicked negligence of the printers.

So had his son, our excellent, most virtuous, and blessed King Henry – Heaven preserve him for many a year! – who granted you, as you told me, his privilege and special protection, to be exercised on my behalf against my slanderers. This good news you were so kind as to confirm to me in Paris, as you lately did when visiting My Lord Cardinal du Bellay, who had retired to recuperate after a long and tiresome illness to

1. This refers to passages in Chapters XXII and XIII of the Third Book in which *âne*, donkey, appeared for *âme*, soul, in the First Edition. Whether this was a misprint or was intended by Rabelais is uncertain.

Saint-Maur: a place – or more correctly a paradise – of health, charm, serenity, comfort, and delights in which all the pleasures of rural and agricultural life are to be found combined.

That is the reason, My Lord, why now, free from all fears, I give my pen its wings. For I hope that in your kindness, you will take my part against my calumniators, like a second Gallic Hercules in knowledge, wisdom, and eloquence, a *Hercules defensor* in virtue, power, and authority. For I may truthfully speak of you what the wise King Solomon said in the forty-fifth chapter of *Ecclesiasticus*, about that great prophet and captain in Israel, Moses: as 'A man fearing and loving God, who found favour in the sight of all flesh, beloved of God and men, whose memory is blessed. God made him like to the glorious saints and magnified him, so that his enemies stood in fear of him. For him he did marvellous and terrible things; he made him glorious in the sight of kings. By him he has declared his will to the people, and by him shewed forth his light. He sanctified him in his faithfulness and meekness, and chose him out of all men. Through him he made his voice to be heard, and to those who were in darkness he caused his law of life and knowledge to be proclaimed.'

In conclusion, I promise you that if I meet any readers who congratulate me on the gaiety of my writings, I will tell them that their entire obligation is to you. They shall thank you alone, and pray Our Lord for Your Eminence's preservation and increased prosperity. To me they shall attribute no merit except my humble obedience and voluntary subservience to your commands. For, by your most honourable encouragement, you have given me both courage and inspiration. But for you, my heart would have failed me and the spring of my animal spirits would have remained dry. May Our Lord keep you in his holy grace. Paris, 28 January 1552.

> Your most humble and obedient servant
> François Rabelais, Physician.

PROLOGUE OF THE AUTHOR

FRANÇOIS RABELAIS
TO THE FOURTH BOOK OF THE HEROIC DEEDS AND
SAYINGS OF PANTAGRUEL

TO MY KINDLY READERS

G O D *save and keep you, good people. But where are you? I can't see you.
Wait till I put on my spectacles. Ha, ha! Fair and softly Lent goes by! Now
I can see you. So what next? You've had a good vintage, so I have been told,
and I should be the last person to be sorry. You've found an inexhaustible
remedy against thirst of all kinds. That was a splendid piece of work. You,
your wives and children, your family and relations, are as healthy as you
could wish. That's very good, that's fine, that's delightful. May God, the
good God, be eternally praised for it, and – if such is his wish – may you continue so for ever. For my part, by his holy favour, I'm in the same condition
and give you greeting. I am, thanks to a little Pantagruelism – which, as you
know, means a certain lightness of spirit compounded of contempt for the
chances of fate – I am, as I said, sound and supple, and ready to drink, if you
will. Do you ask me why, good people? There is one irrefutable answer: it
is the will of the mighty and beneficent God, on whom I rely, whom I obey,
whose most holy message of good news I revere. By this I mean the Gospel
where, in* Luke iv, *the physician who neglects his own health is told, in
bitter mockery and biting derision, 'Physician, heal thyself.'*

*Though Claudius Galen had some feelings for the Holy Bible, and had
known and conversed with the saintly Christians of his time, as appears from*
lib. II. De usu partium; lib. II. De differentiis pulsuum, cap III; et
ibidem, lib. III cap. II; et lib. De rerum affectibus – *if this last is by
Galen – it was out of no such reverence that he preserved his health, but out
of fear of exposing himself to vulgar and satirical jibes:*

> *He boasts of healing poor and rich,*
> *But is himself just one large itch.*

*Indeed he makes the proud boast that he would not claim any reputation as a
physician if he had not been completely healthy, except for a few light and
passing fevers, from his twenty-eighth year into his ripe old age; although by*

nature he was none of the healthiest and was well known to have a weak stomach. For, as he says, lib. V, De sanit. tuenda, *a physician who is neglectful of his own health will not easily be credited with care for the health of others.*

Asclepiades, the physician, made the still prouder boast of having made a bargain with Fortune that he should be counted no physician if he were to fall ill from the day he began to practise the art till his extreme old age, which he reached, vigorous in all his limbs, and triumphant over Fortune. In the end, without any previous malady, he exchanged life for death by accidentally falling from the top of an ill-constructed and rotten staircase.

If by some disaster Health has slipped away from your Lordships and hidden away somewhere, upstairs or down, in the front or back, right or left, inside or out, near or far from your territories, may you with our blessed Saviour's aid quickly find it again! If you should be lucky enough to do so, then challenge it, claim it, seize it, and take possession of it immediately. The law permits it, the King desires it, and I advise you to do so. For you have the same authority as the legislators of old gave to a master to claim his run-away slave wherever he might find him. Praise be to God and all good men! Is it not set out in the old customs of our most noble, most ancient, most beautiful, most flourishing, and most wealthy kingdom of France, that the dead shall seize the quick – that is shall, before dying, confer his properties upon him? Is this not common practice? Refer to the recent statements of the good, the learned, the wise, the most humane, most noble, and most just André Tiraqueau, counsellor of the great, victorious, and triumphant King Henry, second of that name, in his most dreaded High Court of Paris. Health is our life, as Ariphon of Sicyon sagely declares. Without health life is not life – is not worth living : ἀβίος, βίος, βίος ἀβίωτος. Without health life is a decrepitude; life is only the image of death. So, when you are deprived of health – that is to say dead – seize the quick, seize health, which is life.

I put my trust in God, that he will hear our prayers, in view of the firm faith in which we offer them, and that he will grant this wish of ours, seeing that it is a modest one. The wise men of old have called moderation golden, that is to say precious, universally praiseworthy, and pleasing in all places. Go through the Holy Bible, and you will find that those who have prayed with moderation have never had their prayers rejected, Zacchaeus is an example, the little man whose body and relics those holy scoundrels of Saint-Ayl near Orléans boast of possessing; they call him St Sylvanus. All he desired was to see our blessed Saviour at Jerusalem. It was a modest wish such as any man might have, and nothing more. But he was too small; he was lost among the crowd; he could not manage it. So he stamped and jumped and pushed and struggled, and in the end climbed up a sycamore tree. Our gracious Lord perceived his sincere and modest desire, and presented himself before him. But Zacchaeus did not only see the Lord. He heard him speak. For he visited the little man's house and blessed his family.

One of the sons of the prophets in Israel was splitting wood near the River Jordan – as is written in Kings II. vi – when the iron worked loose from his hatchet and fell into the river. He prayed God kindly to restore it to him. It was a modest request; and in full faith and confidence he threw – not the hatchet after the helve, as certain censorious, scandalous and ill-bred devils proclaim – but the helve after the hatchet, as you properly say. Suddenly a double miracle occurred. The iron rose out of the deep water, and fitted itself to the helve. Now would this Israelite have been heard if he had prayed to mount up into the Heavens in a flaming chariot like Elijah, or for his seed to multiply like Abraham, or to be as rich as Job, as strong as Samson, or as handsome as Absalom? I doubt it.

On the subject of modest wishes in the matter of hatchets – let me know when it's time to drink – I will tell you a story from the Fables of the wise Aesop the Frenchman – the Phrygian or Trojan I should say, following Maximus Planudes. However, according to the most reliable chroniclers, we noble French are descended from those peoples – so no matter. Actually Aelian writes that he was a Thracian; and Agathias, following Herodotus, that he was a Samian. It's all the same to me.

In Aesop's time there was a poor villager living at Gravot by the name of Ballocker, a feller and splitter of timber, who picked up a poor living, one way and another, by this poor trade. Now he happened to lose his hatchet, and if ever a man was in a stew or a jam it was he. For on his hatchet depended his life and his livelihood. By his hatchet he lived respected and honoured by all the rich wood merchants. Without his hatchet he would die of starvation. If death had met him without his hatchet a week later, he would have mown him down with his scythe and weeded him out of the world. In this plight, he began to wail, and to beg, implore, and call on Jupiter, in the most beautiful prayers – for, as you know, Necessity was the inventor of Eloquence – raising his face to the skies, kneeling on the earth, bareheaded, with his hands raised to Heaven, and his fingers outspread, tirelessly crying at each refrain of his litanies: 'My hatchet, my hatchet! Only

that! Only my hatchet, Jupiter, or the money to buy another! Alas, my poor
hatchet!' Jupiter was holding a council on certain urgent matters, and old
Cybele – or the young and bright Phoebus, if you like – was delivering an
opinion. But Ballocker's clamouring was so loud that, to the general amazement, it penetrated to the council and consistory of the gods.

'What devil is it, down there,' asked Jupiter, 'howling so horribly? By
the powers of the Styx, haven't we had enough troubles already? Don't we
find it hard enough at present to deal with all these important and contro-
versial problems that are in front of us? We've resolved the dispute between
Presthan, King of the Persians, and the Sultan Soliman, Emperor of Constantinople. We've stopped the quarrel between the Tartars and the Muscovites. We've answered the Sherif's petition. We've done the same for
Dragut-Rais's. The question of Parma is solved. So are those of Magdeburg,
of Mirandola, and of Africa – which is the mortals' name for the town on the
Mediterranean Sea that we called Aphrodisium. Owing to some carelessness,
Tripoli has changed its master. Its hour had come anyhow. Now here are the
Gascons swearing and demanding the restoration of their bells. In this corner
are the Saxons, the Easterlings, the Ostrogoths, and the Germans, once invincible peoples, but now kaput, and governed by some little man who is a
complete cripple. They are calling on us for vengeance, help, and restitution
of their former integrity and freedom. Then what are we to do with these
men Ramus and Galland, who are setting the whole University of Paris upside down, with their crews of scullions, hangers-on, and henchmen? I'm very
puzzled indeed. I haven't decided yet which side to back. In other respects,
both of them seem to me good ballocky fellows. One of them has Sun-crowns,
which tip the scales; and the other would be glad to have some too. One of
them has a little learning; the other is not ignorant. One of them likes honest
men; and the other has honest men's liking. One is a sly and wary fox; the
other slanders the old philosophers and orators with tongue and pen, and
barks at them like a dog. Tell me what you think about it, Priapus, you
great asspizzle. I've often found your counsel fair, and your advice to the
point; et habet tua mentula mentem.'[1]

'King Jupiter,' replied Priapus, taking off his hood, and raising his red,
flaming, cocksure head. 'You have compared one to a barking dog, the other
to a cunning fox. My opinion is therefore that, without more trouble or ado,
you deal with them as once you did with a dog and a fox.' 'How was that?'

---

1. For you have intelligence in your tool.

asked Jupiter. 'When? Who were they? Where was it?' 'What a fine
memory!' mocked Priapus. 'Our venerable father Bacchus, over there in
front of you with his crimson face, wanted to take vengeance on the Thebans.
So he created a magic fox that could never be caught or wounded by any
animal in the world, whatever harm or damage it did. The noble Vulcan
here had forged a dog of Monesian brass, and by hard blowing had given it
breath and life. He presented it to you, and you gave it to your darling
Europa. She passed it on to Minos, Minos gave it to Procris, and Procris
finally gave it to Cephalus. So the dog was as magical as the fox and, like
one of our modern lawyers, it seized on every creature it came across; nothing
could escape it. Now these two beasts happened to meet – and what happened?
The dog was bound, by fated destiny, to catch the fox; the fox, by its destiny,
could not be caught. The case was brought before your council. You protested
that you could not cross the fates. The fates were contradictory. The final and
faithful resolution of two such contradictions was declared to be, by Nature,
impossible. You were sweating with perplexity, and as your sweat fell to the
earth, there arose a crop of round-headed cabbages. Then, for want of a categorical resolution, this whole noble assembly was seized with a miraculous
thirst. At that sitting more than seventy-eight hogsheads of nectar were
drunk. You took my advice. You turned both beasts into stones; and immediately you were out of your difficulty; immediately a truce to thirst was proclaimed over the whole of great Olympus. That was in the year of flabby
balls, near Teumessus, between Thebes, and Chalcis.

'My advice is that you follow that precedent, and petrify this other dog and
this other fox. The metamorphosis is not unknown. They are both called
Peter. And since, according to the Limousin proverb, it takes three stones to
make an oven's mouth, you can add Master Peter de Cognières, whom you
petrified long ago for the same reasons. Then these three dead stones can be
placed in the form of an equilateral triangle inside the great temple in Paris,
or in the middle of the porch. It will be their job to put out candles, torches,
tapers, rushlights, and lighted flares, as in the game of Snuff-it-out. For when
alive they most ballockishly lighted the flames of faction, feuds, ballockish
sects, and divisions among the idle scholars. Let this be a perpetual reminder
to the world that these testicular little self-admirers were rather scorned than
condemned by your court. I have spoken.'

'You are being kind to them, in my opinion, fair Master Priapus,' said
Jupiter. 'You don't treat everyone so favourably. For seeing that they are so
anxious to perpetuate their names and memory they would certainly prefer

to be transformed like this, when they are dead, into hard stone and marble, rather than return to earth and decay.

'Do you see there, behind us, around that Tyrrhenian Sea and in the towns near the Apennines, what tragedies are being stirred up by certain Pasto- phores? The fury will burn for a time, like a Limousin oven, and then go out; but not so quickly. We shall get plenty of amusement out of it yet. But there is one drawback that I can see. We have had a very small stock of thunderbolts ever since the time when you, my fellow gods – with my per-mission, of course – amused yourselves by throwing them so wastefully at the new Antioch. Since then the doughty champions who undertook to de-fend the fortress of Dindenarois against all comers have imitated your example. They exhausted all their ammunition, firing at sparrows, and then had nothing to defend themselves with in time of need. So they valiantly sur-rendered the place and gave themselves up to the enemy, who were just on the point of raising the siege. For they were frantic and despairing, and their one urgent thought was to beat a swift retreat, though it would mean utter disgrace.

'See that my orders are carried out, Vulcan my son. Wake up your sleep-ing Cyclops, Asterops, Brontes, Arges, Polyphemus, Steropes, and Pyrac-mon – and set them to work. See that they have enough to drink, by the way. On fire-workers you must never spare wine. Now let's deal with that bawler down there. See who he is, Mercury, and what he wants.'

Mercury peered down the trap-door of Heaven, through which they hear what is said here on earth, and which is very like the hatch of a ship, though Icaromenippus compared it to the mouth of a well. He saw that it was Bal-locker crying for his lost hatchet and reported the fact to the council. 'Really,' said Jupiter, ' this is a nice how-d'you-do. As if we had nothing else on our agenda at this moment but the return of lost hatchets! Still, we'll have to give it him back. It's written in the book of fate, you understand, just as surely as if the wretched article were worth the whole Duchy of Milan. Actually, his hatchet is as valuable and important to him as a kingdom would be to a king. There, there, let him have the thing back, and let's have no more talk about it. The next item before us is to put an end to the quarrel between the clergy and the molehill of Landerousse. Where had we got to?'

Priapus had remained standing in the chimney corner. But when he heard Mercury's report, he could not restrain a polite but somewhat hilarious com-ment on the subject : 'King Jupiter, in the days when, by your ordinance and special favour, I was keeper of the gardens on earth, I noted that this word hatchet *was in several ways equivocal. It signifies a certain instrument used for cutting down and splitting timber. It also signifies – at least it did so of old – a female frequently, soundly, and unceremoniously laid on her back. In fact every good fellow called the girl who gave him his pleasures,* my hatchet. *For they employ this tool'* – and as he spoke he displayed his nine-inch knocker – *'so boldly and stoutly to drive in their wenches' helves, as to free them forever from a fear which is endemic among the female sex: the fear that these helves may perpetually dangle from below men's bellies down to their heels through lack of being suitably contained. And I remember, for I've a member – a very good memory I should say, large enough to fill a butter-pot. As I was saying, I remember hearing some musicians singing one day during the Tubilustria, on the feast of our good Vulcan here, in May it was. The musicians were Josquin des Prez, Ockeghem, Hobrecht, Agricola, Brumel, Camelin, Vigoris, de la Fage, Bruyer, Prioris, Seguin, de la Rue, Midy, Moulu, Mouton, Gascogne, Loyset Compère, Penet, Fevin, Rouzée, Richardfort, Rousseau, Consilion, Constantio Festi, and Jacquet Berchem. They were singing melodiously, and this was their song:*

> Long Tibbald on the day he wed,
> Before he lay with his new wife,
> Placed on the floor behind the bed
> A hefty mallet – on my life!
> "Oh my dear love," she said, "what's this?
> What is this mallet for?" Said he,
> "To wedge and splice you better with."
> "You need no mallet, dear," said she.
> "When Big John to my bed does come
> He only shoves me with his bum."

'Nine Olympiads and one intercalary year later,' continued Priapus. 'Oh, what a fine member – I mean memory – I've got. I often commit a solecism in the symbolization and association of those two words. – I heard Adrian Villaert, Gombert, Jannequin, Arcadelt, Claudin, Certon, Manchicourt, Auxerre, Villiers, Sandrin, Sohier, Hesdin, Morales, Passereau, Maille, Maillart, Jacotin, Heurteur, Verdelot, Carpentras, Lhéritier, Cadeac, Doublet, Vermont, Bouteiller, Lupi, Pagnier, Millet, Dumoulin, Alaire, Marault, Morpain, Gendre, and other jovial musicians, in a private garden, beneath a lovely arbour, and behind a rampart of bottles, hams, pasties, and dainty morsels in veils and skirts, singing most charmingly:

If hatchets unhelved are quite useless,
And tools without hafts useless too,
Let us make the one fit in the other,
I've a helve. Let the hatchet be you.

So we must find out what kind of hatchet this noisy Ballocker's shouting for.'

At these words all the venerable gods and goddesses burst out laughing, like a microcosm of flies, and Vulcan with his twisted leg performed three or four pretty little jigs on the daïs, for the love of his mistress.

'There, there!' said Jupiter to Mercury, 'go down at once, and drop three hatchets at Ballocker's feet; his own, another of gold, and one of solid silver, all of the same size. Give him the choice of the three, and if he picks his own and is grateful, let him have the other two. But if he picks either of the two others, chop off his head with his own. That's the way I want you to deal with all these hatchet-losers in future.'

When he had spoken, Jupiter twisted his neck like a monkey swallowing pills, and made such a terrible grimace that all great Olympus quaked.

Mercury, with his pointed cap, his hood, his heel-wings, and wand, dropped through the trapdoor of Heaven and cleft the airy void. He came lightly down to earth, and threw the three hatchets at Ballocker's feet. 'You've bawled enough to need a drink,' said he. 'Your prayers have been granted by Jupiter. See which of these three hatchets is yours, and take it.'

Ballocker picked up the golden hatchet, examined it, found it rather heavy, and said to Mercury: 'Lord bless me, this isn't mine and I don't want it.' Then he did the same with the silver hatchet. 'It isn't this one,' he said. 'You can keep it.' Then he picked up his own hatchet, looked hard at the wooden helve, and recognized his mark on it; upon which he bounded with joy, like a fox who has found some hens astray, and his face split in a grin: 'God's turds!' said he. 'This one's mine. If you'll leave it for me, I'll make you a sacrifice. I'll give you a great big pot of milk all covered with fine straw-berries, on the Ides – that is to say the fifteenth – of May.' 'My good fellow,' said Mercury, 'of course I'll leave it for you. Take it. And since you've been moderate in your wishes and chosen wisely, by the will of Jupiter I give you the two others into the bargain. Henceforth you've got enough to make you a rich man. Be an honest one as well.'

Ballocker politely thanked Mercury, paid a reverence to great Jupiter, tied his old hatchet to his leather belt, and slung it on his rump, like Martin of Cambrai. The two other, heavier hatchets he hung round his neck, and went *swaggering about the country, with a broad smile for all his neighbours and fellow-parishioners, to whom he would say, repeating Patelin's little phrase: 'And haven't I got some?'*

Next day he put on a white smock, loaded the two precious hatchets on his back, and went off to Chinon, a famous town, a noble town, an ancient town, in fact the finest town in the world according to the opinion pronounced by the most learned Hebrew scholars. At Chinon he exchanged his silver hatchet for good testers and other silver money; and his golden hatchet he turned into fine angels, beautiful Agnus Dei crowns, good Dutch ritters, honest reals, and gleaming Sun-crowns as well. With these he bought several farms, lands, houses, cottages, huts, and summer-houses; several fields, vineyards, woods, ploughlands, pastures, ponds, mills, gardens, and willow plantations; a number of oxen, cows, ewes, sheep, goats, sows, hogs, donkeys, horses, hens, cocks, capons, pullets, geese, ganders, drakes, ducks, and small fowl. In a short while, indeed, he was the richest man in the district, even richer than the limping Lord de Mauleuvrier.

The bumpkins and yokels of the district were astounded at this turn in Ballocker's luck, and the sympathy and pity that they had felt for the poor man in the old days turned to envy of his great and unexpected wealth. So they began to run about, inquiring and searching to find out by what means, where, on what day, and at what hour, this great treasure had come to him. When they heard that he had got it through losing his hatchet, they said: 'Ho, ho, so we only need to lose a hatchet to become rich men, do we? That's easy enough and costs very little. So the revolution of the heavens, the constellation of the firmament, and the aspect of the planets are at present such that whoever loses his hatchet will immediately become a rich man? Ho, ho, ho, my dear hatchet, you're going to get lost, if you don't mind. Lost you shall be, by God!' So they all lost their hatchets. There wasn't a devil among them that kept a hatchet! There wasn't a mother's son in the district who didn't lose his hatchet. No more trees were felled, no more wood was split throughout the whole country, through lack of hatchets.

The Aesopian fable goes on to say that certain predatory little gentlemen of the lowest class, who had sold Ballocker some small meadow or small mill so as to cut a fine figure at the Grand Inspection of the militia, also heard of his good luck. When they learnt that this fortune had come to him so simply and just like that, they sold their swords to buy hatchets, so as to lose them as the peasants had, and by their loss gain whole piles of silver and gold. They might have been mistaken for those little pilgrims to Rome, who sell all they have and borrow from others to buy piles of indulgences from a newly elected Pope. Now there was such a crying and praying and lamenting and calling on Jupiter – 'My hatchet, my hatchet, Jupiter! My hatchet here, my hatchet there, oh, oh, oh, Jupiter, my hatchet!' – that the air all around rang with the bawlings and howlings of these hatchet losers.

Mercury was quick to bring them hatchets. To each one he offered his own lost one, a gold one, and one of silver; and each one chose the gold one, picked it up, and gave thanks to Jupiter, the great donor. But as each one was lifting it from the ground, while he was still bent and stooping, Mercury cut off his head, as Jupiter had decreed. The number of heads chopped off corresponded exactly to the number of hatchets lost. You see how it is. You see what good fortune attends those whose wishes are simple, and who choose in moderation.

But you scurvy devils from the low countries, who say that you wouldn't forego your wishes for ten thousand francs a year, take warning by this. Let none of you speak so rashly in future as I have sometimes heard you do, with your: 'Would to God I had at this moment seventy-eight millions in gold. How I should triumph!' May you get a plague of chilblains! What more could a King, or an Emperor, or the Pope himself wish for?

So you see by experience that by framing immoderate wishes all you get is the itch and the scab, but not a penny in your purse. You do no better, in fact, than that pair of true Parisian cadgers, one of whom wanted as many good Sun-crowns as have been spent, acquired, or disposed of from the time when the first foundations of the city were laid till the present day; the whole computed at the rate, price, and value of the dearest year during that period. Wasn't he a dainty fellow, don't you think? He'd eaten sour plums without peeling them, hadn't he? And were his teeth set on edge? The other wished for the church of Notre-Dame brimful of steel needles from the pavement to the height of the arches, and to have as many Sun-crowns as could be stuffed into as many sacks as could be sewn by each and every one of those needles, till they were all blunt or broken. That was a wish, that was! What do you think of it? Now what came of this? By evening each one of them had chilblains on his heels, a little sore on his chin, a bad cough in his lungs, the catarrh in his gullet, a large carbuncle on his seat, and devil a crust of bread to clean his teeth with.

So wish in moderation. What you ask will come to you, and better things too, if you toil hard at your own work in the meantime. 'Oh,' you say, 'but God might just as easily have given me seventy-eight thousand as the thirteenth part of a half. For he is all-powerful. A gold million is as little to him *as a farthing.' Come, come, come! Who taught you to argue like this about God's power and predestination, you poor creatures? Peace! Hush, hush, hush! Humble yourselves before his sacred countenance and recognize your imperfections. It is on moderation, my gouty friends, that I base my hopes. I firmly believe that if it pleases the good God, you will get your health, seeing that health is all that you ask for at present. So wait a little longer, exercise half an ounce of patience.*

That is not the habit of the Genoese. In the morning, in their offices and counting-houses, they discuss, weigh up, and decide what person or concern they can extract money from that day. Having decided who is to be fleeced, rooked, cheated, and swindled, they go on to the Exchange, and greet one another with: Sanita e guadagno, Messer.[1] They are not content with health. They wish one another profit as well, that is to say as many crowns as Cadaigne. Hence it arises that often they get neither.

So then, since you are in good health, give a good cough for me, toss off three bumpers, give your ears a good shake, and you shall hear marvels of the noble and excellent Pantagruel.

1. Good health and good profit to you, sir.

CHAPTER I: *How Pantagruel put to sea to visit the Oracle of the Holy Bacbuc*

In the month of June, on the day of Vesta's feast, that same day on which Brutus conquered the Spaniards, and on which the covetous Crassus was beaten and destroyed by the Parthians, Pantagruel took leave of his father. Following a praiseworthy custom of the primitive Church, practised among the early Christians, the good Gargantua offered up a prayer for the prosperous voyage of his son and all his company. Pantagruel then put to sea from the port of Thalassa, accompanied by Panurge, Friar John of the Hashes, Epistemon, Gymnaste, Eusthenes, Rhizotome, Carpalim, and other old domestics and servants of his; and with them went Xenomanes, the great traveller and journeyer by perilous ways, who had arrived some days before, at Panurge's command. For certain good reasons Xenomanes had left with Gargantua his great and universal hydrographical chart, on which was marked out the route they were going to take on their visit to the Holy Bottle of Bacbuc.

In the third book I gave you the number of their ships. But these were escorted by triremes, long barges, galleons, and Liburnian galleys equal to them in number, well equipped, caulked, and provided, also supplied with Pantagruelion in plenty. The officers, interpreters, pilots, captains, mates, galley-officers, oarsmen, and sailors met on the *Thalamège*, which was Pantagruel's great flagship, on the stern of which, as an ensign, stood a great and capacious bottle, half of smooth and polished silver, and half of gold enamelled with crimson dye. Thus it was easy to tell that white and claret were the noble traveller's colours, and that the purpose of the journey was to learn the word of the Bottle. High over the stern of the second ship was hung an old-fashioned lantern ingeniously cut out of specular or transparent stone, a sign that the expedition was to pass by Lanternland. The device of the third was a fine, deep porcelain drinking-mug. On the fourth was a golden jar with two handles, in the shape of an antique urn. The fifth carried a famous tankard of bastard emerald. The sixth, a monk's leather bottle made of four metals welded together. The seventh, an ebony funnel all embossed and inlaid with gold. The eighth, a very precious ivy goblet, damascened with gold leaf. The ninth, a toasting-cup of pure refined gold. The tenth had a bowl of sweet-smelling agalloch – you call it aloe-wood – edged with Cyprian gold worked in the Persian fashion. The eleventh, a gold vintage-basket of mosaic-work. The twelfth, a firkin of dull gold, decorated with a scroll of large Indian pearls in the shape of a bush.

Thus there was nobody, however sad, cross, sour, or melancholy he might be – no, not even if he were another Heraclitus the Weeper – who was not filled with fresh joy, and whose spleen did not yield to laughter when he saw this noble fleet of ships with their devices. There was no one who did not exclaim that the travellers were all worthy boozers, and who did not feel prophetically certain that the journey out, and also the journey home, would be performed in health and happiness.

So the general assembly was on the *Thalamège*, and there Pantagruel gave them a short and pious exhortation on the subject of navigation, wholly based on arguments drawn from Holy Writ. When this was over, prayers were raised to God in high clear tones, distinct enough to be heard and understood by all the burgesses and citizens of Thalassa, who had rushed out on to the mole to witness their departure. After the prayer, there was a melodious singing of that psalm of the blessed King David which begins, *When Israel went out of Egypt*. Then, after the psalm was finished, tables were set up on deck and the meats promptly served. The Thalassians, who had sung this psalm with them, sent to fetch a quantity of food and wine from their houses. All drank to them; they drank to all. That is why not one of the assembly was sick or had any qualms in his stomach or his head from the rolling of the sea. They would not have warded off this trouble so easily by drinking salt water for several days beforehand, either pure or mixed with wine; or by eating quince pulp, or lemon rind, or the juice of sourish pomegranates; or by keeping a long fast; or by covering their stomachs with paper; or by following other remedies that foolish physicians prescribe for those going to sea.

After drinking again and again, everyone retired to his own ship, and soon they set sail before a fine East wind. The captain of the fleet, Jamet Brahier by name, had set the course and fixed all the compass-needles accordingly. For his advice, and Xenomanes's also, was that since the Oracle of the Holy Bacbuc lay near Cathay, in Upper India, they should not take the ordinary Portuguese route. The Portuguese sail through the Torrid Zone, past the Cape of Good Hope at the southern tip of Africa, and far below the Equinoctial Line; an enormous voyage in which they completely lose sight of the guiding Pole Star. The advice of these two was that they should follow as closely as possible the Parallel of India aforesaid, and take a circular course around this same Pole in a westerly direction. In this way, clinging to the Pole Star, they would stick to the latitude of the port of Olonne, but work no further north for fear of striking the Arctic sea and becoming ice-bound. By following this regular route along a fixed parallel, they would have on their starboard and to the east what as they sailed out of port had been on their port bow.

This plan proved of inestimable advantage to them. For they made the voyage to Upper India in less than four months, without shipwreck, without danger or loss of crew, in great calm – except for one day off the Macreons' – or, Longlivers' – Island. The Portuguese, on the other hand, would scarcely make the trip in less than three years, and this with countless troubles and innumerable dangers. In my opinion, with all due respect to better judges, this lucky route of theirs was the one followed by those Indians who sailed to Germany and were honourably entertained by the King of the Suevi, at the time when Metellus Celer was Proconsul in Gaul. Their visit has been described by Cornelius Nepos, and Pomponius Mela, also by Pliny, after them.

CHAPTER 2: *Pantagruel buys many fine things on the Island of Medamothy*

FOR the first day out and the two following, they saw no land or anything new. For they had ploughed these seas before. On the fourth they sighted a land called Medamothy, or Nowhere Island, which was a fair and pleasant sight. For it had a great number of lighthouses and high marble towers, adorning its whole coastline, which was no less in circuit than that of Canada.

On inquiring who was the ruler of this land, Pantagruel was told that it was King Philophanes the Inquisitive, who was away at the moment at the wedding of his brother Philotheamon the Curious with the Infanta of the Kingdom of Engys – or Nextdoor. He landed at the harbour, while the ships' crews were taking in water, and looked at various pictures and tapestries, various animals, fish, birds, and other strange and exotic merchandise, displayed along the harbour road and in the markets of the port. For it was the third day of the great annual fair, which brought all the richest and best-known merchants of Africa and Asia to this place each year. From this display Friar John bought himself two rare and costly pictures. The first was a life-like head of a plaintiff in the Court of Appeal, and the other the portrait of a servant looking for his master, with every detail correct: gestures, bearing, features, gait, expression, and feelings. It was an original painting by Master Charles Charmois, painter to King Megistus; and he paid for it in monkey-money.

Panurge bought a large painted picture copied from the tapestry made in ancient days by Philomela for her sister Procne. Its subject was her deflowering by her brother-in-law Tereus, and his cutting out of her tongue in order that she should not reveal his crime. I swear to you by the handle of this lantern that it was a spirited and remarkable painting. Don't imagine, for a moment, that it was just the picture of a man astride a girl. That would be too ridiculous and far too crude. This painting was of a very different order, a far more sensible piece of work. You can see it at Thélème, on the right-hand wall, as you enter the high gallery.

Epistemon bought a picture too, a lifelike representation of Plato's Ideas and the Atoms of Epicurus; and Rhizotome bought another, a portrait of Echo in her natural shape. Pantagruel, for his part, commissioned Gymnaste to purchase the life and exploits of Achilles in seventy-eight pieces of high-warp tapestry, twenty-four feet long and eighteen feet wide, all of Phrygian silk, embroidered with gold and silver. The work began with the wedding of Peleus and Thetis; going on to the birth of Achilles, to his youth as described by Statius Papinius, his exploits and feats of arms, as described by Homer, and his death and funeral, as described by Ovid and Quintus Calaber, and concluded with the appearance of his ghost and Polyxena's sacrifice, as described by Euripides.

He also commissioned the purchase of three fine young unicorns, a male with a burnt sorrel coat and two dapple grey females; also a

tarand, which was sold him by a Scythian from the country of the
Geloni. A tarand is an animal the size of a young bull, with a head like
a stag's, only a little larger, with huge many-branched antlers. It has
cloven hooves, and a long coat like a great bear's, with skin almost as
tough as armour. The Gelonian said that only a few tarands were to
be found in Scythia, because it changes colour according to the place
where it lives and grazes, taking on the hue of the grass, trees, bushes,
flowers, landscapes, pastures, rocks, and generally of everything that
it approaches. This trait it shares with the marine polyp or sea-
anemone, with the lynx and the painted wolf of India, and with the
chameleon, which is a sort of lizard, so remarkable that Democritus
has devoted a whole book to its shape, anatomy, properties, and
magical qualities. I myself have seen it change colour with its feelings.
What we found most remarkable about this tarand was that not only
its head and skin, but its whole coat also, took its colour from its surroundings. Beside Panurge, in his rough cloth cloak, its coat became
grey; beside Pantagruel, dressed in his scarlet mantle, its skin and coat
went red; beside the captain, who was dressed like the priests of Isis
or Anubis in Egypt, its coat appeared pure white. These last two hues
are impossible in a chameleon. When it was free of all fear and emo-
tion, the tarand resumed its natural colour, which was like that of the
donkeys of Meung-sur-Loire.

CHAPTER 3: *How Pantagruel received a Letter from his Father
Gargantua, and of a strange way of getting very speedy News
from distant Countries*

WHILE Pantagruel was busy with the purchase of these strange animals, ten salvos of culverins and small cannon were heard from the
mole, together with a great and joyous shout from all the ships. Pantagruel turned back towards the harbour, and saw that it was the *Cheli-
donia*, one of his father's swift dispatch-boats, which had on its prow
a flying-fish, or sea-swallow, modelled in Corinthian brass. This fish
is as large as a Loire dace, fleshy and scaleless, with cartilaginous wings,
like those of bats. These are very broad and long, and with their aid
I have seen these fish fly more than six foot above the water for more
than the length of a bowshot. At Marseilles they call them landoles.

This vessel, indeed, was as light as a swallow and seemed to fly rather than to sail over the sea. In it was Malicorne, Gargantua's squire and carver, whom he had sent expressly to get news of his good son Panta-gruel's health and state of mind, and to bring him letters of credit.

After the first salutation and short embrace, Pantagruel did not open his letter, but before broaching any other subject, inquired of Malicorne: 'Have you brought the *gozal*, the heavenly messenger?' 'Yes,' he answered, 'she's packed in this basket.' This was a pigeon, taken from Gargantua's dovecot, which had just been hatching her young at the moment when the dispatch-boat was leaving. If ill-luck had befallen Pantagruel, black jesses were to have been tied to her legs. But since everything had gone well and prosperously with him, when they took her out of her basket they tied on a white taffeta ribbon in-stead. Then without further delay they at once let her go absolutely free. The pigeon flew off immediately, cleaving the air with incredible speed. For, as you know, there is no flight as swift as a pigeon's, when she has eggs or young. For Nature has endowed her with a persistent urge to be with her offspring and to protect them. So in less than two hours she travelled by air a distance which the dispatch-boat had needed three whole days and nights to cover, using both oars and sails and with a continuous following wind. When she arrived, Gargan-tua's servants saw her fly into the dovecot, to find her young in her own nest, and informed their noble master that she carried the white ribbon. He was delighted to be thus reassured of his son's safety.

This was the practice of the noble Gargantua and Pantagruel, when they wanted prompt news of anything to which they attached great interest and importance, such as the issue of a battle on land or sea, the capture or continued resistance of a fortress, the settlement of some important dispute, the delivery or miscarriage of a queen or great lady, the death or recovery of their sick friends or allies, and other such matters. They would take a *gozal* and dispatch her from hand to hand, by postal relays, to the place from which they wanted news. Then, on her return, carrying a black or white ribbon, according to events or occurrences, the bird would relieve their minds, after travel-ling further through the air in one hour than thirty posts could do overland in a whole day. This was redeeming and gaining time in-deed. So, as you can readily suppose, in every month and season of the year you would have found pigeons in plenty in all the dovecots of their farms, either hatching their eggs on their nests or rearing their young. This hatching out of season can easily be managed with the help of rock saltpetre and the sacred verbena plant.

After the release of the *gozal*, Pantagruel read his father's letter, which ran as follows:

My dearest son,

The natural affection which a father feels for his beloved son is so much increased in my case by my regard for and my appreciation of the particular gifts bestowed on you by divine election that since your departure it has more than once driven every other thought from my mind. Only one care and fear has remained with me, that some misfortune or difficulty may have followed your embarkation. As you know, good and sincere love is always accompanied by some fear. So because, as Hesiod tells us, a good beginning in anything is half the battle and, as the common proverb runs, it's when you put it in the oven that the loaf gets its crust, to free my mind of this anxiety I have expressly sent Malicorne, so that I may have news by him of your welfare during the first days of your voyage. For if they have been as prosperous and as good as I hope, it will not be difficult for me to foresee, prognosticate, and judge of the rest.

I have collected some amusing books, which will be given you by the bearer. Read them when you want a rest from your more serious studies. The same bearer will give you fuller news of all happenings at this court. May God's peace be with you. Give my greetings to Panurge, Friar John, Epistemon, Xenomanes, Gymnaste, and the rest of your servants, who are my good friends. From your paternal house, this thirteenth of June.

Your father and friend, GARGANTUA

CHAPTER 4: *Concerning Pantagruel's Letter to his Father Gargantua, and the several valuable Curiosities which he sent him*

AFTER reading this letter, Pantagruel had a long conversation with the squire Malicorne, and was with him so long that Panurge interrupted him: 'When are you going to drink?' he asked. 'When are we going to drink? When is the worthy squire going to drink? Haven't you talked long enough to need a drink?' 'You're quite right,' answered Pantagruel. 'Have some refreshments prepared at that inn

over the way, which has a mounted satyr for its sign.' And in the
meantime he wrote the following letter for the squire to carry back to
Gargantua:

Most gracious Father,

    The unexpected arrival of your squire Malicorne has greatly moved
and affected me. For our senses and faculties suffer more violent and over-
whelming surprises in this transitory life from unsuspected and unforeseen
events than from those expected and anticipated. In fact, the soul is often reft
from the body by such shocks, even though the sudden news may be as satisfactory as we could wish. I did not expect to see any of your servants, or to
hear any news from you before the end of this voyage of ours. Indeed, I was
quietly contenting myself with the sweet memory of your august Majesty,
which is so deeply inscribed – or rather sculpted and engraved—on the hindmost lobe of my brain, that often I have been able to call up your likeness in
its true living shape.

    But you have made me unexpectedly happy by the favour of your gracious
letter, and by your squire's report have greatly heartened me with the news of
your health and prosperity, together with that of all your royal house, I must
first – as I have most willingly done in times past – praise the blessed Saviour
who, in his divine mercy, keeps you in this long enjoyment of perfect health
and, secondly, send you my undying thanks for the warm and deep-rooted
affection that you bear towards me, your most humble son and profitless
servant.

    Long ago a Roman named Furnius obtained from Caesar Augustus the
promise that his father, who had been one of Anthony's party, should be pardoned and restored to favour. 'To-day, by doing me this kindness,' said Fur-
nius, 'you have reduced me, sire, to utter shame. For in life or in death, I
shall be considered an ungrateful man, since I have not the power to show my
gratitude.'

    I can say in the same way that by the excess of your paternal affection I
should be reduced to the painful straits of having to live and die in ingratitude, were I not acquitted of this crime by a maxim of the Stoics. They
used to say that a kind act is made up of three parts: firstly, the giver's,
secondly the recipient's, and thirdly the rewarder's; and that the recipient
amply rewards the giver if he willingly accepts the gift and keeps it perpetually in his memory. He is, on the other hand, the most ungrateful man in the
world if he scorns or forgets the favour bestowed on him.

Being overwhelmed, therefore, by infinite obligations, all proceeding from your immense kindness, and being powerless to make you the slightest return, I can at least clear myself from the imputation of ingratitude by never allowing the remembrance to be expunged from my memory. My tongue, also, shall never cease to confess and protest that to render you worthy thanks is something that is beyond my powers and faculties.

I have, moreover, complete confidence that, with the compassion and help of Our Lord, the end of this voyage of ours will be as prosperous as its beginnings, and that we shall enjoy happiness and perfect health throughout. I shall not fail to keep a complete record of it in commentaries and log-books, so that on our return you can read an accurate account of all that befalls us.

I have found here a Scythian tarand, a strange animal remarkable for the variations in colour of its skin and coat, which conform to its surroundings. Please accept it as a present. It is as tractable as a lamb, and as easy to feed. I am also sending you three young unicorns, which are tamer and more domesticated than kittens. I have talked to your squire, and told him how to treat them. They cannot graze in the fields on account of their long frontal horn. So they have to feed off fruit trees, or from special mangers, or to be fed by hand with grass, sheaves, apples, pears, barley, or wheat, or indeed with any kind of fruit or vegetable. It surprises me that our old writers speak of them as so wild, fierce, and dangerous, and say that they have never been seen alive. If it pleases you, you have evidence to the contrary. You will find that they are the gentlest beasts in the world, provided that they are not teased.

I am also sending you the life and exploits of Achilles in fine elaborate tapestry; and I promise you that any strange animals, plants, birds, or stones that I may find and collect during the course of our voyage, I will, with God's aid, bring back to you. I pray God too to preserve you in his holy grace.

From Medamothy, this fifteenth of June, Panurge, Friar John, Epistemon, Xenomanes, Gymnaste, Eusthenes, Rhizotome, and Carpalim, after humbly kissing your hand return your greeting with a hundredfold interest.

Your humble son and servant, PANTAGRUEL

While Pantagruel was writing this letter, Malicorne was feasted, toasted, and repeatedly embraced by all. Gracious, how merry they all were, and how many messages he promised to deliver for everybody! When his letter was finished, Pantagruel pledged the squire, and gave him a great gold chain, weighing eight hundred crowns, at every seventh link of which were large diamonds, rubies, emeralds, turquoises, and pearls set alternately. Each of Malicorne's sailors received five hundred Sun-crowns; and to his father Gargantua, Pantagruel sent the tarand, in a satin coat brocaded with gold, together with the tapestry of the life and exploits of Achilles and the three unicorns caparisoned in embroidered cloth-of-gold.

So they sailed from Medamothy, Malicorne to return to Gargantua, and Pantagruel to continue his voyage. When they were at sea, he had Epistemon read him the books his father had sent him, of which I would gladly tell you the contents, if you pressed me to do so. For he found them both pleasant and entertaining.

CHAPTER 5: *Pantagruel meets a Ship with Travellers returning from Lanternland*

ON the fifth day, as we were gradually beginning to circle the Pole, and departing further from the Equinoctial Line, we sighted a merchant ship approaching us on our port side. There was great rejoicing both on their part and ours; on ours, since they brought us news of the sea, and on theirs because we could tell them of *terra firma*. As we drew close to them, we learnt that they were Frenchmen from Saintonge; and after we had held some conversation with them, Pantagruel discovered that they were returning from Lanternland. This gave him a new burst of joy, and equally delighted the whole fleet. On inquiring about conditions in that country and the customs of its people, we were informed that at the end of the following July a general assembly of the Lanterns was due to meet, and that if we arrived then – which we should find it easy to do – we should see a fine, honourable, and jolly assembly of Lanterns. For already they were making such preparations that it looked as if the lanternization was going to be tremendous. We were also told that if we touched at the great kingdom of Gebarim – or the warriors – we should be honourably received and welcomed by King Ohabé the Friendly, the ruler of that country, who spoke the French of Touraine, as did all his subjects.

While we were listening to all this news, Panurge started up a quarrel with a dealer from Taillebourg, named Dingdong. The occasion of the quarrel was a remark of this Dingdong's. Seeing Panurge without his codpiece and with his spectacles tied to his bonnet, he had said to his companions: 'Here's a fine figure of a cuckold!' Panurge, because of his glasses, had far better hearing in his ears than usual. So, having overheard this remark, he demanded of the merchant: 'How the devil could I be a cuckold, seeing that I am not yet married? But if I'm to judge by your ugly mug, you certainly are one yourself.'

'Indeed I am,' said the dealer, 'and I wouldn't be otherwise for all the spectacles in Europe, and all the goggles in Africa as well. For I'm married to one of the prettiest, most attractive, most virtuous, and chaste women in all the country of Saintonge, with all due respect to the rest. I am bringing her back from my travels a fine eleven-inch branch of red coral as a birthday present. But what's this got to do with you? What are you interfering for? Who are you? Where do you come from, you goggle-eyed son of Antichrist? If you're of God's party, answer me.'

'I should like to know,' said Panurge, 'what you would do if, by the consent of all the elements, I were to ficfacfuckforum that most pretty, attractive, virtuous, and chaste wife of yours, so thoroughly that Priapus, the stiff garden god, who dwells here at liberty, unhampered by any attached codpiece, were to stay inside her. Suppose he were so jammed in that he would never come out, and that he would be there for ever, unless you were to extract him with your teeth, what would you do then? Would you leave him there for all eternity? Or would you pull him out with those handsome teeth of yours? Answer me, you ram-dealer, you son of Mahomet. For I'm sure you're of the devil's party.'

'I'd slash you with this sword on that ear where you wear your spectacles,' answered the dealer, 'and I'd fell you like a ram.' With this he pulled at his sword. But it stuck in his scabbard because, as you know, the excessive nitrous moisture of the sea-air readily rusts all weapons.

Panurge ran to Pantagruel for help. Friar John clutched at his newly ground cutlass and would have slain the merchant out of hand if the captain of the ship and some other passengers had not begged Pantagruel to prevent any such outrage on board. So their quarrel was patched up, and they shook hands. Then Panurge and the dealer drank one another's healths most heartily, in sign of perfect reconciliation.

CHAPTER 6: *The Quarrel being over, Panurge bargains with Dingdong for one of his Sheep*

THE quarrel being quite settled, Panurge whispered to Epistemon and Friar John: 'Just go a little way off, and you'll be very tickled by what you'll see. There's going to be a high old game, if the rope doesn't break.'

Then he turned to the dealer, and pledged him once more with a full mug of good Lantern wine. The dealer cheerfully redeemed his pledge, in all honour and courtesy. Then Panurge begged him kindly to sell him one of his sheep.

'Alas, alas, dear friend and neighbour,' replied the dealer, 'how clever you are at tricking poor folk. You are a strange customer indeed, and a mighty fine sheep-buyer! Blow me if you don't look more like a cut-purse than a dealer in sheep. Holy Nicholas, mate, I shouldn't like to stand near you with a full purse at a tripe-dresser's in a thaw. You'd fool anyone who didn't know you, that you would. Now take a good look at him with those spectacles of his! Haw, haw, my friends, doesn't he look every inch the history writer?'

'Patience,' said Panurge. 'But, by the way, as a special favour, will you sell me one of your sheep? How much, now?'

'My dear friend, my dear neighbour,' answered Dingdong, 'do you know what you're asking? These are long-haired sheep. Jason took his golden fleece from one of them. The Burgundian order of the Golden Fleece was derived from them. These are Levantine sheep, pedigree sheep, fatted sheep.'

'All right,' said Panurge. 'But sell me one, if you please, and let's be done with it. I'll pay you promptly in Western crowns, low-bred and with no fat on them.'

'My dear friend, my dear neighbour,' answered the dealer, 'just listen a moment with your other ear.'

PAN. At your service.

DEAL. You're going to Lanternland, are you?

PAN. Certainly.

DEAL. To see the world?

PAN. Certainly.

DEAL. To amuse yourself?

PAN. Certainly.

DEAL. I believe your name is Robin Mutton.

PAN. As you please.

DEAL. I mean no offence.

PAN. I understand that.

DEAL. I believe you're the King's jester.

PAN. Yes, I am.

DEAL. Shake on that. Ha, ha, you're going to see the world, you're the King's jester, and your name's Robin Mutton. D'you see this sheep? Its name's Robin, like yours. Robin, Robin. Bah, bah, bah, bah. There's a fine voice for you.

PAN. Very fine and harmonious.

DEAL. Now let's make a bargain, my dear friend and neighbour. You, Robin Mutton, shall sit on this scale of the balance. My sheep Robin shall sit on the other. I bet you a hundred Arcachon oysters that he will have it over you in weight, price, and value, and that he'll pull you up, short and sharp, exactly as you'll be hung up and suspended, one fine day, on the gibbet.'

'Patience,' said Panurge. 'You would be doing a real kindness to me and to your posterity if you'd sell me that one, or one not quite so grand. Sir, master, I pray you to do so.'

'My friend and neighbour,' replied the dealer, 'the fleeces of these sheep will be made into fine Rouen cloth. Compared with them, cloths woven from the skeins of Leicester are mere fustian. The skins will be made into splendid moroccos, which will be sold as moroccos from Turkey, or from Montélimar, or as Spanish produce at the worst. The guts will be turned into violin and harp strings, which will fetch as high a price as if they came from Munich or Aquileia. What do you say now?'

'If you will kindly sell me one,' said Panurge, 'I shall be under a perpetual obligation to you. Look, here's spot cash. How much do you want?'

As he said this he displayed his purse, full of new Henricuses.

CHAPTER 7: *Continuation of the Bargain between Panurge and Dingdong*

'My friend and neighbour,' replied the dealer, 'they are meat for none but kings and princes. Their flesh is so delicate, so savoury, and so tasty that it's like balm. I'm bringing them from a country where the very pigs, so help me, feed only on myrobalan plums. The sows when they're with litter – begging the company's pardon – are fed on nothing but orange blossom.'

'But sell me one,' said Panurge, 'and I'll pay you like a king. Take a pawn's word for it. How much?'

'My friend and neighbour,' answered the dealer, 'these are sheep bred from the stock of the very ram that carried Phrixus and Helle over the sea called Hellespont.'

'Hell and damnation,' exclaimed Panurge, 'you must be *clericus vel adiscens*, a priest or a budding novice.'

'*Ita*, that means cabbages,' replied the dealer, 'and *vere* are leeks. But rr, rrr. rrrr. rrrrr. Ho, Robin, rr. rrr. rrrr. You don't understand that language. But, to the point. In all the fields where they piss, the wheat springs up as fine as if God himself had pissed there. It needs no other marling or manuring. And that's not all. The alchemists make the best saltpetre in the world from their urine. With their turds – pardon my coarseness – the physicians of our country cure seventy-eight kinds of complaints, the least of which is St Eutropius's Evil, the dropsy – from which Heaven preserve us! Now, what do you think, my friend and neighbour? And what's more, I paid a nice price for them.'

'Never mind the price,' said Panurge. 'Just sell me one, and I'll pay you well for it.'

'My friend and neighbour,' replied the dealer. 'Consider for a moment what wonders of Nature are displayed by these animals before you, even in a member that you might consider of no consequence. Now take these horns here, and pound them gently with an iron pestle or andiron, I don't mind which. Then bury them wherever you like, so long as it's in a sunny spot, and water them often. In a few months you'll see the most delicious asparagus in the world spring up, as good even as the best plants from Ravenna. Don't you tell me, gentlemen, that your cuckold's horns have virtues like that, or such miraculous properties!'

'Patience,' was Panurge's only answer.

'I don't know whether you're a scholar,' said the dealer. 'I've seen plenty of scholars, and famous scholars, that were cuckolds. I have indeed. But if you were a scholar, let me tell you, you'd know that in the lower limbs of these divine animals – in their feet that's to say – there's a bone – the heel, or the astragal, if you'd rather – with which they used to play at the royal game of *bones*. There wasn't any other animal that would do except the Indian ass and the Libyan gazelle. There was an evening when the Emperor Octavian Augustus won more than fifty thousand crowns at that game. But you cuckolds could never hope to win as much as that.'

'Patience,' said Panurge. 'But let's get on.'

'How can I ever tell you the true merits of the internal organs, my dear friend and neighbour?' asked the dealer. 'The shoulders, the haunches, the legs, the neck, the breast, the liver, the spleen, the tripes, the paunch, and the bladder, which they play ball with, and the ribs which they use in Pygmy-land for making little bows to shoot cherry-stones at the cranes, and the head, to which they add a little sulphur to make a marvellous decoction for loosening the bowels of constipated dogs.'

'Piss and shit,' said the ship's captain to the dealer. 'There's far too much haggling here. Sell it to him if you're going to. But if you don't want to, stop playing the fool with him.'

'I will though,' said the dealer, 'just to oblige you. But he shall pay three pounds apiece for them, three pounds minted at Tours. Then he shall have his choice.'

'That's a lot of money,' said Panurge. 'In our country I could buy five, or even six, for that amount. See that you're not overcharging me. You're not the first man I've met who's wanted to get rich too quickly and make his way in the world, but has fallen down into poverty, and sometimes even broken his neck.'

'May the ague rot you, you great dolt,' cried the dealer. 'By Christ's foreskin of Charroux, and that's a solemn vow, the poorest of these sheep is worth four times as much as the best of those that the Coraxians sold in Tuditania – a part of Spain – for a gold talent apiece, in the old days. And what do you think a gold talent was worth, you prize idiot?'

'My sweet sir,' said Panurge, 'you're getting hot round the collar, I can see that plainly enough. But here, take your money.'

When Panurge had paid the dealer, he chose out of the whole flock one fine big ram, and carried him away bleating and crying. The rest of the sheep bleated and cried in concert, as they watched their companion being led away. Meanwhile the dealer was saying to his shepherds: 'That customer knows how to make a good choice. He's a good judge, he is, the rogue! I was reserving that one – honestly and truly I was – for the lord of Cancale, since I know his taste exactly. He's as merry and jovial as can be when he's got a nice tempting shoulder of mutton in one hand, like a left-handed racquet, and a good sharp carving-knife in the other. God knows, he wields a pretty knife.'

CHAPTER 8: *Panurge drowns the Dealer and his Sheep in the Sea*

ALL at once – I don't know how; things happened so swiftly that I hadn't time to watch them – Panurge without another word threw his crying and bleating sheep out into the sea. Then all the rest of the flock, crying and bleating on the same note, began to fling themselves into the water after him, one after another. In fact they all jostled one another to be the next to leap after their companion. It was impossible to keep them back. For, as you know, it is the nature of sheep to follow the leader, wherever he goes. Aristotle says, in fact, in his ninth book *De histor. anim.*, that the sheep is the stupidest, silliest animal in the world.

The dealer, in his alarm at seeing his sheep perish by drowning, tried to prevent them and held them back with all his might. But it was useless. They all jumped into the sea, one after another, and were drowned. Finally Dingdong clutched hold of one great, strong ram by the fleece. He was up on the forward deck, and thought that if he could hold this one back he would save the rest. But the ram was so strong that he carried the dealer overboard with him in much the same way as the sheep of Polyphemus, the one-eyed Cyclops, carried Ulysses and his companions out of the cave. Dingdong was drowned, as were the rest of the shepherds and drovers, who seized the sheep, some by the horns, others by the legs, and others by the fleece, and were dragged into the water also, where they perished miserably.

Panurge stood beside the galley with an oar in his hand, not to help the drovers but to prevent them from clambering aboard and escaping their death; and all the time he preached to them as eloquently as the little Friar Olivier Maillard, or like a second Friar John Bourgeois. With rhetorical flourishes, he pointed out to them the miseries of this world, and the blessings and felicities of the other life, affirming that the dead were luckier than those who lived on in this vale of tears. He promised to erect to each one of them a fine memorial and honourable tomb at the top of Mont Cenis, upon his return from Lantern-land. However, in case they were not yet weary of living among mankind and so found drowning unwelcome, he wished them good luck and hoped that they might meet a whale, which would return them after three days, safe and sound to some Satinland, as happened to Jonah.

When the ship was rid of the dealer and his sheep, Panurge asked: 'Are there any other sheepish souls left? Are there any followers of Thibault the Lamb or of Reynauld the Ram, who are sleeping while the others graze? I'm sure I don't know. That was an old trick of war. What did you think of it, Brother John?'

'Anything you do is good,' replied Friar John. 'I can only find one fault with it. I think it was the old custom in war, on the day of the battle or assault, to promise the soldiers double pay for that day. If the battle was won, there would be plenty to pay them with. If it was lost, it would be disgraceful of them to claim the money, though those runaway Swiss from Gruyère did so after the battle of Cerisoles. Well, to be consistent you ought to have deferred payment till the end. Then the money would have stayed in your purse.'

'I had some shitten good fun for my money!' answered Panurge. 'Why, that joke was worth more than fifty thousand francs. But let us sail on. The wind is favourable. Listen to me, Brother John. No man ever did me a good turn without getting a reward, or at least an acknowledgement. I'm not an ungrateful man, I never was, and never will be. And nobody's ever done me a bad turn without being sorry for it, either in this world or the next. I'm not such a fool as that.'

'You're damning yourself like an old devil,' answered Friar John. 'It is written: *mihi vindictam*, etc. – Vengeance is mine. It's breviary stuff, that is.'

CHAPTER 9: *Pantagruel reaches the Island of Ennasin, and of the strange Relationships there*

THE west wind went on blowing, changing occasionally to that breeze from the south-west which is called the *garbino*, and a whole day passed without our discovering land. On the third day, however, at the flies' noon, we sighted a triangular island, very similar in shape and situation to Sicily, called Alliance Island. Its inhabitants resemble the red-painted Picts, or Poitevins, except that they all, men, women, and children alike, have noses shaped like the ace-of-clubs. For that reason the ancient name of the island was Ennasin. They were all kindred and related to one another, a fact of which they boasted. Indeed, the Governor of the place openly proclaimed to us: 'You people from another world consider it a remarkable thing that from one Rome family – the Fabii – on one day – the 13th of February – from one gate – the Porta Carmentalis, formerly situated at the foot of the Capitol, between the Tarpeian Rock and the Tiber, and since called the Scelerata – there went forth against certain enemies of the Romans – the Veintes from Etruria – three hundred and six knights, all related, with five thousand other soldiers, all vassals of theirs, who were killed to a man – near the river Cremera, which flows out of Lake Baccano. But from this country, in case of need, more than three hundred thousand could march, all related to one another, and all of one family.'

Their relationships and degrees of kinship were of a very strange kind. For they were all so related and intermarried with one another that we found none of them who was a mother or a father, an uncle or an aunt, a cousin or a nephew, a son-in-law or a daughter-in-law, a god-father or a god-mother, to any other; except indeed for one tall noseless old man, whom I heard calling a little girl of three or four, Father, while the little girl called him, Daughter.

The degrees of relationship between them were such that one man called a woman, dear Octopus, and the woman called him, you old Porpoise. 'Those two must feel a hot tide rising,' said Friar John. 'when they've rubbed their bacon together a little.' Another of them called out with a smile to a stylish young baggage: 'Good day, young pretty currycomb,' and she answered him with, 'A grand morning to you, my chestnut steed.' 'Ha, ha!' cried Panurge, 'come and see a steed currying favour. I bet there'll be some fine warm work, for the chestnut steed with the black stripe must have his cock combed good and often.' Another man called to his fancy-girl: 'God bless you, dear desk,' to which she called back: 'The same to you, old brief.' 'By St Trinian,' exclaimed Gymnaste. 'That brief must often be lying on its desk.' Another called his girl, 'Old stagger', and she called him, 'You worm'. 'His worm will have given her plenty of fits of the staggers,' said Eusthenes. Another saluted a female relative with: 'Good day to you, hatchet,' and she replied: 'The same to you, helve.' 'God blast my belly,' cried Carpalim. 'That hatchet's well helved and that helve's well hatcheted. Do you think he's got the big tip that Roman whores are so fond of? Or perhaps he is a Franciscan friar with a good one.'

As we went on, I saw a lecherous fellow who greeted his female relative as, 'My mattress', and she called him, 'Eiderdown', and indeed he looked a downy old bird. One man called his girl: 'Sweet doe', to which she answered: 'Old Crust', 'Shovel' and 'poker'; 'clog' and 'slipper'; 'boot' and 'shoe'; 'mitten' and 'glove', were other names exchanged between relatives of different sexes. One man in particular called his woman his rind, to which she replied: 'Dear bacon': and their relationship was that of bacon to rind.

Two similarly allied persons called one another 'Omelette' and 'My egg', and they were as much of a piece as an egg and an omelette. Similarly, one man called his wench, 'You old tripe', and she called him a Savoury Faggot. We could not discover, by reference to our own customs, what degree of alliance, relationship, affinity, or consanguinity existed between this pair. But it was explained to us later that she was the tripe that had gone to the making of that faggot. 'Hullo, my shell,' was one man's greeting to his woman friend, and she replied: 'Blessings on you, oyster.' 'That oyster knows how to slide into its shell,' commented Carpalim. Another said: 'A good life to you, dear pod,' and the girl answered: 'May yours be a long one, my dear pea.' 'There's a pea in a pod for you,' exclaimed Gymnaste. Another great ugly beggar, clattering on high wooden clogs, met a great, fat, squat wench, and said to her: 'God bless my peg-top, my spinning-top, my humming-top.' 'The same to you, dear whip,' she answered proudly. 'By the blood of St Francis,' cried Xenomanes, 'is he a tough enough whip to lash that top?'

A learned professor, with sleekly combed hair, who had been chatting for some time with a lady of rank, took his leave of her with the words: 'Thank you indeed, fair lady.' To which she replied: 'But the debt's all on my side, you unlucky gambler.' 'Lucky in love and unlucky at cards, isn't an ill-fitting match,' observed Pantagruel. A not so newly fledged graduate called to his young inspiration: 'Hullo, hullo, it's a long time since I saw you, dear bag.' 'I'm always glad to see you, my jolly pipe,' she answered, 'Couple them together,' said Panurge, 'and blow up their arses. Then you'll have a bagpipe.' Another man called a girl his sow, and she called him her grass; and it struck me that this sow liked being turned out to grass. I saw a mincing little hunchback, quite close to us, salute a girl relation of his: 'God save my Peg.' 'Ho,' said Friar John. 'She's just a great hole, I imagine, and so he's the peg. It would be interesting to know if this peg's capable of entirely stopping that hole.'

Another man called to a woman relation of his: 'Good-bye, dear coop,' and she called back: 'Good day to you, you goose.' 'It's my opinion,' said Ponocrates, 'that that goose spends a lot of time in his coop.' One smutty fellow talking to his piece of goods, said: 'Don't forget, poop,' and she replied: 'I shan't fail you, fart.' 'Do you call these two relations?' Pantagruel asked the Governor. 'I think they're more like enemies than allies. He just called her a poop.' 'My dear visitors from the other world,' answered the Governor. 'You have few relatives that are as close kin as this poop and this fart. They emerged invisibly from the same hole, and at the same instant.'

'You mean that the north-west wind had set their mother's lantern swinging?' asked Panurge. 'What mother do you mean?' asked the Governor. 'That relationship belongs to your world. They've got no father or mother. Fathers and mothers belong to the world overseas, to the world of hayseed folk.' The good Pantagruel was watching and listening to everything, but at these remarks he felt almost abashed.

After most carefully inspecting the island's situation and observing the customs of the Ennasian people, we went into an inn, to take a little refreshment, and found them holding a wedding there in their local fashion. They were making high good cheer, I promise you. In our presence they celebrated a marriage between a pear – a very luscious female she seemed to us, though those who had felt her said she was rather over-ripe – and a young, downy-haired cheese with a

somewhat reddish complexion. I had heard talk of such marriages before, and several had taken place in other parts of the world. Indeed,
they still say in our pastures that never was there such good cheer as
the wedding of cheese and pear. In another room I saw them marrying
an old female boot to a supple young buskin. They told Pantagruel
that the young buskin was only marrying this old boot because she
was oncoming, in good condition, and well greased for household use,
especially for one fond of fishing. In another lower room I saw a neat
young pump married to an old slipper; and we were told that he had
not taken her for her charm or good looks, but out of greed and
avarice for the crowns that were sewn thick inside her.

CHAPTER 10: *Pantagruel goes ashore on the Island of Cheli,
whose reigning Monarch is St Panigon*

THE south-west wind was still behind us, when we said good-bye to
those unpleasant Alliancers with their ace-of-clubs noses, and put out
to sea. As the sun went down we disembarked on Cheli or the Isle of
Compliments, a large, fertile, rich, and populous island whose king was
Panigon, or All-things to-all-Men. Accompanied by his children and
the princes of his court, this King came down to the harbour to receive
Pantagruel, and led him up to his castle, where, as they entered the
donjon-gate, the Queen appeared, escorted by her daughters and the
court-ladies. Panigon desired her and all her suite to kiss Pantagruel
and his men, as was the courteous custom of that country, and Friar
John alone escaped this compliment, by slipping off and hiding among
the King's officers.

Panigon tried, by every possible argument, to keep Pantagruel with
him for that day and the next. But Pantagruel excused himself on the
plea that the weather was calm and the wind favourable: a state of
things that travellers desire more often than they get. One must make
use of one's good fortune, he said, when it comes, for it doesn't come
always, or as often as it is wanted. Panigon accepted this excuse and
allowed us to depart, after we had drunk twenty-five or thirty mugs
all round.

When Pantagruel came down to the port, however, he could not
discover Friar John. So he asked where he was, and why he was not

with the company. Panurge did not know what excuse to make for him, and was about to return to the castle to fetch him, when Friar John rushed up, with a broad smile on his face, and cried out in high good spirits: 'Long live the noble Panigon. By the dead ox's belly, he keeps a fine kitchen. I've just come from it. Everything's served in full ladles, and I had good hopes of stuffing my paunch and lining my frock in the good monastic way.' 'So, my dear friend,' said Pantagruel, 'you're at your kitchens again!' 'Cock's body,' answered Friar John, 'I know the customs and ceremonies there better than all this fiddle-faddling with the women, *magni, magna, shittery-shattery*, bow, repeat, the same again, the embrace, the tight squeeze, kiss Your Ladyship's hand, kiss Your Highness's. You are most welcome, *tiddly-posh tiddly-push*. A turd, I say! You may kiss my arse. All shit and piddle! I don't say, of course that I don't like a quick cuddle on the quiet sometimes when I've a chance to introduce my what's-its-name. But all this shit-ten bowing business plagues me worse than a fast she-devil – I mean to say a two-day fast. And St Benedict was right about that. You talk of kissing young ladies. By the holy and worthy frock I wear, I fight shy of that, for fear the same thing might happen to me as happened to the Lord of La Guerche.'

'What was that?' asked Pantagruel. 'I know him. He's one of my best friends.'

'He was invited,' said Friar John, 'to a sumptuous and magnificent banquet, which was given by a relative and neighbour of his, and to which all the gentlemen, ladies, and young ladies of the neighbour-hood were also invited. While they were waiting for him to come, these ladies disguised the pages of the company, dressing them up as fair and attractive young women, and when he arrived these petti-coated pages were waiting for him beside the drawbridge. He kissed them all most courteously, with a magnificent bow for each. But when he had done, the ladies who were waiting for him in the gallery burst out laughing and signed to the pages to take off their finery. However, the good gentlemen was so ashamed and so annoyed by this that he refused to kiss the real ladies. He said that seeing he had been so taken in by pages disguised as women, these might quite likely be servants even better disguised.

'By almighty God – pardon my swearing,' cried Friar John, 'why don't we remove our human selves into some grand kitchen, and there consider the turning of the spits, the sweet music of the jacks, the placing of the bacon fat, the temperature of the soups, the preparation of the dessert, and the order of the wine service? *Beati immaculati in via*.[1] That's breviary stuff, that is.'

CHAPTER 11: *Why Monks love to be in Kitchens*

'THAT's spoken like a true monk,' said Epistemon, 'a true monking monk, I mean, not one that's just monked over. You remind me now of something I saw and heard in Florence, about twenty years ago. We were a pleasant band of studious fellows, very fond of travelling and most anxious to visit the learned men, the antiquities, and curiosities of Italy. At the particular moment I have in mind we were carefully contemplating the position and beauties of Florence, the structure of the Duomo, and the magnificence of its churches and grand palaces. Indeed, we were beginning to compete as to who should find the fittest words with which to praise them, when a monk from Amiens, named Bernard Lardon, burst out partly in anger, partly in curiosity: 'I can't think what the devil you find here to praise so much. I've kept my eyes as wide open as you have, and I'm no blinder than you are. But, after all, what is there here? A few fine houses, and that's all. But God and our good patron, the blessed St Bernard, be with us if I've seen a single cook-shop in the whole town, and I've looked around me carefully enough. Yes, I tell you, I've spied about me, I've kept my eyes open, and I have been waiting to count how many I should see on the left and how many on the right. I wanted to see how many cook-shops we should see cooking, and on which side of the road there would be more of them. Now, in Amiens, in a quarter – or let's say a third – of the distance we've covered in our walk, I should be able to show you more than fourteen cook-shops, all ancient and aromatic. I don't know what pleasure you've had in seeing the lions and the Africans – I think that that was the name you gave to what they call tigers – near the belfry; or in staring at the porcupines and ostriches in the Lord Filippo Strozzi's palace. But, by my life, boys, I'd rather see a good fat gosling on a spit. All this porphyry and marble is very beautiful. I've nothing to say against it, but our

1. Blessed are the undefiled in the way.

cheesecakes at Amiens are more to my taste. These ancient statues are well carved, I can quite believe that. But by St Fériol of Abbeville, the little wenches in our country are a thousand times more seductive.'

'What's the meaning of this,' asked Friar John, 'and why is it that you always find monks in kitchens? You never find kings, popes, or emperors there.'

'Do you think there's some latent virtue,' put in Rhizotome, 'some specific and hidden property, in kettles and spits that draws monks there as the magnet attracts iron, but never draws emperors, popes, or kings to it? Or is there some natural and magnetic quality inherent in frocks and cowls that automatically drags good monks into the kitchen, even though they neither wish nor choose to go there?'

'Form following matter is what he means,' said Epistemon, 'that is a phrase from Averroës.'

'You're right, quite right,' said Friar John.

'I'll tell you,' said Pantagruel, 'though I won't solve that problem. It's a bit of a thorny one, and you could hardly touch it without getting pricked. I remember reading once that Antigonus, King of Macedonia, went into his camp kitchen one day, and found the poet Antagoras there, frying a conger-eel and holding the pan himself. "Was Homer frying conger when he described Agamemnon's great deeds?" asked the King very gaily. "Do you think, sir," answered the poet, "that Agamemnon bothered to find out if anyone in his camp was frying conger when he was performing his great deeds?" To the King it did not seem right that the poet should be frying this dish in his kitchen. But the poet objected that it was far more improper for a king to be found in the place.'

'I'll crown that story,' said Panurge, 'by telling you how Breton of Villandry answered the Duke of Guise one day. They were talking about one of King Francis's battles against the Emperor Charles the Fifth, in which Breton had been magnificently armoured down to his reinforced greaves and steel shoes, and grandly mounted as well, but had never been seen to fight. "I was there, I swear," asserted Breton; "I could easily prove it. Yes, I was in a spot where you would never have dared to come." The noble Duke considered this speech both rash and a good deal too insolent and, somewhat offended, broke off the conversation. But Breton easily calmed him down by saying, to the general amusement: "Yes, I was with the baggage, a place in which your Grace would never have dared to hide, as I did." '

Thus gossiping, Panurge and his party went down to their ships, and departed from the island of Cheli.

CHAPTER 12: *How Pantagruel passed through the land of Clerk-ship, and of the strange customs among the Bum-bailiffs*

CONTINUING on our course, we came next day to Clerkship, a much-blotted and blurred country, which I could make nothing of. We saw sharks of the Court and Bum-bailiffs there, men who will hang their fathers for a shilling. They did not invite us to eat or to drink, but with an endless multiplication of learned compliments, informed us that they were always at our service – so long as we paid them. One of our interpreters described to Pantagruel the very strange way in which these people earn their livings – quite the opposite way to that of our modern Romans. At Rome, an infinite number of people gain their livelihood by poisoning, beating, and killing. But the Bum-bailiffs gain theirs by being beaten. In fact if they were to remain for any length of time without being beaten, they would die of hunger, and their wives and children also.

'They are like the people Claudius Galen describes,' said Panurge, 'who cannot erect their cavernous members in an equatorial direction without being well whipped. By St Thibault, a beating like that would have the contrary effect on me. Devil take me if it wouldn't thoroughly lower my mast.'

'This is how they work,' said the interpreter. 'When a monk, priest, money-lender, or lawyer has a grudge against any local gentleman, he sends one of these Bum-bailiffs to him. Master Bum-bailiff will summons him, writ him, insult him, and shamelessly abuse him, according to his brief and instructions. Then, unless the gentleman is as stolid as an ox and has less brains than a tadpole, he will be compelled either to punch the fellow and crack him over the head, or to give him a good hiding or, better still, to throw him over the battlements or out of the window of his castle. Whereupon Master Bum-bailiff's as rich for the next four months, as if a beating were his natural harvest. For he receives a good wage from the monk, money-lender, or lawyer, and damages from the gentleman, which are sometimes so excessively heavy that they will cost a man all he has got, and he'll be in danger of miserably rotting in prison, as if he had struck the King.'

'I know a very good remedy against that sort of nuisance,' said Panurge – 'the one employed by the Lord of Basché.'

'What's that?' asked Pantagruel.

'The Lord of Basché,' said Panurge, 'was a courageous, virtuous, generous, and chivalrous gentleman. On returning from a certain long war, in which the Duke of Ferrara, with French aid, valiantly defended himself against the fury of Pope Julius the Second, he was writted, summonsed, and visited every day by the Bum-bailiff, at the whim and pleasure of the fat Prior of St Louant. One day, as he was breakfasting with his men – for he was a kindly and hospitable person – he sent for his baker Loire and his wife, and for the vicar of the parish, whose name was Oudart, and who acted also as his butler, as was the custom of the time in France. Then, in the presence of his gentlemen and other servants, he addressed them. "You see, my children, the annoyances I suffer every day from these wretched Bumbailiffs. But I've made up my mind. If you don't help me I seriously intend to leave this country, and enter the Sultan's service, devil take me if I don't. Next time they come here you must all be ready. You, Loire, and your wife must appear in my great hall in your best wedding clothes, as if you had just been betrothed and were about to be married. Now here's a hundred gold crowns for you, to get your finery furbished up. You, Master Oudart, must appear without fail in your best surplice and stole, with the holy water, as if to marry them. You, Trudon – this was his drummer's name – must be here too, with your pipe and drum. When the service is over and the bride has been kissed to the sound of the drum, you'll all give one another something to remember the wedding by, a little tap or two, I mean, with your fists. It will only make your supper taste the better. But when it comes to the Bum-bailiff's turn, you must thresh him like green rye. Don't spare him, I beg of you. Slap him, punch him, and hit him hard. Look, here are some jousting gloves covered in kids' leather. Don't count your blows, but hit out at him, left and right. The one who punches him hardest I'll count as my best friend. Have no fear of receiving a summons for this. I'll stand surety for you all. His beating will just be the usual horse-play that you have at every wedding."

' "Very well," said Oudart, "but how shall we recognize this Bum-bailiff? For here, in your house, there are visitors every day, coming from everywhere."

' "I've provided for that," answered Basché. "When a man comes to the door, either on foot or on some miserable nag, with a great fat silver ring on his thumb, that'll be the Bum-bailiff. The porter will usher him in politely and then he'll sound the bell. At that signal get ready, and come into the hall to play the comedy with the tragic end-ing that I've outlined to you."

'That very day, as God would have it, a fat, old red-faced Bum-bailiff appeared at the gate. When he rang the bell, the porter recog-nized him by his clumpish leggings, his wretched mare, his canvas bag full of writs, which hung from his belt, and – surest sign of all – by the thick silver ring which he wore on his left thumb. He greeted the visitor politely, courteously showed him in, and then sounded the castle bell. When they heard it ring, the baker and his wife got into their fine clothes and appeared in the hall, successfully keeping straight faces. Oudart donned his surplice and stole, emerged from his pantry, and drew Master Bum-bailiff in to have a good long drink while everyone around was putting on gloves. "You couldn't have come at a better time," he told him. "Our Lord's in a grand mood. We shall be making great cheer in a moment, and the drink will go round in bucketsful. We're having a wedding in the hall. Drink this down, and be merry."

'While the Bum-bailiff was drinking, Basché was in the hall, seeing that all his people were properly equipped; and when they were ready he sent for Oudart, who entered, carrying the holy water. Master Bum-bailiff followed him in and, after making the proper number of obeisances, duly served his summons on Basché, who treated him with the greatest cordiality, gave him a gold piece, and begged him to witness the marriage-contract and the wedding; which he did. Towards the end blows began to be exchanged. But when it came to the Bum-bailiff's turn, they treated him to such a lusty hammering with their gloves that he was knocked out and bruised all over. They turned one of his eyes into a poached egg in black butter, fractured eight of his ribs, knocked in his breast-bone, cracked his shoulder-blades in four places, and smashed his jawbone into three pieces; and all the time they laughed as if it were a joke. God knows what a hiding

Oudart gave him, with his great ermine-lined steel gauntlet, which was covered by his surplice sleeve. For he was a powerful fellow.

'So Master Bum-bailiff returned to the Isle Bouchart, looking as if he had been clawed by a tiger, yet quite pleased and delighted with my Lord of Basché. And thanks to the good surgeons of that region he lived as long as you would expect. What is more, nothing further was said about the incident, the memory of which died out with the sound of the bells that chimed at his burial.'

CHAPTER 13: *The Lord of Basché praises his Servants after the manner of Master François Villon*

WHEN the Bum-bailiff had left the castle and climbed on to Blind Bess – which was the name he gave his one-eyed mare – my Lord of Basché called his wife, her ladies, and all his people out into the arbour of his private garden. Then he sent for the luncheon wine, and for plenty of pasties, hams, fruit, and cheese to go with it, and they all drank together in high glee. At the end of the meal he told them this story:

'In his old age Master François Villon retired to Saint-Maixent in Poitou, under the protection of a worthy churchman who was abbot of that place. There, for the people's amusement, he undertook a production of the Passion play in the Poitevin manner and dialect; and when the parts were distributed, the actors rehearsed, and the theatre ready, he told the Mayor and aldermen that the Mystery could be acted at the end of the Niort fair. It only remained to find dresses to suit the characters. So the mayor and aldermen settled the date.

'Now Villon requested Friar Stephen Fliptail, the sacristan of the local Franciscans, to lend him a cope and stole, to dress up an old peasant who was playing God the Father. But Fliptail refused, on the excuse that by their provincial statutes they were strictly forbidden to give or lend any article to an actor. Villon replied that the statute only applied to farces, mummeries, and bawdy games, and that he had seen such loans allowed at Brussels and elsewhere. Fliptail, nevertheless, peremptorily told him to find his costumes elsewhere, if he pleased, but to expect nothing from his sacristy. For most certainly he would get nothing from there. Villon reported his refusal to the actors in high indignation, adding that God would take vengeance on Flip-tail very soon, and deal him an exemplary punishment.

'On the following Saturday Villon got news that Fliptail had gone to collect alms at Saint-Ligaire, and was riding a young mare who had not yet been covered, which they called the monastery filly. He was due to return at about two in the afternoon. So Villon led a parade of his devils through the town and the market, all dressed up in wolves-, calves-, and ram-skins, surmounted by sheeps' heads, bulls' horns, and great kitchen hooks, with stout leather belts round their waists, hung with large cow-bells and mule-bells, which made a horrible din. Some carried black sticks full of squibs; others waved long lighted firebrands, on to which, at every street corner, they threw great hand-fuls of powdered resin, which produced terrible flames and smoke; all of which amused the crowd and quite terrified the small children. Now, when this parade was over, Villon led his actors out to drink at a little inn outside the gate, on the Saint-Ligaire road, and as they reached the place he saw Fliptail in the distance, riding back from his begging mission, whereupon he recited these macaronic lines:

> Hic est de patria, natus de gente of cadgers
> Qui solet antiquo scrappas portare in wallet.

"As God's my life," cried the devils, "that's the man who wouldn't lend God the Father so much as a cope. Let's give him a good fright." "That's a grand idea," said Villon. "But let's hide until he passes. In the meantime prepare your squibs and firebrands."

'When Fliptail came up, they all rushed tumultuously into the road to meet him, throwing fire from all directions at him and his mare, clanging their bells and howling like real devils: "Hho, hho, hho, hho, brrrourrrourrrrs, rrrourrrs, rrrourrrs! Hou, hou, hou. Hho, hho, hho! Don't we make fine devils, Brother Stephen?"

'The mare, thoroughly scared, began to trot, broke into a gallop, reared and plunged, and broke away, all the time dealing her rider double kicks, and farting with terror. This was too much for Friar Stephen, who was flung from his seat although he clung to the pom-mel of the pack-saddle with all his might. But his stirrup-straps being of rope, the leather thongs of his right sandal became so entangled in them that he could not get it free of his stirrup. So he was dragged along on his arse by the mare, who kept on kicking out at him and dashing over hedge, bush, and ditch, wild with terror. In the end she broke his skull open, so that his brains fell out near the Hosanna Cross. Then his arms and his legs snapped off, one after another, and his trailing bowels were left to feed the crows. In the end his mare returned to the monastery, bringing nothing of him back except his right foot and shoe, which were still entangled in the stirrup.

'When Villon saw that his plan had succeeded, he said to his devils: "You'll play your parts well, my dear devils. You'll act splendidly, I promise you. Oh, you *will* act splendidly! I defy the team of devils of Saumur, Doué, Montmorillon, Langeais, Saint-Épain, Angers, and even the Poitiers troupe in their great hall, by God, to put on as good a show. Oh, you'll act splendidly indeed!"

'Similarly, my dear friends,' said Basché, 'I foresee that you'll play this farce with a tragic ending splendidly in future, seeing that at the first trial and rehearsal you gave this Bum-bailiff such an eloquent banging, thumping, and tickling. From now on, I double all your wages. You, my dear,' said he to his wife, 'do whatever honours you think fit. All my wealth is in your hands to keep. For my part, first I'll drink all your healths, my good friends. Come, the wine is nice and cool. Secondly, take this silver bowl, steward; it's a present. And you, my squires, here are two silver-gilt cups for you, and you're not to whip your pages for the next three months. My dear, give them my best white plumes with the gilt buckles. Master Oudart, this silver flagon is for you; the other one is for the cooks. This silver basket is for my valets. This silver-gilt bowl is for the grooms. These two dishes I give to the porters, and there are ten porringers for the muleteers. You, Trudon, take all these silver spoons and this comfit-box. This large salt-cellar is for you lackeys. Serve me well, my friends, and I'll show my gratitude. Also take my word for it that I'd rather receive a hundred mace-blows on my helmet, by God, in war and in the service of our worthy King, than accept so much as one summons from those dogs of Bum-bailiffs, for the amusement of that pot-bellied prior.'

CHAPTER 14: *More Bum-bailiff-bashing at my Lord of Basché's*

FOUR days later another Bum-bailiff came to summons Basché, on the instructions of that fat prior. This one was young, tall, and thin, and on his arrival he was quickly recognized by the porter, who rang the bell. At this sound everyone realized what was afoot. Loire was kneading his dough; his wife was sifting the flour; Oudart was minding the pantry; the gentlemen were playing tennis; my Lord of Basché was playing three-hundred-up with his wife; the ladies were rattling the bones; the officers were playing at nap, and the pages at 'How many fingers?' Suddenly everyone realized that there was a Bum-bailiff in the land. Oudart hopped off to put on his robes, and Loire and his wife to don their finery; Trudon to play his flute and beat the drum; and all the rest started to laugh, to get ready and – On with the gloves!

Basché went down to the courtyard; and the Bum-bailiff, when he met him, fell on his knees before him, begging him not to take offence at his bringing him a summons from the fat prior. He pointed out to him in an eloquent speech that he was a public official, a servant of the Monkery and summoner on behalf of the mitred abbot, but that he was willing at any time to act in the same capacity for my Lord of Basché, or even for the humblest member of his household, in any business he might be pleased to entrust to him. 'Now come,' said my Lord. 'You aren't going to serve me with a writ before you've drunk some of my Quinquenais wine, and attended a wedding I'm just going to celebrate. Master Oudart, make him drink and refresh himself. Make him drink deeply, and then show him into the hall. You will be very welcome, sir,'

'After eating and drinking his fill, the Bum-bailiff came into the hall with Oudart; and there were the actors in the farce, in their places and well prepared. When he entered they all began to smile, and the Bum-bailiff grinned back amicably, as the mystic words were pronounced over the bridal pair, as their hands touched, as the bridegroom kissed the bride, and all were sprinkled with holy water. Whilst the wine and spices were being brought in, blows began to be exchanged. The Bum-bailiff dealt Oudart a slap or two. But Oudart had his gauntlet hidden under his surplice and slipped it on like a mitten. Then they started thumping the Bum-bailiff, and bashing the

Bum-bailiff, and blows fell on the Bum-bailiff from all directions. "The wedding, the wedding," they cried. "The wedding, and this will make you remember it!" And they dealt with him so thoroughly that blood spurted out of his mouth and nose and ears and eyes. In short, he was thoroughly thumped and battered and pounded, head, neck, back, chest, arms, and all. Believe me, the young men of Avignon never played such a sweet game of Slash-him at Carnival time, as my Lord of Basché's men played on that Bum-bailiff. Finally he fell down. Then they threw copious wine in his face, tied a beautiful yellow-and-green fool's favour on the sleeve of his jacket, and set him up on his snotty beast. I don't know whether he was well bandaged and nursed by his wife and the doctors when he arrived at the Isle Bouchart. Nothing has been heard of him since.

'Next day, since evidence that the writ had been served was not to be found in the Bum-bailiff's bag or pouch, the same comedy was repeated. A new Bum-bailiff was sent, on behalf of the fat Prior, to serve a new writ on my Lord of Basché, with two beadles as escort. When the porter rang the bell, the whole family rejoiced, for they knew it was a Bum-bailiff. Basché, who was at table, dining with his wife and his gentlemen, sent for the Bum-bailiff, sat him down beside him, and placed the beadles next to the ladies. There they dined cheerfully and well. The Bum-bailiff got up from table and, with the two beadles for witnesses, served his writ on Basché, who politely asked him for a copy of his warrant. It was produced, my Lord accepted service, and four crowns were duly paid to the Bum-bailiff and his beadles. By now everyone had retired to prepare for the comedy, and Trudon began to beat his drum. Basché then invited the Bum-bailiff to be present at the wedding of one of his officers, and to draw up the contract, for which he promised him good and proper pay. The Bum-bailiff was most courteous. He took out his writing-case, promptly produced some paper, and kept his beadles beside him. Then Loire came into the hall through one door, and his wife with the ladies through the other, all in their wedding clothes. Whereupon Oudart, in his priestly robes, took them by the hand, asked them their intentions, and gave them his blessing, with a liberal sprinkling of holy water. The contract was signed and sealed; wines and spices were brought in through one door; quantities of orange and white favours through another; and through a third the gauntlets were quietly introduced.'

CHAPTER 15: *Some ancient Wedding Customs are revived by the Bum-bailiffs*

'AFTER tossing down a great cup of Breton wine, the Bum-bailiff said to my Lord: "Sir, what's the meaning of this? Don't you celebrate weddings here in style? God bless my soul, the good customs are dying out. You don't find hares in their forms any more; true friendship's dead, and in many churches they have forbidden the ancient tipplings to the blessed Saints after the singing of the anthems at Christmas. The earth's in its dotage. The end of the world's approaching. Now come on – The wedding, the wedding, the wedding!"' With this he began to hit Basché and his wife and, after them, Oudart and the ladies.

Then the gauntlets got busy. The Bum-bailiff's head was split in nine places, one of the beadles had his forearm wrenched out of its socket, and the other had his upper jaw so dislocated that it fell half over his chin, and exposed his uvula, with notable loss of incisors, molars, and canines. At a signal from Trudon, who varied the note of his drumming, the gloves were whipped away, quite unperceived, and sweetmeats handed round again with renewed laughter, all the jolly company drinking to one another, and everyone pledging the Bum-bailiff and his beadles. But Oudart swore and cursed at this wedding custom, complaining that one of the beadles had entirely dislocathing-umabobbed one of his shoulders. All the same he drank the fellow's health gaily. The beadle with the broken jaw clasped his hands and speechlessly begged his pardon – for he could not speak. Loire complained that the beadle with the unsocketed forearm had given such a punch on one of his elbows that he was bruisedblueandcontused on his heel.

'Look,' said Trudon, covering his left eye with his handkerchief, and showing his drum knocked in on one side, 'What harm have I done them? And yet they haven't been content to bashscuppercand-dashblackwhiteandblue my poor eye; they've knocked in my drum into the bargain. It's usual enough to beat the drum at weddings, but it's not usual to beat the drummer. He's used to being very well treated. May the devil take my drum for his nightcap!'

'Brother,' answered the one-armed beadle, 'I'll give you a fine, large, old Royal Patent, that I've got in my bag, to mend your drum with. Forgive us, in God's name. By Our Lady of Rivière, the fair Lady, I meant no harm.'

One of the squires came hobbling and limping up, giving a telling imitation of the noble Lord of La Roche-Posay and, turning to the beadle whose jaw hung down like the beaver of a helmet, asked him: 'Are you one of the Flagellants, or the Flagellators, or the Fly-flaps? Weren't you satisfied to have deathanddamnationcrashandbashibulated all our upper limbs with great clouts from your mittens without deathanddamnationslashdashandpulverizing us on the shins with the fine-pointed toes of your boots? Do you call this child's play? By God, there's no play about it.'

The beadle clasped his hands, and seemed to be begging his pardon. But he could only mumble with his tongue like a marmoset: 'Mon, mon, mon, vrelon, von, von.'

The bride cried and laughed, laughed and cried as she complained that the Bum-bailiff had not been satisfied to thump her without choice or distinction of limbs, but had brutally pulled her hair, and in addition had treacherously dughiskneeandheavedhisfoot into her private parts.

'Devil take it,' cried Basché. 'Of course the King's man – for so the Bum-bailiffs call themselves – had to whack my poor old backbone. I don't feel any grudge against him for that. These are little nuptial caresses. Nevertheless take good note that he has summonsed me like an angel, but drubbed me like a devil. There's something of the Friar Flagellant about him. I drink to him with all my heart, however, and to you too, my worthy beadles.'

'But,' protested his wife, 'why did he give me such a very liberal dose of his fists? What was his quarrel with me? Devil take him if I appreciate that. Indeed, I very much dislike it, that I'll swear. But there's one thing I'll say for him. He's got the hardest knuckles I've ever felt on my shoulders.'

The steward kept his right arm in a sling, as if it had been confracturated. 'It was the devil that persuaded me to come to this wedding,' said he. 'God damn me if I haven't got both my arms smashedgroundandpulverized. Do you call this a wedding? I call it a shitten funeral. I call it a perishing banquet of the Lapithae, as described by Lucian.'

The Bum-bailiff was past speaking. The beadles excused themselves by saying that they had not meant any harm by their thumping, and begged to be forgiven, for God's sake; and so they departed.

A mile and a half from there the Bum-bailiff felt somewhat unwell. But the beadles got to the Isle Bouchart, and publicly announced that they had never met a finer gentleman than the Lord of Basché, or a more hospitable house than his, and that there never had been such a wedding. The fault had been entirely on their side, they admitted, since they had struck the first blows. How many more days they lived I don't know. But from that time it was firmly believed that Basché's money was more pestilential, deadly, and pernicious to Bum-bailiffs and beadles than was the gold of Toulouse in ancient times, or Seius's horse to its possessor. So ever since then my Lord of Basché has been left in peace, and a Basché wedding has become a proverbial phrase.

CHAPTER 16: *Friar John's Investigations into the character of Bum-bailiffs*

'THAT would seem a jolly tale,' said Pantagruel, 'if we weren't bidden never to let the fear of God out of our minds.'

'It would have been a better one,' said Epistemon, 'if that hail of young gauntlets had fallen on the fat Prior. Since it amused him to fritter his money on annoying Basché and getting his Bum-bailiffs beaten, a rap or two over his shaven head would have done him no harm, especially when you think of the extortions we see itinerant judges like him practising nowadays under the village elm. After all, what crime were those poor Bum-bailiffs committing?'

'In this connexion,' said Pantagruel, 'I am reminded of an ancient Roman gentleman called Lucius Neratius. He was of a noble family and was rich in his time, but he had a very tyrannical nature. When he came out of his palace, he had the wallets of his servants filled with gold and silver coins. Then, when he met any spruce young gentleman, more smartly dressed than he, without the least provocation he would gaily give him a hard punch or two in the face. Then, straight away, to appease his victim and prevent his complaining to the magistrates, he would hand him some money. This would satisfy the beaten man, since it would be quite as much as the damages Lucius Neratius would have had to pay for the assault by the Law of Twelve Tables;

and that is how he spent his fortune, paying out his money for the pleasure of beating people.'

'By St Benedict's holy tun,' said Friar John, 'I'll put this idea to the test, here and now.' So he went ashore, plunged his hand into his great purse, and brought out twenty gold crowns. Then, having gathered a large crowd of these Bum-bailiffs around him, he shouted out before them all: 'Who'd like to earn twenty crowns for taking the very devil of a beating?' 'Io, io, io!' they all cried. 'You'll knock us out all right, sir. Sure enough you will. But there's good money in this.' And the whole mob rushed up to see who could get the first date for this precious beating.

Friar John chose out of the whole crowd one red-nosed Bum-bailiff, who wore a great broad silver ring on the thumb of his right hand with a very large toad-stone set in the bezel. But as he picked him out, I heard all the others complaining. One tall, thin young Bum-bailiff, a good and clever scholar who was reported to be a decent enough fellow from the Ecclesiastical Court, grumbled and muttered that Red-nose took all their trade, and that if there were only thirty blows to be had on the whole of their territory, he would take twenty-eight and a half of them. But all this complaining and grumbling was only from jealousy.

Friar John gave Red-nose a thundering good hiding with a heavy stick, on his back and belly, arms and legs, head and all; and I thought he had beaten him to death. Then he threw him the twenty crowns, and the wretch struggled to his feet, as pleased as Punch – or as two Punches. Then the rest of them clamoured around Friar John, saying: 'Sir, sir, Friar Devil, if you would like to beat one or two more of us we would take it at a reduced price. We're at your service, all of us, Master Devil, sir. We're absolutely all at your service, bags, papers, pens, and everything.'

But Red-nose shouted against them, crying as loud as he could: 'God's bloody bones, you cadgers, what do you mean by poaching on my territory? Are you trying to capture my clients and inveigle them from me? I summons you before the Church Courts for this day week in the morning-o. I'll law you and claw you like the devil of Vauverd.' Then he turned to Friar John, and said with a gay laugh: 'Reverend Father in Devilry, if you've found me a good subject, and if it would amuse you to beat me some more, I'll be satisfied with half the price, and reckon it quite fair. Don't spare me, please. I am entirely at your service, absolutely and entirely, Master Devil, head, lungs, guts, and all. I say this, and I mean it.'

But Brother John cut the fellow's speech short, and moved away. The rest of the Bum-bailiffs then turned to Panurge, Epistemon, Gymnaste, and the others, and humbly begged for the honour of a beating for a very small sum, because otherwise they were in danger of a very long fast. But nobody would listen to them.

Later, when we were looking for water for the ship's crew, we met two old She-bailiffs of the locality, miserably weeping and lamenting together. But Pantagruel had stayed on board, and was already sounding the recall. We imagined that they were relations of the Bum-bailiff who had taken a beating, and asked them the cause of all this grief. They answered that they had every reason to weep, seeing that at that hour two of the most honest fellows in all Bum-bailiff-land had just been yanked by the neck on a gibbet.

'My pages often yank a sleeping comrade by the toe,' said Gymnaste. 'So to yank a man by the neck must mean to hang or strangle him.'

'Of course, of course,' said Friar John. 'You speak like St John of the 'Pocalypse.'

When they asked the old women the cause of this hanging, the answer they got was that they had removed a holy treasure and put it in safe keeping.

'That's a very high allegory,' said Epistemon. 'What I think its meaning is that they stole the church plate, and put it in the care of Mother Earth, at the end of their own gardens.'

CHAPTER 17: *Pantagruel passes the Isles of Vacuum and Void, and of the strange Death of Slitnose the Windmill-swallower*

THAT same day Pantagruel passed the Isles of Vacuum and Void, in which they did not find so much as a frying-pan. For the great giant Slitnose had swallowed all the pots and pans, kettles and cauldrons, saucepans and dripping-pans, in the whole land, owing to the lack of windmills, which were his ordinary food. It had happened that shortly before dawn, which was the hour of his digestion, he had fallen seriously ill with a certain stomach disorder. The cause, according to

the physicians, was that the digestive faculties of his stomach, naturally accustomed to absorb windmills with their sails whirring, had not
been able completely to assimilate the pots and cauldrons. He had
digested the kettles and saucepans well enough, as was evident from
the bubbles and sediment in the four barrels of urine that he had filled
that morning on two occasions.

They tried different methods of relieving him, according to their
art. But the malady was stronger than their remedies; and that morning the noble Slitnose had passed away in so strange a manner that
Aeschylus's death will now seem quite a natural occurrence. The
soothsayers, as you'll remember, had fatefully foretold to him that he
would be killed on a certain day by the fall of something which would
strike him on the head. On that day he had gone out of town, and
kept away from all houses, rocks, and other things that might fall and
hurt him as they fell. So he sat down in the middle of a wide field,
trusting himself to the mercy of the clear and open sky, in perfect
safety, as it seemed to him, unless, of course, the sky should fall, which
he believed to be impossible. They say all the same that the larks very
much fear the collapse of the heavens. For if the heavens fell they
would all be caught.

The Celts who lived along the Rhine in ancient days – the noble,
valiant, chivalrous, warlike, and valiant French, that is – dreaded it too.
For when Alexander the Great asked them what they most feared in
the world, hoping that when they thought of his great deeds and victories, his conquests and triumphs, they would say that they feared
only him, they answered that the one thing they feared was that the
sky might fall. They did not refuse, however, to enter into alliance,
league, and amity with this brave and magnanimous monarch, if you
believe Strabo, *Book VII*, and Arrian, *Book I*.

Plutarch also, in his book *Of the Face that appears on the Body of the
Moon*, tells of one Pharnaces who feared that the moon might fall on
the earth, and felt great pity for those who, like the Ethiopians and the
Taprobanians, dwelt right under her. It worried him to think what
might happen to them if such a great mass were to fall on their heads.
He would have been equally afraid for the earth and the sky, if they
had not been securely propped up and supported on the Pillars of
Atlas, as was the opinion of the ancients, according to Aristotle's testimony in his fifth book of *Metaphysics*.

But, notwithstanding all his precautions, Aeschylus was killed by the fall of a tortoise-shell, which descended from the claws of an eagle high in the air, struck him on the head and broke his skull.

You need not wonder either at the death of the poet Anacreon, who choked over a grape-pip; nor at that of Fabius, the Roman praetor, whose breath was stopped by a goat's hair as he was drinking a bowl of milk; nor at that of the timid fellow who so feared to let a fart and make a bad smell in the presence of the Roman Emperor Claudius that he dropped down dead, from holding his wind; nor at that of the man who is buried on the Flaminian Way at Rome, and who complains in his epitaph that he died from a cat-bite on the little finger; nor at that of Quintus Lecanius Bassus, who suddenly died of a tiny, almost invisible, needle-prick on the thumb of his left hand; nor at that of Quenelault, the Norman physician, who suddenly dropped down dead at Montpellier after hacking a fleshworm out of his hand with a penknife.

Philemon's death need not surprise you either. His servant had prepared some figs for his first course at dinner. But while he went for the wine a stray jackass had got into the house and solemnly consumed the figs where they lay. When Philemon came in, he gazed with fascination at this graceful fig-eating ass; and on his servant's reappearance he remarked: 'Seeing that you left the figs for this reverent ass, it's only right that you should give him a drink. Let him have some of that good wine you've just brought up.' After he had said this he became so exceedingly jovial, and burst into such enormous and continuous laughter, that the strain on his spleen took his breath right away and he suddenly died.

Spurius Saufeius's end need not surprise you either, though he died of eating a soft-boiled egg as he came out of the bath; nor need the tale that Boccaccio tells about the man who dropped down dead from picking his teeth with a sage-stalk. You need not wonder either at Philip Placuit, who, being sound and fit, dropped dead in one minute, while paying an old debt, without any previous malady; or at Zeuxis, the painter, who suddenly died of laughing as he looked at the features of an old hag in a portrait that he had painted; or at innumerable others which are recorded for us by Verrius or Pliny, or Valerius, or Baptista Fulgosus, or Bacabery the elder.

The excellent Slitnose, alas, died of choking, while eating a lump of fresh butter at the mouth of a hot oven on his physician's instructions. We also learnt on this visit that the King of Cullan in Void had defeated the satraps of King Mechloth, and sacked the fortresses of Nix.

After that we passed the islands of Nout and Snout, as well as those of Teleniabin and Geneliabin, which are very fruitful in material for suppositories. We also sailed past the islands of Ewig and Einig,[1] which once cost the Landgrave of Hesse some trouble.

CHAPTER 18: *How Pantagruel survived a great Storm at Sea*

THE next day nine transports passed us on the starboard side, laden with monks, Jacobins, Jesuits, Capuchins, Hermits, Augustines, Bernardins, Celestins, Theatins, Egnatians, Amadeans, Franciscans, Carmelites, Minims, and other holy brethren who were going to the Council of Chesil[2] to chew over the articles of faith against the new heretics. When he saw them Panurge was overjoyed. For now he felt certain of meeting with every good fortune, both that day and for many days afterwards in a long succession. So after courteously greeting the holy fathers and recommending the salvation of his soul to their fervent prayers and private devotions, he had seventy-eight dozen hams, a quantity of caviare, saveloys in tens, and hundreds of dried fish-roes, together with two thousand fine angels for the souls of the departed, flung aboard their ship.

Pantagruel stood by, pensive and melancholy; and when Panurge noticed his state of mind he asked him the cause of this unaccustomed depression. But just then the captain, who had observed the fluttering of the weather-pennant on the stern and expected a fierce squall followed by a sudden hurricane, piped all hands on deck. All came up, officers, sailors, shipboys, and passengers. The sails were lowered: the mizzen-sail, mizzen top-sail, lug-sail, main-sail, studding-sail, and sprit-sail. He then had the top-sail hauled down, also the fore-topsail

1. This refers to a quarrel between the Emperor Charles V and the Landgrave of Hesse, about whether the Landgrave had been exempted from perpetual imprisonment, and could be imprisoned for a term of years, or whether his exemption covered all and any imprisonment. The argument hinged on these two words in a document.

2. In Hebrew, the baleful star. This refers to the Council of Trent.

and main-topsail, and lowered the mizzen-mast and all the yardarms, leaving only the ratlins and the shrouds.

Suddenly the sea began to swell and rage from the lower depths. Mighty waves struck the sides of our ship. The nor'-wester whistled through our shrouds, in a wild hurricane, accompanied by black squalls, terrible gusts, and deadly scuds of wind. The heavens thundered above us; it flashed and lightened, rained, and hailed. The sky lost its brightness and became thick, dark, and overcast. Soon there was no glimmer in the heavens but the sheet and forked lightning, and fiery rents in the clouds. Tempests and squalls, whirlwinds and hurricanes were lighted up all around us by thunderbolts, flashes, forked lightning, and other aerial manifestations. Our looks expressed horror and dismay, as the hideous tempests whipped the mountainous waves of the sea. Believe me, we felt that ancient Chaos had come again; that fire, earth, sea, air, and all the elements were in rebellious confusion.

After Panurge had plentifully fed the scavenger fish with the contents of his stomach, he lay hunched up on the deck, in complete misery and depression, and looking half dead. He called on all the blessed saints, male and female, to help him, swore that he would make confession at a suitable time and place, and then cried out in great terror: 'Steward, ho! My friend, my father, my uncle, bring me a little salt pork! We're going to have only too much to drink soon, from what I can see. Eat little and drink much, will be my motto from now on. I would to God and the blessed, worthy, and holy Virgin, that now, at this very moment, I were comfortably on dry land. How blessed, blessed, and four times blessed are those men who plant cabbages in the solid earth. Why, O Fates, did you not spin me a cabbage-planter's lot? Few and signally blessed are those whom Jupiter has destined to be cabbage-planters. For they've always one foot on the ground and the other not far from it. Anyone is welcome to argue about felicity and supreme happiness. But the man who plants cabbages I now positively declare to be the happiest of mortals. And I have better reason for saying this than Pyrrho had when he was in a similar danger to ours and saw a pig on the shore eating scattered barley. He declared the creature to be fortunate in two respects, in having plenty of barley, and in being on dry land in addition. Oh, there is no such divine and lordly habitation as the earth which a cow treads!

Blessed Saviour, this wave will sweep us away! Bring me a little vine-gar, my friends. I'm sweating in my agony. Alas, the halyards have snapped, the anchor-cable is in pieces, the thimbles are breaking, the main-mast top is plunging into the sea, our keel is sky-high, our cables are nearly all destroyed. Alas, alas, where are your top-sails? *Alles ist verloren, bei Gott!*[1] Our main-top has run adrift. Alas, who will claim this wreck? Oh, help me, somebody, on to one of these stout timbers. Lads, your stay-tackling's falling. Oh, oh, don't desert the tiller, or the tackle either! I can hear the rudder-post cracking. Is it broken? For God's sake, let's save the rudder-tackle, and don't worry about the stays. Be-be-be bous, bous! Look to the needle of your compass, for heaven's sake, Master Stargazer, and tell us where this hurricane's coming from. I'm in a fine frenzy, I can tell you. Bou, bou, bou, bous, bous! It's all up with me. I'm shitting myself in an utter frenzy of fear. Bou, bou, bou, bou! Oh, oh, oh, oh, oh, oh, oh! Oh, oh, oh, oh, oh, oh, oh! Bou, bou, bou, ou, ou, ou, bou, bou, bous, bous! I'm drown-ing, I'm drowning, I'm drowning, I'm a dead man! Good friends, I'm drowning!'

CHAPTER 19: *The Behaviour of Panurge and Friar John during the Storm*

FIRST Pantagruel implored the aid of the great God, our Protector, and offered up a public prayer of fervent devotion. Then, on the cap-tain's advice, he clung tight and firmly to the mast. Friar John had stripped to his doublet to help the seamen, and so had Epistemon, Ponocrates, and the others. But Panurge remained squatting on the deck, weeping and moaning. Friar John noticed him as he was passing along the middle deck, and called to him: 'For God's sake, Panurge you calf, Panurge you blubberer, Panurge you coward, come and help us! That would be far better than moaning away there like a cow, squatting on your ballocks like a baboon.'

'Be, be, be, bous, bous, bous,' wailed Panurge, 'Oh Brother John, oh my dear friend, oh my dear father, I'm drowning, I'm drowning, my friend, I'm drowning. It's all up with me, my ghostly father, my friend, I'm done for. Your cutlass couldn't save me from this. Alas,

1. My God, all is lost (German).

alas, now we're higher than the top-note, right out of the scale. Be be be, bous, bous! Alas, and now we're below the bottom C. I'm drowning. Oh my father, my uncle, my all! The water has got into my shoes by way of my shirt collar. Bous, bous, bous, paisch, hu, hu, hu, hu, ho, ho, ho, ho, ho. I'm drowning! Alas, alas, hu, hu, hu, hu, hu, hu! Bebe, bous, bous, bobous, bobous, ho, ho, ho, ho, ho! Alas, alas! Now I'm just like a forked tree, with my legs in the air and my head down. Would to God I were at this moment in that ship with the good and blessed council-bound fathers whom we saw this morning. Such fat and devout and jolly fellows they were, so sleek and so gracious. Heigh-ho, heigh-ho, heigh-ho, alas, alas, that devilish wave – *mea culpa Deus* – I mean God's blessed wave will drive our ship to the bottom. Alas, Father John, my father, my friend, take my confession! Here you see me on my knees. *Confiteor*, your holy benediction.'

'Come, you hangdog devil,' cried Friar John. 'Come, in the name of the thirty legions of hell, come and help us! ... But will he come?'

'Let's not swear at this moment, my friend and father,' said Panurge. 'To-morrow we'll swear as much as you like. Heigh-ho, heigh-ho, alas, our ship's letting water. I'm drowning. Alas, alas! Be be be be be bous, bous, bous, bous! Now we're on the bottom. Alas, alas! I'll give eighteen hundred thousand crowns in rents to anyone who'll put me ashore, all stinking and shitten as I am, if ever a man was in my shitten country. *Confiteor*. Alas, listen to just one word of a will, or a little codicil at least.'

'May a thousand devils leap on this cuckold's body,' cried Friar John. 'In God's name, why talk about wills at this moment? We're in extreme peril, and we must bestir ourselves now or never. Here, will you come, you devil? Bo'sun, my hearty! That was neat work, mate. Here, Gymnaste, up on the bridge! That wave fairly did for us. Look, our light's put out. We're rushing headlong to meet those million devils.'

'Alas, alas,' cried Panurge, 'alas! Bou, bou, bou, bou, bous. Alas, alas! was it here that we were fated to perish? Ho, ho, good people, I'm drowning, I'm a dead man. *Consummatum est*. I'm done for.'

'Magna, gna, gna,' exclaimed Friar John. 'Isn't he a sight, the shitten blubberer? Here, boy, in all the devils' names, look to the pump.

Are you hurt? For God's sake, cling on to one of the stanchions. Here, on this side, in the devil's name! Ho, like this, my boy.'

'Oh, brother John, my spiritual father, my friend, let's not swear. It's a sin. Alas, alas! Be be be, bous, bous, bous. I'm drowning, I'm a dead man, my friends. I pardon everyone. Good-bye. *Into Thy hands*. Bous, bous, bououououos! St Michael of Aure, St Nicholas, help me now or never! Here I make a solemn vow to you and to Our Lord, that if you come to my help now – I mean if you save me from this danger and put me ashore – I'll build you a great lovely little chapel or two,

> Between Candes and Montsoreau,
> Where cow or calf shall never graze.

Alas, alas, more than eighteen bucketsful or more have poured into my mouth. Bous, bous, bous. It's very salty and bitter.'

'By the virtue of the blood, flesh, belly, and head of God,' cried Friar John, 'if I hear you moaning again, you devil's cuckold, I'll maul you like a sea-wolf. By God, why don't we throw the man to the bottom of the sea? That's neat work, you at the oars! Like that, my friend! Hold on tight, up there! I think all the devils are unchained to-day, or else Proserpine's in labour. All the devils are dancing a morris.'

CHAPTER 20: *The Captains abandon their Ships at the height of the Storm*

'Ho, you're committing a sin, Brother John, my former friend,' cried Panurge. 'I said former friend, for now I'm no more and you're no more. It grieves me to say so, since I think that swearing like that is very good for your spleen. Just as it's a great relief for a woodchopper if someone near him cries *H'm* very loud at each stroke; and just as it's a marvellous comfort to a skittles-player who has thrown crooked if some lively fellow near him leans forward and half turns his head and body towards the place where the ball would have hit the skittles if it had been thrown straight. But it's a sin you're committing all the same, my sweet friend. Suppose we were to eat some *cabirotados*, or goat stews, should we be safe from this storm? I've read that the servants of the Cabiri, the Gods that Orpheus celebrates, were never afraid at sea, in times of storms. They were always safe. You can read about them in Apollonius, Pherecydes, Strabo, Pausanias, and Herodotus.'

'He's raving, poor devil,' said Friar John. 'May the horned cuckold be seized by a thousand, a million, and a hundred million devils. Lend us a hand here, my boy. Isn't he coming? Here, on the port. By God's headful of relics, what monkey prayers are you muttering there between your teeth? This devilish sea-calf is the cause of the whole storm, and he's the only one who won't help the crew. I swear that if I get at you, I'll give you the stormy devil's own hiding. Aye, my sailor lad, hold on while I make a double knot. That's a good fellow. I wish to God that you were Abbot of Talemouze and the present Abbot were transferred to Croulé. Brother Ponocrates, you'll hurt yourself there. Epistemon, keep clear of those rails, I saw the lightning strike them.'

'Hoist!'

'That's right. Hoist, hoist, hoist. Clear the long-boat. Hoist.'

'God almighty, what's that? The ship's head's smashed to bits. Thunder away, devils, fart, belch, and shit your worst! A turd for that wave! God's truth, it almost swept me into the sea. I think the devils in their millions are holding their provincial chapter here or squabbling over the election of a new rector!'

'Port, there!'

'Right you are. Mind that pulley there, boy. Ho, for the devil's sake, mind out! Port, port!'

'Bebebebous, bous, bous,' blubbered Panurge, 'Bous, bous be bous, bous, bous, I'm drowning. Alas, alas! We've only got two of the four elements left to us here, fire and water. Bouboubous, bous, bous. If only it had been Almighty God's will that I were in the close at Seuilly at this minute, or at Innocent the pastry-cook's, opposite the painted cellars at Chinon, even if I had to strip to my doublet and cook the pasties myself. Hi, my man, don't you know how to throw me ashore? You know so many good tricks, they tell me. I'll give you my whole property in Salmigundia and the great revenue from my snail-farm, if you'll only contrive to set me on *terra firma*. Alas, alas, I'm drowning. Oh, my dear friend, since we can't come safely to port, let's get into some roads. Anywhere will do. Drop all your anchors. Let's get out of this danger, I beseech you. ... Heave the lead and the line, skipper. Let's know the depth of the deep. Take a sounding, my dear skipper, for God's sake, my friend! Find out if we're not just within our depth. We might be able to drink here without stooping. I almost believe we could.'

'Helm a-lee, ho!' cried the skipper, 'helm a lee! Hands to the halyards. Come, helm a-lee, helm a-lee! Haul at the tackle! Stand off from the sails! Ho, make fast below, make fast there! Ho, helm a-lee, and head on to the sea! Unhelm the tiller and let her drive!'

'Have we come to that?' asked Pantagruel. 'May the good God, our Saviour, help us now!'

'Let her ride,' cried Jamet Brahier, the stout skipper. 'Let her ride, and let every man think of his salvation. To your prayers, all of you, for nothing will help us now but a miracle from heaven.'

'Let's offer up a great fine vow,' said Panurge. 'Alas, alas, alas, bou, bou, bebebebous, bou, bous. Alas, alas! Let's pay for a pilgrim. Come, come, let everyone fork out his pennies towards it. Come, out with your purses!'

'Ho! On this side,' cried Friar John. 'To starboard, in the name of all the devils! Let her drive, for God's sake! Unhelm the tiller, ho! Let her drive, let her drive. Let's have a drink. Some of the best, I say, the best for the stomach. D'you hear me, steward? Produce it, exhibit it. It will all go down to all the hordes of hell, otherwise. Ho, page, bring me my drawer here – for that was what he called his breviary – Now, draw some, my friend, like this. God Almighty, that's fine hail and fine lightning too. When shall we come to All Saints Day? I think to-day's the unholy feast of the million devils.'

'Alas,' cried Panurge, 'Brother John's damning himself most thoroughly in advance. Oh what a good friend I'm losing in him! Alas, alas, now there's worse coming than ever. We're going from Scylla to Charybdis. Ho, ho, I'm drowning. *Confiteor*. One little word of a will, Brother John! Good Master Extractor of the Quintessence, my friend, my Achates! Xenomanes, my all! Alas, I'm drowning. Just two words of a will, here on this mat.'

CHAPTER 21: *The Storm continues, also some brief remarks on the Making of Wills at Sea*

'To make a will at this moment,' said Epistemon, 'when we ought to be stirring ourselves and helping the crew, if we want to avoid being wrecked, seems somewhat out of place to me. Indeed, it's as inappropriate as the behaviour of Caesar's subalterns and favourites on the invasion of Gaul. They wasted their time in drawing up their wills and codicils, lamenting their bad luck, and bewailing the absence of their wives and friends in Rome, when they ought to have resorted to arms and fought their hardest against the enemy Ariovistus. It's as plain folly as the way that carter carried on when his wagon was upset in a stubble-field. He went down on his knees to implore Hercules for help, instead of goading his oxen and putting out a hand to lift the wheels. What good will it do you here to make a will? Either we shall escape this danger, or we shall be drowned. If we escape it'll be no good to you. Wills have no value or authority unless the testator's dead. If we're drowned, won't it go down with us? Who'll take it to your executors?'

'Some kind wave will throw it ashore,' said Panurge, 'as it did Ulysses; and some king's daughter, going for a stroll in the fresh air, will find it. Then she'll see that it's properly executed, and have a magnificent monument erected for me near the shore, as Dido did for her husband Sichaeus; as Aeneas did for Deiphobus, on the Trojan shore near Rhaete; as Andromache did for Hector in the city of Buthrotum; as Aristotle did for Hermeias at Eubulus; as the Athenians did for the poet Euripides; the Romans for Drusus in Germany, and for Alexander Severus, their Emperor, in Gaul; as Argentarius did for Callaeschrus; as Xenocritus did for Lysidice; as Timares did for his son Teleutagoras; as Eupolis and Aristodice did for their son Theotimus; as Onestes did for Timocles; as Callimache did for Sopoles, the son of Dioclides; as Catullus did for his brother; as Statius did for his father; and as Germain de Brie did for Hervé, the Breton captain.'

'Are you raving?' asked Friar John. 'Come here and help us, in the name of the five hundred thousand million cartloads of devils. Help us, may the pox gnaw your moustaches and three wide rows of cankerous sores make you a pair of breeches and a new codpiece. Has our ship struck a reef? For God's sake, how shall we tug it off? There's the very devil of a sea running. We shall never get away, devil take me if we shall!' At this point a piteous prayer was heard from Pantagruel, who cried aloud: 'Lord God, save us. We are perishing. Yet may it not be according to our desires, but Thy will be done.'

'God and the blessed Virgin be with us,' wailed Panurge. 'Alas, alas, I'm drowning. Bebebebous, bebe, bous, bous. Into Thy hands! Dear God, send me a dolphin to carry me ashore like a sweet little Arion. I shall play my harp most beautifully, if it's not ruined.'

'All the devils may take me,' said Friar John. 'God be with us,' muttered Panurge between his teeth. 'But if I come down there to you,' resumed Friar John, 'I'll give you good proof that your balls hang from the arse of a cuckoldy calf, a horned calf with a broken horn. Mgnan, mgnan, mgnan. Come here and help us, you great weeping calf, in the name of the thirty thousand devils. May they leap on your body! Are you coming, sea-calf? Fi, what an ugly blubberer it is!'

'You never say anything fresh,' protested Panurge.

'Now, out with my pretty little appetizer, my sweet breviary, and let me rub up your feathers. *Beatus vir qui non abiit.* Blessed is he that walketh not in the counsel of the ungodly. I know all that by heart. Let's look at the legend of our master Saint Nicholas.

Horrida tempestas montem turbavit acutum.[1]

Tempête was a great whipper of schoolboys at the College of Montaigu. If pedagogues are damned for whipping poor little children, their innocent scholars, he's on Ixion's wheel, I'll be bound, whipping the bob-tailed cur that keeps it turning. If they're saved for whipping innocent children, on the other hand, he must be high above the ...'

CHAPTER 22: *The Storm ends*

'LAND, land!' cried Pantagruel. 'I see land. Pluck up a sheep's courage, my lads, and we'll be safe in port. I can see the sky beginning to clear on the northern horizon. Now wait for a south-easter.'

'Courage, my lads,' said the skipper; 'the swell's dying down.

1. The awful Tempête created hell at Montaigu *or* The awful tempest swept the mountain peaks.

Hands to the main-top! Helm a-weather, helm a-weather! Up with the mizzen top-sail! Man the capstan! Heave, heave, heave. Back with the tiller. Haul hard at the rope-end. Clear the tacks! Clear the sheets! Clear the bowlines! Tack to port! Put the helm under the wind! Pull on the starboard sheet, you son of a whore.'

'You must be very pleased, my good lad,' said Friar John, 'to hear this news of your mother.'

'Luff, luff,' cried the captain. 'Keep her short and full. Right the helm.'

'Right it is,' answered the sailors.

'Cut along, and head straight for the harbour! Now the links! Get the bonnets a-tack! Heave, heave!'

'That's good. He knows his craft, and it's a joy to hear him,' said Friar John. 'Ho, ho, ho, lads, put your backs into it! Good! Heave now, heave!'

'Look lively, on the starboard!'

'That's good and a joy to hear. I think the storm has passed its crisis. I think it is dying down. Glory be, and the Lord be praised for it! Our devils are beginning to scamper off.'

'Gently now!'

'That's good sound sense. He knows his craft. Gently, gently! Here, by God. Come here, my gentle Ponocrates, you lusty fornicator. He'll get none but male children, the lecher! Eusthenes, my brave friend, up with you to the fore-top!'

'Heave, heave!'

'That's right. Heave, in God's name, heave, heave!'

> I shall fear nothing to-day,
> For to-day's a holiday.
> Noel, Noel, Noel!

'That's a fine shanty,' said Epistemon. 'It's not far out either. For to-day is a holiday. I like it.'

'Heave, heave! Good!'

'Oh,' cried Epistemon, 'I've good news for you all. I can see Castor there to starboard. Cheer up, I tell you.'

'Be be bousbousbous,' blubbered Panurge. 'I'm very much afraid it's that bitch Helen.'

'Truly, it's Mixarchagetas,' answered Epistemon, 'if you prefer the name the Argives gave him. Ho, ho, I see land! I can see harbour! I can see a great crowd on the mole. I can see fire on the *obelischolychny*.'[1]

'Ahoy, ahoy,' cried the captain. 'Double the cape and the rocks.'

'Doubled they are,' cried the sailors.

'Away she goes,' cried the captain, 'and so do the rest of our fleet. Drink to the fair weather!'

'That sounds good, by St John,' cried Panurge. 'That's grand to hear.'

'Mgna, mgna, mgna,' muttered Friar John. 'If you ever taste a drop, may the devil taste my blood! Do you hear that, you miserable devil? Skipper, here's a full tankard of the best. Bring up the hogsheads there, Gymnaste, and that thumping great iambic or gammonic pie; legs or hams are all one to me. Mind you bring her in right.'

'Courage,' cried Pantagruel, 'courage, my lads, and let's show our hospitality. For here, almost alongside us, are two coracles, three rowing-boats, five little ships, and eight skiffs, that the good people of this near-by island have sent to save us. But who is that Ucalegon, that useless idler, there below moaning in such distress? Wasn't I holding the mast firmly in my hands, and didn't I keep it straighter than two hundred cables could have done?'

'It's that poor devil Panurge,' replied Friar John, 'who's got the shivering fits. He always trembles with fear when he's full.'

'If he was afraid during that awful turmoil and in the perils of the storm,' said Pantagruel, 'so long as he's acted like a man otherwise I don't think a jot the less of him. It's a dull and cowardly heart that's afraid at every emergency, as Agamemnon was, which is why Achilles ignominiously reproached him with having a dog's eyes and a stag's heart. But not to be afraid when the situation is obviously perilous, is a sign of scant intelligence, or none at all. Now if there is one thing in this life to fear, other than offending God, I won't say that it's death, pure and simple. I don't want to join issue with Socrates and the Academics. Death is not an evil in itself. But I do say that if anything is to be feared it is that particular death by shipwreck. For, as Homer remarks, it is a grievous, beastly, and unnatural thing to perish at sea. Aeneas, in fact, during the storm that surprised his fleet near Sicily, regretted that he had not died at the hands of the brave Diomedes. He declared those who had perished in the fires of Troy three-

1. A lighthouse in the form of an obelisk.

times and four-times blessed. Here on board no one has died. God our
Saviour be eternally praised for that! But truly we're in sad disorder.
All right. Then we shall have to repair the wreck. Mind out that we
don't run aground!'

CHAPTER 23: *How Panurge was the best of companions, once
the Storm was over*

'HA, ha,' cried Panurge. 'All's well. The storm's over. Please let me
be the first to go ashore. I've got some private business that I want to
deal with. Can I do anything for you there? Just let me coil that rope.
I've plenty of courage, you see, and there's not much fear in me.
Throw it over to me, friend. No, no, not a jot of fear. True, that tenth
wave which broke over us from stem to stern made my pulse beat a
bit faster.'

'Lower the sails.'

'That's good hearing. But, Brother John, are you idling there? Is
this the time to be drinking? Who knows if St Martin's footman, the
devil, isn't brewing us another storm? Do you want me to help you
over there? By God, I'm very sorry now, though it's too late, that I
didn't follow the good philosophers' teaching. They say that to walk
near the sea and sail near the land is as safe and pleasant as to walk beside your horse when you're leading him by the bridle. Ha, ha, ha,
all's well, by God! Can I give you a hand again there? Throw it over
to me. I'll see to that all right, or the devil's in it.'

Epistemon had the palm of one hand all raw and bloody from pulling with might and main at one of the cables. But when he heard
Pantagruel's words on the subject of fear, he exclaimed: 'Believe me,
my Lord, I was every bit as frightened and terrified as Panurge. But
that didn't prevent me from helping. I consider that if it's a fatal and
inevitable necessity that we die – and indeed it is – then it rests in
God's hands at what hour and in what manner we meet our death.
Therefore, we must unceasingly implore, invoke, pray, beseech, and
supplicate him. But we must not confine ourselves to that. We must
also make efforts on our own account and, as the Holy Apostle says,
be workers together with him. You know what Caius Flaminius, the
consul, said when Hannibal caught him in a trap, and hemmed him

against the Perusian Lake called Trasimene? "My lads," he said to his soldiers, "you can't expect to get away from here by vows and prayers to the gods. We shall need all our strength and manhood to escape. We shall have to hack our way with our bare swords through the ranks of the enemy." Similarly, as Sallust tells us, Marcus Portius Cato said that the divine aid wasn't to be won by idle vows and womanish lamentations. If you watch and work and struggle your hardest, said he, everything comes out right, and just as you wish it. But if a man is careless, gutless, and lazy in a moment of danger or necessity, it's no good his calling on the gods; he merely provokes and annoys them.'

'Devil take me,' began Friar John.

'I'll go halves with him,' interrupted Panurge.

'Devil take me,' Friar John resumed, 'if the close at Seuilly wouldn't have been stripped and destroyed if I'd only sung *Contra hostium insidias* – that's breviary stuff, that is – as the other devils of monks did, and if I hadn't protected the vineyards against those robbers from Lerné with stout blows with the staff of my cross.'

'On with the vessel,' cried Panurge. 'All goes well. But Brother John's doing nothing there. Friar John Do-nothing, that's his name. He just watches me sweating and toiling here, to help this honest sailor – the first sailor I've ever called honest. Just two words with you, my friend, and don't take what I say amiss. What's the thickness of this vessel's planks?'

'They're a good two inches thick,' answered the captain. 'Don't be frightened.'

'Almighty God, then,' said Panurge. 'So we're always just two inches from death. Is this one of the nine joys of marriage? Ha, Captain, you're right to measure danger by the yardstick of fear. I've no fear myself. They call me William the Fearless. I've enough courage and more than that. I don't mean a sheep's courage. I mean a wolf's courage, a murderer's coolness. I fear nothing – except danger.'

CHAPTER 24: *Friar John proves that Panurge was needlessly frightened during the Storm*

'GOOD-DAY to you, gentlemen,' said Panurge. 'Good-day to you, one and all. I trust that you are all well. Yes, thank heaven, and you? You're all heartily welcome, and you've come just in time. You, coxswains, there, put down the gang-plank, and bring that skiff alongside. Shall I give you a hand again? I feel like working as hard as four oxen. There's a real wolf's hunger in me for work. This is a fine place truly, and these are fine people. Have you anything more you want me to help with, my lads? Don't spare the sweat of my body, for goodness' sake. Adam – who is man – was born to labour and toil, as birds were made to fly. It's the will of the Lord, you understand, that we should eat our bread in the sweat of our brows, not in idleness, like that monk, Friar John, whom you see in his rags, drinking there, half dead with fear. Here's the fine weather. I know now how right that noble philosopher Anacharsis was. You remember his answer to the man who asked him what sort of vessel he thought was the safest. "A vessel in harbour," he said. That was a true and reasonable answer.'

'He made a better reply still,' said Pantagruel, 'when he was asked which were the more numerous, the living or the dead, "In which class do you count those at sea?" he asked. By which he meant subtly to infer that those who sail the seas are so close to the continuous peril of death that theirs is a living death, a deathly existence. Similarly, Portius Cato said that he only regretted three things: that is, having ever told a woman a secret, having ever spent a day in idleness, and having ever gone by sea to any place that could be reached by land.'

'By the worthy cloth I wear, my pusillanimous friend,' said Friar John to Panurge, 'you had no cause or reason to be frightened during the storm. For your fatal destiny is not to perish by sea. You're certain either to swing high in the air, or make a brave bonfire like a Church Father. Would you like a sound cloak against the rain, my Lord? Then don't buy any of your wolf-skin or badger-skin mantles. Flay Panurge, and make a coat of his skin. But don't go near the fire, or pass too close to a blacksmith's forge, for heaven's sake, or you'll find it in ashes in a minute. But you can expose it to the rain, or snow, or hail, as much as you like. You can even dive into the deepest water, by God, and you won't get wet. Make it into winter boots, and they'll never let water. Make bladders out of it, to teach the children to swim. They will learn without danger.'

'His skin, then,' said Pantagruel, 'will be like the herb called Maidenhair, which is never moist or damp, but always dry, even if it's been laid in water for any length of time. Therefore it is called *Adiantos*.'

'Panurge, my friend,' said Friar John, 'never fear the water, I beg of you. Your life will be ended by the opposite element.'

'Yes,' answered Panurge, 'but the devil's cooks are sometimes absent-minded, and make mistakes in their jobs. Often they put something on to boil which was meant to be roasted. Just as in our kitchens here the master-cooks often lard partridges, wood-pigeons, and doves with the probable intention of putting them on the roast. But it very often happens that they boil the partridges with the cabbage, the pigeons with the leeks, and the doves with the turnips.

'But I've something to tell you, my fair friends. I protest before this noble company that when I vowed a chapel to St Nicholas between Candes and Montsoreau I meant a chapel – a flask, that is – of rose-water. Cow or calf will never graze on it, because I shall throw it into deep water.'

'Well, what a rascal!' exclaimed Eusthenes. 'A rascal, and a rascal and a half! He's a perfect proof of the Lombards' proverb:

Passato el pericolo, gabbato el santo.[1]

CHAPTER 25: *After the Storm, Pantagruel visits the Isles of the Macreons*

IMMEDIATELY after this we landed at the port of an island called the Isle of the Macreons, or the Long-lived. The good people of the place gave us an honest welcome; and an old Macrobe – for that is what they called their senior aldermen – invited Pantagruel to their town-hall, to take refreshment, to feast and to rest. But he refused to leave the harbour until all his men had landed. Then, after he had called the roll, he ordered each one to be provided with new clothes, and the ships' provisions to be laid out on shore, so that all the crew could

1. Danger past, we bilk the saint.

have a feast. His orders were promptly obeyed, and God knows how much was eaten and drunk. All the people of the town brought food in plenty, and the Pantagruelists gave them more in return, though it is true that their provisions were somewhat damaged by the recent storm.

When the feast was over, Pantagruel begged everyone to return to duty and get busy repairing the damage. This they all did, and gladly. The job of repairs was much eased for them, however, by the islanders who were carpenters and artisans of all sorts, such as you find in the arsenal at Venice. The great island had only three ports and eight in-habited parishes; the rest was thick wood and waste land, as wild as the Ardennes forest.

At our request, the old Macrobe showed us all the sights worth see-ing in the island. In the shady and unfrequented forest, he pointed out several old ruined temples, several obelisks, pyramids, monu-ments, and ancient tombs, with different inscriptions and epitaphs. Some were in hieroglyphics, others in the Ionic tongue, others in Arabic, Hagarene, Slavonic, and other tongues, which Epistemon carefully copied down. Meanwhile Panurge said to Friar John: 'This is the island of the Macreons. Macreon, in Greek, means old man, a man stricken in years.'

'What do you want me to do about that?' asked Friar John. 'D'you want me to alter it? I wasn't in the country when they baptized it.' 'Now that I come to think of it,' said Panurge, 'I think that's the derivation of the word mackerel. For procuring, like a *maquereau* – or pimp – is an old man's job; the young prefer thigh-play. It's worth wondering if this isn't the original Mackerel Island, the model of the one in Paris. Now let's go and fish for oysters in their shells.'

The old Macrobe asked Pantagruel, in the Ionic tongue, how they had managed to make the port that day. It must have required great skill and efforts, he said, since there had been such terrible winds and such a fearful storm at sea. Pantagruel replied that our heavenly Saviour had taken pity on the simplicity and sincerity of his servants, who were not travelling for gain or to trade in merchandise. One reason, and one reason only, had sent them to sea: the earnest desire to see, to learn, to know, and to visit the oracle of Bacbuc, from which they hoped to receive the judgement of the Bottle on a problem posed by one of their company. Nevertheless they had not got so far without

great hardships and considerable danger of shipwreck. Then he asked
the old man what he thought was the probable cause of that frightful
hurricane, and whether the seas around that island were usually subject to storms, as the straits of Saint-Mathieu and Maumusson were in
the Atlantic, and various places in the Mediterranean, such as the Gulf
of Adalia, Porto di Telamone, Piombino, Capo Melio in Laconia, the
Straits of Gibraltar, the Straits of Messina, and others.

CHAPTER 26: *The good Macrobe tells Pantagruel what happens
on the Deaths of Heroes*

THEN the good Macrobe answered: 'Friends and strangers, this island
is one of the Sporades; not one of your Sporades which are in the sea
of Carpathos, but one of the oceanic Sporades. They were once fertile,
much visited, wealthy, and populous, and a centre of trade subject to
the power of Britain. Now, in the course of time and with the world's
decay, they have become poor and desolate, as you see. In this dark
forest before you, which is more than seventy-eight thousand parasangs in length and breadth, is the dwelling-place of the Demons and
Heroes who have become old. We have seen a comet shining for three
nights on end, but now it has disappeared. So we suppose that one of
them died yesterday and that it was his death that whipped up the terrible storm that came down on you. For while they live there is an
abundance of all good things in this place and on the neighbouring
islands, and continuous calm and fair weather prevail at sea. But when
one of them dies we habitually hear great and piteous lamentations in
the forest, and witness great plagues, disasters, and afflictions upon
earth. Then there are disturbances and darkness in the air, and storms
and tempests at sea.'

'There is some probability in what you say,' said Pantagruel. 'For
whilst a torch or candle is alive and burning, it shines on those near it,
lights up its surroundings, offers its help and brilliance to all, and does
no harm or displeasure to anyone. But the moment it is out, it poisons
the air with its smoke and vapour, offends everyone near it, and dis-
pleases everybody. It is the same with those noble and famous souls.
For so long as they inhabit their bodies, their presence brings peace,
pleasure, profit, and honour. But at the hour of their decease the isles

and the mainland are habitually disturbed by mighty commotions; by darkness, thunder, and hail in the air; by earthquakes, tremors, and horrors upon earth; by storms and tempests at sea, and by lamentations of the peoples, changes of religion, transfers of territory, and over-throws of states.'

'We have recently had experience of this ourselves,' said Episte-mon, 'on the death of the valiant and learned Guillaume du Bellay. Whilst he lived the fortunes of France were so great that the whole world envied her, the whole world sought her alliance, and the whole world dreaded her. Immediately after his death she became the scorn of the whole world, and has been so for a long time now.'

'That explains why after the death of Anchises at Trapani in Sicily the storm gave Aeneas such a terrible tossing,' said Pantagruel. 'And perhaps that's the reason also for the tyrannies and cruelty of Herod, King of Judaea, when he saw himself about to die of a dreadful and revolting disease. For he died of phthiriasis, devoured by lice and worms, as Lucius Sulla had died before him, and Pherecydes the Syrian, the teacher of Pythagoras, and the Greek poet Alcman, and others. He foresaw that on his death the Jews would light bonfires of rejoicing. So he summoned all the nobles and magistrates to his serag-lio from all the cities, towns, and castles of Judaea, under the fraudulent pretext of wishing to inform them of matters of importance concern-ing the government and protection of his province. When they had assembled, each arriving in person, he had them shut up in the seraglio hippodrome. Then he said to his sister Salome and her husband Alex-ander: "I am certain that the Jews will rejoice at my death. But if you will listen to my instructions and carry them out, I shall have an honourable funeral and there will be public mourning. The moment I have passed away, have all these noblemen and magistrates who are imprisoned here killed by the archers of my guard, to whom I have given express commands to this effect. If this is done all Judaea will be mourning and lamenting despite themselves, and strangers will think that it is on account of my death. It will just appear as if some heroic soul has died." '

'A certain desperate tyrant had the same idea in mind when he said: "Upon my death may the earth be enveloped in fire." That is to say, Let the whole world perish. That scoundrel Nero amended those words, as Suetonius testifies, into "During my life", a detestable sentiment, mentioned by Cicero, in his third book on the *Ends of Good Men*, and by Seneca, in his second *On Clemency*, and attributed by Dion Nicaeus and Suidas to the Emperor Tiberius.'

CHAPTER 27: *Pantagruel discourses on the Deaths of Heroic Souls, and tells of the Prodigies that occurred on the decease of the late Lord of Langey.*

'I WOULD not have missed the storm at sea which caused us such trouble and suffering,' said Pantagruel, 'if that had caused me also to miss the tale which the good Macrobe has just told us. I am very ready to believe what he says about the comet seen in the sky for some days before such a decease. For some of these souls are so noble, precious, and heroic that a few days before the event we receive heavenly notice of their impending death and departure. When the prudent physician sees from premonitory signs that his patient is approaching his death, he advises the wife, children, kindred, and friends of the imminent departure of their husband, father, or relative. This is so that, in the little time he has to live, they may exhort him to put his house in order, to instruct and bless his children, provide for his wife's widowhood, make all necessary dispositions for the education of his orphans, and not be surprised by death with his will unmade and his soul and household in disorder. Similarly, the kindly heavens seem to rejoice at the coming arrival of these blessed souls, and to let off fireworks before their decease in the form of comets and meteoric displays. These they intend as a sure prognostic and trustworthy prophecy to mankind that within a few days these venerable souls will forsake their bodies and the earth.

'It was exactly the same in Athens, in ancient times, when the judges of the Areopagus used certain signs to indicate their individual judgements in the cases of criminals on trial. These varied with the sentence, a Θ signifying the death penalty, a T pardon, and an A an adjournment – that is to say that the case was not yet clear. These signs, publicly displayed, relieved the relatives, friends, and acquaintances of those on trial from their doubts and anxieties, and informed them of the probable fate of criminals who were still in prison. In the same way the heavens tacitly say to us by comets, as by notices scrawled on the sky:

"Mortal men, if you wish to know, or learn, to ascertain, understand, or be advised of any matter of public or private importance known to these happy souls, call upon them as speedily as you can and obtain their answers. For the end and resolution of the play is at hand. If you let this moment pass your regrets will be vain."

'They do more. To show the earth and its inhabitants how unworthy they are of the presence, company, and enjoyment of such famous souls, they surprise and alarm us by prodigies, portents, monsters, and other premonitory signs which violate the whole order of Nature. This we saw several days before the departure of the most illustrious, generous, and heroic soul of that learned and valiant knight of Langey, of whom you have spoken.'

'I remember that,' said Epistemon, 'and my heart still shivers and trembles in my pericardium when I think of the many terrible prodigies that we clearly saw five or six days before his death. The Lords D'Assier, Chemant, Mailly the one-eyed, Saint-Ayl, Villeneuf, Guiart, Master Gabriel the physician from Savigliano, Rabelais, Cahuau, Massuau, Majorici, Bullou, Cercu called the Burgomaster, François Proust, Ferron, Charles Girard, François Bourré, and many others, friends, domestics, and servants of the deceased, gazed upon one another in silent dismay, uttering not a word with their tongues, but all assuredly reflecting and foreseeing in their hearts that France would shortly be deprived of this perfect knight, who was so essential for her glory and protection. They knew that the heavens were claiming his return, as their right and natural due.'

'By the tip of my cowl,' exclaimed Friar John, 'I should like to become a scholar in my old age. I've a pretty good intellect, let me tell you. Now allow me to ask you a question. I ask it

> As the king asks his bodyguard,
> And the queen asks her serving man.

Can death be the end of these heroes and demi-gods you tell us about? By Our Lady, in my ruminations I thought that they were immortal, like lovely angels – may the Lord pardon my ignorance. But this most reverend Macrobe says that they die once and for all.'

'Not all of them,' answered Pantagruel. 'The Stoics said that they were all mortal but one, who alone is immortal, incapable of suffering, and invisible. Pindar clearly says that those hard-hearted sisters the

Fates spin no more thread – that is to say life – from their flax and spindles for the Hamadryads than for the trees whose guardian goddesses they are. These are the oaks which, according to Callimachus and Pausanias, *in Phoci*, gave them birth. Martianus Capella, by the way, concurs in this opinion. As for the Demi-gods, Pans, Satyrs, Sylvans, Will-o'-the-Wisps, Aegipans, Nymphs, Heroes, and Demons, many men have from the sum total of the different aeons calculated by Hesiod, reckoned their lives to last 9,720 years. This figure was reached by raising the unity to quadrinity, multiplying the quadrinity by four, and then multiplying the sum five times by solid triangles. See Plutarch in his book *On the Obsolescence of Oracles*.

'That's no breviary stuff,' said Friar John. 'I'll only believe so much of it as you wish me to.'

'I believe that all intellectual souls are exempt from the scissors of Atropos,' said Pantagruel. 'They are all immortal, whether angelic, daemonic, or human. I'll tell you a story about that. It's a very strange one. But it's written down and vouched for by several learned and well-informed historians.'

CHAPTER 28: *Pantagruel's pitiable story about the Death of Heroes*

'EPITHERSES, the father of Aemilian the rhetorician, was sailing from Greece to Italy in a ship carrying a miscellaneous cargo and several passengers. Towards evening the wind failed them near the Echinades, some islands which lie between the Morea and Tunis, and their ship was carried towards Paxos, under the shore of which they hove to. Now, as some of the passengers were sleeping and some awake, as some were eating and some drinking, a voice was heard from the island of Paxos of someone loudly crying, *Thamous!* This cry terrified them all. This Thamous was their captain, an Egyptian. But he was only known by name to one or two of the passengers. The voice was heard a second time, loudly and terrifyingly calling, *Thamous!* No one replied, but all stood silent and trembling. Then the voice was heard a third time, more terrible than before. Upon which Thamous answered: "I am here. Who is calling me? What do you want me to do?"

Then the voice was heard again, even louder, commanding him, when he reached the port of Paloda, to announce the news that the great god Pan was dead.

'Epitherses related that when they heard this speech all the sailors and passengers were amazed and greatly frightened. They debated amongst themselves whether it would be better to say nothing or to proclaim the news they had been given. Thamous gave his decision that if they had a favourable wind behind them they ought to pass by and say nothing, but if they were becalmed he would declare what he had heard. When they came close to Paloda, it happened that both wind and tide failed them. So Thamous climbed on the prow and, facing towards the land, declared, as he had been told to, that the great Pan was dead. No sooner had he spoken the last word than loud sighs, lamentations, and shrieks were heard from the shore, coming not from one person alone, but from many together.

'Since there had been several witnesses, this news soon spread to Rome; and Tiberius Caesar, who was then Emperor, sent for this Thamous. When he had listened to him, he believed his story and, on inquiring from men of learning, who were plentiful at that time at his court and in Rome, who this Pan was, he gathered from their answers that he was the son of Mercury and Penelope, as had been recorded at an earlier date by Herodotus and by Cicero, in his third book *On the Nature of the Gods*.

'I should interpret this anecdote, nevertheless, to refer to that great Saviour of the Faithful, who was shamefully put to death in Judaea through the envy and wickedness of the pontiffs, doctors, priests, and monks of the Mosaic Law, and I do not consider my reading of the story far-fetched. For he can rightfully be called, in the Greek tongue, Pan; seeing that he is our All. All that we are, all that we live by, all that we have, all that we hope for is from him, in him, of him, and by him. He is the good Pan, the great shepherd who, as the lovesick swain Coridon affirms, loves not only his sheep with a great love, but his shepherds also. At his death there were wailings, sighs, fears, and lamentations throughout the whole mechanical universe, throughout the heavens, the earth, the sea, and hell beneath. The date agrees with this interpretation of mine. For that most good and mighty Pan, our Saviour, died outside Jerusalem in the reign of Tiberius Caesar.'

When Pantagruel had finished his story he remained silent, in a profound meditation. A little while afterwards we saw the tears rolling down from his eyes, as big as ostrich eggs. God take my soul, if every word I say isn't the truth.

CHAPTER 29: *Pantagruel sails past Sneaks' Island, where King Lent used to reign*

WHEN the ships of the jovial company were refitted and repaired, and their victuals had been replenished, the Macreons were left thoroughly satisfied and contented with Pantagruel's expenditure on their island. Our men, too, were more jovial than usual when we set sail on the following day, in high spirits, with a sweet and pleasant wind behind us. About midday Xenomanes pointed out Sneaks' Island in the distance, where ruled King Lent. Pantagruel had heard of him in the past, and would have liked to meet him in person. But Xenomanes dissuaded him, because it would take them far out of their course, and also because of the poor tables kept throughout the island and at the king's court.

'All you'll see there for your money,' said he, 'is a great guzzler of dried peas, a great herring-barrel man, a mighty mole-catcher, a powerful hay-trusser, a demi-giant with straggling whiskers, and a double tonsure. He's of Lantern-land stock and has a head full of whimsies. He's the standard-bearer of the Ichthyophagi, the dictator of Mustardland, a whipper of small children, and a burner of ashes. He's the father and patron of physicians, and he's all over pardons, indulgences, and solemn masses; a worthy man, a good Catholic, and thoroughly devout. He weeps three parts of the day, and never attends a wedding. But I must admit that he is the most industrious manufacturer of larding-sticks and skewers in all the forty kingdoms. About six years ago, when passing Sneaks' Island, I picked up a gross and gave them to the butchers of Candes, who thought very well of them and with good reason. When we get back I'll show you a pair of them, hung up on the great door of the church. His principal nourishment is salted hauberks, helmets, and morions, also salted sallets or salads, which sometimes give him a painful hot-piss. His dress is most cheerful, in cut as well as in colour: grey and cold, with nothing before and nothing behind, and sleeves to match.'

'Now that you've told me about his dress, his food, his way of life, and his amusements,' said Pantagruel, 'I'd be glad if you'd describe the shape and configuration of his bodily parts.'

'Yes, please do so, my ballocky friend,' said Friar John. 'For I've found him in my breviary. He comes next to the Movable Feasts.'

'I will gladly,' replied Xenomanes. 'We shall perhaps hear rather more of him when we touch at Savage Island, which is inhabited by the wild Chitterlings, his mortal enemies, with whom he is perpetually at war. If it wasn't for the help they get from their protector and good neighbour, the noble Shrove-Tuesday, that great Lanterner Lent would long ago have exterminated them, and destroyed their homes.'

'Are they male or female?' asked Friar John. 'Angels or mortals? Women or virgins?'

'They are of the female sex,' replied Xenomanes, 'and mortal by nature. Some are virgins and some are not.'

'Devil take me,' said Friar John, 'if I'm not on their side. Is it not a shameful disorder in Nature that men should fight against women? Let us go back and hack that great villain to pieces!'

'What, fight against Lent?' cried Panurge. 'By all the devils in hell I'm not so crazy or so rash as that. *Quid juris*, what would the law say, if we found ourselves caught between the Chitterlings and Lent, between the hammer and the anvil? A pox on that! Get it out of your mind, and let's go. Farewell to you, Master Lent. I recommend the Chitterlings to you, and don't forget the Sausages either.'

CHAPTER 30: *Xenomanes's Anatomy and Description of Lent*

'As for Lent's internal organs,' said Xenomanes, 'he has – or at least he had in my time - a brain of the size, colour, substance, and strength of a male flesh-worm's left ball.

His lobes are like a gimlet.
His vermiform excrescences like a tennis-racket.
His membranes like a monk's cowl.
His funnel like a mason's hod.
The vault of his cranium like a patchwork bonnet.
His pineal gland like a bagpipe.
His miraculous network like a head-stall.

His mammillary attachments like old shoes.
His eardrums like a whirligig.
His temple-bones like feather-dusters.
The nape of his neck like a lantern.
His nerves like taps.
His uvula like a pea-shooter.
His palate like a mitten.
His saliva like a shuttle.
His tonsils like a spy-glass.
The back of his mouth like a porter's hod.
His gullet like a grape-basket.
His stomach like a belt.
His pylorus like a pitchfork.
His trachea like a sickle.
His throat like a ball of tow.
His lungs like a fur-lined hood.
His heart like a chasuble.
His mediastinum like a forceps.
His arteries like a watchman's cloak.
His diaphragm like a cockaded cap.
His liver like a double axe.
His veins like canvas window-blinds.
His spleen like a quail-decoy.
His guts like a bird-net.
His gall like a cooper's adze.
His mesentery like an abbot's mitre.
His hunger-gut like a burglar's jemmy.
His blind-gut like a breastplate.
His colon like a drinking-cup.
His bum-gut like a monk's leather bottle.
His kidneys like a trowel.
His loins like a padlock.
His ureters like a pothook.
His emulgent veins like a pair of squirts.
His spermatic vessels like puff-pastry cake.
His prostate gland like a feather-jar.
His bladder like a catapult.
The neck of it like the clapper of a bell.

His abdomen like an Albanian's tall hat.
His peritoneum like an armlet.
His muscles like a bellows.
His tendons like a hawker's glove.
His ligaments like a hanging purse.
His bones like jaw-breaking biscuits.
His marrow like a wallet.
His cartilage like heath-tortoises or moles.
His neck-glands like a pruning-knife.
His animal spirits like a great punch on the jaw.
His vital spirits like hard flips in the face.
His seething blood like a rain of slaps on the nose.
His urine like a popefig.
His sperm like a hundred carpenter's nails.
And his nurse told me that when he married Maundy Thursday,
   he begot only a number of locative adverbs and certain double
   fasts.
He had a memory like a scarf.
His common sense was like a buzzing hive.
His imagination like a peal of bells.
His thoughts like a flight of starlings.
His conscience an unnesting of young herons.
His deliberations like a sack full of barley.
His repentance like the carriage of a double-cannon.
His undertakings like a galleon in ballast.
His understanding like a ragged breviary.
His ideas like snails crawling down from strawberry plants.
His will like three nuts on a dish.
His desire like six trusses of sainfoin.
His judgement like a soft slipper.
His discretion like an empty glove.
His reason hollow as a little drum.'

CHAPTER 31: *Lent's external Anatomy*

'LENT was a little better proportioned in his external parts,' Xeno-manes continued, 'except that he had seven ribs more than a common man.

His toes were like the keyboard of a spinet.
His nails like a gimlet.
His feet like guitars.
His heels like clubs.
His soles like hanging-lamps.
His legs like snares.
His knees like stools.
His thighs like a crank-arbalest.
His hips like borers.
His potbelly was buttoned up in the old fashion and belted high.
His navel was like a fiddle.
His pubic bone was like a cream cake.
His member like a slipper.
His ballocks like a double leather bottle.
His genitals like a carpenter's plane.
His testicle-strings like tennis rackets.
His perineum like a flageolet.
His arse-hole like a crystal mirror.
His buttocks like a harrow.
His loins like a pot of butter.
The base of his spine like a billiard table.
His back like a large cross-bow.
His vertebrae like a bagpipe.
His ribs like a spinning-wheel.
His chest like a canopy.
His shoulder-blades like mortars.
His breast like a portable organ.
His nipples like cattle-horns.
His armpits like chessboards.
His shoulders like a wheel-barrow.
His arms like round hoods.
His fingers cold as friary andirons.

His wrist bones like a pair of stilts.

His arm-bones like sickles.

His elbows like rat-traps.

His hands like curry-combs.

His neck like a beggar's bowl.

His throat like a punch-strainer.

His adam's apple like a barrel with a pair of bronze goitres hanging down from it, fine pieces which matched and were shaped like an hour-glass.

His beard was like a lantern.

His chin like a toadstool.

His ears like a pair of mittens.

His nose like a high boot, hung on like a small shield.

His nostrils like babies' caps.

His eyebrows were like dripping pans, and beneath the left one he had a mole of the size and shape of a piss-pot.

His eyelids were like fiddles.

His eyes like comb-cases.

His optic nerves like tinder-boxes.

His forehead like an earthenware bowl.

His temples like watering-cans.

His cheeks like a pair of clogs.

His jaws like a drinking-cup.

His teeth were like boar spears; and you will find specimens of his milk-teeth at Coulonges-sur-l'Autize in Poitou, where there is one, and at La Brosse in Saintonge, where there are two hung above the doors of the cellar.

His tongue was like a harp.

His mouth like a horse-cloth.

His misshapen face like a mule's pack-saddle.

His head twisted to one side like a retort.

His skull like a game-bag.

The sutures of his skull like the Pope's seal.

His skin like a gabardine coat.

His epidermis like a sieve.

His hair like a scrubbing-brush.

His whiskers as already described.'

CHAPTER 32: *More about Lent's Anatomy*

'IT is one of the miracles of Nature,' continued Xenomanes, 'to see or hear a description of Lent.

If he spat, it was basketfuls of artichokes.

If he blew his nose, it was salted eels.

If he wept, it was ducks in onion sauce.

If he trembled, it was great hare-pies.

If he sweated, it was stock-fish in butter sauce.

If he belched, it was oysters in the shell.

If he sneezed, it was barrels full of mustard.

If he coughed, it was boxes of quince-jelly.

If he sobbed, it was pennyworths of water-cress.

If he yawned, it was potsful of pea-soup.

If he sighed, it was smoked ox-tongues.

If he whistled, it was hods full of fairy-tales.

If he snored, it was bucketsful of shelled beans.

If he frowned, it was pigs' trotters fried in their own fat.

If he spoke, it was far from being that crimson silk out of which Parysatis wanted whoever spoke to her son Cyrus, King of the Persians, to weave his words. What it was, was coarse Auvergne frieze.

If he blew, it was boxes for indulgences.

If he blinked his eyes, it was waffles and wafers.

If he grumbled, it was March-born cats.

If he nodded his head, it was iron-bound wagons.

If he pouted, it was broken staves.

If he mumbled, it was the law clerks' pantomime.

If he stamped his foot, it was postponements and five-year adjournments.

If he stepped back, it was piles of cockle-shells.

If he slobbered, it was communal ovens.

If he was hoarse, it was an entry of the Morris-dancers.

If he farted, it was brown cow-hide gaiters.

If he pooped, it was Cordova-leather shoes.

If he scratched himself, it was new regulations.

If he sang, it was peas in the pod.

If he shat, it was toadstools and morels.

If he puffed, it was cabbages fried in oil, alias, in the language of
Languedoc, *caules d'amb'olif.*

If he made a speech, it was last year's snows.

If he worried, it was for the bald and the shaven alike.

If he gave nothing to the tailor, the embroiderer did no better.

If he woolgathered, it was of members flying and creeping up walls.

If he dreamt, it was of mortgage deeds.

'It was a strange business; while doing nothing he worked, and
while working did nothing. He kept his eyes open when sleeping, and
slept with his eyes open, like a Champagne hare, not daring to shut
them in case his old enemies the Chitterlings might descend on him.
He laughed as he bit, and he bit as he laughed. When he fasted, he ate
nothing, and when he ate nothing he fasted. He nibbled at a mere
morsel, and drank only in his imagination. He bathed above the high
steeples and dried himself in the ponds and rivers. He fished in the air,
and there caught outsize lobsters. He hunted at the bottom of the sea,
and found ibexes, wild-goats, and chamois there. Whenever he surprised a crow he picked out its eyes. He feared nothing but his own
shadow and the bleating of fat kids. On certain days he hung about
the streets. He made fun of holy relics and girdled friars. He used his
fist for a mallet, and wrote prophecies and almanacs on rough parchment with his great pen-case.'

'That's the villain,' said Friar John. 'That's my man. That's the fellow I'm after. I'm going to send him a challenge.'

'That's a strange and monstrous anatomy of a man, if I should call
him a man,' said Pantagruel. 'What you say reminds me of the shape
and anatomy of Misharmony and Discord.'

'And what shape were they?' asked Friar John. 'I haven't even
heard of them, the Lord forgive me.'

'I'll tell you what I've read about them in the ancient fables,' answered Pantagruel. 'Physis – Nature, that is – in her first delivery
brought forth Beauty and Harmony, without physical copulation.
For she is most fertile and prolific in herself. Antiphysis, who has always been Nature's enemy, was immediately jealous of these beautiful and noble offspring and, to be even with her, gave birth to Misharmony and Discord, by copulation with Tellumon. They had

spherical heads, as round as footballs, and not delicately flattened on either side as human beings have theirs. Their ears were high on their heads, and stuck up like asses' ears. Their eyes stood out of their heads on the ends of bones like heel-bones, without eyebrows, and were as hard as crabs' eyes. Their feet were round, like tennis balls, and their hands and arms faced backwards, in reverse. They walked on their heads, continually turning cartwheels, arse over tip, with their legs in the air.

'Now, just as mother apes – as you know – think their offspring the prettiest things in the world, so Antiphysis was loud in her children's praise, and took great pains to prove that they were prettier and more attractive than Physis's. A spherical head and spherical feet, she said, were the nicest possible shape; and a circular motion, like that of a cartwheel, was not only the most proper and perfect means of travelling, but smacked somewhat of the divine. For the heavens and all things eternal were made to revolve in just that way. To have one's feet in the air and one's head down, therefore, was to imitate the creator of the Universe, seeing that hair in men was like their roots, and their legs were like branches. Furthermore, trees are far more securely attached to the earth by their roots than they would be by their branches. By this argument she claimed that her children were far better off and far better shaped than Physis's, being formed like standing trees, while her rival's offspring resembled trees upside down. As for their arms and hands, she proved that it was more reasonable to have them reversed, since their backs ought not to be left un-defended and their fronts were sufficiently guarded by their teeth. For a man can use his teeth not only for chewing, which requires no help from his hands, but also to defend himself against anything that may harm him. So, basing her argument on evidence drawn from the brute creation, she attracted every fool and madman to her side, and won the admiration of every brainless idiot, of everyone, indeed, who lacked sound judgement and common sense.

'Since that time, she has brought forth the pious apes, holy hypo-crites, and popemongers; the maniacal nobodies, demoniacal Calvins, and impostors of Geneva; the furious Puy-Herbaults[1] – Pfui, how they stink! – the belly-stuffers, church-lice, holy-holy men, cannibals, and other deformed monsters, misshapen in Nature's despite.'

1. Puy-Herbault, a monk who had made a furious attack on Rabelais' earlier writings.

CHAPTER 33: *Pantagruel sights a monstrous spouting Whale near Savage Island*

TOWARDS noon, as we came near to Savage Island, Pantagruel sighted in the distance a huge and monstrous spouting whale, making straight towards us. It was snorting and thundering, and so puffed up that it rode high on the waves, above the main-tops of our ships. As it drew near it sent great jets of water from its throat, which looked like mighty rivers tumbling from the mountains before it. Pantagruel pointed it out to Xenomanes, and to the ship's captain, who advised that the *Thalamège's* trumpets should be sounded. So the alarm call went out: 'Combat formations!' At this signal all the ships, galleons, frigates, and brigantines drew up in order of battle, according to their previous instruction, in the shape of the Greek Y, Pythagoras's letter; which is the formation you will see cranes take when flying. They formed an acute angle, therefore, and at its cone and base was the *Thalamège*, ready to put up a fierce fight. Friar John climbed bravely and resolutely on to the fo'c'stle with the gunners. But Panurge began to wail and cry more loudly than before. 'B-b-b-b-b-b-b-b,' he moaned, 'this is worse than ever. Let's run away. Why I'll be blowed if it isn't the Leviathan described by the great prophet Moses in his life of that holy man Job! He'll swallow us all up, ships and men together, like so many little pills. We shan't take up any more room in his hellish great throat than a grain of spiced oats in an ass's mouth. Look at him there. Let's flee and go ashore. I think it's the same sea-monster that was sent in the old days to gobble up Andromeda. We're all done for. Oh, if only there were some valiant Perseus here to slay him at a blow!'

'I'll be a Perseus to him!' answered Pantagruel. 'Don't be afraid.'

'God's truth, then,' said Panurge, 'remove us from the causes of fear. You wouldn't expect me to be frightened, would you, except in the face of evident danger?'

'If your fatal destiny is as Friar John described it a little while ago, you should be afraid of Pyroeis, Eöus, Aethon, and Phlegon, the celebrated and flammivomous horses of the sun, which breathe fire through their nostrils. But you need have no fear of spouting whales, which only throw up water from their mouths and their blowing-holes. For you'll never be in danger of death by water. In fact that element is more likely to preserve you than to hurt you, more likely to protect you than to do you harm.'

'That be hanged for a tale,' said Panurge. 'It's wasted on me. By all the little fishes, haven't I explained the transmutation of the elements to you carefully enough? Haven't I shown you what a close connexion there is between roasting and boiling, boiling and roasting? Oh, oh! Here it comes. I'll go and hide myself below. We shall all be dead men in a minute. I can see the cruel Atropos on the maintop, with her scissors freshly ground, ready to cut the thread of all our lives. Mind out! Here it comes. Oh, you dread and horrible monster! You've drowned plenty of good men before us, who haven't lived to boast of the fact. Oh, if only it spouted wine – good, appetizing, and delicious wine, white and red – instead of this bitter, stinking salt water, that in a way would be bearable. It would give us a chance of showing calm, like that English lord who was ordered to choose what death he would suffer for the crimes he had been convicted of, and elected to be drowned in a butt of malmsey. Here it comes. Oh, oh, Satan, Leviathan, you devil! I can't look at you, you're so hideously ugly. Go off to the Chancery! Go after the Bum-bailiffs, do!'

CHAPTER 34: *The Monstrous Spouter is slain by Pantagruel*

As the spouter swam into the defensive angle formed by the ships and galleons, it spouted great barrels of water on to the foremost of them, as over the Cataracts of the Ethiopian Nile. Arrows, darts, javelins, spears, pikes, and halberds flew at it from all sides. Friar John did not spare himself. Panurge was half dead with fear. The artillery thundered and flashed like the devil, and did its best to prick it in earnest, but to little purpose. For as the great iron and brass balls sank into its skin they seemed from a distance to melt away, as tiles do in the sun. Then Pantagruel saw the urgency of the situation and put out all his strength. Then he showed what he could do.

You may quote from the written records the story of that scoundrel Commodus, Emperor of Rome, who was so skilful with a bow that he could plant his arrows from far off between the fingers of young children as they held their hands in the air, and never touched them.

You may talk of that Indian archer, at the time of Alexander's conquest of India, who was such a master of the bow that he could send his arrows from a great distance through a small ring, although they were nearly five foot long, and their tips were so large and heavy that he could pierce steel scimitars, stout shields, tempered breastplates, and everything else he struck, no matter how hard and resistant, firm and solid it might be. You may tell us too of the marvellous marksmanship of the ancient Franks, who had the highest reputation of all as bowmen and who, when they hunted creatures black or brown, rubbed the tips of their arrows with a drop of hellebore, because the flesh of game was tenderer, tastier, healthier, and more delicious if they did so, although they had to cut round and remove the part of the beast that was struck. You may also mention the Parthians, who could shoot better behind their backs than other nations could facing forward, and speak with admiration of the Scythians' skill in the bowman's art. You may tell of the occasion long ago when they sent an ambassador to Darius, King of Persia, with the offering of a bird, a frog, a mouse, and five arrows, but no written message. When asked what these presents signified, and whether he was instructed to make any statement, the messenger answered no. Darius was left in utter astonishment, his brains quite benumbed, until Gobryas, one of the seven captains who had slain the Magi, interpreted the meaning to him. 'By their gifts and offerings,' he explained, 'the Scythians tacitly wish to inform you that unless the Persians can fly up to heaven like birds, or conceal themselves in the bowels of the earth like mice, or dive to the bottoms of ponds and swamps like frogs, they will all be sent to their doom by the power and arrows of the Scythians.'

But the noble Pantagruel was incomparably the superior of any of these at the throwing of spears and the shooting of shafts. With his fierce javelins and arrows – which in length, thickness, weight, and ironwork were very like the great beams that sustain the bridges of Nantes, Saumur, and Bergerac, also the Pont-au-Change and the Pont-aux-Meuniers in Paris – he could open oysters from a thousand yards without grazing their shells, or snuff a candle without putting it out. He could shoot magpies in the eye, strip the soles off boots without damaging the leather, take the plumes off helmets without even scratching them, and turn over the leaves of Friar John's breviary, one after another, without tearing one of them.

The first of these arrows, of which there was a great store aboard, he drove so deep into the spouter's forehead that he pierced both its jaws and its tongue, so that it could no longer open its mouth, or draw in or spout out water. With his second shot he gouged out its right eye, and with his third its left. Then, to the great delight of everyone, the spouter was seen bearing these three horns on its forehead, slightly tipped forward, in the shape of an equilateral triangle, and veering from one side to another, staggering and swaying, as if stunned, blind, and going to its death. Not content with this, Pantagruel shot another bolt at its tail, which struck obliquely like the rest; then three more perpendicularly along its spine, which they divided exactly into three equal parts between its nose and its tail. Lastly he shot fifty into one of its flanks, and fifty into the other; after which the spouter's body looked like the hull of a three-masted galleon, mortised together by beams of regular dimensions, which might have been the ribs and chain-wales of the keel. It was a jolly sight to see. Then, as it died, the spouter turned over on its back, like all dead fish; and lying on the water, with its beams beneath it, it looked like that scolopendra, or hundred-legged serpent, described by the ancient sage Nicander.

CHAPTER 35: *Pantagruel goes ashore on Savage Island, the ancient abode of the Chitterlings*

THE crew of the ship *Lantern* towed the spouter ashore on to a neighbouring island, called Savage Island, in order to make an anatomical dissection of it and to gather the fat of its kidneys, which they asserted was most useful and necessary for the cure of a certain disease called by them Lack of Money. Pantagruel thought very little of it. For he had seen others like it, and even more enormous, in the Gallic Ocean. He agreed, however, to go ashore on Savage Island, so that some of his men who had been drenched and fouled by the spouter could dry and refresh themselves. They landed at a small deserted harbour on the south side, which lay in the shelter of a pleasant little wood of fine tall trees, from which there flowed a delicious stream of sweet, clear, silvery water. There they set up their kitchens in grand tents, and they did not spare the fuel. Everyone changed whatever clothes he thought fit. Friar John rang the bell, and at that signal the tables were set up and a meal promptly served.

As Pantagruel was gaily dining with his men and the second course was being brought in, he noticed a few tame little Chitterlings, clambering noiselessly up on to a tall tree, beside the spot where the drink was cooling. 'What creatures are those?' he asked Xenomanes, supposing that they were squirrels, weasels, martens, or stoats.

'They're Chitterlings,' replied Xenomanes. 'This is Savage Island, which I told you about this morning. Between them and Lent, their ancient and bitter enemy, there has been mortal war for a long time. I think that the volleys fired against the spouter have given them a fright and made them suspect that their enemy has come with his forces to surprise them, or to lay waste their island, as he has already made several vain attempts to do. His failure so far has been entirely the result of their care and vigilance. For the Chitterlings are like Dido. She, you remember, was obliged constantly to guard and watch her coasts, because her enemies were bitter and their territory near, as she told the companions of Aeneas when they tried to put in at Carthage without her knowledge or permission.'

'Well, my dear friend,' said Pantagruel, 'if you can see any fair means by which we could put an end to this war and reconcile them to one another, just let me know and I'll deal with the matter most gladly. In fact I'll put everything I have into arranging their differences and settling the dispute between these two parties.'

'That is impossible for the present,' said Xenomanes. 'When I was passing by here and by Sneaks' Island about four years ago, I set about trying to arrange a peace between them, or a long truce at the least. Indeed they would have been good friends and neighbours by this time, if only either party had been willing to yield on a single point. Lent refused to include the wild Blackpuddings or Mountain Bolognies, their good friends and allies from of old, in the treaty of peace; and the Chitterlings demanded that Fort Herring-barrel should be put under their rule and government, as Brine-tub Castle is at present, and that the collection of stinking villains, assassins, and brigands, who occupy it at present, should be driven from it. Over these points they could not agree; both considered the conditions unjust. So no agreement was concluded between them. All the same they remained less remorselessly hostile to one another, and were milder enemies than in the past. But since the national Council of Chesil's denunciations, by which they were prodded, bullied, and summonsed, and by which it was further proclaimed that Lent would be a putrid, broken-down stockfish if he were to make any alliance or agreement whatever with them, their feelings have been exacerbated. In fact, they have become so stubborn and enraged that it is now impossible to remedy the situation. It would be easier for you to reconcile cats and rats, or dogs and hares, to one another.'

CHAPTER 36: *How the wild Chitterlings laid an Ambush for Pantagruel*

WHILE Xenomanes was talking, Friar John saw twenty-five or thirty slenderly built Chitterlings near the harbour, but retiring as fast as they could towards their town, citadel, castle, and fortress of Chimney.

'There's going to be a shindy here. I can foresee that,' said he to Pantagruel. 'These worshipful Chitterlings may chance to take you for Lent, although you are not in the least like him. Let's leave this feasting, and put ourselves into a state to resist them.'

Then Pantagruel got up from table to reconnoitre beyond the edge of the wood. But he came back immediately to inform us that he had discovered an ambuscade of fat Chitterlings on the left, and that on the right, about a mile and a half away, he had seen a huge battalion of great and mighty Chitterlings marching furiously towards us in battle array, along a small hill, to the tune of bagpipes and flageolets, sheeps' paunches and bladders, fifes and drums, trumpets and clarions.

Reckoning by the seventy-eight standards which he counted, we supposed their numbers to be not less than forty-two thousand. The order they kept, their proud gait and their resolute faces convinced us that these were no small fry, but old Chitterling warriors. From the first ranks, as far back almost as the standards, they were all very well armed, with pikes which seemed small from a distance, but were steel-tipped and sharp. The flanks of this army were supported by a large force of game-puddings, stout dumplings, and mounted sausages, all well-built islanders and wild brigands.

Pantagruel was greatly worried, and he had reason to be, though Epistemon pointed out to him that it might be the use and custom in

Chitterling country to come out armed to welcome their friends from abroad. After all, the great kings of France are received and welcomed by the chief cities of their kingdom in just this way on their first entry after they have been raised to the throne and crowned. 'Perhaps,' said he, 'this is the local Queen's ordinary bodyguard, and she has been warned by the young Chitterlings of the watch, whom you saw in the tree, that the fine and proud array of your vessels has come into this harbour. She thinks, no doubt, that you must be a rich and power-ful prince, and is coming to visit you in person.' This argument did not satisfy Pantagruel. He called his council, and asked for their general advice as to what he should do at this crisis when hope was doubtful and the danger clear.

He then briefly explained to them how this kind of armed recep-tion, disguised as a demonstration of politeness and friendship, had often proved fatal. 'This is the way,' he said, 'in which the Emperor Antoninus Caracalla on one occasion slew the Alexandrians and, on another, defeated the bodyguard of Artaban, King of the Persians, under the pretence of coming to find a husband for his daughter. But his treachery did not remain unpunished. For a little later he too lost his life. In this way too the sons of Jacob killed the Shechemites to avenge the rape of their sister Dina. By just such a stroke of hypocrisy the garrison of Constantinople was slaughtered by the Roman Em-peror, Gallienus. Under a similar pretext of friendship Antonius en-ticed Artavasdes, King of Armenia, then had him bound and put in heavy chains, and finally ordered him to be murdered. We find a thousand other such stories in the ancient chronicles. Charles, King of France, the sixth of that name, is praised to this very day – and right-fully so – for his wise treatment of the Parisians on his return from his victories over the Flemings and the men of Ghent. When about to enter this good city, he heard at Le Bourget, in the Île-de-France, that they had come out with their mallets – which had earned them their title of Malleteers – in battle array, to the number of twenty thousand fighting men. So he refused to enter, although they protested that their only reason for arming themselves was to give him a more honourable welcome, and that there was no ruse or disaffection what-ever. He insisted, nevertheless, that they should first retire to their houses and put away their weapons.'

CHAPTER 37: *Pantagruel sends for Colonel Maul-chitterling and Colonel Chop-sausage; also a notable digression concerning the proper Names of Persons and Places*

THE council's decision was that in any event they must stand on their guard. Then, on Pantagruel's instructions, Carpalim and Gymnaste summoned the soldiers from the *Toasting-cup*, whose commander was Colonel Maul-chitterling, and the *Vintage-basket*, which was under Colonel Chop-sausage, junior.

'I'll relieve Gymnaste of that trouble,' said Panurge. 'What's more, his presence is necessary to you here.'

'By my cloth,' cried Friar John, 'you want to avoid the battle, you coward. You won't come back, I swear you won't. But that'll be no loss. For the fellow would only weep and lament and howl and discourage our good soldiers.'

'Friar John, my ghostly father,' affirmed Panurge, 'of course I shall come back, and very soon. While you're fighting I'll pray God for your victory, like that warlike captain Moses, the leader of the children of Israel.'

'The names of those two colonels of yours,' said Epistemon to Pantagruel, 'Maul-chitterling and Chop-sausage, give us an assurance of victory. If these Chitterlings, by any chance, intend to attack us we shall have success and victory.'

'That's the right way to take things,' said Pantagruel. 'I'm glad that you can foresee and prophesy our victory from the names of our officers. That method of prophecy by names is not at all new. It was celebrated and religiously observed in the olden days by the Pythagoreans. Many great lords and emperors have used it in ancient times to their advantage. Octavian Augustus, for instamce, the second emperor of Rome, one day met a peasant Eutyches – that is to say, *the lucky one* – leading an ass called Nicon – which in Greek means *victorious*. Struck by the significance of the driver's name and the ass's, he felt confident of all prosperity and good fortune, also of certain victory. When Vespasian, also a Roman emperor, was alone one day, praying in the temple of Serapis, a servant of his, called Basilides – that is to say *royal* – suddenly came in. When he saw this man, whom he had left as sick a long way in the rear, he took hope and felt certain that he would win the Imperial throne. Regilian was chosen emperor by the soldiers for no other reason, and on no other pretext, than his name. See also the *Cratylus* of the divine Plato.'

'By my thirst,' said Rhizotome, 'I should like to read him. I've heard you quoting him often enough.'

'You'll see there,' continued Pantagruel, 'how the Pythagoreans conclude from their names and numbers that Patroclus ought to have been slain by Hector, Hector by Achilles, Achilles by Paris, and Paris by Philoctetes. My mind is set in an utter whirl when I think of Pythagoras's amazing discovery. For by the odd or even number of syllables in any proper name, he could tell on which side a man was lame, blind, gouty, paralytic, pleuritic, or otherwise defective by nature. That is to say that he associated an even number with the left side of the body, an odd number with the right.'

'I saw his system practised at Saintes,' said Epistemon, 'during a general procession, in the presence of that most excellent, virtuous, learned, and fair-minded man, president Briand Vallée, Lord of Douhet. As a lame, one-eyed, or hunch-backed man or woman passed he was told the person's proper name. If the syllables were uneven in number he immediately declared them to be deformed, one-eyed, lame, or hunchbacked on the right side, and if they were uneven, on the left. And this proved correct. We didn't find a single exception.'

'By this discovery,' said Pantagruel, 'the learned have affirmed that the kneeling Achilles was wounded by Paris's arrow in the left heel. For his name has an odd number of syllables. It is worth noting also that the ancients used always to kneel on the right knee. Venus was wounded by Diomedes before Troy in the left hand, since her name in Greek has four syllables, Vulcan limped on his left foot, for the same reason. Philip, King of Macedon, and Hannibal were blind in the right eye. We could particularize further by the same Pythagorean reasoning, on the subject of sciaticas, ruptures, and headaches in one side of the brain.'

'But to return to names, consider how Alexander the Great, the son of King Philip, of whom we have spoken, achieved his success by the interpretation of a single name. He was besieging the strong city of Tyre, and attacking it with all his power for several weeks, but in vain. His military engines and his assaults were profitless. Whatever he destroyed was immediately repaired by the Tyrians. So, in his

despair, he conceived the idea of raising the siege, though he saw that
a retreat would be singularly damaging to his reputation. In this sad
perplexity he fell asleep; and as he slept he dreamt that a satyr came
into his tent, and skipped and capered on his goatish legs. Alexander
tried to catch him, but the satyr always escaped. Finally he chased the
creature into a corner and captured him. But at this moment he woke
up. When he described his dream to the philosophers and learned men
of his court, they told him that the gods promised him victory and that
Tyre would soon be taken. For if this word Satyros is cut into two,
you have *Sa Tyros*, which means *Tyre is yours*. Indeed, at the next
assault he carried the town by storm and by this great victory sub-
jugated that rebellious people.

'Conversely, consider how the significance of a name threw Pompey into despair. After Caesar had beaten him at the battle of Pharsalia his only means of escape was by flight; and as he fled by sea he
came to the island of Cyprus. Near the town of Paphos he saw on the
coast a beautiful and luxurious palace; and when he asked the captain
its name, he was told that they called it Κακοβασιλέα, that is to say,
Evil King. So frightened and horrified was he by this name that he fell
into a despair, feeling certain that he could not escape, but would soon
lose his life. The passengers and sailors heard his cries, sighs, and
groans; and, as it turned out, a short time afterwards an unknown
peasant by the name of Achillas cut off his head.

'We could carry our argument even further and quote what happened to Lucius Aemilius Paulus, when the Roman senate elected him
Imperator; that is to say head of the army they were sending against
Perses, King of Macedon. Towards evening on that day he returned
home to prepare for his departure, and as he kissed his little daughter
Tratia noticed that she was rather sad. "What's the matter, Tratia
darling?" he asked. "Why are you so worried and sad?" "Oh
Father," she answered, "Persa is dead." This was the name of a little
bitch, which was her great favourite. Her reply gave Paulus perfect
assurance that he would beat Perses.

'If we had time enough to dwell on the sacred books of the Hebrews
we should find a hundred famous passages to demonstrate the religious importance which they attached to proper names and their
meanings.'

As this discourse ended, the two colonels arrived at the head of their soldiers, all well armed and resolute. So Pantagruel made them a short speech exhorting them to show their courage in battle, in case they were driven to fight – though he still could not believe that the Chitterlings were so treacherous. But he forbade them to begin the attack. He gave them as their watchword, *Shrove Tuesday*.

CHAPTER 38: *Why men have no reason to despise Chitterlings*

Now you are laughing at me, my jolly boozers. You do not believe that what I tell you is really true. I don't know what to do about you. Believe me if you like; and if you don't, go and see for yourselves. But I know well enough what I saw. It was on Savage Island. I give you its name. And now recall to your minds the strength of the giants of old who attempted to pile high Mount Pelion upon Ossa, and then to topple Ossa over Olympus, in order to fight the gods and dislodge them from the sky. Theirs was no common or ordinary strength. Nevertheless they were no more than Chitterlings in one half of their bodies, or – to be more correct – serpents. The serpent who tempted Eve was a Chitterling; yet, for all that, it is written of him that he was slyer and more subtle than any beast of the field. So are the Chitterlings. Furthermore, it is maintained in many academies that this tempter was the Chitterling named Ithyphallus, into whose shape good Master Priapus was transformed. He was a great tempter of women in the old days, in Paradise, as it was called in Greek, which in French means the pleasure gardens. The Swiss are now a brave and warlike people. But how do we know that they were not once sausages? I wouldn't put my finger in the fire to prove the contrary. The Himantopodes, a very famous people of Ethiopia, are, according to Pliny's description, Chitterlings and nothing more.

Now if these arguments do not satisfy your lordships' incredulity, go in a moment – I mean after drinking – and visit Lusignan, Parthenay, Vouvent, Mervent, and Pouzauges, in Poitou. You will find there witnesses of renown, old and solidly built, who will swear to you on the arm of St Rigomer that Melusine, their original foundress, had a woman's body down to the prickpurse, and that below that she was a serpentine Chitterling, or perhaps a Chitterlinic serpent. But she had a fine, attractive way of moving for all that, which is imitated even to this day by the Breton dancers when they dance their jigs to the sound of their own singing. And why do you suppose Erichthonius was the first to invent coaches, litters, and chariots? It was because Vulcan begot him with Chitterlings' legs; and to hide them, he preferred to travel in a litter rather than on horseback. For in his time Chitterlings had not yet a good reputation. The Scythian nymph Ora, also, had a body half woman and half Chitterling. Nevertheless Jupiter thought her so beautiful that he slept with her, and had a fine son called Colaxes by her. So now, stop laughing, and believe me that nothing is truer than my tale, except the Gospel.

CHAPTER 39: *Friar John joins the Cooks in an attack on the Chitterlings*

WHEN Friar John saw these furious Chitterlings advancing so boldly, he said to Pantagruel: 'There's going to be a fine puppet-battle here, in my opinion. What honour and what lordly praise we shall win when we gain the victory! I wish you would stay aboard your ship, my Lord, and remain a mere spectator of this engagement. I wish that you would leave me and my men to deal with them.'

'What men?' inquired Pantagruel.

'That's breviary stuff,' answered Friar John. 'Why was Potiphar, who was the chief cook in Pharaoh's kitchen, the man who bought Joseph, and whom Joseph could have made a cuckold if he had wanted to – why was Potiphar, I say, made Master of the Horse for the whole kingdom of Egypt? Why was Nebuzar-adan, King Nebuchadnezzar's chief cook, chosen out of all his captains to besiege and destroy Jerusalem?'

'I'm listening,' said Pantagruel.

'By our Lady's wound,' said Friar John, 'I'd stake my oath that previously they had had Chitterlings to fight, or people of no better reputation. For cooks are incomparably more suitable for attacking, fighting, subjugating, and destroying Chitterlings than are all the horsemen, janissaries, mercenaries, and foot-soldiers in the world.'

'You call to my mind an anecdote that I have read about one of Cicero's smart and witty answers,' said Pantagruel. 'At the time of the civil wars at Rome between Caesar and Pompey, he felt rather attracted to Pompey's side, although he was courted and greatly favoured by Caesar. Hearing one day that the Pompeians had lost a considerable number of men in a certain engagement, he decided to visit their camp. There he found little strength, less courage, and great disorder. Foreseeing, therefore, that they would be utterly ruined and destroyed – as indeed was the case – he began to jibe and mock, first at one party, then at another, making those bitter and stinging observations at which he was such an adept. Some of the captains, being stout, resolute, and confident fellows, took his mockery in good part and replied: "But don't you see how many eagles we've still got?" Eagles were then the Roman ensigns in time of war. "They would be good and useful if you were fighting against magpies," answered Cicero. Well, seeing that we have to fight against Chitterlings, you assume, I see, that it is to be a culinary battle, and propose to make allies of the cooks. Do as you wish. I will stay here and see what comes of your bragging.'

Friar John went straight to the kitchen tents, and said most gaily and courteously to the cooks: 'My lads, I want to see all of you gain honour and victory to-day. You shall perform feats of arms never yet witnessed within our memory. Belly to belly, do men think nothing of the valiant cooks? Come, let's fight these wretched Chitterlings. I'll be your captain. And let's drink, my friends. Here's courage to you!'

'That's right, Captain,' replied the cooks, 'we are under your jolly command. With you to lead us we'll live and die!'

'Live, yes,' said Friar John. 'But die, no. We'll leave dying to the Chitterlings. Now let's get into good order. Your watchword shall be Nebuzar-adan.'

CHAPTER 40: *How Friar John fitted up the Sow, and of the brave Cooks who manned it*

THEN, at Friar John's command, the master engineers fitted up the great sow, which was in the ship, *Leather Bottle*. It was a miraculous contrivance, built of such a size that it fired cannon balls and steel-flighted bolts from the great bombards which were set in rows around it, while inside more than two hundred men could shelter, and play a safe part in the battle. It was copied from the sow of La Réole, with the aid of which Bergerac was captured from the English, when the young king Charles VI was on the French throne.

Here are the numbers and names of the brave and valiant cooks who went into the sow, even as the Greeks did into the Trojan horse:

Soursauce	Greasypot
Jackofalltrades	Fatguts
Cowardycustard	Mortarpestle
Slipslop	Swillwine
Porkfry	Peaspudding
Foulfingers	Goatstew
Mandragora	Carbonado
Lostbread	Gutspudding
Wearybones	Hotpot
Soupspoon	Pigsliver
Soused cod	Slashface
Pancake	Hashface.

All these noble cooks bore on their coats of arms a larding-pin vert on a field gules, charged with a chevron argent, inclined to the left.

Baconrasher	Roundbacon
Bacon	Antibacon
Gnawbacon	Frizzlebacon
Pullbacon	Tiebacon
Savebacon	Scratchbacon
Archbacon	Treadbacon

and one who was called Jobacon, a native of the Rambouillet district. The name of this culinary doctor had been Jollybacon, but by process of syncopation it had become shortened, in the same way as you say Idolater for Idololater.

Stiffbacon	Freshbacon
Selfbacon	Sourbacon
Sweetbacon	Billbacon
Chewbacon	Squatbacon
Finebacon	Nuffbacon

Slicebacon	Peasandbacon
Flybacon	Bladderbacon
Oglebacon	Covetbacon

All names unknown among the Maraños and the Jews.

Ballocky	Greensauce
Plucksalad	Panscraper
Cressbed	Trivet
Turnipscraper	Tallypot
Hogger	Crackpot
Rabbitskin	Scrapepot
Freepepper	Shiverer
Piepan	Saltgullet
Shavebacon	Snaildresser
Freefritter	Drybroth
Mustardpot	Marchsoup
Barberrysauce	Chinepicker
Swillbroth	Renneteer
Gayboy	Macaroon
Pancake	Skewerman

Also Crumb, who was afterwards transferred from the kitchen to the living-quarters, and put into the service of the noble Cardinal Le Veneur.

Spoilroast	Merriman
Ovencloth	Newtool
Headcloth	Flyflap
Firepoker	Conqueror
Longtool	Oldtool
Talltool	Hairytool
Vaintool	Hasticalf
Fleshsmith	Gabaonite
Muttonchop	Clodhopper
Turnmilk	Swillbung
Alpscaler	Jackodandy
Blowguts	Scarface
Skate	Smuttynose

Mondam, who invented Sauce Madame, and in return got this name in the Franco-Scottish tongue

Chattertooth	Antitus
Slobberchops	Chiefturnipeer
Scumpot	Urelelipipingues
Quailsbill	Slovenly
Rincepot	Stuffguts
Wafflemen	Swedeeater
Saffraneer	Puddingbag
Scurvycoat	Pigling

Also Robert who was the inventor of Sauce Robert, which is so wholesome and necessary for roast rabbits, ducks, fresh pork, also poached eggs, salt cod, and a thousand other such dishes.

Coldeel	Salmigundian
Thornback	Poorfish
Gurnard	Pickledherring
Rumblegut	Slapjaw
Beggingbag	Widebeak
Blowhard	Tasteall
Squirrel	Sweetheifer
Tittletattle	Donkeythistle
Pickledbeef	Stickyfingers
Fryingpan	Sowsticker
Lazybones	Handgrill
Calabrese	Cocklicrane
Turnipkin	Assface
Shittail	Coxcomb
Tomturdy	Bullcalf
Crapbreech	Smartster

Into the sow entered these noble cooks, all cheerful, gallant, brisk, and eager for battle. Friar John with his great curved scimitar went in last and shut the sprung doors on the inside.

CHAPTER 41: *Pantagruel snaps the Chitterlings over his Knees*

THESE Chitterlings came so close that Pantagruel could see them stretching their arms and beginning to lower their lances. Thereupon he sent Gymnaste to hear what they had to say, and to see how they would excuse themselves for warring against their old friends without provocation. For they had suffered neither wrong nor slander.

When he came before their front ranks, Gymnaste made a low and sweeping bow and cried out as loudly as he could: 'Yours, we are all yours, all yours, and at your service, all of us. We are all friends of Shrove Tuesday, your old ally.'

I have been informed since that what he actually said was Tove Shrewsday and not Shrove Tuesday. However that may be, at this word a stubby, wild saveloy sprang out in front of their ranks and tried to seize him by the throat.

'By God,' cried Gymnaste, 'you won't get down me except in slices. Why, you'll never get into my mouth, as you are.'

Then he unsheathed his sword Kiss-my-arse – as he called it – with both hands, and cut the saveloy in two. Heavens, how fat he was! He reminded me of the great Bull of Berne who was killed at Marignano on the defeat of the Swiss. Believe me, he had no less than four inches of fat on his belly.

When this brain-sausage had been brained, the Chitterlings rushed at Gymnaste and were villainously overthrowing him when Pantagruel and his men hurried to his assistance at top speed. Then the martial fray began pell-mell. Maul-chitterling mauled Chitterlings; Chop-sausage chopped sausages; and Pantagruel performed the miracle of snapping Chitterlings across his knee. Friar John was lying snug in his sow, seeing and watching everything, when suddenly the dumplings, who were in ambush, charged out most terrifyingly upon Pantagruel. Then, when he saw the disorderly hubbub, the Friar opened the doors of his sow and burst out with his stout soldiers, some of whom were armed with iron spits, others with andirons, racks, frying-pans, shovels, kettles, gridirons, pokers, tongs, dripping-pans, brooms, cooking-pots, mortars, and pestles, all in battle array, like so many house-breakers, and all howling and shouting together most horribly: *Nebuzar-adan! Nebuzar-adan! Nebuzar-adan!* Bawling their cry, they tumultuously charged the dumplings, and went straight through the sausages. When the Chitterlings suddenly caught sight of this fresh reinforcement, they took to their heels at a full gallop, as if all the devils in hell were after them. But Friar John beat them down with belly-blows, like so many flies, and his soldiers did not spare themselves. It was a pitiful sight. The field was all covered with dead or wounded Chitterlings; and history related that but for God's special intervention the whole race of Chitterlings would have been exterminated by our soldiers. But a miracle occurred. You may believe as much of it as you like.

From a northerly direction there flew towards us a great, huge, gross, grey swine, with wings as long and broad as the sails of a windmill, and plumage as crimson red as the feathers of a phoenicopter, which in Languedoc is called a flamingo. It had flashing red eyes like carbuncles, and green ears the colour of chrysolite. Its teeth were as yellow as a topaz. Its tail was long and as black as Lucullian marble. Its feet were white, diaphanous, and transparent as a diamond, and broadly webbed like those of a goose, or as Queen Pedauque's were of old at Toulouse. It had a gold collar round its neck, inscribed with some Ionic lettering of which I could only make out two words: ΥΣ ΑΘΗΝΑΝ – the hog (instructs) Minerva.

The weather was fine and clear. But on the approach of this monster there came such violent thunder from the left that we were all struck with amazement. The moment the Chitterlings saw the hog they threw down their arms and sticks, and all fell on their knees, raising their clasped hands in the air, without a word, as if in adoration. Brother John and his men, nevertheless, went on smiting and spitting them. But at Pantagruel's command the retreat was sounded and all fighting ceased. Then, after flying several times up and down between the armies, the monster threw more than twenty-seven pipes of mustard down on the ground, and disappeared, flying through the air and shrieking continuously: 'Shrove Tuesday, Shrove Tuesday, Shrove Tuesday!'

CHAPTER 42: *Pantagruel's Negotiations with Niphleseth, Queen of the Chitterlings*

As this monster made no further appearance and the two armies remained silent, Pantagruel demanded an interview with the Lady Niphleseth – for that was the Queen of the Chitterlings' name. She was in her chariot beside the standards, and his request was readily granted.

The Queen alighted, graciously saluted Pantagruel, and made him welcome. But he protested against the Chitterlings' attack. She, however, made honourable excuses, alleging that there had been a mistake caused by faulty information. Her spies had reported that their old enemy King Lent had made a landing and was amusing himself by inspecting the spouters' urine. She then implored him to be so kind as to pardon their offence, pleading that there was more shit than spite in the Chitterlings, and offered in return, on her own behalf and on that of all the Queen Niphleseths her successors, to pay him homage for the whole island realm, to be loyal to him and his successors, and to obey his every command. They would be friends to his friends and enemies to his enemies, she said, and furthermore, in acknowledgement of their fealty, they would send him annually seventy-eight thousand royal Chitterlings, to serve him at the first course of his dinner for six months in the year.

All this she duly did. Next day she sent the aforesaid number of royal Chitterlings to the good Gargantua in six large brigantines, under the command of the young Niphleseth, Infanta of the Island. The noble Gargantua dispatched them as a present to the great King in Paris. But owing to the change of air and the lack of mustard, which is the natural balm and restorative of Chitterlings, they nearly all died. Then, at the King's wish and with his special permission, they were buried in heaps in a corner of Paris, which is known to this day as the *Rue Pavée d'Andouilles*, or Chitterling Paved Lane. But, at the request of the royal court ladies, Niphleseth the younger was rescued and honourably treated. She was afterwards married to a good rich husband and had several fine children, for which Heaven be praised.

Pantagruel graciously thanked the Queen, entirely pardoned the wrong, refused her offer of homage, and presented her with a pretty little knife of Perche manufacture.[1] He then questioned her closely about the monster which had appeared. She answered that it was the spiritual embodiment of Shrove Tuesday, their tutelary deity in times of war and the first founder and member of the whole Chitterling race. That was why he looked like a hog. For the Chitterlings were descended from hogs. Pantagruel asked what his purpose was in dropping so much mustard on the ground. Had it some curative value? And the Queen answered that mustard was their Holy Grail and Celestial Balm. If a small quantity were put into the wounds of fallen Chitterlings, in a very short time the wounded were healed and the dead brought to life.

Pantagruel held no further discussions with the Queen, and retired to his ship, as did all his good companions, with their arms and their sow.

CHAPTER 43: *Pantagruel lands on the Island of Ruach*

Two days later we arrived at the Island of Ruach, or Windy Island, and I swear to you by the stormy Pleiades that I found the conditions and customs of its inhabitants stranger than I can say. They live on wind. They drink nothing and they eat nothing but wind. Their only houses are weathercocks, and in their gardens they sow nothing but the three varieties of anemone, or wind-flower. Rue and other carminative herbs they carefully weed out. For nourishment the common people use fans made of feathers, paper, or cloth, according to their means and capacity. The rich live on windmills. When they hold a feast or a banquet they set up their tables under one or two windmills, and feast there as gaily as at a wedding, discussing during their meal the goodness and excellence, the rare and salubrious qualities of winds, as you, my fellow drinkers, philosophize at your banquets on the subject of wines. One praises the Sirocco, another the Besch, another the Garbino, another the Bise, another the Zephyr, another the Galerne, and so on. Others praise smock winds for suitors and lovers. The sick they treat with draughts of air, just as we do ours

1. A trifle. A penknife seems to have been a favourite gift of early voyagers to America. It was, apparently, a cheap way of winning the inhabitants' friendship.

with draughts of sirop. 'Oh,' said one inflated little fellow to me, 'if only I could have a bladderful of that good Languedoc breeze they call the Circius! The noble Schyron, the physician, who passed through that country one day, told us that it is strong enough to overturn loaded wagons. How good it would be for my Oediponic leg! The biggest are not always the best.'

'But,' said Panurge, 'what about a large butt of that good Languedoc wine that grows at Mirevaux, Canteperdrix, and Frontignan!'

I saw a handsome fellow who looked rather dropsical, in a violent fury with a great stout servant of his and a little page, and kicking them devilish hard with his boot. Not knowing why he was so angry, I thought he was acting on his doctors' advice, and that it was a good thing for a master to get into a rage and kick his servants, and for the servants to be kicked. But I heard the fellow cursing his men for robbing him of half a bottle of the best Garbino, which he had been keeping carefully as a most precious food for late in the season. They do not shit, piss, or spit on this island. But, on the other hand, they poop, fart, and belch most copiously. They suffer from all sorts and varieties of diseases. For every malady originates and develops from flatulence, as Hippocrates proves in his book, *On Wind*. But the worst epidemic they know is the windy colic, as a remedy for which they use large cupping-glasses, and so draw off much wind. They all die of dropsy or tympanites; they all fart as they die, the men loudly, the women soundlessly, and in this way their souls depart by the back passage.

A little later, as we were walking about the island, we met three great puffed-up fellows, on their way to amuse themselves by looking at the plovers, who abound in this country and live on the same diet. I noticed that just as you, my dear boozers, carry flagons, leather bottles, and flasks when you go about, so each one of them carried a pretty little bellows on his belt. So if the wind happened to fail them, they could blow up a fresh one with these neat bellows, by process of attraction and reciprocal expulsion. For, as you know, wind in its essential definition is nothing more than air in movement and undulation.

At this moment we received an order, in their King's name, not to let any man or woman of their country aboard any of our ships for the next three hours. For he had been robbed of a full fart of the original wind which that old snorer Aeolus had given to Ulysses of old, to propel his ship in the calm. This he religiously preserved, like a Holy Grail, and with it cured several frightful maladies, merely by releasing and distributing to the sick as much as would be needed to make a virgin's poop – which is the Blessed Sisters' name for a ring at the back-door bell.

CHAPTER 44: *How a little Rain lays a high Wind*

PANTAGRUEL praised their form of government and way of life, and said to their Volatile Magistrate: 'If you accept Epicurus's opinion that pleasure is the supreme good – easy and not toilful pleasure, I mean – then I consider you happy. For your nourishment, being wind, costs you little or nothing; all you have to do is to blow.'

'True enough,' said the Magistrate. 'But nothing is an unmixed blessing in this mortal life. Often when we're at table, feeding on one of God's great good winds, as on celestial manna, happy as so many monks, a little rain will blow up, which lays the wind and robs us of our food. So many of our meals fail through lack of victuals.'

'It was like that with Quinquenais Johnny,' broke in Panurge, 'when he pissed on his wife Quelot's backside, and laid the malodorous wind that issue from it as from a great Aeolian retort. I made a pretty little poem about it, not long ago:

> When Johnny one evening had tested his wine,
> A wine still fermenting, and heady and strong,
> He called his wife Quelot and said: 'Let us dine.
> Just cook us some turnips and don't be too long.'
> They were gay at their meal and were singing a song
> As they went off to bed, where they rammed and lay quiet.
> But John couldn't sleep for the horrible riot
> His wife Quelot made with her blasting behind.
> So he pissed on her bum. Then he cried: 'You will find
> That a very small rain lays a very high wind.'

'What is more,' said the Magistrate, 'we sustain an annual disaster which is very great and destructive. There's a giant called Slitnose who lives on the Island of Vacuum, and every year he transports himself here in the spring, on his doctors' advice, to take a purge. He eats up a great number of our windmills as pills, and also a lot of bellows, of which he is very fond. This causes us great misery, and makes us keep three or four lents a year, not counting certain special rogations and orisons.'

'But don't you know any way of preventing him?' asked Pantagruel.

'On the advice of our Mezarims, or belly-doctors,' replied the Magistrate, 'at the season when he usually arrives we put a lot of cocks and hens in our windmills. The first time he swallowed them it almost killed him. For they crowed and cackled inside him and flew about his stomach, so that he fell into a swoon, had a heart seizure, and then a terrible and dangerous convulsion. It was as if a serpent had crept through his mouth into his stomach.'

'There's an inappropriate and incongruous comparison for you!' said Friar John. 'For I once heard that when a serpent enters a man's stomach it does no harm at all. It comes out again immediately if the patient is hung up by the legs and a pan full of warm milk is placed near his mouth.'

'You were told this,' said Pantagruel, 'and so were they who told it to you. But this cure has never been seen or read of. Hippocrates, in his fifth book *Of Epidemics*, writes that an accident like this happened in his time, and that the patient died suddenly of spasms and convulsions.'

'What's more,' continued the Magistrate, 'all the foxes in the country ran up his throat in pursuit of the hens, and he might have died at any moment if he hadn't taken the advice of a stupid magician and at the moment of the paroxysm flayed a fox – or vomited – as an antidote and counter-irritant. Since then he has had better advice, and cures himself by means of a suppository they give him, made of a decoction of wheat and millet, which attract the hens, and of goose-liver, which attracts the foxes. He also takes some pills through his mouth, made up of greyhounds and terriers. So now you know our misfortune.'

'You need not be afraid for the future, my good people,' said Pantagruel. 'This great Slitnose, the windmill-swallower, is dead, I assure you. He died from suffocation, choked by a lump of fresh butter, eaten at the door of a hot oven by order of his physicians.'

CHAPTER 45: *Pantagruel lands on Popefigs' Island*

NEXT morning we touched at the Island of the Popefigs, who had once been rich and free, and were then known as Jollyboys. But now they were poor and miserable, and subject to the Papimaniacs. This is how it had happened.

One year, on the day of the annual high festival, the Burgomaster, Aldermen, and High Rabbis had gone to amuse themselves and watch the procession in the near-by island of Papimania. One of them, when he saw the effigy of the Pope, which it was the laudable custom to display in public on the highest holidays, made an obscene gesture with his fingers, which in that country is called 'showing a fig', and which is a sign of public contempt and derision. To revenge themselves for this the Papimaniacs, without a word of warning, some days later resorted to arms, and surprised, ravaged, and devastated the whole of Jollyboys' Island, putting every man with a beard on his chin to the edge of the sword. The women and children they spared, on conditions similar to those imposed on the people of Milan by Frederick Barbarossa.

The Milanese had revolted against him in his absence, and chased his wife out of the city, ignominiously mounted on an old mule named Thacor, or *a Fig up your Arse*, and riding reversed; that is to say, with her bottom turned to the mule's head, and her face to its rump. On his return Frederick had beaten them and taken the city, and he had been so quick that he had even recovered the famous mule Thacor. Then, in the middle of the great market square, before the eyes of all the captured citizens, he had a fig placed in the mule's private parts by the common hangman, who proclaimed, in the Emperor's name and to the sound of the trumpet, that if any of them wished to escape death, he must publicly remove the fig with his teeth and replace it in the same position without the aid of his hands. Anyone who refused would be incontinently hanged. Some of the Milanese were so ashamed and appalled by this abominable punishment that they preferred the fear of death, and were hanged. In others the fear of death was stronger than their shame. These, when they had pulled out the fig with their own good teeth, publicly showed it to the executioner, saying *Ecco lo fico*.

The remainder of these poor, unhappy Jollyboys were only spared from death at the cost of a similar ignominy. They were enslaved and made to pay tribute, and forced to take the name of *Popefigs*, because they had shown a fig to the Pope's portrait. Since that time these poor people have not prospered. Every year they have had hail, storms, famine, and all kinds of disasters, as an eternal punishment for the sins of their ancestors and relations.

When we saw their misery and distress, we decided to cut our visit short. We merely entered a little chapel near the harbour to take some holy water and commend ourselves to God. We found the place ruined, desolate, and roofless as the Church of St Peter at Rome. But when we had entered the chapel and were taking the holy water we saw in the sacristy a man, muffled up in stoles and entirely submerged in the tank, except for so much of his nose as he needed to breathe through. Around him were three priests, all shaven and tonsured, reading the book of exorcisms and conjuring away devils.

Pantagruel found this surprising, and asked what games they were playing there. He was informed that there had been such a terrible plague raging in the island for the last three years that more than a half of the country was deserted, and its land unfarmed. After the plague had died down, this man hiding in the sacristy had been ploughing a great fertile field and sowing it with winter wheat. At that very moment a little devil – one who did not know yet how to thunder or hail except over parsley and cabbage, and could not even read or write – had got Lucifer's permission to come to this Island of Popefigs for a holiday and have a little fun. For the devils were on very good terms with its inhabitants, both male and female, and often went to spend some time there.

When this little devil arrived, he went over to the farmer and asked him what he was doing. The poor man replied that he was sowing this field with winter wheat, to help support himself next year.

'Oh, but this field isn't yours,' said the devil. 'It's mine. It belongs to me. For from the moment you showed the Pope a fig, this whole country was adjudged, consigned, and given up to us. Still, sowing wheat is not my business. So I leave you the field, but only on condition that we share the profits.'

'I agree,' said the farmer.

'I mean,' said the devil, 'that we are to divide the land's yield into two parts. One shall be what grows above the earth, the other all that the earth covers. The choice is mine, for I'm a devil of noble and ancient stock, and you're only a peasant. I choose what is in the earth; you can have what's on top. When are you expecting to reap?'

'About the middle of July,' answered the farmer.

'Very well,' said the devil, 'I shan't fail to be here. In the meantime, do your duty. Work away, peasant, work away! I'm off to tempt the noble nuns of Dryfart to the gentle sin of fornication, with the Cowled hypocrites and the Belly-stuffers. I know their fancies pretty well. They have only to meet and the engagement is on.'

CHAPTER 46: *How the little Devil was fooled by a Popefigland Farmer*

HALF-WAY through July, the devil duly appeared, accompanied by a squad of little devils' choristers; and when he found the farmer, he said to him: 'Well, peasant, how have you been getting on since I left you? Now's the time for us to share out.'

Then the farmer and his men began to cut the corn, and the devilkins to root the stubble out of the earth. The farmer threshed his corn in the barn, winnowed it, put it in sacks, and carried it to market for sale. The devilkins did the same, and sat down beside the farmer in the market to sell their stubble. The farmer got a good price for his wheat, and stuffed the money into an old top-boot, which he tied to his belt. The devils made no sale. Far from it. The peasants mocked at them in the open market.

When the market was closed the devil said to the farmer: 'You've fooled me this time, peasant, but next time you shan't.'

'How could I have fooled you, Master Devil?' asked the farmer. 'You had the first choice. The fact is that when you chose you thought you were fooling me. You expected that nothing would spring from the earth for my share, and that you would find the seed I had sown intact in the ground. You meant to tempt the poor beggars and canting skinflints with it, and so make them fall into your snares. But you are very young at your trade. The seed that you see in the ground is dead and rotten, but from its corruption sprang the new crop that you saw me sell. So you made the worse choice, and earned the Gospel curse.' 'Let's say no more about it,' said the devil. 'What can you sow our field with for this next year?'

'To get the best out of the ground,' replied the farmer, 'the proper thing would be to sow beets.'

'Well,' said the devil, 'you're an honest peasant. Put in plenty of seed. I'll guard your beets from storms, and I won't hail on them even once. But understand that I take for my share the part above ground; you can have what's below. Work, peasant, work! I'm off to tempt the heretics. Their souls are very tasty in a carbonado. My Lord Lucifer has his usual colic, and they'll make a tasty snack for him.'

When harvest time came, the devil turned up once more with a squad of devilkins-in-waiting and, on finding the farmer and his men, he began to cut and gather the green tops of the beets. After him the farmer dug and pulled up the great beets, which he put in sacks. So they all went off together to the market, where the farmer got a good price for his beets and the devil sold nothing. What was worse, he was made a public mockery.

'It's quite clear to me, peasant,' said the devil, 'that you've fooled me again. I've had enough of going halves with you. Now, the bargain shall be that we have a scratching match, and the first of us to give in shall forfeit his share of the field. The winner shall take the lot. Our meeting shall be to-day week. Be off with you, peasant, I'll give you a devil of a clawing. I was going to tempt those thievish bumbailiffs and law-suit prevaricators, those double-dealing attorneys, and cavilling advocates. But they've sent a messenger to tell me that they're all mine already. Lucifer is quite sick of their souls, and generally sends them down to his sloppy kitchen-devils, except when they're highly seasoned. You monks say that there's nothing to compare with a student at breakfast, a lawyer at dinner, a vine-dresser at snacks, a merchant at supper, a chambermaid at second supper, and a hooded hobgoblin at any meal at all. That's true enough. In fact Master Lucifer takes goblins for his first course at all his meals, and he used to take scholars for breakfast. But alas, by some misfortune, for the last few years they have been adding the Holy Bible to their subjects of study. For this reason we can't catch any of them for the devil, and I'm afraid that unless the canting priests come to our aid, and by threats or curses, force, violence, or burning, wrench their *St Pauls* out of their hands, we shan't get another taste of them down here. He generally dines on law-twisting lawyers and pillagers of the poor, and he is not short of them. But one gets bored with eating the same meat every day; and he said, not long ago, in full chapter that he would like to eat the soul of a shifty priest who had forgotten in his sermon to recommend himself to the charity of his hearers. He promised double pay and a first-class post to anyone who would bring him one straight off the spit. Each one of us went out in quest of one, but we had no luck. They all remind the noble ladies to remember the monastery. He has given up snacks, ever since he has suffered so terribly from the colic, brought on by the dastardly treatment of his pupils, purveyors, sutlers, charcoal-merchants, and sausage-sellers in the Northern countries.[1] He takes a good supper off usurous merchants, apothecaries, forgers, coiners, and adulterators of merchandise; and sometimes, when he is in a good mood, he makes a second one off chambermaids who have drunk their masters' good wine and filled up the cask with stinking water. Work, peasant, work! I'm going to tempt the students of Trebizond to leave their fathers and mothers, to give up their regular way of life, to exempt themselves from their King's edicts, to live in subterranean liberty, despising the world, mocking everyone and putting on the pretty little cap of poetic innocence, to transform themselves into so many charming will-o'-the-wisps.'

CHAPTER 47: *How the Devil was fooled by an old Woman of Popefigland*

THE farmer was sad and thoughtful as he returned home, and when his wife saw his state of mind she thought he had been robbed at the market. But when she learnt the reason for his depression and saw that his purse was full of money, she gently comforted him, assuring him that no harm would come to him from this scratching-match. He need only leave things to her, she said. She had already thought of a good way out.

'If the worst comes to the worst,' said the farmer, 'I shall only take one scratch. I shall give in at the first blow and leave him the field.'

1. A reference to the Reformation.

'Not a bit of it,' said the old woman. 'You rely on me. Don't you worry, but let me deal with him. You told me that he's only a little devil. I'll make him give in to you straight away, and the field will remain ours. If he had been a big devil, then there would have been something to think about.'

The day we touched at the island was the day fixed for the match. Very early in the morning the farmer had made a thorough confession, taken communion like a good Catholic, and on the vicar's advice had hidden in the sacristy, under the water, as we found him. But just as they were telling us this story, we had news that the old woman had fooled the devil and won the field.

The way it happened was this. The devil came to the farmer's door, where he knocked and called out: 'Hi, peasant, peasant! Now for a good clawing-match!' Then he went briskly and resolutely into the house, but did not find the farmer there, only his wife lying on the floor, weeping and wailing.

'What's this?' demanded the devil. 'Where is he? What's he doing?'

'Oh,' cried the old woman. 'Where is he, the wretch, the butcher, the brigand? He's torn me to bits, I'm finished, I'm dying of the wound he gave me.'

'Why?' asked the devil. 'What's the matter? I'll make him dance for you pretty soon.'

'Oh,' said the old woman, 'he told me, the butcher, the tyrant, the devil-scratcher, that he had an appointment for a clawing-match with you; and to try out his nails, he merely scratched me with his little finger, here between my legs, and tore me quite open. I'm finished. My wound will never heal. Just take a look. But now he has gone to the blacksmith's to have his claws sharpened and pointed. You're done for, Master Devil, my dear friend. Make your escape. He'll be here in a moment. Please, please, run away off.'

With this she lifted her clothes to the chin, as Persian mothers used to of old when they saw their sons fleeing from the battle, and showed him her what's-its-name. When the devil saw this huge and continuous cavity, extending in all directions, he cried out: 'Mahound! Demiurge! Megaera! Alecto! Persephone! He shan't find me here. I'm off like a streak. Very well, I leave him the field.'

When we had heard the final outcome of this story, we retired to our ship, and cut our stay short. Pantagruel subscribed eighteen thousand gold reals to the church building fund, in consideration of the people's poverty and the distress of the place.

CHAPTER 48: *Pantagruel goes ashore on the Isle of Papimania*

HAVING left the desolate island of the Popefigs, we sailed for a day through a most pleasant calm, and at evening perceived the blessed island of the Papimaniacs. No sooner had we dropped anchor in the harbour than, even before we had tied up, four persons in different garbs rowed out to us in a skiff. One was frocked, shitten, and booted like a monk; another dressed as a falconer, with a lure and hawking-glove; another as a law-pleader, with a great sack full of informations, summonses, chicaneries, and postponements in his hand, and the fourth was like an Orléans vine-dresser, with fine cloth gaiters, a pannier, and a pruning-knife at his belt.

The moment they were tied up to our ship, they all shouted out together: 'Have you seen him, good passengers? Have you seen him?'

'Whom?' asked Pantagruel.

'You know whom,' they answered.

'Who's he?' asked Friar John. Then, thinking that it was some thief or murderer or church-robber that they were inquiring for, he added: 'I'll fairly lay him out. Od's my life if I don't.'

'What's this, strangers?' they asked. 'Don't you know the One and Only?'

'Gentlemen,' said Epistemon. 'We don't understand your terms. Explain to us, if you please, whom you mean, and we'll tell you the truth, with no deception.'

'He is who he is,' they proclaimed. 'Have you never seen him?'

'He who is,' replied Pantagruel, 'is by our theological doctrine God. He used those words in declaring himself to Moses. Certainly we've never seen him. He is invisible to mortal eyes.'

'We're not making the very least reference to the Supreme God who rules in the heavens. We are speaking of God upon earth. Have you ever seen him?'

'They mean the Pope,' exclaimed Carpalim. 'Take my word for it.'

'Yes, yes,' answered Panurge. 'Yes, indeed. I've seen three of them, and I didn't get much good from it either.'

'What!' they cried. 'Our sacred Decretals proclaim that there's never more than one living.'

'I mean three one after another,' explained Panurge. 'I've never seen more than one at a time.'

'O thrice and four times happy people,' they cried. 'You are welcome, and much more than welcome!'

At this they knelt before us and tried to kiss our feet. But this we refused to let them do, pointing out they could not do more to the Pope himself, if by good luck he should ever visit them in person.

'Oh yes, we could,' they said. 'We've already decided upon that. We would kiss his bare bum and his ballocks into the bargain. For he's got ballocks, has the Holy Father. We found that out from our great Decretals.[1] Otherwise he wouldn't be Pope. In fact, our subtle Decretaline philosophy tells us that this is a necessary consequence: He is Pope: therefore he has ballocks. And if there ceased to be ballocks in the world, the world would have no Pope.'

Meanwhile Pantagruel asked one of their ship's boys who these personages were. The answer was that they were the four Estates of the island; and the boy added that we would be welcomed and handsomely treated since we had seen the Pope. This remark he addressed to Panurge, who whispered back: 'I swear to God you're right. All's well in the end, if you've only the patience to wait. We've never profited so far from having seen the Pope. But now, by all the devils, it's going to stand us in good stead, as I can see.'

Then we landed, and all the people of the country, men, women, and children, came in a procession to meet us. Our four Estates cried out in loud voices: 'They've seen him! They've seen him! They've seen him!' and when they heard this proclamation, all the people knelt down before us, raising their clasped hands and crying: 'Oh, happy men! Oh, most happy!' And they continued to shout this for more than a quarter of an hour. Then the schoolmaster ran out with all his pedagogues, pedants, and scholars, and gave them all a magisterial whipping, much as they used once to whip little children in our country on the hanging of some criminal, in order that they should

1. Books of pronouncements by Popes in the form of answers to questions put to them.

never forget the occasion. But this annoyed Pantagruel, who said to him: 'Gentlemen, if you don't stop the beating of these children, I shall go away.'

When they heard his stentorian voice they were amazed, and I saw one little long-fingered hunchback who asked the schoolmaster: 'By the Supplement to the Decretals, does everyone who sees the Pope become as big as this man who is threatening us? Oh, how passionately I do long to see him, so that I can grow and be as big as he is.'

Their comments were so loud that Greatclod – which is what they call their bishop – bustled up on an unbridled mule with green trappings, accompanied by his *apposts* – as they call his vassals – and by his *supposts* or officers, carrying crosses, banners, standards, canopies, torches, and holy-water bowls. They too tried with all their might to kiss our feet, as the good Christian Valfinier did to Pope Clement. They said that one of their *Hypothetes*, or backward prophets, the scourer and glosser of their holy Decretals, had left it in writing that, just as the Messiah, whom the Jews had expected so fervently and so long, had finally come to them, so the Pope would one day come to this island; but that until that happy day, if anyone were to land who had seen him in Rome or elsewhere, they must feast him well and treat him with reverence.

However we courteously begged to be excused.

CHAPTER 49: *How Greatclod, Bishop of Papimania, showed us the Heaven-sent Decretals*

THEN Greatclod said to us: 'By our holy Decretals we are enjoined and commanded to visit the churches before the taverns. Do not let us violate this rule, but let us go to church. We will go and feast afterwards.'

'You lead the way, good man,' said Friar John, 'and we'll follow. Your reminder was timely. You're a good Christian, and it's a long time since we've seen one. I feel much rejoiced in my spirit, and I think I shall enjoy my food the better for it. It's a grand thing to meet good men.'

When we came to the church door we saw a great gilt book, all covered with fine and precious stones, spider-rubies, emeralds, dia-

monds, and pearls more valuable than – or at least as valuable as –
those that Octavian dedicated to the Capitoline Jove. It hung in the
air from the sculptured frieze of the porch, suspended by two stout
golden chains. We gazed at it in wonder, while Pantagruel handled it
and turned over its pages, for he could easily reach it. But he told us
that when he touched them he felt a gentle tingling of his nails and a
tautening of his arms, together with a violent temptation to beat up a
sergeant or two, providing they were not tonsured.

Then said Greatclod: 'In the old days the Law was given to the
Jews by Moses, written by the very hand of God. In Delphi these
words were found written by a God above the gate of Apollo's
temple: ΓΝΩΘΙ ΣΕΑΥΤΟΝ[1] and after a certain lapse of time the
syllable ΕΙ[2] was also seen, written by a divine hand, as a message from
Heaven. The image of Cybele too was sent down from Heaven into
Phrygia, into a field called Pessinus. Also in Tauris, if you believe
Euripides, there was the image of Diana. The oriflamme, or standard
of St Denis, was dropped from the skies to the noble and most Christian kings of France, as a weapon against the infidels. In the reign of
Numa Pompilius, the second king of the Romans, the rounded shield
called *ancile* was seen at Rome to descend out of the skies. In ancient
days the statue of Minerva fell out of the empyrean blue on to the
Acropolis at Athens. And here, too, you may see the holy Decretals,
written by the hand of an angelic cherub. Possibly you people from
across the sea may not believe this.'

'We should find it difficult,' replied Panurge.

'And miraculously transmitted to us,' continued Greatclod, 'in that
same manner which caused Homer, father of all philosophy – except,
of course, the divine Decretals – to call the River Nile *Diipetes*, or sent
by Zeus. And because you have seen the Pope, their evangelist and
everlasting protector, you will have our permission to see them and
kiss them inside, should you wish to. But previously you will have to
fast for three days and make a regular confession, carefully sifting and
cataloguing your sins so severely that not a single detail shall fall to the
ground, as the divine Decretals, which you see here, enjoin us. For
that you need time.'

'Most worthy man,' answered Panurge. 'We have seen Excretals –
I mean Decretals – in quantity, on paper, on lantern-parchment, and

1. Know thyself.   2. Thou art.

on vellum, written by hand and printed in type. There's no need for you to worry about showing us these. We are grateful for your kind thought, and thank you accordingly.'

'But truly,' exclaimed Greatclod, 'you've certainly never seen these, which are written in an angel's hand. Those in your country are merely transcribed from ours, as we find from the writings of one of our old Decretaline scholars. I beg and implore you not to consider the trouble to me. Just tell me whether you agree to confess and fast just for three short days. Blessed days they'll be.'

'To cuntfess,' answered Panurge. 'Very well, we agree. But we don't find this the right moment for a fast. For we've fasted so much, so very much, at sea, that the spiders have spun their webs over our teeth. Here's good Brother John of the Hashes' – at this title Greatclod graciously conferred on him the short accolade – 'the moss has grown in his throat, through lack of exercise for his chaps and movement of the jaw-bones.'

'That's quite right,' put in Friar John. 'I've fasted so long, so very long, that I've become round-shouldered.'

'Let's go into the church, then,' said Greatclod, 'and pardon us if we don't immediately sing you God's blessed Mass. But it's past midday, and our holy Decretals forbid us to sing a Mass – a High and proper Mass, I mean – after that hour. But I'll sing you a Low and dry Mass.'

'I should prefer one moistened with a little good Anjou wine,' said Panurge. 'Lay on then, lay on stiff and low!'

'Strike me blue,' exclaimed Friar John, 'I greatly dislike having my stomach empty still. If I'd had a good breakfast and fed my fill like a monk, and he'd happened to sing us a Requiem, I'd have brought him bread and wine in memory of what has gone before. But get along, lay on, go ahead! Be sure and keep it short, though, for fear it dangles in the dirt, and for another reason besides, if you please.'

CHAPTER 50: *How Greatclod showed us the Archetype of a Pope*

WHEN the Mass was over Greatclod drew a huge bundle of keys out of a trunk beside the high altar, and with them opened the thirty-two locks and fourteen padlocks of a strongly barred iron window above it. Then he most mysteriously enveloped himself in damp sackcloth and, pulling back a curtain of crimson satin, showed us an image, which I thought very crudely painted. This he touched with a longish stick, and made us all kiss the point that had touched it. He then asked us: 'What do you think of this image?'

'It represents a Pope,' answered Pantagruel. 'I know it by the tiara, the furred stole, the surplice, and the slipper.'

'You are perfectly right,' said Greatclod. 'It is the archetype of that good God upon earth whose coming we devotedly await, and whom we hope to see one day in our land. O happy, yearned-for, long-expected day! Happy and thrice-happy you also, to whom the stars have been so favourable that you have actually seen that good God on earth in life and face-to-face! For we, by the mere sight of his image, gain full remission of all our sins that we can remember, together with the third part and eighteen fortieths of the sins we have forgotten. We are only shown it, to be sure, on the great annual festivals.'

Thereupon Pantagruel said that it was a work in the great tradition of Daedalus, the first sculptor; and that though ill-proportioned and badly made, still, latently and occultly, it contained a certain divine efficacy in the matter of pardons.

'It was like that at Seuilly,' said Friar John. 'The beggars were supping one high feast day in the hospital, and boasting, one that he had made six farthings, another two halfpennies, and a third seven three-penny bits. Then a fourth fat rascal got up and proclaimed that he had made three whole shillings. "Oh yes," replied his companions; "but you've got God's lucky leg." – as if there were some divine and fortunate power concealed in a leg that was all ulcerated and decayed.'

'When you are going to tell us stories like that,' said Pantagruel, 'please remember to bring a basin. That one nearly made me sick. Fancy using the name of God in such a filthy, abominable context! Ugh, I say ugh! If such misuse of words is the habit in your monkery, please leave it there, and don't bring it with you out of the cloister.'

'Physicians do say,' said Epistemon, 'that there is a certain divine participation in certain ailments. You remember how Nero used to praise mushrooms, and call them in the Greek phrase, *the food of the Gods*, because he had poisoned his predecessor, the Emperor Claudius, with them.'

'I don't think this statue is much like our last Popes,' put in Panurge. 'I have never seen them in stoles, but with helmets on their heads, and a Persian tiara on top; and while the whole Christian realm was in peace and quiet, they alone carried on furious and most cruel wars.'

'But that,' said Greatclod, 'was against rebels, heretics, and desperate Protestants, who disobeyed this great and holy God upon earth. It is not only permissible and lawful for him to wage such wars, but he is commanded to by the sacred Decretals. It is his duty to put to the fire and sword Emperors, Kings, Dukes, Princes, and Republics the moment they transgress his commandments by so much as a jot. He must spoil them of their goods, dispossess them of their realms, proscribe them, and anathematize them, and not only kill their bodies and those of their children and other relatives, but also damn their souls to the bottom of the hottest cauldron in all Hell.'

'But here, in all the devils' name,' protested Panurge, 'there are no such heretics as Raminagrobis was, and as there are now among the Germans and the English. You are proved and sifted Christians.'

'Yes, we are indeed,' said Greatclod, 'and so we shall all be saved. Let us go and take some holy water. Then we will have dinner.'

CHAPTER 51: *Some small talk during dinner in Praise of the Decretals*

NOW note, fellow boozers, that while Greatclod was saying his dry Mass, three church bell-ringers, each with a great bowl in his hand, were passing among the crowd, crying: 'Don't forget the happy people who have seen him face-to-face.' As we came out of the temple, they brought Greatclod their basins, which were quite full of Papimaniac money.

Greatclod told us that this collection was for convivial purposes, and that, in accordance with a miraculous gloss, hidden in a certain corner of their holy Decretals, one half of the contribution would be spent on good drink, the other on good food. This was done, in a very fine tavern, which rather reminded me of Guillot's at Amiens. Believe me, the viands were copious and the drinks numerous.

I made two memorable observations at this dinner: first, that no dish was brought in that had not a great deal of canonical stuffing; whether it was kid, capon, or hog – which is very plentiful in Papimania – pigeon, rabbit, leveret, turkey, or any other meat, it was all the same.

Secondly, that the whole of the first and second courses was served by the young marriageable maidens of the place. They were pretty, I promise you, and most appetizing; sweet little fair creatures, and most graceful. They wore long, white, loose robes with double girdles. Their heads were bare, and their hair plaited with little bands and ribbons of violet silk, embellished with roses, pinks, marjoram, fennel, orange blossom, and other scented flowers, and each time we put down our glasses they invited us to drink again with the neatest and daintiest of curtseys. Friar John took sideways glances at them, like a dog who has stolen a chicken.

As they cleared the first course these maidens sang a melodious epode in praise of the sacrosanct Decretals; and as the second course was brought in Greatclod, in high good cheer, called to one of these master-butlers: 'Here, clerk, bring some light!' At these words one of the girls promptly presented him with a full beaker of *Supplementary* wine. Then, holding it in his hand and sighing deeply, he said to Pantagruel: 'My Lord, and you, my good friends, I drink to you all from the bottom of my heart. You are all very welcome.' When he had drunk and handed the beaker back to the pretty maiden, he exclaimed most ponderously: 'O divine Decretals, it is thanks to you that wine is found to be so good, so very good.'

'That's the best joke yet,' exclaimed Panurge.

'It would be better still,' said Pantagruel, 'if they could turn poor wine into good.'

'O seraphic *Sixth*,' continued Greatclod, 'how vital that book is for the salvation of humanity! O cherubic *Clementines*, how neatly the perfect life of a true Christian is contained and described in that fourth book! O angelic *Supplementaries*, without you all poor souls would perish, who wander aimlessly here in mortal bodies, about this vale of tears! Alas, when will this gift of special grace be vouchsafed to men, that they may forsake all other studies and occupations only to read you, blessed Decretals, to understand you, know you, use you, put you into practice, incorporate you, absorb you into their blood, and draw you into the deepest lobes of their brains, the very marrow of their bones, and the tortuous labyrinths of their arteries? Then, and not till then, so and not otherwise, will the world be a happy place.'

At this Epistemon got up and said quite clearly to Panurge: 'For want of a close stool I'm forced to retire. This stuffing has relaxed my bumgut. I shan't be long.'

'Then,' continued Greatclod, 'there will be no more hail, frost, fogs, or natural disasters! Then there will be an abundance of all good things on earth! Then there will be perpetual and inviolable peace throughout the Universe, an end of all wars, plunderings, forced labour, brigandage, and assassination, except against heretics and accursed rebels! Then there will be joy, happiness, jollity, gladness, sport, pleasures, and delights throughout all human kind! Oh what great learning, what inestimable erudition, what godlike precepts, are packed into the divine chapters of these immortal Decretals! Oh, when you read only half a canon, a small paragraph, a single sentence of these sacrosanct Decretals, you feel the furnace of divine love kindle in your hearts; and of charity towards your neighbour as well, providing that he is not a heretic. You feel a fixed contempt for all fortuitous and earthly things, an ecstatic elevation of your spirits, even to the third heaven, and firm contentment in all your affections.'

CHAPTER 52: *More about the Miracles wrought by the Decretals*

'THERE'S a golden-voiced organ for you, said Panurge. But I believe as little of it as I can. I happened to read a chapter of the stuff once, at Poitiers, at the Scotch Decretalipotent doctor's, and devil take me if I wasn't constipated for more than four, indeed for five days afterwards. I only shat one little turd. But what a turd! I'll swear to you it was like the ones Catullus said his neighbour Furius shat:

> You don't pass ten poor turdlets in a year,
> And even if you break them with your fingers
> And rub them small no dirt or soiling lingers,
> For they are harder than the beans or stones.

'Ha, ha,' exclaimed Greatclod. 'By St John, my friend, you must have been in a state of mortal sin.'

'That's wine from a different cask,' said Panurge.

'One day,' said Friar John, 'when I was at Seuilly, I wiped my bum with a page of one of these wretched *Clementines* that John Guimard, our bursar, had thrown out into the cloister meadow, and may all the devils take me if I wasn't seized with such horrible cracks and piles that the poor door to my back passage was quite unhinged.'

'S'John,' exclaimed Greatclod, 'that was a manifest punishment from God, a vengeance for the sin you had committed in soiling that holy book which you should have kissed and adored, with the adoration known as *latria*, or with *hyperdulia* at the least. The great Panormitanus never lied on that score.'

'John Chouart at Montpellier' said Ponocrates, 'had bought from the monks of St Olary some fine Decretals written on large and handsome Lamballe parchment, to tear into vellum leaves to beat gold between. But he was so strangely unfortunate that not a single piece he beat came out right. They were all torn and full of holes.'

'That was a punishment,' said Greatclod, 'and the vengeance of God.'

'At Le Mans,' said Eudemon, 'Francis Cornu, the apothecary, used a dog-eared *Supplementary* to make up paper bags, and I renounce the devil if everything that was wrapped up in them did not immediately become spoiled, contaminated, and rotten: incense, pepper, cloves, cinnamon, saffron, wax, spices, cassia, rhubarb, and tamarind. In fact there was not a drug, purge, or medicine that wasn't ruined.'

'A punishment,' said Greatclod, 'the vengeance of God, for making a profane misuse of such sacred writings.'

'In Paris,' said Carpalim, 'a tailor called Groignet used an old *Supplementary* for his patterns and templates and, strange to relate, all the garments he cut to those patterns were spoilt. Gowns, hoods, cloaks, cassocks, skirts, short coats, ruffs, doublets, petticoats, riding-cloaks, and farthingales: all turned out useless. When he meant to cut a hood, Groignet made the shape of a codpiece. Instead of a cassock, he would produce a scalloped hat. On the pattern of a short coat he would cut out an amice. From the template for a doublet would come something like a frying-pan, which his workmen would sew up, and jag round the bottom, after which it looked more like a hot-chestnut pan. Instead of a ruff, there came a long boot; on the pattern for a farthingale, he cut out a penitent's hood. When he meant to make a cloak, he would produce a Swiss soldier's hat. In fact the poor man was condemned by the courts to replace his customers' cloth, and to-day he is bankrupt.'

'A punishment,' said Greatclod, 'and the vengeance of God.'

'At Cahusac,' said Gymnaste, 'an archery match was arranged between my Lord of Estissac's men and the Viscount de Lausun. Perotou had ripped up half a *Decretals* belonging to Canon La Carte, and had cut the leaves to make the white of the target. Now I'll give myself, sell myself, or make a free present of myself to the hosts of hell if a single archer in the whole country – and Guienne is famous for its archers – could lodge an arrow in it. They all missed the mark. That sacrosanct target remained virgin, intact, and untouched. What's more, the elder Sansornin, who held the stakes, swore to us on his favourite oath, that he had clearly, visibly, and manifestly seen Carquelin's arrow, going straight for the bull's eye in the middle of the white. "But God's figs," said he, "when it was on the point of striking and piercing, it was deflected six foot to the side, in the direction of the bakehouse."'

'A miracle!' cried Greatclod, 'a miracle, a miracle! Here, clerk, bring me a light. I drink to you all. You seem good Christians to me.'

When they heard this, the girls began to giggle among themselves and Friar John gave a sudden nasal whinny as if ready to play the jackass, or at least the stallion, and leap on them, like famine on the poor.

'I think one would have been safer from an arrow beside that target,' said Pantagruel, 'than Diogenes was of old.'

'What do you mean?' asked Greatclod. 'How? Was he a Decretalist?'

'That be hanged for a tale,' said Epistemon, returning from his errand.

'Diogenes,' said Pantagruel, 'wanting a little amusement one day, visited the archers who were practising at the butts. Among them was one who was such a bad, inaccurate, and clumsy shot that when it was his turn to shoot all the spectators scattered for fear he might hit them. Diogenes watched him send one arrow so wide that it fell a good six foot from the target. So at the second shot, whilst all the people moved off in every direction, he ran over and stood right beside the white. This was the safest place, he declared. For the archer would be more likely to strike any other place. Only the white of the target was quite safe from his arrow.'

'One of my Lord d'Estissac's pages, by the name of Chamouillac,' said Gymnaste, 'discovered the spell. By his advice Perotou removed the white, and made another from the papers of the Pouillac lawsuit instead. After that both sides shot very well.'

'At Landerousse,' said Rhizotome, 'at the wedding of John Delif there was a grand and sumptuous banquet, as was then the custom of the country. After supper they acted some farces, interludes, and comic turns, and danced several morris-dances to the bells and drums. Then masks and mummers of various sorts came in. My school-friends and I had all had fine violet and white favours given us that morning, and we wanted to do the party as proud as possible. So at the end we performed a gay masquerade, in false beards and liberally decorated with cockle-shells from St Michel and with snail-shells too. As we had no arum, burdock, or bugloss leaves and no paper, we made our masks from the leaves of an old *Sextum*, which were lying about there, cutting little holes in them for the eyes, the nose, and the mouth. But strange to say, when our little capers and schoolboy jokes were over, and we took off our masks, we appeared uglier and more repulsive than the Devil's brood in the Doué miracle-play. Our faces were all sore in the places which those leaves had touched. One of us had small-pox, another the scab, another the great pox, another the measles, and another great carbuncles. In fact the one who came off best was the one who merely lost his teeth.'

'A miracle,' cried Greatclod, 'a miracle!'

'It's not time to laugh yet,' said Rhizotome. 'My two sisters, Catherine and Renée, had used this *Sextum* for a press. For it was covered with thick boards and studded with nails. They had put their newly washed wimples and cuffs and collars in it, all white and beautifully starched. Now I swear by Almighty God ...'

'Wait a moment,' interrupted Greatclod, 'which God do you mean?'

'There's only one,' answered Rhizotome.

'One in the Heavens, it's true,' said Greatclod. 'But haven't we another, on earth?'

'Gee up there,' exclaimed Rhizotome. 'I'd forgotten about that, 'pon my soul I had. Well, by Almighty God, the Pope upon earth, their wimples, collars, bibs, head-scarves, and all their other linen became blacker than a charcoal-burner's sack.'

'A miracle,' cried Greatclod. 'Clerk, some more light, and listen to these fine stories.'

'How is it, then,' asked Friar John, 'that people say:

> Since decrees grew tails and wings,
> And knights took trunks to hold their things,
> And every monk rode on a horse,
> The world's been going from bad to worse.'

'Ah, I understand you,' said Greatclod. 'You're quoting one of these newfangled heretics' lampoons.'

CHAPTER 53: *How, by virtue of the Decretals, Gold is subtly drawn out of France into Rome*

'I WOULD gladly pay for a dish of the best tripe a man could guzzle,' said Epistemon, 'if only we could collate with the originals those terrific chapters, *Execrabilis, De multa, Si plures, De Annatis per totum, Nisi essent, Cum ad Monasterium, Quod dilectio, Mandatum,* and certain others that draw a hundred thousand ducats and more every year out of France into Rome.'

'That's no small sum, is it?' said Greatclod. 'Still, it doesn't seem to me a very great one when you consider that the most Christian realm of France is the Roman court's sole nurse. But can you show me any books in the world, books of philosophy, medicine, law, mathematics, polite literature, or even – God help me – of Holy Writ that can extract as much? No, not one. Pooh, pooh! You won't find a speck of this aurifluous energy in any of them, I promise you. And yet these devils of heretics won't read them and learn them. Burn them, nip them with pincers, slash them, drown them, hang them, impale them, break them, dismember them, disembowel them, hack them, fry them, grill them, cut them up, crucify them, boil them, crush them, quarter them, wrench their joints, rack them, and roast them alive, the wicked Decretalifuge, Decretalicide heretics. Why, they're worse than homicides, worse than parricides, these murderers of the Decretals, the devil take them.

'As for you, my good people, if you wish to be called good Christians and to have that reputation, I beseech you with clasped hands to believe no other thing, to have no other thought, to say, undertake, or do nothing, except what is contained in our sacred Decretals and their corollaries: the fine *Sextum*, the magnificent *Clementines*, the splendid *Supplementaries*. What deific books! So you will be glorified, honoured, exalted, and rich in dignities and preferments in this world. You will be universally revered and dreaded, and preferred, chosen, and elected above all others. For there is no class of men beneath the cope of heaven in which you will find persons fitter for all undertakings and affairs than those who, by divine foreknowledge and eternal predestination, have applied themselves to the study of the holy Decretals. Should you wish to select a bold commander, a good captain and leader of an army in time of war, a man capable of foreseeing all difficulties, of avoiding all dangers, of leading his men boldly to the attack, and gaily into battle, of taking no risks, but always winning without loss of life and turning his victories to good account, then, believe me you must take one who knows the Decrees.[1] No, no, I mean the Decretals.'

'That was a big gaffe,' said Epistemon.

'Should you wish in time of peace to find a man fit and capable of undertaking the government of a republic, a kingdom, an empire, or a principality; of maintaining the Church, the nobility, the senate, and the people in riches, friendship, concord, obedience, virtue, and dignity, believe me, you must choose a Decretalist. Should you wish to find one capable, by means of his exemplary life, his rare eloquence, and his holy admonitions, of rapidly conquering the Holy Land without bloodshed, and converting the unbelieving Turks, Jews, Tartars, Muscovites, Mamelukes, and Sarrabovites, then, believe me, you must choose a Decretalist.

'Why is it that in many lands the people are rebellious and uncontrolled, the pages cheeky and mischievous, and the students frivolous dunces? Why, because their governors, squires, and teachers were not Decretalists! But tell me, on your conscience, what was it that founded, strengthened, and gave authority to those splendid religious houses which you now see everywhere, adorning, decorating, and doing honour to the Christian world as the stars do to the firmament? The divine Decretals. What was it that founded, underpropped, and shored up, that now maintains, supports, and nourishes, the devout monks and nuns in their convents, monasteries, and abbeys? To what do we owe these holy folk, without whose continuous prayers, day

1. Pronouncements made by the Popes of their own initiative.

and night, the world would be in evident danger of returning to its ancient chaos? To the holy Decretals.

'What is it that endowed the famous and celebrated patrimony of St Peter with such abundance of all goods, temporal, corporeal, and spiritual, and what is it that daily increases that abundance? The sacred Decretals. What makes the holy apostolic see of Rome so powerful throughout the Universe, that at all times even to this day, willy-nilly, all kings, emperors, potentates, and lords depend on it, pay homage to it, are crowned, confirmed, and lent authority by it? What is it that forces them to come and kiss it, and prostrate themselves before its miraculous slipper, of which you have seen the picture? Why, God's blessed Decretals. I'll tell you a great secret. The Universities of your world generally bear on their crests and coats-of-arms a book, sometimes open, sometimes closed. Now what book do you think it can be?'

'I'm sure I don't know,' said Pantagruel. 'I've never read a word of it.'

'Why, the Decretals, of course,' proclaimed Greatclod, 'without which all the privileges of all the Universities would decay. I've taught you something there! Ha, ha, ha, ha!'

Here Greatclod began to belch, fart, laugh, dribble, and sweat. He handed his great, greasy bonnet with its four codpiece-like corners to one of the girls, who placed it on her head in great delight, having first kissed it most lovingly. For she took this as a sign and promise that she would be the first to marry.

'Hurrah,' cried Epistemon, 'hurrah! *Hoch! Trinken wir!* Let us drink! That was an apocalyptic secret.'

'Clerk,' cried Greatclod, 'Clerk, some light here, and make it two lanterns. Bring in the dessert, girls! ... As I was saying, if you devote yourself in this way to the exclusive study of the blessed Decretals, you'll be rich and honoured in this world. I say therefore, that in the next world, you will infallibly be brought safely into the blessed kingdom of Heaven, the keys of which are in the hands of our good God the Arch-Decretalist. O my good God, whom I adore but have never seen, open to us, of your especial grace, at least at the hour of our death, that most sacred treasure house of our most holy mother Church, of which you are the guardian, preserver, dispenser, administrator, and steward. Give orders that those precious works of super-erogation, those goodly pardons, do not fail us in our need. Then the devils will find no purchase for their teeth in our poor souls, and the dread jaws of hell will not engulf us. If we must pass through purgatory, so be it! It is in your power and discretion to deliver us when you will!'

Here Greatclod began to weep huge hot tears, to beat his breast, to cross his thumbs and to kiss them.

CHAPTER 54: *Greatclod gives Pantagruel some Good-Christian Pears*

As they watched this doleful conclusion of Greatclod's oration, Epistemon, Friar John, and Panurge began to make mewing noises behind their napkins, while at the same time pretending to wipe their eyes, as if they had been moved to tears. The girls were well trained, and offered everyone full glasses of Clementine wine, together with plenty of sweets. So the banquet was gaily resumed.

When the meal was quite finished, Greatclod gave us a large quantity of fine, fat pears, saying as he did so: 'Take these, my friends. They are singularly good pears, and you won't find them as good elsewhere. Not every land grows everything. Only India produces black ebony. Good incense comes only from Saba. The true vermilion is found only in the soil of Lemnos, and only in this island do good pears grow. Set some seedlings from them, if you like, in your own country.'

'What do you call them?' asked Pantagruel. 'They seem excellent to me, and they have a fine flavour. Now if you were to stew them in a saucepan, cut into quarters, with a little wine and sugar I think they would be a very sound food for the sick, and the healthy too.'

'We just call them pears,' answered Greatclod. 'We're simple folk, as it pleased God to make us. We call figs figs, plums plums, and pears pears.'

'Indeed,' said Pantagruel. 'When I get back home – and pray God it be soon – I'll plant and graft some of them in my garden in Touraine on the banks of the Loire, and they shall be called Good-Christian pears. For I've never seen better Christians than these good Papimaniacs.'

'I should be just as pleased,' said Friar John, 'if he would give us two or three cartloads of his girls.'

'What would you do with them?' asked Greatclod.

'We would bleed them half-way between their big-toes with certain prodding tools that work wonders,' replied Friar John. 'In that way we'd graft some Good-Christian children on them, and the race in our land would multiply. It's not too sound at present.'

'No, by God. We'll not do that,' answered Greatclod. 'For you'd be up to your boyish tricks with them. Although I've never seen you before, I recognize you by your nose. Dear, dear, what a simple fellow you are! Would you wish to damn your immortal soul? Our Decretals forbid it. Oh, if only you knew them through and through!'

'Patience,' cried Friar John. 'But *si non vis dare, praesta quaesumus* – if you won't give them, at least lend them to us. That's breviary stuff. On that subject I fear no man with a beard, not even a Crystalline – I should say Decretaline doctor in a three-cornered cap.'

When the meal was over, we took our leave of Greatclod and all the good people. We humbly thanked them and, in return for all their kindness, promised them that when we came to Rome we would plead so hard with the Holy Father that he would hasten to pay them a personal visit. Then we returned to our ship. Pantagruel, in his generosity and out of gratitude for the sight of the Pope's blessed image, gave Greatclod nine pieces of doubly embroidered cloth of gold, to be hung in front of the barred window. He also had the box for the repair and upkeep of the church quite filled with double-slippered crowns, and for each of the girls who had served us at dinner he ordered nine hundred and fourteen gold angels to be set aside, to be used in due course as a dowry.

CHAPTER 55: *Pantagruel, on the high seas, hears various Words that have been thawed*

As we were banqueting, far out at sea, feasting and speechifying and telling nice little stories, Pantagruel suddenly jumped to his feet, and took a look all round him. 'Can you hear something, comrades?' he asked. 'I seem to hear people talking in the air. But I can't see anything. Listen.'

We all obeyed his command, and listened attentively, sucking in the air in great earfuls, like good oysters in the shell, to hear if any voice or other snatches of sound could be picked up; and so as to miss nothing, some of us cupped the palms of our hands to the backs of our ears, after the manner of the Emperor Antoninus. But, notwithstanding, we protested that we could hear no voice whatever. Pantagruel, however, continued to affirm that he could hear several voices on the air, both male and female; and then we decided that either we could hear them too, or else there was a ringing in our ears. Indeed, the more keenly we listened, the more clearly we made out voices, till in the end we could hear whole words. This greatly frightened us, and not unnaturally, since we could see no one, yet could hear voices and different sorts of sounds of men, women, children, and horses.

It was all so clear that Panurge cried out: 'God's my life, is this a trick? We are lost. Let's get away. We've fallen into an ambush. Brother John, are you there, my friend? Keep close to me, I beg of you. Have you got your cutlass? Make sure it doesn't stick in the scabbard. You never scour it half enough. We're lost. Listen. My God, those are cannon shots. Let's run away, I won't say with our feet and hands as Brutus did at the battle of Pharsalia, but with sail and oar. Let's get away. I've no courage on the sea. In a cellar or elsewhere I've more than enough. Let's run away. Let's save ourselves. I don't say this because I'm afraid, for I fear nothing except danger. That's what I always say, and so did the free-archer of Baignolet. So let's take no risks, and we'll get no slaps. Let's flee, and about turn! Turn the helm, you son of a whore! I would to God I were at Les Quinquenais at this moment, even if it meant never marrying! Let's fly. We're no match for them. They outnumber us by ten to one, I'm sure of it. Besides, they're on their own dunghills, and we don't know the country. Let's run away. It'll be no disgrace. Demosthenes said that he who flies lives to fight another day. At least let's retire. Starboard, larboard, to the foresails, to the topsails! We're dead men. In the name of all the devils, let's get away!'

On hearing Panurge make all this uproar, Pantagruel asked: 'Who is that coward down there? Let's see first what people they are. They may happen to be our friends. But still I can't catch sight of anyone, though I can see a hundred miles all round. But let's listen. I have heard that a certain philosopher called Petron believed that there are several worlds touching one another as at the points of an equilateral triangle. The inner area of this triangle, he said was the abode of truth and there lived the names and forms, the ideas and images of all things past and future. Outside this lies the Age – our secular world. In certain years, however, at long intervals, some part of these falls on humankind like distillations, or as the dew fell on Gideon's fleece, to remain there laid up for the future, awaiting the consummation of the Age. I remember, too, that Aristotle maintains Homer's words to be bounding, flying, and moving, and consequently alive. Antiphanes, also, said that Plato's teaching was like words that congeal and freeze on the air, when uttered in the depths of winter in some distant country. That is why they are not heard. He said as well that Plato's lessons to young children were hardly understood by them till they were old.

'Now it would be worth arguing and investigating whether this may not be the very place where such words thaw out. Shouldn't we be greatly startled if it proved to be the head and the lyre of Orpheus? After the Thracian women had torn him to pieces, they threw his head and lyre into the river Hebrus, down which they floated to the Black Sea, and from there to the island of Lesbos, still riding together on the waters. And all the time there issued from the head a melancholy song, as if in mourning for Orpheus's death, while the lyre, as the moving winds strummed it, played a harmonious accompaniment to this lament. Let's look if we can see them hereabouts.'

CHAPTER 56: *Pantagruel hears some gay Words among those that are thawed*

IT was the captain that answered: 'My lord, don't be afraid. This is the edge of the frozen sea, and at the beginning of last winter there was a great and bloody battle here between the Arimaspians and the Cloud-riders. The shouts of the men, the cries of the women, the slashing of the battle-axes, the clashing of the armour and harnesses, the neighing of the horses and all the other frightful noises of battle became frozen on the air. But just now, the rigours of winter being over and the good season coming on with its calm and mild weather, these noises are melting, and so you can hear them.'

'By God,' cried Panurge. 'I believe you. But could we see just one of them? I remember reading that, as they stood around the edges of the mountain on which Moses received the Laws of the Jews, the people palpably saw the voices.'

'Here, here,' exclaimed Pantagruel, 'here are some that are not yet thawed.'

Then he threw on the deck before us whole handfuls of frozen words, which looked like crystallized sweets of different colours. We saw some words gules, or gay quips, some vert, some azure, some sable, and some or. When we warmed them a little between our hands, they melted like snow, and we actually heard them, though we did not understand them, for they were in a barbarous language. There was one exception, however, a fairly big one. This, when Friar John picked it up, made a noise like a chestnut that has been thrown on the embers without being pricked. It was an explosion, and made us all start with fear. 'That,' said Friar John, 'was a cannon shot in its day.'

Panurge asked Pantagruel to give him some more. But Pantagruel answered that only lovers gave their words.

'Sell me some, then,' said Panurge.

'That's a lawyer's business,' replied Pantagruel, 'selling words. I'd rather sell you silence, though I should ask a higher price for it, as Demosthenes did once, when bribed to have a quinsy.'

Nevertheless he threw three or four handfuls on the deck, and I saw some very sharp words among them; bloody words which, as the Captain told us, sometimes return to the place from which they come – but with their throats cut; some terrifying words, and others rather unpleasant to look at. When they had all melted together, we heard: Hin, hin, hin, hin, his, tick, tock, crack, brededin, brededac, frr, frrr, frrrr, bou, bou, bou, bou, bou, bou, bou, bou, tracc, tracc, trr, trrr, trrrr, trrrrr, trrrrrr, on, on, on, on, on, ouououououon, Gog, Magog, and goodness knows what other barbarous sounds. The Captain said that these were the battle-cries, and the neighings of the chargers as they clashed together. Then we heard other great noises going off as they melted, some like drums and fifes, others like clarions and trumpets. Believe me, we were greatly amused I wanted to preserve a few of the gay quips in oil, the way you keep snow and ice, and then to wrap them up in clean straw. But Pantagruel refused, saying that it was folly to store up things which one is never short of, and which are always plentiful, as gay quips are among good and jovial Pantagruelists.

Here Panurge somewhat annoyed Friar John, and put him in a huff. For he took him at his word at a moment when he least expected it, and threatened to make him as sorry for this, as Guillaume Jousseaulme was for having sold the noble Patelin cloth on credit. If ever Panurge married, said the Friar, he'd seize him by the horns like a calf, since Panurge had deceived him like a man. Panurge, in derision, made an ugly face at him, and cried out: 'Would to God that I could have the oracle of the Holy Bottle, without travelling any further!'

CHAPTER 57: *Pantagruel lands at the Home of Messer Gaster, the first Master of Arts in the World*

THAT day Pantagruel landed on an island more admirable than all others, both for its situation and on account of its governor. At first approach, it appeared rough, stony, mountainous, and barren on all sides. It was repulsive to the eye, very painful to the feet, and scarcely more accessible than that mount in Dauphiné which owes its name of Mount Inaccessible to its toadstool shape, and to the fact that no one within human memory has been known to climb it, except Doyac, King Charles VIII's master of artillery, who reached the top with the aid of some marvellous machines, and found an old ram there. It was difficult to guess who had transported the creature to that place. Some said that he had been carried there as a lamb, by some eagle or horned owl, and escaped among the bushes.

After overcoming the preliminary difficulties, with considerable toil and no lack of sweat, we found the top of the mountain so pleasant and fertile, so healthy and delightful, that I thought it was the true Garden and Earthly Paradise, the situation of which causes our good theologians so much disputation and labour. But Pantagruel insisted that this was the abode of Arete – that is virtue – described by Hesiod, though he did not wish to prejudice sounder opinion.

The governor of the place was Messer Gaster, first master of arts in this world. For if you believe that fire is the great prime mover of the arts, as Cicero writes, you are in error and you do him wrong. Cicero did not believe it himself. If you believe that Mercury was the prime inventor of the arts, as our ancient Druids thought, you are greatly in error. The satirist is correct when he says that Messer Gaster – Sir Belly – is the true master of all the arts.

With him resided peacefully Dame Penia, otherwise called Poverty, mother of the nine Muses, from whose former alliance with Porus, lord of Abundance, Love, that noble child and the mediator between Heaven and Earth, was born for our profit, as Plato affirms in his *Symposium*.

To this chivalrous monarch we are all bound to show reverence, swear obedience, and give honour. For he is imperious and strict, blunt and stern, difficult and inflexible. One can convince him of nothing. One can neither remonstrate with him nor persuade him of anything. He does not hear a word. In the same way as the Egyptians said that Harpocras, the god of silence – called Sigalion in Greek – is *astomous* – that is to say mouthless – so Gaster was created without ears. He only speaks by signs. But these signs all the world obeys, more promptly than Praetors' edicts or royal commands. When he calls, he will not admit the slightest stay or delay. You say that when the lion roars, all beasts round about shiver, for as far – that is to say – as his voice carries. That is written, and it is true. I have seen the evidence. But I guarantee that at Messer Gaster's command the whole sky trembles, the whole earth shakes. The words of his command are – Make up your mind to obey immediately, or die.

The captain told us how one day, following the example of the limbs that conspired against the belly, as Aesop describes it, the whole Somatic kingdom mutinied against him, and plotted to refuse him obedience. But they quickly suffered for it and repented, and returned to serve him in all humility. Otherwise they would all have perished of hunger.

In no company where he is present is there any need to discuss rank or precedence; though Kings, Emperors, or even Popes may be present, he always goes in first. At the Council of Basle, too, he took first place, though, as you may hear, it was a disorderly assembly, since there was so much intriguing and contention for precedence. The whole world is busy serving him; the whole world labours to do so. But as a reward, he does the world a service; he invents all the arts, all the devices, all the crafts, all the machines and contrivances for it. Even the brute beasts he instructs in arts denied them by Nature. He makes ravens, jays, parrots, and starlings into poets; he makes poetesses of magpies, and teaches them to pronounce human words, to speak them and to sing them. And all for the sake of the belly!

Eagles, gerfalcons, falcons, sakers, laniers, goshawks, sparrow-hawks, merlins, haggards, peregrines, all wild and rapacious birds of prey, he tames and domesticates. So he will give them their full liberty of the skies when he chooses; send them as high as he will for as long as he pleases; and keep them soaring, straying, flying, hovering, flattering him, and paying court to him above the clouds. Then suddenly he will make them swoop from heaven to earth. And all for the sake of the belly!

Elephants, lions, rhinoceroses, bears, horses, and dogs, he makes to dance, jump, caper, fight, swim, hide, bring him anything he wants, or carry what he wishes. And all for the sake of the belly!

He makes fresh-water fish and those of the sea, whales, and marine monsters, rise from the lowest depths. He drives wolves out of the woods, bears out of the rocks, foxes out of their holes, and snakes out of the ground, in great numbers. And all for the sake of the belly!

So violent is he, in fact, that in his rage he devours everything, beasts and men alike, as witness the case of the Basques, when besieged by Quintus Metellus in the Sertorian wars, and of the Saguntines, when Hannibal besieged them, and of the Jews, when they were besieged by the Romans; and there are six hundred other instances. And all for the sake of the belly!

When his regent Penia rides through the land, everywhere she goes all courts are closed, all edicts are void, all ordinances are vain. She is subject to no law, and exempt from all. All men flee from her, throughout the world, preferring to expose themselves to shipwreck at sea, electing to pass through fire, across mountains, and over chasms, rather than let her catch them.

CHAPTER 58: *Pantagruel's dislike of the Engastrimythes and the Gastrolaters at the Court of this Master of Ingenuity*

AT the court of this great master of ingenuity, Pantagruel met with two sorts of tiresome and over-officious summoners, whom he greatly detested. One lot were called the Engastrimythes or Ventriloquists, the other the Gastrolaters or Belly-worshippers.

The Engastrimythes claimed to be descended from the ancient stock of Eurycles and, to prove this, cited the authority of Aristophanes, in his comedy entitled *The Hornets* or *Wasps*. Whence they were in ancient days called the Eurycleans, as Plato writes, also Plutarch in his book *On the Obsolescence of Oracles*. In the Holy Decrees, 26 *quaest.* 3 they are called Ventriloquists; and Hippocrates calls them this in the Ionic tongue, in his fifth book on *Epidemics* when speaking of the belly. Sophocles calls them Sternomantes. These men were diviners, magicians, and deceivers of the common people, who appeared to speak not from the mouth but from the belly, and to give answers to those who questioned them. Jacoba Rodogina, an Italian woman of low extraction, practised as such, about the year of our blessed Lord 1513. At Ferrara and elsewhere we have often heard the voice of the unclean spirit issuing from her belly, and so have countless others. The sound was low, weak, and small, but always well articulated, distinct, and intelligible, whenever she was summoned or called for by the rich lords and princes of Cisalpine Gaul, who were curious to hear her. To remove all suspicion of fraud or concealed trickery, they had her stripped stark naked, and ordered her nose and mouth to be stopped up.

Her evil spirit asked to be called Curlyhead or Cincinnatulus, and seemed to take pleasure in hearing his name. When he was called by it, he immediately answered the questions put to him. If he were asked about present or past events, he would reply so pertinently as quite to astonish his hearers. But if he were asked about the future he always lied; never did he tell the truth. Often, instead of replying, he seemed to make a confession of ignorance, by letting a huge fart or mumbling a few unintelligible words with barbarous inflexions.

The Gastrolaters, on the other hand, always went about in close troops and bands. Some were gay, dainty, and delicate; others sad, serious, harsh, and gloomy. But all were idle, doing nothing and not attempting a stroke of work. They were a charge and a useless burden on the land, as Hesiod says. For, as far as one could judge, they were afraid of offending and reducing the belly. Moreover they were so strangely masked and disguised, indeed so oddly dressed, that they were a fine sight to see. You say, and several wise and ancient philosophers have written, that Nature's skill is marvellously displayed in the apparent delight with which she has shaped the shells of the sea; there is such a great variety, so many shapes, colours, patterns, and forms that art could never imitate. But we saw no less diversity, I assure you, in the fancy-dresses of these Gastrolaters in their shell-shaped cowls. They all looked up to Gaster as their great God, worshipped him as a God, sacrificed to him as their God almighty, and recognized no other God but him. You would have supposed that it was really of him that the holy Apostle wrote in the third chapter of the Epistle to the Philippians: 'For many walk, of whom I have told you often, and now tell you even weeping, that they are the enemies of the cross of Christ: whose end is destruction and whose God is their belly.'

Pantagruel compared them to the Cyclops Polyphemus, into whose mouth Euripides put these words: 'I only sacrifice to myself – to the gods never – and to this belly of mine, the greatest of all the gods.'

CHAPTER 59: *Of the ridiculous Statue called Manduce, also of how and what the Gastrolaters sacrifice to their Ventripotent God*

As we observed the looks and behaviour of these lazy broad-gorged Gastrolaters, in utter amazement, we heard the ringing of a peculiar bell, at the sound of which they all ranged themselves in battle order, each according to his office, degree, and seniority. In this order they came before Messer Gaster, led by a stout and powerful young Pauncher, who carried a wooden statue on a tall, brightly-gilt pole. It was badly carved and clumsily painted; and such as had been described by Plautus, Juvenal, and Pomponius Festus. At Lyons, in carnival time, they call it the Chewcrust. But these people called it Manduce. It was a monstrous, ridiculous, and hideous effigy, a scarer of little children. Its eyes were bigger than its belly, and its head larger than the rest of its body. It had an ample pair of wide and horrible jaws, well provided with teeth, both upper and lower; and these were made to gnash horribly together, by means of a little cord concealed in the gilt pole, the same device as they use for the dragon of St Clement at Metz.

As the Gastrolaters approached, I saw that they were followed by a great crowd of clumpish servants carrying baskets, punnets, panniers, pots, ladles, and kettles. Then, with Manduce conducting them, and singing some unknown dithyrambs, crapulous anthems, and paeans of

praise, they opened their pots and baskets and made sacrifice to their
god of white Hippocras with soft dry toasts,

white bread,
soft bread,
choice bread,
common bread,
carbonados, of six kinds,
goat stews,
cold roast loins of veal,
    spiced with powered gin-
    ger,
couscous,

brawn,
fricassees of nine kinds,
small pies,
fat early morning soups,
hare soups,
round-headed cabbages in
    beef marrow,
hot-pot,
salmagundi.

And with them they offered an eternity of drink, a good full white
wine coming first, and the clarets and red wines following. These, let
me say, were ice cold, and served and proffered in great silver cups.
Then they sacrificed:

chitterlings, spattered with
    fine mustard,
sausages,
smoked ox-tongues,
saveloys,
salamis,
hams,
smoked meats,

quarters of pork with peas,
fried rashers,
hog's puddings,
boars' heads,
salt venison with turnips,
dainty bits on skewers,
olives in brine,

and all this in close association with perpetual drink. Then they
shovelled into his gullet:

legs of mutton in garlic,
cold pies in hot sauce,
pork cutlets in onion sauce,
roast capons in their own
    gravy,
cockerels,
goosanders,
kids,
fawns and does,
hares and leverets,

partridges and their young,
pheasants and pheasant
    chicks,
peacocks and peafowl,
storks and storklets,
woodcock and snipe,
ortolans,
turkey cocks, hens, and
    chicks,
ringdoves and their young,

pigs cooked in white wine,
duck in onion sauce,
blackbirds and land-rails,
water-hens,
sheldrakes,
egrets,
teal,
divers,
bitterns and spoonbills,
curlews,
grouse,
coots cooked with leeks,
roes and kids,
shoulders of mutton with
    caper sauce,
slices of beef royale,
breast of veal,
boiled fowl and fat capons
    in clear jelly,
hazel-hens,
pullets,
rabbits, young and old,

quail and their young,
pigeons and young pigeons,
herons and hernshaws,
bustards and young bus-
    tards,
fig-peckers,
guinea-fowl,
plovers,
geese and goslings,
wild pigeon,
widgeon,
larks,
flamingoes and swans,
shovellers,
wild-duck and cranes,
sea-duck,
great curlews,
snipe,
turtle-doves,
coneys,
hedgehogs,
water-rail.

With these came reinforcements of wine, and then large

pasties of venison,
of dormice,
of wild goat,
of kids,
of pigeons,
of chamois,
of capons,
bacon pies,
pigs' trotters in lard,
fried pie-crust,
stuffed capons,
cheeses,
Corbeil peaches,
artichokes,

puff-pastry cakes,
cardoons,
shortbread,
fritters,
sixteen kinds of tarts,
wafers and biscuits,
quince tarts,
curds and cream,
eggs in snow,
candied myrobalan plums,
jelly,
red and purple hippocras,
macaroons and stuffed mon-
    keys,

twenty sorts of tarts,
hard and soft sweets in seventy-eight varieties,
comfits in a hundred colours,
clotted cream on straw,
cream waffles with castor sugar.

Fine wines brought up the rear, for fear of the quinsies; also toasts.

CHAPTER 60: *How the Gastrolaters sacrificed to their God, on the interlarded Fast-days*

WHEN he saw this rabble of sacrificers and the multiplicity of their sacrifices, Pantagruel lost his temper, and would have returned to his ship if Epistemon had not begged him to see this farce to the end.

'And what do these scoundrels sacrifice to their ventripotent god?' he asked, 'on the interlarded fast-days?'

'I'll tell you,' answered the captain. 'For his first course they offer him:

caviar,
botargos,
fresh butter,
pease soup,
spinach,
bloaters,
kippers,
sardines,
anchovies,
salt tunny fish,
bean salad,
a hundred kinds of salads, of cress, hops, wild cress, rampion, jews' ears (which is a form of fungus that grows on old elder-bushes), asparagus, chervil, and many other plants,
salted salmon,
salted eels,
oysters in their shells.

At that point he had to drink, or the devil would have carried him off. But they take proper precautions against that, and nothing is lacking. Then they offered him:

lampreys in hippocras sauce,
barbels, great and small,
mullet, great and small,
skate,
cuttle-fish,
sturgeon,
whales,
mackerel,
dabs,
plaice,

fried oysters,
winkles,
crayfish,
smelts,
gurnet,
trout,
lake-trout,
cod,
octopus,
flat-fish,
flounders,
saw-fish,
sea-bream,
gudgeon,
brill,
sparling,
great carp,
sea-pike,
bonitos,
dog-fish,
sea-urchin,
sea-carp,
torpedo,
spider-crab,
lord-fish,
swordfish,
angel-fish,
small lampreys,
perch,
pickerel,
carp,
carplet,
salmon,
salmon-trout,
dolphins,
porpoise,
turbot, ·
white skate,

soles,
dover soles,
mussels,
lobsters,
prawns,
dace,
bleak,
tench,
grayling,
fresh haddock,
cuttle-fish,
stickleback,
tunnyfish,
little gudgeon,
miller's thumbs,
Dublin bay prawns,
cockles,
crawfish,
suckers,
conger eels,
porpoises,
bass,
shad,
muraenas,
prickle-fish,
barblets,
eels, great and small,
turtles,
serpents – that is wood-eels,
john dorys,
sea-hens,
pike,
sturgeon-royal,
loach,
crabs,
snails,
frogs.

If he did not drink after devouring these dishes, he would be within a step or two of death. But proper provision was made against this danger. For there was a further sacrifice of

salted haddocks,	mussels,
dried cod,	whelks,
eggs fried, buttered, poach-ed, boiled, baked in the embers, fried in the pan, scrambled, whisked, &c.,	dried haddock, soused pike,

to aid in the cooking and digestion of which, service after service of wine was provided. As a final sacrifice, they offered:

rice,	skirret,
millet,	cornflower mould,
groats,	frumenty,
almond paste,	prunes,
whipped cream,	dates,
pistachio-nuts, or pistica,	walnuts,
figs,	hazel nuts,
raisins,	water-parsnips,
grapes,	artichokes.

and with them an eternity of liquor.

Believe me, it was no fault of theirs if this same Gaster, their god, was not adequately, luxuriously, and abundantly provided for in these sacrifices. He was certainly better served than the statue of Heliogabalus, and even more liberally than the idol Bel in Babylon, in the time of King Balthazar. Notwithstanding this, Gaster confessed himself no god, but a poor, vile, pitiful creature. Just as King Antigonus the first answered a certain Hermadotus, who had in a poem called him god and a son of the sun, with the words: 'My Lasanophore denies it' – the *lasanon* being an earthen pan used to receive the belly's excrements – so Gaster referred these obsequious apes to his close-stool, to see, to examine and philosophically to consider what kind of god they could discover in his faeces.

CHAPTER 61: *Gaster's Invention of a means of getting and preserving Corn*

WHEN these gastrolatrous devils had retired, Pantagruel turned his
serious attention to Gaster, the noble master of arts. The law of
nature, as you know, has assigned to him for his food and sustenance
bread with its dependent products, and given him the additional
blessing of never lacking the means to find and store it.

So, in the beginning, he invented the blacksmith's art and the
cultivation of the earth by agriculture, so that he might produce himself grain. He invented the art of war and arms in order to defend his
corn; and medicine and astrology together, with the necessary
mathematics, to keep corn in safety for many centuries, and to safeguard it from climatic disasters, the depredations of brute beasts, and
the thieving of brigands. He invented watermills, windmills, hand-
mills, and a thousand other devices, to grind his grain and make it
into flour; yeast to raise his dough; salt to give it savour – for it was
known to him that nothing in the world made men more subject to
disease than unleavened and unsalted bread; fire to bake it, and clocks
and sundials to measure the time of baking the product of his corn,
his daily bread. Now it happened that in one country the corn failed.
So he invented a means of transporting it from one land to another.
His very ingenious method was to mate two kinds of beasts, in order
to produce a third kind, which we call the mule; a more powerful,
less delicate beast than any other, and one capable of harder work. He
also invented carts and wagons, as a more convenient method of
carrying it. Where the sea or some rivers stood in the way of his
transport, he invented boats, and ships propelled by oar and sail – to
the great amazement of the elements – in order to cross the seas,
rivers, and streams, and carry loads of corn from unknown, barbarous, and far-distant nations.

When he cultivated the land it sometimes happened that for some
years the needful rain did not fall in due season, and through lack of
it the seed lay in the soil, spoilt and dead. In other years there was excessive rain, which washed the seed away. In yet others the hail spoilt
it, the wind shook it out of the ear, or storms blew it down. But long
before we arrived he had invented an ingenious method of bringing

down rain from the skies, by merely cutting a herb which is common in the fields but known to few, and which he showed to us. I took it to be the herb of which Jove's priest of old put a single branch in the Agrian fountain, on Mount Lycaeus in Arcadia. That was in time of drought, and it raised a mist. The mist formed itself into thick clouds, and when these dissolved into rain the whole country was watered as liberally as anyone could wish. He invented also a cunning method of arresting the rain, suspending it in the air, and causing it to fall into the sea. He invented a method of destroying hail, suppressing winds, and deflecting storms, in the manner used by the Methanensians of Troezen.

But another disaster befell him. Thieves and brigands stole the grain from the fields and robbed him of his bread. So he invented a method of building towns, fortresses, and castles to lock it up and keep it in safety. There were also occasions when, finding no wheat in the fields, he heard that it was locked up in towns, fortresses, and castles, and more carefully defended and guarded by the inhabitants than the golden apples of the Hesperides were by the dragons. So he invented an ingenious method of assaulting and demolishing fortresses and castles by machines and engines of war, battering-rams, slings, and catapults, of which he showed us the designs which have, by the way, been badly misunderstood by the ingenious architects, disciples of Vitruvius, as Messer Philibert de l'Orme, chief architect to King Megistus, confessed to us. But when these weapons recently became inefficacious, thanks to the malignant subtlety or subtle malignity of the fortifiers, he invented cannons, serpentines, culverins, bombards, and basilisks, which throw iron, lead, or brass balls weighing as much as great anvils. This was effected by the mixing of a terrifying powder, by which even Nature was amazed, confessing herself beaten by art. In this way he totally eclipsed the achievement of the Oxydracians, who conquered their enemies with the help of thunderbolts, thunder, hail, lightning, and tempest, and so struck their enemies with sudden death on the open battlefield. For one basilisk shot is more horrible, more frightening, and more diabolical; it maims, rends, mows down, and slays more soldiers; it stuns more people and smashes down more walls, than a hundred thunderbolts could do.

CHAPTER 62: *Gaster invents an ingenious method of being neither wounded nor touched by Cannon-balls*

THERE were occasions when, after storing his corn in his fortresses, Gaster found himself attacked by his enemies. Sometimes his fortifications were demolished by this most villainous and infernal machine, and his grain and bread seized and snatched from him by Titanic strength. So he invented a cunning method, not of preserving his ramparts, bastions, walls, and defences from such cannonades, not of keeping the balls from touching them, and stopping them dead short in the air, not of preventing them from harming his defences or the citizens defending them, if they touched. He had already taken very good precautions against these dangers, and he gave us a demonstration of them. They have since been adopted by Fronto and are at present in common use as one of the soberer pastimes or amusements of the Thélèmites. The demonstration was as follows – And do not be so incredulous in future when you read about the experiments that Plutarch tells us he performed. If you see a flock of goats, for instance, running away at top speed, put a bit of sea-holly into the mouth of the hindmost, and they will all stop immediately.

Into a bronze falconet, on top of the gunpowder, which had been carefully compounded, purged of its sulphur, and mixed with a proper proportion of fine camphor, he put an iron cartridge of the right calibre, and twenty-four little iron pellets, some round and spherical, others tear-shaped. Then, having taken aim at one of his young pages, as if intending to hit him in the stomach, half-way between the page and the falconet, in a direct line, he strung up a heavy siderite on a wooden gibbet by means of a rope. By siderite I mean ironstone, otherwise called Herculean, and found in ancient times at Ida, in the land of Phrygia, by one Magnes, as Nicander attests. We commonly call it loadstone. Then he applied fire to the falconet, through the touch-hole. When the powder was burnt up, the cartridge and pellets were impetuously ejected through the weapon's mouth, by the air which rushed into the chamber so that there might be no vacuum. For when the powder was consumed there would otherwise have been a void, which Nature cannot tolerate. Indeed, rather than suffer one to exist anywhere in the world, she would prefer the whole fabric of the Universe – sky, air, earth, and sea – to be reduced to its ancient chaos. The cartridge and pellets, thus violently discharged, seemed quite certain to strike the page. But just as they approached this stone, they lost velocity, and all remained floating in the air, revolving around it. So strong was its attraction that not a single pellet got past it and hit the page.

But what Messer Gaster invented was none of these things. He discovered an artful way of making bullets turn back against the enemy, with the same violence with which they had been fired. They returned on the same trajectory, and were as dangerous to the firer as to the man he had intended to hit. Gaster did not find this a difficult invention. For does not the herb called Ethiopis open all locks that it is brought near? Does not the Echeneis, a very feeble fish, stop the mightiest ships afloat in spite of all the winds, and hold them back even when a hurricane is blowing? Furthermore, does not the flesh of this fish, preserved in salt, draw gold out of the deepest wells ever sounded?

Is there not also, according to Democritus's writing and Theophrastus's belief and experiment, a herb at the mere touch of which an iron wedge, deeply and most violently driven into a great hard log, suddenly flies out? It is this herb that the wrynecks – you call them woodpeckers – use, when the entrance to their nest, which it is their habit most laboriously to hollow out of a great tree trunk, has been blocked by the stoutest wedge.

And do not stags and hinds, when severely wounded by darts, arrows, or bolts, eat a little of the herb called dittany, which is common in Candia – supposing of course that they can find some – whereupon the arrows at once fall out, leaving them quite uninjured? With this same herb Venus cured her dearly beloved son Aeneas, who was wounded in the right thigh by an arrow shot by Turnus's sister Juturna. Does not the very scent given off by laurels, fig trees, and seals, deflect the lightning, which never strikes them? Do not mad elephants regain their senses at the mere sight of a ram? Do not mad and uncontrollable bulls become docile when they come near to wild fig trees, and remain motionless with cramp? Does not the fury of a viper die down when it is touched with a beech branch? Did not Euphorion make a statement to the effect that in the island of Samos, before the temple of Juno was built there, he had seen certain beasts called

Neades, at whose mere cry the earth split into chasms and formed an abyss? And likewise do not the more tuneful elder-bushes, those best fitted for the making of flutes, grow in places where no cocks are heard to crow as, according to Theophrastus's report, the sages wrote of old? Indeed the cock's crow seems to dull, weaken, and stupefy the material wood of the elder; and the lion too, strong and resolute beast though he is, becomes utterly stupefied and confounded when he hears this same sound.

I know that others have considered this observation to apply to the wild elder-bush, which grows so far from any town or village that no cock's crow can be heard in its neighbourhood. This kind, of course, should be the one selected for the manufacture of flutes and other musical instruments, and should be preferred to the common sort that grows near barns and ruins. But others have interpreted this statement in a higher sense, not according to the letter, but allegorically, in the Pythagorean manner. As when they said that Mercury's statue should not be made of any sort of wood, indifferently, the disciples of Pythagoras meant that God ought not to be worshipped in the vulgar fashion, but in a special and esoteric way. They also prove to us by this same example that wise and studious people should not devote themselves to trivial and vulgar music, but to the celestial, divine, angelic, and more abstruse branches of the art, which are brought from greater distances; that is to say from a region in which the crowing of cocks is not heard. For we too, when we wish to refer to a distant and almost unfrequented spot, speak of it as a place where no cock has ever been heard to crow.

CHAPTER 63: *How Pantagruel fell asleep near the Island of Chaneph; and the Problems proposed on his Waking*

WE pursued our journey, gossiping the while, and on the following day came off Chaneph or Hypocrisy Island, where Pantagruel's ship could not put in because the wind failed us and there was a calm at sea. Despite the fact that additional bonnet sails had been raised, we could only make headway by heeling with the main lifts, and veering from starboard to larboard. So we were all thoughtful and depressed, down in the dumps and worried, and did not exchange a word together.

In fact, Pantagruel was dozing on a mattress beside the hatchway, with a Greek Heliodorus in his hand. For it was his habit to sleep better by book than by heart. Epistemon was observing the elevation of the Pole with his astrolabe; Friar John had gone off to the galley, and was calculating the probable time of day by the ascendant of the spits and and the horoscope of the fricassees; Panurge was bubbling and gurgling away with his tongue on a Pantagruelion stalk; Gymnaste was sharpening lentisk toothpicks; Ponocrates was dreamily brooding, tickling himself to make himself laugh and scratching his head with one finger; Carpalim was carving a gay, pretty little, whirring windmill out of a walnut shell, with four beautiful miniature sails made out of slips of alder; Eusthenes was drumming with his fingers on a long culverin, as though it were a monochordion; Rhizotome was making a velvet purse out of the shell of a heath tortoise, or mole; Xenomanes was patching an old lantern with a hawk's jesses, and our captain was pulling maggots out of his sailors' noses, when Friar John returned from the galley and saw that Pantagruel had woken up.

Then, breaking this obstinate silence, he asked in a loud voice and in the gayest of spirits: 'What's the best way to raise fine weather in the doldrums?' Panurge quickly seconded him with the question: 'What's the cure for melancholy?' Epistemon came in third with the light-hearted inquiry: 'How can a man make water when he has no urge to?' Gymnaste then heaved himself to his feet and asked: 'What's the cure for dimness of the eyes?' Ponocrates, after rubbing his forehead a little and shaking his ears, inquired: 'How can a man avoid dozing like a dog?'

'Wait,' said Pantagruel. 'We learn from the decisions of the subtle peripatetic philosophers that all problems, questions, and mysteries that demand an answer should be exact, clear, and intelligible. What do you mean by dozing like a dog?'

'I mean sleeping hungry in the midday sun,' answered Ponocrates, 'as dogs do.'

Rhizotome, who was squatting on the gangway, then raised his head and, yawning so widely as to cause all his friends to yawn also out of natural sympathy, he demanded: 'What's the remedy for oscitation or yawning?'

Xenomanes, who seemed most preoccupied with the repairing of his lantern, asked: 'How can a man equilibrize and balance the bagpipes of his stomach, so that it doesn't incline to one side more than to the other?'

Carpalim asked, as he played with his windmill: 'How many natural processes does it require before a man can be said to be hungry?'

When Eusthenes heard the sound of voices, he ran up on deck, and called out from the capstan: 'Why is it that a fasting man is in greater danger of death if he is bitten by a fasting snake, than if both man and snake have fed? And why is it that a fasting man's spittle is poison to all snakes and venomous creatures?'

'My friends,' said Pantagruel, 'one single answer is enough to solve all the doubts and problems you have proposed; one sole medicine will meet all these cases, and cure all these symptoms. The answer shall speedily be given you, without any great circumlocutions or any wordy discourse. The hungry stomach has no ears; it can't hear a word. But you shall be answered by signs, gestures, and demonstrations, which will deal with your questions to your absolute satisfaction. As long ago in Rome, Tarquin the Proud, the last king of the Romans' – as he said this, Pantagruel pulled the cord of the little bell, and Friar John at once dashed to the galley – 'answered his son Sextus Tarquinius by signs, the young man being in the town of the Gabini and having sent an express messenger to inquire how he could complete the conquest of that people and reduce them to perfect obedience. The said king, mistrusting the messenger's loyalty, did not answer him in words. He merely led him into his private garden, and before his eyes cut off the tall heads of the poppies growing there with his cutlass. When the messenger returned without an answer, but told the son what he had seen his father do, Sextus Tarquinius easily understood the meaning of this demonstration. He knew what his father's advice was: that he should cut off the heads of the chief men of the town, in order to keep the rest of the people – the commons that is – dutiful and obedient.'

CHAPTER 64: *Pantagruel gives no answer to the Problems propounded*

THEN Pantagruel asked: 'What sort of people live in this damned isle of dogs?'

'They are all hypocrites,' replied Xenomanes, 'prayer-gabblers, pie-faces, saintly mumblers, bigots, and hermits. They're all poor creatures who live – like the hermit of Lormont, between Blaye and Bordeaux – on the alms they receive from passing travellers.'

'I'm not going there, I promise you,' said Panurge. 'May the devil blow up my arse if I do! Hermits, saintly mumblers, pie-faces, bigots, and hypocrites, in the name of all the devils, get out of my sight! I still remember our fat council-bound fathers of Chesil, and I wish Beelzebub and Astaroth had brought them to take counsel with Proserpine, such a lot of storms and devilries as struck us after we saw them! Listen, my fat rogue, my dear friend Xenomanes, if you please. Can you tell me if these hypocrites and hermits and sneaks here are virgins or married men? Have they any feminine gender? Would it be possible, hypocritically, to have one's hypocritical bit of fun with them?'

'That's a fine and cheerful question indeed,' said Pantagruel.

'Oh yes, of course,' answered Xenomanes. 'There are fine, jovial she-hypocrites, female pie-faces, hermitesses, and women of great religion among them; and there's no shortage of little hypocrites, pie-faced brats, and miniature hermits. ...'

'To hell with them!' interrupted Friar John. 'From young hermit comes old devil. That's a true proverb. Remember it.'

'... otherwise, through failure of the progeny to multiply, the island of Chaneph would long ago have become an empty desert.'

Pantagruel sent Gymnaste in his pinnace to take them their alms; seventy-eight thousand pretty little half crowns stamped with the lantern. 'What's the time?' he then asked.

'Past nine o'clock,' answered Epistemon.

'Just time for dinner,' said Pantagruel. 'For the moment is approaching when the shadow falls on the tenth degree of the dial: the sacred line that Aristophanes so praises in his comedy *The Preaching Women*. Among the Persians, in the old days, an exact hour for taking refreshment was fixed for kings alone; everyone else took his appetite and his stomach as his clock. In fact, in Plautus, a certain parasite complains and rails most bitterly against the inventors of clocks and sundials, since it is a well-known fact that no clock keeps better time than the stomach. When Diogenes was asked at what hour a man ought to feed, he replied: "A rich man, when he's hungry; a poor man, when he has food." The physicians say more correctly that the canonical hours are:

> To rise at five, to dine at nine,
> To sup at five, to sleep at nine.

The famous King Petosiris's magic was different.'

He had not completed this remark when the knights of the belly set up the tables and sideboards, spread them with scented cloths, plates, napkins, and salt-cellars, and brought in tankards, mugs, flagons, cups, beakers, basins, and water-jars. Friar John, together with the stewards, head-waiters, loaf-bearers, cup-bearers, carvers, servers, and tasters, brought in four tremendous pork pies, so large that they reminded me of the four bastions of Turin. Gracious, how they drank and feasted! And they had not come to the dessert when the north-west wind began to fill the sails – mainsail, mizzen, topsails, and all. Then they all sang their separate hymns in praise of the High God of Heaven.

Over the fruit, Pantagruel asked: 'Tell me now, friends, if your questions aren't answered.' 'I've stopped yawning, God be praised,' said Rhizotome. 'My dog's nap is over,' said Ponocrates. 'My eyes are bleary no longer,' answered Gymnaste. 'My fast is finished,' said Eusthenes. 'For the whole of to-day my spittle will do no harm to

Asps,	Arges,
Amphisbaenas,	Ascalabi,
Amerudutes,	Attelabi,
Abedessimons,	Ascalobates,
Alhartraz,	Basilisks,
Ammobati,	Blind-worms,
Apimaos,	Boa-constrictors,
Alhatrabans,	Buprestes,
Aractes,	Cantharides or Spanish Fly,
Asterions,	Caterpillars,
Alcharates,	Crocodiles,

Catoblepes,
Cerastae,
Colotae,
Cychriodes,
Caphezates,
Cauhares,
Cuhersks,
Chelydri,
Craniocolapti,
Chersydri,
Chencryni,
Cockatrices,
Chalcidian lizards,
Deaf-adders,
Dipsades,
Domeses,
Drymades,
Dragons,
Elopes,
Enhydrides,
Fanuises,
Galeotis,
Harmenes,
Haemorrhoids,
Handons,
Icles,
Illicines,
Ichneumons,
Jarraries,
Kesudures,
Leeches,
Mad dogs,
Myopes,
Mantichores,
Moluri,
Myagi,
Miliares,
Megalauni,

Nightmares,
Ptyades,
Porphyries,
Pareades,
Phalanges,
Penphredones,
Pityocamps,
Rutulae,
Rhimories,
Rhagions,
Rhaganes,
Salamanders,
Scytalae,
Sea-hares,
Stellions,
Scorpenes,
Scorpions,
Selsirs,
Scalavotins,
Solofuidars,
Salpugae,
Solifugae,
Sepae,
Spiders,
Stinces,
Stuphae,
Sabrins,
Sangles,
Shrew-mice,
Sepedons,
Scolopenders,
Tarantulas,
Typholopes,
Tetragnaths,
Teristales,
Toads,
Vipers,
Weasels.

CHAPTER 65: *Pantagruel passes the time gaily with his Retainers*

'IN what category of these venomous creatures do you put Panurge's future wife?' asked Friar John.

'Speak ill of women, would you, you fawning, smooth-arsed monk?' cried Panurge.

'By the gormandizer's bladder,' proclaimed Epistemon, 'in the words which Euripides gives to his heroine Andromache, man has, by his own ingenuity or with the help of the gods, discovered a practicable remedy against all poisonous beasts; but against an evil woman hitherto he has found none.'

'That braggart Euripides,' said Panurge, 'was always maligning women. But the gods took vengeance on him, and he was devoured by dogs, as Aristophanes contemptuously observes. Let us proceed. Next man speak!'

'I shall leak in a moment,' said Epistemon, 'enough to sink the ship.'

'I've got my stomach pretty properly ballasted,' claimed Xenomanes; 'it won't heel any further over to one side than to the other.'

'I'm neither short of wine nor bread.'

'Hunger, farewell. Thirst, you're dead,' recited Carpalim.

'I've thrown off my melancholy,' said Panurge, 'thanks to God and to you. I am as jolly as a parrot, as merry as a hawk, as light-headed as a butterfly. Your excellent Euripides wrote the truth when he made that famous boozer Silenus say:

> He's out of his mind, he's raving mad,
> The man who drinks and still feels sad.

We ought undoubtedly to give great praise to the good God, our Creator, Saviour, and Preserver, for this excellent bread, for this grand fresh wine, and for these splendid meats. For over and above the pleasure and delight we get from eating and drinking, we are healed by our victuals of certain disorders both of the body and the mind. But you haven't replied to our blessed and venerable Brother John's question: What's the way to raise good weather?'

'Since you're contented with this easy solution of the questions proposed,' said Pantagruel, 'so am I. But elsewhere and at some other time we will say more on the subject, if you agree. It remains then to deal with the problem put forward by Friar John: how to raise good weather? But haven't we raised it, as fine as you like? Look at the wind-gauge on the scuttle. Listen to the whistling of the wind. Look how taut the stays, the ties, and the sheets are. As we raised and emptied our glasses, good weather has been raised likewise, by an occult sympathy of Nature. Atlas and Hercules raised their burdens in the same way, if you believe the ancient mythologists. But they raised them half a degree too much, Atlas in the jovial entertainment of his guest Hercules, and Hercules to make good the thirst he had suffered in the Libyan deserts.'

'True enough,' said Friar John, interrupting his speech, 'I have heard from several venerable doctors that your good father's butler Tirelupin saves more than eighteen hundred pipes a year by making the visitors and servants drink before they're thirsty.'

'For,' continued Pantagruel, 'just as camels and dromedaries in the caravans drink for the thirst that is past, the thirst that is present, and for the thirst to come, even so did Hercules. So it was that by his excessive raising of the weather the Heavens were subjected to a new movement, that of titubation and trepidation, the causes of which have been so much disputed and discussed by our crack-brained astrologers ever since.'

'This is what the common proverb says,' broke in Panurge.

> While round a fat ham we drink together,
> The storms pass off, and give way to good weather.

'And not only,' said Pantagruel, 'have we raised good weather while feasting and drinking, but we've greatly lightened the ship. We haven't lightened it only in the way that Aesop did his basket – that is to say by emptying it of victuals – but we've also freed ourselves from our fast. For just as a dead body is heavier than a living one, so a man fasting is heavier and more earthy than when he has eaten and drunk; and men going on a long journey are not far wrong when they take a good drink with their breakfast and say: "That'll put a spur on the horses." You know, do you not, that the Amycleans of old, who revered and worshipped Bacchus above all the other gods, gave him the most fitting title of *Psila*? *Psila* in Doric means wings. For as, by the

help of their wings, birds fly lightly aloft into the air, so with the aid
of Bacchus – of good, tasty, and delicious wine, that is to say – the
spirits of humankind are raised on high, their bodies manifestly made
nimbler, and what was earthy in them becomes pliant.'

CHAPTER 66: *How, near Ganabin Island, a Salute was fired to
the Muses, on Pantagruel's instructions*

As the fair wind and this jovial conversation continued, Pantagruel
described in the far distance a mountainous country, which he pointed
out to Xenomanes.

'Do you see that high rock to larboard,' he asked, 'with two peaks
that are much like Mount Parnassus?'

'Yes, that's Ganabin Island, or the Isle of Thieves,' replied Xenomanes. 'Would you like to land there?'

'No,' answered Pantagruel.

'You're quite right,' said Xenomanes. 'There's nothing worth seeing there. The people are all thieves and robbers. There is, all the same,
near the peak to the right the loveliest fountain in the world, and
around it a very fine forest. Your crew could take in wood and water
there.'

'That's good and learned advice,' said Panurge. 'Oh, deary me!
Let's never land in a country of thieves and robbers. I'm sure that
island will be just another Sark or Herm, which are islands that I once
saw between Britanny and England, or like Poneropolis in Philip's
Thrace. They'll be chock-full of outlaws, robbers, brigands, murderers, and assassins, all the outscourings of the deepest dungeons of
the Conciergerie. Let's not land there for a moment, I implore you.
If you don't trust me, at least take the opinion of this good, wise
Xenomanes. 'Ods my life, they're worse than cannibals. They'll eat
us all alive. Don't land there, I beg of you. It'd be better for you to go
down to hell. Listen, I can hear the horrible tocsin sounding, I swear
I can, the way the Gascons used to sound it around Bordeaux, against
the salt-tax collectors and the commissioners. Either I can hear it or
there's a singing in my ears. Let's go right past. Oh, let's give them a
wide berth!'

'Put ashore there,' said Friar John, 'and let's land. Forward, onward, and straight at them. We shan't have to pay for our lodging. Forward, and we'll destroy them to a man. Let us land – and pillage them!'

'The devil can have my share of the loot,' said Panurge. 'This devil of a monk here, this devilish lunatic of a monk is afraid of nothing. He's as foolhardy as all the devils, and does not care a damn for other people. He seems to think that everyone else is a monk like himself.'

'A million devils take you, you purulent devil,' replied Friar John. 'May they dissect your brain and cut it into slices! This damned fool is such a scurvy coward that he shits himself every hour of the day out of utter funk and panic. If you're so perturbed by idle fears, don't land, but stay here with the baggage. Or go and hide yourself under Proserpine's petticoats, down among the hosts of hell.'

At these words Panurge vanished from the company, and slunk off below into the store room, among the crusts and scraps and bread-crumbs.

'I feel an urgent shrinking in my soul,' said Pantagruel, 'something like a voice coming from far away, which tells me that we ought not to land. Each and every time I've had that sensation in my head, it's proved lucky for me. For I've either held back from the undertaking it has warned me against, and passed it by, or else I've gone in the direction it prompted me. I've been just as lucky either way, and never repented of it.'

'That's like Socrates's daemon,' said Epistemon, 'which the Academics sang such praises of.'

'Listen then,' said Friar John. 'While the crews are fetching water, Panurge is as snug as a bug below. Would you like a good laugh? Now, see this basilisk beside the fo'c'stle. Let's have it fired, as a salute to the Muses of this Mount Antiparnassus. The powder in it is spoiling anyhow.'

'That's a good idea,' answered Pantagruel. 'Send up the master gunner.'

The gunner promptly appearing, Pantagruel ordered him to fire the basilisk, and to be sure and charge it afterwards with fresh powder. This the fellow instantly did; and at the first basilisk-shot from Panta-gruel's ship, the gunners of all the other ships, frigates, galleons, and galleys of the fleet also fired one of their big pieces which was loaded. There was a fine din, take my word for it.

CHAPTER 67: *Panurge shits himself out of utter fear, and of the large cat Rodilardus, which he took for a Devil*

PANURGE rushed out of the store-room like a goat with the staggers, clad in his shirt and with nothing else on but one of his stockings, which was half-way down his leg. His beard was all spattered with breadcrumbs, and he was grasping a great sable cat, which was entangled in his other stocking. His jaws were waggling like a monkey's, that is hunting lice in its head. He was trembling, and his teeth were chattering, and he made straight for Friar John, who was sitting on the starboard chain-wales. 'Take pity on me,' he implored the friar, 'and keep me within safe reach of your cutlass. By my share in Papimania, I swear to you, on my sacred oath, that all the devils in hell have broken loose, and I've seen them. Look you, my friend, my brother, my ghostly father, the host of hell are holding a wedding today. You never saw such preparations for an infernal banquet. Can you see the smoke of hell's kitchens?' – As he said this he pointed to the gunpowder smoke that hung above the ships. 'You never saw so many damned souls. And d'you know what? Look you, my friend, how soft and fair and tender they are. It wouldn't be wrong to call them the Stygian ambrosia. I did think, God forgive me, that they were English souls. I believe that the Isle of Horses, near Scotland, has been sacked and gutted by the Lords of Therme and Dessé this very morning, and all the English who had surprised it have been destroyed.'

As Panurge came near, Friar John smelt an odour of some sort which was not gunpowder. So he turned Panurge round, and saw that his shirt was all mucky and newly shitten. The retentive power of the nerve which controls the sphincter muscle – Panurge's arse-hole that is – had been relaxed by the extreme fear which had accompanied his fantastic visions. On top of this had come the thunder of the cannonading, which is more terrifying in the bowels of the ship than on the deck. Now one of the symptoms and concomitants of fear is that it usually opens the gate of the seraglio in which the fecal matter is temporarily stored. A case in point is that of Messer Pandolfo de la Cassina of Siena, who was posting through Chambéry, and stopped at that good fellow Vinet's inn. When he arrived he picked up a stable fork and said: '*Da Roma in qua io non son andato del corpo. Di gratia, piglia in mano questa forcha, et fa mi paura.*'[1] Vinet made several thrusts at him with the fork, as if seriously intending to hit him. '*Si tu non fai altramente,*' said the Sienese gentleman, '*tu non fai nulla. Pero sforzati di adoperarli piu guagliardemente.*'[2]

At this, Vinet gave him such a thrust of the fork between his neck and his collar, that he knocked him head over heels on the ground. 'God's bloody feast,' cried the host spluttering and laughing all over his face, 'that's what we call a Chambéry special, *datum Camberiaci.*' The signor had taken down his trousers just in time. For suddenly he did a bigger pile than you would have expected of nine buffaloes and fourteen arch-priests from Ostia. The Sienese gentleman concluded by offering Vinet his courteous thanks. '*Io ti ringratio, bel messere,*' said he, '*Cosi facendo tu m'hai esparmiata la speza d'un servitiale.*'[3]

Another case is that of the English king, Edward IV. Master François Villon had been banished from France and had come to his court, where he had been received with such favour that not even the smallest details of the King's life were kept secret from him. One day, as King Edward IV was doing his business, he showed Villon a painting of the French coat-of-arms, and said: 'You see what respect I have for your French kings. I keep their armorial bearings in this place only, beside my close-stool.'

'Gracious me,' answered Villon, 'how wise and prudent, and how careful of your health your Majesty is. How well you are served, too, by Thomas Linacre, your doctor! For naturally he sees that in your old age you'll become constipated, and that you'll have to fetch an apothecary to your bum every day. I mean that without a suppository, you'll have no droppings. So he has cunningly made you paint the French arms up here and nowhere else, which was a most singularly providential precaution. For at the mere sight of them you get in such a funk and become so hideously afraid, that all of a sudden you shit like eighteen wild bulls of Paeonia. If they were painted in some other part of your palace, in your bed-chamber, your hall, your chapel, or

1. I haven't had a motion of the bowels since I left Rome. Take up this fork, if you please, and give me a fright.
2. If you don't do better than that it'll do no good. Try to handle it a bit more valiantly, do.
3. Many thanks, my dear sir, many thanks. By that blow you've spared me the cost of a suppository.

your galleries, or anywhere else, good God, you'd shit all over the place the moment you saw them. What's more, if you had the great oriflamme of France painted up here, you'd shit your very bowels out through your bum hole at the sight of it. But h'm, h'm, and three times h'm!

> I am a silly Paris dope,
> A dope from Paris, near Pontoise,
> And dangling on a six foot rope,
> My neck'll know the weight of my arse.

An ill-informed dope, let me tell you, an ignorant dope of poor understanding. For I was surprised when I came to you, to see you take down your trousers in your bedchamber. I actually thought that you kept your close-stool there, behind the tapestry or between the bed and the wall. It seemed a very odd thing to me that you should take down your trousers in your bedchamber and then make a long journey to the family seat. But wasn't that a really doltish thought? The underlying theory is entirely different, by God. You do well to act as you do. You couldn't do better, I assure you. Take your trousers down in good time, and far away, and be careful about it. For if you enter this closet without untying your points, the moment you see these arms, you mark my words, the seat of your trousers will have to serve as bed-pan, chamber-pot, shit-pail, and close-stool, I'll be blessed if it won't.'

Friar John held his nostrils with his left hand, and with his right forefinger called Pantagruel's attention to Panurge's shirt. On seeing his servant thus alarmed, shivering, trembling, bewildered, beshitten, and scratched by the claws of the celebrated cat Rodilardus, Pantagruel could not contain his laughter, and asked: 'What do you want with that cat?' 'With this cat?' answered Panurge, 'devil take me if I didn't think it was a downy-haired young devil that I'd snatched up on the quiet, using my stocking for a mitten, down in the great bread bin of hell. Devil take the devil! He's scratched my skin to shreds a' thin as a shrimp's whiskers.' At this, he threw the cat down.

'Off with you,' said Pantagruel, 'off with you, for God's sake. Take a hot bath, clean yourself, calm your fears, put on a clean shirt, and then get dressed.'

'Do you say that I'm frightened?' asked Panurge. 'Not a bit of it.

I've got as much courage, by God, as if I'd swallowed all the flies that have been put in pastry in Paris, from St John's Day till All Saints'. Ha, ha, ha! But, ho! What the devil's this? Do you call it shit, turds, crots, ordure, deposit, fecal matter, excrement, droppings, fumets, motion, dung, stronts, scybale, or spyrathe? It's saffron from Ireland, that's what I think it is. Ho, ho, ho! Saffron from Ireland! It is indeed. Let's have a drink.'

End of the Fourth Book of the heroic Deeds
and Sayings of the noble
Pantagruel

THE FIFTH AND LAST BOOK

OF THE HEROIC ACTS AND SAYINGS OF

THE GOOD PANTAGRUEL

COMPOSED BY

M. François Rabelais

DOCTOR OF MEDICINE

WHICH CONTAINS THE VISIT TO THE ORACLE
OF THE DIVINE BACBUC
AND THE VERDICT OF THE BOTTLE
THE SECURING OF WHICH WAS
THE WHOLE PURPOSE OF
THIS LONG VOYAGE

TO ALL KINDLY READERS

INDEFATIGABLE boozers, and you, thrice precious martyrs to the pox, while you are at leisure and I have nothing more important on hand, let me ask you a serious question: Why is it commonly said nowadays that the world is no longer gormless? Gormless is a Languedocian adjective, signifying unsalted, saltless, tasteless, and flat. Metaphorically it means foolish, simple, devoid of intelligence, and cracked in the upper storey. But would you say, as might logically be inferred from this, that the world which was once gormless has now turned wise? What conditions, and how many, did it require to make it gormless? And what conditions and how many were necessary to make it wise? Why was it gormless? Why should it become wise? By what signs did you recognize its former folly? By what signs do you affirm its present wisdom? Who made it gormless? Who has made it wise? Which were the more numerous, those who loved it when it was gormless, or those who love it now that it is wise? For how long was it gormless? For how long will it stay wise? What did its former folly spring from? What are the roots of its present wisdom? Why did its ancient folly come to an end at this time and no later? Why did its present wisdom begin now and not before? What harm came of its former folly? What good can we expect of its present wisdom? How can its ancient folly have been abolished? How can its present wisdom have been restored?

Now answer me, if you please, and I'll use no stronger entreaties on your reverences, for fear I may disquiet you, my worshipful fathers. Now do not be coy, but deal confusion to Herr der Teufel, the enemy of Paradise, the enemy of Truth. Take heart, my lads, and if you're on my side, drink three or five cups for the first part of the sermon, and then answer my question. But if you're of the other party, then get out of my road, Satan! For I swear to you by the great Hurlyburly that if you don't help me with the solution of the problem I've propounded, I shall shortly be sorry that I ever put it to you. Indeed, I am sorry already. But I'm in as great a quandary as if I held a wolf by the ears and had no hope of assistance.

Well? Oh, I see; you're not disposed to answer. So I won't answer either, by my beard. I will merely put before you the prediction on this subject made by a venerable doctor in the prophetic vein, the author of a book entitled The Prelates' Bagpipe. *What does the old lecher say? Listen, my Tom Noddies, listen.*

> *Jubilee year, when all the world got shaved,*
> *The supernumerary year thirty-one,*
> *With what irreverent lightness it behaved!*
>
> *How gormless it appeared. Yet with long-spun*
> *Law-cases persevering, it will cast*
> *Its greedy gormlessness, and at the last*
> *Will pluck that fruit whose flower it feared in Spring.*

Now you've heard it. But have you understood? The doctor is ancient, the words are laconic, the sentiments Scotine and obscure. Nevertheless, despite the fact that the subject he is treating is in itself profound and difficult, the best interpreters of this good father explain that the Jubilee year thirty-one signifies the years of this present century up to the year 1550. There will be no need to fear the flower this year. The world will be said to be gormless no more when the spring comes. The fools, whose number is infinite, as Solomon attests, will perish in their madness, and all kinds of folly will cease. That these are countless also Avicenna states, when he says maniae infinitae sunt species. *During the rigours of the winter, folly was driven back to the centre. But now it appears on the surface, and rises like the sap in trees. Experience demonstrates this to us. You know it, and you can see it. What is more, the matter was long ago investigated by that great good man Hippocrates, as he states in his aphorism,* Verae etenim maniae, *etc. As the world is growing wise, therefore, it will no longer fear the flower of the bean in spring; that is to say – as you may piously believe with your glass in your hand and tears in your eyes – a pile of books in time of Lent. These used to appear as flowery, flourishing, and florid as so many butterflies, but were really as tiresome, boring, perilous, prickly, and dark as those of Heraclitus, and as obscure as Pythagoras's numbers – and he was the King of the Beans, as Horace attests. All these books will perish, and come to hand no more. They will be neither read nor seen. Such was their fate, and such their predestined end.*

In their stead have come beans in the pod. These jolly and fruitful books of Pantagruelism, I mean, which are well received and cheerfully bought now-

adays, in expectation of the next Jubilee's coming. All the world in fact is given over to the study of these books, and so it is called wise. Now give a hearty cough or two, and drink nine bumpers off on end, since the vines are fairs and usurers are hanging themselves. They will cost me a lot in ropes if the good times last. For I promise you I'll provide them with plenty, free of charge, on each and every occasion when they decide to hang themselves and save the expense of a hangman.

But so that you may partake of this wisdom in store and be free of ancient folly, please strike out from your scrolls the device of the old philosopher with the golden thigh, by which he forbade you the use and consumption of beans. For you can take it as an established fact, accepted among all good comrades, that his purpose in thus banning the bean was the same as the late fresh-water physician Amer's – the nephew of the advocate and lord of Camelotière – when he forbade his patients the wing of a partridge, the parson's-nose of a chicken, and the neck of a pigeon, with the words:

ala mala, croppium dubium, collum bonum pelle remota,[1]

and so reserved them for his own mouth, leaving his patients only the bones to gnaw. He has been succeeded by certain Hooded Ghouls, who forbid us the use of beans – that is to say of Pantagrueline books – following the ex-ample of Philoxenus and Gnatho the Sicilian, the ancient founders of their monachal and ventral orgies. At a crowded banquet, just when the tastiest morsels were being served, these early cram-guts would spit on the food, so that everyone else should refuse to eat it, out of disgust. In the same way, this hideous, snotty-nosed, catarrhal, and worm-eaten bunch of prayer-mumblers curse these appetizing books in public and private and, in their insolence, villainously spit upon them.

Now though we have to-day in the Gallic tongue, both in verse and in less strict forms, several excellent works to read, and though few relics remain of those snivelling and Gothic times, I have still preferred to hiss and cackle like a goose among the swans, as the proverb runs, rather than count as a dumb spectator among all our delightful poets and excellent orators. In fact I would rather play the part of a yokel among the many skilful actors on our noble stage than appear in the ranks of those who only feature as shadows and ciphers, merely gaping at flies, pricking up their ears like asses in Arcady in time to the music, and thus silently demonstrating that they are in favour of the performance.

1. The wing is bad, the rump doubtful, and the neck good without its skin.

Having made my choice and selected my role, I have decided that there would be nothing unworthy in my tumbling my tub, like Diogenes. You would not say then that I lacked an example. I have been carefully observing a great swarm of minor Colins, Marots, Heroets, Saint-Gelais, Salels, and little Massuaus, and a long line of other Gallic poets and orators; and I see that after hanging for a while around Apollo's school on Mount Parnassus and taking frequent swigs at the Caballine spring, all among the jolly Muses, they contribute nothing to the eternal fabric of our vulgar tongue but Parian marble, alabaster, porphyry, and firm royal cement. They treat of nothing but heroic exploits, great themes, arduous, weighty, and difficult subjects, and all this in a crimson satin style. In their writings they produce nothing but divine nectar, rare, light, and sparkling wines, delicate and delicious juice of the muscat grape. Nor is this glory confined to the male sex. Women have shared in it, among them one born of the blood royal of France, whose name should not be mentioned without a preliminary fanfare of praise. For she has astonished our whole age by her writings and her superb imagination, also by her ornate language and miraculous style. Now imitate these poets if you have the skill. For my part, I should not know how to; not everyone is privileged to haunt and inhabit Corinth. Not everyone could offer handfuls of gold, to the value of a full shekel, for the building of Solomon's temple. And since it is beyond our means to make as great advances in architecture as they do, I am resolved to do as Renaud of Montauban did: to wait on the masons and to put the pot on for the masons. Then, since I cannot be their equal, at least they shall have me as an audience, as an indefatigable audience, for their more than divine writings.

As for the rest of you, little jealous, competitive, envious prigs, I'll frighten you to death. Go and hang yourselves, and choose your own trees for gibbets; you won't go short of rope. I hereby affirm before my Helicon, in the presence of the divine Muses, that if I live so long as a dog, and three crows' lives on top of that, sound in body and mind as did that blessed captain of the Jews, and Xenophilus the musician and Demonax the philosopher – if I live as long as that, I say, I will by pertinent argument and irrefutable reason prove in the teeth of any number of vampers of patchwork poems, of rakers over of material that has been worked a hundred times, of botchers of old Latin tags and dealers in ancient Latin words, mildewed and of uncertain meaning, that our vulgar tongue is not so vile, useless, poor, and contemptible as they suppose. So in all humility I beg that when the treasures are distributed to the great poets, as they were by Phoebus of old, a post may, by special grace, be *found for me, as that of official mythologist was for Aesop. For, like him, I aspire to no higher rank. I merely beg them not to deny me the office of a puny vegetable-painter, a minor turnip-draughtsman of the school of Pyreicus. I am quite certain that they will not deny me that. For they are the kindliest, the most gracious and generous creatures in the world.*

Then all boozers, then all gouty wine-tasters, will wish to have these books for their perfect enjoyment. For when they recite them at their conventicles, when they observe the high mysteries contained in them, they will gain singular profit and great reputation, as did Alexander the Great under similar circumstances, from the books of high philosophy composed by Aristotle. Belly on belly, what pot-wallopings, what crevice-linings, there will be!

Therefore, my dear boozers, I advise you in good time to lay up a fair store of them when the opportunity offers, and as soon as you find them in the booksellers' shops. When the chance comes you must not only shell them, but gulp them down as an opiate cordial and absorb them into your systems. Then you will discover what good there is in them, ready for all gentle bean-shellers to extract. Now here I offer you a fine good basketful, gathered in the same garden as the former crop; and I beg you, reverend sirs – for so I address you – to accept my present gratefully, in expectation of something better at the next coming of the swallows.

CHAPTER 1: *How Pantagruel arrived at Ringing Island, and of the Noise we heard*

ON that day and the two that followed we sighted no land, nor did we see anything new, for we had sailed that way before. But on the fourth day we sighted land. This, our captain told us, was Triphes Island, or the Isle of Delights, and here we heard a noise coming from afar, which was loud and repeated, and which sounded to our ears like the ringing of bells: of large bells, small bells, and middle-sized bells, all ringing together as they do in Paris, Tours, Jargeau, Medon, and elsewhere, on high festivals. The nearer we came, the louder we heard this jangling, and it seemed likely to us that it might be Dodona with its kettles, or the Portico of the Seven Echoes in Olympia, or perhaps the perpetual humming of the Colossus which stands above Memnon's tomb at Thebes in Egypt, or the clanging that was heard of old around a certain tomb on the island of Lipara, one of the Aeolian group. But the topography did not agree with these suppositions.

'I suspect,' said Pantagruel, 'that a swarm of bees has begun to take flight, and that the neighbours are rattling their pots and kettles and basins – the corybantic cymbals of Cybele, the great mother of the gods – to call them back. Let us listen.'

As we came closer, we heard mingled with the perpetual jangling of the bells what we took for the persistent singing of the place's inhabitants. Pantagruel thought, therefore, that before touching at Ringing Island, we ought to land in our skiff on a small rock, beside which we could make out a hermitage and a small garden plot. There we found a nice little hermit called Braguibus, who came from Glatigny. He gave us a full explanation of all this jangling, and regaled us in a very strange way. He made us fast for four days on end, on the excuse that we should not be received on Ringing Island otherwise, since it was the *Fast of the Four Times*.

'I don't understand this riddle of yours,' said Panurge; 'it would be truer to call it the *Time of the Four Winds*, since if we fast we have nothing but wind for stuffing. Have you no other way of passing the time here except by fasting? It seems a thin amusement to me. We could pass our time without your palatal or palatial feasts. We could dispense with them nicely.'

'I can only find three times in my Grammar,' said Friar John, 'past, present, and future. The fourth one here must be a tip for the server.'

'It's an aorist,' said Epistemon, 'derived from the compound pluperfect of the Greeks and Latins, and it refers to times striped and variable. Let us have patience, as the lepers say.'

'It is, as I have told you, obligatory,' said the hermit. 'Anyone who objects is a heretic, and there is nothing for him but the fire.'

'To be frank with you, Father,' said Panurge, 'when I am on the sea I am more afraid of getting wet than warmed, more frightened of drowning than burning. However, let's fast, in God's name. But I've fasted for so long that fasting has whittled away all my flesh, and I'm much afraid that in the end the bastions of my body will decay. But I have another fear as well: that my way of fasting will not please you. For I know nothing about the art, and it doesn't suit me at all, as many people have told me – and I believe them. So far as I am concerned, fasting doesn't bother me, I assure you. There's nothing so easy or convenient. But what I am really afraid of is that I may not be able to fast in the future, since one has to lay up grist for the mill for that. Still, let's fast, in God's name, since we have arrived on such an esurient occasion. I haven't met with one like it for a long time.'

'If we must fast,' said Pantagruel, 'there's nothing for it but to get it over quickly, like a bad bit of the road. In the meantime, I should like to run through my papers, and make sure whether study at sea is as good as study on land. For when Plato wants a word to describe a stupid, incompetent, and ignorant fellow, he compares him to someone brought up at sea, on board ship, as we might say a man brought up in a barrel who had never looked out through the bung.'

Our fasting was hideous and terrible. On the first day we fasted on broken cudgels; on the second, on battered swords; on the third, on molten iron; and on the fourth, on blood and fire. Such was the Fairies' commandment.

CHAPTER 2: *How the Ringing Island had been inhabited by the Siticines, who had turned into Birds*

WHEN our fast was over, the hermit handed us a letter addressed to one whom he called Master Æditus or Sacristan of Ringing Island. But when Panurge greeted him, he called him Master Antitus.[1] He was a little bald old fellow, with a richly purple nose and a ripe crimson complexion; and on the hermit's introduction he gave us a very good reception, understanding that we had fasted, as above described. After we had made a very good meal, he showed us the island's chief features, and told us that it had originally been inhabited by the Siticines or Dirge-singers. However, by Nature's ordinance, by which everything changes, they had been turned into birds.

Hereupon I received a full account of all that Atteius Capito, Pollux, Marcellus, Aulus Gellius, Athenaeus, Suidas, Ammonius, and others, had written about the Siticines and Sicinnists; and we had no difficulty in giving credence to the transformations of Nyctimine, Procne, Itys, Alcyone, Antigone, Tereus, and others. We raised no doubts either concerning the children of Matabrune, who were changed into swans, or the men of Pallene, in Thrace, who were suddenly transformed into birds after bathing nine times in the Tritonic lake.

After this he spoke of nothing else but cages and birds. The cages were large, rich, sumptuous, and marvellously constructed. The birds correspondingly big, beautiful, and sleek, and much like the men of my country. They drank and ate like men, muted like men, slept and trod their females like men. In short, at first sight you would have said they were men. But according to Master Æditus' explanation they were not in any way human. For, as he protested, they were neither secular nor laymen. Moreover their plumage puzzled us. For some were all white, some all black, others all grey, others half white and half black, others all red, others half white and half blue. They were a lovely sight to see. The males he called clerijays, monajays, priestjays, abbeyjays, bishojays, cardinjays, and the popinjay. The females he called clergesses, priestgesses, abbeygesses, bishogesses, cardingesses, and popingesses. In the same way, he told us, as among the bees the idle drones do nothing but eat and ruin everything, so for the

1. Booby.

last three hundred years there had been, for some reason or other, a great number of bigots among these happy birds. These monsters had flown in in the fifth month of each year, and had utterly fouled and bemuted the island; and so hideous were they that everyone shunned them. For they all had wry-necks, hairy paws, the claws and bellies of Harpies, and shitty rumps like the Stymphalides. What was worse, it was impossible to exterminate them. For twenty-four would fly up for every one that died. They made me long for some second Hercules, and Father John was so deep in thought about them that he was oblivious to the world.

CHAPTER 3: *How there is only one Popinjay in the Ringing Island*

WE then asked Master Æditus why, since every other species of these venerable birds multiplied, there was only one popinjay. He answered that this had been so since the beginning and that it was so ordained by the stars; that from the clerijays were born the priestjays and mona-jays without physical copulation, as in the case of the bees. From the priestjays came the bishojays; from them the grand cardinjays, and each cardinjay, if death did not intervene, ended up as popinjay; but of these there is only one, as there is only one king in a hive of bees, and only one sun in the sky.

When the popinjay dies, another is produced in his place out of the whole brood of cardinjays; also, be it understood, without physical copulation. Therefore it is that this species consists of but one individual with a perpetuity of succession exactly like that of the phoenix of Arabia. True it is that about two thousand seven hundred and sixty months ago Nature produced two popinjays. But this was the greatest calamity that the island had ever known. 'For,' said Editus. 'all these birds so pecked and clawed one another that the island was in danger of losing all its inhabitants. One faction of them adhered to one and supported him, another faction stuck to the other and defended him, while part of them remained as dumb as fish and did not sing, and some of the bells seemed to be under an interdict, for they did not sound at all. During these disorderly times they called for the aid of all the Emperors, Kings, Dukes, Marquises, Counts, Barons, and all the world's republics lying on the mainland and on *terra firma*; and this mutinous schism did not come to an end till one of the popinjays departed this life and the plurality was reduced to unity.'

Then we asked what caused these birds to sing so continuously. The Editus answered that it was the bells hanging above their cages, and went on to say: 'Would you like me to make these monajays whom you see swathed in hoods like mulled-wine strainers, sing like so many larks in the air?'

'If you please,' we replied. Upon which he sounded just six strokes on the bell. Then the monajays rushed up, and the monajays started singing.

'And if I were to ring this bell, should I make these ones sing too?' asked Panurge – 'the ones with plumage the colour of a red herring, I mean.'

'Yes, just the same,' said Æditus.

Panurge rang, and immediately these smoked birds rushed up, and sang all together. But they had hoarse and unpleasant voices, and Æditus explained to us that they lived on fish alone, like the herons and cormorants of this world, and that they were a fifth species – the cowljays, newly minted. He added, furthermore, that he had received notice from Robert Valbringue, who had passed by recently on his way back from Africa, that a sixth species would shortly fly in, which he called capucinjays, a more woe-begone, sterile, and loathsome species than any in the whole island.'

'Africa,' said Pantagruel, 'is always producing things both new and monstrous.'

CHAPTER 4: *How the Birds of Ringing Island were all Birds of Passage*

'BUT now that you have explained to us,' said Pantagruel, 'how the popinjay is produced by the cardinjays, and the cardinjays by the bishojays, and the bishojays by the priestjays, and the priestjays by the clerijays, I should very much like to know how these clerijays are born in the first place.'

'They are all birds of passage,' said Æditus. 'They come to us from the other world; part of them from a great land of marvels which is

called Breadlessday, and part from another country which lies towards
the west and is called Toomany-of-'em. These clerijays fly to us every
year in flocks from these two countries, leaving their mothers and
fathers and all their friends and relations behind them. This is how it
happens. Sometimes there are too many children, either male or
female, in some noble house in this latter country, so that if a man
should give an inheritance to all – as reason demands, Nature ordains
and God decrees – the property would quickly be eaten up. Now this
is the moment when the parents get rid of some of them on to this
island, especially if they are of the Bossard or Humped Island brood.'

'That is to say from the Isle Bouchart near Chinon, I suppose,'
broke in Panurge.

'I said Bossard,' answered Æditus. 'For usually they are hump-
backed, boss-eyed, lame, one-armed, gouty, deformed, and bewitched; in fact a useless burden to the earth.'

'That is the absolute contrary of the custom which formerly
governed the admission of Vestal virgins,' said Pantagruel. 'According
to Labeo Antistius, it was strictly forbidden to raise a maiden to this
high rank if she had any vice in her character, any defect in her organs
of sense, or any physical blemish, never mind how small or hidden.'

'What amazes me,' Æditus went on, 'is that the mothers there carry
their children a whole nine months in the womb since they cannot
bear to keep them at home for nine years, and quite often not even for
seven. They just put a shirt over their clothes, and snip a hair or two
from the crowns of their heads, mumbling a few expiatory words to
keep evil at bay as they do so. It was in much the same way that the
priests of Isis were created among the Egyptians, merely by shaving
them and putting stoles over their heads. So it is that, visibly, patently,
and manifestly, by Pythagorean metempsychosis, and without any
wound or lesion, they turn their children into the kind of birds you
see before you. But I do not know, my fair friends, why it is, or how
it happens that the females, whether clergesses, monagesses, or abbeygesses, do not sing pleasant songs or hymns of thanksgiving, such as
were sung to Oromasdes of old by order of Zoroaster, but instead
utter only such curses and lamentations as were formerly addressed to
the demon Ahrimanes. Indeed they hurl continuous imprecations at
their relations and friends who have transformed them into birds, and
this, let me tell you, is the practice of the old as well as of the young.

'A still greater number of these birds come from Breadlessday, which is extremely long. For through lack of sufficient sustenance, also of the skill and will to work at any honest craft or trade, and of the patience to give loyal service to some honourable family, its inhabitants, the Asaphis, are often in danger of falling victims to that evil counsellor hunger; others are crossed in love, or fail in their enterprises and become desperate; and there are others still who have committed some heinous crime and, if caught, will be put to an ignominious death; all of these fly here. Here a certain livelihood is provided for each. Here, though they were once skinny as magpies, they become as sleek as dormice. Here they have perfect security, immunity, and freedom from pursuit.'

'But,' asked Pantagruel, 'once these fine birds have flown away, do they ever return to the world where they were hatched?'

'Some of them do,' replied Æditus. 'In the old days they were very few, and they returned very late and very reluctantly. But since certain eclipses, a great bunch of them has flown back, by virtue of the celestial constellations. But that does not trouble us at all, since now there are more rations for those who remain. What is more, before they flew off they all left their plumage among these nettles and briars.'

We actually found some of these feathers, and as we searched we came by chance upon a pot of roses.

CHAPTER 5: *On the Dumbness of the Gormander-birds on Ringing Island*

HE had scarcely stopped speaking, when there flew quite close to us twenty-five or thirty birds of a colour and plumage that we had not so far seen on the island. Their feathers changed every hour, like a chameleon's skin, or the flower of a tripolion or teucrion. And they all had a mark under the left wing, as of two diameters cutting a circle at right angles, or of a perpendicular line falling on a straight line. It took almost the same form with all of them, but it was not always of the same colour. Some had it white, some green, some red, some violet, and some blue.

'Who are these?' asked Panurge, 'and what do you call them?'

'They're mongrels,' answered Æditus, 'and we call them gorman-ders.[1] They possess a great number of rich gormanderies in your world.'

'Make them sing a little, if you please,' I asked him, 'so that we can hear their voices.'

'They never sing,' he replied. 'But they eat twice as much, to make up for it.'

'Where are their females?' I asked.

'They haven't any,' he replied.

'How is that?' asked Panurge. 'Are they all scabby then, and eaten up with the pox?'

'Yes, this kind of bird is subject to the disease,' said he, 'since they sometimes haunt the sea-shores. The reason for their coming up to you,' he continued, 'is to see if they can find among you a magnificent species of jay or goth, a fierce bird of prey, which does not, however, come to the lure or perch on the glove. They say that there are such in your world, and that some of them wear very fine and precious iesses on their legs, with an inscription on the leather which condemns anyone *qui mal y pense* to be promptly beshitten. There are others who wear a victory over the devil on the front of their plumage, and others still who bear a ram's fleece.'

'That may well be so, Master Antitus,' said Panurge, 'but we know nothing of them.'

'Now that's enough talking,' said Æditus, 'let's go and drink.'

'What about eating too?' asked Panurge.

'Yes,' said Æditus, 'we'll eat and drink lustily, a full feed and double the stakes. There's nothing so costly or so precious as time. So let's spend it on good works.'

He wanted to take us first to the cardinjays' baths, grand, sumptuous, and delightful places, and after we had bathed to have us rubbed with precious ointments by the slaves of the Thermae. But Pantagruel told him that he would drink only too much without that. So Æditus led us into a large and most pleasant refectory, and said to us: 'I know that the hermit Braguibus has made you fast for four days. So you shall stay here four days, as a recompense, and never stop eating and drinking.'

'Shan't we sleep during all that time?' asked Panurge.

'You'll be quite free to,' replied Æditus. 'For he who sleeps drinks.'

Good lord, what cheer we made! He was a splendid fellow!

1. Knights commander of the religious orders.

CHAPTER 6: *How the Birds of Ringing Island are fed*

PANTAGRUEL looked rather glum, and seemed not too pleased with the quatridian stay that Æditus had prescribed for us. And when this sacristan saw this he said: 'My lord, you know that for seven days before and seven days after the winter solstice, there is never a storm at sea. This is because of the elements' respect for the Halcyons, birds sacred to Thetis, which lay and hatch their eggs on the shore at that season. Now here the sea compensates itself for this long calm, and never ceases to rage most horribly for four days on end whenever any travellers arrive. Its purpose in this, as we suppose, is to constrain them to stay here for this period, and to compel them to be feasted on the proceeds of our ringing. So do not think that you are wasting your time here in idleness. You are detained here forcibly, unless you care to fight Juno, Neptune, Doris, Aeolus, and all the maleficent gods. So make up your minds to make good cheer.'

After the first piled platefuls, Friar John said to Æditus: 'In this island you have nothing but cages and birds. They don't dig or cultivate the soil. Their sole occupation is frolicking, warbling, and singing. From what country then do you get your horn of abundance, your store of so many good things and dainty pickings?'

'From all the rest of the world,' answered Æditus, 'except for certain countries that lie under the North wind, which some centuries ago stirred up the bog.'

'Shoo!' exclaimed Friar John.

> They'll live to rue the day, they will.
> They'll live to rue the day.

Come, let's drink, my friends.'

'But from what country do you come?' asked Æditus.

'From Touraine,' replied Panurge.

'You were hatched by no ill jay, and that's certain,' said Æditus, 'seeing that you come from the blessed Touraine. So very many good things come to us every year from Touraine that, as we have been told by some passing travellers from that district, the Duke of Touraine has not enough left of all his revenue to fill his stomach with bacon. And the cause of this is the excessive bounty that his predecessors have lavished on his most sacred birds, so that we here might eat ourselves sick on pheasants, partridges, pullets, turkeys, fat capons from around Loudun, venison of all kinds, and every sort of game. Let's drink, my friends. Just look at this perch of birds. How downy and plump they are, on the revenue that comes to us from there. And they sing finely for their providers. You never saw better mumbling than they do, when they see the two gilt sticks up on high. ...'

'It's a high festival then, I suppose,' said Friar John.

'And when I ring these great bells for them, which you see hanging round their cages,' he continued. 'But let's drink, my friends. To-day is a fine drinking day, indeed, and so is every other day. Let's drink. I drink to you with all my heart. You are extremely welcome. Don't be afraid that wine and food will give out here. For even if the heavens turned to brass and the earth to iron, we shouldn't go short of victuals, not for eight, or even nine years longer than the famine lasted in Egypt. Let's drink together in all good fellowship and charity.'

'What a devil of a lot of comforts you have in this world,' exclaimed Panurge.

'We shall have a great number more in the next,' replied Æditus. 'We shan't fail to pasture in the Elysian fields, at least. Let's drink, my friends. I drink to you all.'

'It was a most godlike and perfect idea of your first Siticines,' said I, 'to devise a means of your having what all mankind naturally strives for, and what is granted to few of them – or more correctly to none. To enjoy Paradise, I mean, in this life, and in the next as well.

> O happy folk! O demi-gods!
> May heaven grant me just your luck.'

CHAPTER 7: *Panurge tells Master Æditus the Fable of the Horse and the Ass*

AFTER we had feasted our fill, Æditus led us into a well-furnished room, hung with fine tapestry and all smothered with gilt. Here he had us served with myrobalan plums and green preserved ginger, with plenty of mulled sack and delicious wine. With these restoratives, as with a drink of sweet Lethe water, he invited us to forget the toils we had suffered on the sea, and to dismiss them from our minds.

He also had a generous quantity of victuals carried aboard our ships, which were lying in the harbour. But we could not sleep, on account of the everlasting jangling of the bells.

At midnight Æditus woke us up to drink; and he himself drank first, saying: 'You people from the other world say that ignorance is the mother of all evils, and you are right. But all the same you do not banish it from your minds for a single moment. You live in it, with it, and by it. That is why so many evils afflict you day by day. You are always complaining and lamenting. You are never satisfied. I can see it at this present moment. For ignorance keeps you here, tied to your beds, as the great god of battles was by Vulcan's art, and you do not understand that it is your duty to be sparing of your sleep, and not to be sparing of the good things of this famous island. You should have consumed three meals already. What is more, you can take it from me that to eat the food of Ringing Island you have to rise very early in the morning. Eaters multiply, but those who are sparing waste away. Plough the field in due season, and the grass will spring up again thicker and richer for the manger. But if you don't mow it, in a few years it will be carpeted with nothing but moss. Let's drink, my friends. Let's drink, one and all. The skinniest of our birds are now singing, and all for us. We will drink to them, if you please. Let's drink, I beg of you. You'll only spit the better for it. Let's drink, one, two, three, nine bumpers, *non zelus, sed charitas.*'[1]

At daybreak he woke us again to drink the early morning soups; and after that we ate only one meal, which lasted all day. We did not know whether it was dinner or supper, luncheon or bed-time snacks. Merely by way of pastime, we took a turn or two about the island to hear the joyous songs of those pretty birds.

In the evening, Panurge said to Æditus: 'I hope you don't mind if I tell you a little story about something that happened in the district of Châtellerault some twenty-three months ago. One morning in the month of April a gentleman's groom was exercising his steeds on some fallow land, and there he saw a gay little shepherd girl

> A-keeping of her lambs
> In the shadow of a wood

and with them an ass and several goats. After a little chat, he persuaded her to mount behind him on the crupper, and come to his stable to

1. Not out of duty, but out of kindness to yourself.

take a country snack with him. Now, as they were talking, his horse went up to the ass and whispered in his ear – for animals could talk all that year in one place and another: "You poor, miserable moke, I feel pity and compassion for you. You must work very hard every day, I can see that by the marks of your crupper. But that's as it should be, for God created you for the service of man. You are an honest moke. But that you shouldn't be rather better rubbed down and combed and caparisoned and fed, that does seem to me somewhat tyrannical – indeed most unreasonable – treatment. You're all rough-coated and dirty and beaten, and here you eat nothing but reeds, thorns, and tough thistles. So my advice to you, moke, is to pace it along with me, and see how those of us are treated and fed whom Nature has bred for war. I promise you a taste of my ordinary fodder."

' "Thank you," answered the ass. "I'll come most willingly, Master Horse."

' "Master Charger to you, moke," observed the steed.

' "Excuse me, Master Charger," replied the ass, "we country folk from the villages are not very good at our language. We haven't been well taught. But I'll obey you willingly and follow you at a distance, through fear of blows – my hide is all criss-crossed with them – since you're so good as to do me this honour and kindness."

'When the shepherdess was mounted, the ass followed the horse, firmly resolved to get a good meal. But when they came to the stable and the groom saw him, he told the stable-boys to welcome him with a fork and give him a good thrashing. On hearing this, the ass commended himself to the god Neptune, and began to scamper off at a lively pace, thinking and reasoning to himself like this: "He is quite right. I'm not of the rank to attend the courts of the great. Nature bred me only to be a help to the poor. Aesop warned me of that clearly enough in one of his fables. This has been presumption on my part, and there's no help for it but to scamper off cheerfully, and in less time than it takes to cook asparagus." With that the ass made off with a trot and a fart and a bound, a rush, a gallop, and another volley.

'When the shepherdess saw the ass make off she told the groom that he was her beast and insisted that he should be well treated, or else she would not come in at all, but would go straight away. So the groom ordered that all the horses should go without oats for a week rather than the ass fail to get his bellyful. But the difficulty was to coax him back. For it was no good the boys calling: "Here, here, moke, good moke, come up!" "I'm not coming," said the ass. "I'm shy." The more wheedlingly they called him, the more stubbornly he made off, galloping and farting the while. They would have been at it still, in fact, if the shepherdess had not told them to toss the oats high in a sieve and call him then. This they did, and the ass suddenly turned back. "Fodder," he cried; "by God the Father, but none of your fork! I'm none of your card-players. I don't say, I pass." So he went back to them, singing melodiously. For, as you know, the melodious voices of these beasts from Arcady are a joy to hear.

'When he got there he was taken into a stable beside the great steed. Then he was rubbed, wiped down, and combed. Fresh litter was thrown to him belly-high and the rack was piled full of hay, the manger was filled with oats also, and as the stable-boys were sifting them he pricked up his ears, as much as to say that he would eat them gladly enough without sifting, and that this was too much of an honour for him. Now, after they had both taken their fill, the horse turned to the ass and asked: "Well, how are you getting along now, my poor moke? How do you like this reception? And yet you did not want to come. What do you say now?"

' "By the fig which one of our ancestors ate," replied the ass, "which made Philemon die of laughing, this is balm to me, Master Charger. But, after all, it's only half cheer. Do you never have a leaping match here, you worthy and horsy gentlemen?"

' "What kind of leaping do you mean, ass?" demanded the horse; "the glanders take you, moke, do you think I'm a donkey?"

' "Ha, ha," answered the ass. "I'm a bit slow in learning the courtly language of you horses. What I mean is, don't you play the stallion here, you noble chargers?"

' "Speak quietly, ass," said the horse. "If the stable-boys were to hear you they'd give you such a mighty hard battering with their forks that you'd have no stomach for a leaping match. We daren't stiffen our pizzles here, even to piss, for fear of a beating. But for the rest, we're as happy as kings."

' "By the pommel of the pack-saddle on my back," said the ass, "you're welcome. You can keep your litter and your hay and your oats. Long live the thistles of the field, for there you can play the stallion to your heart's content. Eat less and always leap your fill, that's my motto. Leaping's hay and fodder to us. Oh, Master Charger, my friend, if you had only seen us at the fairs, when we hold our provincial chapter, how we stallionize all out while our mistresses sell their goslings and pullets!" Such was their parting, and my tale is done.'

Here Panurge ceased, and uttered no further sound. Pantagruel urged him to finish his argument, but Æditus replied: 'One word is enough for a good listener. I perfectly understand the moral you intend to convey by your fable of the ass and the horse. But you *are* a bashful fellow. Let me tell you, however, that there's nothing for you here. Don't mention the matter again.'

'Yet,' said Panurge, 'I saw a white-plumed abbeygess here not long ago, who would be nicer to ride than to lead by the hand. If the rest of them are game-birds, she seems to me a game hen. Pretty and dainty I say, and well worth a sin or two. God forgive me, I mean no harm. But may all the harm I do mean befall me very promptly.'

CHAPTER 8: *How with much difficulty we got a sight of the Popinjay*

THE third day passed with the same feasting and copious banquets as the first two. But on this day Pantagruel earnestly demanded to see the popinjay. Æditus answered, however, that he did not let himself be seen as easily as that.

'What,' asked Pantagruel, 'does he wear Pluto's helmet on his head, or Gyges' ring on his claws, or a chameleon on his breast, to make himself invisible to the world?'

'No,' replied Æditus, 'but he is by nature rather difficult to see. Still I will give orders that you shall see him, if it's possible.'

After saying this he left us at table, still nibbling, and returned a quarter of an hour later to tell us that the popinjay was at that hour visible. He then led us, stealthily and silently, right up to the case in which he was sitting, with two little cardinjays and six great fat bishojays under his wing. Panurge gazed long and attentively at his shape, attitude, and bearing, and then cried out in a loud voice: 'God damn the creature! He looks like a dupe-o.'

'Speak quietly, for God's sake,' exclaimed Æditus; 'he has ears, as Michael de Matiscones sagely observed.'

'So has a dupe-o,' said Panurge.

'If once he hears you blaspheming like this, you're lost, my good people, all of you. Do you see that basin there in his cage? Out of that come thunderbolts, thunder and lightning, devils and tempests, which will sink you a hundred feet below the earth in a single moment.'

'I would rather drink and be merry,' said Friar John. But Panurge remained deep in contemplation of the popinjay and his company, till suddenly he saw a madge-owl beneath the cage and cried out:

'My God, we're all caught in a trap. Here's quick trickery, and slick lock-pickery in this place. Look at that stuffed madge-owl. We're decoyed and done for, I swear we are.'

'Speak quietly, for God's sake,' said Æditus. 'That's no madge-owl. It's a male bird. It's a noble treasury-bird.'

'Make the popinjay here sing to us a little, so that we can hear his fine voice,' said Pantagruel.

'He only sings on his high days,' replied Æditus, 'and he only eats at his own hours.'

'That's like me,' said Panurge, 'but all hours are my hours. Come, let's drink, then, instead.'

'Now you're speaking properly,' said Æditus. 'If you speak like this you'll never be a heretic. Let's go. For I'm of the same mind.'

As we returned to our drinking, we caught sight of an old green-headed bishojay, who was sitting snoring beneath some greenery, with a suffragan and three pelicans, which are gay protonotary-birds. Beside him was a pretty abbeygess, who was singing most charmingly, and who so delighted us that we wished all our members could be transformed into ears. For we were anxious not to miss a note of her song, and to give our whole attention to it without any distractions.

'That pretty abbeygess is singing herself to death,' said Panurge, 'and all the time that fat rogue of a bishojay is just snoring. I'll make him sing a tune this very moment, damned if I don't.'

He then rang a bell which hung above the cage. But the harder he rang it, the louder the bishojay snored. He did not sing a note.

'By God, you old buzzard,' exclaimed Panurge, 'I'll find another way of making you sing.'

Then he picked up a large stone, intending to hit the creature on his

mitre. But Æditus quickly shouted out: 'Smite, wound, slay, and murder all the kings and princes in the world, my good man, by treachery,
poison, or any other way you will; or pull the angels down from their
nests in Heaven. For all this the popinjay will grant you pardon. But
don't touch these sacred birds, if you love your life, your profit, and
your welfare – and not yours alone, but those of your relations and
friends, living and dead. Why, even those who are yet to be born after
them would suffer from his curse. Look carefully at that basin.'

'I'd far rather drink instead,' said Panurge, 'and have a good
feast.'

'He's right, Master Antitus,' said Friar John. 'While we're looking
at these devilish birds, all we do is to blaspheme. But when we're
emptying your bottles and mugs, we do nothing but praise God.
Come, and let us drink instead. O the blessed word!'

On the third day – after drinking, – as you'll understand – Æditus
allowed us to go. We made him a present of a pretty little knife from
Perche, which he accepted more gratefully than Artaxerxes did the
glass of cold water which was offered him by a peasant in Scythia. He
thanked us courteously, and replenished our ships with every sort of
provisions. Then he wished us a prosperous voyage, a sure salvation
for ourselves, and success to our enterprise, and made us swear by
Jupiter that we would return by way of his territory. 'You will notice,
my friends,' he said to us on parting, 'that there are many more ballocks than men in this world. That is something to remember.'

CHAPTER 9: A Landing on Tool Island

AFTER thoroughly ballasting our stomachs we had the wind behind
us. So the mizzen-mainsail was raised, and in less than two days we
arrived at the uncultivated and uninhabited Isle of Tools. Here we saw
a great number of trees on which hung mattocks, pick-axes, hoes,
scythes, sickles, spades, trowels, axes, bill-hooks, saws, grubbing-axes,
shears, scissors, pincers, shovels, augers, and bobbins. Others bore
daggers, poniards, clasp-knives, penknives, punches, swords, rapiers,
back-swords, scimitars, tucks, bolts, and knives. Anybody who
wanted one had only to shake the tree, and they promptly fell down
like plums. What is more, when they touched the ground they struck

a kind of grass called scabbard-grass, and sheathed themselves in it. One had to take good care that as they fell they did not strike one's head or one's foot, or some other part of one's body. For they descended point downwards – in order to sheathe themselves straight – and they would have dealt a man a nasty wound. Underneath some other sorts of trees I saw certain kinds of grass growing in the form of pikes, lances, javelins, halberds, boar-spears, partisans, prongs, forks, and hunting-spears. These pointed upwards, so as to touch the tree on which they found heads and blades, each suitable to its kind. These the trees above held ready for the moment when they grew tall enough, just as you prepare dresses for small children when you intend to take them out of swaddling-clothes. What is more – for I should not like you to reject the opinions of Plato, Anaxagoras, and Democritus (who were no small philosophers, were they?) – I must tell you that these trees looked to us like terrestrial animals, exactly like the beasts, in fact, in that they too had skins, fat, flesh, veins, arteries, ligaments, nerves, cartilages, glands, bones, marrow, humours, wombs, brains, and recognizable articulations. For these they certainly possess, as Theophrastus ably infers. But since they have their heads – that is to say their trunks – downwards, and their hair – that is their roots – in the ground, and their feet – that is their boughs – upside down, it is as if a man were playing at the forked oak.

And just as you poxy fellows feel in your sciatic legs and your shoulder-blades the distant approach of rain, or wind, or good weather, or any sort of change, so in their roots, stems, gums, and marrow, they feel what sort of staff is growing beneath them, and prepare the right heads and blades. True it is that in all things – except the divine – error may creep in, and even Nature is not exempt from this law. For she produces monstrous things and misshapen creatures. So I found some faults in these trees too. For one half-pike, which was growing high from the ground beneath these tool-bearing trees, had struck a broom-head instead of a steel point when it touched the boughs. However, the thing will serve to sweep chimneys. One partisan, too, was fitted with a pair of scissors instead of a blade. But there is a use for everything, and this will serve to rid the gardens of caterpillars. A halberd staff also had struck a scythe-blade, and looked like a hermaphrodite. But that does not matter. It will do for some mower. It's a good thing to put one's trust in God!

As we returned to our ships I observed, behind some bush or other, some people or other doing something or other in some way or another. They were sharpening some tools or other, which they kept somewhere or other. It was a fine business of some sort.

CHAPTER 10: *Pantagruel arrives at Sharping Island*

ON the third day after this we came to Sharping Island, the very image of Fontainebleau forest. For the earth is so thin that its bones – the rocks, that is – stick through its skin. It is sandy, sterile, unhealthy, and unpleasant. But here our captain pointed out to us two little cubes of rock, each with eight equal square faces, which seemed from their appearance either to be of alabaster or to be covered with snow. He informed us, however, that they were of bone, and that in them was the six-storeyed abode of the twenty devils of chance, who are so much feared in our country. The biggest of their combined throws he called the *Double Six*, and the smallest *Amb's-ace*. Those between them, were *Cinques*, *Quaters*, *Treys*, and *Double-twos*; and the others *Six and Five*, *Six and Four*, *Six and Three*, *Six and Two*, *Six and One*, *Five and Four*, *Five and Three*, and so on. Then I observed that there are few gamblers in the world who do not invoke the devils. For when they throw a pair of dice on the table and cry out, in their devotion: 'Double-six, my friend', that's the big devil, and when it is 'Amb's-ace, my lad', it is the little devil; and with 'Four and Two, my hearties', and all the rest they are invoking the various devils by their names and surnames. And not only do they invoke them, but they call on them as their friends and familiars. It is true that these devils do not always come immediately at their bidding. But they have an excuse for that; they were elsewhere, answering a prior call from some other gambler who had invoked them. All the same, it would be wrong to say that they have no ears and senses. They have, I assure you, and very fine ones.

After this the captain told us that there have been more break-ups, shipwrecks, and loss of life and goods on and around these square rocks than around all the Syrtes, and Charybdises, Sirens, Scyllas, Harpies Islands, and whirlpools in all the seas. I could easily believe him. For I remembered that among the wise Egyptians of old, Neptune was designated in hieroglyphics as the first cube, as Apollo was by the one, Diana by the two, and Minerva by the seven, &c.

There also, he told us, was a flask of the Sangraal or divine blood, a thing known only to few; and Panurge was so successful in his fervid entreaties that he persuaded the local magistrates to show it to us. But they made far more ceremonies and were three times more solemn about this than they are at Florence when they show you Justinian's *Pandects*, or over Veronica's napkin at Rome. I never saw so many veils, so many flares and torches, so many links and blessed tapers in my life. What they revealed to us in the end was the muzzle of a roast rabbit.

We saw nothing else worth speaking of there except Good Face, the wife of Bad Luck, and the shells of two eggs laid and hatched by Leda of old, from which were born Castor and Pollux, the brothers of the fair Helen. The magistrates gave us a piece of it in exchange for some bread. On our departure, we bought a bundle of sharping hats and bonnets. But I do not think that we shall make much profit by the sale of them, and I expect that those who buy them from us will make even less by wearing them.

CHAPTER 11: *How we passed the Wicket presided over by Claw-puss, the Archduke of the Furrycats*

HAVING already had experience of Procuration, we avoided the place, and we also passed Condemnation, which is another completely desert island. We passed the Wicket as well, where Pantagruel did not want to land. And he was right, for we were arrested on the orders of Clawpuss, Archduke of the Furrycats, and made prisoners, because one of our people had beaten a Bum-bailiff as we passed Procuration.

The Furrycats are the most ghastly and terrible creatures; they eat little children and feed on marble stones. So just tell me, boozers, whether you would not expect them to have snub noses! The hair of their coats does not grow outwards, but is turned inside, and each and every one of them carries as his badge and symbol an open pouch. But they do not all wear it in the same way. Some have it slung round their necks like a scarf, others on their rumps, others on their paunches, and others at the side; and all this for good and mysterious reasons. They also wear their claws so long, strong, and steel-tipped that nothing escapes them once they have got their paws on it. Some wear on their heads caps ornamented with four spouts or codpieces, some have caps back-to-front, others mortar-boards, and yet others mortified headgear.

As we entered their den a poorhouse beggar, to whom we had given half a teston, said to us: 'Good people, God grant that you may soon come out of that place in safety. Take a good look at the faces of these valiant pillars and flying-buttresses of Clawpussular justice, and remember that if you should live another six Olympiads plus the life-times of two dogs, you'll see these Furrycats lords of all Europe and peaceful possessors of all the estates and domains that are therein, un-less the goods and income unjustly acquired by them suddenly decays in the hands of their heirs. Take this from an honest beggar. They are ruled by the sixth essence, which causes them to seize everything, devour everything, and beshit everything. They hang, burn, quarter, behead, murder, imprison, waste, and ruin everything, without dis-tinguishing between good and bad. For among them vice is called virtue, wickedness is entitled goodness, treason takes the name of loyalty, and thieving is styled liberality. Plunder is their motto, and when they plunder they have the approval of all men except the heretics. They do everything with sovereign and irrefragable authority.

'As proof of my warning, you will notice that here the mangers are above the racks. Remember this one day. And if ever plague, famine or wars, whirlpools, cataclysms, conflagrations, or other misfortunes strike the world, do not attribute or refer them to an evil conjunction of the planets, to the Court of Rome's abuses, to the tyrannies of earthly kings or princes, to the impostures of hypocrites, heretics, and false prophets, to the malignancy of usurers, coiners, and clippers of testons, to the ignorance and carelessness of physicians, surgeons, and apothecaries, or to the perversity of adultresses, poisoners, and infanti-cides. Attribute them all to the enormous, unspeakable, incredible, and inestimable wickedness which is continuously plotted and prac-tised in the Furrycats' workshops. This is no more known to the world than is the Cabala of the Jews; and therefore it is not abhorred, cor-rected, and punished as it rightly should be. But if some day it be plainly revealed and demonstrated to the people, there is not – and never has been – any orator eloquent enough by his art to restrain

them; or any law sufficiently severe and draconian, by fear of punishment to prevent them; or any magistrate powerful enough to restrain
them, from mercilessly burning these creatures alive in their burrows.
Even their own children, the Furrykittens, and their other relations
would loathe and abominate them. That is why, as Hannibal was
commanded by his father Hamilcar, under solemn and religious oaths,
to harry the Romans for the whole of his life, so was I enjoined by my
late father to wait outside this door until the thunder of heaven falls on
this house and burns them to ashes, like those other Titans, the profane enemies of the gods. For men have developed such tough hides
that they neither notice, feel, nor foresee the evil that they have
suffered, are suffering, and will suffer from them, or if they feel it,
dare not, will not, and cannot exterminate them.'

'So it's like that, is it?' exclaimed Panurge. 'I'm not going in. Oh,
no, no, I swear I'm not. Let's turn back. Let's turn back I say, for
God's sake.

> This noble beggar's given me a fright
> Worse than a thunder clap on an autumn night.'

But as we turned back we found the gate closed, and were told that it
was as easy to get in here as into Avernus, but the difficulty was to get
out. There was no possible way of escape, we learned, except by order
and discharge of the court; and the reason for this was that one cannot
get away from a fair as easily as from a market, and that, our feet being
dusty, we were subject to Pie Powder.

The worst of it was when we came in through the wicket. For in
order to get our order and discharge, we were brought before the
most hideous monster that was ever described. He was called Clawpuss, and I could find no fitter comparison for him than to the
Chimaera, or the Sphinx, or to Cerberus, or perhaps to the image of
Osiris, as the Egyptians represent him, with three heads joined together – one a roaring lion's, one a fawning dog's, and one a ravening
wolf's – all interlaced by a dragon biting its own tail, and by fiery
beams, which shot out all round him. His hands were thick with blood.
He had a harpy's claws, a muzzle like a raven's bill, tusks like those of
a four-year-old boar, and eyes like hell's throat. He was entirely
muffled in mortars and pestles, and only his claws showed. His seat,
and that of the wild cats, his collaterals, was a long brand-new rack,

above which, contrary to the usual practice, were fixed fine broad mangers, as the beggar had told us. Above the principal seat was the picture of an old woman, holding a sickle-case in her right hand, and a scales in her left. She wore spectacles on her nose, and the dishes of the scales were a couple of velvet pouches, one full of bullion and hanging down, the other empty and suspended high above the beam. I am of the opinion that this was a portrait of Clawpussical justice; and if it was, their practice was very different from that of the ancient Thebans, who erected the statues of their Dicasts or judges after their death, in gold, in silver, or in marble, according to their deserts, but always without hands.

When we were brought before it, certain men, covered all over in pouches and sacks, with great strips of writing, made us sit down on stools. But Panurge protested: 'My good friends and vagabonds,' said he, 'I'm quite well off as I am, and anyhow your stool is too low for a man with new breeches and a short doublet.'

'Sit down there,' they shouted, 'and don't let us have to speak to you again. The earth will open up this instant and swallow you all alive if you don't give the right answers.'

CHAPTER 12: *Clawpuss propounds us a Riddle*

WHEN we were seated, Clawpuss, from the midst of his Furrycats, addressed us in a furious voice: 'Come on now, come on, come on!'

'Some drink now, some drink, some drink!' muttered Panurge between his teeth.

> A pretty creature, young and fair and slender,
> Conceived, without a sire, a swarthy son
> And bore him painlessly, the little tender
> Suckling, although his birth was a strange one.
> For, like a viper, through her side he bored
> Impatiently, a truly hideous thing,
> And then o'er hill and valley boldly soared,
> Riding the air, or o'er land journeying;
> Which drove the Friend of Wisdom out of his mind,
> For he had thought him of the human kind.

'Come now, answer me that,' said Clawpuss to me. 'Solve this riddle for me on the spot. Come now, do!'

'By God now,' I answered, 'if I had a Sphinx at home, by God now, as Verres had, who was one of your precursors, then by God I could solve your riddle, by God now I could. But I swear to you I've never been to any such place, and I'm quite innocent in this matter, by God now.'

'Come now,' said Clawpuss, 'by the Styx, since that's all the answer you'll give me, come now, I'll show you that you would have done better to fall into Lucifer's paws – come now! – than into ours. Come now, do you see them? Come, you villain, you plead ignorance, do you? As if that were sufficient to excuse you from our tortures. Come now, our laws are like spiders' webs. Your innocent little flies and pretty moths all get caught, come now, but your great horse-flies break them, now, and pass through them now. We don't hunt after the great robbers and tyrants, you see now. For, come now, they're too hard to digest, now. They would hurt us now. But you pretty little innocents, come now, the great devil shall sing a Mass for you. Come now, that he shall, come now!'

Clawpuss's speech was more than Friar John could endure, and he broke in: 'Come Master Devil berobed, how can you expect him to answer in a case that he is ignorant of? Aren't you satisfied with the truth?'

'Come now,' said Clawpuss, 'this is the first time since I've ruled here that anyone has spoken without first being interrogated. Come now! Who has let this wild madman loose on us?'

'You're lying,' said Friar John, without moving his lips.

'Come now, you'll have enough business on your hands; come now, when it's your turn to answer, you scoundrel,' answered Clawpuss.

'You're a liar,' muttered Friar John through his teeth.

'Come now, d'you think you're in the gardens of the Academy, among the idle hunters and searchers after truth? Come now, we have something else to do here. Come now, here you have to answer, I can tell you. Come now, you have to answer, and categorically. Come now, my man, come now, you have to give answers even if you're ignorant. Here you confess what you've done – come now! – even if you haven't done it. Come now, here you swear you know what you never learnt. Come now, come! Here you have to be patient even when you're in a rage. Here we pluck the goose, but we don't let him cackle. Come now, you're speaking without a writ of attorney. Come now, I can see that clearly. A fierce quartan ague take you, come now, and may you be married to it! Come now, come!'

'You devil,' cried Friar John, 'you arch-devil, you universal devil, so you would make monks marry, would you? Ho, ho, ho, I proclaim you a heretic.'

CHAPTER 13: *Panurge solves Clawpuss's Riddle*

PRETENDING not to have heard this accusation, Clawpuss turned to Panurge, and said: 'Come now, come now, come now, stupid, aren't you going to say anything?'

'Devil take it,' replied Panurge, 'I can see plainly enough that the plague's after us here, devil take it now, seeing that innocence here spells no security. I can see the devil sings his Mass here, devil take me if I don't. So I beg you to let me stand surety for everyone, devil take us, and allow us to go. That's all I can say, the devil take it!'

'Go!' exclaimed Clawpuss. 'Come now, no one has ever escaped from here without leaving some hair behind him, now, or his skin more often. Come now! Why now, that would look as if people didn't get fair treatment in this court. Come now, you're a poor devil now. But you'll be a much poorer devil now, if you don't solve the riddle I've put to you, now. Come now, what does it mean now? Come now, tell me.'

'The devil take you,' answered Panurge, 'it means a black weevil born out of a white bean, devil take you, through a hole that it's gnawed, devil take you. This weevil sometimes flies and sometimes crawls on the earth, devil take you! Therefore it was supposed by Pythagoras, the first Friend of Wisdom – or, in Greek, *philosopher* – devil take you, to have received a human soul from somewhere by metempsychosis, the devil take you! Now if you here were human, devil take you, after a shameful death your souls would, in his opinion, enter into the bodies of weevils, devil take you. For in this life you gnaw and consume everything. So in the next

> Like vipers you would gnaw
> Your mothers' bodies through,
> The devil take you!

'Od's my life,' exclaimed Friar John, 'but I heartily wish my arse-hole could be turned into a bean, and be gnawed all round by these weevils.'

After this remark, Panurge threw into the middle of the court a great purse full of Sun-crowns; and at the jingling sound all the Furrycats began to exercise their claws like fiddlers playing a preliminary trill. Then they all cried out loudly: 'Here are the spices. It has been a good, appetizing, well-spiced case. These are excellent people.'

'Come now, that's gold, come now,' said Panurge. 'That's Sun-crowns I say.'

'The court understands that,' said Clawpuss. 'Gold, come now, gold! That's well-come. Come, my children, that's well-come. Come, my children, that's well-come. Now pass *out* and go your ways. But come now, we're not such devils, we're not so black, come now, are we? Come now!'

When we had passed through the wicket we were escorted right down to the harbour by certain mountain clawyers who informed us before we went aboard that we could not go away without first paying the tribute due to Clawpuss's lady and to all the Furrykittens. Otherwise they were empowered to take us back to the wicket.

'A turd!' cried Friar John; 'we'll have to go aside here and scrape the bottoms of our purses, if we're going to satisfy everybody.'

'And don't forget a tip for us poor devils,' said the clawyers, 'to buy wine with, you know.'

'The poor devils,' replied Friar John. 'Their wine's never forgotten. We're reminded of it at all times and seasons.'

CHAPTER 14: *How the Furrycats live on Bribery*

FRIAR JOHN had not finished speaking when he saw seventy-eight galleys and frigates entering the harbour. So he suddenly ran off for news, and to see at the same time what cargo the vessels were bringing in. They were all loaded, as he saw, with venison, hares, capons, pigeons, pigs, kids, chickens, ducks, teal, goslings, and other sorts of game, among which he also discovered some rolls of velvet, satin, and damask. Upon this he asked the travellers where they were carrying

these fine morsels to, and for whom they were intended. They answered that they were for Clawpuss and for the Furrycats, male and
female.

'What do you call these dainties here?' asked Friar John.

'Bribery,' replied the travellers.

'Those who live on corruption,' said Friar John, 'shall perish in
the seed. By God, that's true. Their fathers devoured the good
gentlemen who trained themselves on hawking and hunting, as
their station demanded, so as to inure themselves to the hardships of
war, when war came. For hunting is war in miniature, and Xenophon
was telling the truth when he wrote that all good war leaders come
out of the hunting-field, as the Greek knights did from the Trojan
horse. I'm no scholar. But I've been told that, and I believe it. The
souls of hunters, according to Clawpuss's opinion, enter after their
death into boars, stags, roebucks, herons, partridges, and other such
creatures as they have always loved and pursued during their lives. So,
after destroying and devouring their castles, estates, domains, possessions, rents, and revenue, these Furrycats still seek to have their blood
and souls in the other life. What an honest beggar that was who
warned us of this by telling us of the manger up above the rack!'

'But,' said Panurge to the travellers, 'the great King has had it
proclaimed far and wide that no one, under pain of the halter, may
take stags or does, boars or roebucks.'

'That is true,' replied one of them for the rest. 'But the great
King is so good and kind, and these Furrycats are so furiously hungry
for human blood, that we are not so much afraid of offending the
great King as we are frightened for our lives if we don't keep these
Furrycats supplied with their bribes, especially since to-morrow Clawpuss is marrying one of his Furrykittens to a huge Tybert, a very well-
furred cat. In time past they used to be called Chewgrasses. But, alas,
they chew grass no more. So now we call them Chewhares, Chew-
partridges, Chewquails, Chewpheasants, Chewpullets, Chewkids,
Chewrabbits, or Chewpigs, for they take no other food.'

'A turd, a turd!' cried Friar John, 'next year they'll be calling them
Chewdungs, Chewshits, and Chewdroppings. Now, will you trust
me?'

'Yes, certainly,' cried the company.

'Then let's do two things,' said he. 'First, let's seize all this game that you see here. For I'm quite tired of salt meats. They heat my digestive tracts. Of course we must pay them well for it. Then, secondly, let's go back to the wicket, and plunder all these devils of Furrycats.'

'I'm certainly not going back,' said Panurge, 'I'm a little bit timid by nature.'

CHAPTER 15: *Friar John of the Hashes decides to plunder the Furrycats*

'By the cloth I wear,' said Friar John, 'what sort of voyage is this that we're making? It's a stinker's voyage. For we do nothing but poop and fart and squitter and mope, and idle around. By the holy cape, that's not my nature. If I don't perform some heroic deed every day, I can't sleep at night. Did you bring me as your companion on this voyage just to sing the Mass and take your confessions? Od's feast, the first one who comes to me to shrive him shall get a fine penance. I'll make him jump into the deep sea, for the useless coward he is, to earn a deduction from the pains of Purgatory. He shall go in head first, I say. What brought Hercules his everlasting renown? Isn't he famous because he wandered through the world, freeing peoples from tyrannies, errors, dangers, and distresses? He put all the brigands to death, and all the monsters, all the poisonous serpents and harmful creatures. Why don't we follow his example, and do what he did in all the countries we pass through? He destroyed the Stymphalides, the Lernaean Hydra, Cacus, Anthaeus, and the Centaurs. I'm no scholar, but scholars say so. Now let's follow his example and root out these Furrycats – they're thorough-paced devils – and free this country from tyranny. As I renounce Mahoun, if I were as mighty and strong as he was I shouldn't ask for your help or advice. Come now, shall we go? We shall slay them easily enough, I promise you, and they'll take it lying down. I've no doubt of that, seeing that they've borne more painful abuse from us so far than ten sows could swill as hogwash. Let's go.'

'They don't object to abuse or worry about shame,' said I, 'so long as they have crowns in their pouches, even shit-smeared crowns; and very likely we could destroy them like Hercules, if only we had someone like Eurystheus to command us. That's all we need at present, unless I were to wish that Jupiter could walk among them for two short hours in the shape in which he once visited Semele, the good Bacchus's mother.'

'God was very merciful to us in getting us out of their clutches,' said Panurge. 'For my part, I'm not going back. I still feel disturbed and shaken from the fright I got. I was very much upset, and for three reasons: firstly, because I was upset; secondly, because I was upset, and thirdly, because I was still upset. Brother John, listen with your right ear to my left ballock. Any time you choose to go down to all the devils, and appear before the tribunal of Minos, Aeacus, Rhadamanthus, and Dis, I'm ready to bear you indissoluble company, to pass the Acheron, Styx, and Cocytus with you, to drink a full bumper of Lethe water, and to pay Charon the fare of his bark for us both. But if you want to return to the wicket and don't want to do so alone, find yourself some other company than mine. I won't go back, and on that I stand as firm as a wall of brass. Unless I'm led there by force and violence I won't go near it, for as long as I live, any more than Calpe will cross the straits to Abyla. Did Ulysses go back to the Cyclops' cave to look for his sword? Gracious me, no! Besides, I left nothing behind at the wicket, and I won't go back.'

'Oh,' exclaimed Friar John, 'a firm heart and a good companion, but with palsied hands! But let's pay our shot in speech like Scot, the subtle doctor. Now why was it that you flung that purse full of crowns to them? What moved you to do so? Have we got a superfluity of crowns? Wouldn't it have been enough to throw them a few clipped testons?'

'It was because Clawpuss opened his velvet purse at every point of his address,' answered Panurge, 'and kept on exclaiming: "Come now, come!" I reckoned that we could get free and make a clean escape if we were to throw some gold in. Gold here and gold there, in all the devils' names! For a velvet purse isn't a receptacle for testons and small money; it's a receptacle for Sun-crowns, you see, Brother John, my dear ballocky friend. When you've been as near the fire as I have and been roasted as I have, you'll talk a different language. But by their injunction, we ought now to depart.'

The ragamuffins were still waiting at the harbour, in expectation of some small change; and when they saw us about to raise our sail, they called out to Friar John, telling him that he must proceed no farther without paying for the court-beadles' wine, according to the spicing assessment.

'By the feast of St Shakehole,' cried Friar John, 'are you still there, you devilish clawyers? Haven't I been bothered enough without your pestering me as well? By God, you shall have your wine, and no mistake. I promise it to you here and now.'

Then he unsheathed his cutlass and jumped ashore, resolved to slay them unmercifully. But they galloped off with all speed, and we saw them no more.

However, we were not out of our troubles, all the same. For, while we were appearing before Clawpuss, with Pantagruel's permission some of our sailors had retired to an inn near the harbour, to feast themselves and take a little refreshment. I do not know whether they had paid their reckoning or not. But, seeing Friar John ashore, an old ale-wife made a great complaint to him in the presence of a *coin-stable*, the son-in-law of one of the Furrycats, with two Bum-bailiffs as witnesses. But Friar John lost patience with their talk and their charges, and turned on them: 'My good scoundrels,' he said, 'are you trying deliberately to suggest that our sailors are not honest men? I maintain the contrary, and I'll prove it to you before the Justice, before Master Cutlass here in fact.'

With these words he flourished his cutlass, and the clods made off as fast as they could go, leaving only the old hag, who protested that they had paid her nothing for the bed on which they had rested after dinner, and demanded five French pennies for the said bed.

'Really,' answered Friar John, 'that's cheap. They are an ungrateful pack of scoundrels, and they won't always find such bargains. I'll pay for it willingly, but I should like to see it first.'

So the old woman led him to the lodging and showed him the bed. Then, after praising all its qualities, she declared that she was not overcharging when she asked five pence for it.

Friar John handed her five French pennies. Then with his cutlass he ripped up the pillow and the bolster and scattered the feathers out of the window. The old woman immediately ran down the stairs, shouting 'Help!' and 'Murder!' and got busy picking up the feathers. But Friar John was not satisfied with this. He carried off the quilt and mattress and two sheets to our ship – quite unobserved, for the air was darkened with feathers – and gave them to the sailors. A little later, he told Pantagruel that beds were much cheaper in that country than around Chinon, although there we had the famous Pontille geese. For the old woman had only demanded five pence for the bed, which would be worth quite a dozen francs at Chinon.

As soon as Friar John and the rest of the company were aboard, Pantagruel set sail. But such a violent sirocco blew up that they were driven off their track, and seemed to be drifting back towards the land of the Furrycats. They were driven into a huge gulf, and a terrible high sea was running, and a ship's boy, who was at the top of the mast, called out that he could once more see the dreadful abode of Clawpuss.

Then Panurge, in the grip of fear, cried out: 'Captain, my friend, never mind the wind and the waves, but turn the ship's head about! O my dear friend, don't let's go back to that wretched country where I left my purse.'

A little later the wind carried them close to an island, where we dared not land at first, but lay about a mile off shore, near some great rocks.

CHAPTER 16: *How Pantagruel came to the Island of the Ignoramuses, who have long Fingers and crooked Hands; and of the terrible Adventures and Monsters he encountered there*

As soon as the anchor was dropped and the ship made fast, we lowered the pinnace. Then, after offering up prayers and thanks to the Lord for having saved and preserved him from so great and acute a danger, Pantagruel with all his company climbed aboard it, to go ashore. This was a simple matter. For the sea was calm and the wind had dropped. So they soon came to the rocky coast and, once on land, Epistemon, whilst admiring the situation of the place and the strange shapes of the rocks, spied a group of the inhabitants. The first man he spoke to was dressed in a short, bright, chestnut-coloured coat, with a demi-worsted doublet with satin half-sleeves, which were of chamois leather above the elbow. He wore a cockaded cap, and seemed a presentable sort of man, and, as we afterwards learnt, he was called Fleecem. Epistemon asked him the names of these strange rocks and valleys, and Fleecem told him that the country of the rocks was a colony of Attorney-land's, called the Land of Charges, and that beyond the rocks, after passing a little ford, we should find the Isle of Ignoramuses.

'By the power of the Decretals,' exclaimed Friar John. 'And what do you good people live on here? Should we be able to drink out of your glasses? For the only utensils I can see about you are parchments, inkhorns, and pens.'

'That's all we live on,' answered Fleecem, 'and everyone who has business on this island has to pass through my hands.'

'Why, are you barbers, then?' asked Panurge, 'and do they have to have their crowns shaved?'

'If you mean the crowns in their purses, yes,' replied Fleecem.

'You won't get a halfpenny or a farthing out of me, by God,' cried Panurge. 'But bring us to these Ignoramuses, I beg of you, dear sir. For we come from the Land of the Learned, and I didn't gain much there.'

Chatting on the way, they came to Ignoramus Island, for the ford was soon crossed, and Pantagruel was very much struck by the nature of the dwellings inhabited by the people of this island. They live in a great wine-press, which is approached by nearly fifty steps; and before entering the main press – for here there are small ones, great ones, secret ones, middle-sized ones, and all sorts – you pass through a great colonnade, where you see, in a kind of landscape, the ruins of nearly the whole world, so many gallows for great robbers, so many gibbets and racks that it quite frightens you. When Fleecem saw that Pantagruel was interested in all this, he said: 'Sir, let us pass on. This is nothing.'

'What!' exclaimed Friar John. 'Is this nothing? By the soul of my codpiece – which is getting warm – Panurge and I are shivering from sheer hunger. I had rather drink than see these ruins.'

'Come,' said Fleecem, and led us into a little press which was hidden away behind, and was called in the language of the island, Pithies or the *Tavern Without*.

Do not ask whether Master John and Panurge stood themselves treats here. For here were Milan sausages, turkeys, capons, and bustards, malmsey-wine, and all kinds of good fare, ready and well served. When an undersized butler saw Friar John amorously ogling a bottle, close to the sideboard but separated from the rest of the bottle army, he said to Pantagruel: 'Sir, one of your people, I see, is making love to that bottle. Don't let him touch it, sir, please. It is reserved for their Lordships.'

'What,' said Panurge, 'so there are Lordships here, are there? But it's harvest time with you, I see.'

Then Fleecem led us up a little hidden stair into a room from which he showed us their Lordships, who were in the great press, into which, he told us, it was not lawful for anyone to enter without leave. But we were able to see them through a little squint window, without their seeing us.

From there we saw twenty or twenty-five great gallows-birds in a huge press, sitting round a great table covered with a green cloth and staring at one another. Their hands are as long as crane's legs, and their nails at least two foot to the tip. For they are forbidden ever to bite them, and they grow as crooked as bills or boathooks. Just at that moment a great bunch of grapes was brought in, of the kind that are gathered in that country from the vine called *The Extraordinary*, the fruit of which often hangs in a public square. No sooner had it arrived than they put it under the press, and there was not a single grape of it from which they did not squeeze golden oil. In fact when the wretched bunch was carried away it was drained so dry that there was not a single drop of juice or liquor in it. Fleecem told us that they do not often get these big bunches, but that they always have something in the press.

'Tell me, my friend,' said Panurge, 'do they get grapes of many different growths?'

'Yes,' said Fleecem. 'Do you see that small one there which they are just going to put back in the press? That comes from the *Royal Tithes* stock. They squeezed it the other day to the straining-point. But the oil smelt of the priest's cupboard, and their Lordships didn't find much relish in it.'

'Why are they putting it back in the press, then?' asked Pantagruel.

'To see if there is any juice still left in the skins,' replied Fleecem.

'God save me!' exclaimed Friar John. 'D'you call these people ignorant? Why, the devils would draw oil out of a wall.'

'Oh, they do,' answered Fleecem. 'They often put castles and parks and forests into the press, and extract potable gold from them.'

'You mean *portable* surely,' said Epistemon.

'I said *potable*,' answered Fleecem, 'for they drink many a bottle of it here that they would not drink otherwise; and they draw it from so many vines that no one knows the number. Just come here, and look into the yard. There are more than a thousand bunches only waiting for their squeezing time. There are some from public stocks and some from private; some from fortifications, from loans, gifts, windfalls, crown domains, privy-purse, appointments, offerings, and the Royal Household.'

'And what's that big one over there with all those little ones round it?'

'That is the *Treasury*, which is the best stock in the whole country. When they squeeze bunches from that stock every one of their Lordships reeks of it for six months afterwards.'

When their Lordships had risen, Pantagruel asked Fleecem to take us into the great press; which he gladly did. Once we were inside, Epistemon, who understood all languages, began to explain to Pantagruel the inscriptions on the press – which was large and handsome and made, as Fleecem told us, from the wood of the true Cross – for on each part was written the name of that part in the language of the country. The screw of the press was called *receipts*; the bowl, *expenditure*; the vice, *the state*; the beam, *moneys due and not received*; the supports, *lapsed tenures*; the main timbers, *annulments*; the side-timbers, *recoveries*; the vats, *surplusage*; the double-handled baskets, *the Rolls*; the treading-trough, *discharge*; the vintage-baskets, *declarations of validity*; the panniers, *authenticated decrees*; the buckets, *potentials*; and the funnel, the *quietus*, or quittance.

'By the Queen of the Chitterlings,' cried Panurge, 'all the hieroglyphics of Egypt could not touch this jargon. Why, these devilish words hold together no better than goats' droppings! But what's the reason, my dear friend, my dear old crony, for calling these people ignorant?'

'Because they're not learned in any way,' answered Fleecem, 'and they don't have to be; and because here, by the ordinance, everything has to be managed by way of ignorance. No reasons must be given except: "Their Lordships say so. It's their Lordships' desire. It's their Lordships' order."'

'By God Almighty,' exclaimed Pantagruel, 'since they make so much from the grape, they must swear vintage oaths.'

'Can you doubt it?' asked Fleecem. 'Not a month goes by that they don't swear them; and this is not like your country, where an oath is only worth something to you once a year.'

On our way out, as he led us past innumerable small presses, we noticed another little green table, around which were sitting four or five of these Ignoramuses, as angry and dirty as an ass with a cracker under its tail. They were squeezing one lot of grape-skins after another through a small press which they worked there, and they were called in the language of the country, Auditors.

'These are the most repulsive-looking villains that I have seen yet,' said Friar John.

From the large press, we went through an infinite number of little presses, all besieged by vintagers, who stripped off the berries with instruments that they call *bills of charges*. Finally we arrived at a low hall, where we saw a great cur with a pair of dog's heads, a wolf's belly, and claws like the devil of Lamballe. He was fed on milk of fines, and he owed this delicate fare to a special order of their Lordships. For to every single one of them he was worth the rent of a good farm. In their Ignoramus tongue they called him *Double*. His mother, who was near him, had a coat like her whelp's and was of the same shape. But she had four heads, two male and two female, and she was called *Fourfold*. She was the most savage creature in those parts, and more dangerous than any except her grandmother, whom we saw shut up in a dungeon, and her they called *Refusal-of-Fees*.

Friar John, who always had twenty-five yards of empty guts ready to swallow up a fricassee of lawyers, began to get testy, and begged Pantagruel to think about dinner and bring Fleecem along. So we departed and, as we did so, by the back door, we saw a man chained up. He was half an Ignoramus and half a scholar, a sort of androgynous devil, and was covered with spectacles, like a tortoise in his shell. He only lived on one food, which they called in their dialect *Scrutiny of Accounts*. When he saw the fellow, Pantagruel asked Fleecem of what breed this worshipful master was, and what was his name. Fleecem told us that he had been chained up there from the earliest times, much to the regret of their Lordships, who kept him almost starving. His name was *Review*.

'By the blessed ballocks of the Pope,' said Friar John, 'there's a fine dandy for you. I don't wonder that their Lordships the Ignoramuses find this popeling a very valuable fellow. If you look at him closely, friend Panurge, I'm damned if I don't think he looks very like Clawpuss. These fellows may be Ignoramuses, but to my mind they're as knowing as any of the others. As for me, I'd send him back where he came from, soundly whipped with an eelskin.'

'By my oriental spectacles, Brother John,' said Panurge, 'you're right. To judge by this false villain *Review*'s mug, my friend, he's more ignorant and wickeder than any of these poor Ignoramuses here. They at least glean their grapes as harmlessly as they can, without long lawsuits. In fact, in three short words, they strip the close of its grapes without all these interlocutories and decrotteries; and that thoroughly annoys the Furrycats.'

CHAPTER 17: *How we passed out*

WE at once started on our way *Out*, and gave Pantagruel an account of our adventures,[1] which aroused his very great pity. In fact he composed an elegy or two on the subject, just for his own amusement.

When we arrived we took some refreshment and drew fresh water. We also took aboard some wood for our stores. To judge by the islanders' looks, they seemed good fellows and fine trenchermen. They were all bloated out and bursting with fat, and we noticed – a thing we had seen in no other country that they slashed their skins to let their fat *out*, in just the same way as the young dandies in my country pink the tops of their breeches to let the taffeta push through. They said that they did this out of no glory or ostentation, but because it was their only way of staying in their skins. Moreover they became bigger more quickly by doing so, like young trees whose bark the gardeners have slit to hasten their growth.

Near the harbour was a tavern, which looked fine and stately from the outside; and seeing a great number of the bloated-out of all ages, sexes, and conditions hurrying there, we imagined that some great feast or banquet was being held inside. We were told that they had been invited to the host's bursting, and that, being his close kindred and relations, they were making all haste. We did not understand this

1. Here the story is broken. Pantagruel had refused to visit the Furrycats, but he had inspected the wine-presses. The manuscript was clearly in a muddled state when it reached the printers. Chapter 16 is, perhaps, an interpolation.

jargon, but supposed that in this country a feast was called a bursting, in the same way as, over here, we speak of an affiancing, a wedding, a churching, a shearing, or a harvesting. We learnt that the host had been a sportive fellow in his time, a great lover of good foods, a mighty man for onion soups, a great watcher of the refectory clock, and an eternal diner, like the landlord at Rouillac. Having for the last ten years blown *out* an abundance of fat, we were told, he had now come to his bursting-time. So, according to the custom of the country, he was ending his days with a burst, since his peritoneum and his skin had been slashed for so many years that they could no longer contain his guts. In fact they could not prevent their pouring out like wine from a burst barrel.

'But tell me, my good people,' said Panurge, 'couldn't you neatly bind up his belly with good stout girths, or strong hoops of sorb-apple wood, or of iron, if need be? If he were bound up like that he wouldn't throw out his cargo so easily, or burst so soon.'

Panurge had no sooner finished speaking than we heard a loud, piercing report in the air, as if some mighty oak were splitting in two. Thereupon the neighbours said that the bursting was over, and that this report had been his death-fart.

That reminded me of the Abbot of Chastelliers, who never deigned to roger his chambermaids except in full canonicals. In his old age he was pestered by his relations and friends to resign his Abbey. But he swore and protested that he, the Reverend Father, would not take off his clothes until he went to bed, and that the last fart he would blow would be an Abbot's fart.

CHAPTER 18: *How our Ship was stranded, and how we were aided by some Travellers who carried the Quintessence*

HAVING weighed our anchors and cables, we set sail before a gentle breeze, but when we had gone about twenty-two miles we struck a furious whirlwind, together with shifting squalls. With our foresails and our topsails spread, we were driven about, temporizing only in order not to override our captain, who assured us that these were only gentle breezes, in pleasant rivalry one with another, and that the clear air and mild current promised us neither much good nor much harm.

We ought, therefore, said he, to observe the rule of the philosopher who advised us to *bear and forbear*; that is to say to temporize. This whirlwind lasted so long, however, that at our firm entreaty the captain attempted to push on and return to our previous course. So, hoisting the mizzen and setting the helm true to the compass, he broke away from the whirlwind, with the help of a stiff gale which arose. But our misfortune was as great as if, after avoiding Charybdis, we had fallen into Scylla. For two miles further on our ship ran aground on a sandbank, like those in St Matthew's Roads.

All our company were mightily upset, as the wind whistled through our foresails. But Friar John never gave way to melancholy, and consoled one after another of us with sweet words, pointing out that we should soon have help from Heaven, and that he had seen Castor gleaming above the main-yard arm.

'Would to God,' said Panurge, 'that I were ashore at this moment – that's all – and that each of you who are so fond of sea water had two hundred thousand crowns. I would put a calf up to fatten for you, and have a hundred faggots dried for you against your return. I'd even agree never to marry if only you could put me on land and give me a horse to ride home on; I'd do without a groom. I'm never so well treated as when I'm without a groom. Plautus was telling no lies when he said that the number of our afflictions, troubles, and worries corresponds to the number of our servants, even if they are tongueless. The tongue is the most wicked and dangerous part of a servant, and on its account racking, torturing, and questioning of servants were invented. There was no other reason, although the law-concocters of to-day, outside this realm, have drawn a logical, that is to say unreasonable, conclusion from it.'

At this moment there sailed straight towards us a ship laden with drums, in which I recognized some passengers of good family, among them Henry Cotiral, an old comrade, who wore a great ass's pizzle on his belt, where women wear their beads. In his left hand he held some blotchy fellow's great, greasy, dirty old bonnet, and in his right a huge stump of a cabbage. The very moment he recognized me he shouted to me most joyfully: 'Haven't I got it? Look at this' – he pointed to the ass's pizzle – 'it's the real *algamana*. This doctor's bonnet is our unique elixir, and this' – pointing to the cabbage – 'is *lunaria major*.'

'But,' I asked, 'where have you come from? Where are you going? What are you carrying? Have you smelt the sea?'

'From the quintessence,' he answered. 'To Touraine. Alchemy. To the very bottom.'

'And what people have you there, with you on deck?' I asked.

'Singers,' he replied, 'musicians, poets, astrologers, rhymers, diviners, alchemists, and clockmakers. They all swear by the quintessence. They all have fine long letters-patent from her.'

He had not finished speaking when Panurge burst in, full of furious indignation: 'You who can make anything from fine weather to small children, why don't you take our ship's head and tow us off, straight away, into the current?'

'I was just going to,' said Henry Cotiral. 'This very hour, this very minute, in the twinkling of an eye you shall be afloat.'

With that he had 7,532,810 large drums knocked through on one side, and he set that side towards the prow. Then they lashed the cables fast at every point, took our ship's head on to their stern, and made it fast to their bitts. So at the very first pull they towed us off the sands with the greatest of ease and with some pleasure to us. For the rolling of the drums, together with the soft pattering of the sand and the crew's shanties, made a music for us that was almost as delightful as that of the stars in their courses, which Plato said he heard on some nights in his sleep.

Hating to be thought ungrateful for this kind act, we gave them a share of our chitterlings and filled their drums with sausages. We were in the act of slinging seventy-two skins of wine on to their deck when two great spouting whales made a furious attack on their ship, splashing more water into it than there is in the whole river Vienne from Chinon to Saumur. It filled all their drums, soaked all their yardarms and soused them from head to foot.

Panurge was so overjoyed by this sight that his spleen shook with laughter and he had a colic for more than two hours afterwards.

'I was meaning to give them their wine,' he said, 'but now they've had water instead, and serve them right. They never care for fresh water, and only use it for washing their hands. But this good water will serve them for borax, being salted with nitre and sal-ammoniac in Geber's kitchen.'

It was impossible for us to hold any further conversation with them, since the whirlwind returned and robbed us of power over the helm. The captain begged our permission to let the ship run adrift. He told us to worry about nothing but making good cheer, since temporarily we should have to skirt the whirlwind and yield to the current if we wanted to come safely to the Kingdom of the Quintessence.

CHAPTER 19: *We arrive at the Kingdom of the Quintessence called Entelechy*

HAVING prudently skirted the whirlwind for the space of half a day, we found the air clearer than usual on the third day following, and landed in perfect safety at the port of Mataeotechny – the Home of Useless Knowledge – which is not far from the palace of the Quint-essence. As we landed, we found ourselves confronted by a great num-ber of archers and men-at-arms, who were guarding the arsenal, and on our immediate arrival they somewhat terrified us. For they made us all put down our weapons, and questioned us rudely.

'What country have you men come from?' they asked.

'We are from Touraine, cousins,' replied Panurge. 'We have come from France. We want to pay our respects to the Lady Quintessence, and to visit this most famous kingdom of Entelechy.'

'What did you say?' they asked. 'Was it Entelechy, which means perfection, of course, or Endelechy, which is mere duration in time?'

'We are simple folk and not learned, dear cousins,' replied Panurge. 'You must excuse our rustic speech. For in all other respects we are loyal and true hearted.'

'We had no idle reasons for questioning you about this distinction,' said they. 'A great number of men from your country of Touraine have passed this way before you, who seemed decent enough clod-hoppers and spoke correctly. But some conceited sorts of fellows have come to us from other countries, some of them as stubborn as Scots-men; and they have tried obstinately to argue the point with us on arrival. They got a good dressing-down, I can tell you, despite their rhubarbative faces. Have you got so much time to spare in your world that you don't know any other way of using it except in this sort of talk and argument and impudent writing about our queen? Why did Cicero have to leave his *Republic* to meddle in the matter? And what about Diogenes Laertius and Theodore Gaza and Argyropylos and Bessarion and Politian and Budaeus and Lascaris and all your devilish wise fools? Weren't there quite enough of them, without their numbers being lately increased by Scaliger, Bigot, Chambrier, François Fleury, and goodness knows how many other poxy young wretches? May a nasty quinsy seize them by the throat, and by the epiglottis as well! We'll ...'

'Devilish wise fools,' muttered Panurge, 'well, I'll be damned if he isn't flattering them.'

'But since you haven't come here to back them in their folly,' he resumed, 'and since you have no commission to do that, we'll say no more about the matter. Aristotle, that first of men and pattern of all philosophers, was our Lady Queen's godfather, and he very rightly and properly called her Entelechy. Entelechy is her real name, and anyone who calls her by any other – can go and shit himself! Anyone who calls her by any other name errs by the whole breadth of Heaven. You are most welcome.'

Then they embraced us, which delighted us all. But Panurge whispered in my ear: 'Weren't you a bit frightened, friend, of that attack?'

'A little,' I replied.

'I was more shaken,' he confessed, 'than Ephraim's soldiers were of old when the Gileadites slew them and drowned them for saying Sibboleth instead of Shibboleth. Between you and me, there wasn't a man in all the Beauce who wouldn't have been welcome to plug my arse-hole with a cartload of hay.'

After this their captain led us, in silence and most ceremoniously, to the Queen's palace. Pantagruel tried to engage him in conversation, and since the captain could not reach up to his height he asked for a ladder or a very tall pair of stilts.

'Be patient,' said the captain. 'We should have been as tall as you if our queen had wished it. Indeed when it pleases her, we shall be.'

In the first galleries we met a great crowd of sick people, grouped according to their different maladies. The lepers were apart, those suffering from poison in one place, those with plague in another, those with pox in front, and so on for all the rest.

CHAPTER 20: *How the Quintessence cured the Sick by Music*

IN the second gallery the captain showed us the Queen. She looked young – though she was eighteen hundred years old at least – and was fair, delicately built, and gorgeously dressed, as she stood surrounded by her ladies and gentlemen.

'This is not the moment to speak to her,' said the captain. 'But watch attentively what she does in the meantime. You have some kings in your kingdoms who miraculously cure certain maladies, such as scrofula, erysipelas, and quartan agues, by the mere laying-on of their hands. But our queen heals men of every complaint without touching them, merely by playing them a tune chosen according to the nature of their disease.'

He then showed us the organ with whose music she made her wonderful cures. It was a strange instrument, for its pipes were made of cassia sticks, its sounding board of guiacum, its stops of rhubarb, its pedals of turbith, and its keyboard of scammony. Whilst we were examining the wonderful and novel construction of this instrument, the lepers were brought in by the queen's abstractors, calcinators, masticators, tasters, tabachins, chachanins, neemanins, rabrebans, nereins, rozuins, nedibins, segamions, perazons, chesinins, sarins, sotrins, aboths, cnilins, archasdarpenins, mebins, giborins, and others of her officers. Then she played them a tune – I don't know what – and they were at once perfectly cured. Next those who had been poisoned were introduced, and she no sooner played them a tune than they were on their feet. After that the blind, the deaf, the dumb, and the apoplectic followed. This, not unnaturally, amazed us, and we dropped to the ground, prostrating ourselves like men in an ecstasy, rapt in excessive wonder and admiration at the virtues we had seen emanating from that lady. It was beyond our power to utter a single word; and there we remained on the earth till, by touching Pantagruel with a beautiful bunch of white roses, which she carried in her hand, she recalled us to our senses and made us stand up. Then she addressed us in such silken words as Parysatis desired should be used by whoever should speak to her son Cyrus – or at least in words of crimson taffeta:

'The probity scintillating on the surfaces of your persons gives me perfect assurance of the virtues latent in the centre of your minds. When I view the mellifluous suavity of your discrete reverences, I am easily persuaded that your hearts are infected with no vice, and suffer no privation of liberal and exalted knowledge, in fact that they abound in much rare and strange learning, which is at present more freely sought than found in the commonplaces of the vulgar and imperite. It is for that reason that I, who in the past have mastered all private affections, cannot now prevent myself from saying to you that you are heartily, most heartily, more than most heartily, welcome.'

'I'm no scholar,' Panurge whispered to me, 'answer her if you will.'

I did not answer her, nevertheless, nor did Pantagruel; and we remained silent.

'By this taciturnity of yours,' continued the Queen, 'I recognize, not only that you come from the school of Pythagoras, from which by successive propagation my most ancient progenitors took root, but that you have also, many a moon ago, bitten your nails, and scratched your heads with one finger in Egypt, that famous factory of high philosophy. In the school of Pythagoras taciturnity was the sign of knowledge, and silence was recognized among the Egyptians as a manner of divine worship. For in silence the priests of Hierapolis sacrificed to their great god, without the least noise or the utterance of a word. My purpose is to treat you with no shortage of gratitude, but by a living formality, even though matter should abstract itself from me, to excentricate my thoughts upon you.'

Having concluded her speech, she addressed herself to her officers, saying to them briefly: 'Tabachins, to Panacea.'

At this signal the tabachins told us that the queen would consider us excused if we did not dine with her. For she took nothing for dinner, except a few categories, shecabots, eminins, dimions, abstractions, harborins, chelimins, second intentions, caradoths, antitheses, metempsychoses, and transcendent prolepsies.

Then he led us into a little closet, lined throughout with alarm-bells, and there we were treated, as only God could describe. It is said that Jupiter writes down everything that happens in the world on the Diphtera, which is the skin of the goat which suckled him in Crete and which he used as a shield in his battle with the Titans, whence it derived its name of Aegiochos. But on my oath, my boozy friends, no one could write down on eighteen goatskins a list of the good meats that were served to us, nor of the sweets and good cheer with which we were regaled; no not even if the letters were as small as those of the Iliad of Homer which Cicero claimed to have read; and they were so small that the whole book could be enclosed in a walnut shell. For my part, had I a hundred tongues, a hundred mouths, a voice of iron, and with them the mellifluous fecundity of a Plato, I could not give you a full account in four books of the third part of one moment of it.

Pantagruel told me that when the queen said to her tabachins: 'To Panacea', it was his belief that she was giving them the word that among them symbolized the highest good cheer, just as Lucullus used to say: 'In Apollo', when he wanted to give his friends a singular treat, even though they had taken him by surprise, as Cicero and Hortensius sometimes did.

CHAPTER 21: *How the Queen passed her time after dinner*

WHEN dinner was over, we were led into the queen's hall by a chachanin, and saw her customary way of passing her time after dinner in the company of the ladies and princes of her court. She strained it, sifted it, sieved it, and finally passed it through a fine large strainer of blue-and-white silk. Then we watched them revive some ancient practices and sport together at the Cordax, the Emmelia, the Siccinis, the Iambic, the Persian, the Phrygian, the Victory, the Thracian, the Calabrism, the Molossian, the Cernophorum, the Mongas, the Thermanstry, the Floral, the Pyrrhic, and innumerable other dances.

After this, by her command, we were shown over the palace and saw things so novel, so strange, and so amazing that my mind is even now rapt away at the mere thought of them. Nothing, however, so overwhelmed us as the practices of the gentlemen of her household; the abstractors, perazons, nedibins, calcinators, and others. They told us freely, without the least dissimulation, that the queen, their mistress, did only the impossible and cured none but incurables. They, her officers, did and cured the rest. I saw one young parazon curing those with the pox – of the very finest, or as you might say of the Rouen variety – merely by touching them on the dentiform vertebra three times with a piece of a clog. Another I saw working perfect cures upon the dropsical, and upon those with tympanies, ascites, and

hyposarcides, by striking them on the belly nine times in quick succession with Tenes' axe.

One cured every fever on the spot, by merely hanging a fox's tail
on the left side of the patient's belt. Another calmed toothache by
simply washing the root of the affected tooth three times with elder-
berry vinegar and letting it dry in the sun for half an hour. Another
cured every kind of gout, hot or cold, natural or accidental, just by
making the sufferer close his mouth and open his eyes. I saw another
cure nine good gentlemen, in an hour or two, of St Francis' disease –
or friar's penury – by relieving them of all their debts. He put a rope
round each one's neck and hung a box of ten thousand Sun-crowns on
the end of it. Another, by a magnificent contrivance threw houses out
of windows, and thus purged them of pestilent air. Another cured all
the three sorts of consumptives – the atrophied, the wasting, and the
emaciated – without baths, without country milk, without pitch-
plasters, Galen's dressings, or any other medicine, merely by making
them monks for three months. And he swore to us that if they did not
get in the monastic way of life, they would do so by art or by nature.

I saw another in the company of a great number of women of two
sorts; of attractive tender fair-haired maidens who looked pretty,
kind, and willing to me, and of toothless, bleary, wrinkled old hags,
all sallow and cadaverous. He was, as Pantagruel was told, recasting the
old women, rejuvenating them, and restoring them to the state of the
maidens, whose beauty, figures, elegance, size, and symmetry of limbs
he had entirely renewed to the perfection they had possessed at fifteen
or sixteen. Only their heels he had been unable to bring back to their
former state, and these remained very much shorter than they had
been in their first youth: which was the reason why henceforth these
ladies would be apt to collapse suddenly on meeting with men, and,
in fact, would be very easy to throw on their backs.

The troop of old women were waiting most eagerly for the next
baking and were pulling at the men like mad, pleading that it was a
most intolerable situation when beauty falls short of desire. He had a
continuous practice in his art, and made a considerable profit by it.
Pantagruel asked him whether he could make old men young again
by a similar method of casting. But the answer was no, that their way
of regaining their youth was to live with recast women. For in that
way they caught the fifth or quintessential pox called the Slough, or

in Greek Ophiasis. Thus they change their hair and skin every year, and so youth is renewed for them, as for the Phoenix of Arabia. This is the true Fountain of Youth. There the man who was old and decrepit suddenly gets young, as Euripides said happened to Iolaus; as happened, by the kindness of Venus, to the fair Phaon, who was so loved by Sappho; to Tithonus, by Aurora's aid; to Aeson by Medea's art, and to Jason likewise – for, according to the evidence of Pherecydes and Simonides, he was restored and rejuvenated by her also – and as Aeschylus says happened to the good Bacchus's nurses and to their husbands as well.

CHAPTER 22: *Of the diverse Employments of the Officers of the Quintessence, and how the Lady engaged us in the capacity of Abstractors*

AFTER this I saw a great number of these officers, engaged in the rapid whitening of Ethiopians by merely rubbing their bellies with the bottom of a basket. Others were ploughing the sandy shore with three pairs of foxes in a yoke, and losing none of their seed. Others were washing the colour out of some tiles. Others were extracting water from pumice, or as you would say pumice-stones, giving it a long pounding in a marble mortar, and so changing its substance. Others were shearing asses, and getting long fleece wool. Others were gathering grapes from thorn-bushes, and figs from thistles. Others were milking he-goats, and catching the milk in a sieve; and much good they got by it. Others were washing asses' heads, and losing no soap. Others were chasing the wind with nets and catching monster crawfish.

I saw one young calcinator artificially extracting farts from a dead donkey, and selling them at fivepence a yard. Another was putrefying sechabots or abstractions. The most marvellous meat!

But Panurge fairly threw up his food when he saw an archasdarpenim fermenting a great tub of human urine in horse-dung, with plenty of Christian shit. Pooh, the filthy wretch! He told us, however, that he watered kings and great princes with this holy distillation, and thereby lengthened their lives by a good six or nine feet.

Others were snapping chitterlings across their knees. Others were flaying eels by the tail, and the said eels did not cry before they were hurt as those of Melun do. Others were making great things out of nothing, and making great things return to nothing. Others were cutting fire with a knife, and drawing up water in a net. Others were making lanterns out of bladders, and turning clouds into brass stoves. We saw a dozen others feasting under an arbour and drinking four sorts of fresh and delicious wine out of fine broad bowls, as hard as they could go and with toasts for one and all. We were told that they were raising fair weather in the local manner, and that Hercules of old raised fair weather with Atlas in just the same way.

Others were making a virtue of necessity, and it seemed a fine and proper job to me. Others were picking their teeth while fasting, a form of alchemy which helped very little to fill the close-stools. Others were carefully measuring flea-hops in a long garden. This practice, they assured me, was more than necessary for the government of kingdoms, the conduct of wars, and the administration of republics. They claimed that Socrates, the first man to have brought philosophy down from heaven to earth, and the first to have transformed it from an idle trifling into a useful and profitable pursuit – that Socrates had spent his time measuring the hops of fleas, as Aristophanes the quintessential testifies.

I saw two giborins away on the top of a tower, acting as sentinels; and we were told that they were guarding the moon from the wolves. I met four others in the corner of a garden, bitterly disputing and on the point of seizing one another by the hair. When I asked the cause of their differences I was told that four days ago they had begun to argue three high and metaphysical questions, by the solution of which they expected to gain mountains of gold. The first concerned the shadow of a jackass, the second the smoke of a lantern, and the third the hair of a she-goat, to know if it was wool. We were then told that it did not seem strange to them that two statements contradictory in mode, form, figure, and time, might both be true; a conclusion that the sophists of Paris would rather be debaptized than accept.

As we were curiously considering the amazing performances of these people, the Queen came up to us with her noble retinue; by which time the bright Hesperus was already shining. At her coming our senses were once more overwhelmed and our eyes dazzled. But she immediately saw our alarm, and said to us:

'It is not the supreme power of the effects, which they see to arise from natural causes by the ingenuity of skilled craftsmen, that causes human thoughts to stray through the abysses of wonderment. It is the novelty of the experience, striking upon their senses, which do not previse the facility of the operation unless a calm judgement is associated with diligent study. Keep your brains clear, therefore, and cast aside all fears, should you be seized by any, as you contemplate the acts performed by my officers. See, hear, and watch at your entire discretion, everything that my palace contains, at the same time gradually freeing yourselves from the shackles of ignorance. This conforms to my own wishes; and to assure you of my sincerity in so saying, also in consideration of the studious desires, of which you seem to me to have made signal demonstration in your hearts, I hereby appoint you to the state and office of abstractors royal. You shall be enrolled on your departure from this place by Geber, my first tabachin.'

We humbly thanked her in silence, and accepted her offer of the high rank she conferred upon us.

CHAPTER 23: *How the Queen's Supper was served, and of her way of eating it*

ON concluding her speech, the Queen turned to her gentlemen and said: 'The orifice of the stomach, the common ambassador for the alimentation of all the members, both inferior and superior, importunes us to restore to them, by the application of suitable nourishment, what they have lost through the continuous action of the natural heat on the radical humidity. Calcinators, chesinins, nedalins, and perazons, do not fail to have the tables promptly set up, and generously spread with every legitimate kind of restorative. You also, my noble tasters, in the company of my gentle masticators, my knowledge of your industry and the care and diligence with which you perfect it, forbids me to commend you to perform your duties thoroughly, and to maintain perpetual vigilance. It is enough to remind you to do what you habitually do.'

When she had spoken, she retired for a little with one group of her ladies, and we were told that she was taking a bath, which was as familiar a custom among the ancients as the washing of the hands before meals is with us nowadays. The tables were quickly set up, and covered with most precious cloths; and the order of service was such that the lady ate nothing except celestial ambrosia, and drank nothing but divine nectar. But the ladies and gentlemen of her household – and we with them – were served with dishes as rare, delicious, and costly as ever Apicius dreamed of.

At the end of the meal, in case hunger had not granted us a truce, a gallimaufry was brought in, of such breadth and size that the gold plane-tree which Pythius of Bithynia presented to King Darius would scarcely have covered it. This gallimaufry consisted of different kinds of soups, salads, fricassees, stews, goat-roasts, roasts, boiled meats, carbonados, great hunks of salt beef, grand old hams, deifical smoked meats, pies, tarts, a pile of Moorish cous cous, cheeses, junkets, jellies, and fruit of every sort. All this struck me as good and appetizing. However, I tasted none of it, since I was full to repletion. I must tell you, however, that I saw pasties in paste there – a very rare thing – and these pasties in paste were pasties in pots. And at the bottom of the pots I saw quantities of dice, cards, tarot packs, spillikins, chess, and backgammon boards, with cups full of Sun-crowns for those who wanted to play.

Finally, beneath all this, I noticed a number of mules in fine trappings, with velvet saddle-cloths, and hackneys similarly equipped, for the use of men and women; also litters just as beautiful, lined with velvet – how many I do not know – and some coaches made in Ferrara, for those who wanted to go out and take the air.

All this did not surprise me, but I found the Queen's way of eating rather strange. She chewed nothing, not because she had not good strong teeth, or because her food did not require mastication, but because this was her use and custom. Her masticators took the meats that her tasters had tasted and nobly chewed them for her. They had their gullets lined with crimson satin, with little gold welts and gold braiding, and their teeth were of fine white ivory. Then, when they had thoroughly chewed her food, they poured it into her stomach through a funnel of the finest gold. For similar reasons, we were told, she only sat on the close-stool by proxy.

CHAPTER 24: *How a festive Ball, in the form of a Tournament,
was held in the Quintessence's Presence*

WHEN supper was over, a ball in the form of a tournament – which
was not only worth seeing but eternally memorable – was held in the
lady's presence. Before this could begin, the floor of the hall was
covered with a large piece of pile tapestry, designed in the form of a
chessboard – that is to say in squares, alternately white and yellow,
each one foot across and all perfectly regular. Then thirty-two yellow
personages entered the room, sixteen of whom were dressed in cloth
of gold. These were eight young nymphs such as the ancients painted
in the company of Diana, one King, one Queen, two Wardens of the
Castles, two Knights, and two Archers. In similar order came sixteen
more, dressed in cloth of silver.

Their positions on the carpet were as follows: the Kings stood on the
back line, on the fourth square, so that the Golden King was on a
white square and the Silver King on a yellow square. The Queens
were beside their Kings, the Golden Queen on a yellow square, and
the Silver Queen on a white one, with Archers on either side as a
guard of honour for the Kings and Queens. Beside the Archers were
the two Knights, and beside the Knights two Castle-wardens. In the
rank immediately in front of them stood the eight nymphs, and between the two lines of nymphs were four rows of empty squares.

Each party had musicians, dressed in similar livery, one band in
orange damask and the other in white. There were eight on each side
with various fantastic instruments, all different, yet perfectly tuned to
one another and marvellously tuneful. These changed the tone, mood,
and time of their music as the progress of the ball required; and this
surprised me, when I considered the number and variety of the steps,
back-steps, hops, leaps, returns, flights, ambuscades, retreats, and surprises. It was even more transcendently incredible, as it seemed to me,
that the dancers should so quickly understand the sound that indicated
their advance or retreat. For no sooner had the music given the note
than they alighted on the intended square, even though their moves
were all different.

For the nymphs who stand in the first line, as if ready to start the
battle, march straight forward against their enemy from one square

to the next, except on their first move, when they are permitted to leap two squares forward. They alone can never retire. But if one of them happens to reach the line of the opposing king, she is crowned Queen to her own King, and henceforth moves and takes in the same manner as a Queen. Otherwise they never strike their enemies except obliquely, on the diagonal line and only in the forward direction. Neither they nor any other pieces are permitted to take any hostile piece if, by doing so, they leave their king exposed to capture.

The Kings move and take their enemies in all directions from where they stand, but only pass from a white square to a yellow one adjoining, or contrariwise; although on their first move, if their file is found empty of other officers except the Wardens, they can put one of these Wardens in their place and retire behind him.

The Queens move and take with greater freedom than any of the rest; that is to say into all positions and in every manner of direction so long as it is in a straight line. They can advance as far as they wish, providing that no intervening square is occupied by a piece of their own colour, and can move diagonally, so long as they keep to the colour of the square on which they stand.

The Archers can also go backwards or forwards as far as they like, but they never depart from the colour of their original square. The Knights advance and take by a gallows movement, leaping over a square, even though it may be occupied by one of their own or by an enemy, and coming down on the second square to right or left, of a different colour from the one they have left. This leap is very dangerous to the enemy, and has to be carefully watched for, since they never take except crookedly. The Wardens advance and take in a straight line, to left or right, forwards or backwards, as kings do. But they can advance as far as they will over empty squares, which Kings cannot.

The law common to both parties was that at the final conclusion of the battle they would shut up and besiege the opposing party's King, so that he could not escape in any direction. When he was shut up, and could neither escape nor receive assistance from his party, the game ended and the besieged King had lost. To save him from such a disaster, therefore, there is no member of his own side who will not offer his life for him; and they attack one another from all directions, following the notes of the music. When any of them took a prisoner of the opposite side, he would make him a bow, touch him lightly with

his right hand, take him off the floor, and assume his place. But if one
of the kings happened to be exposed, the opposite party was not permitted to take him. The one who discovered him or held him in
check was rigorously required to make him a deep bow and warn him
by saying: 'God save you, sire', so that he might be rescued or
covered by his servants, or so that he could change his position, if by
mischance he could not receive aid. On no account could he be taken
by the opposing party, but had to be saluted with the left knee on the
ground and the words, 'Good day'. There the tournament came to an
end.

CHAPTER 25: *The Battle between the Thirty-two at the Ball*

WHEN the two companies had thus assumed their places, the musicians began to sound in unison a martial strain, as alarming as the signal for a charge. We saw the two parties quiver and brace themselves
to fight manfully when the hour for combat came and when they
were summoned from their camp. Suddenly the musicians of the
Silver band ceased and only the instruments of the Golden band
played on. By this we understood that the Golden party was going to
attack; which soon happened. For, as the music changed, the nymph
placed in front of the Queen made a complete turn towards the King
on her left, as if begging his leave to enter the battle and at the same
time saluting the rest of the company. Then, in all modesty, she advanced two squares forward and made a half-curtsey to the opposite
party, whom she was attacking. Then the Golden musicians ceased,
and the Silver ones struck up. I must not fail to mention at this point
that after the nymph had saluted her King and her party in order that
they should not remain inactive, they returned her salute by making a
complete turn to the left, except the Queen who turned to the right,
towards her King. This salutation was performed by all movers, and
was the convention observed throughout the whole conduct of the
ball, by both sides alike.

To the music of the Silver musicians the Silver nymph who stood
in front of her Queen stepped forward and graciously saluted her
King and all his company: a salute which they returned as the Golden
party had done, except that they turned to the right and their Queen

to the left. Then she alighted on the second square forward and, after curtseying to the enemy, stood in front of the Golden nymph with no distance between them, as if intending to fight, although these nymphs can only strike sideways. Their companions, both Golden and Silver, followed them in a broken line, and gave the appearance of skirmishing until the Golden nymph who had first entered the field struck the silver nymph to her left with her hand, sent her off the field and occupied her place. But soon, on a new note from the musicians, she was struck in the same way by the Silver Knight. A Golden nymph made him move off; the Silver Knight emerged from the camp, and the Golden Queen placed herself before her King. Then, fearing the Golden King's anger, the Silver King changed his position and retired behind his right-hand Warden, to a place which seemed well protected and defensible.

The two Knights on the left, the Golden one and the Silver, advanced and made large captures of the opposing nymphs, who could not retreat, especially the Golden Knight who devoted his entire attention to the capture of nymphs. But the Silver Knight had greater plans in his mind. He disguised his intentions and, sometimes, when he could have taken a Golden nymph, let her go and advanced further, to such effect that he came close to his enemies, into a position from which he bowed to the Golden King and said: 'God save you, sire'. Upon this warning to protect their King, the Golden party trembled; not that they could not quickly bring him aid, but because in saving their King, they could not avoid losing their right-hand Warden. Then the Golden King retired to the left, and the Silver Knight took the Golden Warden; which was a great loss to the Golden party. They, however, resolved to work their revenge and surrounded him on all sides, so that he could not retreat or escape from their hands. He made countless attempts to get away, and his party tried innumerable tricks to rescue him, but finally he was taken by the Golden Queen.

Deprived of one of their bastions, the Golden party tried desperately, by hook or by crook, to find a way of retaliating. Casting caution aside, they did great damage among the hosts of the enemy. The Silver party assumed indifference and awaited the hour of their revenge. They offered one of their nymphs to the Golden Queen, after laying her a secret ambush, which almost allowed the Golden Archer to

surprise the Silver Queen. The Golden Knight then attempted to capture the Silver King and Queen, and greeted them with, 'Good day!'
The Silver Archer saved them, but was taken by a Golden nymph,
who was captured by a Silver nymph. The battle was sharp. The
Wardens came out of their posts to the rescue. Everything was in
perilous confusion. The goddess of battles had not yet declared herself.
Sometimes all the Silver forces penetrated to the Golden King's tent,
but were quickly repulsed. Among others, the Golden Queen performed mighty deeds. In one sally she took that Archer and, darting
to the side, captured the Silver Warden. At the sight of this, the Silver
Queen advanced and struck with similar boldness, taking the remaining Golden Warden and some nymphs at the same time.

The two Queens fought a long battle, sometimes trying to surprise
one another, sometimes to escape and protect their own Kings.
Finally the Golden Queen took the Silver one, but was immediately
afterwards taken by the Silver Archer. Her King had then only three
nymphs, an Archer and a Warden, and the Silver King no more than
three nymphs and his right-hand Knight; for which reasons they
fought more cautiously and slowly for the rest of the game.

The two Kings seemed grieved at the loss of their beloved royal
ladies, and gave all their thoughts to the winning of new ones. They
strenuously tried, therefore, to raise one of their three nymphs to the
dignity of a bride, promising each to love her joyfully, and swearing
to receive her as the new Queen if she could advance as far as the
enemy King's last line. The Golden nymphs succeeded first, and one
of their number was made Queen. Whereupon a crown was placed
on her head and she was given new robes. The Silver nymphs followed
the same tactics. But only one file remained open for the advance towards a coronation, and this was guarded by the Golden Warden. The
advancing nymph, therefore, stayed still.

The new Golden Queen wanted to show herself brave, valiant, and
warlike, upon her accession, and performed great feats of arms in the
field. But during this by-play the Silver Knight took the Golden
Warden, who was guarding the outskirts of the field; and so a new
Silver Queen was made, who also wished to show her valour upon
her accession. The battle was renewed more fiercely than before.
Countless ruses, countless assaults, and advances were made by each
party, to such effect that the Silver Queen secretly entered the Golden

King's tent, and said: 'God save you, sire'. There was no way of relieving him except by his new Queen, who, without more ado, stepped
in the way and saved him. Then the Silver Knight, leaping in all directions, came up to his Queen, and together they so confused the Golden
King that he had to sacrifice his Queen in order to extricate himself.
Notwithstanding this, the Golden Archer and the two remaining
nymphs defended their King with all their might. But in the end they
were captured and sent off the field, and the Golden King was left
alone. Then the whole Silver company made him a low bow and
said: 'Good day, sire', which signified that the Silver King had conquered. At these words the two bands of musicians began to strike up,
in unison, to proclaim victory, and the first ball was brought so joyfully to a close that we were all beside ourselves with delight, like
people in an ecstasy. Such mighty feats, such dignity of behaviour, and
such rare graces made us imagine – and not wrongly – that we had
been transported to the sovereign bliss and supreme felicity of the
Olympian heaven.

When the first tournament was over both parties returned to their
original places, and began to fight again in the same way as they had
fought before, except that the music was half a beat faster than in the
first battle. The moves also were totally different from before. This
time I saw the Golden Queen, as though grieved at the previous rout
of her army, called out by the music and taking the field among the
first, together with an Archer and a Knight. Indeed, she almost surprised the Silver King in his tent, in the midst of his officers. Afterwards, when she saw that her plan was discovered, she skirmished
among the Silver troop, and so discomfited the nymphs and other
officers that it was a sad sight to see. You would have compared her to
another Penthesilea the Amazon, raging through the Grecian camp.
But the havoc was short-lived. For, exasperated at their losses, but
disguising their grief, the Silver party secretly planted an ambuscade.
They posted an Archer in a distant corner, and with him a Knight-
errant, and by these two the Queen was taken and sent off the field.
The rest were soon defeated. On the next occasion she will be better
advised to stay near her King and not venture so far off. Or, if she
must go, she will take a more powerful escort with her. So the Silver
party were victors once again.

For the third and last dance the two parties stood up as before; and to me they seemed to have a gayer and more determined look than in the two previous ones. The time of the music was faster by more than a fifth, and was in the warlike Phrygian mode invented by Marsyas in ancient days. Then they began to wheel about and engage in a marvellous battle, with such agility that they made four moves to one beat of the music, all with the customary turnings and bows that have already been described. It was in fact just a series of hops, leaps, and curvettings upon the tight-rope, one after another. When we saw them revolving on one leg after making their bow, they looked for all the world like small children's spinning-tops, which are whipped so hard that they seemed to be motionless. For they spin at such a speed that their motion looks like repose and they appear to be quite still, or, as the children say, to be sleeping. If we paint a point of some colour on them, it seems to be not a point, but a continuous line, as Cusanus has wisely observed in his divine work.

Then we heard nothing but hand-clapping and acclamations repeated at each move by both parties alike. Never was Cato so severe, Crassus the grandfather so unsmiling, Timon of Athens so misanthropic, or Heraclitus such an enemy to laughter – which is peculiar to man – that he would not have relaxed his frown at the sight of these young men with their queens and their nymphs, moving, advancing, leaping, vaulting, capering, and wheeling in five hundred different ways to the swift changes in the music; and so nimbly did they move that one never got in the way of the other. The smaller the number of those remaining on the field the greater was our pleasure in watching the tricks and manoeuvres they practised to surprise one another, all in obedience to the indications given them by the music. I will say more. If this superhuman spectacle confused our thoughts, amazed our spirits, and transported us out of ourselves, we were moved even more by the fears and emotions raised in our hearts by the sound of the music. I could readily believe that it was by such harmonies that Ismenias stirred Alexander the Great, when he was dining quietly at table, to leap up and seize his arms. In the third tournament the Golden King was the victor.

During these dances the Lady disappeared unobserved, and we saw her no more. Nevertheless we were taken by Geber's minions and enrolled among her abstractors, as the Queen had commanded. Then we went down to the harbour of Mataeotechny and boarded our ships. For we had been told that the wind was fair, and that if we did not take advantage of it immediately we should hardly have another chance till the moon was in her third quarter.

CHAPTER 26: *We land on the Isle of Odes, on which the Roads go up and down*

AFTER we had sailed for two days, the Isle of Odes hove into sight, and there we saw a strange thing. For the roads there are animals, if Aristotle is right when he says that one irrefragable sign of an animal is that it moves of its own accord. For the roads there move like animals, and some are roads errant, like the planets, others roads passing, roads crossing, and roads traversing. I noticed that travellers frequently asked some inhabitant of the island: 'Where does this road go?' The answer would be: 'From Noon to Fevrolles, to the church, to the town, to the river.' Then, turning on to the right road, without any further effort or bother they would find themselves at their destination, in much the same way as men whom you see travelling by boat on the Rhone from Lyons to Avignon and Arles.

But, as you know, there are difficulties in everything and nothing goes smoothly throughout. So here, we were told, there was a class of people whom they called waylayers and road-beaters, and the poor roads feared and avoided them as if they were brigands. For they would lie in wait for them as they passed, as men do when trapping wolves or catching quail in a net. I saw one of them who had been arrested by the law because, without leave from Pallas, he had taken the school way, which was the longest. Another boasted that he had honestly taken the shortest, and that he had been so lucky in his choice that he had come in first.

Carpalim had said something of the sort once to Epistemon when he had found him with his tool in his fist, pissing against a wall. 'I don't wonder that you're always first at our good Pantagruel's rising,' he had remarked. 'The road you take must be like the thing you're holding. Nothing could be shorter or less used.' I recognized the main road to Bourges among them, and saw it going at an abbot's pace. But I noticed it flying away on the approach of some carters, who threatened to tread it down with their horses' hooves and to pass their carts over its belly, as Tullia passed her chariot over the belly of her father, Servius Tullius, the sixth King of the Romans.

I also noticed the old road from Péronne to Saint-Quentin, and a decent, tidy road it seemed to me. And there among the rocks I recognized the good old road of La Ferrata, mounted on a great bear.[1] When I caught sight of it in the distance I was reminded of St Jerome in the picture – if only his lion had been a bear. For it was all mortified, with a long white ill-kempt beard, which you would rightly have compared to bunches of icicles. It had a great number of rosaries on it too made of badly trimmed pine trees, and it seemed to be on its knees, not entirely standing or entirely lying, and to be beating its breast with great rough stones. It inspired us with mingled fear and pity.

As we watched it a brisk bachelor of that place drew us aside, and pointed out to us a very smooth road, quite white and slightly littered with straw.

'Don't despise the opinion of Thales of Miletus in future,' said he. 'He proclaimed that water was the beginning of all things. And don't forget Homer either, who said that all things derive their birth from the ocean. That road you see there was born of water and will return to it. A couple of months ago boats were passing down it, but at present it carries carts.'

'Really,' said Pantagruel, 'that's too sad! In our world we see five hundred such transformations and more, every year.'

Then, as he watched the goings of these moving roads, he told us that it must have been on this island that Philolaus and Aristarchus had philosophized, and that Seleucus had come to the conclusion that the earth really revolved round the poles, and not the heavens, although to us the contrary appears to be true. It is the same thing on the river Loire. The trees on the banks appear to be moving. Yet it is not they that move but we, with the movement of the boat.

As we returned to our ships we saw them, near the shore, breaking on the wheel three waylayers, who had been taken in an ambush. They were also burning over a slow fire a great ruffian who had beaten a road and broken one of its ribs. We were told that it was the road to the dam or levee of the Nile, in Egypt.

1. The road over the Mont Cenis pass, which was said to have been crossed by King Arthur in the company of a bear.

CHAPTER 27: *How we came to the Isle of Sandals; and of the Order of the Quavering Friars*

FROM here we came to the Isle of Sandals, where they live on nothing but haddock soup. Nevertheless we were well received and entertained by the king of the island, Benius the Third of that name. After we had drunk, he took us to see a new convent founded, erected, and built according to his plans for the Quavering Friars. This was the name that he gave to his religious order, saying that on the continent there lived the little Servite Friars, friends of Our sweet Lady; *item*, the great and glorious Friars Minor, who are semibreves of bulls, the Friars Minim, who are smoked herrings, also the Minim crotchet Friars, who have crooked fingers; and that Quavers was as low as he could go. By the terms of the Bull patent, obtained from the Fifth or Quintessence – who makes a perfect chord – they were all dressed as incendiaries, except in one respect. For as tilers in Anjou have their knees padded, so these friars had their bellies quilted, and belly-quilters were greatly respected amongst them. They had the codpiece of their breeches in the shape of a slipper, and wore two each, one sown on in front and one behind. By this duplicity of codpieces, they affirmed, certain recondite and horrific mysteries were symbolically represented. They wore round shoes like basins, in imitation of those who dwell in the Sea of Sand, and in addition they shaved their chins, and shod their feet with iron. Also, to show that they despised Fortune, they had the backs of their heads shaven and plucked like pigs, from the crown to the shoulder-blades. The hair in front, from the parietal bone forwards, grew freely. So they went against Fortune, like people who cared nothing for the goods of this world; and in further defiance of that perverse goddess they each carried, not in their hands as she did, but at their girdles like a rosary, a sharp razor, which they whetted twice a day and set three times a night.

Beneath their feet they each wore a round bell, because Fortune is said to have one under hers. The flap of their cowls was tied in front instead of behind; and so their faces were concealed and they could mock freely both at Fortune and the fortunate, exactly as our young ladies do when they are wearing those masks that you call the plain girl's friend. The ancients called them *charities*, because they hide a multitude of sins. Since they always had the back parts of their heads exposed, as we expose our faces, they were able to go arse first or belly first, whichever they chose. If they went arse first, you would think that this was their natural way, on account of their shoes being round and of their codpiece preceding them, also because the backs of their heads were shaved and roughly painted with two eyes and a mouth, as you see them on coconuts. If they went belly foremost you would take them for people playing blind man's buff. They were a pleasant sight to see.

This was their way of life. When the clear morning star began to shine over the earth, they booted and spurred one another, out of charity. And thus booted and spurred, they slept, or at least they snored; and as they snored they wore goggles on their noses, or at least spectacles. We found this a strange sort of behaviour. But they satisfied us with their answers. For they pointed out to us that when the last judgement came, men would be taking their rest and sleeping. So to make it absolutely plain that they did not refuse to appear there, as the fortunate do, they held themselves booted and spurred and ready to mount their horses when the trumpet sounded.

When midday struck – and note that their bells; clock-bells, church-bells, and refectory-bells alike – were made according to Pontanus's method; that is to say, lined with fine down and with a fox's tail for a clapper. So, when midday sounded, they woke up and took off their boots. Then those who wanted to piss pissed, those who wanted to shit shat, and those who wanted to sneeze sneezed. But all of them compulsorily and by rigorous statute yawned widely and plentifully and breakfasted off yawns. It struck me as a pleasant sight. For after putting their boots and spurs in the rack, they came down to the cloister, and there scrupulously washed their hands and their mouths. Then they sat down on a long bench and picked their teeth till the Prior made them a sign by whistling in his palm. Upon which each one opened his mouth to its fullest extent and yawned for half an hour, sometimes longer, sometimes less, according to the Prior's estimate of a suitable breakfast for that day in the calendar. After this they formed up in a grand procession, carrying two banners, on one of which was a beautifully painted portrait of Virtue, on the other a handsome picture of Fortune. One Quaverer carried the banner of Fortune in front, and after him walked another, bearing that of Virtue and, in his other hand, a sprinkler dipped in Mercurial water, as described by Ovid in his *Fasti*, with which he continually beat the friar in front, who was carrying Fortune.

'This order does not agree with the theory of Cicero and the Academics, who would have Virtue lead and Fortune follow,' observed Pantagruel. But it was pointed out to us that this was the proper way for them, because their purpose was to give Fortune a beating.

During the procession, they melodiously quavered some antiphons between their teeth – I don't know which, for I did not understand their patter. But in the end, after listening attentively, I discovered that they only sang with their ears. Such fine music it was, and in perfect harmony with the sound of their bells! You'll never find them out of tune. Pantagruel made one admirable observation about their procession, when he remarked: 'Have you noticed the subtlety of these Quaverers? Did you see how when they formed their procession they came out through one door of the church and went in through another. They took good care not to go in where they came out. On my honour, they're a fine-witted lot; fine enough to take gilt, I should say, fine as a lead dagger, not fine refined but fine refining, and passed through a fine sieve.'

'Their subtlety,' said Friar John, 'is extracted from the occult philosophy, and I'll be damned if I can understand a word of it.'

'But it's all the more to be feared because it can't be understood,' replied Pantagruel. 'Because subtlety understood, subtlety foreseen, subtlety revealed, loses the essence and the very name of subtlety. We then call it plain clumpishness. But they know a trick or two, I promise you!'

After the procession was over they took a little healthy exercise, returning on foot to their refectory, placing their knees beneath the tables, and each propping his breast and his stomach up on his lantern. When they were in this posture, a great Sandal came in with a fork in his hand, and gave them each a lick of it. So they began their meal with cheese, and ended with mustard and lettuce, which Martial testifies to have been the usage among the ancients. For in the end, at the conclusion of their dinner, they were each presented with a plateful of mustard.

This was their diet: on Sundays they ate puddings, chitterlings, sausages, veal stews, pork-liver rissoles, and quails, not to forget the cheese at the beginning and the mustard at the end. On Mondays, good peas and bacon with full commentary and interlinear glosses. On Tuesdays, plenty of holy bread, scones, cakes, and well-browned biscuits. On Wednesdays, country fare – that is to say fine sheep's heads, calves' heads, and badgers' heads, which are plentiful in that land. On Thursdays, seven kinds of soups and eternal mustard between. On Fridays, nothing but sorb-apples, and these were not very ripe, so far as I could tell from their colour. On Saturdays they gnawed bones – not, however, because they were poor or in want, for every one of them had a very fine belly-benefice. Their drink was antifortunal wine; which was the name they gave to some local brew or other. And whenever they wanted to eat or drink, they pulled down the flaps of their cowls in front, which served them as bibs.

When dinner was over they offered God a very fine grace, all in quaverings; and for the rest of the day, in expectation of the Last Judgement, they devoted themselves to works of charity: by pummelling one another on Sundays, tweaking one another's noses on Mondays, scratching one another on Tuesdays; wiping each other's noses on Wednesdays, boring the worms out of each other's nostrils on Thursdays, tickling one another on Fridays, and whipping one another on Saturdays.

Such was their regimen when they resided in the convent. But when, on the cloistral prior's orders, they went out, they were strictly forbidden, under frightful penalties, to touch or eat fish if they were on the sea or the river, or any kind of meat if they were on dry land, in order that it should be universally evident that in enjoying the object they did not yield to a sense of power and concupiscence, and could no more be moved by such failings than the Marpesian rock.

All that they did was accompanied by the suitable and appropriate antiphons, always sung with the ears, as we have said; and when the sun set in the Ocean, they booted and spurred one another as before and, with their goggles on their noses, composed themselves for sleep. At midnight the Sandal entered, and up they jumped. Then, after whetting and setting their razors and marching in procession, they pushed their knees under the tables and feasted as before.

When Friar John of the Hashes saw these jolly quavering Friars and learnt the contents of their statutes, he completely lost patience and cried out aloud: 'Look at that great table-rat! I'll smash him, I swear, and run. I wish to God Priapus were here, as he was at the nocturnal rites in Canidia, to see them farting full blast and quavering in counter-fart. Now I'm really and truly certain that we're on the counter-earth or Antipodes. In Germany they're demolishing monasteries and de-frocking the monks; but here they are erecting them upside down and back to front.'

CHAPTER 28: *Panurge interrogates a Quavering Friar, and only gets monosyllabic answers*

EVER since we had come in, Panurge had done nothing but con-template the faces of these royal Quaverers. But now he pulled one of them by the sleeve, a fellow as thin as a red herring, and asked: 'Brother Quaver, Quaver, Semi-Quaver, where's the girl?'

The Quaver pointed downwards. 'There,' said he.

PANURGE. Have you many of them here? – THE FRIAR. Few.

P. How many are there really? – F. Score.

P. How many score would you like? – F. Five.

P. Where do you keep them hidden? – F. There.

P. I take it that they are not all of the same age. But what sort of figures have they? – F. Fine.

P. What about their complexions? – F. Clear.

P. Their hair? – F. Fair.

P. What colour are their eyes? – F. Dark.

P. Their breasts? – F. Round.

P. Their expressions? – F. Shy.

P. Their eyebrows. – F. Smooth.

P. Their charms? – F. Ripe.

P. Their glances? – F. Free.

P. What kind of feet? – F. Flat.

P. Their heels? – F. Short.

P. And their lower parts? – F. Grand.

P. Their arms? – F. Long.

P. What do they wear on their hands? – F. Gloves.

P. And what are the rings on their fingers made of? – F. Gold.

P. What material do you dress them in? – F. Cloth.

P. What kind of cloth? – F. New.

P. What colour is it? – F. Grey.

P. What colour do they wear on their heads? – F. Blue.

P. And their stockings? – F. Brown.

P. And of what quality are all these materials? – F. Fine.

P. What about their shoes? – F. Hide.

P. How do they generally keep them? – F. Foul.

P. And how do they walk about? – F. Fast.

P. Now let's come to the kitchen – I mean the girls' kitchen – and without any hurry let's go thoroughly through their fare. What is there in the kitchen? – F. Fire.

P. What keeps this fire going? – F. Wood.

P. And what sort of wood is it? – F. Dry.

P. What trees do you take it from? – F. Yew.

P. And the brushwood and faggots? – F. Oak.

P. What wood do you burn in the bedrooms? – F. Pine.

P. And any other wood? – F. Lime.

P. I'll go you halves in these girls. But how do you feed them? – F. Well.

P. And they eat? – F. Bread.

P. Of what sort? – F. Brown.

P. And what else? – F. Meat.

P. How cooked? – F. Roast.

P. Do they eat any soups? – F. None.

P. And pastry? – F. Lots.

P. Just my taste. But do they eat no fish? – F. Yes.

P. Well now, and what else? – F. Eggs.

P. How do they like them? – F. Cooked.

P. I mean cooked in what way. – F. Hard.

P. Is that all their meal? – F. No.

P. What else do they have then? – F. Beef.

P. And what more? – F. Pork.

P. And what more? – F. Goose.

P. And gander too? – F. Yes.

P. In addition? – F. Cock.

P. What do they have for seasoning? – F. Salt.

P. And for the dainty ones? – F. Juice.

P. Of the grape? – F. Yes.

P. And for the last course? – F. Rice.

P. And what else? – F. Milk.

P. And what else? – F. Peas.

P. What peas do you mean? – F. Green.

P. And what sort of fruit? – F. Sound.

P. How served? – F. Raw.

P. And what else? – F. Nuts.

P. And how do they drink? – F. Neat.

P. What? – F. Wine.

P. What sort? – F. White.

P. In winter? – F. Strong.

P. In spring? – F. Rough.

P. In summer? – F. Fresh.

P. In autumn and at harvest time? – F. Sweet.

'By the blessed Pope Joan,' cried Friar John. 'How fat these quavering wenches must be! And what a trot they must go, on such good and plentiful fodder.'

'Just wait till I've finished,' said Panurge.

P. At what time do they go to bed? – F. Night.

P. And when do they get up? – F. Day.

'This is the gentlest Quaverer I've ridden this year,' said Panurge. 'Would to God and the blessed St Quaver, and that worthy virgin St Quaveress, that he were the first President of the Paris Court! God's truth, my friend, what a fine dispatcher of cases, shortener of suits, resolver of disputes, ransacker of bags, fumbler through papers and abstractor of documents he would make! But now let's turn to the other victuals, and speak at some length and in all calmness about these said sisters of charity.

P. Now what sort of brief-cases have they got? – F. Big.

P. At the entrance? – F. Fresh.

P. And inside? – F. Hollow.

P. I meant what's the temperature? – F. Warm.

P. What is there on the outside? – F. Hair.

P. Of what colour? – F. Red.

P. And of the older ones? – F. Grey.

P. And the rifling of them? – F. Quick.

P. Their buttock-play? – F. Smart.

P. Are they all wrigglers? – F. Yes.

P. Now what about your tools? – F. Large.

P. And in section? – F. Round.

P. What colour at the tip? – F. Red.

P. And when they've finished, what are they like? – F. Shrunk.

P. And your genitories, what about them? – F. Huge.

P. How are they hung? – F. Close.

P. What are they like when it's over? – F. Limp.

P. Now, by the oath you've taken, when you want to cover them how do you throw them? – F. Down.

P. What do they say when you roger them? – F. Nowt.

P. But they make you very welcome. In fact they attend to the work in hand, eh? – F. True.

P. Do they breed you children? – F. None.

P. How do you lie together? – F. Bare.

P. Now, by that oath of yours, how many times, on a fair reckoning, do you do it each day? – F. Six.

P. And each night? – F. Ten.

'The pox,' exclaimed Friar John, 'the lecher doesn't care to go beyond sixteen. He's shy.'

P. But tell me, could you do as well, Brother John? Why he must be a green leper. Do all the rest do as much? – F. All.

P. Who is the greatest ladies' man of you all? – F. I.

P. Have you ever served a fault? – F. None.

P. That's quite beyond me. When you've emptied and exhausted your spermatic vessels on one day, can you have as much left on the next? – F. More.

P. Either I'm dreaming, or they possess that Indian herb which Theophrastus writes of. But if by lawful impediment or otherwise, during this pursuit there occurs some diminution of member, how are things with you then? – F. Bad.

P. And what do the girls do then? – F. Curse.

P. And if you take a day's rest? – F. Worse.

P. Then how do you treat them? – F. Laugh.

P. And what do they say then? – F. Shit!

P. And how do you answer them? – F. Farts.

P. And how do they sound? – F. Crack!

P. How do you punish them? – F. Hard.

P. And do you get anything out of them? – F. Blood.

P. And what's their complexion then? – F. Red.

P. But how would you prefer it? – F. Dyed.

P. And what do you make yourselves? – F. Feared.

P. And what do they take you for then? – F. Saints.

P. By that same god-damned oath of yours, tell me in what season of the year do you put up the poorest performance? – F. A'ust.

P. And the liveliest? – F. March.

P. And what are you like for the rest of the year? – F. Gay.

'So this is the world's poor Quaver,' said Panurge with a smile. 'Did you hear how resolute and summary and explicit he is in his answers? He only returns you monosyllables. I think he would take three bites at a cherry.'

'Od's my life,' said Friar John. 'He doesn't talk like that to his girls, I'll be bound. He's a polysyllabic enough with them. You talk about three bites of a cherry. By St Francis, I swear he wouldn't make more than two bites of a leg of mutton, or one draught of a quart of wine. Look how bedraggled he is.'

'This rascally fraternity of monks,' said Epistemon, 'are as ravenous for their victuals everywhere, and yet they tell us they have no more than an existence in this world. But what the devil more have Kings or great princes?'

CHAPTER 29: *Epistemon's Displeasure at the Institution of Lent*

'DID you observe,' asked Epistemon, 'how that wicked and miserable Quaverer quoted March to us as the month for lechery?'

'Yes,' answered Pantagruel, 'and what's more it always falls in Lent, which was instituted for the maceration of the flesh, for the mortification of the sensual appetites, and for the restraining of the venereal passions.'

'Now,' said Epistemon, 'you can judge the intelligence of the Pope who first instituted it, when this poor sandal of a Quaverer admits that he is never so beshitten with lechery as in time of Lent, also from the plain arguments adduced by all good and learned physicians. For they affirm that never in the whole course of the year is any food eaten more exciting to the act of concupiscence than at that time. For lenten-fare is: beans, peas, haricots, chick-peas, onions, walnuts, oysters, herrings, smoked fish, pickles, and salads entirely composed of aphrodisiac herbs such as rocket, garden-cress, tarragon, watercress, water-parsley, rampion, horned poppy, hop-buds, figs, rice, and raisins.'

'You would be very much surprised to learn,' said Pantagruel, 'that the good Pope who instituted Holy Lent especially prescribed these foods to encourage the multiplication of the human race. For he knew that to be the season when the natural heat proceeds from the interior of the body, in which it has lain throughout the winter cold, and diffuses itself about the surface of the limbs, as the sap does in trees. What convinces me of this is that in the baptismal register of Thouars the number of children is greater in October and November than in the other ten months of the year; and so by retrospective computation we find that they must all have been made, conceived, and engendered in Lent.

'I am listening to your argument,' announced Friar John, 'and I'm getting no small pleasure from it. But the Vicar of Jambet attributed this copious impregnation of women, not to Lenten fare but to the little hump-backed beggars, and little booted preachers, and dirty little confessors, who at this season of the year damn all erring husbands three fathoms lower in hell than Lucifer's claws. So, in their terror, these husbands give up rogering the servant girls and return to their wives. I have spoken.'

'Interpret the institution of Lent according to your own fancy,' said Epistemon. 'Everyone is full of his own ideas. But all the doctors will oppose its suppression, though I believe it is impending. I'm sure they would. I've heard them say so. For without Lent their art would fall into contempt. They would earn nothing, since no one would be ill. All diseases are sown in Lent. It's the nursing-ground, the native bed, and dispenser of all maladies. What's more, not only does Lent corrupt the body, it drives souls out of their senses as well. Just consider that. Devils try their hardest then; hypocrites come out of doors; and canters hold their great feasts and fairs and stations and sessions and pardons and confessions and whippings and anathematisations. However, I should not like to infer that the Arimaspians are any better than ourselves in this respect. But I know what I'm saying.'

'Now my pious and Quavering ram,' said Panurge, 'what do you say to that? Isn't he a heretic?' – F. Yes.

P. Ought he to be burnt? – F. Ought.

P. And should or shouldn't it be as soon as possible? – F. Should.
P. Without being parboiled first? – F. Yes.
P. In what way then? – F. Live.
P. So that he may end up how? – F. Dead.
P. For he has vexed you and driven you – what? – F. Wild.
P. What do you think he is? – F. Mad.
P. Mad would you say, or raving? – F. Worse.
P. What do you want him to be? – F. Ash.
P. Have others like him been burnt? – F. Scores.
P. Heretics or less than that? – F. Less.
P. Are there still some to be burnt? – F. Lots.
P. Would you save any of them? – F. No.
P. Shouldn't they all be burnt? – F. All.

'I don't know what pleasure you get from talking to that wretched tattered monk,' said Epistemon. 'But if I didn't know you otherwise, I should have a very poor opinion of you. The impression you would make on me would not be to your credit.'

'Let's go, for Heaven's sake,' said Panurge. 'I should like to take him to Gargantua; he pleases me so much. When I'm married he shall serve my wife as a fool.'

'He'll serve your wife all right,' said Epistemon, 'but in another capacity. It's you who'll be the fool.'

'That settles you this time, my poor Panurge,' said Friar John, laughing. 'You'll never escape being made a cuckold, arse high.'

CHAPTER 30: *Our Visit to Satinland*

REGALED by our glimpse of the Quavering Friars' new foundation, we sailed on for two days, and on the third our captain sighted a lovely island, more delightful than all the rest. It was called Frieze Island because its roads were of that cloth; and on it was Satinland, which is so well known to pages at Court. Here the trees and plants never lost their flowers or leaves. For they were made of damask and figured velvet, and the birds and beasts were of tapestry.

We saw many birds, beasts, and trees there similar to those we have over here in shape, size, bulk, and colour. However, they ate nothing, did not sing, and did not bite, as ours do. We saw many also that we had never seen before, amongst them several elephants of different kinds. I especially noted six males and six females which were presented by their trainer in the theatre at Rome in the time of Germanicus, the nephew of the Emperor Tiberius. These were learned elephants – musicians, philosophers, dancers, performers of the pavane, and acrobats – ; and they would sit at table, in complete composure, eating in silence, like so many holy fathers in the refectory. Elephants have a snout three foot long, which we call the proboscis, and with this they suck up water to drink, and pull down palms, plums, and all sorts of food. They also use it as a hand for attack or defence and, in battle, throw men high into the air, making them burst out laughing as they fall. They have very fine large ears, shaped like winnowing fans. They have joints and articulations in their legs; those who have written to the contrary have never seen them, except in pictures. Among their teeth they have two large horns. Juba, at least, called them so, but Pausanias affirmed that they were teeth, and not horns. Still, it is all one to me, provided you understand that they are of real ivory, and are five or six foot long. They are in the upper jaw, not the lower; and if you believe those who maintain the contrary – especially that double-dyed liar Aelian – you will find yourselves wrong. It was, by the way, here and nowhere else that Pliny saw them dancing on ropes with little bells and walking the tight-rope, in this way passing over tables while the feast was going on, without disturbing the drinkers drinking.

I saw a rhinoceros there exactly like the one that Hans Cleberg once showed me, and very little different from a boar I once saw at Limoges except that it had a horn on its snout, a foot and a half long and pointed, with which it dared to do battle with an elephant. With this horn it struck the great beast in the belly – which is the weakest and tenderest spot in an elephant – and laid it dead on the ground.

I saw thirty-two unicorns there. This is an amazingly fierce creature, in every way similar to a fine horse, except that it has a stag's head, feet like an elephant, the tail of a boar, and a black horn on its forehead, six or seven foot long, which generally hangs down like a turkey-cock's comb. When it wishes to fight or use it in any other way, it raises it stiff and straight. I saw one of them in the company of several other wild animals, purifying a fountain with its horn.

Hereupon Panurge informed me that his dangler was like a unicorn's horn, not in its length, indeed, but in its virtues and properties. For just as the unicorn purified the water of pools and springs from any dirt or poison in them, so that these various animals could drink in safety after it, so men might safely bore in after him without fear of chancres, pox, the clap, a peppering of pustules, or any other such small favours. For if there were any trouble in the mephitic chasm, he would thoroughly purify it with his stiffened horn.

'When you are married,' said Friar John, 'we'll make the test on your wife. Give us permission, in God's name. For the instruction you are giving us is most salutary.'

'Very well,' answered Panurge. 'But immediately afterwards you'll be taking into your stomach the little pill that aggregates you to God, and is made up of twenty-two Caesarian knife-thrusts.'

'A mug of some good fresh wine would be preferable,' replied Friar John.

I saw there the Golden Fleece which Jason won. Those who said it was no fleece but a golden apple, because μῆλα signifies both apple and sheep, have made very poor use of their visit to Satinland. I saw a chameleon there, as described by Aristotle, and like the one shown to me once by Charles Marais, a distinguished physician in the noble city of Lyons on the Rhone. Like them, it lived on nothing but air. I saw three hydras there, like those I had already seen elsewhere. These are serpents, each with seven different heads. I saw fourteen phoenixes. I had read in several authors that there is only one of them in the whole world in each age. But, according to my poor judgement, those who have written on the subject – even Lactantius Firmianus – have never seen one anywhere except in Tapestry-land. I also saw the skin of Apuleius's golden ass.

I saw there three hundred and nine pelicans, six thousand and sixteen Seleucid birds, marching in battalions and eating grasshoppers among the corn; also some cynamologi, argatiles, goat-suckers, thynunculi, and crotonotaries – I mean onocrotaries, of course – with their great gullets – also stymphalides, harpies, panthers, dorcades, cemades, jackals, satyrs, cartazoni, tarands, aurochs, monopes, pegasi, cepi, neades, puff-adders, cercopitheci, bisons, sardinian sheep, byturi, ophyri, giant vampires, and griffins.

I saw Shrove-Tuesday on horseback – mid-August and mid-March held his stirrups – also were-wolves, centaurs, tigers, leopards, hyenas, giraffes, and orixes.

I saw a remora – a little fish called Echeneis by the Greeks – beside a large ship, which did not stir, although it was in the open sea with all its sails set. It was in this Satinland, and nowhere else, that Mutianus saw this creature. Friar John told us that two kinds of fish used to abound about the Courts of Parliament in the old days which rotted the bodies and tortured the souls of all litigants, whether nobles or commoners, poor or rich, great or small. The first sort were April fish, which are procurers or mackerel; and the second poisonous remorast an eternity of litigation, that is to say, without final judgement.

I saw there sphinxes, striped wolves, ounces, and cephi, which have fore-feet like hands and hind-feet like a man's feet, also cocrutae and eali, which are as large as hippopotami and have tails like elephants, jaws like boars, and horns that move like asses' ears. Cocrutae are very fast creatures, as large as Mirebalais asses. They have the neck, the tail, and the breast of a lion, the legs of a stag, and a mouth slit right open to the ears. They have no teeth, except one in the upper jaw and one in the lower, and they speak with a human voice, but they never uttered a sound there.

You say that no one ever saw a sacre's eyrie. But I saw eleven of them and took good note of them. I saw left-handed halberds, which I had never seen elsewhere. I also saw some mantichores, very strange beasts. They have the body of a lion, red hair, the face and ears of a man, and three rows of teeth close together, like the fingers of your two hands interlocked. They have a sting in their tail with which they prick like scorpions, and a most musical voice.

I saw catoblepes, savage creatures that have small bodies but disproportionately large heads, which they can scarcely raise from the earth. Their eyes are so poisonous that whoever looks at them drops down dead, as if he had seen a basilisk.

I saw some beasts with two backs, which seemed to me the merriest creatures in the world. They were greater bum-wagglers even than the wagtail. In fact their backsides never stayed still.

I saw some milch crawfish, which I had never seen anywhere else. They marched in very fine order, and it did me good to see them.

CHAPTER 31: *How we saw Hearsay in Satinland, who kept a School for Witnesses*

ON pressing a little further inland into this Land of Tapestry, we saw the Mediterranean Sea parted and revealed to its greatest depth, just as the Red Sea was parted asunder to make a passage for the Jews as they departed from Egypt. There I recognized Triton, winding his mighty shell, together with Glaucus, Proteus, Nereus, and countless other gods and monsters of the sea. We also saw an infinite number of fish of different kinds, dancing, flying, jumping, fighting, eating, breathing, copulating, hunting, skirmishing, laying ambushes, making truces, bargaining, swearing, and sporting.

In a corner close by we saw Aristotle holding a lantern, in the posture of the hermit who lighted St Christopher in the picture, prying, pondering, and putting everything down in writing. Behind him, like a bailiff's bulldogs, were a number of other philosophers: Appianus, Heliodorus, Athenaeus, Porphyrius, Pancreates the Arcadian, Numenius, Posidonius, Ovidius, Oppianus, Olympius, Seleucus, Leonides, Agathocles, Theophrastus, Damostratus, Mutianus, Nymphodorus, Aelianus, and five hundred other equally fine idle fellows, such as Chrysippus or Aristarchus of Soli, who spent fifty-eight years considering the nature of bees, and did absolutely nothing else. Among them I noticed Peter Gilles, with a urine-glass in his hand, in deep contemplation of the urine of these fine fishes.

After a long examination of this Satinland, Pantagruel said: 'I have been feasting my eyes here for a long time. But I can't get any the fuller for it. My stomach is roaring with downright raging hunger. Let us feed, I say, let us have a taste of one of these anacampserotes that is hanging here. Pooh, it is no good at all!'

I then took some myrobalans, which were hanging on the end of some tapestry. But I could neither chew them nor swallow them, and if you had tasted them you would have rightly staked your oath that they were tangled silk and had no taste whatever. Anyone would think that Heliogabulus learnt the art of hospitality there. For his method was as close to that of Satinland as a transcript to a Bull. For when he wanted to feast those whom he had kept fasting for a long time, with the promise of sumptuous, liberal, and imperial banquet at the end, he would feed them on waxen, marble, and porcelain meats, on paintings, and on figured table-cloths.

While searching this land, therefore, to see if we could find any food, we heard a strident and confused noise, like that of women washing linen or the clappers of the mills at Basacle, near Toulouse. Without any delay we went over to the place where it came from and saw a little old hunchback, all misshapen and monstrous. His name was Hearsay, and his mouth was slit to the ears. In his throat were seven tongues, and each tongue was slit into seven parts. Nevertheless, he spoke on different subjects and in different languages, with all seven at the same time. He had also, spread over his head and the rest of his body, as many ears as Argus of old had eyes. But, for the rest, he was blind and his legs were paralysed.

Around him I saw innumerable men and women listening to him attentively, and amongst the group I recognized several with very important looks, among them one who held a chart of the world and was explaining it to them succinctly, in little aphorisms. Thus they became clerks and scholars in no time, and spoke in choice language – having good memories – about a host of tremendous matters, which a man's whole lifetime would not be enough for him to know a hundredth part of. They spoke about the Pyramids, the Nile, Babylon, the Troglodites, the Himantopodes, the Blemmyae, the Pygmies, the Cannibals, the Hyperborean Mountains, the Aegipans, and all the devils – and all from Hearsay.

There, as I believe, I saw Herodotus, Pliny, Solinus, Berosus, Philostratus, Mela, Strabo, and a great number of other ancients, together with Albertus Magnus the Dominican, Peter Martyr, Pope Pius the Second, Rafael de Volterra, Paulus Jovius the Valiant, Jacques Cartier, Chaiton the Armenian, Marco Polo the Venetian, Ludovico Romano, Pedro Álvarez, and I do not know how many other modern historians, hiding behind a piece of tapestry and stealthily writing down the grandest stuff – and all from Hearsay.

Behind a piece of velvet embroidered with leaves of dupe's-mint, I saw, close to Hearsay, a great number of men from Perche and Maine, good students and fairly young. When we inquired what branch of learning they were studying, we were told that ever since their youth they had been learning to be witnesses, and that they profited so well by their instruction that when they left this place and returned to their own provinces, they lived honestly by the trade of bearing witness. For they would give sworn evidence on any subject to whoever would pay them the highest wage by the day – and all this from Hearsay. Believe it or not, they gave us slices of their cake and we drank liberally from their barrels. Then they advised us, in the friendliest fashion, to be as sparing of the truth as possible if we wanted to get preferment at the courts of the great.

CHAPTER 32: *How we came in Sight of Lanternland*

AFTER our poor reception and poor feeding in Satinland, we sailed on for three days, and on the fourth, with good luck, we came to Lanternland. As we approached we saw certain little fires flitting over the sea. For my part I thought that they were not lanterns but fish, that with their flashing tongues struck fire out of the sea; or perhaps Lampyrides, which you call glow-worms, gleaming out there, as they do in my country when the barley is getting ripe. But the captain informed us that they were watchlights, set out around the place to mark the land, and for the safe piloting in of some foreign Lanterns who, like good Franciscans and Dominicans, were coming to attend the Provincial Chapter. Some of us suspected that they might be there as storm-warnings, but the captain assured us that he was right.

CHAPTER 33: *We land at the Port of the Midnight-oilers and enter Lanternland*

WE entered the Lanterns' port immediately, and there upon a high tower Pantagruel recognized the lantern of La Rochelle, which gave us a good light. We also saw the lanterns of Pharos, of Nauplion, and that one on the Acropolis at Athens which was sacred to Pallas. Near the port is a little village inhabited by the Midnight-oilers, who live on lanterns as the lay brothers in our country live on nuns. They were worthy and studious people, and Demosthenes had once burnt his oil with them. From this place to the palace we were escorted by three Obelisk-lights, military guards of the harbour, with tall hats like Albanians. To them we explained the cause of our visit and our purpose;

which was to obtain from the Queen of the Lanterns a Lantern lass[1] to guide us on the journey we were making to the oracle of the Bottle. They promised to oblige us and gladly, adding that we had come there at a good moment, for this was the occasion of their Provincial Chapter, and that while they were holding it we should have a good choice of Lanterns.

When we came to the royal palace we were presented to the Queen by two Lanterns of Honour – namely, by the Lantern of Aristophanes and the Lantern of Cleanthes. Panurge explained to her in Lanternese the reasons for our journey, and we were made welcome. In fact she commanded us to be present at her supper, in order to facilitate our choice of the Lantern who would best suit us as a guide. This greatly pleased us, and we were not backward in noting and considering everything about them: their actions, their dress, and their bearing, also the order of service.

The Queen was dressed in virgin crystal, all inset with damascene work, and trimmed with great diamonds. Of the Lanterns of the Blood, some were dressed in rock-crystal and some in talc. The rest wore horn, paper, and oiled cloth. The Cressets also were clad according to their rank and the antiquity of their houses. I noticed a single pot-shaped one of earthenware, parading among these gorgeous objects, and this greatly surprised me. But I was told that this was Epictetus's Lantern, for which three thousand drachmas had once been refused.

I carefully examined the shape and mechanism of Martial's many spouted Lantern, and paid even greater attention to that of Eicosimyx, which was once consecrated to Canopa by the daughter of Critias, and I took careful note also of the hanging Lantern, once taken from the temple of Apollo at Thebes and transported by Alexander the Conqueror to the town of Cyme in Aeolia. I noted another which was remarkable for the fine tuft of crimson silk that it wore on its head; and I was told that this was Bartolus, the Lantern of the Law. I noticed two others, which were equally remarkable on account of the suppository-bags which they carried on their belts; and I was told that one was the Great, and the other the Little Light of the Apothecaries.

When supper time came, the Queen sat down in the chief seat, and the others took their places according to their rank and dignity. For

1. The Lanterns were female, and the Cressets male.

the first course, they were all served with fat moulded candles, except the Queen, to whom they brought a great stiff flaming taper of white wax, slightly red at the tip. The Lanterns of the Blood-Royal were also given exceptional treatment, as was the Provincial Lantern of Mirabalais, who was provided with a walnut-oil candle, and the Provincial of Lower Poitou, to whom I saw them give a candle decorated with coats of arms. And Heaven knows that after that they gave out a glorious light from their wicks; with the exception, however, of a number of young Lanterns, who were under the care of a single fat one, and who did not shine like the others, but seemed to me to cast a lascivious glow.

After supper we retired to rest, and next morning the Queen commanded us to choose one of the most eminent Lanterns as our guide. We picked out the great Master Peter d'Amy's friend whom I had formerly known very well, and chose her. She recognized me with equal ease; and she seemed to us a more divine, heavenly, learned, wise, eloquent, kindly, gracious, and suitable guide for us than any other member of the company.

After humbly thanking the royal lady, we were escorted to our ship by seven acrobatical young torches, beneath Diana's clear light; and as we were leaving the palace I heard one great bandy-legged torch exclaim that one good-night was worth as many good-mornings and more as there have been chestnuts in goose-stuffing since Ogyges' flood. By this he meant to convey that there is no good cheer except at night, when the lanterns are out in the company of their noble Cressets. Such cheer the sun cannot gaze on with his eye, as Jupiter proved when he lay with Hercules's mother Alcmena, and eclipsed the sun for two days on end. For not long ago that good orb had revealed the wickedness of Mars and Venus.

CHAPTER 34: *How we arrived at the Oracle of the Bottle*

WITH our noble Lantern leading and lighting us, we arrived most joyfully at the island of our desire, in which was the Oracle of the Bottle.

As Panurge landed he cut a neat caper on one leg and said to Pantagruel: 'To-day at last we have what we have been seeking with so much toil and labour'. He then paid a gracious compliment to our

Lantern, who ordered us all to be of good cheer, and not to be in the least frightened, whatever might appear to us.

As we approached the Temple of the Holy Bottle, we had to pass through a large vineyard planted with all sorts of vines, such as Falernian, Malmsey, Muscadine, Taggia, Beaune, Mirevaux, Orléans, Picardent, Arbois, Coussy, Anjou, Graves, Corsica, Verron, Nerac, and others. This vineyard was planted by Bacchus of old with such a blessing that it bore leaves, flowers, and fruit at all seasons, like the orange trees of San Remo, and here our grand Lantern commanded us to eat three grapes each, to put vine-leaves in our shoes, and to take a green branch in our left hands. At the far end of the vineyard we passed under an antique arch, on which was the memorial of a drinker, most delicately carved; that is to say that in one place there was a long row of flagons, leather-bottles, bottles, flasks, cans, barrels, firkins, pots, tankards, and old-fashioned pitchers, hanging from a shady trellis. On another were a great number of garlics, onions, shallots, hams, botargoes, cheese-cakes, smoked ox-tongues, old cheeses, and suchlike delicacies, intertwined with vine-leaves, and most cunningly tied together with vine-stalks; on another were a hundred shapes of glasses, such as glasses on feet and glasses on horseback, rummers, tumblers, beakers, mazers, bowls, cups, goblets, and other such Bacchic artillery. On the face of the arch, under the frieze, were inscribed two verses:

> Ere you pass this postern, pray
> Get a lantern on the way.

'Well, we've provided for that,' said Pantagruel. 'For in the whole country of Lanternland there's no better or more divine Lantern than ours.'

This arch ended in a fine wide arbour, entirely formed of vine-stocks, hung with grapes of five hundred different colours and of five hundred different shapes, which were not natural but produced by the science of viticulture. They were yellow, blue, brown, grey white, black, green, and violet; streaked, spotted, long, round, triangular, bag-shaped, crowned, bearded, club-headed, and mossy. This arbour was closed at the end by three old ivy-trees, very green, and all loaded with berries; and there our most illustrious Lantern commanded us each to make himself an Albanian hat of this ivy and to cover his head with it; which we did without hesitation.

'Jupiter's pontiff of old would not have passed beneath this arbour like this,' said Pantagruel.

'There was a mystical reason for that,' said our excellent Lantern. 'For if he had, the wine – that is to say, the grapes – would have been over his head and he would have seemed to be, so to speak, mastered and dominated by wine. This signifies that pontiffs and all persons who devote and dedicate themselves to the contemplation of things divine must keep their minds calm and free from all perturbation of the senses: a disturbance which is more present in drunkenness than in any other passion. For similar reasons, therefore, you would not be re-ceived in the Temple, having passed beneath here, if Bacbuc, the noble priestess did not see that your shoes were full of vine-leaves. For that condition is altogether and diametrically opposed to the other, and clearly signifies that you despise wine, have trodden it underfoot, and have conquered it.'

'I'm no scholar,' said Friar John, 'and I'm sorry for it. But I read in my Breviary, in the Book of Revelations, that a woman was seen with the moon under her feet, and that it was reckoned a marvellous sight. The significance of it, as Bigot explains to me, is that she was of a differ-ent race from the rest of women, who are quite contrary by nature. They have the moon in their heads and consequently their brains are always moon-struck. And that makes it easy for me to believe what you say, my dear Lady Lantern.'

CHAPTER 35: *How we approached the Temple of the Bottle by an Underground Way, and why Chinon is the finest City in the World*

THEN we went underground, through a plaster-lined vault, roughly painted at the entrance with a dance of women and satyrs around an old laughing Silenus on his ass.

'This entrance reminds me of the painted cellar in the first city in all the world,' said I to Pantagruel. 'There are paintings like these there, and they are just as fresh as these.'

'Where is this first city you refer to?' asked Pantagruel, 'and which city can it be?'

'Chinon – or Cainon –' said I, 'in Touraine.'

'I know where Chinon is,' said Pantagruel, 'and I know the painted cellar. I've drunk many a glass of fresh wine there, and I don't doubt that Chinon is an ancient city. Its motto proves the fact, for it runs:

> Chinon, Chinon, Chinon, Chinon,
> Little city, great renown,
> Perched upon its rocky brow
> The woods above, the Vienne below.

But how can it be the first city in the world? Where do you find that written? What makes you suppose so?'

'I find in Holy Writ,' I replied, 'that Cain was the first builder of cities. Now, it is very probable that he called the first one of all after his own name Cainon, as all other founders and restorers of cities have done since his time, in imitation of him. For Athene – that is, in Greek, Minerva – gave her name to Athens, Alexander to Alexandria, Constantine to Constantinople, Pompey to Pompeiopolis in Cicilia, Adrian to Adrianople, Cana to the Canaanites, Saba to the Sabaeans, Assur to the Assyrians: and there are also Ptolemais, Caesaria, Tiberias, and Herodium in Judaea.'

As we were thus chatting, the great Flask – our Lantern called him the Flash – Governor of the Holy Bottle, came out, escorted by the Temple guard, who were all French bottle-men. Seeing that we bore vine-leaves, as I have said, and were crowned with ivy, and recognizing our illustrious Lantern as well, he brought us safely in, and commanded that we should be led straight to the Princess Bacbuc, Lady-in-waiting to the Bottle and priestess of all the mysteries; and this was done.

CHAPTER 36: *Our Descent of the Tetradic Steps; and Panurge's fright*

THEN we descended an underground marble staircase, and came to a landing. Turning to the left, we went down two other flights, and came to a similar landing. Then there were three more to the right, ending in a similar landing, and four to the left again.

'Is it here?' asked Panurge at this point.

'How many flights have you counted?' asked our splendid Lantern.

'One, two, three, and four,' answered Pantagruel.

'How many is that?' she asked.

'Ten,' answered Pantagruel.

'Multiply this result by the same Pythagorical tetrad,' said she.

'That's ten, twenty, thirty, forty,' answered Pantagruel.

'How many does that all make?' she asked.

'A hundred,' answered Pantagruel.

'Add the first cube,' said she, 'which is eight. At the end of that fore-ordained number of steps we shall find the Temple door. And note most carefully that this is the true psychogony of Plato, which was so highly praised by the Academicians, but so little understood. The half of it is made up of unity, of the first two plain numbers, two squares, and two cubes.'

In descending these numbered stairs underground we had good service from, firstly, our legs, for without them we could only have rolled down like barrels into a cellar; secondly, our illustrious Lantern, for we saw no other light as we descended, any more than we should have done in St Patrick's Hole in Ireland, or in the cavern of Trophonius in Boeotia. When we had gone down seventy-eight stairs, Panurge cried out to our most luminous Lantern:

'Most wondrous lady, I beg of you with a contrite heart, let us turn back. For, by God's truth, I'm dying from sheer fright. I agree never to marry. You have taken great pains and trouble for me, and God will reward you for it in his great rewarding-place. I shan't be ungrateful either, when I get out of this Troglodytes' cave. Let's turn back, if you please. I'm very much afraid that this is Taenarus, which is the way down to hell. I think I can hear Cerberus barking. Listen, that's he, or I have a singing in my ears. I've no liking for him at all, for there's no toothache so bad as when a dog has got you by the leg. And if this is only Trophonius's cave, the ghosts and goblins will eat us alive, as they once devoured one of Demetrius's bodyguard, for lack of scraps. Are you there, Friar John? I beg of you, old paunch; keep close to me. I'm dying of fear. Have you got your cutlass? I haven't any weapons at all, offensive or defensive. Let's turn back.'

'I'm here,' said Friar John. 'I'm here. Don't be frightened. I'm holding you by the collar, and eighteen devils couldn't get you out of my hands, even though you aren't armed. Arms never failed a man in his need, if he had a stout heart and sturdy muscles. They would rather rain down from heaven, as stones did of old on the fields of La Crau, near Marius's canal in Provence, to help Hercules when he had no other weapons to fight the two sons of Neptune with. But tell me, are we just going down here to the Limbo of Little Children – they'll shit all over us, I swear – or is this the way to hell, and to all the devils? By God, I'll give them a good drubbing for you, now that I have vine-leaves in my shoes. I shall put up a stiff fight! Where do we go? Where are they? I'm afraid of nothing but their horns. But the thought of the horns that Panurge will wear when he is married will keep me quite safe from them. I can see him there, in my prophetic mind, like a second Actaeon, horned, horny, and hornified.'

'Beware, Frater,' said Panurge, 'that when the time comes for monks to marry, you don't wed the quartan ague. And if you do, may I never return safe and sound from this Hypogaeum if I don't stuff her for you, merely to make you cornigerous and cornipetous. What's more, I think the quartan ague is a pretty nasty baggage. For I remember that Clawpuss wanted to marry her to you, but you called him a heretic.'

Here the conversation was interrupted by our splendid Lantern, who remarked that this was the place where we must observe a holy silence, both by suppression of words and by curbing of tongues. For the rest, she categorically assured us that we were in no danger of returning without hearing the Word of the Bottle, since we had already lined our shoes with vine-leaves.

'Let us go on, then,' said Panurge, 'and charge head foremost through all the devils. We can but perish, and that is soon done. I have always been preserving my life for some battle. Let's move, let's get moving, let's press onwards. I have enough courage and more. It's true that my heart is pounding. But that is from the chill and staleness of this cave. It's not fear, oh no, it's fever. Let's move, let's move on, let's pass on, push on, piss on. My name's William the Fearless.'

CHAPTER 37: *How the Temple doors opened of themselves, in a marvellous Manner*

AT the bottom of the steps we found a fine, jasper portal, designed in the Doric style, and built in that manner. And on the face of it was written in Ionian letters of the purest gold, the following sentence, ἐν οἴνῳ ἀλήθεια, that is to say, *In wine lies Truth*. The two doors were of a metal like Corinthian bronze. They were massive, and decorated with little scrolls of vine-tendrils in relief, delicately enamelled to the details of the moulding, and they closed against one another, fitting exactly edge to edge, without any lock or chain or any other fastening. The only thing that hung down was an Indian loadstone, the size of an Egyptian bean, set in refined gold at two points, hexagonal in shape, and quite symmetrical, on each side of which, close to the wall, was suspended a bunch of garlic.

At this point our noble Lantern asked us to accept her excuses for guiding us no further. We had now only to obey the instructions of the priestess of Bacbuc, she said. For she herself was not permitted to enter, for certain reasons which it was better to pass over in silence than to reveal to mortal men. But, come what might, she commanded us to keep our heads, to have no fears or alarms of any sort, and to rely on her for our return. Then she pulled the loadstone which hung at the joint between the doors, and threw it to the right, into a box expressly designed for the purpose; and at the same time drew from the hinge of each door a crimson silk cord nine foot long, on which the garlic hung. These she fastened on to two gold buckles, which were fixed at the sides for that express purpose, and withdrew.

Suddenly the two doors opened of their own accord, without anyone touching them; and as they opened they made no loud noise, or horrible creaking, as rough and heavy bronze doors usually do, but a soft and delightful murmur, which echoed through the vault of that temple. Pantagruel at once perceived the cause of this. For he saw beneath the end of each door a little roller, which was secured to the door by its axle, and which revolved, as the door moved towards the wall, over a hard serpentine stone, which was rubbed smooth and polished all over by its friction. This was the cause of this sweet and musical sound.

I was greatly puzzled to know how the two doors had opened of themselves, without pressure from anyone; and to solve the mystery, I cast a glance between the doors and the wall, once we were inside, to see if I could learn what force or instrument was closing them again. I suspected that our kind Lantern had applied to their closing edge the herb Aethiopis, by means of which anything that is shut can be opened. But I noticed that, at the point where the two doors closed on the inner lock, a fine steel plate was let into the Corinthian bronze.

I also noticed two squares of Indian loadstone, about two inches across and bluish in colour, well smoothed and polished. They were completely inset in the Temple wall at the places where the doors stopped against it when fully open. So, thanks to a wonderful and mysterious provision of nature, the steel plates were set moving by the violent attraction of the loadstone; and in this way the doors were slowly pulled back; not always, however, but only when their own loadstone was removed. For once this is taken away the steel is released from its natural submission to it. The two bunches of garlic, which our jolly Lantern had removed on the crimson cord, had also to be hung some distance away, because they neutralize the magnet and rob it of its powers of attraction.

On one of these loadstone squares, to the right, was exquisitely carved in ancient Latin characters, the Senecal iambic verse:

Ducunt volentem fata, nolentem trahunt.[1]

On the other square, to the left, was elegantly engraved in capital letters this sentence:

ALL THINGS MOVE TO THEIR END.

CHAPTER 38: *The marvellous Emblems on the Temple Pavement*

WHEN I had read these inscriptions, I turned to contemplate the magnificent temple, and examined the marvellous complexity of the stone floor, to which no work which is now, or ever has been, beneath the firmament can rightfully be compared. No, not the floor of the temple of Fortune at Praeneste, in Sulla's day, or that Grecian pavement called Asarotum which Sosistratus laid in Pergamum. For

1. Fate leads the willing, but the unwilling drags.

it was a tessellated floor, made up of little squares, all of fine and polished stones, each in its natural colour. One of the varieties used was red jasper charmingly flecked in different colours; another was serpentine, another porphyry, another lycophthalamy, powdered with golden spots the size of atoms, another was agate, streaked with little confused and irregular waves of a milky colour, another very precious chalcedony, another green jasper, with a few red and yellow veins; and these were arranged in diagonal lines.

Under the porch the floor was made of a mosaic of small stones jointed together, each of a single colour. These made up a figured design, and it was as if a handful of vine-leaves had been strewn on the floor without any great care. For in one place they seemed to lie thickly, and in another less so. This foliage was wonderful all over, but particularly so in certain places. In one of these some snails were seen, in half shadow, climbing over the grapes; in another some small lizards were scampering over the leaf-clusters; and in yet another were shown grapes, some half ripe and some wholly so, which were so cunningly designed and so skilfully executed by the artist that they would have deceived the starlings and other small birds as did the painting of Zeuxis of Heraclea. However that may be, they thoroughly deceived us. Indeed, where the artist had scattered the vine-leaves thickest, we lifted our feet and took long strides, for fear of entangling ourselves in them. In fact we walked as men do over rough and stony places.

After this I looked up and studied the Temple vault and walls, which were entirely covered with a mosaic of marble and porphyry, forming a series of pictures extending from one end to the other. These were very finely executed, and represented good old Bacchus's victory over the Indians. They began on the left-hand side of the entrance and were made up as follows:

CHAPTER 39: *Bacchus's Victory over the Indians, as represented in the Mosaic-work of the Temple*

AT the beginning various towns, villages, castles, fortresses, fields, and forests were shown all fiery and ablaze. In this same picture some frantic and depraved women were seen furiously tearing to pieces live calves, sheep, and ewes, and consuming their raw flesh. This picture was meant to convey how, in his invasion of Indis, Bacchus put everything to fire and sword. The Indians, nevertheless, thought so little of him that they did not deign to go out and meet him. For they had had certain information from their spies that there were no warriors in his army, but a little effeminate old man who was always drunk, accompanied by a crowd of naked yokels, who did nothing but leap and dance and wore tails and horns like young goats, and by a great horde of drunken women. So they resolved to give them free passage and offer no armed resistance, thinking that a victory over such people would bring them shame rather than glory, and would redound to their disgrace and dishonour rather than to their honour and glory. Thus despised, Bacchus conquered one territory after another, and set everything ablaze. For fire and thunder are Bacchus's paternal weapons, and even before he was born Jupiter saluted him with the thunder, on the occasion when his mother Semele and his maternal house were burnt up and destroyed by fire. He also slaughtered far and wide, since it is his nature to make blood in peace-time and to shed it in time of war. As is proved by that field on the Island of Samos which is called Panaema – that is to say *all bloody* – where Bacchus overtook the Amazons, who were flying from the country of the Ephesians, and put them all to death by phlebotomy, so that this field was all covered and soaked in blood. This explanation will make it plainer to you henceforth than Aristotle made it in his *Problems*, why the common proverb used to be: 'Neither eat nor plant mint in time of war'. The reason is that in war-time blows are usually dealt haphazard, and if a man who is wounded has touched or eaten mint that day, it is impossible, or very difficult, to staunch his blood.

The next mosaic picture represented Bacchus advancing into battle, on a magnificent chariot drawn by three pairs of young leopards harnessed together. His face was like a young child's, as a sign that no good drinkers ever grow old, and red as a cherub's, without a single hair on his chin. He had pointed horns on his head, and on top of these a fine crown made of grapes and vine-leaves, and a crimson-red mitre. On his legs he wore gilded buskins.

There was not a single man in his company; his whole army and bodyguard consisted of Bassarids, Evantes, Euhyades, Edonides, Trieterides, Ogygies, Mimallonides, Maenads, Thyades, and Bacchae, wild, furious, and raging women, with live dragons and serpents round their waists instead of girdles, with their hair floating in the breeze, and wearing fillets of vine-leaves. They were dressed in stag and goatskins, and carried in their hands little axes, thyrsi, spears, halberds with blades in the form of pine-cones, and a certain kind of small shield which clanged loudly at the least touch. These they used, on necessary occasions, as cymbals and drums. There were seventy-nine thousand two hundred and twenty-seven of these women.

The vanguard was led by Silenus, a man in whom Bacchus placed entire confidence, and whose virtue and very great courage and prudence he had recognized in the past in many engagements. He was a little, tremulous old man, bent, plump, and pot-bellied, and had large, upstanding ears, a pointed, aquiline nose, and thick, unkempt eyebrows. He rode a jackass and carried a staff in his hand, on which he would lean and with which he would fight manfully, if he had to dismount. He was dressed like a woman, in a yellow robe, and his company consisted of young countrymen, with horns like goats and as cruel as lions. They were all naked, sang continuously, and danced the cordax. They were called Tityri and Satyrs, and their numbers were eighty-five thousand, one hundred and thirty-three.

Pan led the rearguard. He was a horrific and monstrous man. For the lower parts of his body were like a he-goat's, his thighs were hairy, and he had horns on his head, which pointed straight to Heaven. His face was red and swollen, and his beard was extremely long. He was bold, courageous, and daring, and easily roused to anger. In his left hand he carried a flute, and in his right a bent stick. His forces were similarly made up of Satyrs, Hemipans, Aegipans, Sylvans, Fauns, Fatui, Lemurs, Lares, Elves, and Hobgoblins, to the number of seventy-eight thousand, one hundred and fourteen. The battle-cry common to them all was 'Evohé'.

CHAPTER 40: *The good Bacchus's attack on the Indians as shown in the Temple Mosaics*

THE next picture showed the good Bacchus's attack upon the Indians. Here I saw Silenus, the leader of the vanguard, sweating huge drops and heavily belabouring his ass. The ass, in its turn, opened its jaws fiercely, whisked its tail, and struck out with its heels in a most horrible fashion, as though it had a hornet under its tail. The satyrs, captains, sergeants of companies, detachment leaders, and corporals, wildly sounding the charge with their goat's horns, rushed furiously around the army, leaping and prancing like goats, farting, kicking, and plunging, as an encouragement to their companies to fight valiantly. Everyone in the picture was shouting: '*Evohé!*' First, the Maenads charged the Indians with horrible cries and a terrible beating of their drums and shields. The whole sky resounded, and this was so well illustrated in the picture that henceforth you need not be so violent in your admiration of Apelles, Aristides the Theban, and those others who have painted thunder, lightning, thunderbolts, winds, words, manners, and spirits.

Next came the host of Indians, apparently warned that Bacchus was devastating their country. In front were the elephants, with towers on their backs, and with them a countless horde of warriors. But their whole army was in rout; their elephants had turned against them and were trampling them down, scared by the horrible onrush of the Bacchae and by panic terror, which had driven them out of their senses. There you would have seen Silenus, spurring his ass fiercely and making flourishes with his stick in the old fencing fashion, and the ass prancing after the elephants with his mouth open as if to bray. Indeed, he sounded the charge with a martial bray, as loud as he gave of old when he woke the nymph Lotis at the height of the Bacchanalian feast, just as Priapus, full of priapism, was about to priapize her as she slept, without so much as a *by your leave*.

There you would have seen Pan, leaping bandy-legged around the Maenads, exciting them with his rustic pipe to fight bravely; and, next in order, you would have seen a young satyr leading seventeen kings as prisoners, a Maenad dragging forty-two captains bound with her snakes, a little Faun carrying twelve banners captured from the enemy, and the excellent Bacchus riding safely over the field in his chariot, laughing and rejoicing and drinking toasts to each and all. Finally, there was a picture, in this same mosaic, of good old Bacchus's trophy of victory and of his triumph.

His triumphal chariot was all covered with ivy, gathered on Mount Meru, and this on account of its rarity – which enhances the price of everything – since it is especially rare in India. Alexander the Great afterwards copied him in this detail on his Indian triumph.

The chariot was drawn by yoked elephants, a detail which was afterwards copied by Pompey the Great in his African triumph at Rome; and on it rode Bacchus, drinking from a bowl, a practice which was afterwards imitated by Caius Marius, after the victory which he won over the Cymbri at Aix-en-Provence. Bacchus's whole army was crowned with ivy. Their thyrsi, shields, and drums were covered with it, and even Silenus's ass was harnessed with it. Beside the chariot walked the captive Indian kings, bound with great chains of gold. The whole brigade marched with godlike pomp, in inexpressible joy and delight, carrying innumerable trophies, banners, and spoils of the enemy, and singing gay triumphal chants, little country catches, and loud dithyrambs.

At the very end was a picture of the land of Egypt, with the Nile and its crocodiles, cercopitheci, ibises, apes, crocodile-birds, ichneumons, hippopotami, and other native beasts. And Bacchus was marching through that country drawn by two oxen, on one of which was written in letters of gold *Apis*, and on the other *Osiris*, because neither an ox nor a cow had ever been seen in Egypt before Bacchus's coming.

CHAPTER 41: *The wonderful Lamp which lit the Temple*

BEFORE I embark on a description of the Bottle, I will describe to you the shape of a wonderful lamp, which threw such plentiful light all over the Temple that although it was underground we could see as well there as one sees the sun at full midday, clearly and serenely shining up on earth.

In the middle of the vault was fixed a massive gold ring, the size of a clenched fist, from which hung three silver chains, a little less stout and most cunningly made. These were two and a half foot long, and in the triangle they formed they held a fine round gold plate, so large that it was more than three foot and three inches in diameter. On it were four buckles or holes, to each of which was firmly secured an empty ball, hollow inside and open at the top, like a little lamp. These balls were about eight inches in circumference, and were entirely made of precious stones: one of amethyst, another of Lybian carbuncle, the third of opal, the fourth of topaz. Each one was full of spirits, five times distilled in a serpentine retort, and as inexhaustible as the oil that Callimachus once put into Pallas's golden lamp on the Acropolis at Athens. It had a flaming wick, partly of asbestine flax – such as was once in the temple of Jupiter at Ammon, where it was seen by that most studious philosopher Cleombrotus – and partly of Carpasian flax, both of which are renewed rather than consumed by fire.

About two and a half feet below this lamp, the three chains, which still hung in the same line, were fastened to three handles, which protruded from a large round lamp of the purest crystal, with a diameter of two foot six inches, and an eight-inch opening at the top. In the middle of this opening stood a vessel of the same crystal, in the shape of a gourd or like a urine-glass, which reached right to the bottom of the great lamp, and which contained such a quantity of the same spirit that the flame of asbestine flax burnt right under the centre of the great lamp. Thus it seemed as if the whole spherical body were burning, indeed as if it were entirely alight, since the fire was at its centre and middle point.

It was as difficult to fix one's gaze firmly and continuously on it as it is to stare at the sun's disk, because the crystal shone so marvellously, and the whole thing was made so subtly transparent by the reflection of the different colours peculiar to each of the precious stones of the four small lamps which hung above the large one, and because the glow of these four wavered and flickered throughout the whole temple. Moreover, when this uncertain light fell on the polished marble, with which the whole interior of the temple was inlaid, such colours appeared as we see in a rainbow, when the bright sun strikes the rainclouds.

It was a wonderful design, and it seemed still more wonderful to me that the sculptor had chiselled around the body of the crystal lamp a brisk and jolly battle between little naked boys, mounted on little

hobby-horses with little whirligig lances and shields cunningly made
of grape-bunches, interlaced with leaves. So ingeniously had he conveyed their childish gestures and struggles that Nature could not have
done better than art had done here. They did not seem to be carved in
material, but to stand out in relief, or at least in grotesque work,
thanks to the varied and soft light inside which shone out through the
incisions.

CHAPTER 42: *The Priestess Bacbuc shows us a curious Fountain
     inside the Temple*

WHILE we gazed in ecstasy at this wonderful temple and its remarkable lamp, the reverend priestess Bacbuc appeared with a radiant face,
followed by her attendants; and when she saw that we were dressed as
I have described, she made no objection to leading us into the middle
of the temple, where beneath the afore-mentioned lamp was the beautiful and curious fountain, of more precious material and workmanship than ever Daedalus dreamt of. Its edge, base, and substructure
were of the purest and most transparent alabaster, a little more than a
foot high, heptagonal in shape, and divided into equal parts on the
outside, with a number of column-bases, miniature altars, mouldings,
and Doric undulations all round it. Inside, it was absolutely circular,
and at the middle point of each angle on the edge was placed a hollow
column, in the form of an ivory circle or balustrade. Modern architects call them *portri*, and they were, in all, seven in number, corresponding to each of the seven angles. Their height, from the base to
the architrave, was just under twenty-eight inches, which agreed
exactly with the length of a diameter passing through the centre of
the fountain's interior circle from circumference to circumference.

These columns were so placed that when we put our eye behind the
hollow of any one of them to look at the others opposite, we found
that the pyramidal cone of our line of vision ended at this same centre,
and there, with the two opposites, formed an equilateral triangle, the
two sides of which exactly intersected the column, which we had set
out to measure. Then, passing on either side of two columns which
were clear, a third of the way up the interval they struck the basic and
fundamental line; which by a test-line, drawn to the universal centre

and equally divided, exactly bisected the distance between the seven columns. And it was impossible to strike another column opposite with a straight line, departing from the obtuse angle on the edge. For, as you know, in any figure with an odd number of angles, one angle is always found to occur between two others.

This was a tacit proof to us that seven half-diameters in geometrical proportion, breadth, and distance are a little less than the circumference of the circular figure from which they are taken; that is to say, three whole diameters with an eighth part and a little more than a half, or with a seventh part and a little less than a half, according to the instructions given of old by Euclid, Aristotle, Archimedes, and others.[1]

The first column – that is to say, the first that struck our eyes as we came in to the Temple – was of a heavenly blue sapphire. The second was of hyacinth – with the Greek letters A and I carved on it in various places – of the exact colour of the flower into which the choleric Ajax's blood was transformed. The third was of anachite diamond, dazzling and glittering as the lightning. The fourth was of male spider ruby inclining towards amethyst, with its flame and sparkle tailing off, in fact, into a purplish-violet, like that of amethyst. The fifth was of emerald more than five hundred times more magnificent than that of Serapis in the Labyrinth of the Egyptians; and glowing more brightly than those which took the place of eyes in the marble lion which lay on the tomb of King Hermias. The sixth was of agate, more gaily varied in colour and markings than the stone which Pyrrhus King of the Epirots loved so well. The seventh was of transparent moonstone, as white as beryl and as clear as Hymetian honey; and in it the moon could be seen just as she is in the sky, the same in shape and in movement, whether full, waxing, or waning, and always silent.

These are the stones assigned by the ancient Chaldeans and Magi to the seven heavenly planets; and in order that we should understand this in a less subtle sense, above the first and exactly perpendicular to the centre of the sapphire hung a figure of Saturn holding his sickle with a golden crane at his feet, most cunningly enamelled in the proper colours of this Saturnine bird, in their proper order. Above the second, or hyacinthine, was Jupiter in Jovetian tin, facing left, with a golden eagle enamelled in its natural colours on his breast. Above the

1. This seems to be a description of an attempt to inscribe a heptagon in a circle. It is not at all easy to follow in the original.

third was Phoebus in refined gold, with a white cock on his right hand. Above the fourth, in Corinthian bronze, was Mars with a lion at his feet. Above the fifth Venus in copper, the same metal as that of which Aristonides made the statue of Athamas, the pink of which expressed the shame he felt when gazing on his son Learchus, who died of a fall. At her feet was a dove. Above the sixth was Mercury in quicksilver, fixed, firm, and malleable, with a stork at his feet. Above the seventh was Luna in silver, with a greyhound at her feet. And these statues were a little more than a third of the height of the columns on which they stood, and so admirably constructed, in true mathematical proportion, that Polycrates' canon – in the making of which he was said to have made art with the aid of art – could hardly have been accepted as a comparison.

The bases of the capitals, architraves, friezes, and cornices were of Phrygian goldsmith's work, solid, and of purer and finer gold than is to be dredged from the Lez near Montpellier, the Ganges in India, the Po in Italy, the Hebrus in Thrace, the Tagus in Spain, or the Pactolus in Lydia. Each of the small arches between the columns was of the stone of the column from which it sprang; that is to say that the first was of sapphire right up to the hyacinth of the next column, and the next of hyacinth right up to the diamond, and so on in order. Above the arches and the capitals of the columns, on the inner face, was a cupola erected to cover the fountain. This began heptagonally behind the planetary figures, and gradually took a spherical shape. It was of crystal so pure and transparent, so smoothly polished, and so uniform all over – without veins, blotches, flaws, or streaks – that Xenocrates never saw anything to compare to it. In its thickness were exquisitely carved, in their due order, the beautifully outlined shapes of the twelve signs of the Zodiac, the twelve months of the year with their symbols, the twin solstices, the two equinoxes, and the ecliptic line, with certain of the more important fixed stars around the Antarctic pole and elsewhere, portrayed with such skill that I thought it the work of King Nechepsos or of Petosiris, the ancient mathematician.

On top of this cupola, and above the centre of the fountain, were three long pearls of uniform size and of a spiral shape exactly like that of a teardrop. These hung together in the form of a fleur-de-lys, and were so large that the flower was more than four inches across. From its calyx protruded a carbuncle the size of an ostrich's egg, cut with seven facets – a favourite number of Nature's – which was such a prodigious wonder that we were almost blinded when we gazed up at it. For it seemed to us to flash and sparkle more brilliantly than the sun's fire or the lightning. In fact, to any fair judge that fountain and those lamps would indubitably have appeared to contain more riches and rarity than are to be found in Asia, Africa, and Europe put together. It would as easily have outshone the fiery red stone of Iarchas, the Indian magician, as the sun outshines the stars at noonday.

Now let Cleopatra, Queen of Egypt, boast of the two pearls that hung from her ears, one of which she dissolved in vinegar and water and swallowed in the presence of Antony the Triumvir, and the pair of which were valued at six million sesterces. Now let Lollia Paulina pride herself on her dress entirely woven of alternate emeralds and pearls, which aroused the admiration of the whole population of Rome: the city that was then called the hiding-place and store-house of the robbers who had conquered the whole world.

The fountain was emptied by three tubes and channels formed of fine pearls and placed at the three equilateral angles on the outside, which have been described already; the channels being corkscrew shaped and double.

When we had contemplated these wonders, we were just about to turn our gaze elsewhere when Bacbuc told us to listen to the flowing of the water. It was a marvellously musical sound, though dull and broken, as if it came from the far distance and underground. But, much as our spirits had been charmed through the windows of our eyes by all the sights I have mentioned, there was as much delight still in store for our ears in the sound of this music.

Then Bacbuc said to us: 'You philosophers deny that motion can arise from the power of figures. But listen now, and you will admit that you are wrong. Merely by that corkscrew figure that you see there in two parts, combined with a five-fold pattern of leaf-work which moves at every inward joint – as the hollow vein does at the point where it enters the right ventricle of the heart – this sacred fountain is emptied, and a harmony produced that mounts up to the sea of your world.'

CHAPTER 43: *How the Water of the Fountain tasted of different Wines, according to the imagination of the Drinkers*

SHE then ordered mugs with lids, cups, and goblets to be handed to us, of gold, silver, crystal, and porcelain; and we were graciously invited to drink of the water that gushed from that fountain; which we willingly did. For, to be frank with you, we are by nature different from a herd of cattle, who – like the sparrows, which only feed when you tap their tails – never eat or drink unless you whack them hard with a big stick. We never refuse anyone who courteously invites us to drink.

Bacbuc then asked us what we thought of the liquor, and we answered her that it seemed like good fresh spring-water to us, more limpid and silvery than the water of Argyrontes in Aetiolia, of Peneus in Thessaly, of Axius in Mygdonia, or of Cydnus in Cicilia; which last Alexander of Macedon found so beautiful, so clear and cool in the midst of summer that he preferred the luxury of bathing in it to the harm that he saw would ensue for him from this transitory pleasure.

'Ha,' said Bacbuc, 'that is what comes of not reflecting, and of not understanding the movements of the muscular tongue, when the drink flows over it on its way down, not into the lungs by the tracheal artery, as was supposed by the good Plato, Plutarch, Macrobius, and others, but into the stomach by way of the oesophagus. Are your throats lined, paved, and enamelled, noble strangers, as Pithyllus, nicknamed Theutes, had his of old, that you have not recognized the taste or savour of this godlike liquor? Bring me those scourers of mine,' she called to her ladies-in-waiting, 'so that we can rake, clear, and clean their palates.'

Then there were brought fine, jolly great hams; fine, jolly, great smoked ox-tongues, excellent salt-meats, saveloys, botargoes, caviar, excellent venison sausages, and other such gullet-sweepers; and, by her command, we ate of these until we confessed that our stomachs were thoroughly scoured and that we were now pretty grievously tormented by thirst. Upon this she observed:

'As a certain Jewish captain of old, a learned and valiant man, was leading his people across the desert in utter famine, he received manna out of the skies, which to their imagination tasted exactly as food had tasted in the past. Similarly here, as you drink of this miraculous liquor you will detect the taste of whatever wine you may imagine.'

This we did, and Panurge cried out: 'By God, this is the wine of Beaune, and the best that ever I tasted, and may a hundred and six devils run away with me if it isn't! How grand it would be to have a neck six foot long, so as to taste it longer, which was Philoxenus's wish; or as long as a crane's, as Melanthius desired!'

'I swear as a Lanterner,' exclaimed Friar John, 'that it's Graves wine, gay and sparkling. Pray teach me, lady, the way you make it like this.'

'To me,' said Pantagruel, 'it seems like wine of Mirevaux. For that's what I imagined before I drank. The only thing wrong with it is that it is cool. Colder than ice, I should say, colder than Nonacris or Dirce water, colder than the fountain of Cantoporeia in Corinth, which froze the stomach and digestive organs of those who drank it.'

'Drink,' said Bacbuc, 'once, twice, and three times. And now again, changing your thoughts, and each time you'll find the taste and savour of the liquor just as you imagined it. After this you must confess that to God nothing is impossible.'

'We never said that anything was,' I replied. 'We maintain that he is all-powerful.'

CHAPTER 44 : *How Bacbuc dressed Panurge, to listen to the Verdict of the Bottle*

WHEN this talk and tippling were over, Bacbuc asked: 'Which of you is it who wants the Verdict of the Holy Bottle?'

'I,' said Panurge, 'your humble little funnel.'

'My friend,' said she, 'I have only one thing to say to you. When you come to the oracle, be careful to listen to the verdict with one ear only.'

Then she wrapped him up in a green gaberdine, tied a fair white nun's snood round his head, muffled him in a mulled wine-strainer, on the end of which, instead of a wool-tuft, she tied three skewers, put two ancient codpieces on his hands for gloves, gave him three bag-pipes tied together for a belt, bathed his face five times in the fountain, and after that threw a handful of flour in his eyes, stuck three cock's feathers on the right-hand side of his mulled-wine hood, made him turn nine times round the fountain, take three pretty little jumps, and give seven bumps with his bottom on the ground. All the time she was muttering some spells or other in the Etruscan tongue and sometimes reading from a book of ritual, which one of her mystagogues carried beside her.

To be brief, I believe that neither Numa Pompilius, second king of the Romans, nor the Caerites of Etruria, nor the blessed Jewish captain ever invented as many ceremonies as I saw then. Nor did the soothsayers of Memphis in Egypt ever perform such rites for Apis, nor the Euboeans in the city of Rhamnusia, nor the ancients for Jupiter Ammon or to Feronis, as those that I witnessed there.

When he was dressed she took him from us, and led him by the right hand through a golden door, out of the temple into a round chapel built of glistening clear stone, which admitted the sun's light through its transparent thickness. The chapel had no window or opening, but the light streamed down through a cleft in the rock which covered the greater temple, so easily and so abundantly that it seemed to come from some internal source rather than to enter from without. This edifice was every bit as wonderful as the holy temple of Ravenna of old, or as the one on the island of Chemnis in Egypt; and I must not omit to mention that the architecture of this round chapel was of such symmetry that the diameter of the floor was equal in height to the vault.

In the middle of it was a fountain of fine alabaster, heptagonal in shape, of singular workmanship and carving, and full of water so limpid that it seemed elemental in its purity. Within it was half immersed the sacred Bottle, wholly encased in fine and lovely crystal, and oval in shape except that its lip was rather more raised than a true oval would allow.

CHAPTER 45: *The Priestess Bacbuc leads Panurge into the presence of the Holy Bottle*

THERE the noble priestess Bacbuc made Panurge kneel down and kiss the edge of the fountain, and then ordered him to get up and perform three Bacchic dances around it. After this she commanded him to sit down between two stools, with his arse on the ground. Then she opened her book of ceremonies and, whispering in his left ear, made him sing an old Athenian vintage-song, which goes as follows:

O
Bottle full
Of mystery,
With a single ear
I hark to thee.
Do not delay,
But that one word say
For which with all my heart I long.
Since in that liqour so divine
That your crystal flanks contain
Bacchus, India's conqueror strong,
Holds all truth, for truth's in wine.
And in wine no deceit or wrong
Can live, no fraud and no prevarication,
May Noah's soul in delights dwell safe and long,
Who taught us use in moderation
Of our cups. Be kind to me,
Let the fair word be said.
From misery set me free
Then no drop, white or red
Shall perish. There shall be no waste of thee.
O Bottle full of mystery,
With a single ear
I hark to thee.
Do not delay.

When this song was sung, Bacbuc threw something into the fountain, and suddenly the water began to boil fiercely, as the great cauldron at Bourgueil does when there is a high feast there. Panurge was listening in silence with one ear, and Bacbuc was still kneeling beside him, when there issued from the sacred Bottle a noise such as bees make that are bred in the flesh of a young bull slain and dressed according to the skilful method of Aristaeus, or such as is made by a bolt when a cross-bow is fired, or by a sharp shower of rain suddenly falling in summer. Then this one word was heard: *Trink*.

'By God almighty,' cried Panurge, 'it's broken or cracked, I'll swear. That is the sound that glass bottles make in our country when they burst beside the fire.'

Then Bacbuc arose and, putting her hands gently beneath Panurge's arms, said to him: 'Give thanks to heaven, my friend. You have good reason to. For you have most speedily received the verdict of the divine Bottle; and it is the most joyous, the most divine, and the most certain answer that I have heard from it yet, in all the time I have ministered to this most sacred Oracle. Get up, and let us examine the chapter in whose gloss this great verdict is interpreted.'

'Let us go,' said Panurge, 'in Heaven's name. I'm no wiser than I was last year. Enlighten us; where is the book? Turn it over; where is the chapter? Let us see this merry gloss.'

CHAPTER 46: *Bacbuc's interpretation of the Verdict of the Bottle*

BACBUC threw something into the basin, and the water immediately ceased to boil. Then she led Panurge back to the middle of the larger temple, where the fountain of life played. There she pulled out a huge silver book shaped like half a hogshead or the quart book of *Sentences*. This she dipped into the fountain, and said to him:

'The philosophers, preachers, and doctors of your world feed you with fine words through the ears. Here we literally take in our teaching orally, through the mouth. Therefore I do not say to you: Read this chapter, understand this gloss. What I say is: Taste this chapter, swallow this gloss. Once upon a time an ancient prophet of the Jewish nation swallowed a book, and became a learned man to the teeth. Now you must immediately drink this, and you'll be learned to the liver. Here, open your jaws.'

Panurge opened his mouth wide, and Bacbuc took the silver book – which we thought really was a book, because of its shape, which was that of a breviary. But it was a true breviary and natural flask, full of Falernian wine, which she made Panurge swallow.

'That was a notable chapter,' said Panurge, 'and a most authentic gloss. Is that all that the verdict of the thrice-great bottle intended to convey? I like it very well indeed.'

'That is all,' answered Bacbuc, 'for *Trink* is a panomphaean word. It speaks oracles, that is to say, in all languages, and is famed and understood by all nations. To us it signifies: Drink. You say in your world that *sack* is a noun common to all tongues, and that it is rightly and justly understood by all nations. For, as Aesop's fable has it, all human beings are born with a sack round their necks, being by nature needy and begging from one another. There is no king under the firmament so powerful that he can do without other men's help. There is no poor man so proud that he can do without the rich, not even Hippias the philosopher, who could do everything. And if one cannot do without a sack, even less can one do without drinking. So we maintain that not laughter but drinking is the proper lot of man. I do not mean simply and baldly drinking, for beasts also drink. I mean drinking good cool wine. Note, my friends, that by wine one grows divine; there is no surer argument, no art of divination less fallacious. Your Academics affirm this when in giving the etymology of wine they say that the Greek οἶνος is like *vis*: force or strength. For it has the power to fill the soul with all truth, all knowledge, and all philosophy. If you have noticed what is written in Ionic characters above the gate of the temple, you may have understood that the truth lies hidden in wine. The Holy Bottle directs you to it. You must be your own interpreters in this matter.'

'It would be impossible to speak better than this venerable pontiff does,' said Pantagruel. 'I told you that much when you first spoke to me on the subject. *Trink* then. What does your heart tell you, when cheered by Bacchic enthusiasm?'

'Let us drink,' said Panurge.

> Come, *trink*, by Bacchus let us tope,
> Ho, ho, for now I truly hope
> To see some round and juicy rump
> Well tickled by my carnal stump
> And stuffed with my humanity.
> For what says my paternity?
> My paternal heart tells me
> That not only shall I be
> Soon comfortably wedded,
> But when my wife is bedded
> She'll love the sport. By Venus,
> What bouts there'll be between us!
> God, I'll plough that field at leisure,
> And I'll take my fill of pleasure.
> I'm a well-fed man, I am,
> And 'The Good husband' is my name,
> The best of all good ones. Io Paean,
> Io Paean, Io Paean!

Io marriage, three times dear.
Listen, Brother John, I swear
My true and intellectual oath
That this oracle speaks truth.
It's certain, and it's fateful – both.

CHAPTER 47: *How Panurge and the rest rhymed in a poetic
Frenzy*

'HAVE you gone mad or are you bewitched?' asked Friar John.
'Look how he's foaming! Listen to the doggerel he's spouting! What
in all the devils' names has he been eating? His eyes are rolling in his
head like a dying goat's. Won't he go away a bit? Won't he go and
do his shit a bit further off? Or won't he eat some dog's grass to relieve his corporation? Or perhaps he'll do as the monks do, and ram
his fist down his throat to the elbow to clear his digestive tubes. Will
he take some more of the hair of the dog that bit him?'

Pantagruel turned angrily on Friar John, and said:

'Believe me, it's the fit divine,
Poetic frenzy. This good wine
Has dimmed his brains, and made him bawl;
    For there's no doubt
    His wits are out,
    And put to rout
    By what he takes.
    He cries, he laughs;
    He laughs, he quaffs,
    And not by halfs
    His heart he makes
    Rhetorical
    Lord over all
    Our grins and scoffs.
And since his brain's inspired by wine
'Twould be the act of a mean thinker
To mock at such a noble drinker.'

'What!' exclaimed Friar John. 'Do you rhyme also? By God almighty, we're all infected. I wish to goodness Gargantua could see us
in this state! I don't know what to do. I swear, whether to rhyme like
you or not. I don't know anything about the job, but here we are in

rhyming country. So, by St John, I'll rhyme like the rest. I can feel it coming. Listen, and accept my apologies if I don't spout like a laureate:

> Oh God, who by Thy power divine
> Turned the water into wine,
> Make a lantern of my bum,
> That I may light my neighbour home.'

Panurge, however, continued his poetizing as follows:

> 'Never did the Pythian god
> Grant by his divine tripod
> Answer surer or more certain.
> I believe that to this fountain
> It was specially conveyed
> From Delphi by the priestly trade.
> Had honest Plutarch drunk from here
> He'd have never been so queer
> As to ask why Delphi's oracle
> Is as dumb as any coracle,
> And never more is heard to speak.
> The reason isn't far to seek.
> The fateful tripod and austere
> Is not at Delphi; it is here.
> Here too all things it presages.
> Athenaeus, in his pages,
> Proves it was a one-eared bottle,
> Full of wine up to the throttle.
> Of wine? No, of the truth most pure.
> For there's no certainty so sure
> In the whole art of divining
> As the deep and subtle meaning
> Of the Bottle's holy word.
> Brother John, now that you've heard
> I beg of you, before we go,
> To ask the question, and to know
> Of the Bottle Trismegist
> If any obstacle exist
> Why you also shouldn't marry.
> And for fear the answers vary
> Dance a little Bacchic jig,
> And from my leafy hose and wig
> Just fling in a little flour.'

Friar John answered in a fine poetic rage:

> 'Marry! By the mighty power
> Of St Benet's boot and gaiters.
> All my friends and fellow fraters
> Know I'd rather be unfrocked
> Than to a petticoat be yoked,
> Rather be shaven close and harried
> Than go so far as to be married.
> Why, I should lose my liberty,
> And for ever and a day,
> To a single wife be tied!
> No, by God, sir, truly I'd
> Not tie myself to Alexander,
> Caesar or the best commander
> That ever in the world was seen.'

Throwing off his gaberdine and his mystical paraphernalia, Panurge replied:

> 'Then you shall be, beast unclean
> Like the wicked serpent cursed.
> But me they'll portcullis-hoist
> Merrily up to paradise.
> From which vantage I shall piss
> Down on you, you wretched scum.
> But listen; when in time you come
> To the old devil's lowest hell,
> As it's probable you will,
> And Dame Proserpine, all forlorn
> Feels the pricking of that thorn
> That lies hidden in your breeches,
> When she's sweet on the caprices
> Of your rare paternity,
> And there's an opportunity
> For a tune or two together
> Before you ride her, hell-for-leather,
> Don't tell me you won't send in haste
> For wine to furnish a repast
> For that old dotard Lucifer,
> From the finest tavern there.
> She's kind, and never yet turned down
> A friar, black or white or brown.'

'Go to the devil, you old fool,' said Friar John. 'I can't rhyme any more. The rheum has got me by the throat. Let's talk of giving satisfaction here.'

CHAPTER 48: *How we took leave of Bacbuc and left the Oracle of the Bottle*

'Do not worry about giving satisfaction here,' replied Bacbuc. 'All will be perfectly satisfactory if you are satisfied with us. Down here, in these circumcentral regions, we place the supreme good, not in taking or receiving, but in giving and bestowing. We count ourselves lucky not if we take and receive a great deal from others, as is perhaps the rule with the sects of your world, but if we can always be bestowing and giving things to others. All I ask of you is to leave us your names and countries written in this register.'

Then she opened a fine, large book, in which one of her ministrant mystagogues drew to our dictation with a golden stylus some lines in imitation of writing; but there was no writing apparent to us.

When this was done she filled three small leather vessels with the miraculous water, and put them into our hands, saying: 'Go, my friends, under the protection of this intellectual sphere, the centre of which is at all points and the circumference at none, and which we call God; and when you come to your country bear testimony that great treasures and wonderful things are hidden beneath the earth. It was not without reason that Ceres lamented so grievously for her daughter when she was carried down into our subterranean regions – Ceres, who was worshipped by the whole universe for being the first to demonstrate and teach the art of agriculture, and by the invention of corn to put an end to the bestial eating of acorns among men. For she accurately foresaw that her daughter would find more blessings and excellencies underground than her mother had ever created up above. What has become of the art of calling the thunder and the fire of heaven out of the sky, which was invented of old by Prometheus the wise? You have certainly lost it. It has departed from your hemisphere, but it is in use down here. Sometimes you are unreasonably dismayed at the sight of towns set alight and consumed by thunder and celestial fire. You do not know from whom, by whom, and for what purpose came this disaster, which is so terrible in your eyes, so useful and beneficial in ours. Your philosophers who complain that everything has been described by the ancients, and that nothing new is left for them to discover, are only too patently wrong. So much as you can see of the heavens, and which you call the *Phenomena*, so much as the earth reveals to you, so much as the sea and all the rivers contain, is not to be compared with what is concealed in the earth.

'It is only right therefore that, in almost all languages, the Ruler of the Underworld has been known by epithets implying riches. When your sages devote their labours and studies to a diligent examination of this lore, having first implored that sovereign deity, whom the Egyptians of old called in their tongue Isis – that is to say the Veiled, the Hidden, the Concealed, by which name they begged and prayed her to manifest herself and appear to them – she will enlarge their knowledge both of herself and her creatures, and give them a good Lantern for guide. For all ancient philosophers and sages have reckoned two things to be necessary for safe and pleasant travel on the road of wisdom and in the pursuit after knowledge; God's guidance and the company of men.

'Thus, among the Persians, Zoroaster took Arimaspes as companion in all his mysterious philosophy; Hermes Trismegistus, among the Egyptians, took Aesculapius; Orpheus in Thrace had Musaeus; and there, too, Aglaophemus had Pythagoras; among the Athenians Plato had first Dion of Syracuse in Sicily, who died, and after that took Xenocrates; Apollonius had Damis.

'So, when you philosophers, with God's guidance and in the company of some clear Lantern, give yourselves up to that careful study and investigation which is the proper duty of man – and it is for this reason that men are called *alphestes*, that is to say searchers and discoverers, by Homer and Hesiod – they will find the truth of the sage Thales's reply to Amasis, King of the Egyptians. When asked wherein the greatest wisdom lay, Thales replied: "In time". For it is time that has discovered, or in due course will discover, all things which lie hidden; and that is the reason why the ancients called Saturn or Time the Father of Truth, or Truth the Daughter of Time. They will also infallibly find that all men's knowledge, both theirs and their forefathers', is hardly an infinitesimal fraction of all that exists and that they do not know.

'From these three leather bottles which I now give you, you will derive knowledge and judgement and, as the proverb has it, will come to know the lion by his claws. By the rarefaction of our water, contained within them, and by the intervention of the heat of the heavenly bodies and the warmth of the salt sea, according to the natural transmutation of the elements, a most salubrious air will be engendered inside, which will serve you as a clear, serene, and delightful wind. For wind is nothing but floating and undulating air. With the aid of this wind you will sail straight if you wish, without touching any land to the port of Olonne in Salmondais. By letting as much air as you think sufficient blow into your sails through this little golden vent, which you see placed here as on a flute, you can travel at full speed or slowly, and always pleasantly and safely, free from storms or danger. Do not doubt this, or imagine that storms arise or proceed from the wind; it is the wind that arises from the storms, which are called up from the gulfs of the deep. Do not imagine either that the rain falls because of the heavens' inability to hold it and the heaviness of the hanging clouds. It falls when evoked by the subterranean regions, as by the evocation of the heavenly bodies it has been imperceptibly drawn up to the clouds from below. And this the King and Prophet testifies to you when he sings that Deep calleth unto Deep. Of these three bottles, two are filled with this water, and the third has been taken from the well of the Indian sages, which is called the Barrel of the Brahmans.

'You will, in addition, find your ships well and properly provided with everything that may be useful and necessary for your other requirements. Whilst you have been here, I have had very good care taken of that. Go, my friends, with joyful hearts, and carry this letter to your king Gargantua. Give greetings from us to him and to the princes and officers of his noble court.'

When she had concluded her speech she handed us some closed and sealed letters and, after we had returned her our undying thanks, she showed us out through a door beside the transparent chapel, where Bacbuc summoned her people to propose questions twice as high as Mount Olympus.

And so we passed through a country full of all delights, pleasanter and more temperate than Tempe in Thessaly, healthier than that part of Egypt which faces towards Libya, better watered and greener than Themischyra, more fertile than that part of Mount Taurus which faces towards the North, or than the Hyperborean Island in the Judaic Sea, or than Caliges on Mount Caspius, sweet-smelling, smiling, and delightful as the country of Touraine; and at last we found our ships in the harbour.

End of the Fifth Book of the Heroic Deeds
and Sayings of the noble
Pantagruel